'Bonne Espérance endured. Over immense stretches of time it had survived the passions that had torn first a family and then a country apart. Housing the living with the dead, still it called Katinka back . . .

Katinka watched her granddaughter slip away like a breath of wind. Since the day she'd stolen the baby and had been imprisoned in the house and garden, there was something very different about Rebecca. Like a tiny caged bird, she sat inside an invisible glass bubble, whistling to check if there was anybody left on the outside. But Rebecca had been locked away to protect her from the outside world. She'd become the focus of attention as the small town placed her in the centre of their quest for the devil's playground. It was a place Katinka knew well, and she wondered if it was time Rebecca learned that the world for which she longed was as hostile as her own.'

Born in the town of Luanshya, Zambia, and educated at Elmhurst Ballet School and Webber Douglas Drama School in the UK, Luanshya Greer has been a professional writer of TV drama, films and stage in the UK and Europe for 24 years. She started her career as an actress with many roles on TV and film, before turning successfully to writing. Her first novel, *Reap the Whirlwind*, has been produced as a major TV series. Luanshya Greer is married to actor John Carson and with their children Ben and Suzanna they now live in South Africa.

ALSO BY LUANSHYA GREER
Reap the Whirlwind

SHADOWS IN THE WIND

Luanshya Greer

ORION

An Orion paperback
First published in Great Britain by Orion in 1993
This paperback edition published in 1994 by Orion Books Ltd,
Orion House, 5 Upper St Martin's Lane, London WC2H 9EA

A CIP catalogue record for this book is available from the
British Library.

ISBN: 1 85797 445 X

Printed in England by Clays Ltd, St Ives plc

*To the memory of my mother and father:
Mavis Greer, who sacrificed so much to give
her children opportunity, and Bryce Greer,
whose unconditional love taught us how.*

ACKNOWLEDGEMENTS

Without the many South Africans of all races in whom I've seen so much forgiveness, courage and hope, even in the eye of the storm, this book could not have been written. To them and the following people who have given their help in a variety of ways — thank you.

My wonderful husband, John, for his constant love and patience as he copied my often unreadable manuscript onto his computer: our children, Ben and Suzanna for always 'being there'.

Mewe Oiliphant, Peter and Elizabeth Maname, Themba and Mildred Nyati, Samuel Oiliphant, Elizabeth and Basil Harris, Xoliswa Makaka, Rev. Peter Fox, Joy Daniels, John Alwood, and Lydia Steinke for their help with custom, culture, feelings and facts.

My sisters, Wendy Bennet and Robyn Davies, for being such a strong source of encouragement.

To a small girl called Portia*, whose short life crossed mine, and helped many more.

The Gibbons family and many locales, who aided my research when I visited Zambia, most especially Kalolo Mulenga, through whom I discovered so much more than I expected.

For an understanding of the politics and events of the time against which I set the story, the books 'A Newspaper History of South Africa' by Vic Alhadeff (Don Nelson), 'The Rise and Fall of Apartheid' by Peter Joyce (Struik), and 'The Readers Digest Illustrated History of South Africa' were extremely helpful.

Isabelle Laffont of Editions Robert Laffont for her patience and total commitment throughout. Those at Orion Books for their care in bringing the book to publication, most importantly my editor, Yvette Goulden, with whom I found such empathy. My agent, Felicity Bryan, for bringing everything together so neatly.

And last, but by no means least, for their powerful and constant support — 'The Monday Girls'.

Thank you all.

* 'Portia's Khaya' is a real children's home that we opened after her death, and which is run by the local African peoples, housing over sixty children in need.

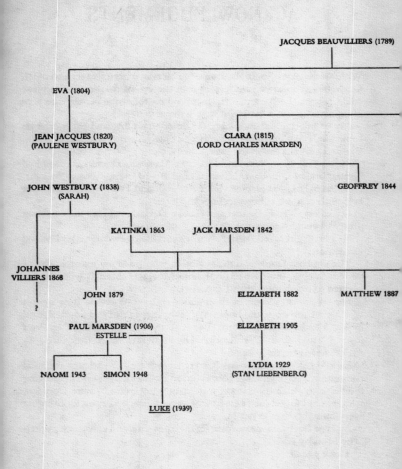

JACQUES BEAUVILLIERS (1789)

EVA (1804)

JEAN JACQUES (1820)
(PAULENE WESTBURY)

CLARA (1815)
(LORD CHARLES MARSDEN)

JOHN WESTBURY (1838)
(SARAH)

GEOFFREY 1844

KATINKA 1863   JACK MARSDEN 1842

JOHANNES
VILLIERS 1868

?

JOHN 1879

ELIZABETH 1882   MATTHEW 1887

PAUL MARSDEN (1906)
ESTELLE

ELIZABETH 1905

NAOMI 1943   SIMON 1948

LYDIA 1929
(STAN LIEBENBERG)

LUKE (1939)

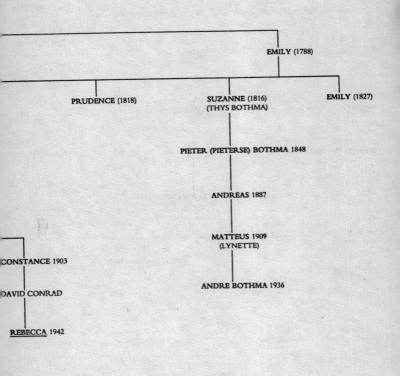

EMILY (1788)

PRUDENCE (1818)   SUZANNE (1816)   EMILY (1827)
                   (THYS BOTHMA)

PIETER (PIETERSE) BOTHMA 1848

ANDREAS 1887

CONSTANCE 1903   MATTEUS 1909
                  (LYNETTE)

DAVID CONRAD

REBECCA 1942   ANDRE BOTHMA 1936

'. . . and all the ends of the earth shall see the salvation of our God.'

Isaiah LII. 10

CHAPTER ONE

The baby screamed as the pram rocked dangerously from side to side. Her eyes level with the shiny black undercarriage and her arms stretched high to reach the handlebar, the seven-and-a-half-year-old girl moved faster over the rough ground. She was heading towards a winding footpath up ahead, making for the railway sidings on the edge of the small mining town.

'Shh!' She pushed up on tiptoe, stretching her neck till her chin propped itself on the hard edge of the pram. 'It's all right.' The baby's kicking feet tossed a blanket into her face and she dropped back on her heels, spitting fluff from her mouth. 'You'll be happy now I've found you,' she assured the dry stony ground that skimmed under the wheels. Her eyes burned black with excitement and trickles of sweat forced her dark hair into sticky pigtails. Her skirt whipped between her legs, clinging to her thighs as if trying to stop her; but the small girl pushed the pram on faster.

Rebecca had stolen the baby from outside Bernstein's grocery store. The afternoon sun had burned down from a dry African sky and the small town had dozed in its buzzing heat. She'd leaned her bicycle against a flaking pillar that held the verandah roof over the shops, and it was then that she'd spotted a large black perambulator. Rebecca had never seen that particular pram in the small town before and her heart had turned a somersault as she peeped at the baby inside it.

Moving quickly into the damp cool of the shop, she'd forced her eyes to adjust quickly to the sudden darkness. Bernstein's sold everything from needle and thread to twenty-pound sacks of sugar and fifty-pound sacks of mealie meal. She'd felt the powdery grit of the meal under the soles of her bare feet. It crept between her toes as it dribbled its way out of the sacks in dusty waterfalls before spreading across the red polished floor.

'You're in early, Rebecca.' Mrs Bernstein's voice came at her through the dark cool of the shop. She was serving a stranger at the counter and on the wall behind her hung a calendar. Under the year – 1949 – was a picture of a lady in a black swimming costume. Rebecca's father had a picture of the lady, too. It hung in the hoisthouse of Stork shaft where he worked. 'Stand back there and wait, dearie.' A dismissive wave of Mrs Bernstein's chubby hand had added to her command.

'Yes, Mrs Bernstein.' Rebecca moved back obediently, tightening her nose against a sickly-sweet smell. It was the perfume the shopkeeper poured down her ample bosom as if a thirsty monster lived in her cleavage, demanding Eau de Cologne 4711. After feeding it the perfume, Mrs Bernstein silenced the monster with a handkerchief embroidered with blue daisies. It looked worse than the one Rebecca had embroidered for her mother last Christmas and it certainly smelt worse.

Through the musty merchandise that stretched between them, dark whispers and hushed laughter reached among Rebecca's thoughts. The stranger Mrs Bernstein was serving had glanced round and Rebecca knew the two women were talking about her. Her entire life had been punctuated by the hostile whispers and hollow laughter of grown-ups.

'Don't mess the floor, dearie.' Mrs Bernstein's voice had snatched Rebecca's attention away from the big-toe drawing of the perfume monster she'd made in the mealie meal under her feet.

'I'll come back later.' Rebecca had run outside to the pram, no longer interested in the pastel fruit drops she'd come to buy.

The blistering hot stones between the railway lines forced Rebecca to lift her feet quickly as she struggled across them with the pram. A large, corrugated-iron warehouse was just ahead of her and to the side of that was an abandoned railway carriage. It was the second most important place in her world.

'Come on!' Rebecca urged the enormous front wheels of the pram over the glinting hot line, pushing her shoulder under the carriage to lift it. 'Don't cry!' she shouted and, picking up each scorching foot in turn, she rubbed them on the calves of her legs to stop the blood boiling over. Her mother said it would if she went without shoes.

'Oh, no!' She jumped back in horror as the pram toppled to the right and a small bundle rocketed out. It landed in the sand on the other side of the line and the moment of silence that followed seemed an eternity. Rebecca didn't move. She didn't feel the red-hot pebbles singeing their way into the soles of her feet. All she saw was a dusty, dead baby.

'*Wah!*'

The baby's lungs emptied themselves in a powerful yell and it snatched a fresh breath as Rebecca picked it up, dusting it down as its face screwed up in renewed anger.

'Don't cry,' she suggested hopefully, picking wet sand from its wide mouth with her finger.

'Hey!' She stared at the baby. Its mouth had tightened around her finger and toothless gums, hard as wood, sucked as she watched in astonishment. It was devouring her finger while blowing bubbles through its nose. 'Wait!' Rebecca remembered how African women sat passively while babies sucked at their huge black breasts and she was terrified. She'd be swallowed alive if the baby searched for a breast on her and she tried to extract her finger as it hung on tight.

'Let go,' she begged as she remembered her mother's Bendix washing machine. It had just arrived from England and its suction was so strong that it had had to be nailed to the floor to keep it in place. The whole town had turned out to watch its alarming performance.

'Have you got a bottle?' She inched her finger out but the baby yelled its indignation, latching on tighter. 'Look!' Rebecca lifted one scorching foot from among the dusty pram sheets on the ground, a glass bottle balanced across her arch. Milk tilted sideways in a wobbly white line, dripping from the teat like a leaking glass banana.

Once safely in the warm darkness of the empty railway carriage, Rebecca studied the baby's face as it drank. Tiny pink fingers curled round the bottle and its mouth sucked hard as delicate blue eyelids lifted like butterfly shutters. The baby was staring at her from contented eyes and Rebecca felt totally at peace. Even the enormous spider's web, lit by a shaft of light between wooden slats, didn't disturb her. The spider hung like a black dustball from eight hairy legs, pretending to be dead. Rebecca knew it was waiting to pounce, but she didn't mind. A surge of warmth had crept from her innermost being, falling in a blanket of love over the tiny bundle in her arms.

'My baby!' The stranger Mrs Bernstein had been serving screamed as she stood on the empty spot where the pram had been. 'The natives have taken my baby!' Her voice ripped from her guts, darting zigzag down the dusty street outside Bernstein's store. 'They'll kill my baby!' Her mind swam with stories of Mau Mau atrocities in Kenya.

'I'm sure it's all right,' Mrs Bernstein lied, her head swinging from side to side on top of her beef-roll neck. The deserted street looked suddenly threatening as the English newcomer screamed aloud the fears everyone else kept to themselves. Mrs Bernstein had also read about the Mau Mau in Kenya and she snatched the embroidered hanky from her cleavage to wipe away the beads of sweat that bubbled on her forehead. Her heavy make-up had cracked like scorched paint and a thread of red drew a line from her lips to her chin. 'There must be an explanation.' She sniffed at the Eau de Cologne on the handkerchief, dabbing a blue daisy under her eyes to catch her melting mascara. 'Maybe your husband took the baby ...'

'He's underground on shift,' the pale Englishwoman whispered through floods of tears. 'Why did we come here? They're savages!' she screamed. 'Oh God ... my baby!'

Mrs Bernstein enveloped the hysterical woman in her arms, unsure how to comfort her. Newcomers from England always imagined the place to be swarming with black savages, but she knew the reality was far worse. The blacks had grown smart. Some even wore sunglasses and they'd learned from the white man to be truly dangerous.

'Mr Mathieson!' Mrs Bernstein waved over the bowed head of the trembling woman in her arms. 'Over here,' she gestured to the tall angular man with a deeply tanned face who'd stopped on the stone kerb across the road. He hesitated, looking out for cars before crossing the deserted street, his face hidden in the shadow of a wide-brimmed felt hat. Mr Mathieson had seen the emotion pouring from the woman in Mrs Bernstein's arms and wished he'd stayed where he was for a second beer. The cool of the hotel verandah was suddenly exactly where he wanted to be.

'Is there something the matter, Mabel?' he asked in a broad Scottish accent, removing his hat and examining the sweat band inside it very carefully. 'You not well?'

'Her baby's gone.' Mrs Bernstein's agitated whisper rode on a nod of her head in the direction of the missing pram. 'It was outside, and it's gone.'

'Her bairn's gone?' Mr Mathieson stared blankly at the empty pavement with little idea of what it was that should have been there. It would be a good thing if the mine did some work on the pavement, he thought. A gang of blacks could sort out the rough patches with a roller in a couple of days. 'Where to?'

'She's been stolen!' the woman screamed at him as she pushed away from Mrs Bernstein. 'The natives ... they've taken my baby!'

'Natives?' Mr Mathieson was unsure what to say next so he put his hat back on his head. 'Aye.'

'Give me my baby! Please, give me my baby!' The woman had run down the street shouting. She was hysterical.

'Well?' Mr Mathieson turned to Mrs Bernstein helplessly. 'Do you not think you should go after her, Mabel?' He looked at the stranger from England who'd stopped at the end of the street. She stood motionless and silent on the red sand of the road as it disappeared into a fringe of buzzing brown bush.

'And say what?' Mabel Bernstein peered at the dumbfounded Scotsman from under arched pencil eyebrows and her breath seeped out slowly. There was nothing to say. The woman was moving back to them.

'When the wee bairn was left, was there nobody else around?' Mathieson tried to ask an intelligent question.

'Nobody,' Mrs Bernstein assured him. She'd forgotten all about Rebecca Conrad. She was looking directly at the deserted bike that leaned against the pillar outside her shop as she spoke, but she'd forgotten.

The baby was sound asleep in Rebecca's arms as she leant against the side of the open carriage door. Her left leg dangled over the wooden edge and her eyes moved carefully over its face. The tiny pert nose twitched as a fat fly buzzed too close and Rebecca pulled the warm bundle of life closer to herself.

'I love you.' She rubbed her cheek against the fluffy tuft of blonde hair on the baby's head. 'I always wanted a baby b –' She stopped. Her hand lifted the skirt of the lace nightdress, revealing the edges of a towelling napkin underneath it and quickly she peeked inside.

'– sister.' Leaning her head back against the hard wood of the carriage, Rebecca's mouth spread into a wide smile. The world, until that moment a planet of cosmic loneliness, was, quite suddenly, safe.

'What time is it?' a man's voice growled, searching for its true pitch as it stirred between sleep and waking. 'Did the boy let you in?'

Wally Craine, the solitary policeman in charge of the Roan Antelope Copper Mining town, pushed a crumpled khaki shirt over his swollen belly. Tucking it into the short khaki trousers that hung perilously low on his behind, he eyed Mathieson heavily. 'I told Isaac I was asleep.' He held his breath as he pushed the two surviving fly buttons through fraying button-holes. 'Don't listen to a bloody word!' His voice blew out on the escaping air of irritation. 'Well?'

Mr Mathieson had never spoken to Wally Craine on a police matter before and found himself at a sudden loss for words.

'You wanted something, Jock?' Wally Craine wiped his hand over his bald head and brought it on down his nose with a sniff.

'In town.' Mathieson nodded towards the swinging gauze door that led out of the small police office and on down a dusty path to the road. The only decoration in the room was a Union Jack and he turned back to study it carefully. 'It's Mrs Jenkins. You know who I mean?' He pulled

5

his eyes away from the crisscross of red and blue. 'They just arrived from overseas.'

'A kaffir rape her?' Wally Craine's jowls fell back in a rubbery roll under his chin as he laughed.

'It's her bairn,' Mathieson called after the representative of law and order as he walked away with little interest. 'The wee bairn's gone, Wally, and she's fair certain the natives took it.'

'Then you tell her no black would ever touch a child. Tell her that and then check her neighbours didn't pick the brat up.' Wally Craine pushed his shirt into his trousers again, tucking his anger away with his stomach. 'She more than likely asked them to and forgot, Jock – they're always doing it.'

'She's gey upset.' Mathieson wondered how any man could let his body get so out of shape and pulled in his own stomach quickly. 'She's with Mabel in the shop now.'

'Mabel Bernstein?'

'She's waiting on you.' Mathieson had spotted a gleam of pleasure in Wally Craine's eye at the mention of the town's merry widow, and he jumped on it. 'It was Mabel Bernstein sent for you.' He pushed the gauze door open casually with his foot as he moved to go and the door swung closed on him.

'Mabel seeing to her, is she?' Wally Craine was clearly delighted and held the gauze back as he reached him at the door. 'You coming, Jock? We better see what we can do.'

'Got to get a wee rest in. I'm on shift.' Mathieson excused himself quickly. Women's business always disturbed him and today's was no different. 'They're at the shop, waiting for you.'

'Yeh, yeh, yeh.' The gauze door groaned as it flattened back against the wall to allow the policeman's large frame through. 'Want a lift?' Wally Craine kicked a metal Coke bottle cap out of his way as he stepped outside. 'You going home?'

'Thanks.' Mathieson side-stepped the rolling piece of metal with jagged edges. 'Aye.' He moved after him towards a battered Dodge motor car with the fading emblem of the Northern Rhodesian police on its door. 'You can drop me across the road.' He had time to return to the cool of the hotel verandah for another beer and he slid into the cracked leather seat with relief.

A long line of African women moved slowly down the railway line towards the old carriage and Rebecca pulled herself deeper into the shadows of her hiding place as she watched them.

'Maybe they live out there in the bush,' she said to the baby as she looked towards the end of the railway line. It came to a sudden end that was reinforced by a heavy wooden buffer, and the dense bush beyond plagued Rebecca with questions. She'd always wondered what lay deeper in the long dry grass and short trees, which twisted their branches together in a heavy canopy, conspiring to conceal their secret. 'That's why they tie their children on their backs,' she went on to the sleeping baby, dismissing her thoughts quickly. 'So they don't lose them out there in the bush.' She shuddered and pulled back into the dark of the carriage as the African women moved past the open doors.

Brightly coloured material was tied around their waists and bare black bosoms jiggled in the sun. With their backs rigidly straight, the women balanced piles of wood on top of their heads and some had babies strapped to their backs – wide-eyed babies who watched the world pass by from a great height.

A woman paused in front of the open carriage and as she leaned forward, Rebecca held her breath. In one movement, with the baby impossibly balanced on her back and the wood on her head, the woman swung the child under her arm, catching it in the curve of her elbow as it latched on to her breast like a rubber dart.

'Wow!' Rebecca exclaimed in fright as she remembered her own narrow escape, and pulled back quickly. The woman had turned and was looking at her. Her look was direct and unquestioning. What a small white girl with a baby was doing in a disused railway carriage was not her right to question.

'Hullo.' Rebecca smiled into the woman's dark brown eyes. They looked out from black velvet skin that stretched across high cheekbones with a wide flat nose between. 'Where are you going?' Rebecca asked, but the woman rebalanced the wood on her head and walked on in silence.

'We'll go home now.' Rebecca's voice was quite suddenly matter-of-fact as she stood up with the sleeping baby. 'They'll be back soon.' She knew her father would be home from the mine day-shift at three o'clock and her mother would return from shopping in Kitwe soon afterwards. 'I wonder what Granny Cat will say.' An image of the little old lady she adored jumped into her mind and she smiled in anticipation. Rebecca knew her grandmother would be pleased she'd found the baby at last.

'Mrs Jenkins wasn't in the shop long at all.' Having repaired her make-up with a fresh layer of pancake, Mabel Bernstein shrugged and her round white bosoms winked at Wally Craine, daring him to pluck the hanky from between them. 'Isn't that right?' She turned towards Mrs Jenkins, who sat distraught in front of ten large cartons of Ideal milk. 'Then it was gone – just like that!'

'Mmm.' Wally Craine tore his eyes away from the source of delight that held the hanky in place and turned to Mrs Jenkins. How English she looked. A bit of sun and a few pounds of flesh would help, he thought. 'You didn't see anybody else when you came in, Mrs ... er ...'

'Jenkins,' Mabel whispered.

Unable to speak through the throbbing pain in her right temple, the English newcomer looked up from swollen eyes and her lips trembled.

'It was only two o'clock. I'd just opened up.' Wally Craine's eyes sidled back to Mrs Bernstein and she took a deep breath to swell her bosom as she spoke. 'Exactly two, it was.' She held a flat box of cigarettes out to him. With a quick lick of her bright red lips she flipped the top open and he shook his head as she took one. 'Most of the town's asleep then.' The cigarette stuck to her bottom lip and wagged as she spoke while Wally Craine struck a match. Holding the flame low, he forced her to bend forward to reach it while pretending to count the daisies on the hanky. 'Thank you.' Mabel Bernstein took a long draw on her cigarette and blew the smoke into beautifully formed rings. They floated gently over his bald head as he peeled his eyes away from the glorious swell of her bosom. 'It's terrible to think of.' She examined the red circle of her lipstick on the cigarette tip and wiped a small flake of tobacco from the corner of her mouth. 'Thank goodness my children are grown up and off my hands.'

'Yes.' Wally Craine had been delighted the day the merry widow's last son had moved into the mine single quarters. 'Well,' he turned to Mrs Jenkins, tucking his stomach away as Mabel's eyes settled on him in an exquisite moment of interest. 'The pavement, you said.' He moved to the door of the shop and gazed into the heat outside, but didn't go out into it. 'You're certain nobody picked the baby up?' He wondered if Mabel would be free for a drink at the mine club later and turned to her with a smile. 'It's not something that's happened in town before. That right, Mabel?'

'I don't believe it.' Wally Craine's thoughts were pushed abruptly aside by the anger that had exploded inside the thin Englishwoman. 'My baby has disappeared in this godforsaken town and you stand around talking rubbish while she's murdered by black people! By Mau Mau!'

'There are no Mau Mau here, lady.' Though Wally Craine was taken aback by her sudden attack, he leapt to the defence of the African people. 'I'm sorry, lady. Sorry for what's happened. But so long as I've lived here, I've never known a native to ...'

'What kind of place is this?' Mrs Jenkins' voice screeched as she stared at the overweight man in front of her. 'Back home, the police would have scoured the whole area by now. They'd have found my baby. She'd be safe!'

'Sorry about that.' Wally Craine could hardly control his anger and Mabel Bernstein was aware of trembling flesh pushing at his shirt-buttons. Comparison of the small African town's one-man police force with Scotland Yard was something she knew he hated and she took a long draw on her cigarette to calm her nerves. Holding Mrs Jenkins back in the doorway firmly, Wally Craine spoke very quietly. 'I'll need to get more details from you, Mrs Jenkins. If you'd accompany me to the station . . .'

'Get your hands off me!' The newcomer from England tried to pull her arm away but he held on to her tightly. 'Did you hear me? Let go of me, you idiot!' But Wally Craine wasn't listening. He'd suddenly noticed a small black bicycle leaning against the pillar and he knew who it belonged to.

'Isn't that the Conrad child's bike, Mabel?'

'What's that?' Mabel Bernstein stopped dead as she saw it. Her hand, tipped with bright red fingernails, moved to her face. Her eyes blinked against the stream of smoke from the cigarette between her fingers and she stared at the small black bicycle.

'Rebecca was in this afternoon.' Mrs Bernstein's voice was hushed in the stillness. She'd always known that child was peculiar.

'I'm not allowed to go under there, but I do,' Rebecca informed the sleeping baby as she carried it past four wooden railway houses. 'There's snakes under there.' The houses were built on stilts and the dark world underneath often served as a hiding place in times of trouble. 'My mother won't let me speak to the people who live there. They're Afrikaans, that's why,' she added. 'But Mrs Viljoen's nice. She gave me a *koeksister* once.' She looked towards the horizon of squat, flat trees which imprisoned her in the African bush. 'Granny Cat comes from where Afrikaans people come from. My mother too, I think. It's a long way away.' She lifted the baby higher on her arm. 'It's a wine farm.' Her arm was beginning to ache. 'Granny Cat says they've got horses there too, but I've never seen a horse.' She moved to the right, stepping off the foot-trodden path she followed as a long line of army ants marched towards her in formation. 'If you stand on a Matabele ant it stinks. I bet you didn't know that.' The long grass pricked at her legs and caught at her hem, pulling loose a long white thread that stretched behind her as she walked. 'And these ones! My dad says army ants could eat a person alive.' She drew in her breath with a hiss. 'The Africans eat ants sometimes – and locusts. I've seen them.'

Rebecca looked towards the wide dirt avenue of houses ahead of her. It was Z Avenue on which she lived, at number 123.

'One two three Z,' she told the baby. 'That's where I stay. We've got the biggest ...' The words dried in her throat and her legs froze in mid-stride. She was looking towards a square brick house with a red corrugated-iron roof. Beside it, towering over it and dwarfing the house completely was an enormous ant hill with a tree growing impossibly out of the top. But Rebecca wasn't looking at the ant hill. Although it was the most important place in her world, she wasn't looking at it. Her eyes had settled on two cars parked in the driveway of 123 Z. One was the Dodge belonging to Wally Craine, the policeman, and the other was Mrs Bernstein's Morris Minor.

Katinka Marsden had woken to find Macaroni the cook peering down at her from a gaunt dark face. The tightly curled hair on his head formed a pure white halo round his ebony face and his voice was gentle as he touched her shoulder. The old lady was very special to Macaroni. She was eighty-six, twenty years older than himself, and he held her in the deepest respect. He would never interrupt the afternoon sleep she took on the verandah each day unless it was imperative.

'Bwana Craine here, mama.' His words were gentle, nudging her from sleep.

'What time is it?' Katinka peered into the face that had welcomed her back into the waking world. 'What does he want, baba?'

'Bwana Craine say he want to speak to you.' Macaroni's dark eyes flicked towards the gauze that enclosed the verandah and Katinka stretched her neck to see through it. The group of three people waiting outside disturbed her and she rubbed her neck where it had stiffened in sleep.

'Is my daughter back yet?' Katinka was too tired to speak to anyone. Tired, and for some reason afraid. 'The bwana, is he back?'

'Nobody here, mama.'

'Where's Rebecca? She must be home.' Katinka screwed up her eyes to see the pocket watch that hung upside down from Macaroni's white jacket. She'd given him the watch for Christmas and he loved it more than anything else. 'She was in from school before I went to sleep. I'm sure she was: I saw her.'

'Rebecca out playing, mama.' Macaroni looked towards the white people who waited outside. They were muttering to one another impatiently and staring through the gauze directly at him. 'What I tell them?'

'All right.' Katinka tried to push herself off the sofa but looked up with a small shrug of defeat. 'Could you help me please, baba?'

Macaroni's strong dark hands moved gently under her arms and lifted her to her feet. She was as light as a feather and her tiny bones felt as fragile as birds' eggs under his hands. Waiting till she stood erect he dusted her dress where he'd touched it, as if wiping away any sign of himself.

'You ready now, mama?'

'Thank you.' Taking the walking stick Macaroni held out to her, Katinka looked up at him with a sudden twinkle in her eyes – eyes that shone brightly from a face darkened with age. 'Are you sure it's not *you* Bwana Craine's after?' she grinned. 'You done something bad, baba?'

Macaroni's shoulders lifted high as he chuckled and his voice rolled like warm liquid on pebbles. 'Not Macaroni, mama.'

Walking to the front door, Katinka leaned hard on the carved lion-head handle of her cane and she peered through the gauze flyscreen ahead of her.

'Hullo,' she smiled, nodding politely at Mabel Bernstein and the woman beside her whom Katinka had never seen before. 'Mr Craine.' She turned to him with a smile that couldn't disguise her curiosity and he looked down, clearing his throat. 'You wanted something?'

'Is Rebecca here, Mrs Marsden?' Mabel Bernstein had stepped closer and her wide pink tongue swept her lips quickly before she went on. 'She left her bicycle outside the shop.'

'She's such a forgetful girl.' Katinka wondered why it took a policeman to report a forgotten bicycle. 'When she comes in I'll send her for it.' She hadn't opened the gauze door that stood between them and Mabel Bernstein's face pressed against it in apparent astonishment.

'She's not in?' Her plucked eyebrows lifted and she glanced at Wally Craine knowingly.

'Nor's my daughter, I'm afraid. Or my son-in-law.' Katinka spoke through their silent look. 'But I'll pass the message on and Rebecca will fetch her bike. Thank you.' She turned to move away with the closed gauze door still between them.

'But I'm afraid it's more serious than that, Mrs Marsden,' Wally Craine said quickly.

'Pardon?' Katinka looked back at him blankly. His face was distorted as it pushed against the gauze and the look behind his eyes disturbed her.

'It's more serious than that, I'm afraid.' He raised his voice to ensure the old lady heard him clearly. 'You see, there's a baby missing, Mrs Marsden, and we have reason to believe Rebecca might know about it.'

'My baby's been taken from outside the shop and these people think she might have gone off with it,' Mrs Jenkins blurted out, pushing forward beside Wally Craine. 'They think she could help find my child.'

'She?' Katinka looked from one face to the other. Blank with tension, they stared back at her through the fine mesh of gauze. 'Are you looking for Rebecca or your baby?'

'Rebecca stole my baby!' Mrs Jenkins raved and Katinka's mind emptied. Voices droned in her ears but she was no longer listening. She was thinking about her tiny granddaughter, Rebecca. She could feel the anger and accusation aimed at the child and was at sea in great depths of despair. Stepping back, her hand went to her head, digging at the temple as if trying to force sense into what was happening.

'That child has never been normal.' Mrs Bernstein's voice broke through Katinka's confusion. 'Everybody in town knows Rebecca's odd – quite peculiar and not to be trusted at all.'

'How dare you!' Katinka was shaking with rage. Her body had drained of strength, about to splinter into a million tiny pieces.

'You only have to look at the child,' Mabel Bernstein went on as if the wall of a cesspool had cracked in her throat. 'I've heard what the teachers at school say about Rebecca. The whole town knows what she is. She's got no friends and she hangs around the railway line with natives all day, doing heaven knows what. Maybe she feels at home with them but we don't. We don't like it. Every time something happens round here we all know who's at the back of it.'

'Be quiet!' Katinka screamed from the depth of her heart, and the sweet smell of silence covered the stench of Mabel Bernstein's words. But the silence had come too late. Rebecca had heard everything from her hide-out on top of the ant hill.

She'd run round the back of Z Avenue and through the sanitary lane behind the houses. Slipping round the garage at the side of the house, she'd at last reached the ant hill and, clutching the baby tightly, she'd climbed as high as she could. Then higher, until she'd pushed herself up into the tree. There, from the safety of her perch among branches that held her above the rest of the world, she'd watched the three grown-ups talk to her grandmother at the door of 123 Z. She'd heard every spiked word and realised what she already knew – that these were the hushed whispers that passed between grown-ups whenever she was around. Whispers that said she was odd, that that was why she didn't have any friends in the small town.

Clinging tightly to the baby as it made a slight sound, she immediately felt better. She wasn't alone any more. She had somebody – a tiny somebody who snuggled against her for comfort. The sound of a car pulling up in the driveway attracted her attention and she looked down on the tops of the three grown-ups' heads as they turned and watched her mother climb out of the car.

'Hullo, Mabel, Wally,' Rebecca's mother smiled, nodding at the stranger who stood with them. 'It's Mrs Jenkins, isn't it? I've been meaning to ask you over for a sundowner. I'm so sorry I haven't got round to it.'

'Do you think I could have a word in private, Mrs Conrad?' Wally Craine said, and Rebecca craned her neck to watch his bald head between the branches of the tree. Everybody seemed suddenly tiny and she felt like a bird on a rooftop.

'Can I speak to you, Constance?' Katinka's voice called from the house, and Constance moved towards her, looking back at Wally Craine curiously. The silence from the tight red lips of Mabel Bernstein made her uncomfortable and the strain on the face of the newcomer from England disturbed her.

'Maybe we should all go inside.' Constance glanced back at the visitors as she moved to her mother in the doorway. 'What is it, Mother?'

'Get rid of them,' Katinka whispered.

'But . . .'

'Go on.' Katinka turned back into the house.

'What's going on, Mother?' Constance moved after her quickly. 'Will you please tell me what's happening,' she called as Katinka's hunched figure headed for the kitchen.

'May we come in?' But Mabel Bernstein had pushed her way inside the house with Wally Craine and Mrs Jenkins before Constance could answer.

'Oh.' She turned back to the people who'd crowded the house with their presence. 'Would you like tea? Macaroni — tea, please,' she called, confused by the strange scene that had greeted her.

'She there, mama.' Macaroni looked at Katinka nervously. Beads of perspiration had gathered on his forehead and his bare feet were powdered with dust. He'd been to see if Rebecca was hiding on the ant hill as Katinka had requested. 'She there,' he repeated quietly, and as Katinka's eyes begged him to answer her unasked question, he nodded. The child Macaroni had just seen high up a tree on the ant hill was indeed clutching a stolen baby. The small girl Rebecca, whose life was a series of lonely days punctuated by invasions of the kind he'd just witnessed, was in deep trouble.

'Take your time making tea, baba.' Katinka laid a hand on his black arm. 'I'll speak to Rebecca.'

'You not go up there, mama!'

'You think I can't climb an ant hill?' A familiar flicker of challenge lit Katinka's eyes and she went out through the back door.

As a slow line of steaming tea poured into a cup, Constance listened to the accusations coming from the people who'd barged into her home.

She was burning with rage. She'd brought Rebecca up strictly. Her daughter had been disciplined in every way possible, yet still there was an area of her child's life she seemed unable to control.

'Just because Rebecca's bicycle is outside the shop doesn't mean she's stolen your baby,' Constance tried to smile at Mrs Jenkins. She could understand how the woman felt but had to ensure she didn't think her daughter was in any way involved. 'Do you take sugar?'

'But where *is* Rebecca, Constance?' Mrs Bernstein looked at her with apparent concern. 'Surely you know where she is?' As she took her cup of tea a small slop dribbled over the edge of bone china and she smiled. 'I'll manage.' Mrs Bernstein remembered the cups. They were from England and she'd sold them to Constance the year before. She'd noticed that Constance Conrad never bought anything unless it was from England, and this had always amused her. 'Playing with her little black friends, is she?'

Constance hadn't missed the sharp edge of Mabel Bernstein's question, but she smiled into the face plastered with make-up. The shopkeeper was not a woman normally invited into the house for tea.

'I must say I find it quite extraordinary that I should arrive home to find such a commotion, just because Rebecca left her bicycle outside your shop. I can only presume that somebody actually saw her with the baby?' Constance allowed her question to hang in the silence for a moment.

'Well no, but . . .'

'No?' Constance's voice rose with indignation and she turned an ice-cold gaze on Wally Craine. 'David will be very surprised to find you here in that case, Wally. Very surprised.' She glanced at her watch as the policeman shifted uncomfortably in his seat. 'He's due home any minute so we'll wait, shall we?' Fixing each of them with a look of distaste, she added the threat of her husband's anger as she held out a plate of biscuits. 'I don't think he'll be pleased.'

'Rebecca?' Katinka peered up at the ant hill that towered above her. Twice as big as the house it stood beside and gripping a huge tree by its roots, the solid form of misshapen earth was a small mountain. Baked as hard as rock by a burning sun and pitted with deep snakeholes, the ant hill was a bizarre monument to millions of tiny ants whose spit and labour had built it over the centuries. Katinka had never seen anything like it among the gentle folds of the Cape of Good Hope and still she found it strangely disturbing. It was alive.

'Rebecca!' The old lady had caught sight of the child's skirt high in the tree and she cupped her hands to call again. 'It's Granny Cat, Rebecca.'

'I'm not coming down,' Rebecca's voice crept down the bumpy slopes of hard earth and touched her. 'Go away, Granny. Go away, please.'

'Are you crying, little one?'

'No!' Pushing away the tears that ran down her cheeks, Rebecca whispered in desperation as the baby opened its mouth to yell, 'Please don't. Please!'

'What have you got up there, Rebecca?' Katinka held her hand against the sun as she peered among the branches of the tree. 'My word – good heavens! Is that a baby?'

Rebecca bit her lip, bouncing the baby as it began to cry. 'It's Mummy's baby,' she yelled down to her grandmother. 'It's the sister Mummy told me she lost – *my* sister!'

Katinka closed her eyes as her mind jumped back to the last time there'd been mention of a sister for Rebecca. Constance had told her daughter that she was sorry, that she'd tried to give her a sister but had kept losing the babies.

'God,' Katinka whispered and closed her eyes. 'Lord, hold that little girl tight in your love.' Her prayer floated silently heavenward.

'It's mine!'

'Yes.'

'What?' Rebecca's puzzled voice pushed nervously at the silence that followed Katinka's unexpected acceptance.

'I said yes, Rebecca. I said yes, it's yours.' The baby had quietened and Katinka knew she had to keep Rebecca's presence on the ant hill a secret until the people had gone. 'Shall I send Macaroni up with a biscuit for you? We could warm up some milk for the baby too, if you like. It sounds a little hungry.' Katinka peered into the tree that reached halfway to heaven; her neck ached and her head felt dizzy. 'I'm not going to tell them you're there, Rebecca.' She turned away from the ant hill, balancing herself on ground that spun under her feet. 'Take good care of the baby, won't you.' Slowly Katinka walked away towards the back door of the house, aware that her granddaughter was watching her every move.

'It's going to be all right,' Rebecca murmured to the baby, stroking its face gently as she laid it in the curve of the tree to rest her aching arm. 'Granny Cat will tell them, you'll see.'

The short walk to the back door of the house seemed a million miles long and every year of Katinka's long life was carried on her back. An invisible weight held her spirit in the pit of her stomach and her body bent double under the darkness that hovered over her. She understood what Rebecca had done and she understood why she'd done it, but Katinka also knew there was not another person in the small town who would. They didn't understand her grandchild because she was different.

Like Katinka herself, Rebecca was darker than a white world could accept.

Macaroni watched Katinka silently as she moved back inside. Though his slow brown eyes were filled with questions he asked none.

'I'll sit with you in the kitchen till they've gone, baba.' Katinka patted him gently on his arm.

'Yes, mama.' Macaroni knew the old lady was protecting her grandchild from the violence of accusation he'd recognised among the white people outside. 'I make you a cup of tea too.' He led her to a chair at the kitchen table and placed a cup and saucer in front of her. 'It still warm, mama.' He took her walking stick and hung it on the back of the chair as she sat down.

The baby's nappy soaked into Rebecca's bare legs as she watched the three visitors leave. From her hiding place in the tree she'd seen her father arrive on his motorbike and it hadn't taken him long to get rid of them. Somehow he always managed to wipe out problems and she rubbed her nose against the tiny pink blob of the baby's to stop herself wondering if that was true this time.

'I said Daddy would make everything all right, didn't I?' she told the small wet bundle who held her very life in its hands.

'No, Constance, that's not what I'm saying,' Katinka looked up at her daughter as she stood beside her in the kitchen.

'Then what *are* you saying, Mother? That you don't know where Rebecca is?' Constance glanced at her husband in irritation. David was pushing his boots off in the doorway and Macaroni quickly picked them up, glad to find an excuse to leave the kitchen. 'For heaven's sake, what are you all trying to do? Tell me, Mother – are you trying to protect Rebecca or something?'

'Perhaps.'

'From what?'

'From you.'

'*Me?*' Constance stared at Katinka in amazement. 'You heard what Wally Craine said – it's possible Rebecca has stolen that baby. Don't you know what that means? For heaven's sake, wake up to what's going on here!'

'Constance.' David's voice was gentle but firm. He turned to Katinka. 'We must find Rebecca, Gran. I don't believe what they're saying any more than you do, but we have to find her to prove it.'

'It's true.' Katinka's words brought everything to a jarring halt and Macaroni stopped dead in the back doorway. With David's boots held in one hand, he backed out quickly, needing to disappear before the silence exploded.

'What did you say?' Constance's voice was very quiet as she leaned across the table to her mother.

'Rebecca has the baby.'

'*What?*' As Constance's voice reached for a scream, a line of hanging cups touched one another in a rippling scale of surprise. 'She's got that baby? Are you telling me you know Rebecca has got that baby and you've sat here denying it?'

'The baby's quite safe,' Katinka's body felt like lead and her tongue was cotton wool but she knew she had to protect her grandchild and forced herself on. 'It's Rebecca I'm worried about.'

'You tell me my child's stolen a baby, and then you ... What's going on in this house? Good grief, I go out for a minute and I come back to all this! Can't I trust anybody?'

'Stop thinking about yourself, Constance!' Katinka's sudden anger clipped her daughter around the ears and Constance stared at her in surprise. 'Your little girl has found herself a baby who she's decided is her sister. For years Rebecca's been looking for a sister, Constance. Looking for any one of the babies you told her you lost.'

'What babies? What are you talking about?'

'The babies you miscarried. The babies you told her you had "lost"!' Katinka peered into her daughter's eyes. She could see a deep well of fear behind them and knew that fear concerned her as much as it did Rebecca. 'That child's entire life is a lie, Constance – but all she did was believe you.'

'So she stole a baby?' Constance was astounded and her voice rang on a false laugh. 'What on earth has that got to do with me? What on earth are you talking about, Mother?'

'She believed your lie,' Katinka repeated.

'You think I should have told her my babies died – is that it? That they were all dead before they were born?' Constance's voice had cracked on the bank of a river of tears but she held them back. 'Is that what you think?'

'You should have told her the truth before someone else did.' Katinka snatched a quick breath. 'You should have trusted your child.' She felt dizzy but went on. 'Constance,' She put her hand gently over her daughter's as it lay clenched on the table, 'Listen to me.' Katinka's voice softened as she felt her daughter's tension. 'Rebecca doesn't know she's done wrong. She's not the monster those people say she is. She's lonely.'

'She steals a baby because she's lonely?' Constance's voice was quiet and ice-cold.

'And unloved.'

Pulling her hand away, Constance stood erect and challenged Katinka. 'Tell me where Rebecca is!'

'And what then? What will you do then, Constance?' Katinka's voice was a melody of hopelessness. 'What will you do to comfort your child in a world that hates her *because she's not quite white*?'

Turning abruptly, Constance moved to the door as Katinka's words uncovered the truth she herself had never faced.

'I know where Rebecca is. She's exactly where she is not allowed to go. Rebecca!' Constance yelled as she swung towards the back door.

'David?' Katinka's voice was soft but David understood the desperation behind her quiet cry and he moved after·his wife quickly.

'I'll fetch her, Constance.' He restrained his wife in the doorway.

'Don't listen to Mother, David. She protects her all the time. Every time something like this happens she . . .'

'I said I'll fetch her, Constance.' David spoke firmly. He knew Katinka had touched on a truth that concerned them all.

As David stepped through the back door, Macaroni looked up from where he was squatting by the garden tap, his long legs bent wide, bare toes digging into the hard grass. The brass spout ran water into a large pot Macaroni held under it and the water spilled over, dripping on to the square concrete base before twirling its way in a silver corkscrew down the drain. His lean body uncurling like a length of rope, Macaroni made his way towards the bottom of the garden: towards the small building that hid behind a wall of mango trees and that seemed suddenly essential to reach. The old man knew Katinka would be silently praying for her grandchild and he tilted his head back as his spirit found hers. Peering into the hot sky, he looked for the God the white missionaries had told him about.

'Great God.' Macaroni's words reached out majestically on his low African voice. 'Have mercy.' He added his prayer to the one he knew would be rising from Katinka's heart.

Standing still in front of the stool beside the piano, Rebecca felt the hard edge of wood that formed a flat circle into a seat. It dug into the back of her knee and she rubbed her calf against the curved wooden trunk of the carved elephant that supported it. Her arms were so tired she wanted to cry and her stomach clung to itself like an empty balloon, but she held tightly to the screaming baby.

Her father hadn't taken it away from her even when he'd reached her in the tree on top of the ant hill. David had admired the baby. He'd wondered if perhaps it was crying because it needed changing. He'd told her how often he'd changed her nappies when she was a baby, and how she'd screamed as he did so.

Even as Rebecca had slid down the ant hill on her bottom, even then her father hadn't taken the baby from her. He'd stayed beside her, he'd slid down with her – but he hadn't taken the baby away.

'Maybe I should change it.' Constance looked across the room at Rebecca with a tense smile. 'Then you could hold it and it won't cry. Don't you think that would be a good idea, darling?'

Rebecca kept her eyes down, clutching the squalling infant tighter as her mother tried to reason with her. The baby's face was red with anger and the soggy nappy dripped down her dress.

'This is ridiculous!' Constance was suddenly beside her daughter. 'Give me that child.' She snatched for it but Rebecca swung away quickly, holding the baby even tighter.

'Constance, stop it.' David moved to her quickly. 'Leave her!'

'You've tried it your way, David, and now she will let that baby go.' Constance made another grab. 'Give me that baby before I smack you!'

'It's mine,' Rebecca shouted, her eyes blazing.

As Katinka watched her daughter trying to tear the baby away from her grandchild, an ache dug its way from her back into her chest. 'Rebecca?' She forced herself to her feet. The baby roared in terror as it was pulled between them and David turned away from the horror that filled the house. He knew the agony his daughter felt but he didn't understand it. He'd spent hours of the time he was supposed to be sleeping before nightshift trying to convince the small girl that she was loved – that it didn't matter if nobody seemed to like her; she was special to him. But the baby his wife and daughter tore apart now represented only the yawning gap of unspoken truth that threatened them all.

'Will you give the baby to me?' Katinka stood firmly beside her grandchild and with the silent command of a look, ordered Constance to let the baby go. 'Will you give it to me, little one?'

Katinka watched the pulse in the small girl's slender neck throb as Rebecca turned away from her quickly, hugging the baby tighter as Constance released it. Dark wisps of hair stuck to her neck before falling in a mass of shining black silk over her face and her slim body heaved with emotion.

'I haven't held a baby since I held you.' Katinka leaned her face around to Rebecca's. 'May I hold this one?' She smiled into the dark moist eyes that had turned to stare at her. Tiny freckles spread in a crooked mat across the bridge of Rebecca's nose and her wide mouth was defiantly straight. 'It's very noisy, isn't it?' Katinka chuckled, covering her ears as the baby caught a fresh breath and let it out in another burst of anger. 'My word!'

'Yes.' Rebecca's voice was quiet. It was filled with failure and took Katinka totally by surprise. Rebecca was looking at her grandmother cautiously, unsure whether she could trust her but longing to.

'Are you certain?' Katinka didn't take the baby as she watched her grandchild for a flicker of assent.

'Yes,' Rebecca nodded. Her arms were tired, her back ached and her entire body shook. She'd come to the end of a dream and held the baby out to her grandmother in silence.

'Thank you.' Gently Katinka took the child and laid it across her shoulder, patting it on the back as she walked away. 'My, it's wet,' she said quietly as she moved towards her chair.

Digging her toes into the carpet Rebecca looked down through a moist film of tears and the pattern jumped at her in a jeering dance.

'You know that isn't your baby sister, don't you, Rebecca?' Constance was standing in front of her and Rebecca noticed dust on the toes of her mother's high-heeled shoes. She longed to brush it off. To throw her arms around her mother. To say she was sorry and be comforted. But she couldn't.

'I don't think we need go on about it.' David was wrapping his arms round them both in an attempt to wipe out the past. 'Why don't you have a wash and get changed, Rebecca. Maybe we could go out somewhere. We'll go for a drive – would you like that?'

'You do know it's not your sister?' Constance twisted her fingers through Rebecca's dark hair as she moved closer to her daughter. 'Do you know that, Rebecca?'

Rebecca did know. She'd always known. It was something she didn't want to admit but she found herself nodding as she looked into her mother's face.

'I didn't want to believe them.' Even now her words reached out for a denial of the stories she'd been told.

'Who, darling?' Constance drew on a deep well of love for her child, love she always held back in case Rebecca was snatched away as her other children had been. 'Believe who, darling? I don't understand.'

'At school.' Rebecca watched her mother carefully and quite suddenly she threw herself into her arms, whispering into the longed-for warmth. 'They said you only had dead babies.' Rebecca's voice was smothered in the folds of her mother's dress and Constance held her tightly as she wept.

'Shh,' Katinka murmured, her voice reaching for a slow lullaby to calm the baby in her arms. It was a Cape Malay lullaby she remembered from somewhere deep in a forgotten past.

CHAPTER TWO

Hard tufts of short grass dug into Rebecca's knees as she tapped a dry twig on the ground, her concentration centred on a small piece of matted grass. It was the secret lid of an underground world and she tapped the twig in the erratic movements of a grasshopper, her legs prepared for a fast retreat. Suddenly the grass lid flipped back and with a flurry of jointed black legs, an enormous spider grabbed the twig, tugging it under its fat body and going for the kill. From the distance that one leap backwards had placed between them, Rebecca watched in fascinated horror. Moving from foot to tingling foot, she clutched her skirt with clammy hands as the angry spider untangled itself from the twig. Ducking back into its hole, it snapped the trapdoor down behind it and a surprised grasshopper nearby stretched an angular leg in relief.

The garden hedge of 123 Z had become the walls of Rebecca's prison. It was eighteen months since she'd stolen the baby and she was nine years old. Though nobody had mentioned it since, the event had changed her life and only her short ride to school offered any escape. The world of railway sidings, wooden houses on stilts and the wide dusty street of shops were no longer hers, and Rebecca was more aware of her confinement that day than ever before.

The circus had arrived. In a blaze of colour it had come from a place beyond the whispering browns of her small world and she knew the tent would be rising from the ground at any moment. The swarthy people with a strange accent and secret dark eyes would already have claimed the bare patch of ground that spread between 123 Z and the church – ground she now only crossed in the company of her parents en route to the Sunday service.

Dropping back on to her bottom, she lay down and stretched her legs flat. Spikes of grass pricked the soft skin behind her knees and she watched

21

two fluffy clouds chase each other across an endless backdrop of sky. She heard the roar of a lion and imagined the huge cat pacing the cage which held it prisoner in the land of its birth. She longed to sit quietly nearby and watch the flurry of preparation, to see the handsome trapeze artiste swinging through the dry air before somersaulting to his feet. His partner always had the longest legs in the world and Rebecca wanted to be her, to be a part of the excitement which lay just outside her boundaries.

Tucking her hands palm-down under her head she pushed her body up in a back bend. Arched high over the ground she drew her feet closer and in short backward steps, moved across the grass.

'Hullo,' she said, as she spotted the upside-down image of Macaroni moving towards her. 'I didn't hear you coming,' she smiled at the tall man who stood on his head in the sky.

'Your grandmother she want to see you.' Rebecca spun through Macaroni's slow brown words as she kicked her legs over her head and stood up to face him.

'Did you see what I did, Macaroni?' She ran beside him as he led her towards the house. 'I can do a somersault too.' She watched her bare feet spread flat beside his on the warm stone paving that drove a straight path to the front door of the house. 'Like the clowns in the circus.' Her eyes sparkled as she looked into those of the man who kept his distance beside her. Never measured and never spoken, it was the official distance between black servants and their white employers. 'What's Granny Cat want?' Rebecca glanced over her shoulder towards the shouts of men hauling on tent-ropes. She could imagine the huge white canvas rising from the ground like a mushroom balloon. She could see strings of bright flags fluttering before snapping tight into bright triangles that stretched down from the peak of the tent. 'Are you going to the circus, Macaroni?'

'No, donna Rebecca.' Macaroni shook his head with the firmness of decision. 'Uh, uh!'

'Are you scared to go?' Rebecca asked with a teasing smile. 'You're scared, aren't you!'

Macaroni's thin shoulders lifted high as he chuckled. It was easier to pretend he was scared than explain. She wouldn't understand that he saw white people doing strange things every day free of charge.

'What have you been doing, Rebecca?' Katinka stood in the front doorway, peering at her through the gauze. 'I think it's too hot outside now, isn't it?'

'Yes, Granny.' Rebecca slipped through the door, allowing it to bang closed on the circus outside – the reason she'd been called into the house. 'Do you want a glass of lemonade?' Taking her grandmother's hand she led her across the red polished floor to the couch. 'I'll get you a glass now.'

Rebecca loved squeezing the enormous yellow lemons which appeared like magic on the tree, no matter how many times it had been picked clean. She'd push her hand under the food in the enormous icebox that stood in the pantry. She'd crunch the ice into a glass with white sugar, and then, when the ice and sugar formed a crunchy sweet pile on the bottom, she'd tip the pure lemon juice on top. She loved watching the mist which spread up over the sides of the glass before forming drops that raced down its sides.

'Won't you sit down for a moment?' Katinka asked.

'Why?' Rebecca turned back. Her grandmother seemed to get smaller every day. Though Katinka had told her that it was she who was growing, she didn't believe that. Rebecca had decided that people shrank before they died so they'd fit into a grave. 'Are you going to tell me about Bonne Espérance?' Rebecca loved hearing her grandmother's stories of her childhood, and she jumped on to the sofa beside her.

'What do you want to hear today?' The mention of Bonne Espérance had cast Katinka backwards through her life. It was a life still woven into the fabric of the place her great-grandfather Jacques Beauvilliers had built a century and a half before. Bonne Espérance, a prosperous Cape vineyard, was the home in which she'd loved her husband Jack and given birth to his children.

In her mind's eye Katinka could see the gracious curves of the driveway that led through an enormous white arch, cutting a path between vineyards that surrounded the Cape Dutch house sheltering at the foot of folding mountains. Red flagstone steps climbed to the heavy wood carving of the front door. Dark shutters held themselves back against rough, whitewashed walls, ever ready to snap wooden lids on watching eyes. Broad yellow-wood floorboards reached the length and breadth of a *voorkamer* – the entrance hall in which generations of family celebrations had been held under sparkling chandeliers. To the right and left, solid wooden doors opened into sitting rooms, kitchens, pantries and bedrooms that stretched back in two extending wings. Built on over the years, the bedrooms had housed the growing Beauvilliers family, and a steep wooden staircase led higher to an attic room, a tiny room that hid in the eves of the house. Tucked under the warmth of dark thatch, it hid the very heart of Bonne Espérance. And it wasn't the vineyards or buildings that drew Katinka's mind back now, it was that throbbing heart. The land Jacques Beauvilliers had cultivated so long ago, still fed the vines from the love he'd poured into it. 'The mother that never dies', as he'd called the red African earth, was still alive with the tread of his feet. It was as if the walls, earth and cobblestones had soaked up the Beauvilliers' lives and breathed them still. The air was heavy with the gasps of the sixteen-year-old slave girl, Eva, as she gave birth in 1820 to her half-caste baby, Jean Jacques. It echoed with the lonely cries of that son of Jacques Beauvilliers, and groaned with the hatred he'd hatched in the heart of his older half-sister, Clara.

Bonne Espérance endured. Over immense stretches of time it had survived the passions that had torn first a family and then a country apart. Housing the living with the dead, still it called Katinka back. She could feel her limbs strengthen as her mind coloured in the heavy greens of vineyards and purple mountains among which she'd once ridden bareback on her horse, Shasaan. Inside the hunched frame that sat beside her grand-daughter on a verandah in Central Africa now, that beautiful young girl lived on ... a woman whose body had trembled with the touch of Jack Marsden's hand.

'Go on, tell me about Bonne Espérance.' Rebecca's voice nudged Jack out of Katinka's head and, tucking the young girl she still was into the secret place of an old woman's heart, she smiled and millions of wrinkles pulled tightly round her eyes.

'You want to hear about Bonne Espérance?'

'Tell me again about the people who lived there when you were little.'

Katinka's long white hair was pushed on top of her head in a tight bun and Rebecca hoped she'd allow her to comb it while she listened.

'Have you done your homework? You know how cross your mother gets if you haven't done it.'

'Yup.' Rebecca knew exactly how cross her mother would get. 'Go on, Granny Cat.' She folded her feet beneath her and waited for a story that might lead her away from the circus she wasn't allowed to see. 'I'm listening.' Rebecca marvelled at the way her grandmother told stories. It was as if she took her by the hand and led her into another world, the world of Bonne Espérance that held so many dark secrets. 'You were telling me about that old lady – the bad one ...'

'Clara?' Katinka looked down at Rebecca as she leaned against her. 'Did I say Clara was bad?'

'She was.'

'Why?' Katinka wondered what the small girl had picked out from among the stories she'd told her. She'd tried to keep certain memories away, especially those in which Clara was 'bad'. 'What did I say to make you think that?'

'You said she didn't like that boy, what was his name? He was her brother or something.' Rebecca stared at Katinka keenly. 'You remember!'

'Are you talking about Jean Jacques?'

'Mmm.'

'He was my grandfather – like my husband Jack would have been to you. He was Jac[...]

'What's a half-[...]

'I was going to t[...]

'You don't want to[...]

'I was going to tell y[...] avoiding the shadows of n[...] sisters, you see. There was [...] remember, I told you she w[...] suddenly back at Bonne Espéra[...] forget, but couldn't. 'Aunt Em[...] Emily's face into her mind. All sh[...] from the thatched roof of a white ga[...] son alive.

'Maybe a glass of lemonade would be [...] [b]ack from the flames.

'What's wrong?' Rebecca peered into he[...] s face as she felt her body tense beside hers. 'Why won't y[...]

Katinka's eyes remained closed and a small bl[...] water found a route among the wrinkles, running a zigzag path to her chin.

'I'll get some lemonade.' Rebecca wiped her grandmother's tear with her finger and ran towards the kitchen quickly. She hated seeing her cry. They were leftover tears of those shed before she'd even existed. 'I'll put lots of ice in because it's hot today.'

Katinka watched her granddaughter slip away like a breath of wind. Since the day she'd stolen the baby and had been imprisoned in the house and garden, there was something very different about Rebecca. Like a tiny caged bird, she sat inside an invisible glass bubble, whistling to check if there was anybody left on the outside. But Rebecca had been locked away to protect her from that outside world. She'd become the focus of attention as the small town placed her in the centre of their quest for the devil's playground. It was a place Katinka knew well, and she wondered if it was time Rebecca learned that the world for which she longed was as hostile as her own.

'The war hadn't really touched our lives at Bonne Espérance, you see.' Katinka took another sip of the lemonade Rebecca had made and pushed a pip from behind a tooth on to her tongue. Carefully she removed it with the tip of a finger and, without a word, Rebecca passed it from Katinka's finger to her own. 'When the war ended, many of our Boer neighbours who'd been fighting came back to their farms.'

'Yes?' Rebecca wiped the pip on her dress. 'I'm listening.' Her words echoed in her empty glass as she stretched her tongue into it, reaching for

25

he English were fighting

nans?' She'd failed to reach the

alfway down the glass.

e recent war with Germany would achieve

War had. 'Suzanne Beauvilliers had become a

was Emily and Prudence's sister – English, like us, but

an Afrikaner called Thys Bothma. Oh, what a love story

he was Clara's sister, too.' Rebecca noticed that Granny Cat had left Clara out. 'The bad one,' she added, to remind her.

'Thys and Suzanne were separated so many times, it was as if their love was never to be – but it was,' Katinka smiled. 'Oh yes, it was.' She remembered her own love for Jack Marsden. 'Many years before they were married, Thys' father had been hanged by the British.' Katinka went on quickly: 'Emily told me once that Thys swore to kill every Englishman he ever saw when they hanged his father.'

'And did he?' Rebecca was most impressed.

'No.' Katinka couldn't help smiling as she remembered the one and only time she'd seen Suzanne Beauvilliers. 'Suzanne was very beautiful,' she chuckled. 'I remember when I was a little girl, she said I shouldn't go in the sun. I couldn't understand what she meant, because I didn't – my mother wouldn't allow me to.'

'Why?'

'The sun's not good for you.'

'But you look as if you've been in the sun. You look like me and I go in the sun.' Rebecca lifted Katinka's hand and examined it carefully. It was very brown, browner even than her own dark skin and she'd often wondered why.

'Do you want me to tell you a story or not?' Katinka pulled her hand back quickly, hiding it in the folds of her dress. The one thing she would never tell the child was why she had eventually left Bonne Espérance to join Rebecca's family in Northern Rhodesia. It had a great deal to do with whether she was brown from the sun or not . . .

'The fighting had been further north than Cape Town in the Boer War, you see,' Katinka went on, distancing them both from the colour of her skin. 'We'd heard of some terrible things.'

'Like what?'

'The British soldiers burned the Boer farms: they said they wanted to stop the women feeding their husbands. The Boers lived in the bush – they were guerrillas and they depended on their women for food. The British even put some of them into camps, like those concentration camps that were found in Germany. Thousands of women and children died in them, of measles and starvation.'

Katinka stopped as she heard an Afrikaans voice in her head. It was shrill. A man was yelling through the darkness as she pushed her way into a burning house to rescue her small son, Matthew. Pieter Bothma was screaming revenge for the death of his parents, Suzanne and Thys, and quickly Katinka retreated from the nightmare that still blazed in her mind.

'You remember Suzanne, the Beauvilliers sister I told you loved the Afrikaner Thys?'

'Yes, you just told me.'

Katinka took a deep breath, trying to pull the teeth of her memories. 'Well, one day when Suzanne was all alone, as Thys was far away on the land and their son Pieter was fighting with the Boers . . .' Katinka stopped. 'I don't think you want to hear this story.'

'But I do,' Rebecca pleaded. 'Tell me.'

'They say,' Katinka paused as she remembered the extraordinary tale that had spread through the winelands on whispers of wonder. 'Their love was so strong. They lived only for one another and no matter how many times they were separated, always love won. Anyway, they say that when the British arrived on their farm, Suzanne sent a young black man they looked after to fetch Thys from the land.' Katinka's hand pressed against her temple as she tried to keep her own searing memories at bay. 'It's such a strange story. Such a love story.' She paused and Rebecca watched in silence as Katinka's eyes grew puzzled. 'Suzanne brought two chairs to the front of the house. She sat on one and she watched as the British soldiers burned their house to the ground.' Taking a deep breath, Katinka sighed. 'She'd been very sick, you see. Suzanne was well over seventy – an old lady like me, that's what they said. Then, when Thys got back later that day, he found their house burned to a shell with Suzanne sitting quite still in her chair.'

'What did he do? Did Thys kill all the soldiers?'

'Suzanne was dead.'

Katinka fell silent and Rebecca stared. She was waiting for the story to continue but couldn't hold back any longer.

'But what did Thys do?' She urged her grandmother to go on as her imagination threw up an image of Thys riding after the British; to kill them all as he'd promised.

'Well,' Katinka paused again. 'They say Thys just sat beside Suzanne. Death had tried to separate them before, you see, and Suzanne was the very air Thys breathed, so he sat down on the chair beside her.'

'And?'

'He died.'

27

'What?' Rebecca's face was filled with disbelief. 'How?'

'The Lord took him.'

'God?'

'Yes.'

'But how? Nobody just dies. Not even God can just "die" somebody!'

'He stopped living.' Katinka nodded slowly. 'He couldn't live without Suzanne, so he just stopped.'

'But he wasn't burned! You said Thys was out on the farm when the soldiers set fire to their house!'

Katinka was no longer listening. She could feel the heat of flames herself. They were pushing her back. She was at the door of her own house on Bonne Espérance, and her small son Matthew was screaming inside. She could feel her oldest son, John and his sister Elizabeth pulling at her skirts to stop her and she could hear Pieter Bothma's voice over the roar of fire.

'God damn the Beauvilliers family to hell!'

As if God had heard him, an enormous beam, crackling with fire, had crashed down from the roof and barred her way to her son.

'I can't get to him! Flames − everywhere there are flames!' Katinka was screaming and Rebecca flinched in terror. Her grandmother was in another world. She was lost in a world of fire and she couldn't reach her.

'*My baby!*' Katinka's voice lifted on a long cry. '*Matthew!*'

'Granny Cat!' Rebecca blinked back her own tears. 'It's all right, Granny.'

'He said we'd killed his grandfather − his mother and his father. Pieter Bothma said we'd killed his family in the camps − his wife, his children!' Katinka's face filled with horror as she stared into the past.

'No, Granny. Nothing's happened. We're here, it's all right.'

'There was a knife. My servant, "I Titus", he leapt out of the dark at Pieter Bothma and he plunged a knife into him.' Katinka stared down at the verandah floor as if Pieter Bothma's body lay at her feet.

'I Titus killed Pieter Bothma?' Rebecca wanted to cheer. 'Good!'

'No, Rebecca. It wasn't good.' Katinka stepped back from the nightmare into which she'd slipped. 'They hanged him.'

'I Titus?' Rebecca was on the edge of her seat and she peered at her grandmother, demanding an answer. 'Why?' Her eyes flooded with tears at the thought of I Titus being hanged. 'Why did they hang him?'

'He was black.' Katinka's words were flat, as if closing the subject forever.

'But why?' Rebecca searched Katinka's face for an answer. 'He tried to help you. He saved you from Pieter Bothma!'

'Enough little one.' Katinka moved her shoulders in small circles, easing the tension that gripped her. 'Do you want to comb my hair?' She tried to change the subject.

'But I Titus didn't do anything wrong, Granny Cat.'

'Now come along, Rebecca. I thought you liked doing my hair for me.' She pulled a clip out of her hair and a lazy white coil rolled down her back. 'I shouldn't have told you that story. Your mother would be very cross with me.'

'Would they kill Macaroni too?'

'Rebecca, please!'

Though she struggled to hold on to the present, Katinka was back in the past once again. Her white neighbours were dragging I Titus towards a tree and she could see his family standing nearby. A young black woman with two small boys, watching in silent acceptance as a noose was pushed over their father's head.

'If Macaroni tried to save Mummy from a white man, would they kill him too? Would they kill Macaroni?' Rebecca rose to the defence of a black man hidden in her grandmother's past, as if knowing they shared the outer edge of a world reserved for others. 'Why did they kill I Titus?' She demanded an answer.

'You wouldn't understand, Rebecca. They were farmers, Boer farmers who'd been fighting a war.' Katinka couldn't explain the hatred she'd seen in the eyes of her Boer neighbours as they'd looked at her. Lynching a black man on an English farm was only a small part of its expression. A terrible sickness had spread through the land since the bloody war had ended. It had contaminated the soul of man and broken the neck of I Titus.

'They hanged I Titus and that's all there is to say.' Brushing the skirt of her dress though it wasn't dirty, Katinka brought herself firmly back to the present.

'But why?' Rebecca wouldn't give up. 'Tell me why.'

'That's enough, child!'

'Pieter Bothma killed Matthew because he was trying to kill *you*.'

'Did you hear me, Rebecca? I said, no more!'

'Why?' But Katinka kept her mouth firmly shut and Rebecca's voice, when it came again, was quiet. 'You said Bonne Espérance was beautiful.' Without another word she walked away.

'There'd been a terrible war between the Afrikaners and the British, Rebecca,' Katinka called after her receding figure. Her grandchild's back was straight and her head high. 'Men were scarred by that war. A lot of things happened that weren't right. Rebecca!'

But Rebecca wasn't listening and didn't come back. She'd overheard her mother and father talking in their bedroom only the night before.

They'd been discussing going to live on Bonne Espérance and Rebecca had liked the idea then. But now she'd decided they would have to go without her.

'The people in this town will drive me to distraction.' Katinka looked up as Constance banged her way through the front door loaded down with large shopping bags. 'Where's Rebecca?'

'Inside.' Katinka was looking down at the hands in her lap. Rebecca was right: age had darkened her skin as it had lightened her spirit.

'Do you know what Mrs Harrison said to me today? You know the one, Rebecca's teacher.' Constance dropped the paper packages on to a wooden chair, sitting down on the sofa beside her mother. 'She said it might be an idea if we sent Rebecca to a boarding school.' A flush of anger rose in her cheeks, as it had when Mrs Harrison had faced her. 'How dare the woman say such a thing. She was suggesting Rebecca had a bad effect on the other children – mine kids, with no more in their heads than getting out of school to the swimming bath.' She rubbed at a dirty mark on the sofa. 'When did Macaroni last have this cover washed?' Constance knew exactly why her mother was watching her with such a questioning look and she turned away. 'We will not go to Bonne Espérance, Mother. We've made our decision and it's final.'

'What about Rebecca, Constance? It's not good for the child to live like a prisoner.' Then, remembering her hair was loose, Katinka tried to push it on top of her head in an effort to gain assurance.

'What is it, Mother, is there something wrong?' Taking her mother's hair gently between her hands, Constance coiled it into a bun. 'Clip?' She took the one Katinka held out to her. 'Is it Rebecca?' She spoke with the clip between her teeth as she held the hair firm. 'Why do you look so unhappy? You're not sick, are you?' She fixed the clip into her mother's hair.

'I'm fine.' Katinka patted her daughter's knee. 'And no doctors, please.' She pushed herself to her feet, looking round for her stick as Constance held it out to her. 'I think I'll lie down for a while.' Turning away, Katinka moved to leave the room, tapping two brown bags on the chair with her stick. 'Dresses?'

'Mother, I must know if you're not well.'

'Dresses from England?'

'Just arrived.' Constance reached out to hold her mother's hand, keeping her back for a moment. 'You really don't look well. What is it?'

'Read that letter from Paul again, Constance.' Katinka moved towards her bedroom. 'I don't think it's an opportunity you should let pass by.'

As she watched Katinka hobble slowly away, Constance realised quite suddenly just how much her mother had aged. It was as if she'd let the brakes off on the downhill road to death and no longer cared. Pushing her shoes off, Constance opened her handbag on the floor. The letter her mother had referred to was inside and slipping it out between two fingers, she allowed it to swing sideways. Neat handwriting on the envelope addressed the letter to *Mr and Mrs David Conrad, 123 Z Avenue, Roan Antelope Copper Mines, Northern Rhodesia* and the handwriting belonged to Constance's nephew, Paul Marsden.

Paul was the son of her older brother, John Marsden; and John was Katinka and Jack's first child – twenty-four years older than Constance. She was what people in the Cape called a *laat lammetjie* – a late lamb, born after Katinka had lost their smallest son, Matthew. Many years later, John Marsden's wife Anne had died giving birth to Paul, and Katinka had brought him up with Constance like a brother.

That was, until one day in 1943.

Constance had gone down to Bonne Espérance for her brother John's funeral and there, on a Monday, she'd met Paul's new wife, Estelle.

'Nice to meet you at last.' Constance had held out her hand to the young woman who'd sat erect in a chair. It was the chair Constance remembered her mother always used. It had sat under a painting of Jacques Beauvilliers and his family for as long as she could remember, but now the painting had gone. So too had the heavy brocade curtains that had spread their warmth across the window all her life. They'd been changed for modern prints that Constance despised.

The house reeked of spirit and polish, each piece of furniture a monument to cleanliness. Laughter had vanished with the dust and the home Constance remembered with such warmth had been cool. Her mother, Katinka, like the heavy Cape Dutch furniture she remembered as a child, sat lost and alone in one corner.

'I'm sorry it had to be on such a sad occasion that we've met, Estelle,' Constance had added, remembering the look on her brother John's face as she'd last seen him in his coffin. He had seemed to be trying to tell her something. Trying to warn her.

'We thought perhaps your mother would be happier if she stayed with you up North.' Estelle spoke immaculate English although she was Afrikaans, and Constance noticed at once that she referred to Katinka as 'your' mother.

'Why?' she'd asked with direct challenge, challenge which swelled like a spring tide when injustice crept in. 'Mother's happy in Bonne Espérance, isn't she? At least she was when my brother John was alive. After all, Bonne Espérance is her home.'

'Not now.' Estelle's face had been strong and her dark hair tightly pulled back. 'Things have changed and she really shouldn't be here now.'

31

Constance had seen for herself how much things had changed in the country of her birth since the war with Germany had begun. Nazi sympathisers in the Afrikaner nation had risen against Jan Smuts and his 'English war'. Their own war against the British was still an open sore and the division between Afrikaner and British was wide. 'Politics have changed, you mean?' Constance had prompted Estelle. The newly formed Afrikaner government had determined to break all ties with the darker people of Africa. The whites clung tightly to the top rung of a newly built racial ladder, standing on the fingers of those underneath – people like Katinka, to whom colour had clung.

'Does my mother embarrass you?' The English arrogance behind Constance's voice had tweaked at the still-raw nerves inside Estelle as she'd dared her to answer.

'If you want your mother to be happy, I suggest you take her away.' Estelle had walked out of the room without another word and they had never spoken since.

But now Paul's letter offered Constance a chance to protect her daughter from the small town that persecuted her. He'd asked them to come back to the Cape and run Bonne Espérance. He and his wife were moving to the Transvaal and had no interest in the family vineyard any longer. But Constance could not say yes: there was no way she would allow her mother to walk in the shadow of such evil again.

'Are you going to try them on?' Rebecca's voice tapped Constance on the shoulder as she stepped into her mother's bedroom. 'Can I watch?'

Rebecca loved to watch Constance try on the new dresses which arrived from England once every six months. She loved the smell of the material and the pleasure in her mother's eyes as a dress nipped neatly into her waist to hang perfectly just below her calves.

'Why is it that only the English can make decent dresses?'

'But you make me lovely dresses.' Rebecca stood beside her mother as she looked at herself in the full-length mirror. 'This one used to be lovely.' She held up the limp skirt of her own dress. 'I remember when it came nearly down to my knees.'

'You haven't been out today have you, Rebecca?'

'No.' Rebecca threw herself backwards on the big double bed. Pushing the pillows apart, she dropped her head between them and pulled the soft corners over her face to avoid the question. 'It's dark in here,' her voice struggled through a mouthful of pillow.

'How's school?' Constance wanted to know if Rebecca was in any way to blame for the teacher's comments. 'You are being good, I hope.'

'Of course.' Rebecca pushed the pillows away from her face, tossed

one to the bottom of the bed and jumped on it. 'I don't speak to anyone.'
Her elbows sunk into the soft feathers as she cupped her chin in her
hands. 'Just like you said.'

Constance's heart sank. No child should grow up in a silent town and
she knew her mother was right.

'Do they speak to you?' she asked carefully.

'Nope.'

Pulling the dress over her head quickly to hide the sudden hurt she felt
for her child, Constance turned away.

'Your strap's twisted.' Rebecca leapt off the bed and straightened her
mother's brassière strap. Her back was pure white, smooth as satin and
without a mark. 'How did Granny Cat get brown like she did when she
didn't ever go in the sun?'

'People always go darker when they get old.' But Constance didn't
want the subject opened and pulled another dress out of the packet
quickly. It was pale green. The material had a sheen and it clung to her
hand with gentle pricks of electricity. 'Do you like this one?'

'Mmm.' But Rebecca wasn't looking at the dress. She was looking at
her mother's legs – at the nylon stockings that fascinated her, the way
they shone. There was a small ladder running up the back of the right leg
and she pointed at it. 'You've got a ladder.'

'Damn, that's the second one this week.' Constance bent over backwards and peered at the offending ladder.

'Are you going to change your stockings?' Rebecca hoped she would.
She loved watching her roll the nylon up her leg till it stretched tight and
firm. Then she'd push a white button at the bottom of her suspender
through a loop and it would go brown like the nylon. 'I think you should.'

'Nobody's coming round.'

'Daddy will be back soon.' Rebecca dived down the bed on to her
stomach and her toes ploughed into the pillow on the bottom. She didn't
want to look at her mother. She knew what often happened when her
father came home for a sleep after work. Constance would suddenly get
tired herself and for some strange reason her parents would bounce up
and down on the bed. Together. Quickly she jumped off the bed and
straightened the cover.

'What would happen if Macaroni killed a white man?' Rebecca asked
suddenly.

'What on earth are you talking about?' Constance smiled as she looked
at the green dress in the mirror. 'Macaroni wouldn't kill a fly.'

'If someone wanted to kill you and he tried to stop them. If he killed
them to stop them killing you.' Constance felt herself tense. She couldn't
understand why Rebecca was asking such strange questions and wondered

33

if there really was something peculiar about her child, as people said.

'I don't want you spending so much time at the bottom of the garden, Rebecca.' Rebecca knew her mother didn't really mean the bottom of the garden. She meant Macaroni's small house.

'Why?'

'Because I told you.' Constance pulled the green dress up over her head and the material smothered her voice.

'All right.' Rebecca decided she wouldn't argue and with luck her mother would forget what she was cross about. She loved sitting on her haunches in the small circle of sand outside Macaroni's house at the bottom of the garden. His *khaya*, as he called it. Though Macaroni's wife would sit beside her for hours on end, stirring a great pot of mealie meal, she wouldn't say a word. They didn't need words. They had something else that was altogether wonderful and silent.

'You did come straight home from school today, didn't you?' Constance glanced at her in the mirror as she straightened her hair and Rebecca decided her mother's golden hair was just like Suzanne's. Suzanne who had married Thys Bothma in the olden days. Suzanne and Thys who'd both died for no real reason, and whose son, Pieter Bothma, had been killed by I Titus.

'It's not right that a black man gets hanged just because he kills a white man.'

'Stop all this talk about hanging and see if Macaroni's pressed Daddy's clean shirt.' Constance wondered if she was going to have to think again about Bonne Espérance. 'Go on, there's a good girl.' She paused and changed her mind. There was no way she could ever take her mother back to a place where the seeds of fear sown generations earlier had blossomed into racial laws. 'Go on! Ask Macaroni about Daddy's shirt.'

Twisting the ball of her bare foot on the wicker mat in the centre of the red polished floor, Rebecca spun it, jumping off quickly before she ran out.

'The bwana's shirt in the cupboard, donna Rebecca. Tell your mother.' Macaroni was peeling potatoes in the kitchen and Rebecca pulled on the curling ribbon of peel till it snapped and swung between her fingers.

'Yuk! It tastes of dirt.' She yanked the potato peel out of her mouth and tossed it at the dustbin like a flying snake. It missed, and Macaroni nodded for her to put it in the bin.

'What would you do if you killed a white man, Macaroni?' Rebecca watched him over her shoulder as she tried to push the ringlet of potato skin off her finger and into the bin. The bin was full of peapods. They smelt nice and she picked one out to eat.

'Uh, uh.' Macaroni nodded towards the white enamel sink and the six peapods on the side that he always saved for her. 'They clean.'

Rebecca had noticed that Macaroni was avoiding her question so she put it differently. With the peapod disappearing slowly into her mouth as she crunched it, she looked him directly in the eye.

'What if . . .' Quickly Macaroni averted his look as he always did and she ducked her face under his, catching him. 'If someone — if a white man — was trying to kill Mummy, what would you do?' Macaroni's face didn't change and she realised she might as well not have spoken.

'Your mother not like you in the kitchen too long.' Macaroni tried to get rid of the small girl who always asked strange questions. 'Or in the sanitary lane.' He added strength to his words with the point of the vegetable knife in his hand. 'You want I tell her you ride home from school that way?'

'No.' Rebecca gulped at the stringy wedge of peapod and stared at Macaroni in horror as it settled halfway down her throat. The short ride down the sanitary lane on her way back from school was her only freedom and she could see it vanishing in front of her eyes.

'She be cross.'

'You won't tell her? Please!' It seemed a long, long moment before Macaroni's comforting nod calmed her and the frayed sludge of pod slid down her throat. 'What would happen if you killed a white man?'

'Go to jail.' Macaroni answered at last, knowing Rebecca never gave up once she asked a question.

'And then you'd be hanged!'

'I go to jail.' Macaroni glanced at her wide-eyed, trying to make her laugh. 'To King George's Hoteli.'

'It isn't King George's Hoteli!' Rebecca hadn't laughed. 'It's prison — where they hang people.'

'Food. Soft bed. No work.' Macaroni nodded his head from side to side with a wide grin.

'Rebecca!' Rebecca swung round as her mother called and, rushing to the kitchen door, she clung on to the handle and lifted her feet off the floor.

'If you were in Cape Town they'd hang you!' The door swung forward with her weight and she jumped round its swinging edge before it closed.

It was October, the month grown-ups called 'suicide month' although Rebecca had never understood why. To her it was the most exciting month in the year as everything waited for the rains to break. She looked up at the heavy dark clouds as she rode home from school on her bike and a streak of lightning drew a jagged yellow line through them. Six slow counts behind it came a thundering roll and she decided she had plenty of time to ride her special way. The rain was six miles distant.

Holding her feet high off the pedals, Rebecca freewheeled down the sand surface of Fifth street, glancing over her shoulder towards the low brick school. A crowd of children she didn't speak to, and who didn't speak to her, were riding out a long way behind. They wouldn't see her, she decided, and quickly pulled the handlebars left, bumping down into the sanitary lane she loved so much. She hadn't noticed the fourteen-year-old girl in straight pigtails who'd hidden behind a tree to watch.

With a jerk of her elbow, Rebecca swung her school satchel under her arm and hitched it higher on to her back as she rode the bumpy path. A pencil slipped through the gap in the cardboard lid of the satchel and hid under a jutting rock in the ground, but she didn't see it. It had her initials engraved on it: R.O.C. The O stood for her middle name, Olivia, which she hated.

The sanitary lane was crowded with Africans. Some were on lunch-break from the houses on either side of the lane and others were gardeners from the same houses. The rest were simply a part of the colourful marketplace erected between rows of toilets and showers. It was these Africans her parents constantly warned her about. They belonged nowhere and because of that they were uneducated and untrustworthy, they told her. But Rebecca knew differently. They were businessmen. Well educated in the finances of sanitary lanes, they brought their wares to sell to those who had no time to shop. On their heads they carried large baskets of fruit, enormous sacks of mealie meal and large bags of sugar. Spooning the sugar into sheets of old newspaper for their customers, they'd twist it into sweet powder bag bombs and Rebecca always longed for one to explode. The men also had birds sometimes, live birds they caught to sell at the high price of one shilling and sixpence – more pocket money than she got in two months.

'Can I see that?' Rebecca pulled her bicycle to a skidding stop. A tall African man sat on the ground with a round basket of fruit held between his knees and long khaki trousers reaching up to a bare black chest. She nodded at the small bird he held tightly in his hand. One wing stood out strangely and the bird squawked in terror as the man gesticulated during an argument over the price of sugar, ignoring Rebecca. But the bird's eyes had fixed on hers with a plea for help and her heart reached out to it.

'Let me see.' She held out her hand with a smile, one she hoped would convey her intention to buy the bird. 'How much?' She was scared but wanted to save the creature. She knew her father could fix its wing and then he'd let it go free as he always did. 'Can I have it?' she asked through a slow rumble of distant thunder.

'*Hayi Khona.*' The black man shook his head, pulled the bird closer to his chest and waved her away. '*Foetsek,*' he muttered under his breath, and Rebecca wondered if he'd even heard the bird's cries.

The rubber handlebar grip of Rebecca's bike dug into the dirt as she dropped it on the ground, approaching him with another sweet smile. Her eyes were fixed on the bird and her heart thumped so loudly she was scarcely able to speak.

'*Mina Funa,*' she pointed at herself as she spoke in Chicabunga. It was the language used between white masters and black kitchen servants, but not in hers. Macaroni spoke English.

'*Hayi Khona!*' The African shook his head at her request for the bird and turned away towards another African, shouting at him in machine-gun Chibemba.

'Hey, Ladiwell.' Rebecca recognised the man he spoke to as the gardener her father employed when he was sober. 'Ladiwell,' she moved closer to the man who sat on his haunches in front of a large wooden bucket of frothing African beer, 'it's me. Hi!' Rebecca knew she'd cornered him the moment he pushed the bucket behind him and sat on it, grinning innocently as he held an open tin can in his hand. 'Tell that man I want to look at his bird,' Rebecca pointed at the man in question.

'Uh, uh,' Ladiwell shook his head. His beer was hidden beneath his backside and he felt quite safe with a tin labelled *Clingstone Peach Halves* in his hand. '*Hamba.*' He waved at Rebecca, ordering her to leave their territory.

'*Wena hamba!*' Rebecca glared at him, not noticing the white girl with straight pigtails who stood at the top of the sanitary lane spying on her. '*Wena hamba!*' she repeated, telling Ladiwell to go away himself and poking at the bucket beneath him with her toe. 'I'll tell the bwana about the beer you're drinking.'

'*Hayi Khona!*' Ladiwell jumped off his bucket of beer, pushing it clear to the other man's feet. 'Not Ladiwell beer. *Hayi Khona!*'

'I can smell it,' Rebecca challenged him. 'Why won't he let me see the bird, anyway? It's a scrawny-looking thing. Nobody would buy it 'cos it would be bad when they got home, and then they'd eat it and they'd die too.' She didn't care if the Africans understood what she was saying, but added just to worry them, 'Then you go to King George's Hoteli – all of you. You'll all go to jail.' She made an enormous gesture that included everyone and turned back to the trader in charge of the bird. '*Wena hamba King George's Hoteli.*'

But the man stared back at her silently. He was looking directly into her eyes and quite suddenly Rebecca was afraid. No African had ever looked directly into her eyes before.

'Uh, uh!' Ladiwell kicked the man in his side, shouting at him in Chibemba. His look had obviously worried Ladiwell too but the African man said nothing as he pushed Ladiwell to one side and moved towards the toilets nearby. A wide trickle of smelly water ran across the concrete floor of the toilets to form a small stream that found its way down the step, circling back to seep under the fence into the garden of 117 Z Avenue.

'Hlala!' Urging the African to wait, she grabbed his arm before he disappeared into the toilet and at that moment a shaft of lightning lit the sky. She still hadn't seen the girl with skinny pigtails who watched from the top of the sanitary lane; she hadn't seen her nose twitch with disgust at the sight of Rebecca Conrad moving into a toilet with an African man. She wouldn't see the girl when she turned back, either. With pigtails flying straight behind her she had raced away to tell her mother what the evil Rebecca was doing now. She'd even picked up the engraved pencil to prove she hadn't made it up.

The African man was caught by surprise as Rebecca's white hand on his arm was lit by lightning. Relaxing his grip on the squawking bird, he tried to duck out of her reach but, quick as a flash, she grabbed the bird. Running to her bike, she yanked it up and, dragging it behind her, she tore away towards the back garden of 123 Z. Africans shrieked after her in a mixture of delight and shock. Their hands flew to their faces and their eyes opened wide shouting their warnings in English and Chibemba, as the black trader made to hold Rebecca off her bike, Ladiwell trying to hold him by the top of his pants before he broke free.

Heaving her bicycle over the ditch between the sanitary lane and her own back garden, Rebecca squeezed herself through a small hole in the hedge as he chased her and the whole world shook with thunder. Racing on to the house with the bird clutched to her body, she pushed through the swinging back door. She knew her father would be sleeping for his nightshift on the mine hoist, but she had to wake him. Things had gone badly wrong. The tall African man who'd looked her directly in the eye had shoved through the hedge after her, and his anger screamed louder than the thunder.

'Wake up!' The bird pecked Rebecca's finger as she held it tightly, shouting at David again as she heard a loud banging on the back door of the house. 'Daddy, please wake up!' She shook him in terror.

With a bird in his face and thunder rattling the gauze of the window, David stared at his daughter in the confusion of disturbed sleep.

'What time is it?' He looked at the clock, certain it couldn't be time to get up. 'What are you doing with that bird, Rebecca? What's all the noise?'

'He was going to kill it!'

'Who?' David lay back on the bed to sort out what was happening as the loud shouts of the African man reached into his mind.

'I found the bird. It's hurt.' Rebecca spun round to the window as the man's voice grew closer. He was just outside. He was screaming at her with no more than thin gauze between them, and her father was still half-asleep.

'Who's that?' David Conrad climbed out of bed, giving up the idea of more sleep. 'What do you want?' he called through the wire-mesh across the open bedroom window and the African shouted back in Chibemba. He was shouting at Macaroni too as he tried to pull him away from the house. 'Tell him I'm coming, Macaroni.' David understood the Chibemba language and he knew exactly what the man wanted. Turning to his small daughter he looked at her sadly. 'You were in the sanitary lane, Rebecca.'

'No, I ...'

'Rebecca!' David knew exactly what she'd done and gently he took the bird.

'Don't give it back to him, Daddy, he'll kill it!' Rebecca urged her father as he pulled his dressing gown on.

'Stay inside!' David left the room with the bird and quickly she ran back to the window. Through the gauze she could see the man whose bird she'd stolen and he was angrier than the stormy sky above him. Pushing Macaroni in the chest, he shouted for retribution. Even as David reached him with the bird in his hand, the African man's eyes blazed. The huge avocado pear tree that reached above them strained against a sudden howling wind, its branches threatening to crush them on the spot but the man's anger screamed on even as David spoke. Together they examined the bird and together they argued as Rebecca's father held out one shilling. Angrily rejecting it, the African shouted again but David stayed totally calm. Adding another shilling to the one in his palm he smiled and the man snatched it. But as he went, he shouted again. It was a shout so full of fury that Rebecca trembled as it touched her. Though she didn't understand what he'd said, Rebecca knew she'd never seen such pain before. She'd never before seen the wound a small white girl could open in the heart of an African man.

A little later, she sat quite still in the kitchen, watching her father fix a matchstick splint on to the bird's wing. Rebecca was enthralled. How calm the bird looked as it sat motionless in his hands, and how calm her father had been in the face of such danger. She adored him. Her heart was bursting with love for the gentle man who somehow always made things come right.

'Has he gone?' Katinka asked from the kitchen door. She'd been taking an afternoon nap when she'd heard the commotion in the garden.

'Everything's fine.' David looked up. 'When did Constance say she'd be in, Gran?'

'She's at the library, but she should have been back by now.' Katinka glanced at her watch and Rebecca hoped her mother would stay away a little longer. Maybe she'd get lost in one of the books as she read it. Her mother often did that, even in her homework books. She'd be asking Rebecca questions and quite suddenly she'd disappear inside the book itself. Lost. Trying to picture her mother in the tiny library with the only stairs in town leading up to it, Rebecca willed her to pick up a book and become absorbed in it. It wouldn't take long for her father to finish with the bird and then she could put it in a box in her room and her mother would never know.

'Rebecca?' Constance's voice carried the tone of trouble as it drew closer to the kitchen. 'Rebecca, where are you?'

'We're in the kitchen,' David called and as he reached the kitchen door, Macaroni changed his mind about coming inside. He'd heard the tone of his mistress' voice and knowing what Rebecca had done, he ducked away towards the safety of his own house.

'You were in the sanitary lane!' Constance was rigid with anger as she stared at Rebecca from the doorway. She was more upset than she should have been, Rebecca thought, and quickly she moved to her father for protection.

'I got this bird – it was hurt. But it wasn't in the sanitary lane.' She tried to pour safe words on her mother's temper.

'Don't lie!' Constance had moved right beside her and waves of anger spilled over Rebecca. Her mother had grabbed the collar of her dress and pulled her close to her face. 'Is this yours?' She pushed a pencil in front of Rebecca's eyes and she squinted at the three letters of her initials that warned her not to lie again.

'Yes.' She wished she could rub the letters out, especially the one in the middle that stood for Olivia.

'Go to your room, Rebecca.' David tucked the bird gently under his arm and stood up. The bird was still quiet, its bright yellow eyes looking from one to the other as if understanding itself to be the source of trouble.

'But I –'

'Go.' David gave Rebecca a small wave and her head bowed under the weight of guilt as she left the room.

'She was in that filthy lane with an African man, David. Can you imagine how I felt when Mrs Bekker shouted for me to stop outside her house? "Do you know what your daughter's doing now, Mrs Conrad? I doubt you would, of course. The shame of it! And in the sanitary lane!" Do you know what they all think of our daughter now, David? Do you know what they say about Rebecca when they see her with Africans in lavatories?'

The realisation that even a prison couldn't keep her daughter safe had hit Constance hard and anger crumbled into the confusion of guilt.

'Why does she do things like this? How can we control her? What should we do now?' Constance dropped on to a chair at the kitchen table and David turned away. He already knew what they were going to do and gently he stroked the bird's head with a finger as it closed one eye.

'We'll talk about it tomorrow, Constance.'

'No, now!' She looked up at him, begging for his support. 'We can't go on like this, we've got to do something. What makes her hang around sanitary lanes and Africans? It's not normal.'

'She was trying to help this bird.' David's voice remained quiet as he looked at his wife. 'I don't think there's anything strange about a little girl trying . . .'

'*They* know that, do they, the people in this town?' Constance dropped her head into her hands and her body heaved with released emotion. 'I can't go on any longer. I can't bear it!'

'Then go.' It was Katinka's voice and it was very quiet. 'In Bonne Espérance Rebecca can start again. You can, too.'

'Never.' Constance stood up abruptly. 'Don't mention Bonne Espérance ever again, Mother, please. I never want to hear the name of that place again.'

'Constance,' David called after her as she tried to escape.

'I will not go back to that place, David!'

'Can we talk quietly, Constance? I don't want Rebecca to hear us.'

Rebecca didn't hear. With her knees pulled up under her chin she sat on the verandah. She was trying to work out which child had seen her in the sanitary lane and she was chewing the end of the pencil, determined to eat her initials away.

A clap of thunder and lightning struck at once, scorching the verandah with a bright white light as the gauze blazed with sparks. Rebecca could smell the sweet scent of thirsty earth that greeted the first heavy blobs of rain and she longed to run outside. She wanted to watch the fat flying ants squeeze out of their holes, see them reach up in a mass of fluttering wings to grab a few moments of life before they drowned in the rain that had brought them. She longed to be high in the tree on the ant hill, daring the lightning to strike her dead. But Rebecca had sensed that even dead she would still be the centre of her family's problem and she lay back on the couch, pulling a cushion over her ears. Her parents were arguing quietly somewhere and she didn't want to hear any more about the problem she was. Their worried whispers all led to Bonne Espérance and the grown-up mystery that was buried there with I Titus.

'There's no point in pretending any more.' David had sat Constance down on a chair in the sitting room and he spoke quietly. 'We can't go on like this – not Rebecca, nor any of us.'

'What about Mother? I can't take *her* back to Bonne Espérance,' Constance argued.

'Your mother wants to go, Constance. It's her home.'

'She's just saying that because –' Constance tried to swallow her tears as David lifted her face to his, his eyes filled with the gentle care that always comforted her. 'What are we going to do, David? How can we protect our child?' She was completely broken and wept openly as he held her.

'Our tickets are booked.' David's words were quiet and matter-of-fact, and Constance stared at him in blank surprise. She looked from him to her mother, Katinka, who was standing quite still in the doorway, smiling and nodding.

'I gave my notice in six months ago, and we leave for Bonne Espérance on the twenty-fourth.' David looked down at the small bird which sat quietly in his hand, both wrinkled eyelids now tightly shut. 'I guess I had better see to you.' He moved away to find a box in which he could keep the small bird safe until it was ready to fly free.

Pulling the cushion out from under her, Rebecca giggled as her head dropped back on the couch with a thud. At last her parents had stopped whispering and she'd planned her own sweet revenge. She'd decided that when she went to school the next day she'd leave notes everywhere. They would say that someone in the school stole pencils from sanitary lanes and that somebody else knew who that somebody was!

We are in the very heart of darkness.

The words were written in a large leatherbound diary and above them was a date: *21st August, 1878.* Katinka held the old book very carefully, reading it by the small lamp at her bedside. She'd read it many times before and though her eyes could hardly see the words, her mind ran through them easily.

Why is it men speak abusively about things they don't understand?

Emily Beauvilliers had written the words on the night Katinka's father,

John Westbury, had been murdered during a political meeting. But they could have been about that very Tuesday in 1951, Katinka thought – about her granddaughter, Rebecca. Was it really seventy-three years? she wondered. She could still smell the fear of that day on Bonne Espérance.

How is it that Katinka, a mere slip of a girl, has been able to draw on such a deep well of forgiveness?' Emily's handwriting continued. *Forgiveness is God's greatest gift. Father once told me my mother had said that.*

'Jacques Beauvilliers.' The name of Katinka's grandfather slipped in a gentle whisper from her lips and she looked towards the dark gauze that stretched across her bedroom window. A tiger moth, big as a bird, battered against the gauze as it tried to reach the light of the lamp beside her. There was such light in forgiveness, Katinka remembered. Light that had wiped away her tears and brought peace.

Closing the diary, she watched the heavy pages flop lazily one on top of the other till their yellow edges clung tight, as if aware of the secrets they held. Secrets which must never be lost to the descendants of those hidden between the worn leather covers. Now her family were going back among those same people and there was much still to forgive on Bonne Espérance. Rebecca must keep Emily's diaries, Katinka decided and, pushing the old book on to the bedside table, her fingers reached for the switch to turn out the lamp. The heavy brushing on the gauze stopped and, as if its life depended on light, the moth spread its wings wide and clung flat.

CHAPTER THREE

Though Bonne Espérance hovered on the horizon of the next day and the house was emptying in front of her eyes, still Rebecca didn't believe they were leaving.

'*Hayi Khona!*' the large white man with a leather face yelled as his gang of four African men struggled to lift the Bendix washing machine off the kitchen floor. '*Yini lo ndeba for ka wena!?*' He demanded what was wrong with them. Wiping the sweat from his brow he pushed his grubby hanky back into his shorts' pocket and it waved at the floor like a dirty cotton flag.

'*Fanakalo!*' He showed them how to lift the machine in an over-acted mime.

'Did you remember that it's bolted to . . .?' Rebecca broke in as she watched from the kitchen door.

'Go away, girlie,' The man in charge of their household removals waved his dirty flag at her and prepared to wipe his brow again.

'You did remember to strap the drum securely, did you?' Constance asked as she leaned over Rebecca in the doorway. She balanced a pile of books on Rebecca's head and Rebecca peered up at them with the touch of her mother's soft body against her back.

'He's forgotten about . . .'

'Yes, lady,' The man from Ndola brushed away their interruptions, wondering what made women so untrusting and blacks so stupid. '*Thatha lupha!*' He indicated that the Africans should grip the machine under the edges of its base. '*Lupha!*' He pointed to the rusty base once again.

'Ask him if he remembered it's bolted to . . .'

'He just told me he remembered, Rebecca. Now please don't get in the way.' Constance moved off with the books.

'OK.' Taking a slight breath, Rebecca parked one bare foot on top of the other and folded her arms. She couldn't think of anywhere more interesting to be.

'Right?' The white man tucked his shirt into his short pants and shouted again. '*Hamba!*' He gave the gang of labourers their starting orders and obediently their long black fingers curled under the rusty edges of the Bendix washing machine. The palms of their hands pressed hard against the white enamel sides. Their shoulders strained, biceps rose, gleaming black slabs of muscle on their backs quivered and Rebecca put her hands to her ears. She'd heard the sound of tearing metal long before the white enamel casing of the machine lifted free of the base which was bolted firmly to the floor.

Nobody moved in the silence that followed. Obediently the Africans held the empty casing in their hands and looked at their boss for further instruction. But the man with the leather face didn't say anything. The drum of the washing machine was carefully laced to the engine on the base and rubber hoses reached like hollow snakes for the casing which had been so suddenly torn free. A hard dry ball of child's sock bounced down the outside of the dimpled drum and Rebecca exploded in a spray of spit and laughter.

'That's the sock I lost.'

'My washing machine!' her mother screamed. A pile of books tumbled at Rebecca's feet and, clambering over them, she ran outside before her giggles pushed their way through her nose in rubbery streamers. 'You idiot!' Constance yelled as she stared at the remnants of her washing machine from England and, dropping everything, the Africans fled after Rebecca. In silent panic they crowded round the water tap outside, crumbling in terrified laughter as Rebecca hiccuped.

'*Kom hierso!*' The leather-faced man yelled for them to come back, carrying the blame in the palm of his hand and ready to swipe it across their faces. 'Bloody Munts,' he called to Constance, unprepared for the attack about to be launched on him in the doorway. 'Amos!' he yelled as her fists landed on his head in a flurry of blows.

But Amos had backed away to Rebecca and, tripping over the brass tap, he shook his head with a nervous laugh.

'No, bwana.'

'You idiot – you *stupid* idiot!' Constance's words hailed down on the head of the man from Ndola as hard as her blows. 'You'll pay for this, you imbecile!'

Rebecca wiped the last glueball from her nose on to her skirt and turned the brass tap on with a smile. There was no way her mother would go to Bonne Espérance without her Bendix washing machine from

45

England, and happily she swallowed mouthfuls of cool water to stop her hiccups.

'And then there's the horses.' Rebecca sat on a blanket spread over the grass beside Katinka's chair and listened as her grandmother tried to make Bonne Espérance sound appealing.

'How many horses?'

'Lots.'

'How do you know I'll like horses when I see them, anyway?' Rebecca threaded her toes through the woollen fringes on the blanket's edge. 'Maybe I won't like horses at all.' She pulled her toes through the soft wool ropes, determined not to give in and Katinka poked her walking stick into Rebecca's side.

'Do you know, I spent every day on my horse, Shasaan. My husband Jack and I would ride for miles through the vineyards.' From the corner of her eye Katinka had spotted that Rebecca was listening, no matter how she tried not to. All her grandchild had ever seen was photographs of horses and all she wanted was one of her own. Tsetse fly made it impossible to keep one in Northern Rhodesia but Bonne Espérance was different.

'When we get there you'll see the horses for yourself,' Katinka promised.

'I told you, I'm not going.' Rebecca lay back and, holding her legs straight in the air, she counted her toes against the sky. 'I'm staying here with Macaroni. I'm going to sell peanuts from Macaroni's Coca Cola stand. Roasted peanuts.' She wondered why her knees were as knobbly as the leftover bone of Sunday's roast lamb and examined them carefully. Unfortunately, the washing-machine disaster hadn't been the answer from heaven that she'd expected it to be. Her father had simply promised her mother a new one from England and desperately Rebecca had hunted for another way out.

'See,' she pointed to her knees. 'I couldn't ride anyway. Look!'

'At what?' Katinka peered at the leg. 'Where?'

'There.' Rebecca lowered her stretched leg in front of her grand-mother's face. 'You see my knees? They're knobbly.'

'There's a hair.' Katinka had caught sight of a single fine hair on Rebecca's suntanned leg. 'You're growing into a woman.'

'Never!' Rebecca rolled on to her stomach in case Katinka looked under her arms for more signs of womanhood, wondering if that single hair was responsible for the decision to go to Bonne Espérance. 'Who'd teach me to ride, anyway? If I even wanted to ride a stupid horse, that is.'

'Luke will teach you.'

'Who's Luke?' She peered under her arm at Katinka. The name had sent a tingle through her body and she didn't know why. 'That name's

46

worse than Olivia.' She pushed a sudden and very strange sensation in her body away as quickly as she could.

'It's a nice name. And Luke's nice, too.'

'Bet he's not.'

'You'll like him.'

Katinka leaned back in her chair and Rebecca dropped her face into the blanket, trying to breathe through it. 'How can I like him?' She came up for air. 'You can't like someone you can't play with.'

'Why not?'

'Don't be silly, Granny Cat.' She rolled over and looked keenly into Katinka's face. 'How can you like someone if you can't talk to them? You know I'm not allowed to talk to anyone.'

At last Katinka had the answer and with a smile she pushed a fine dark hair away from Rebecca's eye. 'Who says you can't play with these children?' Rebecca's mouth dropped open and the crooked eye-tooth her mother worried about stuck on her bottom lip. 'Of course you can play with Luke. You can play with all the children.'

'All?' Rebecca had stopped breathing and she stared at her grandmother in silent amazement.

'There's Luke, and there's Naomi, and there's Simon – well, perhaps not Simon.' Katinka peered at Rebecca as her face turned bright red. 'Are you all right?' Rebecca's held breath escaped in a burst and she jumped to her feet.

'I'm still not coming to Bonne Espérance.' She ran away quickly. She needed privacy to think about things like friends. About Luke, Naomi and Simon. She had to be in her special place on the ant hill to decide if Luke, Naomi and Simon were part of the grown-up mystery of Bonne Espérance. Especially Simon. Simon who had 'perhaps not' in front of his name.

'Rebecca,' Constance called as she stood at the front door. She could see her mother in the chair she'd put her in out of the way, but Rebecca was nowhere.

'She'll be back in a minute,' Katinka replied quietly, knowing that at last she'd aroused Rebecca's interest in Bonne Espérance.

'Where is she?' Constance scanned the large square garden for her daughter.

'Up the ant hill. Thinking about something.' As Constance reached her chair, Katinka felt her tense and gripped her daughter's arm. 'Let her be, darling.' Constance had looked towards the ant hill, spotting Rebecca's leg dangling over a branch of the tree and Katinka patted her hand. 'She'll be fine and you must be tired with all the packing.'

'I am.' Constance rubbed her neck.

'Do you know, I'm really quite excited.' Katinka tried to convince her daughter. 'It's been eight years since I saw Bonne Espérance.' She held a long-distant memory of her home close to her heart and didn't want to go back to find it shattered. But she smiled. 'Don't worry. Rebecca will come round to the idea soon.'

As Constance walked back to the house, her head disappearing under the verandah roof, Rebecca leant back against the sturdy branch of her tree. She hadn't forgotten the last time she'd watched people from up there and her breath came out in a small huff of disbelief. Stealing a baby was the most childish thing she'd ever heard of. It had spoiled everything and had led to Bonne Espérance.

'Luke, Naomi and Simon.' She mouthed each name carefully as a vast horizon of friendship tugged at her intention to sell peanuts.

'I'll just stand beside you and sell my peanuts. Roasted ones,' she explained her plans to Macaroni as he swept a pile of dust into each corner of the echoing house. Though the contents and curtains were packed in large boxes and the furniture stood in a queue ready to leave the next morning, Rebecca was still looking for a way out. 'Everyone likes peanuts. Just like they like Coca Cola.'

'Where you live?' Macaroni asked, with a long sweep at her feet. 'You go! Go with your granny.' Rebecca jumped as the broom slid under her on straw tentacles, landing with one foot on each side of the long handle before Macaroni tipped her off.

'Why should I go, anyway? Luke's a horrible name! I bet I won't even like him.' She jumped back on to the broom before he could move it away.

'Are you coming?' Rebecca spun round with David's voice, every part of her suddenly on tiptoe.

'Wait!' she yelled as she raced after him through the house, her bare feet ploughing through Macaroni's neat piles of dust. 'Sorry,' she called back to him. 'Where are we going?' she questioned her father as Macaroni reorganised the spread dust back into a neat pile.

'Hang on!' David shouted over the roar of the black Matchless motorbike beneath them, and Rebecca leaned to the left as the bike rounded a sharp bend. 'Good girl.' She felt the tread of her father's words through his back and held him tighter still, wishing tomorrow would never come.

Two ribbons of deep blue tarmac snaked through the African bush; a conveyor belt of rocks running beside it on an endless journey in the opposite direction. Up ahead, like a giant Meccano set, the hoists of Stork shaft drove their way through the flat tops of trees while heavy wheels turned slowly against the evening sky of her father's world.

'Becky!' a man's voice called through the roar of engines and Rebecca narrowed her eyes as she looked up towards the cool iron roof of the hoist-house. Dewi Hawkins waved from a glass box on stilts and through the distance between them she felt the warmth that poured down from the chubby Welshman on afternoon shift.

'Where've you been, bach? You haven't come to see your Uncle Dewi in a long time.' Dewi Hawkins was a winding-engine driver like Rebecca's father, and the soft Welsh lilt of his voice seemed ready to launch into song at any moment.

'I'm coming now.' Rebecca reacted to the familiar comfort that Dewi's presence in her life always brought. 'Can I go, Dad? Uncle Dewi said I could.' She turned back to David before racing up to her Welsh friend.

'So my little girl leaves tomorrow.' Dewi Hawkins pushed a book off his lap to make room for Rebecca, knowing it would be the last time that he did so. He adored the small child whom the women of the town had ostracised and, placing one hand on each of her delicate shoulders, he challenged her with a grin. 'How many bells?'

'Three?' Rebecca looked in wonder towards the array of switches and lights in the wheelhouse. Dewi Hawkins, like her father, held many lives in his hands when he worked. She'd never ceased to wonder at how they drove a steel cage filled with men miles into the depths of the copper mine, their only guide a ringing bell and marks on a steel cable.

'Is it going to ring now?' she shouted over the sudden roar of engines.

'Maybe.' A wide smile lit Dewi Hawkins' sunburnt face and Rebecca covered her ears as his hand reached forward to a huge lever. Driving its way between her protective fingers a bell rang sharply. It rang three times and Rebecca tensed as Dewi's grip tightened on the handle. His eyes were fixed on the steel rope that ran down from the wheelhouse before passing back up through a square hole in the roof. It was a hidden world that Rebecca was a part of for the very last time. She knew the steel cage would be racing down the deep rock shaft very, very fast. Only the lights on the miners' hats would be visible as darkness sucked them towards the centre of the earth, to the solid core where they'd blast and dig for copper.

'Are they there yet?' she shouted over the roar of the engine, and her voice echoed in her head.

'Almost,' Dewi smiled. 'There!' He hung one arm around Rebecca's shoulder, having secured the cage at the base of the shaft.

'So. Are you going to miss me?' he asked.

'I'm not going.' Rebecca hugged him quickly. She was suddenly sad and wanted to get away. 'See you soon, Uncle Dewi.' She climbed down to her father quickly as he waited at the bottom.

'Don't forget to write, will you?' Dewi Hawkins called after them both as the bells demanded his attention again and his hand moved back to the lever.

'Never,' David answered, and for the first time Rebecca realised the truth: men like Dewi Hawkins shared a part of her father's life which neither she nor her mother could ever replace. She knew that he didn't want to go to Bonne Espérance either.

'We can unpack the boxes. We don't have to go.' She looked up into her father's strong face as she reached him. His jawline was clean and firm, his nose classically straight, and his eyes a deep blue. 'You don't want to go either, Daddy. I know.'

'You think I'm going to give this back to them?' David held his wrist out to her with a canny smile. The gold Rolex given to him by the mine looked suddenly worthless. It had been exchanged for the friendships of years. 'Of course I want to go.' David tucked his small daughter under his arm and walked her towards an enormous square doorway cut into the high iron walls of the hoist-house.

Tickey stood alone outside, holding a large watering can as he tended a small patch of runner beans and cabbages. He looked up in delight as Rebecca ran to him, holding her foot under the cool spray that came from the can. He saw her mouth form the English words of greeting that he'd learned to read on lips and he nodded with a wide grin, his dark cracked fingers reaching to the enormous straw hat on his head.

'Enjoy them, Tickey.' David held the African man's shoulder firmly in one hand and pushed a pound note into the torn pocket of his trousers. 'You won't get vegetables like these again.'

Shaking his head with a silent laugh, Tickey bowed his body low. Holding his left hand across his right arm he held his hand out to David and it was then that Rebecca saw tears in her father's eyes. The goodbye was final and she knew that whatever she'd done to cause them to leave the small town must be terrible. The dark mystery that lay deep in Bonne Espérance drew them back against their will, no matter how she tried to stop it.

Leaning over David in the bed, Constance tucked her head into his neck. She could hear the regular beat of his heart and hoped he wanted her. Wrapping her leg across his stomach she curled her foot under his back, longing to disappear in the safety of his love. 'Are you awake, David?' she whispered.

'Mmm.' David pulled his eyes away from the ceiling and brushed his wife's hair from his nose. He'd been awake all night. Though he came from an English farming family, he wasn't certain that running an African vineyard was something he'd adapt to easily, but Bonne Espérance wasn't the problem that had kept him from sleep. It was the laws of separation being written into the constitution by the new Nationalist Government in South Africa. Strict separation of the races had come down on the people like a sword. Families had been divided with a stroke of the pen and David knew theirs could be among them. In the gentle stream of moonlight that shone through the bare gauze window he could see the longing in his wife's face and felt his own body respond. Pushing the delicate strap of her nightdress off her shoulder he kissed her soft white skin.

'Everything packed?'

'Even the food.' Constance felt his lips move towards her breasts and pushed her hand through his thatch of thick brown hair. As much as her muscles ached with the days of packing, they ached now for him. In the honey warmth of their lovemaking she knew she'd find the courage to face the coming day. The seconds ticked noisily across the face of the clock towards five and there was only half an hour before it would herald morning.

'David?' She leaned over him, holding his face between her hands. She longed for him and felt his desire rise under her body as she brushed her lips against his. Making love had never become routine. Each time their bodies joined together they were still young and still in love. Even under the weight of problems that had piled up against their marriage, she still felt the familiar spark of excitement as their skin touched. She felt his hand run down her buttocks to grip her thigh and pulled her knee up as he slipped his hand under her, a slow ripple of pleasure rising in her loins.

'David,' she whispered as he pushed her back on to the bed, his mouth moving to her stomach.

'You're beautiful.' Through the dark his eyes passed over the familiar lines of her body and though Constance knew she didn't look beautiful, he had made her feel it.

Yanking her sleeping bag high over her head Rebecca burrowed deeper as she heard her mother cry out in pleasure. Why did they have to bounce when 123 Z was about to disappear behind the tail end of a train, she thought angrily, and tried instead to think about that train. She wondered what it would be like to sleep in a bunk and, pushing the soles of her feet into the bottom of the bag, she straightened her legs to peek out of the top for air. Everything was quiet as she glanced backwards over her head to the thin partition wall that separated her bedroom from her parents' and she wondered why. She wondered what hour the cuckoo clock in the lounge would sound if it hadn't been packed. Was the cuckoo in or out when it had been wrapped in paper and packed in a box, she puzzled. She looked at the new dress that hung from the picture-rail and tried to think about that instead. It was a beautiful dress. Her mother had made it. And she'd made it longer than any Rebecca had ever had before. But where would she hang it on the train? It took four days and five nights to get to the Cape, and her mother had said it was only for wearing on and off the train. She hoped it would still look good when she met Luke. Maybe it wasn't such a bad name after all, she thought as her body tingled. The partition behind her began to shake and quickly she wriggled her way back into the safety of her sleeping bag, pulling it closed over her face to escape. Her heart beat so fast she thought she was going to die. Die all alone in the dark while her parents bounced on the bed and a bell announced that day had arrived.

Looking up at the ant hill, Rebecca pushed the new white sandals which went with her new long dress deep into the wet of dew that covered the grass. Katinka had told her she would never see an ant hill like it again and still she couldn't believe it was true.

'Are you sure there are no ant hills in Cape Town?' She turned to Katinka who stood quietly beside her. 'None at all?'

'There are mountains, beautiful purple mountains all round Bonne Espérance. You'll love them. They're much much bigger than ant hills.' Katinka took Rebecca's hand in hers and squeezed it. 'We must say goodbye to Macaroni now.'

'I don't want to.' Rebecca pulled her hand free, turning her back on Katinka. No matter how hard she squeezed her eyes shut, the tears still threatened to find a way out and she bit her lip to hold them back. 'He'll cry.' She swung round as her mother stepped out of the front door with the last small bag. 'We're going now, Mummy,' she called. But Constance had stopped in front of Macaroni as he stood silently outside the house looking towards Rebecca and Katinka.

'Well,' Constance smiled. 'I suppose this is it, Macaroni.'

'Yes, donna.' Macaroni's face expressed no emotion. It was as if he'd died inside the angular black body dressed in David's long khaki trousers and shirt. The trousers were gathered by a belt at his thin waist and hung in pleats that reached halfway down his calves.

'Whenever I have a Coca Cola I'll think of you.' Constance tried to break down the wall she'd built between them as mistress of the house.

'Yes, donna.' She'd never understood why Macaroni didn't call her 'mama' as he did Katinka. It was an expression of endearment and he'd reserved it for her mother.

'Goodbye then.' Constance turned towards the Humber Super Snipe parked behind the large removal truck in the driveway as David climbed into it. They needed the entire day to load their goods and the car on to the train before it left Ndola station that evening.

'Goodbye, Ladiwell. Don't forget to water!' Constance waved as she saw Ladiwell, the gardener. He stood round the side of the house at a loss and she hoped David had made sure he was financially secure. 'Come on, Mother. Rebecca!' she called as she moved to the car. Katinka was dressed in a long black skirt with a fitted black jacket, and on her head was a small black hat. A feather stuck out of it at a jaunty angle and Constance knew her mother had dressed to look happy.

'Did you know there aren't any ant hills on the other side of the Zambezi, Macaroni?' Rebecca turned towards Macaroni, who stood silently a little way away, and holding back her tears, she tried to smile. 'Can you imagine anywhere so plain? It'll be like your apple pie without custard.' She forced a laugh, but Macaroni didn't say anything.

'Now you just remember to make sure you take the empty Coca Cola bottles back, Macaroni.' Katinka's eyebrows lifted and the feather on her hat dipped as she glanced down at his feet. 'What have you got on?' she said in amazement.

'Shoes.' Macaroni tried to move his toes in the hard confines of David's patent leather evening shoes. One lace was cut in half and looped under the soles to be tied over his arch in a fancy bow.

'Don't you know how to do laces up?' Rebecca bent down to the wide feet squashed so proudly into her father's black patent leather. 'Where's the other lace?'

'In other shoes.' Macaroni's eyes crinkled closed in a smile. 'Brown brogues.' He described David's other shoes with carefully enunciated pleasure.

'I'll write to you.' Rebecca stood up and watched the old man's long upper lip stretch straight before he nodded. 'I'll send it to the post office.' She knew that in some magical way her letters, addressed simply to *Macaroni*, would find their way from the post office to the village he was going to with his family. He'd sit beside his Coca Cola stand and look at the letters, she thought. He wouldn't read them – he couldn't. But he'd look at them.

'Bye bye,' Rebecca said suddenly, and ran away towards the waiting car.

'You take care, baba.'

Katinka tilted her head back and looked up into his eyes. They were filled with tears which hadn't yet fallen. 'I wonder if we'll recognise each other?' she said on a whisper, and Macaroni nodded. He knew exactly what she was talking about.

'*Hamba gashli, mama.*' His hand reached out to her and she looked at it. It was shaking. '*Hamba gashli.*' He repeated his wish that she go well and Katinka took his bony black hand between hers.

'*Hlala Khale.*' Her wish that he stay well was like a prayer and Macaroni's being cracked as tears rolled freely down his dark cheeks.

'May the Great God be with you, mama,' he whispered and turned away.

'Goodbye, Macaroni.' Rebecca's voice slipped past Katinka, reaching out to touch the old man's back. But he didn't turn. Nothing could bring him to say goodbye to the small child he'd known since the day she was born and he walked away without looking round. Macaroni had a large part of Rebecca tucked into the pocket of her father's trousers and he knew that tears could never release the pain.

'Look at that!' David held his daughter's hand tightly as they trod on the loose pebbles beside the train that stood in Ndola station. 'It's the compartment we're in, see?' He held the train tickets out to Rebecca and she looked up at him in amazement. Tucking her under his arm, David moved her closer to the steps between the carriages and whispered in confidence, 'You take the tickets and find the two coupés we're in, then call to me from the window. I'll wait here with our bags.'

'OK.' Rebecca pulled herself up on the iron bars that ran alongside the steps, jumping on to the rusty red platform between the carriages. It was the first time she'd been part of a long journey and her father had made her feel very important. She looked down between the enormous rubber hoses that linked the carriages like umbilical cords. She was engulfed by new and strange sensations; the smell of soot, polish and coffee and she jumped back against the wooden walls of the carriage as a steward in a white suit moved towards her. A tray of coffee and cups was balanced magically on his upturned hand.

'You lost, ducks?' he asked with a wide grin. ''Ave a gander at your tickets and tell me where you want to be.'

'What?' The cockney accent of the short man was totally foreign to Rebecca. 'I'm looking for our compartment. These ones.' She held out the tickets and he squinted at them through the cups on the tray. 'My dad sent me to find them,' she confided proudly.

'And they're right behind you, sweetheart,' the steward smiled, pushing open the compartment door behind her with his foot. 'Next one along's yours too. Back in a tick and I'll settle you in.' He moved away with the tray and Rebecca stared ahead into the little wooden room on wheels. It was the place she'd be occupying with Katinka for the next two days and the scent of wood and leather filled her with excitement.

'Rhodesian Railways,' she murmured as she saw the initials R.R engraved on the window.

'Rebecca!' Her father was calling her from outside the compartment window and she moved to it quickly, flattening her nose against the glass. 'Is it nice?' David asked as he saw her. 'Push the window down from the top. You'll see a piece of metal – push it down.'

Rebecca wondered how her father knew so much about Rhodesian Railway trains. She reached up to the metal but it wouldn't budge. Hanging on to it as hard as she could, she swung on it and slowly the window slid down with her weight.

'It's lovely,' she told her father through the sudden opening. 'It's got leather seats – and look! It says R.R. for Rhodesian Railways. Here! In here!' she called as she spotted Constance bringing Katinka towards the carriage from the ladies' toilets on the platform. Quickly she crossed her legs. The journey was going to be long and she wished she'd remembered to go herself, but she was busy right now. 'We're in this one, Granny,' she shouted at Katinka, jumping on to the open bottom bunk as she reached for the wooden base of the bunk above. The top one would be hers and she couldn't wait to try it.

'Here,' David pushed a bag through the open window and she tugged till it slipped inside with a sudden bang. It bumped down on to a small bowl with a silver cover and she stared at the letters R.R. engraved on that too.

'A basin.' She stared in amazement as she lifted the silver lid. Dropping it back, she stuck her head out of the window and yelled, 'We've got a basin, too! We've got a silver basin with taps!'

'Get ready to help Granny up,' Constance called as she led Katinka to the steps. 'Come and help granny, darling. We need you.'

'I'm coming.' Rebecca turned to the door.

'Another bag, Rebecca.' She swung back to her father outside the window. 'I need you to take that end and pull.'

'I'm coming!' she shouted in excitement with the sudden demands for her attention. 'Wait, Granny. Wait, Dad.'

Rebecca was part of a very important happening and quite suddenly she realised the strong ties to her past had snapped. 'I don't know what to do first,' she giggled. 'You'll all have to wait – all of you.' She commanded them to be silent as she tried to bring order to the beginnings of their new life.

It was evening by the time the train's departure was announced with a smoking toot from the engine, and Rebecca stood silently with her father on the small viewing platform at the rear of the train. 123 Z, Macaroni, and an ant hill with a tree on top were already lost in the bush, and her new life had begun as they pulled out of Ndola station.

'Mrs Bernstein! Hey,' she shouted through the growing distance between them as she suddenly spotted her. 'Sorry I didn't see you before I left.' She leaned over the railings and waved. She was going to miss the perfume monster that lived in Mrs Bernstein's cleavage. 'I'll miss you too!' she yelled.

Mrs Bernstein stood dumbfounded. She couldn't conceive how the child could possibly think she'd come to say goodbye to her, when she'd only come to the station to collect a parcel. Though Mrs Bernstein had insisted to all and sundry that she'd had nothing to do with the family's departure, she heaved a sigh of relief as she watched the train chug away into the distance. She didn't know Rebecca had silently vowed that one day she would return to 123 Z.

'Tell me again.' Rebecca's voice reached down to Katinka who lay half-asleep in the bunk beneath her own later that night. 'You said Luke wasn't my sort of cousin like the others. Why'd you say that?' She tucked the heavy crisp sheet under her chin and pushed her toes to the bottom of the bunk.

'Because he was born before his mother married your Uncle Paul.'

Katinka had been answering Rebecca's questions ever since they'd climbed into their bunks and she was completely exhausted by the child's sudden interest in Bonne Espérance. 'Luke has another father.'

'Who?'

Katinka didn't know how to explain that Luke's mother had given birth to him without being married. That her grandson Paul, with a heart he seemed to wear on his sleeve, had married Luke's mother more out of pity than love. She could picture Estelle's face when they arrived at Bonne Espérance. Her nose would be thin, as with the rise of a bad smell, and Katinka wasn't sure she could face her. She'd seen the distaste Estelle felt for her many years before, but now it was backed by law.

'Tell me, Granny Cat.'

'He's dead,' Katinka said quickly. 'Luke's father died a long time ago and now it's time we went to sleep.' Rebecca's face hung upside down over the edge of the top bunk. 'Goodnight.' Katinka closed her eyes.

'But what about Naomi and "perhaps-not-Simon"?' Rebecca didn't want Katinka to disappear into sleep and her loose black hair swung from side to side with the movements of the train. 'What happened to their father?' she asked between the regular clatter of wheels on the line.

'He's Uncle Paul. Now you go to sleep.'

'OK,' Rebecca pulled herself back up to her bunk and lay down. The pillow felt hard under her head and she punched a small circle around the embroidered R.R. in its centre.

'What's wrong now, Rebecca?' Katinka asked the banging wooden base of the bunk above her.

'Go to sleep, Granny.' Rebecca dropped her head back into the pillow and allowed the rhythm of puffing steam and clattering wheels to take over the rhythm of her body. She was glad Luke wasn't her sort of cousin. It meant she didn't have to like him.

Katinka had been asleep on the bottom bunk all day and the blinds were pulled down, making the small compartment dark and hot. Her grandmother had said she was still tired and Rebecca wondered how that was possible. They'd slept all night and she herself was bored, not tired.

'Why make a fuss about me being tired?' Katinka had argued. 'It's a long journey and we're all tired.'

Peering down between her legs as they dangled over the edge of the top bunk, Rebecca watched her grandmother. Katinka was still sound asleep, leaving her alone with her thoughts. She knew her parents would be talking about schools and money in the compartment next door, so she'd rather not be with them. She'd explored every inch of the train with R.R. engraved all over it and she'd gazed for hours at the miles of spreading bush through which the train puffed its slow route. She'd screeched with delight as she'd seen an enormous red billboard in the middle of nowhere. *Drink Coca Cola* had been written across it in bold black letters.

'Look!' she'd shouted to Katinka. 'They're telling everyone about Macaroni!'

But only as she'd seen many other similar billboards along the train's route had she decided she was wrong. There had to be other black men whose bwanas had given them a Coca Cola franchise before leaving. They couldn't all be for Macaroni.

Watching her new dress swing happily from a hanger above the compartment door, Rebecca smiled proudly. It was the longest dress she'd ever had and she wished she could wear it again. But it was only for getting on and off in. Her mother had reminded her of that fact constantly. The old shorts and shirt she had on were very dirty, almost black from soot. Her eye was still sore from the tiny speck of charcoal which had zoomed into it as she'd stuck her head out of the window, and her bottom ached from being sat on. Leaning back against the wall behind her she stretched her legs up, hanging them by the toes from the top edge of the metal window-frame. A small dead moth stuck to her toe and she wiped it off on her other leg, examining its squashed remains carefully. She remembered how they'd woken in the middle of the night, unable to breathe in the cloud of moths that had found their way through the ventilation grills. She remembered how the train had stopped while the cockney steward had wiped 'the little buggers' away. The natives had used the time for chopping trees in the bush to stoke the engine's fire and their voices had risen with their swinging axes, but Rebecca was bored.

She lowered her toe towards the bottom edge of the blind and lifted it to peek outside. The painted letters R.R. vanished in the fold of material as it doubled back, but she still couldn't see. It was getting dark and her mind slipped slowly backwards over the journey so far, over the magical names of the small places the train had been through: Bwana Makuba, Kapirimposhi. The train would be stopping at Bulawayo the next day. There they would bath and change, her mother had told her, before they got on to another train for the rest of the journey into South Africa. And then she'd get to wear her new dress!

The bathroom in Bulawayo station was enormous, and large fluffy white towels declared that they too were the property of Rhodesian Railways. They hung over rails that ran around the walls of the square white room and Rebecca held one gently to her face.

'This one's yours, Granny Cat.' She'd been told to share the bathroom with her grandmother and to make sure she helped Katinka wash. Though it was usually the other way round, Rebecca had accepted that everything had changed and felt suddenly very grown-up.

'Come, Granny Cat,' she said as she turned towards Katinka, ready to help her into the bath. Katinka was sitting fully dressed on the closed lid of the toilet and gazed back in innocent silence. 'You said you were going to take your clothes off, Granny.'

'I forgot.' Katinka sat quite still on the toilet. 'You go first, darling.'

Lying back in the deep warm water Rebecca watched as a steady stream of charcoal dust seeped upwards, spreading into a grey film on top of the water.

'I'm filthy,' she chuckled with delight and drew patterns in the charcoal tornadoes that surrounded her. 'I want to be really clean.' She glanced up at her new dress that hung on the towel-rail and sunk deeper till the water lapped around her chin. 'This is the best bath I've had in my whole life.' She glanced round at Katinka, hoping she might have tempted her to wash, but her grandmother hadn't moved from the closed toilet seat.

'Good,' Katinka said with little interest.

The white towel was enormous and Rebecca tried to walk across the concrete floor with it wound round herself, the way they did in films. But she tripped. Naked and gleaming, she giggled.

'Your turn, Granny. You can get in now.' Katinka moved to the bath and Rebecca pushed herself along on the towel with her feet, pretending she was in a sack race. 'Hey, what are you doing?' She turned back with the sound of water vanishing down the plughole as Katinka sat on the toilet seat once again.

'That was your bath, Granny Cat!'

'Yes,' Katinka smiled sweetly.

'You're not shy, are you?' Rebecca looked at her grandmother in amazement. They'd had many baths in one another's company before and Katinka had never been self-conscious about her tiny wrinkled body. She loved to bath. 'Do you want me to leave you? Do you want to be on your own?'

'Whoopsie!' Katinka jumped off the toilet seat, pulled down her pants and sat down again in the nick of time. 'That's better,' she said, as a slow waterfall flowed through the silence.

'I'm ready.' Katinka stood up and pulled her pants up from the floor, but she stopped halfway. Silently she tilted her head up towards Rebecca as the child tugged her new dress over her head.

'Look what you've done, Granny,' Rebecca said through the material stretched across her mouth, and she pulled it down under her chin, wriggling her body into the dress. 'You've got your skirt in your pants.' She moved to her, her damp feet sticking to the floor. 'You're being very naughty today, Granny Cat. You were supposed to get undressed, not dressed!'

Rebecca didn't see Katinka look the other way and gasp for breath, trying to heave her pants up while Rebecca heaved them down.

'You are naughty,' Rebecca finally realised that her grandmother had no intention of bathing. 'Will you do my dress up, please?' She turned her back on Katinka and waited as she pushed the solitary button at the neck through the button-hole.

'It looks very beautiful, little one,' Katinka said quietly as Rebecca spun her way across the bathroom, her skirt filling out in soft waves. 'You won't tell Mummy that I didn't bath, will you?' Katinka's voice was soft but insistent.

'No.' Rebecca shook her head as she looked at the old lady who'd turned to her for help. 'But maybe I should wash your face before she sees you.'

The new train was exactly the same as the old train except for the engraved letters and the new stewards. The letters had changed to S.A.R., which Katinka told Rebecca stood for South African Railways, and the amiable cockney steward had been replaced by a man who didn't seem to like them. He was Afrikaans and Rebecca wondered if the Boer War was still on. Perhaps it had slipped her grandmother's mind. Katinka had forgotten a lot of things since they'd climbed on the train in Ndola.

'Are we the enemy or them?' she asked her grandmother later, wondering which side they were on now – if they were goodies or baddies. Perhaps Bonne Espérance was one of those camps where the British had locked up the Boers. 'Who's winning?' She had to know if it was they who'd be locked up this time.

'The war's over, child. A long time over,' Katinka answered, but Rebecca's mind jumped nervously back to the man in uniform who'd stamped their British passports on the border with South Africa. She'd thought the little round hammer dipped in ink was going to go straight through her new blue book. She hoped it wouldn't because she liked her British passport. It said that if she wasn't allowed to pass 'without let or hindrance' they'd have to answer to the King of England, and that made her feel safe. She could find out what 'let or hindrance' meant later.

'Look, Granny,' Rebecca shouted to Katinka as she dozed on the bottom bunk. Rebecca was gazing out of the window at the platform outside. The sign said MAGALAPI. It was night and a band was playing on the station platform, their enormous brass instruments reflecting the gawdy colours of lights that strung electric ribbons over their heads. They were playing *Blue Moon* and Rebecca knew it was her mother's favourite tune.

'Mummy!' she shrieked in surprise as Constance spun across the platform in a flying silk dress from England. She was held tight in David's arms and the platform was a whirl of twirling skirts and pressed trouser legs. It seemed as if everyone on the train had emptied out to dance under a wide black sky as millions of African stars watched. 'Oh,' Rebecca sighed into her cupped hand. She longed to be outside with them and wished she could slip into her new dress. She'd dance like her parents were dancing. She'd spin across the platform like the trapeze artiste's partner in the circus.

'Go on.' Katinka's voice started her and she looked round at her grandmother blankly. She nodded towards Rebecca's new dress. 'What are you waiting for?'

Held between her mother and father, standing on her father's new black patent leather shoes, Rebecca felt the warm night air brush past her as they twirled to the strains of *The Blue Danube*. Crickets joined in with a scratchy chorus and she was certain that everyone had noticed what a beautiful dress she wore. Even the small black pikinins, watching wide-eyed from the dark, even they would say it was the most beautiful dress they'd ever seen, she decided. Also the longest.

*

'What is it?' Rebecca had heard her grandmother make a slight noise and she leaned over the edge of her bunk, looking down at her now. 'Did you call me, Granny Cat? Are you awake?' Katinka's mouth was moving and Rebecca could hear something but couldn't quite make it out. Swinging down from the bunk in a half-somersault, she looked at Katinka carefully. She'd been sleeping for ever it seemed, and still she was asleep. 'I didn't hear you, Granny. What did you say?'

'Johannes.' Katinka's eyes opened sleepily and she looked up into Rebecca's face. Then tears flooded her eyes. 'Johannes Villiers,' she whispered.

'Who's that?' Rebecca didn't know her grandmother was back in time. That she was with her own mother. That Katinka's mother Sarah Westbury was dying.

'Johannes,' Katinka murmured again as her mind looked into the memory of her dying mother. 'What is it?' Katinka was leaning over her mother. She was trying to understand what her mother was telling her, but she couldn't hear her properly. 'Brother?' Katinka heard the word she'd never expected to hear. She didn't have a brother. 'Who's Johannes? I don't have a brother.' She moved her ear closer to her mother.

'Cape Town ... Suzanne ... brother ... Johannes Villiers. My son.' Katinka spoke the few lost words she'd picked out from her mother's dying confession and Rebecca's face grew puzzled.

'Who is Johannes?' Her voice walked through her grandmother's dream as Katinka tried to pull herself out of the cotton-wool sleep that cocooned her. She needed to speak to the small child who was looking at her now, as she had once looked at her dying mother.

'Find him!' Katinka's words reached towards her granddaughter on a whisper. 'Johannes Villiers – my brother. *Find him!*'

Rebecca scratched her head, deciding that Granny Cat must be talking in her sleep. She often did, but never before about a brother. In all the stories Katinka had told her, her grandmother had never told her she'd had a brother called Johannes.

'Cape Town.' Katinka's whispered voice interrupted Rebecca's thoughts.

'Who's in Cape Town, Granny Cat?'

But Katinka couldn't hear her grandchild any more. She was in a narrow street. It ran down from Adderley Street in Cape Town and she was surrounded by dark children. Lost in a sea of strange faces, she was looking for her brother, Johannes Villiers.

'Gone. War,' Katinka murmured and Rebecca froze. She must warn her parents that the Boer War wasn't over yet. But quite suddenly fear gripped her by the throat and she shook Katinka by the shoulders.

61

'Wake up, Granny. Wake up!'

'Yes?' Katinka pulled herself up the slippery sides of her dream and, peering over the edge, she stared at her granddaughter's face. 'What's wrong, Rebecca?'

'It's you, Granny. You said about a brother. Wake up!' Rebecca tried to hold her grandmother back from sleep and Katinka's eyes fixed on her in a split second of terror. It was a look Rebecca had never seen before and she pulled away from it quickly, but then with the gentlest of smiles, Katinka's eyes softened and her hand reached out to her grandchild.

'You're dreaming, Rebecca. Go back to sleep.' And drifting back into sleep herself, Katinka left Rebecca alone on the shore.

But in her head the child held a small piece of information which she wasn't sure was real or just part of an old lady's dream.

'Granny Cat?' Rebecca whispered nervously, but Katinka said no more.

Climbing back into her bunk, unable to sleep, Rebecca toyed with the information she'd gleaned. 'Johannes Villiers. Brother. Cape Town.' She pushed her back firmly against the wooden wall of their compartment, certain she'd stumbled on a small part of the mystery that surrounded Bonne Espérance. It was definitely a grown-up mystery and that made it much more interesting.

A sharp rap on the door startled Rebecca back to the present and she looked hard at the tall Afrikaans steward as he stepped in, uninvited and carrying a bundle of sheets and pillows.

'I'll do it,' she said quickly, not wanting the enemy to make her bed. 'My granny's asleep.' She jumped down and took the bundle of sheets with S.A.R. embroidered on them. 'Thank you,' she said in answer to the foreign words he muttered and closed the door on him quickly. Rebecca had something important to think about and had no intention of letting war get in the way.

'Are you all right, Rebecca?' Her mother's voice interrupted her thoughts. She was on the outside of the door, banging on it as she struggled against the lock. 'Mother? Rebecca? It's time to eat – let me in.'

'She's asleep, Mummy,' Rebecca called through the closed door, holding the sheets tightly under her arm. 'Whoopsie!' she whispered as two pillows slipped from the roll, dropping softly on to her feet. 'Granny said she doesn't want anything to eat, and neither do I.'

'You've got to eat, Rebecca. Come along,' Constance argued.

'Granny got me something before,' Rebecca lied. Everything was happening at once and she wanted to be alone to sort out the information she'd gathered. 'Night night, Mummy.' She turned and looked at Katinka, glad she was sound asleep and hadn't heard her lie. 'You've got to keep yourself tucked in, Granny Cat.' Katinka's hand had slipped off her chest and Rebecca gently lifted it back. 'I'll cover you up in case you get cold.' She dropped three sheets on the floor as she held the folded edge of one. Carefully she spread the sheet over Katinka and tucked it carefully under her chin. 'Night, Granny.' She kissed her on the forehead. 'You are cold!' She picked up a second sheet, tucking that over the first. 'You really must be tired.' Katinka's hand slipped down again and Rebecca put it firmly back on her chest. 'I won't talk any more, 'cos I'm tired too.' Rebecca flung the last two sheets and a pillow on to the top bunk. She looked at the spare pillow she was standing on and wondered whether to push it under her grandmother's head. Deciding she wouldn't disturb her, she tossed it up to join the other.

With her body wound in the sheets and both pillows propping up her head, Rebecca tried to piece together all she'd heard. She'd sort it out now and check it with Granny Cat in the morning. As her mind played marbles with the information she'd collected, Rebecca felt her eyes grow heavy. She was falling asleep among rolling glass balls, and each one bore a name.

A key turned the lock of the compartment door from the outside and the door slid quietly open. Constance had tried to wake Rebecca and her mother by banging on the door loudly, but she'd achieved nothing. David had decided to call the steward to unlock the door for them and they'd brought plates of food, determined to make sure they ate.

'It wasn't such a good idea, putting them in a coupé together after all. They're as obstinate as one another,' Constance grumbled as they entered. 'They're both children.' But quite suddenly her voice filled with fear as she looked at her mother. Katinka was still neatly tucked into the bunk as Rebecca had left her, but her hand had slipped free once again and it hung limply to the floor.

'David.'

'What is it?' David stepped into the compartment behind his wife. He held a tray with two plates and on each sat a yellow omelette in a puddle of oil. He looked at Katinka in silence, understanding the tone of Constance's voice and carefully he put the tray on the basin cover. He didn't need to check but he did. Leaning his face down to Katinka's he listened for any sign of life and slowly he stood up, turning to Constance. She had her back to him. 'I'm sorry,' he said.

Constance felt the train judder to a sudden halt under her feet as she realised her deepest fears had materialised and her mind leapt to her small daughter.

'Don't wake Rebecca.' She turned to her mother, holding her small, cold body close to her own. She knew Katinka's death would devastate her child and she wanted to protect her for as long as possible. 'Please don't wake Rebecca, David.' Constance moved away, holding back her own grief as David pulled the sheet over Katinka's face.

Strange noises had stirred Rebecca's already fitful sleep as she turned over in the top bunk. The train had stopped and she lay still, trying to adjust to the missing sounds she'd learned to use as a lullaby.

'Hold it!' A strange man's voice crept out from somewhere in the dark and she decided the railway men must be collecting wood for the engine again. The train often stopped while men went into the bush to cut down trees for fuel and, satisfied with her own sleepy explanation, she rolled over to face the wall. She wanted to slip the time in sleep and reach Bonne Espérance quicker. There were so many things she had to check out. Listing them in her head once again, she drifted back into a deep sleep.

'Careful.' Her mother's voice woke her with sudden fright. Something had banged in the compartment and Rebecca tried to work out what it could be. Then she smiled to herself. Her mother must still be banging on the door, trying to get them to eat, she decided, and lay totally still. Constance would go away when she was sure they were both asleep and as silence closed around her, Rebecca's ears prodded it for tell-tale signs of her mother. Then she listened more keenly. Her grandmother had once told her you could hear God in silence and she hoped it was true. Maybe He would tell her about Johannes Villiers.

'Granny?' The silence had gone on too long and everything was far too still. 'Are you awake?' She decided her grandmother must be awake. She could hear someone crying and she knew it wasn't God. The Bible said there were no tears in heaven.

Leaning her head down over the edge of the bunk, Rebecca peered through the darkness. Granny Cat was sitting up. She was crying and Rebecca wondered why she was crying in the dark.

'Why are you crying, Granny? It's silly. Crying in the dark's a waste of time.' Rebecca pulled herself over the edge of the bunk and slid her body down till her feet reached the wooden edge of the bottom bunk. 'I've been waiting for you to wake up all night. I didn't sleep because I kept thinking about what you said ...' Rebecca's words ran to a slow halt as she realised it was her mother who was sitting there.

Her mother was crying and her grandmother had gone.

'Where's Granny?' She peered at Constance curiously through the dark. 'Why are you crying, Mummy?' She turned as she felt someone behind her. 'Where's Granny?'

'Rebecca.' Her father was very close. He stood in the small carriage and in his hand he had a ring. It was a gold wedding ring.

'Where is she?' Rebecca asked very carefully. Everyone had changed places without her knowledge and she was suddenly quite lost in a mystery. 'Why've you got Granny's ring? Where's Granny Cat?'

'Granny Cat's dead, Rebecca.' As he told his small daughter that the only person she hadn't said goodbye to had gone, David's words were very gentle.

CHAPTER FOUR

Luke Marsden pushed his horse faster towards the outer reaches of Bonne Espérance. He wished the wind would blow his mother's words away, but even the thunder of his horse's hooves didn't drown them.

'Your future doesn't lie in the Cape, Luke, no more than your father's does.'

His mother was wrong. Luke knew there was no other place in the whole world for him. His future nestled among the spreading green vines of Bonne Espérance where he'd spent all his thirteen years. Bonne Espérance was a haven in a sea of troubles and he didn't want to leave it.

'Luke!' His name trailed after him on the distant voice of Thabo. 'Luke!' His friend's voice chased him again and he pulled his horse up sharply. Spinning in a small cloud of dust he faced back the way he'd come.

'What is it?' Luke yelled between cupped hands, and his eyes searched for his black friend among the straight paths that drove their way between the vines. 'Is it Simon?'

'Yes,' Thabo's voice called back and Luke dug his heels in, riding back the way he'd come. His small brother Simon meant even more to him today than he had yesterday.

'He cross,' Thabo informed Luke as he reined his horse.

Simon, Luke's three-year-old brother, was caught in a whirlwind of anger that was made more frightening by his mongoloid features. His tiny feet banged the wooden base of a handmade cart and his arms swung wildly at Thabo as he tried to hold him. Dropping his reins and leaping down beside him, Luke took his young brother and held him firmly.

'He don't want the cart,' Thabo explained. 'He very stubborn.'

'I'm coming back soon, Simon.' As he tried to reassure the tiny mongol boy, Luke turned him away from the wooden cart he and Thabo had made for him. 'It's all right.' Luke peered into Simon's dark slanting eyes, searching for a moment of reason in his brother's jumbled mind. 'You stay with Thabo.' He pressed Simon's face against his own. 'OK?'

'He OK,' Thabo grinned, tilting his head from side to side under Simon's face to make him laugh. 'You try to frighten Thabo?' The child's tongue stretched towards Thabo over Luke's shoulder, uncluttered affection reaching for his brother's friend. 'OK now.' Thabo took Simon and held him.

'Don't say anything.' Luke touched his friend on the arm. 'Huh?'

'Uh uh.' Thabo shook his head quickly and firmly. Luke's mother insisted the young black boy wasn't to go anywhere near the child and Thabo wasn't about to tell her he had. 'He laughing now,' Thabo said as Simon's face spread into a lopsided smile, spilling over in chortles of delight. 'He fool us!'

Glancing towards the white gabled house in the distance, Luke moved back to his horse. He knew his mother would be making sure every inch of the Cape Dutch home was swept and scrubbed although it was already clean. The wood, glass and silver would be gleaming under the hard rubbing of black hands and he knew it wasn't to welcome the relations arriving that day from Northern Rhodesia. It was to put them in their place.

'I won't be long,' Luke called back to Thabo as he rode away. There was still a great deal he had to think about and his young brother Simon was a very large part of it.

'Go,' Thabo urged, swinging Simon's chubby body on to his back and holding his wrists tightly round his neck. 'Simon ride like Luke.' Thabo galloped among the vines and the small boy shrieked his excitement. 'Simon riding,' Thabo called through the curious sounds he'd learned to recognise as laughter.

Over the years Thabo had spent with his friend, in a world built outside the reach of Luke's mother, he'd grown sensitive to Luke's need for solitude. He knew Luke had many problems and the family due to arrive later that day would add to them. Thabo knew that among them would be an old lady who used to live on Bonne Espérance – a frail old lady who'd once told Thabo that she'd known his ancestor, I Titus. I Titus was a man around whom many myths had grown, and Thabo found it hard to believe that Katinka had walked in that time.

'Hold on,' Thabo called to the laughing child on his back and his heart ached. It had been only the night before that he'd heard what was going to happen to the mongol child, the child whom his people said was touched by God.

'*Thabo.*' He'd heard Luke's hushed call through the night air of yesterday and had looked towards the lit window of Luke's bedroom. It was in an extending wing at the back of the house. The other wing was boarded up and unused except as a secret meeting place. All of that day, Thabo had known something was happening inside the big house and that somehow it affected him, but he'd had to wait till night-time to find out what it was . . .

'Come on.' Luke pushed his bedroom window wider and leaned out, looking at Thabo through the darkness, his straight blond hair tumbling over his eyes. 'I've got things to tell you.'

Thabo ran silently across the cobbles in front of the house. Suddenly, he flattened his black body against the white walls that ran up in a gable over the front door, and froze motionless. The curtains on the window beside him had swished open and he'd wished Luke's bedroom wasn't so close to his parents'. If Estelle Marsden ever caught him in her son's bedroom, Thabo knew that he and his family would be thrown off Bonne Espérance for good.

'Here.' Luke's arm stretched over the windowledge and grabbed his hand. Thabo's strong black fingers locked with Luke's and he swung his body over the edge of the window sill.

'Eee,' Thabo whispered as the hard edge of the window frame dug into his stomach and a rose bush grabbed at his bare legs. 'Your mother's awake,' he hissed at his friend, and a looming image of Estelle filled his mind. 'She kill me!'

'Simon's going,' Luke said as Thabo landed head-first on the floor. 'They're sending him away.'

'Yes.' Thabo pushed himself up off the floor and rubbed his hands on his pants. 'He go with you to Johannesburg?' He glanced back towards the window and spoke quickly in Xhosa. 'One day your mother will be out there with her gun, waiting for me.'

'Listen.' Luke joined Thabo in the Xhosa language they often shared, a language that slipped off his tongue more naturally than English. Luke's first memories were couched in the comforting clicks and long-drawn-out vowels of his Xhosa nanny, Sophie. 'My mother's putting Simon into a hospital, Thabo. He's going to be locked up because she says we can't take him.'

'Locked up?' Thabo's father had once been taken to the jail in Cape Town and he'd never forgotten his eyes as they'd peered at him from behind iron bars. 'No!' Thabo shook his head violently. 'He die!' In his mind's eye the small boy's distorted face peered at him, a steel bar dividing it in two. 'Those people mustn't come here – they must go!' Thabo blamed all the changes that were sweeping through their lives on the family he'd been told were taking over Bonne Espérance. 'We don't want them here.' His eyes narrowed as he turned to Luke and he spoke in quiet, determined Xhosa. 'The child Simon is God's child and our people must never harm him, Luke.'

'Do you think it's what I want?' Luke pulled a crisp loaf of bread from under his pillow. He dug his teeth into it and ripped off a hunk before passing the rest to Thabo. 'Do you think I want to go?' He leaned over the edge of the bed and pulled an open tin of condensed milk out from under it. The jagged edges met like sharks' jaws, hard drips of dried milk forming teeth. 'Maybe we can make my aunt and uncle change their minds and go back.' Luke's eyes lit up with that exciting possibility as Thabo pushed the tin lid back, dipping his own finger into the white sweetness. 'We could frighten their kid!'

'Who?' Thabo pulled his finger out of the can and an elastic thread of milk stretched down towards his open mouth. 'Your cousin?' he said through the sweetness that spread over his tongue before covering the roof of his mouth. 'What's her name?'

'Rebecca,' Luke told him as they dug into a feast of condensed milk and bread. 'It shouldn't take much to frighten her. She's only nine like Naomi.'

Lost in their Xhosa conversation, the two young boys hadn't heard Estelle approaching Luke's door.

'Luke?' her voice called suddenly. Before his friend had time to react, Thabo had grabbed the condensed milk tin and dived under the bed, pulling his bare feet after him.

'Who were you talking to?' Estelle asked, coming in. The striped bottom of the ticking mattress pressed down on Thabo's head as he lay flat on the floor beneath it.

'My history – I'm learning it out loud.' Luke pushed a schoolbook off the bed and Thabo tilted his head to read it as it dropped to the floor beside him. He'd already learned Luke's history himself and he closed his eyes as the lovely smell of school paper drifted into his nose. 'Why can't Simon come with us?'

'I've told you before.' Estelle's white feet appeared at the edge of the bed and Thabo pulled back quickly. 'It'll be better for him. He'll be much happier with his own kind.'

There was a moment's pause and Thabo tensed. Estelle had said that about him once, too. When Luke had asked why Thabo couldn't sleep with him in his bedroom, she'd said that Thabo was happier with his own kind.

'That boy hasn't been in here has he, Luke?' Estelle's words peeped under the bed at Thabo.

'Who?'

'You know the boy I mean.'

'Thabo hasn't been here.'

'I thought I smelt something.'

Thabo watched Estelle's feet turn and move away. He heard the door close behind her and wondered how it was that she never remembered his name, but always his smell.

A stream of wet kisses pulled Thabo out of the long night he'd spent in Luke's bedroom and he swung Simon off his back, holding him in front of him. The slanted eyes, strangely alight in the round face, peered at Thabo intently. It was as if Simon had been in on his memories and wanted to know Thabo's decision.

'I escape you,' Thabo whispered, wondering how he'd find his way into a white hospital. 'I take you like so.' He tucked Simon under his arm and ran down a narrow path between the vines. 'We go far away!' Simon squealed with laughter and his chubby legs kicked uselessly as Thabo held him.

'Why are you doing that?' Naomi, Luke's nine-year-old sister, stood in the kitchen doorway and watched Sophie. Sophie sat at the large wooden table polishing the silver, turning a gleaming knife in her hand till she caught sight of herself in the blade. 'They probably don't even use knives and forks,' Naomi informed her.

'Your mother say.' Sophie ignored the child. It was more than her life was worth to argue with her mistress Estelle.

'My mother say what?' Naomi imitated her and moved closer, watching Sophie's chubby hands pick up a fork. 'I bet they eat mealie pap in their fingers like you.'

Sophie nodded at the dull coat of polish covering the fork in her hand. She'd never seen white people eat mealie pap before and wondered what part of Africa the visitors were coming from.

'Maybe your mother she teach them.' Sophie pushed her bottom lip forward. Estelle had managed to teach her all kinds of useless manners but none to her daughter Naomi, she thought.

'Huh!' Naomi swung away, turning in a small circle that spread her starched skirt wide. 'I bet Rebecca still wears short dresses.' She looked down at her own skirt. It fell halfway down her calves and she pushed it flat to make it longer. 'Socks too, probably.' She wriggled her bare toes in the open white sandals on her feet. 'Or maybe no shoes at all!' Naomi swung away across the kitchen, pausing to admire herself in the gleaming copper bottom of the large pot that hung over the huge wood stove. 'When are they coming? I'm bored.'

'You tell your brother he better not dirty his clothes.' Sophie looked at

Naomi through narrowed eyes, wondering that the child was so different from Luke. 'He changed yet, like your mother said? She be cross with him if he out riding again, in good clothes.'

'Will you stay with them – that Rebecca and her family? You going to work for them now?' Naomi looked round at Sophie, running her index finger down the marble kitchen surface beside her. 'Ugh!' A tiny spot of jam had stuck to her finger and she held it out to Sophie in disgust, pushing it under her nose. 'Jam.' Sophie squinted at the straight white finger that pointed between her eyes and pulled it down, wiping it on the apron that spread tight across her bosoms. 'You'd better clean it.' Naomi nodded at the offending marble and dropped back on her heels, looking down at her sandals. 'Are you sure you cleaned my shoes today?'

'Haven't you finished the silver yet, Sophie?' Estelle interrupted as she entered the kitchen. 'Outside!' She pushed Naomi towards the kitchen door. Estelle's dark hair was scraped back into a neat bun at the nape of her neck and what beauty there might once have been was bound by pretension. 'You haven't even polished the front step yet. I told you to do it first thing, Sophie.'

'I clean the silver like you said, madam.' Sophie sat firmly on her stool, venting her silent rage on the fork. 'Like madam told me.' A prong poked through the rag and jabbed her finger.

'And I told her they don't use knives and forks anyway,' Naomi added as she moved to the door. 'They probably live in mud huts.'

'That doesn't mean we lower *our* standards.' Estelle didn't correct her daughter. 'If they're to live in this house I intend to show them exactly how it's to be looked after.'

And that was precisely what Estelle had been doing since she'd woken early that morning. She was determined that her English sister-in-law Constance would never make her feel inferior again. Estelle had spent her entire life convinced she was second class. An Afrikaner mother had meant Afrikaans was her mother tongue; until she went to school. There Estelle had learned that Afrikaans was the language of donkeys and she'd spent many hours in the corner for daring to speak it. Under the sharp eye of the Englishwoman who'd taught her, she'd stood for hours with a board pinned to her chest and a dunce's hat on her head. The board stated that she would no longer speak her own ugly Dutch language and shame had quickly taught her English.

'You don't really consider this clean?' Estelle held a gleaming spoon out to Sophie.

'I do the step now.' Sophie pushed her plump body off the stool, sliding the wooden seat under the table with an angry bare foot. 'I hope the old lady she not slip on the polished step,' she added, as a warning note to her mistress.

'Where's the master?' Estelle moved after her towards the back door. 'Find him, and don't forget to change your uniform.' She tugged at the material of Sophie's overall, holding her back for a moment. 'This is filthy.'

'Yes, madam.' Sophie looked down at the striped uniform she'd only just washed.

'They're forty minutes late already.' Estelle pushed her on with complaints. 'Don't they have any regard for time at all?'

'It bad, madam,' Sophie said, ducking out of her path quickly as she made for the safety of her own small room outside.

'Ma told you to wash and change long ago.' Naomi's nasal voice reached for Luke as she peered into the dark of the stables, her nose held tight against the smell. 'Did you hear me, Luke?' Luke ducked under the horse's belly and ran the hard grooming brush firmly down its chest without acknowledging his younger sister. 'You must stink of horses!' Naomi backed into the doorway, checking that her skirt hadn't been dirtied. 'I bet that Rebecca still wears short dresses.' She twirled proudly in the doorway. 'Oh no!' She brushed angrily at a piece of straw that clung to the material. 'Anyway, Ma says she steals babies.'

'Go away, Naomi.' Luke dismissed her inane chatter and moved round to the horse's face. 'Girls,' he muttered, and Salu's large eyes blinked as he undid the horse's halter. 'Now there's another one coming.' He pulled the halter over the horse's head and stopped dead as he tripped over the words his sister had left behind.

'*She steals babies.*'

Striding through the sitting room, Naomi called for Sophie to clean her skirt. 'Sophie!' she yelled through the house, irritated that the black servant hadn't answered at once. 'Daddy.' She spotted her father and went over to stand by him as he gazed out of the window. 'Why can't we go to Johannesburg straight away?' she whined. 'That Rebecca's funny and I'm glad she's not in my room. I don't want to see her.'

'Naomi.' The tone of her father's voice stopped her briefly. 'You'll be kind to Rebecca when she arrives – do you hear me?'

'Why should I?' Naomi's bottom lip pushed out and her head tilted back. 'Ma says she's not nice, that she should be in jail.'

Paul Marsden knew his wife disliked his family and in many ways he understood why, but he wanted to welcome them. Though Constance was in fact his aunt, when his mother had died in childbirth they'd been brought up by Katinka as brother and sister. He could still remember

Constance's last remark as she'd left Bonne Espérance with Katinka eight years earlier, and it touched his pride once again.

'*I hope you'll take hold of your own life one day, Paul.*'

Outside his wife's knowledge, Paul had taken hold of his own life — but now even the brief moments in which he felt like a man as he lay in the arms of another woman, even they were to be taken from him.

'Whatever your mother might say, you will treat Rebecca and her family with respect,' he told the tight-lipped face of his daughter. 'Do you hear me?'

'Why should I?' Naomi lifted her foot and rubbed at a small mark on the white sandal. 'You know she's funny, and that's why they're coming.' Naomi turned away sharply, swinging her slim body out of the room. 'Sophie!' she yelled. She'd learned to dismiss her father just as her mother did.

'Don't they know what a telephone is?' Estelle's voice snatched Paul's attention and instinctively his mind crept away into the arms of Elize. 'Or don't they have such things in mine quarters?' Estelle reduced Constance and her family to the level of migrant labourers.

'I'll drive into Cape Town and see what's kept them.' Paul grabbed at this way out of the suffocation of his own home. He could make a small detour to Stellenbosch, he thought. Just the gentle touch of Elize's hand and the warmth of her voice would help the sudden insecurity he felt. 'I'll go.'

'Don't be ridiculous!' His wife's voice held him back like a small dog on the end of a lead. 'They're probably lost and you'd never find them in Cape Town.' Her eyes fixed on Paul's, as if assuring him that she knew exactly where he'd intended to go. 'Stay here until they arrive.' Estelle was determined her husband would be at her side when Constance arrived. Marriage to Paul Marsden had ensured she was no longer second class. 'Have you made sure Luke's changed yet, Sophie?' She moved towards the door.

Alone at last in the highly polished room, Paul wondered again if perhaps his wife knew about Elize. Her determination to move the family north to the Transvaal might not be to secure their future as she'd said, but he smiled. For the first time in his life he was one step ahead of her. Then his smile faded. A cheap copy of Van Gogh's sunflowers on the wall had caught his eye, the picture that had long since taken the place of the family portrait of Clara Beauvilliers' wedding. All the young life that Paul had shared with Constance, Jacques Beauvilliers and his family of daughters had stared down at him from that space on the wall. They'd watched him constantly and he'd made up endless stories for Constance about the eagle-eyed Jacques Beauvilliers. Many was the time they'd run in terror

73

as Katinka had threatened to call him down to punish them.

Where had those days gone, Paul wondered now. Long days. Bright blue days. They'd vanished when he'd married Estelle, for whom he'd felt no more than pity. They'd been wiped out as the Nationalist Government's grasping hand closed round the throat of his country and Bonne Espérance itself seemed to have died. Though he hadn't cared for the vineyard as his father and grandfather before him had, Paul loved it in a curious way. He watched Thabo leap across the cobbled square in front of the house, his agile body like a fleeting shadow, and Paul wondered if that black child had ever had any bright blue days in his life.

'What is it?' Thabo called in Xhosa as he reached the stables and squeezed his body through a narrow gap in the crumbling wall. 'Your mother's calling for you, Luke. You must go.'

Luke's eyes were sparkling with the excitement of an idea, and Thabo felt his heart lift without understanding why. 'I know what to do about Simon,' he said.

'Your mother's looking for you,' Thabo said again. 'She'll shoot me if she finds me in here.' Thabo ignored Luke as his imagination threw up an image of Estelle aiming a shotgun straight at his head. 'I go now.'

'She won't find you.' Luke calmed his friend with the assurance that his mother would never come into the stables. 'We're going to steal Simon.'

'*What?*' Thabo peered at his friend in amazement. 'Uh, uh.' He shook his head. 'Uh, uh,' he repeated, and turned and looked towards the light that poured through the open doors; in his mind's eye, Estelle's shotgun became a machine gun. 'You go to your mother.' He tried to leave quickly but Luke grabbed his shoulders, turning him back to face him. 'What you doing, Luke?'

'I'm serious, Thabo.'

'Uh, uh.' Thabo pulled himself free. 'You want they hang me?' He spoke in broken English as his mind pounced on the myth of I Titus, waving it at him in warning. 'I go.'

'Wait!' Luke grabbed the top of Thabo's short trousers and they slipped down over his bare backside. 'Listen to me.' He pulled his friend's trousers back on to his hips and turned him to face him. 'Do you want Simon locked up?' Thabo shook his head but kept silent. Every time they'd broken the rules he'd been blamed and not Luke. 'I'll say I did it.' Luke understood Thabo's reluctance but still he persisted. 'Please, Thabo. We've got to do something for Simon.'

The tug of Luke's pleading caught Thabo off-balance and he lowered his head with a shrug. Though he was two years older than Luke he

74

always felt younger and he'd decided it was because Luke went to school while he didn't.

'That girl who's coming today – you know the one I mean?' Luke jumped on Thabo's moment of vulnerability. 'Rebecca.'

'Your cousin.' Thabo nodded. He was nervous and lapsed back into the safety of his own Xhosa language.

'Naomi says she steals babies!' Thabo's face grew puzzled as his mind struggled with the curious image Luke's words had thrown up. 'So?' he shrugged, wondering what school Luke's cousin had learned that in.

'Luke!' Estelle's voice pushed its way towards the stables and Thabo spun round to the safety of the gap in the wall.

'See you later,' Luke called after his friend's slim body as it pushed its way through the crumbling opening. 'Don't say anything!'

'Huh.' Thabo's deep-throated exclamation slipped back and Luke smiled.

'I'm coming to wash and change now,' he called as he ran towards the stable doors. 'Won't be long.' He grinned at Estelle as he ran on past her towards the house; the excitement of his plans lifting him in springing strides. The anger he'd felt at strangers taking over Bonne Espérance had spiralled into hope.

'Yea, though I walk through the valley of the shadow of death, I will fear no evil. Thy rod and Thy staff they comfort me.' The priest's words passed over Rebecca's head, unheard as she stared into the dark of the oblong hole at her feet. On long black cords, Katinka's narrow wood coffin was being lowered into a freshly dug grave and a large part of Rebecca wanted to crawl down with her.

'Johannes Villiers.' Her grandmother's whispered words crept through the lid of the coffin. 'Find him, Rebecca!'

Searching among the headstones in the small graveyard, Rebecca's eyes settled on a simple cross at the head of a grave further away.

The name *Emily Beauvilliers* was cut into the stonework and Rebecca's mind lifted in a moment of recognition, leaping back into the pages of the diaries she'd found among Granny Cat's possessions. They'd been written by the name on the gravestone. *Emily Beauvilliers. Born 1827, Died 1899.* Rebecca wondered how anybody could have lived and died so long ago and she glanced round towards the white gabled house in which Emily once lived. The house disturbed her. It was large and curiously empty, surrounded by deep purple mountains that threatened to crush them all. Bonne Espérance had none of the warmth her grandmother had described, and all she wanted to do was to run home.

'Thou preparest a table before me in the presence of mine enemies . . .'

The mellow sound of the priest's voice rolled on and Rebecca's eyes moved cautiously over the group of strangers who'd gathered round her grandmother's grave. They were all members of the same family, Constance had told her. Descendants of the man Jacques Beauvilliers, who'd once tended the red earth that drew Granny Cat to its heart now. Though dressed in the black of mourning and standing in sombre silence, nobody cried. Only in the eyes of her older cousin, Lydia, could Rebecca see the glisten of threatening tears. The beautiful dark-haired woman was watching her, and quickly Rebecca looked away. Beside Lydia was her husband, Stan Liebenberg and he was an Afrikaner. The enemy stood right there on Bonne Espérance and Rebecca was very unsure, as unsure as she was of the young boy who stood on the other side of the grave. It was Luke Marsden. Luke, whom she'd thought about in the tree on top of the ant hill at 123 Z. Unable to look at anyone, she fixed her attention on the wooden casket that settled itself deep in the crumbling red earth in front of her. She concentrated her mind instead on the long black cords that pulled her grandmother free of the world forever.

'Thou anointest my head with oil. My cup runneth over.'

Granny Cat had vanished in the ground and Rebecca felt curiously lonely. She was loose in God's pocket. Abandoned in a foreign place where the enemy lurked, she was alone with the secret of Johannes Villiers.

As if sensing comfort in Luke, her eyes ventured towards him again. He was very handsome. He watched her from under a heavy fringe of blond hair and Rebecca could hardly breathe.

'I told you her dress would be short.' Naomi's hard sandal dug into Luke's ankle, giving weight to her whisper and Luke silenced her with a quick kick on the shin. He felt strangely protective towards the small dark-haired girl who stood across the grave from him.

'Surely goodness and mercy shall follow me all the days of my life. And I will dwell in the house of the Lord forever.' The priest's words were drowned by the heavy clatter of earth falling on Granny Cat's coffin.

'Salt?' Estelle raised her eyebrows as she held a silver cruet out to Constance. 'We don't use too much in our cooking.' She'd noticed that Rebecca still hadn't taken her napkin from its silver ring and she smiled condescendingly. 'You can use the napkin, dear.'

'Thank you.' Rebecca blushed under the gaze of Naomi who sat opposite her and, pulling the starched white napkin free of the silver ring, she tucked it into the collar of her new dress.

'Look at her!' An explosion of laughter spat peas from Naomi's mouth across the table and on to the immaculate bodice of her own dress.

'See what she did to my dress!' Naomi excused herself to her mother

76

as she picked the peas from her bodice, pushing them off her finger on to the side plate.

'If you put your napkin in properly like she did, it wouldn't have happened.' Luke pushed Naomi's napkin into the collar of her dress and, as Naomi boiled, Rebecca bit her lip to hide her pleasure.

'Paul will be showing you round after lunch.' Estelle glanced at David, removing the attention from her daughter. 'It's a little run down,' she smiled, 'but Paul isn't a farmer, of course.' She turned her cool gaze on to Constance. 'Perhaps I could show you round the house.'

'I was born in it.' Constance's voice was very quiet and Estelle's mouth tightened into a straight line as Constance held her breeding high in front of her.

'I'm sorry you were put to the trouble of preparing for my mother without reason.' Constance tried to quieten her anger as her mind slipped back to her mother's tiny body being measured by the undertaker.

'It seems so sudden.' Paul turned to her, needing to know exactly what had happened to the person he'd always considered his own mother. 'I thought she was well. The last time we spoke she sounded fine.'

'Yes.' Constance looked down, uncertain whether she could hold back the emotion that blocked her throat. The practicalities of moving Katinka's body into the goods van before Rebecca woke, the formality of undertakers the moment they'd arrived in Cape Town; nothing had yet woken Constance to the reality of her mother's death. Deep down she still blamed the cold woman at the head of the dining table.

'It might have been easier if you'd let us know what had delayed you.' Estelle's voice was as angular as her body and Constance listened without expression. 'We could have arranged for a local undertaker. It would have been a lot simpler and we'd have saved so much delay.' She paused. 'When's your furniture due to arrive?'

Unable to bear Granny Cat being discussed like a piece of furniture they'd lost en route, Rebecca got up suddenly and ran out of the room.

'Your napkin!' Naomi called after her and Luke kicked her as he got up himself.

'Excuse me.' He moved after Rebecca and Naomi yanked the napkin from her collar.

'Sit down, Luke.' Estelle tried to restore order but Luke had left without turning back. 'Do you think it's wise for Rebecca to be in the midday sun, Constance?' she asked quietly. 'She's so like your mother, isn't she?' She paused, knowing her meaning was abundantly clear. 'You were saying?'

'I believe you were saying.' Constance lowered her eyes, digging her fork into the tasteless food she couldn't eat. 'About undertakers, wasn't it? Is that your family's line of business?' She lifted eyes filled with challenge and stared at Estelle in silence.

'Wine?' Paul held a bottle high, trying to break the growing tension between the two women. 'Do you like it, David? It's one of ours.'

'Yes.' David glanced at the label as the two men steered the conversation away. 'Bonne Espérance, Cabernet Sauvignon. It's good.'

An ancient slave bell stood like a monument to the beginnings of Bonne Espérance and Rebecca was standing motionless beside its flaking white base, her head lowered. Even from the house Luke could see she was crying and he waited in the doorway, unsure what to do. Girls' tears confused him, and spotting Thabo further away, he signalled for him not to come closer.

Unaware of either Luke or Thabo, Rebecca's eyes moved from the slave bell to the cellars. Through a veil of tears she looked at the stables, the barn and the servants' quarters that formed a square around the courtyard in front of the house. They were not the sparkling white that Granny Cat had described. They were grubby and ugly. They were hideous buildings in a hideous place that was filled with hideous people.

'Don't cry.'

Rebecca turned away sharply as Luke's voice reached her. Wishing he'd leave her alone, she tilted her head back and fixed her eyes on the enormous bell that hung above her head. She didn't want to cry. Hoping the tears would run back into her eyes, she held her chin high to help them along.

'What's that bell?' she asked, sniffing loose tears that had run back up her nose.

'It's the slave bell. Here.' Luke pulled the napkin out of Rebecca's collar and held it out to her.

'I know.' Rebecca looked at the napkin nervously, taken aback by Luke's kindness. 'Granny Cat said there were slaves here once – that Jacques Beauvilliers owned people.'

'Go on, blow your nose.' Luke nodded at the napkin. 'That's what it's for. Why are you crying, anyway?'

'Jean Jacques was a slave,' Rebecca said quietly as she wiped her eyes, prepared to talk about anything except the reason she was crying. 'Jean Jacques was Eva and Jacques Beauvilliers' son.' She poked her chin forward, daring him to argue.

'Oh.' Luke turned away. 'I don't know about the slaves. It was long ago. Nobody knows.'

'Granny Cat did. And I Titus was hanged.' Rebecca added that fact quickly. She knew she couldn't tell Luke the secret of Johannes Villiers, the secret Katinka had entrusted to her, but she had to take her mind off crying.

'Have you got a horse?' She turned to Luke and as she did so, suddenly felt nervous. That tingling sensation had touched her once again and she wanted to run away. 'Granny Cat said you had horses. Have you? Do you ride?'

'Yes.'

'Where's Simon? Why isn't he here?'

'He's asleep.' Luke ducked her question. He knew his mother would keep Simon out of sight for as long as possible. 'OK now?' He watched Rebecca as she blew her nose loudly on the napkin, squeezing it into an embarrassed ball in her hand.

'I'll wash it,' she said quietly.

'You can keep it.' Luke turned away. He didn't know why he was still talking to Rebecca now she'd stopped crying. There were more important things to do. 'Do you want to see him?'

'Simon?'

'My horse.'

'Yes.'

'Come on then,' Luke called over his shoulder as he moved quickly towards the safety of the stables. He was glad to be away from the grown-ups and the curious tension that had filled the house since Rebecca and her parents had arrived. But talking to Rebecca hadn't proved much easier. 'Can you ride?'

'Of course.' Rebecca watched Luke's long tanned legs stride ahead of her towards the stables. 'A bit,' she added, as the sound of a neighing horse reached her.

'Come on then.' Luke stood inside the stables next to an enormous black horse and Rebecca hung back. She had no idea horses were so big and all she could see was a row of enormous bodies pushing uncomfortably against one another. 'You can ride this one.'

'No.' Rebecca backed away from both Luke and the animal with gleaming muscles rippling down his flank. 'He's too big.'

'Come on!' He took her hand, leading her back towards Salu. The bones in Luke's hand were hard, but somehow his grip was gentle and the tingling sensation inside her curiously comforting. 'Say hullo to Salu.'

Rebecca looked up into the melting brown eyes of the horse and all at once felt safe. Luke's hand was flat against the arch of her back and she knew he was in total control as he spoke gently to the horse.

'This is Rebecca, Salu. You're going to be friends. She's going to ride you.'

'Maybe.' Cautiously Rebecca stretched her hand towards the horse's nose. 'Hey!' Her shoulders lifted with nervous delight as Salu buried his nose in her palm, blowing bubbles of soft, warm air into it. 'Oh he's lovely. His nose is all soft. Look at his eyes!'

'Don't they have horses where you come from?' Luke stared at her in amazement and she burned with embarrassment. 'Haven't you ever seen a horse before?' He laughed at the thought.

'Have you seen an ant hill?' Rebecca countered, her chin held high as her dark eyes flashed. 'With a tree on it?'

'Of course.' Luke was taken aback by the sudden anger behind her eyes. They were black and as deep as the sea.

'I don't mean those silly little lumps on the ground you've got here. I'm talking about an ant hill as big as a house.' Rebecca clung tightly to the confidence the ant hill instilled in her. 'You don't get ant hills as big as mine on this side of the Zambezi. All you've got is molehills!'

'So?' Luke shrugged. 'Can you ride a horse?'

'No more than you could climb my ant hill!' Rebecca swung away and ran to the stable door. She was fleeing from the strange feelings Luke's presence had roused inside her and she pulled her skirt down, wishing it was as long as Naomi's.

As Luke watched her go, his breath came out in a long whistling sigh. He'd been right in the first place. Rebecca was no different from his sister and he dreaded the long month he'd have to spend in her company before leaving for the Transvaal. He hated the fact that a girl who knew nothing about horses and everything about ant hills would be taking his place on Bonne Espérance.

'She say yes.' Thabo's voice crept through a gap in the stable wall ahead of him. 'Nombeko say yes.' Thabo's eyes were alight with achievement but Luke was no longer interested.

'Forget it. It won't work.' Luke leant back against the horse, Salu.

'You let them lock Simon up?' Thabo stared at his friend in amazement. 'Rebecca no good? She not steal babies?' He lapsed into English as he talked of the young white girl he'd just seen run out of the stables.

'She's just a girl.' Luke turned away and propped his chin on the horse's back. 'If Naomi doesn't spill on us then she will. They're all the same.'

'But you say Rebecca she know how to steal babies,' Thabo reminded him.

'What's that got to do with anything?' Luke turned to face him, slipping back into the Xhosa language. 'We won't be able to move with two girls watching us all the time. It was a stupid idea.' He pushed himself away from Salu and moved to the doors. 'I'll be spending my time teaching her to ride my horse and then she'll get to keep him. She didn't even know what a horse was.' Luke left a trail of frustrated anger behind him as he walked away and Thabo watched in grim silence.

Even if he had to do it alone, Thabo was determined to make sure Simon was not locked up. The pure love that poured from the mongol child was a light in the world and he treasured it. The old woman, Nombeko, had promised to help and Thabo knew her name meant 'to be honest'.

Rebecca stopped beside the open doorway to the sitting room as she heard the sound of a small child. Peering through the slit in the door frame, her face grew puzzled. Her mother was holding a small boy in her lap and he was laughing, but there was something wrong. Though she couldn't see his face she sensed there was something strange about him.

'Take him away now, Miriam.' Estelle's voice broke through the child's laughter.

'Yes, mam.' Sophie's daughter Miriam bent down to take Simon. 'I take him back to his room now, mam.'

'Is that Simon?' Rebecca ran into the room but stopped dead as she saw the baby who peered at her over Miriam's shoulder. His face was distorted and quite suddenly she was lost inside fear of the unknown.

'He's spitting again,' Naomi said flatly as she poked at the piano tunelessly.

'Put him to bed,' Estelle ordered and turned to the piano sharply. 'Stop that, Naomi!'

'I'm practising,' Naomi whined and Rebecca moved quickly after Miriam. Simon's face had lit with a crooked smile and her fear had vanished inside it.

'Can I hold him?' she asked, understanding for the first time why Granny Cat had called him 'perhaps-not-Simon'. A sliver of spit crept from the corner of the child's mouth and his tongue pushed out, hanging over his lips. But Rebecca wasn't afraid. His eyes were curiously alight and he looked at her with a tenderness she'd never experienced before.

'Take the child away, Miriam,' Estelle repeated.

'Please, I want to hold him,' Rebecca argued.

'Take him, Miriam!' Estelle wanted her shame out of sight where it belonged and Constance signalled Rebecca to be quiet as she turned to Estelle gently.

'You'll find a good school for him in Johannesburg, I expect,' she smiled. 'I believe they've advanced a great deal with the treatment of these children.'

'He'll be staying in Cape Town.' Estelle picked up the silver coffee pot and her shoulders relaxed as the door closed behind Miriam and Simon.

'Coffee?' she asked through the stream of silent questions aimed at her by Rebecca.

'Is he going to your family in the Cape?' Constance asked. 'No, I won't have any more coffee, thank you.'

'My family's in the Transvaal.' As Estelle watched a steaming black stream of coffee pour into her cup, she was deeply angry. Her private disgrace had been displayed in front of people she despised and now they dared to question her. She knew that Simon was God's punishment for the sin she'd committed when she married Paul. Like the rest of the Beauvilliers family, Paul wasn't white even though he looked it. Theirs was a marriage Estelle's church would have condemned if they had known the truth of her husband's ancestors. 'Simon's going into a children's home,' she said firmly, hoping to close the subject once and for all.

'What home?' Rebecca's dark eyes searched Estelle's face carefully.

'Naomi, please!' Estelle shouted as her anger snapped, and the tuneless piano music stopped at once.

'But you'll never see him again. He's only little.' Rebecca tried to swallow the hard lump in her throat as she watched Estelle's eyes for just a glimmer of hope. 'You can't send him away. That's mean.'

Constance could see a deep well of emotion rising in Rebecca, and she had noticed Estelle straighten with anger. Glancing quickly at Naomi, who sat rigid on the piano stool with her long skirt spread over her knees, Constance spoke quietly. 'Why don't you play outside with Rebecca, Naomi?'

'Because I don't want to.' Naomi's voice was flat and nasal.

'It's OK.' Rebecca ran out of the room. The thought of 'perhaps-not-Simon' with his crooked smile and big tongue being locked up was more than she could bear and she needed to be alone.

With her legs stretched straight on the narrow bed in the small attic room of the house, Rebecca twiddled her toes, watching them carefully. Her mind ran over and over the things she'd heard about Simon and she felt like a mouse in a maze as she looked for answers. What kind of home was 'perhaps-not-Simon' going to? Was it a boarding school like the one she'd been threatened with once? Was it an orphanage? She shook her head quickly, dismissing the orphanage. Perhaps-not-Simon had parents. And a brother and sister. She could hear Luke somewhere outside and quickly she jumped off the bed and ran to the small window in the sloping roof.

'Ow!' She banged her head as she tried to look out of it. Luke was dragging a small wooden cart across the yard below and she tapped on the window, but he didn't look up. She pushed the small brass lever fixed under a latch and shoved it again, but it wouldn't move. 'Hey, Luke,' she called with her mouth pressed against the glass. A haze of mist spread over the window pane and, pulling the napkin out of her pants she wiped it clean quickly. 'Luke!'

Thabo nudged Luke as he moved past him with a large bucket of water in one hand. 'Rebecca, she wants you.' He pointed up at the tiny window in the thatched eaves of the house, the room that had once concealed the heart of Bonne Espérance and now held Rebecca. Glancing up, Luke caught sight of a white napkin waving and he dropped the handle of the small cart to wave back, but then he turned away.

'We take Simon in that,' Thabo winked, nodding at the cart as he passed Luke. 'We and she.' He looked up at the attic window, beckoning to Rebecca out of Luke's sight. Thabo had sensed that the girl who stole babies was their only answer. Everyone knew babies were women's business.

'I told you, she's a girl,' Luke objected.

'Nombeko she say yes.' Thabo made sure Luke knew he hadn't given up yet and he walked away.

Thabo's beckoning wave had called Rebecca into a world shared by two boys and she took the narrow wooden stairs that led down from her attic room three at a time. She was sure Luke would have the answers she needed.

'You're not allowed to run on the stairs,' Naomi commented through tight lips as Rebecca brushed past her at the bottom. 'Or go without shoes!' she shouted as Rebecca disappeared barefoot through the front door.

'Who was that?' Rebecca asked as she skidded to a stop beside Luke. 'With the bucket. Him.' She pointed after Thabo as he disappeared into the barn.

'Just someone,' Luke said calmly and tilted the cart to one side, spinning the old pram wheels he'd fixed to it.

'Is he a slave?'

'What?' Luke laughed at Rebecca's stupidity and turned back to the cart.

'What's that?' She touched the cart with her bare foot, unsure how to ask the question she needed answering.

'What do you think it is?'

'Looks like a cart.' Luke watched her blank-faced, and her eyes flashed with anger. 'I'm not stupid.' Her look held him on the end of an elastic thread, assuring him she could pull him right inside her head at any moment. 'I wanted to ask you about Simon.'

'What do you want to know?' Luke bent down to the cart to escape Rebecca's look.

'Why does your mother want to give him away?' Luke's heart tripped over an extra beat with Rebecca's words.

'My mother said.' Luke unexpectedly found himself protecting Estelle. 'He's a mongol. Simon's sick.'

'What's a mongol?'

'He's not normal.' Luke's anger rose as her questions probed his decision not to help Simon. 'Children like Simon get locked up all the time. They have to be locked up.'

'Why?' Rebecca hadn't given an inch and she stared her challenge. 'Has he killed someone?'

'Don't be stupid.' Luke's frustration grabbed him by the collar and swung him away from her. 'What do you know about it, anyway! He's not your brother, is he?'

'He's yours.' Rebecca's voice brought Luke to a skidding stop and he closed his eyes. His foot pushed the cart gently backwards and forwards on the cobbles and he gazed down at it blindly. 'That's for Simon, isn't it?' Rebecca watched the small cart that rolled between them. 'You've made it for him.'

'So?' Luke turned to face her. 'What's it got to do with you? What's anything got to do with you? This isn't your place, Simon isn't your brother. All this —' his arms spread wide in a gesture that included everything he loved and was about to lose '— none of this is yours!'

'No.' Rebecca could feel the unfamiliar friendship she'd forged in a moment slip out of her grip as he accused her of taking something she didn't even want.

'Damn!' Luke kicked the small cart and it rolled away over the cobbles as Rebecca ran back to the house. 'Damn!' He ran after the cart and kicked it again.

'Rebecca help us, Luke.' Thabo's voice chased after the sound of wheels against cobbles. 'Come. We must make plan.' He beckoned Luke into the barn.

The rest of the week passed slowly. Nobody mentioned Simon again and Rebecca was forced to unpack her case under Naomi's piercing gaze. As her family unpacked, so Estelle's family packed. While modern furniture and drapes were exchanged for those that Constance remembered from her own past, Rebecca had been locked in a curious game of oneupmanship.

'Do you want to see mine?' Naomi had asked, her nose in the air as Rebecca showed her the grubby rag doll she'd loved all her life.

Like soldiers in long frilly dresses, Naomi's dolls stood on a large white shelf over her bed and every one had shiny blonde hair. They had shiny faces too, rosy cheeks and rosebud mouths just like Naomi.

'See?' Naomi said smugly as she turned a doll on its back. 'It cries like a baby.' The doll made strange noises that sounded nothing like a baby and Rebecca's mouth had turned down in disgust. 'And this one walks.' Naomi took down another doll whose short fat legs were pushed up frilly holes in her pants. 'See?' she said arrogantly as the doll took slow clumping steps across the floor.

'Did Frankenstein give you that?' Rebecca had smiled as she remembered the film which had frightened her half to death. 'Are the bolts up her pants?' She'd deliberately antagonised Naomi and at last she'd got away from her.

Rebecca was glad she'd been sent to bed without supper that night. Another meal lost in a display of silver wasn't something she relished and she wondered if Estelle had ever noticed the absentee napkin. But she missed Luke, and she patted the napkin where she kept it up the leg of her pants.

Pulling Emily Beauvilliers' old leather diary up into her lap, she gazed at the immaculate writing, trying to find something that would make Bonne Espérance her home. She'd persuaded her mother that Granny Cat had said that the diaries were to be hers and now they were.

I swear I will protect Jean Jacques' son and never allow Clara to know of his existence.

Rebecca leaned her chin on her hand, her elbow digging into the mattress as she wondered why Jean Jacques' son had had to be kept a secret. Leafing quickly through the pages, she searched for an answer but found no clues. The fact that Jean Jacques was the son of a slave meant nothing to Rebecca and she pulled another diary from the box beside her bed. Flicking through it speedily, she suddenly stopped, and turned back two pages.

What is it about that old key?

Emily's handwriting was not as neat as it had been in the other diaries, but Rebecca didn't notice that. She'd stopped breathing as she read the words. Words about an old key that had been part of an oath to kill Jean Jacques – an old key that had been buried somewhere on Bonne Espérance by Jack Marsden, her grandmother's husband.

'That's it!' she shouted out loud as she decided that the key Emily wrote about was the same one Luke had threatened her with earlier that day.

They'd gone with her mother to Cape Town and Rebecca had been terrified by the numbers of people in the streets. She'd hung on to Luke's arm, frightened of being pulled away by the tide of bodies, and he had been irritated.

'What's wrong with you?' He'd pulled his arm free. 'They're just people. Haven't you seen people before, either?'

Rebecca's eyes had moved quickly among the faces that crowded round her on the pavement. Some were dark, not black as she'd expected, but dark. A drunk man had reeled towards her with a lopsided smile seeping its way through alcohol. A woman had clipped him sharply behind the ear, yelling abuse and secretly Rebecca wished Cape Town was as quiet as the mining town in which she'd grown up. Mrs Bernstein's shop was suddenly very appealing.

'Look at that!' she'd exclaimed as she stared into a window full of washing machines.

'That's what we've come to buy.' Constance had disappeared into the shop ahead of them and reluctantly Luke followed with Rebecca. They'd stared at each other for hours across the tops of machines. Her mother had seemed determined to know everything about every machine in the shop and the assistant had been equally determined to sell them. Rebecca had glanced at Luke, bored to tears as he slumped in front of a row of machines and she'd wondered again why he'd so suddenly turned against her.

'What's that?' Rebecca had shrieked with excitement as they left the shop and immediately she'd regretted it.

'Haven't you even seen the sea before?' Luke asked this with more than a little disdain, turning his back on the amazing miles of deep blue water that spread out ahead of them.

'Of course I've seen it before.' Rebecca tried to be equally dismissive and turned away from it. 'It's just water with salt in it.'

Luke's grunt of dismissal had angered Rebecca more than she'd expected, and quite suddenly she'd pushed him as he stood on the sea wall that surrounded the docks. He'd stumbled, reeling on the edge for a terrifying moment before Constance grabbed his shirt and hauled him back.

'If you ever do that again *I'll get the key!*' Luke had yelled at Rebecca in a mixture of fright and anger.

'What key?' She'd shrugged away quickly, trying to hide her shame.

'*The key!*' He'd given the word a significance far beyond anything else. 'There's nothing that key doesn't know about – and that includes you,' he'd whispered menacingly. 'And tell me about your stupid ant hill now.' He'd pointed behind her with great arrogance and Rebecca's eyes had opened wide in amazement, as she turned to look.

Silver granite rose high in a solid slab and dark rivers of rock flowed motionless downwards. The city of Cape Town curled at the feet of an enormous mountain and a tablecloth of cloud dipped over its flat grey top.

'Has that been there all the time?' Rebecca's voice was a whisper of amazement. She'd been underneath the vast flat mountain all day and she hadn't seen it. Table Mountain had appeared out of nowhere. It had watched her secretly from its hiding place among the clouds and her confidence had soaked through the soles of her feet, spilling into the sea. Rebecca's ant hill, her personal pride which stood so grandly at 123 Z was nothing in comparison. When the ant hill had assured her it was the most splendid creation in the entire world, it had lied. Faced by the awesome majesty of Table Mountain, Rebecca felt suddenly naked.

What is it about that old key and why did Jack bury it like that? Now, confined to her bedroom, Rebecca reread Emily Beauvilliers' words. They'd been written almost eighty years before, on the day of her sister Clara's funeral, yet they spoke of the same key Rebecca had heard about that very day.

'What key? Where is it?' Rebecca mumbled to herself, scratching her head. It seemed the key Luke had threatened her with really did exist.

'Are you all right?' Constance poked her head round the edge of the door and Rebecca shut the diary quickly. The key had taken on great importance and she didn't want her mother to know about it.

'For you.' Constance held out a thick jam sandwich wrapped in paper and she sat beside Rebecca on the bed. 'How are you getting on with Luke now?' she asked. 'You haven't tried to drown him again, I hope.'

'Nope.' Rebecca dug her teeth into the sandwich. 'Was there a key to Bonne Espérance when you were little?' she asked casually, pushing blobs of strawberry jam into her mouth. 'A big key?'

'Lots of them. My father had a great big bundle of keys for the cellars and store rooms.' Constance remembered how her father, Jack Marsden, had loved Bonne Espérance; and how she'd loved him. But she was glad he couldn't see the vineyard now and, picking up the diary to remove her thoughts, she glanced at it. 'Why are you reading these old books? What are they about?'

'I'm not.' Rebecca shrugged. 'I think I'll go to sleep now.' She pushed the remainder of the sandwich into her mouth and lay back, hoping her mother wouldn't dive between the pages of Emily's diary and enter the secret world she'd found. 'I'm tired,' she said through a mouthful of bread and jam, closing her eyes tight.

'Goodnight, darling.' Constance kissed her on the forehead, stroking her hair back. 'Remember how much I love you.' Her voice was quiet and Rebecca wondered what was going to happen. Her mother often said that just before a real disaster.

As the light went out Rebecca looked at the slanted white ceiling above her. It was held in place by enormous dark beams and she wondered again about the key Emily talked of in the diary. Was it the same key Luke had threatened her with? The key to all knowledge? To Johannes Villiers, perhaps? Or maybe it was the key to the room she was in? The room Emily Beauvilliers had said Jean Jacques was thrown out of by the bad sister, Clara.

Rebecca shook her head as she looked around, deciding that such an old room would never be as clean. But then she remembered her Aunt Estelle and decided it was just possible and, pulling the sheet over her head, she hoped the ghost of Jean Jacques wasn't still there.

In the dark afforded by the sheet, Rebecca listened to the new sounds to which she wasn't yet accustomed. There were crickets but they were much quieter than the ones outside 123 Z. Like everything else about Bonne Espérance, the crickets were gentle as her grandmother had said. She pushed the sheet back in sudden fright and looked around the room. No, it wasn't gentle. Nothing about Bonne Espérance was gentle! Her mind had jumped back to the black man, I Titus, who'd been hanged just outside. And which part of the house had her grandmother's little Matthew died in, she wondered. So many people had died in this house. She'd seen their gravestones. There was Clara – the bad one that Granny Cat wouldn't talk about. There was Jacques Beauvilliers: the stone on his grave was so old she'd hardly been able to read it, and next to it was another stone that she couldn't read at all. Then there was a small one tucked beside it, which bore just one word: *Eva*. She counted the gravestones she could remember on her fingers and suddenly she was terrified. She'd remembered eleven. Eleven dead people had once lived in the house and all of them might come upstairs to check her out.

A loud crack on the window startled her and she pulled the sheet back over her head with a small scream. Lying totally still under the bedclothes she listened. Another crack on the window chased her deeper down the bed as she realised that ghosts didn't need to use stairs. Windows would be fine for them.

'Rebecca!' She froze as her name crept under the sheet towards her. 'Rebecca,' the voice called again and her entire body shook. There was no way a ghost would pass by a shivering sheet without looking under it, she told herself in horror. 'It's Luke, Rebecca.' Her breath pushed the sheet off her face as it escaped in a mixture of joy and terror. 'Open the window,' his voice called again, and she shouted her relief.

'I'm here!' She jumped out of bed and ran to the window. Luke's face was pressed against the glass outside as he clung to the window-ledge like a flying goldfish.

'Open it,' he mouthed.

'I can't.' She pushed uselessly at the windowlatch.

'Pull.' Luke nodded at the small brass lever. 'Pull it.'

Rebecca pulled the lever and it slid gently out from under the latch. The bottom half of the window slid up in front of her and Luke heaved himself through, jumping into the room.

'OK, Thabo,' he hissed back down into the night and Rebecca watched him carefully. 'We want to talk to you,' Luke whispered without looking at her, and Rebecca felt her knees weaken. 'We need your help.' Thabo's black face appeared at the window and a gleam of white teeth greeted her.

'You be hungry,' he said, passing a brown paper bag through the window ahead of him.

'Yes.' She took the bag of food quickly, aware that boys didn't like being wrong.

David had woken with a sound outside the bedroom window and he moved to it, pushing the curtains back.

'What's the matter?' Constance sat up in bed and watched her husband.

'I thought you were asleep.' He moved back to the bed and sat on the edge. Leaning her elbow into the dip his weight made, Constance ran her fingers down his back.

'Is it going to be all right, David? After they've gone?' She was thinking about the sad neglect that hung over Bonne Espérance. She knew she could restore the house to the bright, warm home it had once been, but the pain that screamed from the earth was David's problem.

'What about Rebecca?' David looked down at his feet, wondering where his slippers had gone. 'I'll go up and see if she's all right.' He made a move to go but Constance wrapped her arms around him from behind.

'She's fine.' She leant her face against her husband's back. They hadn't made love since they'd left Northern Rhodesia and she longed for him to hold her. To secure her. 'Do you think Paul and Estelle ever make love?'

'Did you go up to Rebecca?' David avoided her question. He'd gathered that Paul was certainly not making love to his wife, but it didn't interest him. 'Has she eaten?'

'She's fine, David. I gave her a sandwich.'

'That child's a pest. Naomi.' He got up and went back to the window, looking into the darkness made up of mountains, trees and vineyards.

'She's like her mother.' Constance lay back and gazed up at the ceiling. Estelle had put them into Katinka's old room as if they might not mind. It was the room Katinka had often taken both her and Paul to bed in when they were afraid of the dark. 'Estelle's mother's Afrikaans, of course. Paul told me.'

'What's that got to do with anything?' David yawned and leaned his elbows on the window-ledge. A stick insect stood motionless on thorn legs and he pushed the window open, throwing it out. 'Happy landings,' he called to the flying twig.

'I don't know who she thinks she is anyway,' Constance went on regardless. 'Just because she speaks English she thinks she is English, but it's quite obvious that her place is up there with that Broederbond mob in the Transvaal. That's why they're going, you know.'

'Her politics have nothing to do with us.' David closed the window and stretched with another yawn. His wife's continual digs at Estelle had begun to bore him. They had little to do with the work that lay ahead of him. 'I wonder who's moved into 123 Z?'

'What she says about Rebecca is our business!' Constance was tense and her voice rose. 'I told you what she said about Rebecca staying out of the sun, about her being like my mother — as if I didn't know exactly what she was getting at! That's what I had to take my mother away from, David, and I'm not so sure the kettle should be calling the pot black in the first place.' Constance's anger had risen as she defended her mother and daughter from Estelle's suggestion that they were rather too dark for Bonne Espérance.

'Does it matter?' Paul's mind had wandered back north to Stork shaft and he glanced at his Rolex watch. It was eleven o'clock. 'Dewi Hawkins will be on my shift tonight.'

'And what's wrong with Paul?' Constance wasn't listening. 'He doesn't look too happy to me. Why hasn't he taken better care of the vineyards? His father loved this place just like mine did, and it was Paul's responsibility to look after it.'

During their long walks around the estate, David had gathered that Paul's interest lay somewhere outside the vineyards, with another woman, but that didn't interest him either. As he gazed into the darkness he could hear hoist bells; he could see a steel cable stretching high into the black night and he wished he was there.

'Do you think you'll be happy here?' Constance's voice pulled him back.

'Of course.' David went back to the bed and climbed into it. 'Goodnight,' he said quietly and, as Constance ran her hand gently over his body, he turned away. He was wondering if Tickey had eaten the vegetables or sold them.

*

'Are you sure you want to do it?' Luke watched Rebecca carefully. Any sign of fear and he'd call the whole plan off.

'Yes.' Rebecca's voice was thin with excitement. For the first time in her life she was part of a tight circle of friendship and there was nothing Luke could ask that she would refuse. 'But what is it?' She looked into his bright face as he stared back at her intently. 'I don't know what it is you want me to do yet.'

'We want to make sure Simon doesn't get sent away.' Luke glanced at Thabo with a nod.

'We take him away,' Thabo explained. 'We hide him with the old lady, Nombeko. Her name it mean honest.'

'We're going to make them change their minds,' Luke told her. 'We'll take Simon away until they do. They'll have to agree that we take him with us then.'

'We're going to kidnap Simon?' Rebecca's eyes were enormous. She'd seen a film about a woman being kidnapped once and she'd never forgotten it.

'Just till they promise he won't get locked up,' Luke assured her.

'Nombeko she look after him. Simon special. My people say.' Thabo felt suddenly awkward in English and turned to Luke quickly, nudging him in the ribs. 'You.'

'Eat some of that first.' Luke dug into the brown paper bag and held out a piece of bread and a half-finished tin of condensed milk. 'You dip it in, see.' Luke dipped a piece of bread in the tin and held it out to Rebecca, catching the drips on his finger. 'Eat it.' He licked his finger and Thabo watched.

'Hey,' Rebecca chewed on the bread and condensed milk, 'this is nice.' She'd gone without supper but never eaten as much. 'Why do you want me to help you?' She held the bread and condensed milk out to Thabo. 'Want some?'

'You're a girl,' Luke said with a shrug. He wasn't really sure it was a good enough reason and added quietly, 'They say you did it before. You stole a baby.'

'What?' Rebecca was suddenly embarrassed. 'That was years ago. I was only seven. I was stupid then.' She stared at Luke as quite suddenly she realised what he was after. 'You want me to steal Simon?'

'We can't do it on our own. Babies need girls.'

'You not tell anyone.' Thabo watched her seriously, running his finger across his throat.

'I don't know.' Rebecca licked the sweetness off her lips and looked at each boy in turn.

They watched her. They waited. Very seriously they stared at her and all at once Rebecca felt totally calm. Luke and Thabo depended on her answer and for the first time in her life she was necessary. Slowly she nodded and the boys' faces lit with delight. With her mouth turned up at the corners, she joined in their pleasure, looking directly at Luke.

'I know about the key!' Rebecca's eyes shone with the excitement of at last being part of Luke's world, but it was as though he hadn't heard. He took her hand between his own and she trembled as he held it.

'You'll have to be brave.' He allowed his eyes to be drawn into hers. 'They'll punish us to find out where we've hidden Simon.' Rebecca nodded. 'They'll torture us.' She nodded again. 'You won't give in, will you?' She wasn't sure if she still had a voice so she shook her head.

'You OK!' Thabo clasped his hand over Luke's and tingling spirals of delight ran through Rebecca as she became a part of their secret bond. She wasn't sure she'd ever wash her hand again.

CHAPTER FIVE

Looking out of her attic window, Rebecca rubbed her bare feet nervously up each leg and waited for Luke to signal her with three flashes of a torch. She'd never known a night as black. Her dressing gown was over her dress, her hair tied in two bunches ready for sleep and she'd convinced her mother she was doing just that.

It had been hard to get her parents to leave the room that night. It was almost as if they'd known what was about to happen. They'd talked for hours about their new home in Bonne Espérance, promising her it was going to be wonderful. It already was wonderful, but she couldn't tell them that. The freedom she'd found in her friendship with Luke and Thabo, the freedom of a shared and dangerous plan, was even more than Granny Cat had led her to expect.

She jumped back as a small light appeared like a firefly in the darkness outside. Then another and another. Her heart raced and she thought her head would explode as she ran through her part in the plan. Moving away from the window to the door, she listened. There were no sounds in the house at all and she glanced back at the lump in the bed that pretended to be her. Peeling off her dressing gown, she tossed it on top and pulled a small cloth bag out from under the bed. It was Luke's school bag. Very quietly she opened the door and her teeth bit into her lip as her eyes moved down the narrow stairway. She closed the door again quickly and leant back on it. A light was on in the hallway and she couldn't understand who was awake at two o'clock in the morning. Her heart thumped as she cautiously opened the door again and peered down. Nothing moved anywhere and her breath slipped out with relief as she remembered: her mother had told her the light would be left on at night so she would have no fear of marauding ghosts.

Carefully she started downstairs, her attention fixed on the door that led off the hall at the bottom to the wing of the house where Estelle and her family slept. Where Simon slept. Luke had told her that Miriam would have checked Simon was all right at midnight and then she would have gone outside to her own room. Rebecca hoped and prayed that Simon wouldn't make a noise when she reached him, and froze as a broad yellow-wood floorboard creaked under her weight. Her foot lifted quickly and she held it poised just above the floor. Holding her breath as if that might lighten her step, she slipped into the dark passage.

Outside the closed door of Simon's room Rebecca waited. She was sure the whole house would wake with the thunder of her heart and gritted her teeth in anticipation. Though she'd spent hours with Simon, making friends with him out of sight of Estelle, she was still a little afraid of him. She closed her eyes and thought instead of the love that poured from his eyes. Thabo's people were right: he was special.

'Simon,' she whispered as she padded gently into the room, leaving the door a little ajar so she could see from the light in the hall. 'Simon!' She leant over the small bed with cot sides and tickled his nose with her finger. Tossing his head from side to side against the pillow, Simon's swollen tongue hung loosely in his mouth and the dim light revealed only the disfigurement of his features. 'You've got to come with me,' Rebecca whispered, holding tight to her daytime memory of him. 'Wake up.'

Simon's eyes flew open and he stared at her. She froze as the slanted dark eyes narrowed, then suddenly he smiled, his arms pushing out to her in welcome.

'I'll get your things,' She picked up the half-empty baby's bottle that lay in the bed. 'Wait,' she whispered as he kicked his feet impatiently and, snatching two nappies from a large pile on the dresser, she pushed them into Luke's bag with a bottle.

Simon was very heavy and for a moment Rebecca struggled to hold him, but she smiled, trying not to let him sense her fear.

'You're fat, you know that?' She bounced him higher in her arms and he laughed in anticipation of a game. 'Shh!' She put her finger on his mouth and a slobbery 'shh' blew back against it in reply.

The passage seemed longer than on her way in and she looked towards the light in the hall. The door leading to Paul and Estelle's room was slightly ajar and she wondered if Estelle was always on guard.

Suddenly the door next to her opened and Rebecca flattened herself against the wall, pulling Simon tight. Naomi had wandered out of her room, brushing silently past Rebecca in her long nightdress. Her hand was pressed tightly between her legs as she sleepwalked towards the bathroom.

'Hope she wets her pants,' Rebecca muttered as she tiptoed away.

'Give him to me.' Luke's voice greeted her outside the kitchen door and he grabbed Simon, turning to run. 'Come on!'

'Your sister's gone to the toilet,' she whispered nervously.

'Come,' Luke called again quietly and she ran after him, glancing back at the house. The kitchen door was still open and she ran back to close it.

'Wait for me,' she called after Luke's shadowy figure as it was swallowed up by the dark. 'Wait,' she called again, running into the blackness. 'Luke!' The bag with Simon's belongings banged against her legs and she screamed as someone grabbed her from the dark bush of rhododendrons. A hand pressed over her mouth and Thabo looked at her with wide eyes.

'You not scream.' He took her hand and pulled her after him.

'Over here,' Luke called softly as Thabo dragged Rebecca behind him while Simon chortled.

'Ow!' Rebecca shouted as a thorn lodged itself in her foot, and she hopped after Thabo, her voice hiccuping her explanation. 'It's a thorn.' Her words bounced with her each hop. 'In my foot.' Luke's bag knocked against her.

'Shut up.' Luke had appeared in front of her out of the blue. 'Be quiet.'

'Then take the thorn out of my foot.' She held her foot out to him angrily.

'Carry the cart till we're far enough away, Thabo.' Luke ignored her and turned to go.

'You want I get it out?' Thabo shone the torch at her feet.

'I'll do it.' Rebecca dropped to the ground holding her foot in front of her as she peered at the dirty sole. 'Boys don't know how.'

'There it is.' Thabo waved the torch at her foot.

'Boys aren't stupid enough to go barefoot in the dark,' Luke quipped.

'And I'm not stupid enough to clump downstairs in shoes,' she hissed angrily, waving her foot in circles to keep it in the light of Thabo's torch.

'Ouch!' Rebecca yelped as Thabo yanked a devil's thorn from the sole of her foot. Three sharp spikes formed a miniature ship's anchor. It was impossible for anyone to tread on it without being caught and that's why the devil had claimed it, she thought.

'You'd better stay here,' Luke grabbed Thabo's arm. 'I'll get the cart.'

'Wait!' The hissing anger behind Rebecca's voice stopped Luke in his tracks and he turned back in surprise. 'I'm coming with you,' she said firmly.

'On one leg?' Luke dismissed her.

'Give Simon to me,' she demanded. 'I'm in charge of him – you said so.' She challenged Luke. 'That's why I'm here.'

Thabo switched off the torch and looked away. He knew how much Luke disliked girls but he wasn't quite sure what would happen next.

He'd seen the look in Rebecca's eyes in his own girl cousin's eyes once, and Thabo had never been the same again.

'Put him on my back.' Rebecca bent over to take Simon and as she did so, Luke's bag fell unnoticed to the ground, hiding in a bush. 'What are you waiting for?' Luke glanced at his friend for reassurance but Thabo wouldn't meet his eye. 'Come on,' Rebecca whispered and reluctantly Luke placed Simon on her back. The small boy screamed with delight, banging his hands happily on her head as he prepared for a midnight piggyback.

'Go on, Thabo,' Luke urged, trying to remove himself from Rebecca's dominance. 'Take the cart.' Thabo grabbed the rope tied to the small wooden cart, wound it round his arm and lifted the cart over his head to cross the rough ground ahead of them.

'Are you sure your foot's OK?' Luke called back to Rebecca as he ran after Thabo.

'What do you care?' Rebecca's voice warned him not to try anything. Her foot was very sore and Simon was heavy but there was no way she'd give in. 'Where's the torch gone?' she called softly into the darkness, and Luke yanked it out of Thabo's pocket and turned it on. Driving a narrow beam through the long grass, it settled on a surprised mole which stood on its head instantly, disappearing in a mound of dry sand.

'We'll get on to the tarmac in a minute,' Luke whispered. 'When we're far away from the house.'

As they reached the narrow blue road that led to Cape Town, Luke moved back to Rebecca and Simon. 'Are you tired?' he asked as Rebecca dropped to the ground holding Simon by the legs.

'Of course not,' she gasped between deep breaths. Her legs ached with the effort of carrying Simon on one good foot and she thought she'd punctured her lungs. 'How much further now?'

'How much further?' Luke's voice reflected his amazement as he picked Simon up. 'Miles and miles – we told you.'

'I only asked.' Rebecca rubbed her foot angrily. 'Can't I ask?'

'No.' Luke moved towards Thabo as he prepared the cart to carry Simon. 'You ready yet?'

'Put him in,' Thabo instructed in Xhosa, holding the cart steady on the ribbon of blue tarmac.

'Where's the rope?' Luke slipped into his friend's language. 'Have you got it?'

Thabo held up one end of a rope and together they looped it round Simon's kicking body. He'd spotted the cart and wanted to get into it at once.

'Keep still,' Thabo shouted in Xhosa again and Rebecca glared at them.

'Don't think I don't know what you're talking about,' she challenged as she reached them on one hopping foot.

'What?' Luke and Thabo secured Simon to the base of the cart.

'Don't you even know what you're talking about?' Rebecca bent down over Simon. 'You drive,' She laid his chubby hands on the small pram-wheel fixed at the front of the cart. 'Good boy!' she said as he leaned forward, hugging the pram-wheel to his chest, while his tongue wrapped round it. 'We've got to do something.' Rebecca's hands plonked on her hips as she looked at Simon.

'What?'

'He's untidy.'

'He's in his pyjamas.'

'His face is untidy.'

'What?' Luke tested the rope to see it was securely tied to the base of the cart before shining the torch into Simon's face. 'What's wrong with it?' His little brother looked exactly the same as he always did and Luke was impatient. 'What's untidy about it?'

'His tongue.' Rebecca remembered her own reaction when she'd first seen Simon, and she didn't want Nombeko to be as afraid as she'd been. 'Can't we hide it or something?'

'How?' Luke glanced at Thabo and Simon gazed at the three children who studied him. Delighted by their attention, he laughed and his tongue pushed further out of his mouth.

'Take this.' Luke handed Thabo the torch and carefully he rolled Simon's tongue back into his mouth, closing it quickly. 'That better?' He glanced round at Thabo and Rebecca as he held Simon's mouth closed.

'Yes,' Rebecca smiled.

Simon's cheeks had puffed out like red balloons and his eyes popped as he watched them, unable to breathe.

'Hey!' Luke slapped the open palm of his hands against Simon's cheeks and his tongue popped back out in an explosion of spit as he grabbed a breath. His tongue lolling happily from the corner of his mouth, Simon banged his hands on the sides of the cart, demanding the game continue.

'Now he cross.' Thabo turned his back on Simon as he moved to pull the cart.

'What's wrong now?' Luke turned to Rebecca. She was standing absolutely still, staring ahead at the road that snaked its way into the solid mouth of night ahead of them. 'You don't have to come,' Luke said gently and an owl hooted close by, sounding Rebecca's fears.

'Let's go.' She tilted her head back, determined not to be afraid. 'What are you waiting for?'

A cloud whisked itself off the face of the moon and the extraordinary little group stood in silhouette against the sudden light. The hum of a still night was broken only by the rumble of the cart's wheels on tarmac and Simon's strange chortles.

'You OK, Thabo?' Luke shouted ahead as the small cart trailed its cargo in Thabo's footsteps.

'What's that?' Rebecca's blood ran cold as a high-pitched scream raced towards them. But before she could run, Luke had pushed her down into the bushes beside the road. Thabo had already lain low over the cart in deep shadow up ahead and the torchlight went out as two yellow eyes took its place. Covering her face in terror, Rebecca pushed herself down into the dry grass. She screamed as the high-pitched whine of an invisible bat flew towards her, its leather wings whipping past her face as they sucked the air away.

'Wow!' Luke was on his feet. 'Did you see that?' He watched the two red tail-lights of a car vanish into the night. 'What kind of car was that?' he shouted to Thabo as he reorganised himself and the cart back on the road. Neither had noticed that Rebecca was still face-down in the dirt. 'Did you see it, Thabo?'

'Of course!' Thabo said.

'Did you see it, Rebecca?' Luke was still looking after the car which had long since disappeared. 'Hey, Rebecca.' He looked at her. 'What's the matter with you?'

'Nothing,' she said in a thin voice as she stood up. 'Nothing at all.' She tried to reassure herself as she sauntered away. If the boys wanted to pretend a giant bat was a car, it was fine with her, she decided.

Looking ahead into the pool of light the torch threw on to the blue tarmac, she decided there must be another million miles still to go. Though her heel had rubbed raw from taking the weight off the ball of her foot, she wouldn't let Luke know how much she longed to be back in her bed.

'Water?' Thabo passed an old flagon to Rebecca. Luke was pulling the cart up ahead now and Thabo held the torch while Simon slept, his head lolling from side to side against the pramwheel.

'Thank you.' Rebecca drank a mouthful of water and wiped the wooden top with her hand, passing the flagon back to Thabo. 'We've gone a long way already, haven't we?' she said hopefully.

'Long ways.' Thabo nodded though he knew there were miles yet to travel before they'd reach Nombeko.

'Duck!' Luke yelled as headlights appeared in a half-moon over the horizon.

'Get down.' Thabo pulled Rebecca off the road after him and Luke dragged the cart into the long grass up ahead. 'I'll take him.' Thabo ran to the kerb as Luke raced back to Rebecca, shouting over the noise of the engine that drove the headlights closer.

'Keep right down.' Luke's face had softened in the light of the torch that shone underneath it. 'Are you OK?'

'Put that torch out!' Thabo yelled back in Xhosa and Luke switched it off but still Rebecca didn't breathe.

Luke's face was right beside hers and she could feel his warm breath in her ear. She wanted to run but her body was shaking and Luke's grip tightened around her. The sound of the engine drew closer and her body tensed as it stopped. There were voices. Laughing voices. Voices that used the same language Thabo and Luke used. Thabo was lit by the headlights as he stood up and Rebecca peered out from under Luke's arm. Thabo was showing Simon to a group of black men. They'd stopped laughing and were examining Simon curiously, nodding at one another with deep sounds of concern as they spoke to Thabo.

'It's OK,' Thabo yelled back at his friends and Rebecca turned to Luke in panic.

'What's happening?'

'They're taking us on the lorry.' Luke pulled her up by the hand, dragging her after him through the long grass and back to the road. 'They're taking us to Nombeko's village. They know where it is,' he said and Rebecca's heart swelled. The Africans were passing Simon from one to the other and they were smiling.

With its cargo rattling, the lorry moved forward and a harmony of African voices fell on Rebecca's aching body like warm oil. Thabo was singing with them and Luke, leaning against him, was asleep. Simon was in the arms of an enormous black man and he banged his fists on the man's legs in time with the singing. His entire body, misshapen and topped by an untidy face, seemed suddenly perfect, caught up in the rhythm of song.

'Jo!' The Africans called out in laughing unison as the packed black bodies surrounding Rebecca leaned over her. The lorry had turned off the main road and bumped its way over a dirt track that led to a small village. Rusty iron and mud shacks huddled together as narrow lanes wound their way among them. A man wrapped in a blanket scratched his head sleepily as he emerged from a shack and made his way towards the edge of the settlement.

'Nceba!' Thabo called to him, the name springing from a quiet click in his throat as he jumped down from the lorry and ran after him. Turning back with a smile and a nod of his head Nceba walked on, as if lorryloads of curious people arrived every night at about this time.

'Thabo.' A very old woman stepped out of the deep voice that had

99

slipped through the corrugated-iron door of a shack. She pulled a length of bright material over her head and walked with Thabo towards the lorry. Her eyes peered among the black bodies with a smile of expectation teasing her lips and she tutted.

'Simon?' she called up, with a solid African vowel ending the name. She clapped her hands slowly as the large African man held Simon down to her over the edge of the lorry. Luke jumped down beside the woman, tugging the little cart after him as she took his brother.

'Nombeko,' Thabo informed Luke, nodding at the old lady who held his brother in her arms. It was as if they'd brought her a child she'd been waiting for all her life and Nombeko turned, circling Simon tighter in her arms as she moved towards the shack.

'He hasn't cried.' Luke looked at Thabo in amazement.

'He knows,' Thabo answered as Rebecca jumped down beside them. Straightening her dress she waved to the Africans in the back of the lorry as they continued on their early morning journey to work. 'You OK?' Thabo asked.

'Yup.' Rebecca folded her arms over her chest and shivered. It was the first time she'd noticed the cold and her bare feet were frozen but she didn't react to the pain. 'What do we do now?' she whispered to Luke.

'In there.' He held his hand out to her. 'You're OK.' He smiled his congratulations and Rebecca looked down quickly. She wanted to hide the hot flush that had rushed to her cheeks with his words but she couldn't.

'You are too,' she said quietly and moving with Luke after Thabo, she looked at his out-held hand but didn't take it.

The inside of the tin walls that formed Nombeko's small shack were papered with fruit-box labels and posters. A fire blazed in a small circle on the sand floor and Rebecca's eyes passed over the scene in amazement. Oranges, apples and pears hid among enormous bunches of grapes. Bananas hung hand in hand down the join in the walls and together they transformed the room into a garden of paper fruit.

'Come, girl.' Rebecca turned with Nombeko's voice and the old lady smiled to reveal pink gums that held a few stray teeth in place. Her eyes wrinkled tightly under a mop of fuzzy white hair and she beckoned Rebecca as she held Simon close. 'Come.'

'What does she want?' Rebecca turned to Luke nervously and he shrugged.

'You know this baby, girl?' Her English was clear and Rebecca felt the old woman's hand grip her arm.

'Yes.' Rebecca turned to Luke quickly. 'But Luke's his brother.'

'A boy!' Nombeko laughed. 'If Nombeko to care for God's child,

Nombeko must know all about God's child.' The old lady moved to the small bed which was balanced on a pile of bricks at each corner. She sat on it, bouncing Simon on her knee as he laughed, holding his arms out to her.

'Sit, girl,' she ordered Rebecca and the two boys looked at each other with a shrug. Their place in the operation had been taken over by Rebecca and the reason behind her part in the plan had been vindicated.

'Let's go.' Luke moved to the door but Thabo grabbed his arm and held him back. The old lady had fixed her eyes on Luke and he looked down sheepishly as she turned back to Rebecca.

'What the child eat?' Rebecca automatically turned to Luke but the old lady tapped her on the arm. 'Nombeko ask you, girl.'

'Food,' Rebecca answered stupidly. 'But he likes these too.' She held out a half-eaten roll of fruit drops. 'See?' she said as Simon reached for them.

'So child like sweet. And pap? He eat mealie pap?'

'Yes,' Thabo said quickly. He'd fed Simon on mealie pap once when Luke had left him in charge and knew he liked it. '*Ewe*,' he repeated in Xhosa.

'And the child like milk?' Nombeko asked Rebecca.

'Cow's milk,' Luke said quickly, wondering why Rebecca was so silent, why she looked so stupid. 'You've got his stuff, Rebecca. Give it to her!' He glared at her impatiently and realised suddenly that she didn't have anything in her hands. 'Where's my school bag?'

'I must have dropped it.' Rebecca's mind raced back to the road. 'When that bat ... I mean that car ...'

'You dropped it?' Luke whispered his terror. If his bag was found he knew it would be recognised immediately. 'You idiot!' he shouted and Rebecca looked down as a lump rose in her throat.

'Simon very wet.' The old woman pushed her mouth forward like a corrugated paper clip and hooted with laughter as she lifted Simon off her lap. Drips fell slowly to the floor and she looked at Rebecca with wide eyes. 'What Nombeko do about that, girlie?'

'This.' Rebecca held her hand out quickly, trying to cover her terrible mistake. In her hand was the napkin she'd washed and kept as a keepsake of Luke.

'That?' Nombeko's laughter threatened to bring the iron house down on their heads. 'I think it better God's child water the floor.' She pulled Simon's rubber pants down and a soggy nappy fell on the floor between her legs. 'OK.' She plonked his bare behind on the sand floor. 'You keep the dust down.' She roared with laughter again and Rebecca glanced at Luke.

'He'll be all right,' she whispered apologetically. Rebecca felt strangely secure, as if revisiting a happy dream. Though the old lady spoke English as well as she did herself, she lived in a hut made of tin and paper. Everything was quite extraordinary but somehow Rebecca felt as safe as she had in Macaroni's *khaya*.

'You think Nombeko not know how to look after Simon?' The old lady brushed her tight white curls back with the flat of her hand. 'Nombeko have nineteen babies. Seven they live.' She leaned back against the rusty iron wall behind the bed, one leg on either side of Simon as he sat on the sand floor. Her feet were wide and flat, the soles like scorched leather and the toes, ten sleeping snails.

'This is his favourite thing,' Luke pulled the small cart into the room. 'We made it for him to play in,' he said in Xhosa.

'And Nombeko she look after God's child till it right he go back to his mother.' She closed her eyes and began to sing a tuneless hushed song as she rocked Simon between her feet. 'You go now, children.'

'But . . .' Rebecca stopped as the old lady's eyes opened, fixing on her like lit darts. 'OK.' She turned away quickly, following Thabo and Luke outside.

A gentle mist rose from the tin roof as the first glimpse of sunlight touched it and Nombeko's voice droned on as the children stood in an uncertain clump, looking back at the shack.

'We must go quickly,' Luke whispered. His eyes had settled on the distant horizon, a warm glow hinting that morning hid behind it. 'We've got to find that bag!'

'I'm sorry,' Rebecca bit her lip in shame.

'You did OK.' Luke shrugged his forgiveness and they walked away. Their tread was light and their hearts warmed by their achievement as Nombeko's village disappeared behind them in the dark.

'Did I really do OK?' Rebecca longed to hear again that Luke thought she'd done well even though she'd lost his school bag. 'I'll find it, Luke.' She swallowed hard as they moved towards the day on which the grown-ups would discover Simon had gone.

The ticking of the large clock in the hall pecked its way endlessly through the silence. A long stream of sunlight stretched through the open sitting room door and across the wide yellow-wood floorboards. A fine line of ants wound their way through a crack in the frame of the closed front door, forming an arc as their tiny feet reflected in black waves on the gleaming wood.

'*Mewe!*' Sophie's voice called through the silence of early morning and a bird imitated the call – 'may where' – its throat opened wide.

'*Ntombi!*' Miriam's voice called back. 'Nnn tomby,' the bird echoed, and a tiny mouse scattered the thread of ants as it dived into a neat round hole in the skirting board.

Sophie pushed the large key into the kitchen door of the house and it turned with an awkward groan. She glanced back into the gentle morning mist that spread out a few inches above the ground and two black feet appeared below the soft cloud.

'*Invula.*' Miriam breathed deeply as she reached her mother at the door, sniffing the strong scent of salt on the air and knowing it would bring rain that day.

'*Ewe!*' Sophie nodded, her wide nostrils drawing in a long breath of salty air. It filled her chest and she smiled as her bosoms formed soft pillows under her chin. She knew she wouldn't have to polish the windows today.

Moving through the kitchen, Miriam pulled a scarf tight over her hair. She pushed down the starched white of her overall and licked her lips clean as she stopped at the door. She didn't know why, but every part of her was suddenly on edge and she looked back at her mother as she filled a copper kettle. Sophie's large behind sat square under the ties of her apron. It formed the soft seat Miriam had spent her childhood on and the calm in her mother's body scattered her moment of warning.

Moving across the yellow-wood floor of the hall Miriam's bare black feet trod through a beam of daylight and she wiped a dead ant from her foot on to her ankle.

Sophie heard the familiar click of her daughter opening Simon's bedroom door and she glanced automatically at the large white clock on the kitchen wall above her. As the stark black hand juddered its way to the half hour, the small hand pointed an accusing finger between five and six and Sophie's shoulders lifted as her body prepared itself for a new day. And then she froze. The scream that ran through the house clutched at her throat. It scuttled across the floor and up the walls as Miriam's terrified voice burst into every room in Bonne Espérance. Her cry of '*Simon!*' crawled under the sheets of every bed and the gentle mist of a new day exploded with her discovery that the mongol child had gone.

Rebecca stood in her nightdress beside her mother in the open doorway of the house and watched without a word as every man on the estate searched the stables, the cellars, the servants' quarters and the barn. She could feel her mother watching her, but avoided her eyes.

'You don't know anything about this do you, darling?' Constance's voice was filled with the fear Rebecca had heard in it so many times before, and her mind leapt back to the ant hill at 123 Z.

'What do you mean?' She gazed at Constance innocently. Though her throat was as dry as parchment and her knees weak, she held her chin firm. 'What are you saying?'

Constance wrapped her arm around her small daughter's shoulder and pulled her into her. Though the ugly minds and watching eyes of the small mining town they'd left seemed to stare at them once again, Constance smiled. 'Of course you don't know anything about it, darling.'

'He must be somewhere out there, Paul.' Estelle's angry words leapt at them from the courtyard as she challenged her husband. 'He's nowhere inside. Every inch has been searched so Simon has to be out there somewhere.'

Rebecca knew that Estelle's concern was not for Simon but for later that day, for the time when Simon was due to be taken away to the children's home, and her mouth drew itself straight across her teeth. Silently she renewed her vow to say nothing, not even when tortured.

'He's not in there.' Luke stepped out of the stables, shrugging his shoulders towards his mother and father, but his eyes touched Rebecca as she stood beside Constance at the door. Nobody else in the world would know what he was saying with that look, Rebecca thought.

'I'll get changed so I can help them.' She turned to her mother but stopped. Naomi was standing on the stairs that led to Rebecca's attic room. Her pure white feet shone as clean as her face and her toes curled smugly over the edge of the bottom step as she barred the way.

'Excuse me.' Rebecca moved to the stairs but Naomi didn't budge, her eyes fixed in a beam of accusation. 'I want to change.' Rebecca pushed past her and ran up the stairs to get away. Reaching the top she stopped and looked down. Naomi was looking up at her. Her slim white neck was arched, a long fair plait pointed straight down her spine and through the distance between them Rebecca could hear her silent accusations.

Peering down from her small attic window on to the scurry of agitated people below, Rebecca felt the hard bark of her tree on the ant hill as it pushed behind her knees. She could see the tiny baby she held in her arms and she could hear grown-up voices below.

'*She hangs around the railway line all day, doing heaven knows what! Everybody in town knows she's odd – peculiar.*'

Mrs Bernstein's words bounced against one another in Rebecca's head and she fixed her eyes on Luke as he stood beside his father. She forced the energy she felt draining through the soles of her feet to concentrate on him. To fix on him and gain the strength to cope with what was coming.

Rebecca had seen a black man move to Estelle. He was holding Luke's school bag in his hand and a nappy poked through its gathered top.

'I knew it!' Estelle's voice rang towards the window of Rebecca's room and banged on the glass pane. 'Where's Rebecca?'

Luke looked at his mother in amazement as she flew towards the house. 'No!' he shouted, running after her. 'It's my bag! It's not hers, it's mine!'

From the height of a slow dream Rebecca watched Paul try to hold Estelle away from the house as Luke chased them both. Her feet moved backwards across the matting on the bedroom floor and the hard edge of the wooden bed dug into the skin behind her knees as her hand gripped a blanket for security.

'Get back into bed, Rebecca.' Rebecca heard her father's gentle voice behind her. 'There's nothing to worry about.' David picked her up and tucked her into the bed. 'It's all right.' He pushed her shaking legs down under the blanket and sat beside her. 'Nobody will accuse you of anything,' he said firmly.

'It wasn't her!' Luke's voice broke through the wood of the closed bedroom door and he pushed through it after Estelle as her angular figure loomed towards Rebecca. 'Listen to me, Ma. It's my bag – it's my fault!'

'You slut! You bloody little half-caste!' Estelle reached for Rebecca but then reeled back against the door as David shoved her away. 'I know about that child of yours,' Estelle screeched wildly as he stood in front of Rebecca, barring her way.

'Stop it, Ma.' Luke's razor-sharp words cut through Estelle's voice. 'I took Simon.' His voice rose above his mother's. *'I took Simon!'*

The air in the room was hot and still. Rain ran in twisting streams down the windows and the gleaming furniture stood to attention as the tiny brass knobs on the desk stared blindly at Luke.

'I'll ask you once more.' Paul's voice was quiet but very firm. 'Where is Simon?' Luke's mouth held its straight line. His bright blue eyes looked into his father's but he blinked as he felt his mother move towards him.

'Tell us what you've done with him!' The hard edge of Estelle's voice banged against Luke's skull but he remained silent. 'You have one more chance – just one more.' His mother's open hand moved beside her leg. 'Do you want me to get the whip?'

'Estelle!'

'Don't "Estelle" me, Paul. He's lying. Can't you see the boy's lying to protect the girl?'

'I'm not lying.' Luke's voice was quiet, the hush of rage held tightly behind it.

'Then where is Simon?' Estelle demanded, and the sharp slap of her hand made Luke gasp.

Catching her breath, Rebecca stood totally still outside the sitting room door. Naomi was at the bottom of the stairs once again. She'd changed into a clean pink dress but it was as if she'd never moved.

'Madam?' Miriam's voice called and Thabo's dark face appeared around the door to the kitchen. His usually wide eyes were squeezed tight and Miriam's black fingers curled around the top of his left ear as she dragged him towards the sitting room. 'It Thabo too!' She assured Estelle of her son's guilt.

'And me.' Rebecca gazed straight into Naomi's eyes as she moved past her into the sitting room.

'Go away,' Luke whispered. He knew that neither Thabo nor Rebecca had any idea of the anger within his mother.

'I took Simon too,' Rebecca said firmly. 'We took Simon away together and it was me who had Luke's bag.'

'Rebecca,' Constance called as she ran into the room catching her daughter's words. She had believed that for once her daughter was not a part of the problem and her voice lifted in desperation. 'You don't have to lie to protect Luke.'

'But it's the truth.' Rebecca's dark eyes fixed on her mother. She wanted Constance to understand that the 'mystery' of her short life had been explained to her at last. Though Rebecca had no idea what 'half-caste' meant, Emily had written those words in her diary about Jean Jacques and at last she'd understood whose loneliness she shared.

'No, Rebecca, please!' For a moment the pain in her mother's voice made Rebecca hesitate but her eyes moved back to Luke and Thabo. Being a part of their friendship meant more than anything else. It cancelled the loneliness Estelle had screamed out loud.

'We took Simon away because you were going to lock him up.' Rebecca's words drove their way towards Estelle on a hard flat note. 'Thabo, Luke and me. We took him.' She noticed the red mark of Estelle's hand across Luke's cheek. 'You can do what you like to me too, but it's true.' The room was silent as she walked to Thabo. Taking his hand in hers, she moved with him towards Luke and they stood silently beside him.

'Simon's safe and when you promise not to send him away we'll bring him back.' Luke's words bounced like an arrogant ping-pong ball across the room before rolling away to hide in a corner. 'Please,' he added quickly, the three children facing the grown-ups as one.

The rain had eased to a soft mist as Paul brought his leather belt down across Luke's damp back and he winced himself. Estelle was watching from the door of the house and Paul knew that if the young boy didn't tell him what his mother wanted to know, her whipping would be far worse than his own.

'Tell her where Simon is, Luke,' Paul whispered between the sharp cracks of his belt.

Out of the corner of his eye Luke had seen Thabo step out from the low door of the small room he shared with his mother Miriam. Thabo's back was bent and he rubbed his head as if trying to wake himself up. Luke knew that when Thabo was beaten by his own people it was in hard whacks across the head. He also knew that Thabo had not given in and as the crack of Paul's belt ran a deep line down his back once again, Luke clenched his teeth in silence.

'I can't go on with this.' The young boy's courage had touched Paul deeply and he moved away from the child who was not his own. As he reached Estelle he pulled the belt tightly around his trousers, forcing the buckle closed as he buckled tight his knowledge of Estelle's true frustration.

The three children had halted her plan to dispose of their small mongol son and Paul could no longer punish Luke for his own failure.

'It's time we talked about Simon.' He reached his arm out to take Estelle's and she pushed it away violently. As if years of buried hatred crept from the solid white walls of Bonne Espérance to join her, she moved towards Luke.

'That girl put you up to it, isn't that true?' Estelle grabbed Luke's hair, yanking his head back. 'Tell me!'

'Never.' Luke's voice was very quiet.

Rebecca had sat tight-lipped for two hours. She'd listened to the crack of the belt across Luke's back and she'd heard Estelle's continued screams of accusation against her, but still she hadn't told her parents where Simon was. Though each had noticed the other was secretly proud of their daughter, Constance and David were unsure what to do next.

'I need the toilet.' Rebecca looked at her mother for permission, then walked quietly out of her bedroom. All she wanted to do was run outside to Luke, to tell him how brave he was and how much she loved him. But instead she walked to the toilet.

'My mother will whip you till you tell.' Naomi's acid words curdled Rebecca's thoughts as they crept up the stairs towards her. 'If she doesn't kill you, God will,' Naomi added spitefully before turning to rush away, and Rebecca wondered how God could possibly be in cahoots with Estelle.

As she sat on the closed toilet seat she thought back to Granny Cat in Bulawayo station. She wondered what her grandmother would have done now. Rebecca was totally unaware that Bonne Espérance had been invaded by truth.

Everyone had turned to look down the long drive that twisted through a dark aisle of oak trees. A very old horse clopped slowly towards the house, dragging a rattling wagon behind it. In the wagon was a group of Africans and among them was Nombeko with Simon tied to her back in a blanket.

Thabo lifted his thundering head from his hands as the wagon-wheels ground to a halt in front of Estelle, Paul and Luke. Sitting under a tree further away, he watched as Nombeko took the hand of a woman beside her and carefully climbed down. Thabo knew that word of trouble took no account of time or distance as it travelled among his people. He was sure his silent cry for help had carried on the wind and stirred the heart of Nombeko.

The old lady's eyes passed over the large white house. They passed over the group of silent white people who stared at her and finally they settled on Estelle.

'Your child is all right, madam.' Nombeko spoke slowly as her bare feet trod the damp cobbles towards Estelle.

Rebecca skidded to a stop beside the window, staring through it as her mother and father stood beside her.

'Nombeko,' she whispered, turning to run as David caught her arm.

'We'll all go, Rebecca.' There was a curious tone in her father's voice and a flicker of wonder lit his eyes.

'The children they bring God's child to me.' Nombeko drew a deep breath and her hand pushed Simon higher as he slept in the blanket that tied him to her back. 'We ask you, madam. In the name of our Great God, have mercy.'

From thousands of miles away, Macaroni's words echoed in the soft mist of rain still falling. As though her spirit reached out through years of bitterness, Nombeko lifted her hands to a higher hope.

'Have mercy on us Almighty God,' she cried.

'Get that woman out of here,' Estelle ground out, her voice edged with steel. 'Get that heathen off this property!' She stepped backwards as Nombeko moved closer. The old lady's head was held to one side and she peered curiously at Estelle without blinking.

'Forgive me, madam,' she said gently, directly into the face of Estelle's hatred. 'God bless you when He give you this child.' She swung Simon under her arm. The brightly coloured blanket fell to the ground and she held him out to his mother like a rag doll. 'Take God's blessing, madam.'

'Blasphemer,' Estelle yelled into the black face in front of her.

'I talk of God, madam.' Though Satan had raised a victory flag over

Estelle's head, Nombeko smiled. 'Your people brought the Great God Jesus Christ to me, madam, and I hold His mighty cross of love out to you.' Simon's head fell forward and his tongue hung loosely from his mouth as Nombeko lifted him closer to his mother.

'Get rid of her!' Estelle's words scuttled across the courtyard on rat's feet. 'Burn Simon's clothes and get rid of that woman!' she screamed into the light that shone from Nombeko and spilled on to her.

Luke watched as his mother darted away like an angry scorpion but he knew the sting in her tail hadn't yet found its prey and tears ran down his cheeks in streams of inadequacy.

'I'll take him.' Rebecca crossed the cobbled courtyard and stopped in front of Nombeko, holding her hands out to Simon.

'Yes, girl.' Nombeko pressed Simon into her arms and his head lolled to one side as he snatched a sudden breath. Reaching her hand gently towards Rebecca's face, the old lady touched her cheek. 'The child is yours.' Slowly she turned and moved back to the wagon, picking up the blanket as she went. 'Simon, he like this.' Nombeko's face lit with a sudden smile as she pulled the small wooden cart off the back of the wagon. It clattered to the ground, rolling its way over the cobbles towards Rebecca as the old woman was helped back into the wagon. The black driver pushed his mouth forward in a gentle click and the old horse lifted its hanging head reluctantly as, with a slow wheeze, it tugged its load forward.

'Look,' Rebecca said softly as she moved to Luke, holding Simon tightly in her arms. 'It's stopped raining.' Thabo's dark body slipped round the edge of the white stable wall as he joined Luke, Rebecca and Simon.

'How dare you tell me what to do!' Estelle's eyes were fixed on Constance, who had suggested that Estelle should leave Simon with her at Bonne Espérance. Now Estelle's back pressed hard against the chair as her nails dug into the palms of her hands. 'It was your daughter who was behind what happened. Say what you like, but Rebecca's no good and there's no point in denying it.' Estelle tried to shift the shame of what had just taken place on to Constance. 'We know why you finally agreed to come down to Bonne Espérance. We know all about that baby your daughter stole. Don't think we haven't heard all about your child and her goings-on up north!'

Years of pent-up anger bubbled inside Constance and she wanted to silence Estelle's foul mouth forever but she spoke quietly.

'We came down here for your sake, Estelle. You and Paul want to go to the Transvaal and I'm offering to help. I can't believe you'd rather bury your child than be shamed by him. Maybe the children were right. Maybe that black woman was right, too.'

'A black?' Estelle scoffed. 'It's your daughter who took Simon to that native!'

'Rebecca tried to help Simon. They all tried to help your child.' Though Estelle had lit a fuse deep inside her, Constance held her temper.

'By taking him to a black woman?' Estelle's face filled with disgust.

'That black woman took better care of Simon than you ever did. Admit it, Estelle.'

'Then send yours to live with her. Send Rebecca back where she belongs.' Estelle's words spat into Constance's face and she could hold herself back no longer.

'God help me but I hope you drown in your own vomit.' She lurched towards Estelle. 'Keep your bloody tongue away from my child!'

'Get your family out of here, Paul, unless you want us all to live like blacks!' Estelle screamed back.

'Do you think I *want* to live in the filth of this house? You can polish and scrub and bleach all you like, Estelle, but you can't kill the stench of hatred you've brought with you into Bonne Espérance!'

'Get her out, Paul,' Estelle shouted.

'He doesn't have to throw us out, Estelle. You've cleaned my home out of love and poured your filth on to my child with your lies ...'

'Lies?' Estelle's voice rose on an hysterical laugh.

'Lies!' Constance's voice matched hers and David tried to hold his wife back as she reached for Estelle. 'No, David.' Constance swung back to him. 'It's time things were said. Time words were spoken out loud in this house instead of sweeping them under the carpets.' She faced Estelle. 'I grew up under the gaze of women just like you – our neighbours. Do you remember them, Paul?' Constance turned to him as he kept his distance from both women. 'Tell her what it was like for my mother and your grandmother, Paul – what women like your wife did to her until the last thread of her dignity snapped. Do you think I don't know what Estelle's saying about Rebecca?' Tears choked Constance's words and bubbled in her throat. 'Do you think I'll stand by while she insults my child?' She spun back to reach for Estelle and collapsed into David's arms as he held on to her. A lifetime's pent-up emotion had broken and Constance wept like a child. 'Tell her, David. Tell her the truth!'

'Rebecca needs you.' David tried to lead his wife away but Constance struggled free.

'This is my home and I won't live with the hatred your guilt hides behind,' she screamed at Estelle. 'Lock Simon up if that's the only way you can face what you really are, but don't expect me to play housekeeper for you.' Her voice dropped to a whisper. 'I can't lower myself to the level you require.'

Naomi's bottom lip quivered as she stood alone in the hallway. The adult game she'd tried to join had backfired and she was lost in a sea of conflicting emotions.

'Damn you!' Estelle's voice chased Constance as she rushed out of the room, pushing past Naomi in the doorway. 'Damn you to hell!'

With her mother's voice racing after her, Naomi ran to the front door. The platform on which she'd built her life had collapsed beneath her, and tears poured down her face. But she stopped as she saw Rebecca, Luke and Thabo outside. They sat under the slave bell in a small circle which held Simon in its centre and they were laughing. Each time they pushed Simon's tongue into his mouth, he poked it out and their joy echoed against the mountains.

'Naomi,' Luke called as he saw his sister standing alone in the doorway of the house. 'Come here!'

'Go to hell!' Naomi screamed and ran away into the distance.

Balanced on a tightrope of diplomacy strung between Paul and David, the next week passed slowly and dangerously. Estelle had convinced Paul that they should leave for the Transvaal sooner than planned and it had been agreed that Simon would be staying on at Bonne Espérance. A silent truce had been called between the two women and they busied themselves with the practicalities of their respective moves, their anger buried in hard work.

'Hey, Luke,' Rebecca called as she slipped her foot into a stirrup, hauling herself up on to Salu's back. 'You know what I've read happened here before? About that key you told me about?' In the time they had left to share, Rebecca spent every daylight moment with Luke and each night she spent buried in Emily Beauvilliers' diaries.

It had been in one of those glorious daylight moments with Luke that Rebecca's life had taken on a new intensity. The terror of the night on which they'd stolen Simon had mellowed into a warm glow of success. Shared joy bubbled between them in small bursts of unexplained excitement and they'd sat close on a rock that clung to the mountains above Bonne Espérance. Unfamiliar emotions had transported them into the beyond of their understanding, hope settling between them like a nervous butterfly.

'This place will always be yours, Luke.' Rebecca's words had expressed his deepest longings and as he'd turned to her, his love of Bonne Espérance encompassed her in its arms.

'One day, when we're grown-up and nobody can tell us what to do, I promise I'll come back and we'll live here together. It'll be ours.'

'When?' Rebecca's voice had been so quiet it hadn't broken the spell that held them and Luke had bounded ahead recklessly, stampeding into a future of childhood dreams.

'We'll get married. We'll take care of Simon together and we'll have dozens of kids.' Unaware he'd lit a consuming fire inside Rebecca, he went on quickly: 'We'll make Bonne Espérance a great vineyard again, like you said it was in those old diaries. We'll import vines from France and Germany. We'll have hundreds of horses and we'll rebuild the house so ...' His words trailed to a halt as Rebecca stared at him. 'What's wrong?'

'You said we'd get married.' Like a wisp of wind Rebecca's voice had dislodged Luke from the plateau of his dreams and colour flushed his face.

'We can't!' Luke tried to laugh. 'We're cousins.' To hide the embarrassment that burned his cheeks he stood up quickly. 'We'd better go down now.' He held out his hand and Rebecca smiled as she took it.

'OK.' She kept silent her knowledge that Luke was not her cousin. 'I'll race you!' She ran ahead of him down the mountain slope. Though Luke had taken back his words, she clung tightly to their promise ...

'I don't want to hear any more of your stories.' The last day he'd spend on Bonne Espérance had arrived and Luke mounted the grey, turning him towards the stable doors. 'I'm going down to the river. Thabo's waiting for me.' Though he'd had to admit that Rebecca was no ordinary girl, Luke didn't want to be left alone with her again in case she reminded him of his promise.

'It's not stories. I showed you those old diaries and it's all true,' Rebecca insisted as she followed behind him on Salu, ducking under the low beam in the centre of the stables. Luke had taught her to ride every day of the past week and it had helped keep the children away from the adult tensions in the house. 'You told me yourself these stables burned down a long time ago, and Emily Beauvilliers said that in her diary. She said Clara set fire to them because Jean Jacques –'

'Who's Clara?' Luke called back, though he wasn't really interested.

'You know about her. She's our ... well, she's our great-great-great-aunt – or something.' Rebecca looked down at the horse's mane and ran her fingers through it. She'd discovered that Luke didn't know Paul wasn't his father, that he wasn't part of the Beauvilliers family, and she'd decided to keep it that way.

'Are you coming or not?' Luke urged his horse forward across the yard and towards the mountains. He wanted to be with Thabo. They'd planned to spend the last day fishing and it was as much to keep from being alone with Rebecca as anything else. She had a presence that disturbed Luke, no matter how hard he tried to ignore it.

'Salu won't move,' Rebecca called after Luke's galloping horse as Salu stood firm. 'Go on,' she nagged uselessly. 'Luke – wait!'

'Kick him,' Luke shouted back, and Rebecca dug her heels into Salu. With an angry snort the horse reared, stretched out and galloped across the cobbles after Luke.

'Wait for me,' she called again, wanting only to cement the close tie Simon had forged between herself and Luke. 'Go on, Salu!' Leaning low on the horse as it galloped underneath her, Rebecca's mind rolled back to Emily Beauvilliers' diaries, back among the yellowing pages in which she'd discovered that there really *was* a key hidden somewhere in Bonne Espérance. She believed that somehow, that key could unite Luke and herself forever, and she wanted to find it before he left in the morning . . .

Thabo looked up as Luke raced towards him with Rebecca hard on his heels. He could hear her distant calls for Luke to wait and understood the threat of separation that drove her. Looking down among the slow curves of pebbles that hid in the dark waters in front of him, Thabo searched for his own answers.

'*Yaybo!*' He called his greeting to Luke, lifting his voice to conceal his sadness at the glimpse of tomorrow that lurked behind the sun.

'Have you caught anything?' Luke jumped down, his eyes moving immediately to the river, as if afraid to look at his friend.

'Thabo will tell you those stories are true.' Rebecca's breathless voice reached them and Luke pulled a face at Thabo. 'Tell him, Thabo.' She swung one leg over the horse's back and slid to the ground beside them. 'You tell him what your people say about the things that happened here in the olden days.'

'Do you know what you've just done, Rebecca?' Luke was smiling as he looked at her.

'I'm talking to Thabo.' She dug a big toe into Thabo's back. 'Tell him!'

'You galloped,' Luke chuckled. 'You're not bad on a horse after all.' Rebecca turned and stared at Salu. Her determination to reach Luke had carried her on a galloping horse without fear and she was amazed. She hadn't noticed the sudden tension her talk of the key had caused Thabo.

'I galloped!' Her hands flew to her face in astonishment.

'Big deal.' Luke squinted against the sun and closed his eyes.

'We can't fish with her making all that noise,' Thabo spoke quiet Xhosa to his friend and Rebecca poked her big toe in his back again.

'What did you say?'

'Nothing,' Thabo and Luke shared secret boys' smiles and Rebecca exploded.

'I hate it when you do that!' She was suddenly on the outside of a boys' barricade and wasn't sure how to break it down. 'It's only because you're too scared to believe the key really is here.'

'So I'm scared.' Luke watched tadpole shapes dance on the pink backdrop of his eyelids. 'Do you see things in your eyes when you look at the sun?' he asked Thabo, opening one eye. 'Like tadpoles?'

'It's true, Luke,' Rebecca yelled. 'I know the key's here.'

''Cos you're mad.'

'Don't call me that.' Rebecca stared down at him and Luke opened both eyes. She was outlined against the glare of sunlight and cast a cool shadow over his face. 'It's in one of those diaries.' She paused, looking at him curiously. 'Are you listening?' Luke snored twice and Rebecca threw herself on top of him, pummelling his chest. 'I'll tickle you.' She dug her fingers under his arms and quite suddenly Luke rolled over, pushing her away.

'Don't do that!' He was strangely angry.

'Do what?' Rebecca's voice was quiet. She'd never seen Luke look at her like that before and she turned to Thabo for reassurance, but he looked back at her blankly. He'd also seen the look in Luke's eyes and at that moment he'd known that their friendship wasn't just threatened by the distance between the Transvaal and Cape Town, it was threatened by the distance a girl could place between two boys.

'He doesn't like it.' Thabo avoided getting involved in more talk about the key. He'd managed to keep its whereabouts a secret from Luke all his life but he wasn't sure he could manage that with Rebecca.

'You care about Bonne Espérance, don't you, Luke?' Rebecca snatched at the one thing she knew held them together. 'You promised me you'd come back one day.'

'Don't be stupid.' Luke moved away before she could mention his promise of marriage. 'And you'd better forget about that key. It doesn't exist!'

'But what if I can prove it does? That it makes dreams come true! That it's buried somewhere on Bonne Espérance?'

Luke didn't like the sensation that Rebecca's closeness had stirred in him and he shrugged, dismissing her.

'There is no key. I told you — I just made it up to frighten you. Like Thabo's father made it up to frighten us when we were kids.' Luke knew the key didn't exist. He and Thabo had searched every inch of Bonne Espérance for it. Thabo's father had said the key held all knowledge — knowledge of everything that ever happened in Bonne Espérance, especially what they did wrong. 'Forget about the key — It was make-believe.' He glanced at Thabo. 'Ask him — he knows there's no key.'

'And I know there is.' Rebecca was about to turn away, but she noticed the slightest flicker in Thabo's eyes and fixed her look on him. 'So does he.'

'Those fish they get too clever.' Thabo pulled his line from the water and swung it towards himself, catching the hook with a half-eaten worm on it. 'See?' He held the hook up, pausing as his eyes met Rebecca's. She was smiling. 'We go now.' He turned away.

'OK,' Rebecca said happily, turning to mount Salu.

'Girls,' Luke sniggered as he glanced at Thabo, wondering why Rebecca had suddenly eased up. 'Come on.' He pulled himself on to his horse's back, holding a hand down for Thabo to climb up behind him.

'You can think Thabo's father made up stories about that key to scare you, but I'm not that stupid,' Rebecca called after them. 'And I know where it is too!' she lied, looking directly at Thabo.

'You know nothing!' Though Thabo laughed he was suddenly afraid. The key his father had woven into a tapestry of myths about Bonne Espérance terrified him, and Rebecca had guessed that he knew its hiding place.

'You won't mind if I find it, then?' There was a gentle tease in her voice as she kept her eyes on Thabo.

'Why should I mind, if it doesn't exist!' Luke glanced round at his friend curiously. 'You OK, Thabo?'

'You won't mind then that it'll be a promise between us? A bond that we can never break?' Rebecca fixed her eyes on Luke as Salu trod the ground nervously under her. 'You won't mind that?'

'Anything you want.' Luke dug his heels into his horse's flanks and Thabo held on to his back tightly. 'I'll promise anything. OK?'

'OK!' Rebecca shouted happily and raced after them. She couldn't see that Thabo had closed his eyes as he leaned his face against Luke's back. She didn't know that Thabo's father had told him the world would come to an end if the old key was ever removed from its hiding place. That deep down, Thabo had sensed that the end was very near, and that Rebecca controlled it.

Thabo was balanced on the old wooden chair with one broken leg and Miriam watched her son suspiciously. His eyes were bright but fear underlined his words.

'My wages will help you,' he explained through a mouthful of leftovers that his mother had brought from the big house. 'I'll go to school too.' The normally sharp clicks of the Xhosa language buried themselves in the mushy potato and peas that puffed out his cheeks. 'There's lots of work in Cape Town.'

'Cape Town?' Miriam's eyes were dull, lit only by the flickering candle on the table between them. The day her husband had disappeared down the long road to Cape Town was still clear in her mind. In the five years that had followed she'd seen him only once, and that had been through the bars of a prison cell. 'What do you want in the city, boy?' The slim yellow flame of the candle bent double on her breath. 'Trouble – like your father?' She clipped Thabo smartly behind the ear and a small lump of potato, fringed with pea green, shot out of his mouth. 'Then where you go? To Johannesburg? Down the mines like a rat?' She wiped angrily at the tiny pile of soggy food on the table.

'Yes.' Johannesburg was a safer distance from Rebecca and Thabo was pleased that his mother had thought of that for herself. 'I'll go to Johannesburg like Luke.'

'Now you think you white?' Miriam clipped him behind the other ear, wondering why she hadn't done the same thing to her husband. 'You stay here and look after your mother, boy!' Moving to the solid wooden door she pushed it open with her foot and ducked outside, refusing to listen to any more.

As Thabo waited for the ringing in his ears to die down he turned his head from side to side, surprised to discover it was still fixed to his shoulders.

'Thabo?' Rebecca's voice mingled with the bells in his head as her nose pressed against the window pane. The white of her face was outlined clearly against the dark outside and her eyes were large. In one movement Thabo slipped off the chair and disappeared under the table, grabbing the three-legged chair as it toppled after him, trying to hide behind it.

'I can still see you, Thabo.' Rebecca's voice teased a singsong route under the table and Thabo reached quickly round the table's edge. Pulling the candle down he blew it out, losing himself in the darkness. 'Are you scared of me or something?' Rebecca's voice mocked him again and he held his breath against the stream of waxy smoke that drifted into his nostrils. Thabo had managed to avoid Rebecca ever since they'd got back from the river but now she'd trapped him in his own home.

'You looking for Thabo, Missy Rebecca?' His grandmother's voice came at him suddenly and the door pushed wide. Lit by a narrow shaft of moonlight, Sophie's spreading bare feet had stopped at the edge of the table. 'Thabo!' her voice searched the room for her grandson.

'He's under the table.' Rebecca's white feet stepped into the yellow beam of light beside Sophie's. 'Why does he sit under the table?'

Thabo stared blankly at his grandmother's face as she peered at him upside down.

'Why you got the candle under the table, boy?' she asked.

'Why's he got the candle under the table?' Rebecca's dark hair swept the concrete floor as her face appeared beside Sophie's. She was smiling the wrong way up and Thabo was very angry. 'Is he hiding?'

'What you hiding from, boy?' Sophie's face disappeared as she stood up and Rebecca's tongue poked out at him quickly. 'You come out from there, Thabo,' his grandmother ordered and Rebecca's head disappeared.

Reluctantly Thabo crawled from under the table and strolled as casually as he could towards a shelf above an old chest in the corner of the room.

'The candle went out,' he assured his grandmother in Xhosa, aware he could never satisfactorily explain the truth. 'I was looking for the matches.' He pulled a small yellow box of matches open and struck one, holding it out to the wick. Putting the lit candle on the table he quickly moved away from its circle of flickering light.

'What do you want?' he asked Rebecca flatly as she smiled at him.

'To show you something.' Rebecca's hand pushed into the pocket of her dress and Thabo's eyes widened. In one move he was at the door and pushing his way through it. A long green tail hung over the edge of her pocket.

'Thabo!' His grandmother's sharp voice stopped him. 'You go with Missy Rebecca, and you mind your manners,' she hissed in Xhosa.

'Luke's waiting for me.' Thabo's eyes were fixed on the chameleon that backed its way cautiously out of Rebecca's pocket.

'But Luke's not allowed out. He's packing.' Rebecca had picked Luke's name from Thabo's rattling Xhosa and shrugged with a quick nod at her pocket.

As the chameleon's eyes rolled independently, its attention fixed on both children at once, Thabo tried to pretend he wasn't afraid. With its split green feet curled around Rebecca's finger as she held it in front of Thabo's face, it puffed itself angrily, its mouth opening wide with a slow hiss of warning.

'I don't know.' Thabo repeated his innocence, his attention held by the tiny monster in front of his face. 'Keep it away,' he pleaded as its body darkened, swelling with the fear it disguised as rage.

'I know you know where that key is.' Rebecca peered at him over the chameleon's dinosaur back. 'I know you do.' 'She pushed the creature closer to his face and it reared up on spindly back legs, its body swaying dangerously near Thabo's eyes. Sweat trickled down his temples and Thabo stopped breathing: the secret of the old key's hiding place was more than his life was worth to give away.

'You're not going to tell.' Rebecca's breath came out in a huff of defeat. She'd guessed Thabo would be as afraid of chameleons as Macaroni had been, but still she hadn't discovered the whereabouts of the key. 'I'll stick it in your bed!' She pushed the chameleon towards his face again and he pulled back sharply.

'They cursed,' Thabo whispered, holding his head back from the little creature round whom as many myths had been woven as the key itself. 'But I not tell you.' He fixed his eyes on Rebecca in defiance.

'You're so stupid.' Rebecca moved deeper into the musty dark of the cellars. Wooden vats lay in long dark rows, laced together by spiders' webs as a slow drip punctuated the silence. 'Don't you care that Luke's going away tomorrow? For ever.' Through the clammy dark of the cellar she could sense Thabo's very real terror and Rebecca felt suddenly guilty. 'I'm sorry.' She held the chameleon up to a low beam that ran the length of the cellars. 'You can go now,' she told it as one roving eye settled on her, the other fixed on Thabo. 'I won't put it in your bed. Promise.' Thabo's held breath seeped out and his shoulders relaxed. 'Luke will never come back, you know. Not ever.' Rebecca lifted a foot towards a vat and kicked it hard. The spread of silvery spider web between the vats shook and the spider clung tight in its centre. Like a knot in a hank of silk thread, it bounced and swung in the shivering web.

'The grave.' Thabo's words were so quiet they slipped past Rebecca unnoticed and she went on.

'Luke would have promised to come back if I'd found the key.' She stopped, realising quite suddenly that Thabo had spoken. 'What did you say?'

'The key.' His jaw tightened as he spoke words which might lead to the end of the world. 'The bad lady, Clara. Her son. My people, they say Master Jack Marsden bury the key in his mother's grave.'

Only the chameleon moved as Rebecca stared at Thabo. Each spindly leg hovered above the beam before cautiously treading its tightrope to safety.

Why did Jack bury the old key like that?

Emily Beauvilliers' words spread across the yellowing paper in black ink.

'Why?' Rebecca mumbled as she sat cross-legged on the bed, the large diary balanced on her spread knees as she stared at it. The entire household was preparing Luke's family for their departure early the next morning and she knew she'd be left alone to unravel the mystery of the old key. Quickly she flicked backwards through the pages in search of a clue.

The evil that clings to Clara has invaded Bonne Espérance. All she wants is to kill our half-brother, Jean Jacques and she holds that old key like a threat.

Rebecca pushed that diary aside and heaved another on to her knees, flicking hurriedly through its pages.

Clara's hatred spilled on to Father even as he died. Even as he drew his last breath, Clara tortured him. All she wanted was Bonne Espérance.

Rebecca snapped the diary shut. Every mention of Clara's name warned her not to disturb her grave and she pushed the diary away. Moving to the window she peered out into the darkness and tensed. A wind had sprung up outside and it blew a dry storm over Bonne Espérance. Holding huge trees by their roots, it swung them wildly in agitated circles and through the groans of tortured oaks Rebecca heard her grandmother call.

'Come, Rebecca.' Katinka's voice flew at the window on the wings of the wind and Rebecca moved to the door obediently.

The full moon hung low, casting the shadows of dancing leaves on headstones. It was as if the lid of every coffin was slightly ajar and the dead waited for Rebecca to take one step too close.

Nervously she moved that step closer. Her eyes were fixed on the stone that bore the name *Clara Marsden* and her heart banged loudly against the wall of her chest. A dusty tornado whipped at a pile of leaves round her feet but Rebecca held back her fear, moving closer to the grave on which her attention was centred.

'What she want?' Sophie's sleepy voice reached through the darkness as Thabo crept back into the room, pulling the door closed on the whipping wind outside. 'What you been doing?' The wind rattled the door on its hinges, threatening to rip it wide.

'Nothing.' Thabo moved quietly towards the window, wondering how his grandmother could be awake when he'd heard her snores from outside.

'You be careful how you play with a white girl, boy. They smarter than you.' Sophie's words came to an end with a snatched snore.

'It's not white that makes you smart.' Thabo rubbed at the mist on the glass and waited until his grandmother's breath had rolled back into deep snoring waves. Carefully he clicked open the lock and pushed the small window back.

The sound of a spade grating on rock pierced the night air and he pulled the window shut quickly. His heart threatening to burst free of his body, his lips moved in a quick prayer of repentance. He'd been forced to tell Rebecca where the key was, he reminded his ancestors, adding the truth quickly: 'I don't want Luke to go away forever.'

Rebecca stood absolutely still. She was certain the noise of the spade had woken the whole house and she glanced nervously towards her grandmother's grave for reassurance. The loose earth that covered it had settled in a red mound.

'You told me I'd like Luke, Granny Cat. You said we'd be friends.' The clear glass ball of a tear formed in the corner of her eye and she pushed it away roughly. 'He's the only friend I've got and he's going away. I've got to find that key, Granny! I love Luke. I'll find Johannes Villiers like you ...' Rebecca stopped in mid-sentence and her attention swung back to Clara's grave, her eyes settling on the cold grey of the headstone. She'd remembered the day of her grandmother's funeral. She'd asked her father that night why they hadn't put a headstone on Katinka's grave, like the others. David had told her that a stone could only be laid once the earth had settled. Quite suddenly, Rebecca understood.

Her bottom lip pulled back under her crooked eye-tooth and she stared at Clara Beauviliers' old headstone. Jack Marsden couldn't have buried the key inside the grave itself – not with everyone watching. He must have buried it under the headstone *before it was laid*. Dropping to her hands and knees beside the stone, Rebecca felt jagged rock tear at the tips of her fingers as she pulled at the hard earth round its base, but she didn't stop. Her entire being was centred on the key, driving her on regardless of pain.

Thabo pulled himself back into the heavy night shadow of the stable wall and he froze. Lights had snapped on in every window of the big house and his mother and grandmother were making their way towards it for the start of the day.

'Rebecca,' he called in a hushed voice, running across the grounds towards the graveyard in an effort to stop her plundering the dead. 'They awake,' he called again as she scratched under the headstone of the grave. 'They coming. You stop now!' Rebecca pushed the spade into the small tunnel she'd dug around the bottom edge of the tombstone. 'You mustn't – no!' Thabo touched her on the shoulder but he leapt back as she swung round on him. Her eyes were burning with a determination he'd never seen before.

'Go away!' Rebecca's voice was threatening and her body curled round the gravestone possessively.

'No,' Thabo whispered as the iron edge of her spade dug into the rock again.

'Go away if you're scared.'

Rebecca leaned her weight against the spade, forcing it deeper under the headstone. Hearing another sound, Thabo spun round to look towards the house. The front door was open, and Paul was heaving an enormous trunk through it.

'Leave it, Rebecca,' Thabo urged frantically, but he pulled back as she dropped the spade and pushed her fingers deeper into the earth.

'Thabo?' Luke was crossing the cobbled courtyard, heading for Thabo's room and Rebecca's hands kept clawing at the earth.

'Help me, Granny Cat!' She dug her fingers under the headstone as Thabo fled in terror. Ducking low among the rows of vines, he tried to reach his room before Luke.

'Will you take care of Salu?' Luke watched Thabo's hand shake as he fumbled with a match. His friend's usually soft brown eyes were brittle as the candlelight touched them and his breathing was fast. 'Are you OK?' Luke had noticed small beads of sweat standing proud on Thabo's dark skin.

'Yes.' Thabo looked at Luke, fixing him in a steady gaze, as if printing his image on his mind. 'And I take care of Simon.'

Luke nodded, moving deeper into the small room in which they'd spent many years together as children. The familiar smell of sleep trapped on warm air, held tight between four walls, carried him suddenly back in time. Luke was snug in Sophie's arms as she rocked him to sleep on the slow melody of a Xhosa lullaby while Thabo sat at her feet.

'You were right about Simon, Thabo.' Luke pulled himself free of memory and smiled at his friend. 'What we did for Simon was right.' Thabo knew nothing was right and he looked at Luke in silence. The world they'd once occupied together was being brought to an end by Rebecca and he wasn't sure how to warn his friend. 'She's not bad, that Rebecca.' Luke's words stepped into Thabo's thoughts and the candle flickered as an icy breeze passed between them. 'For a girl anyway,' Luke added with a smile.

'Will I see you again?' Thabo peered into Luke's eyes as if looking for the answer there.

'Of course.' Luke smiled but his eyes were empty. ''Course we'll meet again. When we're grown-up.'

'No! You must come back before we grow up.' Thabo's words ran to a slow halt as he realised that Luke had already gone. Fear had filled the space his friend had occupied and Thabo knew that their world had already come to an end. Apartheid was a grown-ups' disease.

Rebecca's fingers tightened around a piece of metal that was caught under the jagged base of the headstone and she pulled. It didn't move. Jamming her shoulder against the stone she wriggled her hand in deeper till she gripped the metal against her palm but still it didn't budge and quickly she grabbed the spade.

'Luke's going, Rebecca!' She didn't hear her father's call. She didn't hear the long blast of the car hooter or the sudden shouts of, 'Goodbye!'

'Say goodbye to Rebecca for me,' Luke's voice called over the sound of the car engine as it pulled away, whipping loose stones from among the cobbles of the courtyard to hurl them back at the house. 'Tell her to write to me, Uncle David.'

The spade snapped back and a piece of metal flew past Rebecca's face. She swung round and stared at the dark shape that lay on the grave behind her. Caked in years of rust and with solid earth barnacles distorting its shape, a key had flown free of the grave.

'Rebecca,' her mother called as she spotted the darting shadow of her daughter ducking through the vineyards. 'What are you doing? Luke's going.' Rebecca pulled her dress free of a grabbing vine, ignoring her mother's calls as she ran on towards the stables. Her eyes were fixed on the straight yellow beam of headlights that drove their way towards the gates of Bonne Espérance and her hand clutched the old key.

'Salu,' she shouted as she ran toward the horse with the key gripped tightly in her hand. She pulled herself on to his bare back and dug her heels into his flank.

'Rebecca,' Constance shouted as the horse squeezed past her through the open stable doors. 'Rebecca – come back.' But the horse's hooves thundered over the cobbles, galloping into the darkness with Rebecca no more than a flying shadow on its back.

'Wait for me!' Rebecca screamed, propelling the horse towards the fence that protected Bonne Espérance from the tarmac road that led to the outside world. 'Luke!' she yelled after the two red tail-lights that were disappearing into the dark ahead of her.

'Dad,' Luke said. 'It's Rebecca.'

'Don't stop, Paul,' Estelle intervened, but the car came to a halt. The engine rose on a high whine as it reversed back down the road and Rebecca stood still on the inside of the fence. A curly stream of exhaust fumes spread low on the blue tarmac in front of her and Luke's bare feet stepped in to it.

'Where were you?' he asked, and Rebecca held her clenched hand out to him in silence. Slowly, with the fence between them, she opened her fingers. The long dark piece of metal lay in the palm of her hand.

'The key.' Rebecca's voice was a whisper of mystery. 'You said you'd promise me anything if I found the key.'

Luke's attention was drawn from the key to Rebecca's face. The small girl with a mat of freckles across her nose had gone, and a woman looked back at him, her eyes reaching for his soul.

'Promise you'll come back.' Rebecca's voice was firm and Luke lowered his head, trying to snap the taut thread that stretched between them.

'It's only a key,' he said quietly, not daring to lift his eyes to hers again.

'No. It's not just a key.' Rebecca's voice was filled with wonder. 'It's our key, Luke.'

'We're going. Come on, Luke!' Estelle's impatient voice broke between them but it was ignored by both.

'Open your hand.' Rebecca's voice was gentle and Luke's eyes lifted to hers as she laid the rusty old key in his open palm. 'This will make our promise come true.' Though Rebecca had never again mentioned Luke's talk of marriage, he was trapped in the dark uneasy sea of her longings. 'No matter what happens, we'll be together one day.' She paused. 'You can go now.'

With a sudden smile she set him free and turned away, but Luke didn't move as the old key lay in his hand.

CHAPTER SIX

A large brass key hung just above the desk in Luke's new bedroom in Johannesburg and his mind was back on the night, four years ago when Rebecca had placed it in his hand. But it wasn't Rebecca that Luke thought about now. He was trying to find Bonne Espérance, desperately trying to conjure up an image of the place that had held the only peace he'd ever known. The secure white house that stood at the foot of dark blue mountains . . . he could feel it. No matter the dramas that had played out around and inside it all his life, Bonne Espérance had remained aloof. Like the arms of a mother it had always secured him and he longed to nestle in its warmth once again.

'If you think you can bring the filth of that bloody woman into my house you're wrong!' The black and white border collie at Luke's feet looked up at him questioningly as Estelle's voice splintered the silence of his bedroom. Luke had tried to bury himself in homework when he'd got back from school that day. He'd forced his ear flat against the palm of his hand, leant his elbow on the small desk in his bedroom and tried to drown the sounds of his mother's screams with historical facts.

'Do you imagine you're the only man she whores with? I'll tell you who else climbs in and out of that woman's bed – kaffirs. And you're a kaffir-lover like the rest of your family.'

The dry Johannesburg air crackled with electricity and Luke pushed the window above his desk open. Climbing on to the desk, treading through books and papers, he dropped gently into the garden outside and the dog peered at him hopefully.

'Stay,' Luke said firmly, turning to go. Though his mother's screams had become part of life as she regularly hurled abuse at Paul, Luke knew things were different this time. Estelle's cries were filled with the knowledge of defeat and they threatened everyone.

'I hate him.' Naomi's cool voice reached Luke as he walked across the lawn towards the bottom of the garden, and he turned on hearing the creak of a swing. With her legs neatly crossed in front of her, Naomi swung backwards and forwards on a small wooden seat. Her face was filled with righteous indignation and she repeated her mother's words. 'He's a kaffir-lover!'

'Why don't you go and see Lynette?' Luke caught the wooden base of the swing as it flew towards him.

'No.' Naomi turned her body and looked at him coldly. 'It's Pa who has to go away.' Luke tipped the base of the swing and Naomi clung to the ropes that hung from the branches of a jacaranda tree. 'You should go too,' she yelled. The grown woman was clearly visible in the body of a twelve-year-old girl and Naomi's words were spiked with distaste. 'You're no different from him!' Luke let the swing go and moved back across the lawn as Estelle's voice reached after him.

'Get out of this house and never come back, you bastard!'

Luke kicked at the purple carpet of jacaranda flowers that spread themselves at his feet.

'You're a kaffir-lover just like him and I hate you too!' Naomi yelled after her brother and pushed herself off the swing, running back to the house.

Stopping under the enormous fir tree at the bottom of the garden, Luke leaned his head back against it, gazing up its tall trunk. Weaver birds' nests hung like Christmas decorations among its branches and the flurried activity of a small male bird caught his attention. Putting the finishing touches to the upside-down nest to which it clung, the feathered master-builder chirped nervously. A nearby female fixed a critical eye on his efforts and Luke wondered if the bird stood any more chance than his father.

'Luke.' Estelle's voice raced towards him through an open window. 'I want you here to witness your father's lies.' The window slammed shut and Luke's heart sank. He'd been hauled in many times to bear witness to his father's evil, and each occasion had left him a shivering jelly of helplessness.

'Ma wants you inside, Luke.' Naomi's bedroom window flung wide as her voice sang like a ventriloquist's dummy. 'Luke!' she screamed after him as he disappeared through a gap in the wooden fence at the bottom of the garden.

Making his way across the bare patch of ground behind the house, Luke glanced up at the dark clouds that collected overhead. He was trying to remember a time when hatred didn't burn like a bush fire between his parents. At sixteen he was old enough to know that their marriage had never been happy, not even at Bonne Espérance, but the gentleness of the Cape had somehow protected him from it.

Stepping off the pathway in front of Luke, an African man touched his cap politely, allowing Luke through as if it was his right.

Thabo must be sixteen like you, but he says he doesn't know how old he is. Is that 'cos he's black?

Rebecca's last letter jumped into Luke's mind and with it, an image of his friend, Thabo. But Thabo wasn't black. He had no colour. He was neither white nor black in the colour-blind shades of their childhood friendship.

'In here, Luke,' a girl's voice called in Afrikaans as a sheet of lightning lit the charcoal clouds from behind. 'Quick.' Her shout was drowned by a sudden clap of thunder. Hard balls of ice pounded down on his head as a hailstorm broke free of the sky. 'I didn't see you leave school today.' Althea Strydom lowered her eyes as Luke stepped in beside her under the verandah roof of the Bowling Club. 'I was at sports.' She explained her white shorts and shirt, rubbing one plimsole up the side of her bare leg before bending down to pull up her sock. 'I'm in the hundred-yard relay.' She tugged the edges of her white shorts down as she stood up. 'What are you doing here?'

'Nothing.' Luke turned away, looking back at the thick white covering of hail on the ground. Althea attended the same Afrikaans school as he did. Her father was in the Civil Service and Luke's mother continually reminded him how important that was. Important enough for him to be sent to an Afrikaans school against his father's wishes.

'Have you been studying?' Althea looked at him shyly, wrapping her arms across her chest as he turned to her. 'It's cold.'

'It's not cold.' Luke turned away again, balancing his bare feet on the wooden edge of the verandah floor. His toes curled over it, reaching for the small balls of ice underneath them.

'Did you get my letter?' Althea moved closer and her index finger ran down Luke's spine.

'Yes.' Though Luke nodded he kept his face away. Althea's letter had been handed to him by a giggling fourteen-year-old on his way out of school that day. He'd read it secretly behind the bicycle sheds and was deeply embarrassed as Althea brought the subject out into the open.

'What I said, it's true,' she whispered and Luke moved quickly to escape. 'Luke!' She held his arm to detain him, and he waited, watching her curiously. Althea's head was lowered and her cheeks were bright pink. 'I thought it's what you wanted.' She turned away to face the wooden wall of the clubhouse, her long fingers curling between the slats of wood. 'I've never done it before, not with anyone.'

'I know that.' Luke's eyes passed over Althea's back and on down the length of her suntanned legs. He'd kissed her once. Outside the school changing rooms her mouth had opened to his and he would never forget the surge of excitement as their bodies touched.

'Don't you want to?' Althea turned to him, her wide pink mouth open, just a little. 'There's nobody here and there's a window open at the back. We can get inside and . . .'

'No!' Luke ran. He ran away across the ground towards the back fence of his house. He ran through the thick layer of hailstones that crunched under his feet and quite suddenly the sun burned an accusing path through the clouds, directly on to him.

'Luke!' Althea's voice was filled with failure as it chased him and he felt suddenly sick. Sick of the desires that teased his body even as his mother's words turned them to searing guilt.

'Go home, Althea,' he shouted back as his bare feet pounded the bubbles of ice.

'Ma?' The house was quiet as Luke opened the back door of the kitchen. 'Ma,' he called again, remaining outside. 'Shh!' He bent down to the dog as it skidded across the lino floor towards him, its entire body wagging with delight. 'Where's Ma?' The dog tilted its head to one side with its ears pricked against the silence, as if listening in terror for Estelle.

Reacting as something dropped on the hall floor, Luke moved through the kitchen and then stopped. In the hall, Paul pushed a cupboard door closed with his foot, picked up a large empty suitcase and looked at him silently.

'What are you doing, Dad?' The sight of the suitcase had thrown Luke into sudden panic. 'Dad?'

Paul's face was ashen and his eyes were totally empty. He longed to reach out to the young boy who stood on the threshold of life, precariously balanced on the outer edge of childhood, but he couldn't.

'Do you want to talk?' Paul asked quietly.

A one-eyed teddy bear, its head attached its body by a single black thread, peered blindly from the pillow as Luke sat on his bed and Paul stood uneasily beside the desk.

'Where did Ma go?' Luke asked quietly and Paul shrugged. 'And Naomi?'

'With your mother.' Paul watched Luke carefully. He wanted to try and explain what had happened between himself and Estelle but wasn't sure he had the right. 'Love isn't something you can order, Luke.' Paul rolled a pencil under the ball of his foot before bending down to pick it up. 'Maybe it would be easier if it was.'

'Did you ever love Ma?' Luke's fingers dug into the dog's thick fur as it sat on the floor beside him, its warm brown eyes fixed on him. 'Did you ever love her? When you had me – did you love Ma then?'

'It's got nothing to do with you, Luke. You must understand that.' Paul moved to the edge of the bed. He could see the tension in Luke's jaw and longed to put his arm round him, to tell him the truth. But he didn't. 'I'm not sure it's even got anything to do with your mother.'

The dog nudged Luke's leg with its nose and laid its head across his knees, pressing him to acknowledge his presence.

'Then it's because of that woman?' Luke met his father's eyes. He'd stated the existence of a woman he'd grown to hate without even knowing her and the dog waited patiently to regain his attention. 'Do you love her?'

'Elize?' Just the sound of her name touched an emotion in Paul that only she had ever tapped, and he rolled the pencil between his thumb and middle finger. He studied it carefully as if he'd never seen a pencil before. 'Yes.' He moved away suddenly.

'That's why.' Luke went after Paul quickly and the dog looked up, surprised he'd been so suddenly abandoned. 'That's why you're leaving? Because of that woman – because you're going to her?'

'I love Elize.'

'And me? Naomi?' A lump had formed in Luke's throat and choked his words. 'I know what Ma's like, but you're married to her, Dad! Doesn't that mean anything?' Luke's words tumbled out in a confused heap at Paul's feet.

'I can't explain.'

'Try!' The pleading in Luke's voice was balanced on a platform of anger that Paul had never heard before. 'Where does your love begin and end for me? Tell me!'

'You're not involved, Luke.'

'How much more involved can I be?' Luke's voice rose on a cry. 'I'm your son!' Paul tossed the pencil on to the desk and went to the door, gripping the handle as he tried to hold back from the truth. He'd been trapped by the lie spun round Luke's birth and he felt suddenly more ashamed of that than of anything else. 'Tell me, Dad! *Why?*'

An invisible wall of silence stood between them and the dog pulled the garrotted teddy bear off the pillow, chewing its ear with low mutterings of disquiet.

'Dad?'

'My love for you hasn't changed, Luke.'

128

'But you're going to walk out of here. Do you call that love?'

'Yes, dammit, that is what I call love.' Paul swung round on Luke, catching him by surprise. 'I've stayed all this time *because of you*! I've put what I found with Elize at risk *for your sake*! Everything I've done has been "for the children"!' Paul paused, his head dropped and he peered up at Luke as he tried to explain what he knew the boy could never understand. 'But now the anger and pain is destroying everyone. Can't you see? I ...' he shrugged '... for the sake of the children.' He moved closer to Luke and the dog looked up with a whimper as the teddy bear's body swung on a thread from its mouth. 'My staying has achieved nothing, but it's destroying everything.' The dog's head tilted to one side and the teddy bear's thread neck stretched longer. 'Don't I have the right to love as well, Luke?' Paul's shoulders lifted. He knew he could never explain the truth or his feelings without revealing the truth of whose son Luke really was. 'I need to be loved just like anyone else.'

'Ma must have loved you once.' Luke's voice cracked as tears pushed their way to the surface. 'What did you do to stop Ma loving you?'

'Became less necessary, perhaps.'

'How?' Luke didn't know why he was pushing his father for answers. He didn't want answers any more than Paul wanted to give them, but he couldn't stop himself. 'Tell me the truth, Dad.'

The dog trod through the silence that followed, the teddy bear's body dragging between its feet as it chewed one ear. A small whimper announced the offering of its head as the dog's brown eyes fixed on Luke's face and the thread snapped free.

'I'll pack my things.' Paul couldn't answer Luke's question and he moved to the door.

'Please don't go.' Luke was suddenly beside him. 'Please, Dad.' His arms wrapped round him and his firm young body clung tight.

'Paul!' Estelle's harsh voice snapped the moment and the teddy bear's head dropped from the dog's mouth.

Luke's eyes hadn't moved from the highly polished black shoes of the Dutch Reform minister who stood behind him in the centre of the sitting room. From the invisible pulpit his self-righteousness had built underneath him, the man in a high white collar spoke in booming Afrikaans.

'Look at your son, man.' The power of the dominee's voice blew against Luke's neck as he turned him by the shoulders to face Paul. 'Do you want this young man to follow the path you've chosen, or will you repent and take up your responsibilities like a God-fearing man? Push that woman and the lusts she has aroused within your flesh back to the pit of hell where she belongs, and repent!'

'Why did you bring him here, Estelle?' Paul's voice was quiet as he looked at his wife. She stood rigidly beside her newfound ally and Naomi was next to her, her face a miniature copy of her mother's martyrdom. 'You took Naomi with you to fetch him?'

'Your daughter knows what you are. The whole church knows and you stand condemned.' Estelle pushed past Luke as she moved to the minister. 'Tell my husband what God thinks of him, Dominee Trichard.'

'Ma!' Luke's voice rang through the room like a clear brass bell and Estelle swung round in surprise as her son faced the implacable church minister.

'Why are you here, sir?' he asked in English.

'Your mother came to seek the Church's guidance on . . .'

'English!' Luke yelled, his body trembling as he stared up at the lantern-jawed man who'd spoken Afrikaans. 'My father is English and you will speak English in his house.'

'It's all right, Luke.'

'It's not all right, Dad.' He faced Estelle. 'What does God say about Dad, Ma? Tell me what you last heard God say about anything. When did you last set foot in a church – to marry Dad? To christen me? Hellfire or blessing to be called down when it suits you – is that what God means to you, Ma?'

'You talk to me of God. You know about God?' Estelle's nails dug into Luke's skin as she grabbed his arm and her voice rose as he pulled free. 'You know what your father has done?'

'Ma.' The Dutch Reform Church minister looked down uncomfortably as Luke swung back at the door, his voice a wail of helplessness as it choked on flooding tears. 'You say you love Dad. How, Ma? Like you loved Simon? Is that how you love people?'

'Bastard!' Estelle turned on Paul in self-defence. 'You see what you've done now – what your whoring with that woman has brought us to?'

'Let him go!' Luke's face was that of a small boy as he peered at his mother through eyes that begged for understanding. 'Please, Ma. Let Dad go.'

Elize moved away from the window, and the white lace curtain fell back across the glass in gentle folds. Tall and slender, Elize's fair hair fell loosely over one eye and she pulled her dressing gown tighter as she turned towards the bedroom, gliding silently across the bare parquet floor. Elize had moved to Johannesburg from the Cape to be near Paul. The love she felt for him leading her into a life of lies and adultery. Their relationship was far outside the bounds of everything she'd once believed in – but she also believed in Paul. He was a man who'd lost his way. He'd stooped to help Estelle in a moment of pity and his life hadn't been his since that moment. But now he'd left Estelle. Forced to abandon his children as his wife had abandoned Simon, it was only now that Elize had seen Paul bleed.

She'd noticed the young man waiting outside in the street every morning for the past week and although she knew Paul had also seen him, neither had said a word.

'Your breakfast's ready.' Paul sat on the edge of the bed, doing up his shoelaces, and automatically he wrapped his arms around Elize as she drew close. 'He's there again today.' She stroked his hair back as he looked up at her, his face puzzled and lost.

Elize had seen the same look of bewilderment in Paul's eyes for the entire week the young man had stood alone outside their small flat. She'd noticed that even after Paul had gone to work, the fair-haired boy of sixteen had stayed on, his eyes never leaving their window as he leaned on a bicycle. The guilt Elize felt every time she'd seen him outside was something she'd still not got used to. She wanted to help but didn't know how.

'What does he want?' Paul looked into Elize's slow green eyes and she shrugged an answer. 'Every time I go outside, he's gone. If he doesn't want to see me, what does he want?'

A pulse beat gently in the delicate arch of Elize's neck and her tongue passed over her lips before she smiled. 'Perhaps Estelle's sent him to spy.'

'We've got to talk about it, Elize.'

'It's him you must speak to. You.' Paul lowered his head and sat in total silence as Elize watched him. 'I put cheese in the scrambled egg.' The warmth that had held their love constant throughout the years spilled on to Paul as she released him from obligation.

'I went to the embassy, Elize.' She stopped at the door and turned back, unsure she wanted Paul to go on. 'I can get a British passport through my great-grandfather. We can go to England as soon as we like.'

'England?' Elize's eyes moved over his face in delicate questioning glances, as if searching for the place he talked about.

'Estelle will never give me a divorce. She'll use the kids as weapons if we stay here. Our lives and theirs will never be our own.' Paul bent down to his shoe and tugged at the laces, trying to push back his last memory of Estelle's defiant screams.

Elize had wiped away the years of insignificant days that had paraded as married life with Estelle and for the first time he felt like a man. He couldn't face losing her. Her constant love, uncompromising and unconditional was the very air that he breathed. He had found himself in Elize and wanted Luke to share that security, to allow the radiance of Elize's love to touch Naomi, for Simon to be accepted by her as a real person for the first time in his short life ... But Paul knew it was impossible.

'The kids have got to be free of the bitterness, Elize. We have to make a fresh start and they have to as well.' Paul stood up, pulling her close and in an instant he was lost in her peace.

Pulling his bicycle back quickly, Luke watched as Paul's car drove out from behind the block of flats and, ducking quickly around the corner, he moved behind a large van. As the sound of the car drew closer he bent down. Looking underneath the van he watched the wheels of Paul's car drive past, making no move to stop it.

The school tie around Luke's neck felt suddenly tight as his throat swelled with tension and he pushed his thumb inside the knot to loosen it. Looking back towards the window on the third floor he saw the soft folds of lace drop back behind the glass and he knew she had seen him again.

Elize watched Luke's singularly lonely figure as he wheeled his bicycle towards the small wall in front of the flats. His figure bent in strange shapes through the gathering pleats of lace and she was strangely nervous. Pushing her hair back, she tried to calm herself and turned towards the front door of the flat. She could hear Luke's feet on the concrete steps outside and found herself taking a step backwards. A figure had stopped on the other side of the mottled glass in the top half of the front door and she cleared her throat.

'It's open,' Eliez said, watching the motionless shadow that waited on the other side of the glass. Her voice was soft and she smiled as the door clicked open.

'Come in, Luke.' Elize held her hand out towards a chair but he didn't step inside. 'Would you like some coffee?' She watched the young boy about whom Paul talked with more love than most fathers showed for their own sons, and Elize felt suddenly sad. Luke looked out of place in his own body. His navy-blue school blazer, though spotlessly clean, was too small. Faded lines stretched between the closed brass buttons and the cuffs shone with age as they stopped short of his wrists. 'Or maybe you'd like a cold drink? I think we've got some Coke.'

'I don't need anything.' Luke's shoulders lifted as he gazed at Elize. There was a serenity about her that he'd never seen before, and wilde-set eyes held him in a gaze of welcome. 'I'm sorry.' Luke looked down. Sketched with the sharp edge of his mother's words and darkened by the humiliation of rejection, his image of Elize had been totally wrong. The woman who stood in front of him was beautiful in a way he'd never imagined, and coming face to face with Elize, he'd bumped into his father's reality for the first time.

'I shouldn't have come here. I'm sorry.'

'I'm just sorry I'm not dressed yet.' Elize held her hand out to a chair. 'Won't you sit down?'

Luke shook his head as he stood uncomfortably in the doorway. 'I wanted to see Dad . . . I must have missed him.'

Elize longed to reach out and pull close the young man who stood on the edge of her life with Paul. To comfort him as he reached out for a father who wasn't his.

'You've been waiting outside for a long time and you haven't spoken to your father yet, Luke. Why go now?' Elize moved to a heavy wooden armchair and sat down. 'Would you believe I've wanted to meet you for a long time? That's why you're here, isn't it? You're as curious about me as I am about you.'

Elize was aware of Luke's eyes passing over her carefully and she smiled. 'Paul tells me you're sitting Matric next year. He says you're going to be a lawyer and he's very proud of that.'

Luke looked down quickly. He hadn't known Paul was proud until then and he buckled under the sudden warmth of acceptance. Elize waited, her eyes passing over the clump of blond hair that fell over Luke's eyes. His firm young hands were clenched at his sides and his voice came out in a whisper.

'He didn't say you were so beautiful.' Luke spoke in Afrikaans and Elize laughed.

'Yes, Luke. I am Afrikaans.' Her eyes danced on a bright smile. 'Just like your mother.' She knew he would have wondered if the growing distance between the English and Afrikaner was why Paul had left his mother. 'And I know how difficult this must be for you, Luke, coming face to face like this. Would you believe it is for me too?' As Luke looked up she smiled and lifted her hands. 'Please don't say you're sorry again. Sorry would never explain how I feel.'

A smile crept into Luke's eyes and he scratched his head. 'Thank you.' He held out his hand, tugging at his school blazer. 'I'll be late.'

'Did you find out what you wanted to know?' Luke nodded as she moved to the door and took his hand. 'There's something else I think you should know.' She was about to turn a key that would either free him, or lock him in permanent despair and she paused for a moment.

'There is nothing I want more in the world than to be with Paul, to marry him and be his wife. But,' she paused, holding tight to Luke's hand, 'I can never take the place of your mother. Can you understand what I'm saying?'

Luke's eyes narrowed in puzzlement before his face spread with a wide smile and he nodded.

'I also understand Dad.'

Although the letter had arrived with the morning post, Estelle hadn't opened it till much later that afternoon. She'd recognised Paul's handwriting and the English stamps postmarked *Chiswick, London*. The same English king had stared at her from the stamps of the last letter she'd received from England, sixteen years earlier, but that letter had come from Luke's real father, Edward Lawson. As Estelle's hands moved in squeaking circles of polish on wood, Paul's letter had remained unopened in her pocket all day.

She'd gazed down at her own reflection in the shining table top and Edward's face had formed beside it as her memory roamed the past.

You wouldn't be happy in England, Estelle. Every word Luke's father had written was scored across her memory in indelible ink. *You'd be out of place with English people.* Estelle's teeth had clenched as the familiar feeling of inadequacy flooded her mind. She'd known exactly what Edward had meant, as he pinned her Afrikaans beginnings to her like a second-class badge and her mind whipped back to the day she'd met him.

'Hullo, love!' She'd never forgotten Edward's warm English voice. He'd stayed on in Africa after a two-year contract with the gold mines had ended and he'd said there was no place in the world like the Transvaal.

'Forget about him,' Estelle's mother had advised her later. Though she'd served the Englishman with tea and perfect round cookies, Estelle had known at once that her mother hadn't trusted him at all.

'Please don't.' Estelle felt her body shiver as her mind whipped further back to another distant memory. She was in the bush with Edward. He was leaning over her. His mouth was brushing her face and his weight pushed her against the sunbaked earth as her body reached for his.

'A virgin?' Edward had smiled in surprise as he looked down at her. 'I'd heard different about you little Afrikaans *meisies*!'

Estelle had responded to Edward's lovemaking with a passion that had surprised even him, and only when she'd got home that night had she felt any guilt. Her mother had looked straight through her as she'd crept back into the house.

'Wash before you go to bed,' she'd said, adding a tablespoon of Dettol to the bathwater to ensure that Estelle knew there was no point in lies.

'We're going to get married,' she'd told her mother in defence.

'Oh yes?' Her mother's voice had been amused as she turned off the bath-tap. 'Taking you to England with him, is he?'

'He's staying here! We're going to live here.'

'And what will he do when you get pregnant?' The guttural edge of her mother's Afrikaans had stung Estelle with the one truth she'd avoided.

'They think Afrikaans girls are only good for sex – like blacks!'

Estelle had been pregnant for four months.

'Of course I want the baby, love.' Edward seemed surprised that she'd even questioned him. 'Just let me get back home and find us somewhere to live, will you?'

'You said you were staying here.'

'There's a war on and there are too many Afrikaner Nazis in this place for my liking.'

'I'll come with you.'

'Bang, bang – war! Get it, love?'

Though Edward had held her tightly in his arms and promised he'd send for her, Estelle had heard only her mother's voice ringing in her ears: 'They think Afrikaans girls are only good for sex – like blacks!'

And finally Edward's letter had arrived, pinning the second-class badge to Estelle once again.

You're Afrikaans and you'd be out of place with English people.

Estelle wiped at the tear that dropped quite suddenly on to the polished table in front of her, and automatically her hand went to Paul's letter as it hid in her pocket. It was his face that looked at her from the table now. Paul was in a warehouse with her. She hadn't known where he'd come from, but quite suddenly Paul had been there beside her.

The streets of Cape Town, where her mother had sent Estelle to avoid the shame of an illegitimate child, had been filled with English and Australian soldiers that day. On their way to and from the war in Europe they'd streamed through Cape Town and she'd hoped to find Edward among them. Then, as the last Englishman had trooped off the ship in the docks, Estelle had gone into labour. Like a small frightened animal she'd hidden herself in a warehouse as she gave birth among wooden boxes labelled *Live Vines*.

'Are you all right?' Paul had looked down at her as if sent by God Himself and with her newborn son, Luke, he'd taken her back to his home on Bonne Espérance.

Ripping the envelope open at last, Estelle looked at Paul's letter without reading it and her mind returned to Katinka. Estelle was back in Bonne Espérance on the day she'd first learned why Paul's grandmother, Katinka, seemed dark for a European. She was listening in amazement as Paul told her without shame, of his family's beginnings, about his great-grandfather, Jacques Beauvilliers – a man who'd loved a Malay slave and fathered a child called Jean Jacques. Jean Jacques, the slave and illegitimate son of Jacques Beauvilliers who was Katinka's great-grandfather.

Estelle, the letter began in Paul's neat handwriting and she felt the familiar surge of anger rise on an acid bubble in her stomach. She'd done all she could to lift Paul and his family beyond the shame of colour that ran in his blood, but deep down she still remembered her mother's words.

Paul had proved to be no different from his ancestor, Jacques Beau-villiers. Too late, she'd realised that that was the reason he'd married her, taking on her illegitimate child, Luke. From that moment, in an effort to ensure her position as his wife, Estelle had become more English than Paul himself.

I decided it was best that Elize and I came to live in England. Estelle didn't read any more of Paul's letter.

'Is that you, Luke?' she shouted in Afrikaans as the back door opened. English had not been spoken in the house since the day Paul had left and her pride clung to the growing strength of the Afrikaner Government as they took hold of the country. 'Luke?' she called again, moving towards the kitchen.

Naomi dropped her school satchel on the floor and pulled the fridge door open, ignoring her mother as she stepped into the kitchen. 'He's probably with Althea. My friend says they fu –' Naomi stopped herself quickly, kicking out at the border collie as it followed her. '*Voetsek!*'

'Why didn't you answer me?' Estelle snapped.

'Because I'm not Luke. Ugh!' Naomi lifted her foot and examined her leg. 'You've slobbered all over me.' The dog turned quickly to the door as it heard the familiar sound of Luke's bicycle, escaping another kick from Naomi's hard school shoe.

'Tell Luke I want to see him.' Estelle's eyes narrowed as Naomi opened her mouth to argue. 'Now!' She moved back to the sitting room, her anger riding the acid ball in her stomach.

'I've got to study for the exams, Ma.' Luke poked his head around the sitting-room door. 'What do you want?'

'Forget your exams. Forget everything except what you're going to do now, boy!' The acid bubble in Estelle's mouth had burst.

'OK.' Luke dropped his satchel in the doorway, unsure what he'd done wrong this time.

'Pick it up!' Luke turned back and picked up the satchel. Each day he came home from school he faced accusations and rebuke from his mother and he knew he'd earned them all on the day he'd stood up for his father against the Dutch Reform minister.

'You see this?' Estelle held the folded letter out towards him, pulling it back as he moved to take it.

'Do you want me to read it or not?' Luke's voice was calm. The gamut of emotions he'd battered his way through like an obstacle race had given him a maturity beyond his years.

'Your father's run away and taken that woman with him to England.' Estelle advanced on Luke suddenly, her anger sweeping over him like a hot desert wind. 'I expect you think that's right, too.'

'What difference does it make?' Luke pulled back as his mother's tongue lashed out at him. 'Can't we just talk about it, Ma? Must you always scream about Dad and "that woman"? Maybe she's OK. Maybe . . .'

'She's a whore and I'll tell you what we're going to talk about.'

'Can I ride to the café and get an ice cream?' Naomi's voice whined from the doorway behind them.

'Well, Luke.' Estelle turned to him with a sudden smile. 'Answer her question.'

Puzzled, Luke glanced round at Naomi, then turned back to his mother curiously. Naomi shrugged and, crossing her right leg over her left, she tucked it in position on the toe of her shoe.

'Go on. Tell your sister yes or no.'

'What are you talking about?' Luke realised the game had changed and he was on edge.

'You don't know?' Estelle's gaze turned on him like a searchlight. 'I thought you wanted to be in charge. Wasn't it you who encouraged your father to leave?' Luke was lost in an icy sea of confusion. 'Now's your chance.' Estelle straightened the wedding ring she still wore on her finger. 'You'll be leaving school and taking a job.' A sudden current dragged Luke deeper into the sea into which he'd fallen. 'You'll forget all your plans and take up the responsibilities you claimed for yourself.'

'But I'm doing Matric next year.' Luke broke into English and Estelle's eyes fixed on him sharply. 'I'm going to University, Ma.' He returned to Afrikaans quickly. 'I don't understand what you're saying.'

'But you understood your father.' Estelle clung to the lie of Luke's birth and pushed a stray hair back into the bun at the nape of her neck. 'It's simple. Your father has given you no choice.'

'Because he's in England doesn't mean he won't . . . Ma!' Luke's voice rose and the maturity he'd gained drained through the soles of his shoes. 'I know Dad won't stop supporting us. He knows I'm going to university. I know it's what he wants!'

'And I knew he wanted us.' Estelle faced her son.

'But you knew different, didn't you Luke?' Naomi's voice floated towards Luke on a note of triumph. 'I bet you even like Dad's whore!'

'Can I trust you to shoulder your responsibilities?' Estelle forged another link in the chain she bound around her son but Luke didn't resist. 'Or are you so like your father you'll run away too?' She padlocked the chain and Luke couldn't move.

CHAPTER SEVEN

Rebecca peered through the narrow slit in the oblong red box outside Stellenbosch post office, squinting into the cool dark that filled it.

'Anything there?' David called as he waited in the car.

'Coming!' Turning the tiny key in the lock, Rebecca opened the small metal door and light reached in to reveal an envelope. It lay face-down on the rusty bottom of the post office box and, holding her breath, she stretched her fingers towards it, turning it over. Luke's stylish handwriting addressed the letter to her and she pulled it out quickly, pushing it deep into her school uniform pocket. Her satchel bobbed up and down on her back as she ran across the stubbly brown grass of the pavement towards her father. Her long brown legs stretched out in leaping strides and a dark plait of hair trailed under a straw hat, held tight by a stretch of elastic under her chin.

'Nothing for me?' David asked as his daughter climbed into the brown leather seat beside him. Though he'd noticed Rebecca slip the letter into her pocket, he pretended he hadn't.

'Nope.' The leather seat squeaked as Rebecca's back slid down it, her hand feeling the edges of the envelope that hid in the dark of her pocket.

'How was school?' David put the car in gear, pulling away from the stone kerb as children raced past on their way home.

'Can you go fast today?' Rebecca slid deeper into the seat. She'd spotted a young girl in the same red and white check uniform that she wore; the girl was waving and Rebecca wanted to avoid her. 'Go, Dad, please!' The car seat pushed her straw hat forward, the brim dropped over her eyes and a red ribbon dangled over her nose. 'I've got lots of homework.' She held the hat elastic away from her chin and it snapped back with a sting. 'Ouch!'

'From Luke is it, the letter?' David held his hand out to her, waiting for the post-box key. 'How is he?' He pushed the key into his pocket and looked at his daughter. Rebecca's bottom lip pushed forward and, slipping the elastic between her teeth, she chewed on it silently. 'Fast, you said,' David smiled and drove on.

Collecting Rebecca from school in Stellenbosch had become a welcome part of David's daily routine at Bonne Espérance. The broad streets reminded him of the small mining town from which they'd come, and if he closed his eyes against the surrounding mountains and oak trees, he was back in Central Africa.

'Don't stop to talk to Mr Viljoen, please,' Rebecca begged through a mouthful of elastic as a man in khaki shorts waved at David. 'Go on!' Her eyes fixed on the speedometer. The long black hand with a crooked arrow pointed proudly at a shaky forty miles an hour. 'You're allowed to do fifty. Go on!'

'Maybe I don't want to.' David glanced at her. Though she was twelve years old, Rebecca was still his baby. 'Do you want to steer?' He lifted his hands off the wooden wheel and she leaned across to it quickly. Holding it tight she zigzagged down the blue strip of tarmac towards Bonne Espérance.

'Faster!' Rebecca yelled as she steered the car home. She wanted nothing more than to be in the privacy of her room with Luke's letter. Since the Monday before, Rebecca had always wanted to get home from school quickly. It had been then that she'd got back to find Paul Marsden with her mother and a woman called Elize, and it was a day she'd never forget.

Paul had come to take Simon away to England and with him had been Elize. Rebecca had sensed tension the moment she reached the sitting room door and it had lived with her ever since.

'Simon's happy here, Paul,' Constance had argued, holding the child tightly by the hand as he tugged to get outside. 'He's part of the family and we all love him.'

'He's my son, Constance,' Paul had countered gently. He'd come in an effort to wipe out a moment in his life which still haunted him. The decision to send Simon away had been one of many Estelle had made without consulting him, and guilt plagued him. It had been Luke's courage that had touched Paul, stirring his own as it hid deep inside him. 'Elize and I are going to live in England and Simon would have a better chance of help over there.'

'To do what, Paul?' Rebecca had hung back behind the slightly open door as her mother spoke. 'Simon's never going to change; he's never going to be normal. You know that, don't you?' Rebecca had felt suddenly angry with her mother but she'd kept silent. She'd known that one day Simon *would* be better. He'd no longer be 'perhaps-not'. 'I love Simon.

We all do.' Constance's words had been touched by grief. 'He's become our child. Is there any reason to change that, Paul? Except to ease your guilt.'

Rebecca had never felt a silence as deep as the one that followed her mother's words, and in it she'd sensed Paul's loneliness.

'You and Elize are looking to find a new life – isn't that why you're going to England?' her mother had gone on, determined to convince Paul he was wrong.

'You don't understand, Constance!' Paul sounded almost desperate. 'What happened to Simon was my fault. Estelle didn't want him from the moment he was born. In all those years I never stood up to her.' Rebecca had shivered as Estelle's face loomed in her mind's eye. 'But Luke – *he* stood up to his mother. That boy ... that child,' Paul's voice had fallen to a whisper and Rebecca's heart rattled just with the mention of Luke's name. 'Luke showed me how wrong I'd been. A young boy showed me what a coward I've been all this time.' He watched Constance carefully. 'I owe it to Simon.'

'To prove you're no longer a coward? That's not what you owe Simon, Paul. You owe him the *love*, not the *proof* of it.' Constance's voice was filled with the tears that flowed freely down her cheeks. 'Luke believes you're his father because you love him, Paul – not because you've ever tried to prove it. Isn't that what you owe Simon?'

It had been then that Simon's place in Rebecca's life was confirmed.

Two rickety wooden chairs balanced precariously on the bumps in a square of sand that was swept smooth around them. Thabo had prepared the patch of shade under the old oak tree behind the cellars very carefully, as he did each weekday. Every morning he worked in the vineyards, waiting impatiently for the afternoons when his day really began. With Simon beside Thabo on the wooden chairs, Rebecca would teach them everything she'd learned in school.

'Rebecca!' Thabo assured Simon that it was she he'd spotted in the ageing Humber Super Snipe that turned into the curved driveway of Bonne Espérance. 'You ready?' Simon sat on one of the chairs and quickly sucked his tongue back into his mouth as Thabo glared at him. His chubby legs dangled over each side of the flat seat and a wide smile lit his eyes as they followed the car to a stop.

'Becka!' he called and Thabo held on to the chair as Simon's entire body waved at her. But the small boy's smile slowly vanished. Rebecca had slipped out of the car and was running towards the house without even looking at them.

'Becka!' he called again in puzzlement and Thabo moved to the sand square in front of him. REBECCA, he wrote in the sand with a sharp stick. Watching Thabo with serious determination, Simon's tongue swung backwards and forwards over his bottom lip like a searching earthworm, but no sound came from his mouth. His eyebrows lifted questioningly, his eyes moved to Thabo's and his mouth turned up in a hopeful smile.

'Rebecca,' Thabo informed him before wiping the word from the sand with his bare foot as he looked towards the house.

Through the window of Rebecca's bedroom he could see her sitting in a small curled ball on the ledge and her attention was buried in something she was reading.

I've got a job now so I won't be doing Matric. I won't be coming to Bonne Espérance either.

Rebecca stared at Luke's letter as she fingered a black and white snapshot in her hand.

I've got a job in the City Hall in Johannesburg now.

Rebecca's eyes moved back to the words which had pricked her bubble of excitement as she'd read the letter.

I won't be coming to Bonne Espérance. I'm sorry.

'We ready.' Thabo's face appeared on the outside of the window and Rebecca swished a curtain closed in front of it.

'Gone!' Simon's exclamation exploded in a spray of spit as he stood bowlegged beside Thabo. The inside-out pattern of pink and white flowers had folded together against the glass in rippling waves and shut them out.

'She come soon,' Thabo assured Simon as he took the six-year-old mongol child's hand and, leading him back towards the chairs like a careful toddler, sat him down. 'We wait.' Thabo had guessed the letter Rebecca was reading was from Luke; he wanted to hear the news, but decided to wait as patiently as he could.

The time that the three children shared was a time of magic, practised in the lengthening shade of late afternoon. The curious threesome would trail around Bonne Espérance on routes of discovery that had been opened to them by the yellowing pages of Emily's old diaries.

They re-measured the steps the small Emily had taken as she strode the distances across the cobbled courtyard between the house, the cellars, the barn and the stables. Rebecca had sat in the wheelbarrow pretending to be paralysed, as Emily had been, and Thabo had pushed, amazed at just how paralysed Rebecca could be when she wanted.

They followed routes that led not only among the buildings and vineyards of Bonne Espérance, but deep into the graves of the Beauvilliers family. The children had trod cautiously through their own vivid imaginations and the past had been brought into the present with their dreams.

Even the deepest beliefs Thabo held, beliefs that had been wound into the fabric of his life by his grandmother, Sophie, had begun to stir with questions.

'But it's the same I Titus Granny Cat told me about.' Rebecca had looked at Thabo indignantly one hot summer's day a year earlier. 'The one that was hanged by the Boer farmers who lived over there.' She pointed to the distant boundaries of Bonne Espérance.

'No,' Thabo had argued. 'I Titus not hanged!' He was equally certain of his facts and faced Rebecca determinedly.

'Don't be stupid! I Titus was hanged because he killed a white man.' Rebecca remembered clearly the day she'd sat on the verandah of 123 Z and Granny Cat had told her the terrible story of I Titus.

'He not hanged!' Thabo knew this story as well as he knew those of the old key and chameleons, and there was no way he'd give in to Rebecca's arrogant claims. His grandmother had told him the true story of I Titus, and *her* grandmother, Rosita, had told her the same when she'd been a child. 'He not hanged,' Thabo stated with total conviction. 'God take I Titus away.'

'God?' Rebecca looked at him in wide-eyed amazement and Simon bellowed 'God Save the King' from the wheelbarrow in which he sat. 'Don't be stupid, Thabo.' Although the tips of Thabo's ears had singed his hair in anger at this dismissal, he had kept his temper under control.

'It was the Boer farmers who killed I Titus,' Rebecca had gone on. 'Granny Cat told me, and that means it's true.'

'And my grandmother she tell me God take him!' Thabo decided that Rebecca hadn't noticed the smoke that curled up from behind his ears. But Rebecca had known one thing for certain: she'd known that the best way to get Thabo to talk was by challenging him.

'So, go on. What *did* your grandmother tell you?' she demanded.

'The house it burning. Big flames they reach to the sky from the roof.' Thabo gazed in wonder at the thatched roof of the big white house as he recalled the story Sophie had told him when he was a child. 'Flames so high they touch heaven.'

'Granny Cat's little boy was inside the house,' Rebecca added quietly as she gazed at the white house that showed no sign of the flames of which they talked. The enormous tears that had rolled from her grandmother's eyes when she'd told her about the fire were still clear in Rebecca's mind.

'From far away, I Titus he see the flames.' Thabo's voice had dropped to a whisper and he stared into the distant mountains. 'He come fast. His feet they like wings, and he . . .'

'Wings?' Rebecca collapsed in giggles.

'You want I tell you?' Thabo's eyes were very dark and he stared at

Rebecca till she shrugged. 'I Titus, he an angel,' his whispered words crept towards her on tiptoe and Rebecca shivered. 'I Titus, the angel of the beautiful white lady of Bonne Espérance.'

'Granny Cat's angel?'

Having caught Rebecca's attention at last, Thabo went on quickly: 'From far away, I Titus, he see the devil swoop down on Bonne Espérance. He see the devil go to kill the white lady!'

'Go on.' Rebecca was all ears. In her mind's eye saw an enormous black angel fly down with wings on his feet. 'What happened then?' she asked, on tenterhooks.

'The devil, he turn to I Titus. His eyes they red, burning like coals. The Devil he lift his arm to kill him, but I Titus, he kill the devil first!' Thabo's arm swung down towards an imaginary body, plunging an invisible knife into it. 'Then he fly away.' Thabo smiled suddenly. 'God, He take I Titus to heaven and no one ever see him again!'

Through the long silence that followed his words, Thabo watched Rebecca very carefully. He didn't really know if he believed the story himself any more, but it had seemed that Rebecca might.

'Now you tell me what you learn in school today.' He quickly reminded her of their bargain then, as he did now.

'Fifteen.' Thabo answered Rebecca's question and she drew a large tick beside the sum she'd drawn on the sand blackboard he'd prepared.

'Now you.' Simon's eyes opened wide as Rebecca's attention turned to him. 'What's one plus one?' This was the question she asked him every day. She watched him, waiting for his answer, and Simon watched her. He waited too.

'Put your fingers away, Thabo.' Rebecca smacked his hand as he waved two fingers at Simon. 'What is it, Simon?'

'Is it, Simon,' Simon echoed.

'Tell me, Simon.'

'Me Simon,' he repeated, laughing with delight as Rebecca threw her arms in the air in frustration.

'You're too stupid, Simon!' He stared at her solemnly from the chair as she moved to him.

'Stupid Simon,' he mumbled and threw his arms around her neck, covering her with sloppy wet kisses.

'You get a letter today?' Thabo asked casually. He'd spotted the edge of a white page sticking out of Rebecca's skirt pocket and seized the opportunity to ask. 'It from Luke?'

'Come on.' Rebecca avoided Thabo's question as she lifted Simon off the chair, struggling to carry him towards the old wheelbarrow.

'Tell me.' Thabo moved after her as she dropped Simon into the barrow. 'What Luke say?' He held the wheelbarrow handles and, tipping it back, he rolled Simon into its centre. 'Luke OK?'

'This way.' Rebecca ran on ahead but Thabo had stopped where he was. He'd seen the direction she was taking. 'What's wrong now?' she called back in frustration. 'Come on.'

'I not go there again.'

'You scared of two skinny kids?' She tilted her head back. 'What you scared of, sissy?'

'Trouble.' Thabo eyed her.

'From who?' She plonked her hands on her hips and Thabo nodded in the direction of Rebecca's father, David. He was walking towards the cellars beside a man. The man was Christian du Toit. He was the wine-maker David had employed on Bonne Espérance and he lived with his family in a house on the outer edge of the farm – the farm that had once belonged to Granny Cat's family.

'So what? He's here and we'll be there. Come on.' Rebecca tugged Thabo's arm to come with her but still he didn't budge, his bare heels burying themselves in loose sand.

'Why we go there anyway?' Thabo asked the question he'd wanted to ask since their adventures together had begun.

'I told you – because Emily wrote about it in those diaries.'

'What's it matter?'

Rebecca stared at Thabo in horror. Emily's diaries led deep into a past that contained Rebecca at its very centre and when Emily had written of the old Westbury farm, her pen had been dipped in the dark ink of secrecy.

The diary told of the truth of Jean Jacques' and Paulene Westbury's son. He was Katinka's father and Rebecca's great-grandfather, John Westbury. It was his blood, the blood of Jacques Beauvilliers' half-caste child that had shamed the Westbury family into living a lie. It was that baby's cries for recognition that still reached out to touch them on Bonne Espérance.

John Westbury had looked white, allowing Paulene's mother to avoid the shame of her daughter's love for Jean Jacques and she'd pretended he was her child. But the outer layer of his white skin had been peeled back by Clara Beauvilliers. She'd revealed John Westbury's coloured blood to a fearful world and the assassin's hand that killed him might have been her own.

Rebecca sensed that the truth of Johannes Villiers lay inside the small house in which Christian du Toit and his family now lived. Behind the walls of the small house lay the very beginnings of someone Emily had not known and Rebecca had determined to find.

'You don't know what it means?' She stared at Thabo in amazement and Simon tugged at her skirt impatiently.

'What?'

'Johannes Villiers! I promised Granny Cat that I'd find Johannes Villiers. I told you, it's where it all began. Don't you see? It's the house Jean Jacques's son was born in.' But Rebecca said nothing about the word which had begun her desperate search in the pages of Emily's diaries. The word *half-caste* that Estelle had screamed at her, echoing Clara's scream at Jean Jacques a hundred and thirty years before.

As Thabo hid behind the enormous tree on the Westbury farm, with Simon in the wheelbarrow and Rebecca beside him, he wondered why she always seemed to get her own way.

'He's coming,' Rebecca whispered, and Simon echoed from the wheelbarrow, 'Coming.'

'Get out of here,' a voice yelled in Afrikaans as a toothless old man appeared behind the window of the house they were watching. He banged on it loudly, his mouth opening and closing like a drowning fish. 'Get!' he yelled in threatening Afrikaans. 'Get off my land!' He waved violently through the suddenly opening window. 'Riaan! Willem!' he shouted to nobody.

'Ready?' Rebecca whispered with a quick glance at Thabo, knowing the old man's troops were on the way. Thabo held up one of a small pile of rocks stacked in the wheelbarrow at Simon's feet, assuring her he was ready as he waved it over his head.

'Mine.' Simon's chubby hands pushed at Thabo till he placed the rock in Simon's open palm and reached for another.

'Now,' Rebecca called. She'd spotted two young boys of her own age peering round the side of the house. 'Fire!' she yelled and Simon threw his rock.

'*Sidenge!!*' Thabo shouted in Xhosa as the rock dropped on his foot. 'Stupid!' he yelled at Simon again, dancing on one foot with the other held tightly in his hands.

'*Domkop, domkop.*' A singsong Afrikaans chant came from the side of the house and two dusty bodies curled backwards as they hurled rocks at the enemy behind the tree.

'Round the back,' Rebecca whispered. 'We'll attack from behind.' Thabo was about to follow her orders but he stopped.

'What are you waiting for?' Rebecca hurled a stone in the direction of the two young boys as they rummaged on the ground for more ammunition. 'Go on, Thabo.'

'No.' Thabo was fed up with Rebecca being in charge of manoeuvres. She'd grown in confidence over the years and thought she knew as much about fighting as he did. 'You go,' he ordered defiantly.

'Me?' Rebecca was amazed by Thabo's sudden mutiny and didn't notice Simon collect another rock from the bottom of the wheelbarrow. 'They're Afrikaans,' she whispered to Thabo, hoping that might spur him on, but then she stopped dead in her tracks. A rock, launched by Simon, had smashed through the window in front of the old man's face and a gaping hole of jagged glass stared back at them. Silence fell on both sides of the armed forces and they looked at each other in horror. The old man had vanished and the hole in the window, where his head had once been, gazed back at them blindly.

Thabo's eyes grew wide and he suddenly felt sick. In a flash he'd seen himself swinging from a gallows with a very old, very white and very dead man at his feet.

'*Oupa!*' The bare feet of the two dusty boys pounded the dry ground as they raced towards the house, raising a trail of tiny dustballs behind them.

Rebecca and Thabo stared at one another, her dark eyes searching his for the next move as Simon's tongue hung out of his mouth with guilt.

A wild banshee scream ripped through the air from behind and the children spun round in terror. The old man, a rifle waving in his hand as angry Afrikaans snapped through his platypus mouth, was running straight towards them.

'My father owns this land!' Rebecca yelled stupidly as she backed away, and Thabo grabbed the wheelbarrow handles. Whipping the barrow round sharply he turned to run and Simon spun inside it like a wobbly top.

'This way,' Rebecca urged as the angular figure with chomping gums steamed towards them like a runaway windmill. 'No – the other way,' she contradicted herself and Thabo spun back but then stopped dead. The two small boys had leapt out at them from either side, leaving them outmanoeuvred and out-flanked.

'*Kom hierso, roinek!*' The boys' singsong of victory challenged the 'rednecked' invader, Rebecca, to take them on.

'*Kom Engelse, kaffir!*' Clenched fists moved in erratic circles in front of their skinny chests as they turned their challenge to Thabo.

'Split!' Rebecca screamed, moving to the right as Thabo ducked to the left. 'Oh no.' The wheelbarrow toppled, tipping Simon in a helpless heap at the bare feet of their challengers. Swinging round in panic to face the onslaught of the old man coming up behind, Rebecca stopped in amazement. He was doubled up in a fit of coughing, struggling for breath in a clutching dustcloud.

'*Kyk daar!*' The young boys hooted with laughter, their attention fixed on Simon. He struggled on his back in the sand like an upturned tortoise while they danced around him.

'No, Thabo!' Rebecca shouted. Thabo's eyes were burning with rage and he lunged towards the enemy as their bodies twisted in hideous contortions, imitating Simon.

'You not do that.' Thabo stopped in front of them, speaking quietly though his entire body shook with rage.

'Don't, Thabo.' Rebecca ran to him quickly as the old man struggled for fresh breath to continue his attack.

'*Kom pikkenien!*' The younger boy beckoned Thabo forward with a jeer.

'*Mabhulu yiza!*' Thabo yelled for the Boer to come to him instead. 'Ayeee!' he screamed, pulling the boy towards him while raining hard blows on the top of his head.

'Leave him, Thabo,' Rebecca pleaded as the boy's eyes disappeared under his fast flattening scalp.

'*Oupa!*' The boy screamed to his suffocating grandfather for help.

'*Kom Oupa!*' The other boy ran towards the old man in retreat and Rebecca's right arm whipped out, landing a crack to his left eye.

'That wasn't the pikkanin, boer!' she yelled. 'That was me – the roinek!' Rebecca grabbed the wheelbarrow as Thabo picked up Simon. 'Run!' she screeched as Simon spat small pellets of sand from his mouth while Thabo pulled him up on to his back. Roaring with laughter Simon clung tightly round Thabo's neck and the three children raced homeward as threats of revenge chased their tails.

'You tell me now what Luke say in his letter,' Thabo insisted between gasping breaths as they ran towards the old Humber Super Snipe and safety.

'Where is he?' Rebecca was looking for Christian du Toit, son of the suffocating old man and father of the enemy. She was certain that this time their raid on his territory would rouse the gentle Afrikaner winemaker. 'Is he in the cellars?' Thabo nodded towards the door of the cellars which was slightly ajar. 'OK.' She moved away with him towards the old Humber Super Snipe.

'Luke's got a job.' At long last Rebecca answered the question Thabo had asked ever since she'd returned from school that day. 'That's all he said.' She climbed into the driving seat of the old car and Thabo heaved

Simon on to his lap as he got in beside her. 'Where do you want to go?' she asked.

'Cape Town,' Thabo said, and Simon leaned out of the window to wave from the stationary car. 'Luke tell you where he work? What about school? He pass Matric?'

'Where in Cape Town?' Rebecca turned the steering wheel, pushed down the indicator switch and Simon roared with laughter. A flickering yellow arrow had poked out of the car beside his head and he pointed at it in open-mouthed fascination.

'The bioscope.' Thabo grabbed Simon's arm as he tried to snap the yellow arrow off the car.

'You can't go to the cinema. You're black.' Rebecca swung the car wheel in the other direction as she stated no more than a fact. 'So where do you want to go?'

'I don't know.'

'Where can you go?'

'I don't know.'

'You must be allowed to go somewhere.'

'I don't want to go.' Thabo leant his head back against the car seat and stared at the dirty windscreen. 'What else Luke say?'

'I told you.'

'You not tell me.'

'OK.' Rebecca's breath escaped in resignation. 'Luke's got a job. He's working in the City Hall in Johannesburg, and he sent me this picture.' She pulled a narrow photograph out of her pocket and passed it to Thabo.

'Who's there?' Thabo asked as he peered curiously at the snapshot. It had been cut in half and Simon stared at it with him, cross-eyed. 'Where Luke's arm gone?' Thabo peered more closely at the photograph.

'Where?' Rebecca glanced at it. 'Oh,' she said casually, 'that was Naomi.'

Luke had told Rebecca in his letter that the girl in the picture with him was Althea, but she'd had two formidable bumps on her chest where Rebecca had none, so she'd cut her out.

'Luke coming to see us? He come Bonne Espérance like he say?' Thabo watched Rebecca carefully, waiting for her answer to the only question that mattered to him.

'Yup.'

'When?'

'I don't know.' Rebecca's mind was back on the two bumps on the girl's chest and she squinted down the front of her own dress. She hoped something had happened today. Something to explain the strange feelings that had begun a few weeks before.

'Luke.' Simon blew the name on a hollow whistle.

'He not coming,' Thabo said flatly as Rebecca's answer confirmed his worst fears. 'What you looking for?' He glanced at her curiously. Her chin was tucked into her neck as her eyes searched the flat front of her chest.

'I didn't say Luke wasn't coming.' Rebecca gave up her search and stared at the windscreen. It was covered in dust and she switched the windscreen wiper on, her eyes following the blade as it smudged squeaking halfmoons of red earth across the glass. 'He's not coming,' she confirmed at last.

Silence fell and Simon waited patiently for the yellow arrow to reappear.

'Why?' Thabo asked and Rebecca shrugged.

'I don't know.' Her face was filled with defeat but her eyes still denied her loss. Her mind had concentrated on the old key. She knew Luke had kept it as he'd promised.

A smile of achievement waited on the lips of Christian du Toit as he watched David Conrad sip white wine from a tasting glass.

'What do you think?' The winemaker spoke in gently accented English, his dark eyes sparkling with pride. An Afrikaner of Huguenot descent, Christian du Toit was the driving force behind David's efforts to restore the vineyard. Christian's family estate had been lost during the Depression of the 1930s and he'd adopted Bonne Espérance as his own two years earlier. David had never questioned the absence of a wife in the house over the hill and that had enabled Christian du Toit to keep his pride, as well as his father and sons.

'I'm not a good judge of wine, Christian.' David's eyes passed over the cellars before he glanced back at the young man beside him. 'That was why I hired you.'

The Afrikaner winemaker had been the answer David had needed if he was ever to rebuild the vineyard to its former glory. He knew nothing about viniculture himself and had used his mine annuity to improve Bonne Espérance only as the winemaker suggested. Under Christian's guiding hand, David had introduced cold fermentation and their white wines had exceeded even their own expectations. Bonne Espérance had slowly regained its name among the better Cape vineyards and both men had in some small way regained their pride.

'Have you ever thought of trading that in?' Christian du Toit glanced at the old Humber Super Snipe, pulling his cap down against the sudden sunlight, as the two men stepped out of the cellars. 'Looks as if they've been at my place again.' He smiled as the three children leapt out of the car, fleeing to the stables.

'What do they do there?' David asked casually, watching Rebecca's bare heels disappear through the stable door.

'What kids do.' Christian laughed. 'Old men do it too!'

'What's that?' They reached the car and David swung the door closed.

'Fight for territory, I think.' Christian glanced at him. 'My dad still swears he'll get the British back.' Christian shook his head with a smile. 'Even the postman has a hard time. It's the crown on his cap Pa doesn't like.'

'And the kids?' David kicked a small stone out of his path as he moved round to close the other car door. 'What do they fight about?'

'Ach! They just hurl insults at each other. They learn some pretty good ones at school, you know.' He glanced at David, amusement sparkling behind his eyes. 'But Willem and Riaan are scared to death of your Rebecca. Do you know that?'

'Riaan?' David chuckled. 'He must be twice her size.'

David knew Rebecca had grown like a wild rose as her roots dug deep into their new home, but still he thought of her as a lonely child on an ant hill and had never tried to cut her back, though Constance said he should.

'Seems like yesterday this old car was new.' David wiped dust from his hand, his mind moving back to 123 Z and the day the Humber had arrived from England. The smell of new leather and the gleam of the wooden facia were fresh in his memory and he wanted to climb back into that time.

'David, have you seen Rebecca?' Constance called. 'Miriam says she's outside somewhere. Have you seen her, darling?'

'No.' David winked at Christian as they moved on towards the house. Though both men had spotted Rebecca and Thabo, neither said a word.

'I bet he knows.' Rebecca's voice was almost hopeful as they stepped out of the stables, and the shadow of the opening doorway of the house swallowed her mother, her father and the winemaker. Christian du Toit had trampled among her thoughts, stirring deep-seated longings of which she had been unaware, till recently.

Rebecca's feelings both shamed and excited her. Though she'd loved Luke since the day he'd drawn her into his circle of friendship with Thabo, everything was different now. A curious need had driven her into a fantasy world and when she saw Christian du Toit, she saw Luke.

The accidental brush of the winemaker's hand would be Luke's, reaching deep to stroke the woman inside her and consuming her with pleasure that turned to instant regret. As Rebecca lay alone in her bed on still nights, imagination stretched Luke beside her, naked as she was. But it wasn't her angular girl's body that felt the touch of Luke's hand. He caressed the soft curves of a woman that wasn't yet her, and throbbing with the pulse of adult passion, Rebecca choked on the guilt of a child.

'Luke working now, so he never come back. I know that.' Thabo's mind clung only to what he had to do now as he too teetered on the threshold of the adult world.

'Luke will come back!' Rebecca's chin was high with determination, her eyes dark with longing. Now more than ever she had to believe that the power of the old key was as strong as the power that raged inside her.

'Luke,' Simon whistled, and dropping his weight between their hands, he laughed at the swirling dustcloud that clung to his dragging feet. 'Luke,' he whistled again with no idea who he was calling.

Miriam's expression of resigned acceptance did not alter as Thabo explained his plans to her later that night. She'd always known that her son would leave the farm and move into the world outside it one day. It was a world she'd never lived in, and it terrified her. But she'd buried her fears in Thabo's dreams and now she faced up to the inevitable.

'You will stay with my brother, Sibonda. He will help you get a pass.' Miriam tried not to heed the tension the word 'pass' brought to her heart. 'You will need a pass to be in Cape Town. The Government, they will give you one.' She explained: 'Sibonda, he will show you what to do.' Miriam unwrapped the turban on her head as she talked, pulling a tightly wrapped bundle of pound notes from inside it. 'There is three pounds.' She handed the tiny green roll to Thabo. 'I have saved it for this day and I ask that you spend it wisely, my son.' Moving closer to Thabo she pulled his head into her body, holding him tightly as her body rocked. 'You will respect your uncle as you have been taught to respect all your elders, my child. You will listen closely to his words, and you will not go against his wisdom.' Miriam passed on to her son the strong code of respect for elders that stood at the centre of her people's culture. She'd heard from her brother in Cape Town that the younger generation in the city had now lost that respect and she knew that without it there'd be nothing left.

'No matter what the others do, my son, you will always remember what I've taught you. And your grandmother! What Sibonda says, that you will do.' She held tight to the meaning of her brother's name. Sibonda – the one who looks after the family. 'The money you will put in these shoes.' Miriam moved to a small enamel cupboard beside the narrow bed that stood in the corner of the room. It had once been in the kitchen of the big house and she'd collected it from the rubbish tip when Estelle had thrown it out. Removing a package from inside it, she carefully unwrapped the newspapers to reveal a pair of shiny black shoes, shoes which she polished every month, wrapped in fresh newspaper and put away again to wait for the right time. 'They will fit you now.' She brushed a thin film of dust from the toes. 'You will need shoes in the town.' She passed them to Thabo.

'My father's!' Thabo stared at the shoes in wonder, pushing the newspaper to one side. Turning them upside down he examined the clean shining soles, attached in broad stitching to the uppers. The shoes were hardly worn and he lifted his bare foot against the sole of one. 'They fit,' he said as the shoe stretched on past his toes. 'My father's shoes fit.' Thabo smiled at his mother proudly. On every passing birthday he'd secretly tried on the shoes and at last they fitted; not his feet but his dreams.

'You are a grown man, my son,' Miriam said proudly.

'And I'll wear them to school.'

'School?' She looked at him, puzzled. 'You go to work.'

'When I finish working,' Thabo added quickly. He could see himself behind a wooden desk, exactly like the one Rebecca sat at in her school classroom. She'd told him that the top of the desk opened like a lid and an inkwell was sunk in one corner. He could see his father's shoes tucked neatly under just such a desk and his heart warmed in anticipation.

'When I have sent you enough money, then I will go to school.' He confirmed his ambition to his mother in proud Xhosa.

'Huh,' Miriam chuckled as she took the shoes back to give them a final polish. 'There will be no time for school.'

'I'll make time. I will go to school and learn.' Thabo's determination hadn't waned in ten long years. Since the day he'd watched Luke leave for his first day at school, Thabo had told himself that one day he'd go to school himself. He'd touched the stiff khaki of Luke's new trousers in wonder. He'd examined the brand new school bag with *Luke Marsden* embroidered on it and he'd smelt the newly sharpened pencil in Luke's pocket. The soft pink rubber on its end was a magic ball and it was then that Thabo had made his decision.

'The money you earn will go also to your grandmother in our village, Thabo. She is old and has worked long years for her children. Now she has many grandchildren to look after and it is you who must help.' Miriam told her son his responsibilities once again.

'Of course.' Thabo held tightly to the confidence the shoes had given him. 'I will look after them all *and* I will go to school.' As he flattened the old newspaper to put it away, fear snatched at his throat. He'd spotted a picture in the paper of a man called Dr Verwoerd and slowly he read the words underneath it, as Rebecca had taught him.

The words said that the Minister of Native Affairs was Doctor H. F. Verwoerd. It said he worked in the City Hall in Johannesburg and Thabo felt suddenly unbalanced. The City Hall in Johannesburg was where Rebecca had said Luke worked.

'You will take care, my son.' Miriam rubbed a rag at the heel of the right shoe. 'You will keep away from trouble.' She wasn't sure which trouble she meant. There were two kinds in the cities, and both could claim her son's life. The police and the black gangs who fought them were something she'd never had to face before. 'You will keep your mind on God, Thabo. It is God who will help you in times of trouble.'

'There won't be any trouble.' Thabo took the polished shoes back from her, smiling reassuringly. He was suddenly pleased that Luke wouldn't be coming back to Bonne Espérance after all. He flattened his mother's life savings of three pound notes under the sole of his right foot and pushed it into his father's shoe. Thabo was about to take his first steps into manhood and was glad he wouldn't see Luke till he'd achieved his dream.

As Rebecca ran her hand down his neck, Salu's warm brown eyes watched her. She'd listened to Thabo's plans and she'd admired his father's shoes as they shuffled forward loosely with each proud step, but Rebecca was terrified. She'd heard her parents talking in the night several times since they'd been at Bonne Espérance. They'd talked about the Afrikaner Government and the ever-increasing apartheid laws that bound the country tighter each day. Though Rebecca didn't understand all she'd heard, she knew those laws were aimed directly at Thabo.

'My father says the Government wants the black people to get out of Cape Town. He says they're going to knock their houses down and move them away. Maybe even your uncle's house will be knocked down so you couldn't stay there anyway. Don't go, Thabo!' Rebecca's words tumbled out in a mixture of fear and loss. He'd told her his plans and she wanted to change them. 'My father says the police lock black people in jail if they catch them. Sometimes they even kill them! Please don't go.' She clung to him, begging him not to leave her. 'Think about Simon.' She used the only weapon she could think of that might work. 'Simon would never understand why you left him and then he'd die.'

'I want to go to school, Rebecca.' Thabo's eyes melted as he looked into hers. He'd never realised she cared, and hoped she'd understand why he was leaving. 'You go to school. You learn things at school and if I not learn I stay stupid.' His eyes fixed on hers, driving his reasoning home. 'I must get education too. So I grow. Then I come back. I promise. I come back when I grow.'

'That's what Luke said.' Rebecca swung away and Thabo looked down. He didn't know how to explain that his dreams of school had a great deal to do with Luke. He'd woken Rebecca to tell her his plans in the hopes she'd be pleased, but she wasn't.

'When I wear my father's shoes I take his place with my life, Rebecca. My father not go to school, so I must go. I not want to die in a ditch because I too stupid to learn to climb out.'

'They hanged I Titus, Thabo.' Rebecca's eyes shone with tears as she snatched at the only means she knew to stop him leaving. 'I Titus didn't go to heaven on wings like you say. White people hanged him.' She tried to shake his determination. 'They hanged him just because he was black.'

'Yes,' Thabo said quietly and Rebecca stared.

'You know that?' she whispered and he nodded. 'Then why are you going?'

'Because I must be a man.'

'But they won't let you.' Rebecca's world was emptying around her again. Once again she could feel the wide silence of loneliness and she screamed into it.

'You're black, Thabo and blacks are "boys"! They don't grow into men!'

Rebecca stopped as she caught a flash of anger in Thabo's eyes but, wiping her tears with the back of her hand, she pressed on. 'It was here in the stables that Emily said goodbye to Jean Jacques, Thabo. Do you remember what I read to you?' Her eyes passed over the restless line of horses in the stable. 'Jean Jacques told Emily that he wanted to be a man too, like you. He joined the army to be a man, but they killed him. If Jean Jacques had stayed here, he wouldn't have died. Thabo? Don't you understand?'

As Thabo listened he realised that in all their time together Rebecca had never sensed his feelings of inadequacy. She'd never understood what his total dependence on her family had done to his soul. Rebecca had no idea that being a man didn't mean growing up. It meant removing his name from the long list of his ancestors. All those, like I Titus, who'd lived and died on Bonne Espérance without ever becoming more than a 'boy'.

'I Titus, he was hanged. Yes, you are right, Rebecca.' Thabo looked at her keenly. He knew he couldn't explain without unravelling a part of himself, but he went on. 'The story my people ... the story they tell about I Titus, they tell that story from shame, Rebecca.' Thabo lowered his head, searching for the English words he needed now. 'God took I Titus, they say. I Titus really an angel, my people say.' Slowly Thabo looked up and into Rebecca's eyes. 'It better to say that than the truth – that his life not his own to fight for.'

CHAPTER EIGHT

A high wire fence clung tight to bits of waste paper as it stretched a bizarre washing line round Langa township, just outside Cape Town. Rows of tumbledown houses leaned against one another in raggedy lines and the setting sun lit their rusty tin roofs in a hazy red glare. Sand streets, piled high with litter and crammed with people, wound their way lazily through the sprawling town and a marmalade dog, its skin glued to its bones, followed Thabo closely.

As Thabo had walked out through the gates of Bonne Espérance that morning, he'd felt two extra pound notes tucked between the sole of his foot and his father's right shoe.

'You'll do well, Thabo,' David had patted him warmly on the back, pressing two notes into his hand. 'And don't forget you can always come back here. We'll always find a job for you.'

'And if you need help ...' Constance had given him a small piece of paper with a number on it. 'Just telephone us. We'll look after you.'

'I be a man now, madam,' Thabo had told her proudly. 'I look after myself.'

But as he'd stood on the other side of the gates, looking back through the high white arch that framed the big house in the distance, Thabo had been aware that eyes peered at him from every angle and he'd no longer felt grown-up. The men in the vineyards had stopped their work and watched him in silence. His mother had stood alone at the kitchen door and Rebecca had gazed at him from the distance of her bedroom window.

But it had been Simon's eyes that had driven deep into his soul. Thabo had known that one day the small mongol boy would realise that he had never walked back up the long driveway to Bonne Espérance and for the rest of his life Simon would wonder why he'd left him.

'You looking for someone?' A man's voice called to Thabo and he moved towards him now, the dog a clinging shadow at his heels. 'Where do you come from, boy?' The African barber who'd called Thabo flashed a row of gleaming white teeth in welcome as he sat at the open door of a small tin house. In a crooked window beside him was a picture of Tony Curtis. With his hair plastered in Brylcreem, the film star's face hung lopsided as the picture swung by just one glued corner.

'You new in Langa?' the barber asked, as his razor-sharp blade peeled another strip of tight black curls off the scalp of the man in front of him.

'I'm looking for my Uncle Sibonda,' Thabo smiled nervously, his eyes fixed on the broad strip of shiny black scalp the blade left behind it.

'Sibonda. Ah!' The warm tone of the barber's voice rose in admiration of Thabo's mother's brother and the blade ploughed on through his client's hair. 'You want a *cheesekop* too?' He nodded at the fast balding head in front of him with a wide grin. 'Nice and cool!'

'No.' Thabo's scalp tingled with the thought. 'Do you know where my uncle lives?'

'I'll take you.' A youth with a cracked leather jacket over his shoulders was quite suddenly beside Thabo. His eyes passed over Thabo's clothes, settling on his father's black shoes. 'You a stranger? You new in Langa?'

The dog growled into Thabo's heel as the young man touched his shirt-sleeve. Miriam had pressed the shirt carefully the night before Thabo had left and it was still stiff with starch. Even the collar had been turned, the worn material of the secondhand shirt concealed by his mother's care.

'It's all right. I know the way.' Thabo had spotted the slim bulge of a knife in the youth's trouser leg and his toes curled protectively round the pound notes in his shoe as he turned to go. 'Thank you.' His mother's warnings of *amahodi* still rang in his ears as he walked quickly away from the township gangster.

'That's the wrong way.' The leather jacket shrugged higher on the youth's shoulders. 'And don't forget your dog.' With a last growl, the dog's scrubbing-brush tail gave Thabo a wave of success as the youth disappeared among the shacks.

'*Foetsek!*' Thabo was suddenly angry with the emaciated animal which had claimed him the moment he'd reached the outskirts of Langa. 'Go away!' The dog's back legs crumpled and it sat in a shivering framework of bones that weren't going anywhere.

'You've got to kick him,' a woman's voice called cheerily from behind, and Thabo spun round. A plump woman, lighter-skinned than himself, smiled and winked broadly. Her hair was bound on top of her head in tiny rollers and she wore a tight red dress. 'You want a beer, handsome? Jabulani?' The group of men in the doorway of the shebeen behind her watched the young stranger silently over the frothing tops of tin cans.

'I don't drink beer.' Thabo turned to move away but stopped quickly, catching the dog in a bony question mark at his feet. The leather-jacketed youth was waiting a little way up the sand street. A cigarette hung from his lips, his eyes were screwed tight against the smoke that wound its way into them, and he whistled quietly to himself.

'Are you lost, child?' A white-haired man had stepped in front of Thabo and the young woman slipped away with a shrug. 'You are looking for someone?' The old man's smile reached for his ears and a slim black finger stroked the grey curls on his chin.

'I'm looking for my uncle.' Thabo noticed the youth had vanished too and he looked round curiously. 'His name is Sibonda.' He spun round at a sudden roar of laughter from the men who drank outside the shebeen. Their eyes were lit with secret amusement and Thabo felt suddenly very stupid.

'Your uncle?' The old man's eyes sparkled with humour. 'Has anybody round here seen Sibonda?' He turned in a small circle towards the men and they doubled over in mirth once again, yellow rivers of beer tumbling down the sides of their tin cans before the sand sucked it under their feet.

'Sibonda?' Thabo stared at the old man in amazement. 'You are Sibonda?' His eyes danced quick sweeps over the old man's face as he tried to place his mother's older brother.

'And you are Thabo?' Sibonda's warm voice curled round the stem of a pipe he pushed into his mouth, and his hands lifted high in pleasure. 'Welcome, my child.' He wrapped his arms round his nephew, turning him in the direction of his home as the dog kept two paces behind.

'First you will go to the Administration Office here in Langa and they will give you a form. Then you will fill in that form and take it to Native Affairs in Observatory, Cape Town. There they will take your photograph.'

'Photograph?' Thabo's eyes were alight as his uncle spelt out the way to achieve a pass. 'A photograph of me?' He dipped a hard ball of mealie pap in the gravy bowl at his feet and pushed it into his mouth. Maria, Sibonda's middle-aged daughter, watched silently as the yellow pap squeezed between Thabo's lips before pushing gravy from the corners of his mouth. She sat quite still on the bed in the corner of the room, with Sibonda beside her.

'And then I will get my pass?' Thabo's tongue ran over his lips to wipe his gravy moustache and he smiled. His spirits had lifted with the township jazz that pushed its way through the rusty metal windows of Sibonda's home and his feet moved to the rhythm of the new life that had opened up before him.

'Then you will take the photograph back to the Administration Office.' Sibonda tapped his empty pipe on his knee and looked at Thabo keenly. 'Until you have your pass you will sleep in the bushes. Up there!' He pointed through the back wall of the house and his eyes sparkled with humour. 'The police they are not stupid. They raid when we sleep.' He chuckled into his beard.

Maria nodded at a yellow and red striped blanket rolled up on the bed beside her. She said nothing, but Thabo knew she was telling him the blanket was for his use in the bush. His mother had told him her brother's house had blankets. They were a sign of welcome. A sign they were not too poor to receive visitors.

'For how long?' Thabo pushed the last hard ball of mealie pap round the insides of the gravy bowl before pushing it into his mouth. 'Will it be a week to get my pass?' The mealie-pap ball rolled round each word before it left his mouth.

'A week?' Sibonda's laughter shook the patchwork tin roof over their heads. 'To get a pass takes many months, boy. Sometimes years and sometimes never.' His laugh turned to coughing and Maria thumped him hard on the back. 'A *dompass* is gold here in Cape Town,' he spluttered, waving his hand at his daughter to stop her hitting him.

'I'll get mine quicker than that.' Thabo's confidence had risen as his dreams took shape in Sibonda's reality. 'And then I'll go to school.'

'School?' Sibonda gasped breathlessly as Maria's hand hovered over his back. 'Your mother has money enough that you go to school?' His voice crept out on the gritty edge of the cough he held back in fear of his daughter's walloping hand.

'When I have earned the money. When I have sent money home to my mother and grandmother, then I will go to school.' Thabo announced his intentions with a proud smile, wiping his mouth with his hand.

'Ah!' Sibonda pushed himself off the low bed, moving away from his daughter in case he coughed again. 'Shoo!' He waved at the bag of bones with a marmalade coat that lay in the open doorway, but the dog didn't move. 'Your mother, she has given you money? You will need money for a pass.' He sank into the sagging armchair beside the open door and the sack bottom pressed down on the concrete floor. 'You sure that dog's not dead?' he asked.

'I have money.' Thabo's foot secretly pressed down on the pound notes in his shoe and he glanced at Maria. She'd never stopped watching him since he'd arrived and he wasn't sure he trusted her.

'And you? How old now?' Sibonda sucked on his pipe, holding a shaky match over the bowl he'd half-filled with tobacco.

'Seventeen,' Thabo said and Sibonda's slow whistle of admiration pushed a dreamy spiral of smoke towards the roof. Picking up the empty plate in front of Thabo without a word, Maria took it away to wash.

'Then you will return to our village?' Sibonda's eyes questioned Thabo through somersaulting smoke rings. 'You will go to Herschell and see the elders?'

'Yes.' Thabo knew his uncle referred to *ukwaluka* – the initiation ceremony for young Xhosa men, to be taken when he was eighteen. 'But first I must get my pass.' He spotted the marmalade dog creeping silent and arch-backed after Maria and the empty bowl. '*Foetsek!*' The dog stopped with Thabo's voice and one crooked back leg scratched its left ear, assuring him that an itch was the only reason it had moved.

'Sssss!' Maria tossed a bone at the dog. Picked clean and boiled to a gleaming white, the bone disappeared as the dog's long snout snatched it. Its body curled back the way it had come and its crooked legs carried it on tiptoe past Sibonda.

'It is your dog?' Sibonda gazed at the animal as it lay down across the doorway like a bumpy mat; the bone was held tight between its front paws and it licked it tenderly.

'Yes.' Thabo had no idea why the dog had chosen him and he'd been unable to lose it. But perhaps it was good, he decided, remembering the gangster who'd followed him all the way to Sibonda's house.

Stepping out of the brick-built Administration Office the next day, Thabo saw the familiar figure of the youth in a leather jacket. He was leaning against a wall in the deep shadows of afternoon and, as he saw Thabo, his foot pushed against the crumbling bricks as he moved after him.

'There's something you want?' Thabo stopped and turned to him. Holding a clean white form in his hand, his fingers clutched it tightly. He'd queued in the crowded Administration Office all day to get the form and was glad to be free of the pressing bodies that had surrounded him. All he wanted now was to go back to Sibonda's house to fill it in.

'I can get you a pass.' The young man rubbed his fingers together with a keen smile and Thabo's toes curled under the edges of the pound notes. 'It's easy if you've got money.' A low growl came from the shadows to the side of the road and the marmalade dog peeled itself off a sheet of black shade. Moving carefully to Thabo's feet, it pinned its eyes on the youth and growled again. 'OK – you don't want a pass.' The young man raised his hands innocently and the jacket slipped off his shoulders. 'Sleep in the bushes for the rest of your life.' With a low sweep of his arm he lifted the jacket, dropping it on to his shoulders as he departed.

With the dog's teddy-bear nose stuck to his heels, Thabo walked on towards Sibonda's home once again. But he was uneasy. The youth in the leather jacket had pushed his mind back to the night before. Back among the long dry grass of Zone Eight, where he'd slept.

'Keep your head down.' Thabo's heart beat a little faster with the memory. 'Down,' a man beside him had hissed as he'd pushed Thabo deeper into the grass till it had rustled over his head in a wicker canopy. Wrapped in the yellow and red striped blanket Maria had given him, Thabo had slept in the bushes that night, as he had every night since his arrival. But on that night the black stillness around him had exploded with the roar of police cars and trucks. Headlights had driven bright steel rods into the sleeping town and ripped the houses wide. Children's screams had burst through doorways and searchlights had danced like giant fireflies among the shapes of scattering people.

'Where's your pass?' a policeman's voice had growled in Afrikaans as he'd grabbed a fleeing man by his hair. 'You bloody kaffirs think you can live where you want!' He'd kicked the man in the back and sent him reeling towards a police van, Alsatian dogs snatching at his heels.

That night Thabo had felt the slow pulse of hatred quicken in Langa township and the look in the eyes of the white police had terrified him. They were looking for people who had no *dompass*, as his uncle called the piece of paper that still eluded Thabo.

Scooping white froth from the surface of soapy water in which Miriam laundered clothes outside the kitchen door, Rebecca asked again about Thabo. Since he'd gone to Cape Town she hadn't been able to picture him and many times she'd decided he might as well have been dead.

'But what's Thabo waiting for now?' Rebecca wiped the soft soap bubbles on to the brown of her arm, watching them burst in the bright sunlight. 'Hasn't he got his pass yet?'

'He still try.' Miriam's soft shoulders lifted before another thundering thud of wet clothes on the side of the iron washtub. 'You heard from Luke?' Miriam knew it wasn't just her son the young girl missed. Though teetering on the verge of womanhood, Rebecca was still a barefoot child. But like a mother, Miriam had sensed their shared moments would soon come to an end as Rebecca spurned childhood affections. 'You got another letter from him?'

'Yes.' Rebecca had kept Luke's last letter under her pillow with all the others, every word safely stored in the private, secret places of memory. 'If Thabo can't get a pass why doesn't he come back here?' She changed the subject and though Miriam wanted her son safely under her wing once again, she shook her head.

'He make his own life now. Like Luke.' Catching the fleeting expression of sadness that crossed Rebecca's eyes, Miriam went on quickly, 'He must get a pass.' Her face spread in a sudden smile and she glanced at Rebecca. 'You want I tell you what we black women do in the old days? When the white police they come to the door for our pass?'

'OK.' Rebecca shrugged. She wasn't really interested but needed to break free of endless days that ran into one another without change. Though schoolwork had become more demanding in the year before Matric and afternoons were spent teaching Simon to ride, any unoccupied moment filled quickly with thoughts of Luke. 'What did you do?' Rebecca daubed soapy bubbles on to her chin and a frothy beard dripped into the sand at her feet.

'The police they come to our place always in the night. They smart! Catch us with no pass when we sleep. So,' Miriam paused, catching her breath between the pounding of clothes, 'I tell my child, Thabo, he must whistle when he see them.' Miriam burst into gales of laughter as she dropped a knot of wet clothes into the tub, glancing at Rebecca. 'When those white police come banging on my door you know what I do?'

'What?' Rebecca dipped her big toe into the tub of soapy water.

'I take off all my clothes and I open the door! "Yes?" I say.' Miriam collapsed into rolls of howling laughter, unable to speak as Rebecca twisted a shirt-sleeve round her foot. '"You want something?" I say.' Wiping tears from her eyes with the back of her hand Miriam giggled and a smile threatened the corners of Rebecca's mouth.

'You opened the door with nothing on?'

'Nix!'

'What did they do?' Untangling her foot from the sleeve, Rebecca's laughter joined Miriam's.

'They run.' Miriam's eyes lit with delight. 'Backwards they run and I stand like this.' With legs spread and one arm leaning against an imaginary doorframe she relived her moment of naked triumph and Rebecca roared. She could see the look of horror on the white policemen's face as they were confronted by yards of bare black skin, threatening to envelop them. But quickly Rebecca's laughter died. As a child Thabo had watched the degrading spectacle of his mother's efforts to survive the pass laws and he still lived in that world. Luke lived in a world far away and Rebecca sensed she belonged to neither.

In his letters Luke said little about the Transvaal, reaching instead for Bonne Espérance. Through Rebecca he was trying to hold on to a past that had evaporated with time, as if knowing it held the person he once was. All reference to Bonne Espérance was a form of goodbye and nowhere could Rebecca find mention of his new life. He didn't talk about his father's departure with Elize. He didn't mention the work he did for the

Department of Native Affairs, as if by ignoring it he could invalidate its claim on his spirit. It was as if Luke had died somewhere en route to the Transvaal, and Rebecca was his only link with life.

'Wipe that smile!' The flip English of the black man who hid behind a camera fought its way through the dark cloth over his head and Thabo's lips closed over his teeth. 'What's that?' The bored face of the African behind the camera ducked out from the small black tent as he looked round the lens at Thabo. 'Take it off!' Thabo's hand reached reluctantly for the warm woollen hat on his head and he whipped it away, tucking it neatly between his knees.

'Why can't I smile?' he asked and the man's mumbled answer was swallowed by the camera. 'Hey!' Thabo ducked as a light exploded and the man looked up, the black cover drooping over his eyes.

'You want a pass?' The man's voice was slow and deliberate.

'That thing.' Thabo pointed at the camera still threatening him with one blind eye that shot fire. 'Poof!' He imitated the sound of the flash. 'It catch fire!' He joined the man in English and moved cautiously back to his seat, wiping it quickly with his woolly hat before he sat on it.

'OK.' Before Thabo could duck a second time, the camera flashed and the man moved away to the door of the cubicle. 'Come back at five o'clock.' He threw the words at Thabo and was gone.

Thabo sat quite still in the empty cubicle, staring at the silent black box on a stand in front of him. He wondered if there was a picture of himself inside it and moved to it cautiously, his body turning sideways and his woolly hat ready to swipe, if need be.

'I said five o'clock.' The man stepped back into the cubicle followed by another. 'Hat off,' he ordered and the new subject obediently pulled a woolly hat off his head.

'Don't forget to duck,' Thabo grinned, and darted outside.

With the experience of being photographed tucked neatly under his belt, he strode down Main Road in the Cape Town suburb of Observatory and, like a newly crowned king, he surveyed his domain.

The street was lined with shops and their windows bulged with an array of shining goods. He stopped beside a large sheet of glass and his nose pressed against it in amazement as music blared from the other side. Tables and chairs were spread out on a highly polished wood floor inside and white youngsters chatted as they drank enormous pink and lemon drinks through straws. Slowly Thabo's feet began to move instinctively to the rhythm of Elvis Presley's voice and gradually his entire body came to life. He'd never heard anything like it before. As Presley sang about his blue suede shoes, Thabo gazed down at his own black ones. Four pounds and one ten shilling note were still tucked safely inside them and life was good. He peered towards a large juke box in the shop as lights flashed and the music came to an abrupt end. A young white boy pushed a coin into a silver slit at the side of the machine and Thabo stared as a grabbing metal arm snatched a small black disc away before replacing it with another. He didn't breathe in the silence that followed, jumping back as a voice blared out.

'*One o'clock, two o'clock, three o'clock rock!*'

'What do you want, boy?' A white man was in the doorway beside him, watching blankly as Thabo danced on the pavement.

'The music,' Thabo grinned. 'It's good,' he shouted over Bill Hayley's voice, his body pulsating with the rock and roll rhythm and his smart black shoes grinding the pavement.

'You like it?' the man asked without reaction to the joy in Thabo's eyes as his look passed over him suspiciously.

'It's good.' Thabo twisted and turned in the doorway, his entire being caught up in the thundering beat that came from inside.

'Get your black backside out of here!' the man bellowed in his face, and Thabo pulled back startled. 'You cheeky munts are all the same.' The white man turned away without noticing the small piece of Thabo's pride at his feet and he trod on it. '*Voetsek!*'

The last remnants of Thabo's person vanished as the door swung closed in his face. *Whites Only* was printed across it in bold lettering.

Though every street Thabo walked for the rest of the day was lined with bright shop windows, he didn't look at them again. All he could see were signs – on doorways, on benches, and at bus stops. Everywhere Thabo looked: *Net Blankes, Whites Only,* spelt out his inferiority. In two languages he was told he had no place and he wondered how he'd never seen them before.

'You don't like the picture?' Thabo asked as he sat in front of his uncle later that night.

'It's good,' Sibonda said uncertainly, staring at a photograph that showed nothing but the whites of Thabo's eyes. 'You take it tomorrow with your form and then you get your pass, maybe.'

'Maybe?' Thabo glanced at the dog at his feet and it gazed silently back from eyes that seemed to understand. 'Not maybe.' Thabo's voice was firm. 'I *will* get my pass – tomorrow. Then I will get work and then I will go to school.' He clung tightly to the only thing that lifted his spirits above signs that declared him unfit to sit on a bench.

'Eat.' Maria pushed a bowl of mealie pap and gravy in front of Thabo and the dog's nose twitched. Its head was balanced on two front paws and its eyes were innocently closed.

'You must forget about school, Thabo.' Sibonda leaned back in his chair, watching the slow stream of pipe smoke that passed in front of his eyes. 'School won't get you money and you need money. There's work in the factories. Not all the work in Cape Town is reserved for coloureds, and you don't need school for that work.' Thabo slipped a small ball of mealie pap to the dog and it disappeared into its mouth.

'You think I want to work in a factory all my life?' Thabo jumped back as Maria snatched the bowl from his hands and the dog's flat tongue wiped its chops clean.

'You so smart, you earn money to feed that dog!' she shouted, stomping off with angry mutterings as the dog hid its face between its paws.

'Give it back to him,' Sibonda said quietly, his authority filling the room in an instant. His daughter looked straight at him, arms akimbo and the bowl of mealie pap balanced on her hip. 'Give the boy his food,' he ordered again.

'To feed the dog?' Maria challenged her father's authority and Sibonda wondered how she'd grown as stupid as she was fat.

'I'm not hungry,' he said as Maria passed the bowl back to him. Sibonda winked at the dog and with its marmalade coat standing on end in shivering surprise, it licked the bowl clean as Thabo lowered it to him.

'When's he going to pay for his food?' Maria grumbled from the corner and Sibonda smiled.

'The dog?' he asked with another wink and she whipped round as it crept away guiltily towards the doorway. With a giveaway lump halfway down the dog's rope neck and its tail clinging between its back legs, she chased it with a broom.

'You'll get used to it, Thabo,' Sibonda laughed, pushing himself deeper into the old armchair as he turned his mind back to the real problem. He knew well why his nephew hadn't been hungry after his first day in the streets of Cape Town. 'Soon you won't even see those signs.'

The man behind the counter of the Administration Office in Langa pointed a thick white finger at a question printed in Afrikaans. 'You see that?' His finger pushed the form across the wood surface, stopping it in front of Thabo with a quick jab. 'It says you must submit your birth certificate.' The man's Afrikaans was matter-of-fact and Thabo tried to keep calm. It was three months since he'd first taken the photograph and completed form back to the same office. Every night of the three months he'd slept in the bushes and every day he'd returned to collect his pass.

'I don't have a birth certificate.' Thabo pronounced the Afrikaans words carefully, as carefully as he guarded the rage that swelled inside him. 'I was born on a farm near Stellenbosch.' His mother had told him he'd been born at Bonne Espérance, but Thabo knew there was no paper to prove it.

'Get the certificate.' The man pushed the form away, looking past Thabo at the man behind. 'Next.'

'I don't have a birth certificate.' Thabo forced his body back in front of the waiting man.

'Your family come from the Transkei, yes?' The white man stayed patient as he looked at Thabo. 'Go to the Transkei. I can't do any more till you have your birth certificate.'

'But I told you I haven't got one.' In desperation, Thabo reverted to Xhosa. 'You can see I'm born. You see me?' He pulled at his clothes angrily. 'You need a paper to say I'm here? Are you blind?'

'I can do nothing for you without the certificate,' the white man replied in perfect Xhosa and Thabo stared. He was unsure what surprised him most – that the Afrikaner bureaucrat spoke Xhosa, or that he insisted Thabo find a certificate which didn't exist to prove he did. 'Next.' The man reverted to Afrikaans and Thabo was shoved from behind as another pushed into his place.

With his mind ajumble, Thabo stepped out of the low brick building into the late afternoon sunlight outside. The laws seemed designed to prevent him from achieving his dreams and he no longer knew what to do. Without a pass he couldn't work. He was illegal in the country of his birth and would be forced to carry on sleeping in the bush rather than risk jail. The excitement which had sprung in Thabo's step as he'd walked into the Administration Office on the first day had gone. His eyes were dull as they searched among the afternoon's long shadows with one last hope. The youth with a leather jacket.

'You said you could get me a pass.' Thabo's Xhosa was quiet as he moved into an alley between a row of tin houses. He could smell the black shoe polish on the cracked leather jacket and tensed as a voice came back at him from among the shadows.

'How much money have you got?'

'Four pounds and ten shillings.' Thabo looked straight into the eyes that had fixed on him and the young man laughed. 'What's wrong?' The youth turned away, his shoulders rising under his jacket in a shrug of dismissal. 'I said, what's wrong?' Thabo grabbed the jacket but pulled back quickly. The youth's dark eyes narrowed on to his and something pushed against his ribs. It was the long silver blade of a knife.

'Give it to me.' The young man's voice was deep with tension and the knife dug a little deeper into Thabo.

'No.' As he pushed forward to get away, a sharp pain drove into Thabo's stomach and he heard the dog growl. *'Sik 'em!'* Thabo shouted, but only a terrified squeal came from the dog as the man's foot caught it in the throat. 'Thief!' Thabo screamed, his arms reaching out from the pain that pulled him back into darkness, his hand grabbing at the black jacket in front of him. But his head jerked back as a knee came up under his jaw and the long line of shanty houses spun in a chaotic dance around him.

'Foetsek!' A voice called through the swirling darkness that pulled Thabo to its centre and somewhere he still heard the sound of the dog. It was still trying to defend him, but its growls of warning had become cries of pain. A pile of stinking rubbish tipped over him as his body was pushed back behind overflowing dustbins and the rancid smell of bad food choked him. Clutching his stomach, Thabo tried to pull himself free of the loud buzzing in his head and a warm wet goo pushed between his fingers. Everything had been wiped out by a narrow blade and all he could hear was the pathetic sound of a dog's cries. Forcing himself to stay conscious, his hands groped desperately over the edge of stones to find his legs.

'My shoes!' His cry raced among the shanty houses, unheard by anyone except the dog.

'Thabo. *Thabo.*' The name bounced over the soft green of the vineyards. Thabo's mother was calling him to eat and he felt warm and safe. 'It's good for you, Thabo.' But it wasn't his mother's voice, it was Sibonda's voice and quite suddenly Thabo realised he was not in Bonne Espérance.

His eyes flew open and the four walls of Sibonda's house tightened around him as he felt the hard bed beneath him. Maria was holding his head and his uncle held a spoonful of soup to his mouth.

'I will go for work. I don't need a pass.' Thabo's voice was weak but he stared into his uncle's face determinedly. 'It'll be all right, I swear it.'

'On what do you swear that, Thabo? Your life?' Sibonda could still see the bleeding and beaten body of his young nephew as he'd found him the night before. 'And what will I tell your mother?'

The marmalade dog had appeared in Sibonda's doorway only barely alive, its throat slit by a knife. It had cried till Sibonda had followed it and, creeping low to the ground through dirty streets, it had led him back to Thabo.

Sibonda could still feel the chill of shock as he'd found his nephew and realised he couldn't take him to the hospital. Thabo didn't have a pass. So Sibonda had carried him back to the house but the dog had not followed. It had crawled away deep into the bushes and hadn't been seen since.

'You must go home, child. Cape Town is not for you.'

'No.' Thabo pushed himself up, holding tightly to his dreams. A clicking crochet hook moved backwards and forwards as Maria's fingers looped through white yarn and she watched them both without expression. 'I can't go back,' Thabo cried. 'I can work without a pass. I can go on sleeping in the bush.' He challenged the truth of Rebecca's last words as they danced among signs on benches and doors.

'Black people don't grow into men!'

'I *will* go to school.' Thabo's eyes moved quite suddenly to the doorway as he realised something was missing. 'The dog?' he whispered.

'The dog is dead.' Sibonda sat down in the old armchair and Thabo stared at him. 'Next time it will be you. You will go back to your mother.'

'I will never get a pass, Uncle. There is no birth certificate.' Bonne Espérance stood like a monument to failure and Thabo pulled away from it. 'I will not go back!'

'My child.' Sibonda's eyes turned on to him calmly. His voice was quiet as he slipped back into a long-distant past. 'I will give you money to go to the Transkei and they will give you a birth certificate. Then,' he took a long and deep breath, as if he knew his words were meaningless, 'then we will go again to the Administration Office to get your pass.'

'There is no paper that says I was born, Uncle,' Thabo repeated, holding his stomach as it screamed with pain. 'Please,' he begged, but Sibonda wasn't listening. He was watching a fly as it settled on his hand, scraping its back legs together nervously. 'I can work without a pass. I will get money to pay for what I eat.' Thabo glanced at Maria but she too had looked away. 'They won't catch me, Uncle,' he cried.

'Nceba said that.' As the name of Sibonda's son sprang from a gentle click of his tongue, Sibonda looked directly at Thabo. His eyes were dull and his voice quiet. 'Then they knew my son had been born. When he was dead, they knew.' A vague smile touched Sibonda's lips. 'You will go back to your mother.'

'Yes, Uncle.' Though his words were obedient, his mind was already made up. The failure Sibonda's demands brought with them was something Thabo refused to accept.

Luke had found Rebecca's letter on the front doormat before he'd left for work that morning but he hadn't read it. Though her letters always brought him a strange comfort, they also disturbed him. He liked the words she wrote and the love she wrote them with, but he'd refused to admit that fact even to himself. Instead, he'd stuffed her letter in the back pocket of his trousers and it had remained unopened all morning, until he sat alone on the park bench in central Johannesburg which he used every lunch-time.

Thabo has been gone for ages and I still miss him. So does Simon. Like I miss you, Luke. Have you seen the film East of Eden? *I've got a picture of James Dean on my wall.*

Luke's mind cast around in his memory to find Thabo; the black friend who lived somewhere in a past that was far removed from the world Luke occupied now. But childhood had gone and Luke couldn't picture Thabo as a grown man. So he thought instead of Simon. His young brother would be almost seven years old now and he wondered what he was like. Rebecca had told him in her letters that Simon walked, that he even talked but often simply echoed what he heard.

You know something? Rebecca's letter went on. *I think James Dean looks like you. He's so gorgeous! I cried all through the film.*

Luke hadn't seen *East of Eden* but he'd heard of James Dean. Everybody of his own age in Johannesburg was talking about James Dean and his photograph was everywhere. But there was no money for extravagances like the cinema, Luke's mother had told him, so he'd forgotten about it. Taking another mouthful of the fishpaste sandwich Estelle wrapped in greaseproof paper for him each morning, he looked back at Rebecca's letter.

Sometimes I get very frightened when I think of Thabo in Cape Town she went on. *His mother says he's OK – that he's staying with his uncle in Langa and that all he wants is to go to school. But Miriam says he hasn't got a pass yet. What's a pass, anyway?*

Luke's mind had unexpectedly latched on to a long-ago image of Thabo. He was in Luke's room in Bonne Espérance and he was looking at one of his schoolbooks. Thabo was trying to read it and Luke was teaching him. Though Thabo had no colour in memory, Luke knew everything was different now. Crunching the greaseproof paper into a hard ball, he tossed it at the small bin beside the bench, as his own life had been tossed aside by his mother. It had become a series of days that ran into weeks, becoming months without change; and it was a life in which Thabo could no longer play a part.

Mapped out by his mother since his father had gone to England, Luke's time was devoted to Estelle's needs. His dreams of university had vanished with his responsibility for the family and his life was a routine of translation work. Though Thabo often interrupted his thoughts as he translated the spider's web of apartheid laws that ruled the country, Luke had quickly learned to push him away. But as he translated Dr H. F. Verwoerd's Afrikaans words on black education, Luke had wondered again about Thabo.

Native education must be controlled to enable it to follow the direction of the state. Race relations cannot be improved as long as the wrong education is given to the natives, turning them into frustrated people who expect from life what South Africa cannot provide.

The Government declared that it was false expectation that had led Thabo to Cape Town in search of an impossible dream and, pushing guilt back quickly, Luke got up from the bench. Only then did he notice the sign he'd translated so many times: '*Whites Only, Net Blankes*'. Only then did he wonder how those words might translate in Thabo's heart.

'Do you think you could handle it, Luke?' Althea's father asked across the immaculate white tablecloth that spread between them. Jan Strydom's heavy face was deeply tanned and though he wore a suit and tie, he might have just walked in from a field of mealies. His Afrikaans was guttural, unlike the softly spoken Cape Afrikaans Luke preferred, but he'd got used to it. 'Of course you will.' Jan Strydom answered his own question, as he always did, and Luke felt Althea's eyes on him as she sat erect in the chair beside him.

'Yes, sir.' They'd just returned from the morning service at the Dutch Reformed church and Althea still wore the high-necked white blouse that was reserved for Sundays. 'Thank you,' Luke smiled, aware that the future his mother demanded of him in the Civil Service depended on Althea's father.

'Good.' Jan Strydom's broad hand pushed into his hair as he lowered his head and the family of seven children followed his lead. Placed round the table in order of their ages, each child bowed in imitation of their father.

'Good Lord,' he began and Luke's eyes passed quickly over the neatly combed heads that never dared question Jan Strydom's authority. 'Bless this the food of Your children and the hands that prepared it.' He commanded God to bless the hands of his wife, Adriana and his words were followed by a chorused 'Amen'. 'I'll speak to Hendrik in the morning,' Althea's father continued as if he hadn't interrupted himself and turned to Luke. 'You would get a rise in salary too. You want the job?'

'Yes,' Luke smiled.

'You've got to help our country, Luke. These people overseas don't even know what apartheid means. You've got to make them understand it's for the natives' own good. Their welfare is ours to ensure and apartheid will do it. It's demanded of us by God.'

'Yes.' Luke agreed with Althea's father again, as he always did. To question the rights or wrongs of apartheid threatened the job his mother demanded he do and Luke had given up his fight.

'It's good, Adriana.' Jan Strydom pushed another forkful of lamb into his mouth and glanced at his wife. 'From Boetie Van Heerden?'

'Yes.' Adriana glared at the small boy beside her and he immediately closed his mouth as he chewed. Her eyes passed on to her husband. His hand was held out and without a word she passed a small salt pot to her youngest son. Silently it was handed down the table to Jan at the head and he took it without thanks.

'We're going to the dam this afternoon,' Althea announced suddenly and her father nodded, pouring a blanket of salt over his food.

'You'll take the *bakkie*?' he asked.

'Yes,' Luke answered him quickly. 'If you're not using it and don't mind.' He was nervous, certain Althea's father had sensed why they were going to the dam.

'Fine.'

Jan Strydom had never refused Luke the use of a vehicle if it meant he was with his daughter. He had four daughters and each would need a husband in time. For that reason he'd helped Luke get ahead. 'It's those students at "Wits" that are half the problem.' His mind returned quickly to the only problem that concerned him. 'They've got nothing better to do than cause trouble. Make them some *padkos*, Ma,' he ordered out of the blue, and Adriana nodded quickly. Glancing at the slivers of meat left on the roast joint in the centre of the table, she decided a few tomatoes would stretch it far enough for sandwiches.

'Did you know those young Communists in Cape Town want blacks in their university?' Jan's voice rose to a high note of amazement. 'How's your mother?' he added unexpectedly. His mind had leapt to the woman who'd married an Englishman and got no less than she deserved in return. Jan had gathered Estelle would be a financial burden on Luke and he often enquired about her health. 'Those damn Communists are behind everything. It's a total onslaught and the sooner we lock them up or throw them out the better.' He jumped back to the real problem.

'We'll have to go.' Luke glanced at his watch, turning to Althea. 'I have to be home before six.'

The rough drive to the dam took at least an hour and he knew he'd need time to pull himself together before he got home. 'Ma likes me to go to church with her at night.' He smiled through the guilt that already clung to him. 'Althea and I walk round the dam.' He assured Jan Strydom that his vehicle was used for nothing but driving.

'I'm ready.' Althea put her knife and fork neatly together as she glanced at her father. 'May I go?' With an abrupt nod from Jan Strydom she dashed out of the room and Luke knew she would change out of her Sunday clothes. She'd put on a loose dress with little underneath it and

Luke's hand felt in his trouser pocket for the small packet he'd brought with him.

'You don't have to use that today.' Althea's eyes smouldered, her lips bone dry as she watched Luke open the packet. 'Please don't.' She held his hand to stop him. 'Maybe it's better without it.' A girl in school had told Althea that boys preferred not to use protection when they had sex and she snatched the packet. Tossing it over the side of the van, she smiled mischievously. 'Let's try!'

As Luke's body moved over hers his eyes peered among the dry bushes to the side of the van. She'd discarded what he used not only as protection from unwanted babies, but his own searing guilt.

'Are you sure?' Luke pushed his thoughts back as desire rushed through his body. Althea's eyes were closed and her lips parted in a small smile. He could feel her body give under his own and moved his face closer to hers, but suddenly he pulled back.

Rebecca's face had flashed in front of him. The small girl, Rebecca, was watching him, as she did each time he was alone with Althea. But now Rebecca was no longer a small girl. Her dark eyes stared as they had the last time he'd seen her and her last words rolled in his head.

This key will keep us together on Bonne Espérance.

Luke pushed Rebecca's image out of his mind and his attention refocused on Althea. Every second Sunday found them in the van in the same area of bush near the dam and on each occasion he wondered why he was there. Luke hated the highveld of the Transvaal. The dry scrubland and arid *koppies* held none of the magic of the Cape. Though his body screamed for Althea, he knew it wasn't her he wanted. He wanted freedom. Release from the constant urge that screamed in his groin, holding within it all the frustrations of his limited life.

'Luke.' Althea pulled his body towards hers, clinging tightly to his back as she wriggled out of her dress. Luke represented the only escape from her father's domination. She was suffocating in a life dictated by the Afrikaner vision of themselves as a chosen people. Drowning in the laws of God, rewritten by the Dutch Reformed Church as they dragged them from the pages of the Bible to suit their own ends. Blind Calvinism had become lids on Althea's mind and blinkers on her eyes. 'Luke?' Her voice was suddenly soft as he dropped the full weight of his body on to hers. Though she'd felt nothing but a little discomfort, at least she knew he'd been satisfied. Her mother had explained that once. In mumbled words of embarrassment Adriana had said that sex was no more than a woman's duty. It was just a small inconvenience that was soon over and, like everything else, it was a sacrifice a good Afrikaner wife made for her man.

171

'One day we won't have to do it in the van,' Althea smiled, breathing gently into Luke's ear as he lay heavily on top of her. 'I'll look after you. Anything you want, I'll do it.' Her eyes shone, knowing that was what Luke wanted too and wondering why her body still throbbed though Luke's didn't.

'Are you sure it's all right?' Luke lifted himself gently off her. He'd caught Althea's meaning and he'd heard wedding bells chime in her heart. 'You want a swim?' he asked. He'd also heard that water was an answer to the problem Althea had caused when she'd thrown the small packet away.

As Althea dived naked into the dark still waters of the dam her skin gleamed, skimming just under the surface. She was beautiful and her body still pleased Luke, but all he felt now was fear. His eyes looked out across the expanse of still waters and his mind leapt back to Bonne Espérance. To the clear bubbling water of the river he'd swum in as a child. To the silver falls that tumbled in shimmering streams down Table Mountain, reaching for wide expanses of white beaches and turquoise sea.

'You want to do it again? In the water?' Althea swum to him, throwing her arms round his neck and longing for him to do to her what other girls talked of. 'Hold me!' With her legs wrapped round the small of his back she hung on, her naked body pressed close to his and her pelvis pushing against him.

'No. We must go.' Though desire had surged through his body again, Luke pushed her away. 'I'll race you!' He swam back towards the muddy grey edge of the dam, pulling her out of the water behind him. All he could see was a small baby with a wedding ring clutched in its hand as Jan Strydom smiled benignly.

'Get dressed,' he shouted as their bodies dried in an instant under the hot afternoon sun. 'I'll have to drive fast.' He tried to explain his hurry as the longing pulse of Althea's body slowed with disappointment. 'Your dad might need the van.' But Luke had decided that driving back fast on a bumpy road might be a more effective answer to his problem than water.

A pair of white underpants were held between Estelle's fingers and her face was blank as a wad of paper tissue dangled helplessly, stuck to the crutch.

'And don't tell me you blew your nose on it.' Estelle's voice was ice-cold as she looked from the tissue to Luke. 'Well?' Luke's mind raced through possible explanations for the evidence of sin his underpants waved from across the room.

'Sies tog!' Naomi's voice called through the open bedroom door as she swanked past, her tiny breasts pushed forward proudly.

'I don't know.' Luke shrugged. 'What do you think it is?' He looked into his mother's eyes and immediately regretted his insolence. She was white with rage.

'Don't you know what that girl's after, Luke? She's like every other young woman in this town. They're trying to get themselves a husband.' Estelle moved a little closer and the hard wad of tissue dropped to the floor as she tossed the pants to one side. The dog, sitting quietly at Luke's feet, tilted his head to one side, about to collect it but Luke kicked him swiftly. 'You can't afford to marry anyone. You have a mother and a sister to support. Unless, of course, you choose to forget that like your father did. Do you want to be just like him? Is that what you want from life – failure, disgrace? Like your father?'

There was little point in arguing. Though Luke knew Paul sent Estelle money from England monthly, it was more than his life was worth to challenge her.

'I'm getting promotion. Mr Strydom says he'll get me into the Broederbond one day too.' Luke knew how much his mother longed for a place in Afrikaans society and he smiled. 'And I'm not marrying anyone.'

Estelle relaxed with her son's words and Luke wondered why he always gave in. He was afraid of his mother, but that wasn't reason enough to allow her to dictate his life. He was almost eighteen years old. Why didn't he walk out of the job that had drained his life away and rubbed out his deepest beliefs? He could leave Althea without a second thought and easily forget the momentary pleasure her body gave him. He could confront Estelle with the lies that tied him to her side as her demands on him grew with every day.

'I won't ever let you down, Ma.' Luke's words sounded like those of a stranger and quite suddenly he realised that they were. The young boy who had grown up on a wine farm and shared dreams with a black friend was dead. He'd died without a whimper many long years before.

Very carefully a middle-aged black man searched through the contents of the dustbin outside an undertaker's red-brick office. It had been on a wet Monday evening two years earlier that Fezile had found a pair of men's wire spectacles among the trash and they'd changed his life. He'd spent every Monday since sifting through the dustbins and he pushed the gold frame of the glasses back on to the bridge of his nose, peering into the bin carefully. His toothless gums chomped together and he wiped his hands to clean them between each article he examined.

'Hey!'

Fezile looked round sharply. The voice had stepped out from behind a brick wall with its owner, Thabo. His eyes large and angry, he held his head erect in challenge and stared at the squat bespectacled man in front of him. 'That's mine.' He nodded to the dustbin and Fezile watched him carefully. Though dressed in rags, barefoot and with dust running up the sides of his legs, he could see a young man's pride fighting for a place among the refuse of Thabo's life.

'This is your dustbin?' Fezile's face could have been carved from ebony as his look settled on Thabo. High cheekbones dipped suddenly into hollow cheeks and his eyes were deepset under an angular brow. 'You own this dustbin?' he asked with a smile.

'Everything here.' Thabo's arms swept a wide circle that encompassed every street in the small Cape Town suburb of Mowbray. It was his territory. For eighteen months he'd slept in its doorways, eating from the bins that lined the sidewalks. Thabo had learned life's lessons in the school of want and anyone who invaded his space was challenged. At nineteen he had total authority over the gang of children with whom he shared the streets and together they stole a living, scuttling in and out of white neighbourhood avenues to outwit the police. Thabo used his newly gained power well and he wasn't prepared to lose it to Fezile or anyone else.

'That dustbin is mine,' he informed the old man one more time. He knew, as Fezile did, that the undertakers' bin often contained good things, only discarded because they couldn't be taken along.

'Where you from, boy? You Sotho?' Fezile had picked up a familiar lilt in Thabo's Xhosa.

'You going to talk all day?' Thabo was impatient with the man who dared to question him and his hand gripped the knife in his pocket. Life was cheap on the streets of Cape Town. Thabo's hunger was kept at bay smoking *dagga* in dark alleys and though Fezile was black, Thabo saw him only as one who threatened the living for which he fought. The *baaskap*.

'Where do you come from? I asked you a question, boy.' Fezile had seen the knife but remained calm in the face of Thabo's obvious resentment.

'Here – I live here. Now you tell me what you want.' In a flash the knife was at Fezile's throat.

'You not going to tell me where you come from?' Fezile talked as if there was no knife threatening him. 'Are you afraid?'

'Of you?' The knife teased the skin in Fezile's neck.

'You're village, boy. Where is your village?'

'You're crazy, old man.' Thabo shook his head and laughed. He didn't want to be dragged back to his beginnings and turned away with a shrug. The streets of Cape Town had no place for the luxuries of a past and he had no time to waste.

'Herschel – that's it, your grandmother's village in the Transkei. Sophie Mayekiso – she is your grandmother? That right, boy?' Thabo swung back, staring in surprise. 'I know your family.' Fezile grinned. He remembered well the small village he'd grown up in himself many years before. 'Your Uncle Sibonda he lives in Langa and ...' As Thabo turned to go he grabbed him by the torn backside of his pants. Holding him back, Fezile's forearm locked under his chin and he took the knife. 'I know he is a difficult man, but perhaps Sibonda is right.' Thabo tried to pull himself free but Fezile held him tight.

'Goodbye.' Quite suddenly the older man let Thabo go, tossing the knife at his feet. 'What I am looking for is not in the refuse today,' he said quietly, knowing Thabo's eyes and attention were still on him as he walked off. 'Nothing round here but trash.'

'Hey, what do you want?' Thabo was beside Fezile in an instant, walking in time with his steps as he pushed the knife back into his pants. He'd spotted a quality rarely found on the streets and Fezile's dignity had drawn him like a magnet.

'What are *you* looking for, son? You tell me.' Fezile turned to him, his eyes searching Thabo's for an answer. 'Dustbins are for rubbish. You are looking for rubbish? You belong with the dustbins now? Not in your village, with your people? Nah, I don't believe it.'

'You use these dustbins too.'

'Yes.' Fezile smiled, poking a finger in the glass lens of his right eye. 'For this, but not for food. I work for food, and I need no knife to get it.'

'And you have a pass? Like a good Bantu you have a pass, yes?' Thabo's voice teased as he danced around Fezile, but still he didn't move away. Still his hand didn't touch the knife again.

Fezile's eyes shone. 'I know how to get work "like a good Bantu"!' Thabo laughed loudly and made to go, but Fezile followed quickly. 'Or does the Bantu I'm talking to like to be trash?'

Thabo stopped and he stood totally still. Since he'd run away from Sibonda rather than face his own failure, nobody had dared criticise him. His authority in the streets had held him aloof and he'd learned long since to outwit people far smarter than Fezile. He'd hold his hand out with a smile, collecting money as insurance that he wouldn't scratch the car of a white driver. Quickly he'd learned that nobody expected any more from him and Thabo had buried his dreams as he'd buried the marmalade dog.

'What do you want, Bantu?' Fezile's eyes gleamed, his mouth pushing forward as toothless jaws collapsed in a pancake sandwich. 'To be stupid like the white men say? Or to be smart?' Fezile turned and walked away. He'd dropped his challenge and could only hope that Thabo would follow and pick it up.

*

The train-ride back to Langa was hot and the carriage reserved for non-whites was crowded to bursting. Pressed between Fezile and a young black woman who kept her nose continually turned away, Thabo wondered why he was there at all – why he'd gone with the arrogant stranger who'd wandered into his life and rekindled a flame he thought had died. He knew the gang of street children he lived with in a hole in the wall of the Liesbeek canal would miss him, but only for a moment. Before night had fallen they would consign him to a mental grave and elect the next eldest boy their leader.

'Where are we going?' Thabo called to Fezile over the rattling thunder of the train. 'Hey, old man! Where we going?' The woman between them turned her head away with irritation as his words echoed round her head.

'Single men's hostel,' Fezile shouted back. 'Zone Eighteen, Langa.' He smiled at the smart young woman who'd turned to glare at him. 'You have my address now, girlie.' He ground his hips with mischievous glee and Thabo was still laughing as Fezile pushed him through the train doors into a tide of disembarking bodies.

'And there is where you will sleep.' Fezile pointed his rough black finger under a concrete table in the centre of a square room. 'The dining room,' he said proudly. 'Where we eat,' He explained its function and led Thabo deeper into the low red-brick building of the single men's hostel in Langa, Zone Eighteen. 'And there is where I cook.' He pointed at one of several primus stoves that stood on another concrete table in a small kitchen. 'And here,' Fezile led Thabo into a small room at the end of a long passage, 'is the bedroom.' A chicken sat on top of an old cupboard. Another balanced precariously on the iron railing at the foot of one of three narrow beds and a third clucked a gentle welcome. 'Here is where I sleep.' A large cockerel, its feathers frayed and sparse, crowed with delight as Fezile spotted him and from its position on an old pillow, it stretched its balding wings in acknowledgement.

'Come.' Fezile clapped his hands and the raggedy bird's spindly legs walked it across the bed towards him.

'Hey,' Thabo shouted as another chicken landed on his head like a feathery helicopter. 'Get off.' He tried to push it away, but it dug its long claws into the mat of his hair. 'Do something!' Thabo glanced at Fezile helplessly as the chicken stretched its long neck down in front of him, clucking an upside-down apology into his face.

'Shoo.' Fezile clapped his hands and the chicken took off in a whirr of dusty feathers, a chunk of Thabo's hair held in its beak. 'With these I make business.' He watched the chicken crash-land on the floor. 'Fresh chickens are good business in Langa.' He snatched the chicken as it strutted past him, wringing its neck casually as he talked. 'This one is for the fat woman down the street.' He nodded his explanation to Thabo as the chicken's head dropped over his hand on an elastic neck. One eye stared at Thabo accusingly and the small black tuft of hair dropped out of its beak. 'Come.' Fezile turned back to the door and the old cockerel went along behind like a dog on a string lead. 'This way.' Thabo watched in astonishment before following the old man back down the long passage to the kitchen.

'You want a job?' Fezile asked as he plucked the chicken's feathers over an ancient sink, peering at Thabo through his wire-rimmed spectacles. 'What kind of job can you do?'

'I don't want a job.' Thabo watched a delicate white feather cling to Fezile's nose, waving its surrender on his breath.

'You been to school? What standard? Standard eight? You seventeen, eighteen? You in standard eight?'

'School's rubbish!' Thabo's jaw clenched and Fezile's eyes narrowed behind the round wire frames of his glasses.

'There's a clever Bantu speaking. You learn what they want you to learn.' He blew the feather away from his nose and it landed on his top lip. 'Come.' He shook the goose-bumped body of the pink chicken before tucking it under his arm and walked out of the kitchen, Thabo and the old cockerel following close behind.

'You talk rubbish, old man, you know that?' Stepping back inside Fezile's bedroom, Thabo checked round it quickly, looking for something worth stealing before he left. Small faded photographs of black women and children were pinned to the grubby walls above the two beds on the opposite side of the room and a calendar declared proudly that it was still 1957. 'You're as out of date as that old calendar.' Thabo pointed to it, hanging beside an old yellow raincoat.

'But the picture's nice.' Fezile peered at the illustration on the calendar and from one blinking eye the old cockerel peered with him. 'You see the mountains? They're beautiful, yes?' But Thabo had turned away. The picture he looked at could have been of Bonne Espérance.

'It's nineteen fifty-eight! And that's a wine farm in Stellenbosch. Haven't you ever seen a wine farm?' he asked arrogantly, angry that his emotions had been roused by memory.

'You can read?' Fezile laughed at Thabo in feigned amazement. 'Not the stupid Bantu you look, huh? You worked on a wine farm? That's good.' He slapped Thabo across the face with the plucked chicken and pushed it into the brown warmth of an old paper bag. Sitting down on the bed, he tugged at the gumboots on his feet. 'The PSG, that's where I work. Peninsular Security Guards. I can get you work there too, but it's hard work.' Fezile winced as he pulled his boot off and a large black toe peeped at him through an ancient Fair Isle sock. The old cockerel's rubber red headdress wobbled from side to side as he examined the sock with Fezile. 'Only one leg this man had when he died.' Fezile pulled the other boot off and a faded blue sock hung loosely over his toes. 'This one too.' He glanced at Thabo's rag clothes and chuckled. 'You didn't get those in the undertaker's bin.'

'Can you get me work?' Thabo ignored Fezile's chat about the origin of his clothes, latching instead on to the old dream the calendar had resurrected.

'You said you had no pass.' Fezile casually twirled the brown paper bag till it wound tight at the top, the paper clinging to the pimpled plump skin of the body inside it. 'Do you want a pass?'

'I don't need a pass. No white cop will ever catch me.' Thabo's shoulders pulled back proudly and he stared down at Fezile.

'Huh!' Fezile chuckled. The old cockerel had jumped into his lap, scratching himself a place to sleep between his knees.

'You think I've lived on the streets without knowing how to dodge them?' Thabo demanded as his pride rose from a deep sleep. 'You think I want a pass to please the white trash? You think I need one!'

'No.' Fezile stroked the old bird quietly, smiling up at Thabo. 'But I think it's a stupid Bantu who says school is rubbish.'

Between the single men's hostel in Langa and the docks of Cape Town, Thabo and Fezile quickly forged a life together. On weekends Fezile killed and plucked chickens for Thabo to sell in the streets of Langa, and at four-thirty each weekday morning, they'd climb on to the train for Cape Town. There Thabo would fall sound asleep, his body held upright by the crowd as they sang Christian songs on the way to work.

'Don't you believe in God?' Fezile had asked him once.

'He doesn't believe in me,' Thabo had laughed. 'Or you.' He'd watched the squat middle-aged man out of the corner of his eye, and Fezile had laughed too.

'Don't you believe it.' He'd raised his voice louder in song with everyone else. 'Our God reigns,' he'd harmonised his praise with others as the packed train thundered towards Cape Town.

'God will look after you.' Thabo had felt the familiar nudge of his mother's last words.

Maybe God was looking after him, he thought many weeks later, as he handed his wages to Fezile. Fezile had organised it so that when Thabo had earned enough to send back to his mother, he would attend a night-school. It was run after hours by a white Christian couple, Fezile told him, and Thabo had wondered if perhaps he was an angel.

'Me – an angel?' Like a wrinkled glove puppet, Fezile's worn face creased with laughter and his pink gums shone, unashamed of their nakedness. 'My mother tell you that?' he chuckled again. '"Wishes come true", she call me.' He explained again the meaning of his name. 'I think God has good reason to take our parents before they see the name was wrong.' Fezile had banged his hand on his knee and laughed even louder, the old cockerel opening one eye to watch him carefully.

'Hey.' Running to the old yellow raincoat that hung on the wall beside the calendar, Fezile swept the ancient cockerel under his arm as he went. 'Look at this.' With its feet in the air the old bird clucked nervously, moving its legs in imaginary steps as it flew sideways under Fezile's arm. 'No, don't look,' Fezile shouted, as his hand dug into the raincoat pocket, pulling out a small newspaper package.

Life with Fezile had become a constant source of surprise for Thabo and he'd obeyed immediately. The last time Fezile had opened a package, it had contained a fountain pen.

'You can look now.' Fezile's voice sounded strange and when Thabo opened his eyes he knew why. Two rows of gleaming white teeth sparkled between the upward curl of Fezile's lips. 'Our dustbin,' he'd announced with a clatter of teeth. 'Nice?' The teeth had posed in front of his lips before he'd sucked them smartly into his mouth.

'There.' Now Fezile passed a post office savings book in front of Thabo's eyes. They sat together on the dockside, eating the lunch of bread and polony he prepared for them each day. 'Fifty pounds,' he whistled through his new false teeth and quickly pushed them back into his mouth as Thabo took the book, gazing at the figure in wonder. 'Now you will go to the night-school.' Fezile bit into a hard crust of bread, his teeth burying themselves in it. Without comment he removed the bread still gripped by the teeth and, pushing them into his pocket, took another bite. 'I'll keep them for Sundays.'

'And when I've been to school I will buy you your own teeth.' Thabo passed the post office book back to Fezile, riding high on the promised fulfilment of a lifelong dream.

'My own teeth?' Fezile grinned around the hunk of bread and polony in his mouth. 'Teeth that eat?' he spluttered in delight.

'Your very own,' Thabo laughed.

'School – that's all I want, that you go to school.' Fezile reaffirmed his belief that education was the answer to all his people's problems and he smiled widely. 'They are expecting you next week.'

*

As the horn sounded for the end of his day's work loading trucks in the dockyards, Thabo went quickly off to change. Fezile had pressed his trousers the night before under the mattress of his bed and they hung neatly down to his ankles. The brown shoes his friend had bought in the market matched them beautifully and odd socks added a little flair.

'Well?' Thabo waited for his friend's reaction as he stood erect.

'Aye yay!' Fezile's teeth clacked together in approval. 'And the silk tie.' He fiddled with the neat blue tie fastened tightly around Thabo's neck. 'He was an Englishman before he died,' he remarked as he caught sight of the label inside it. 'Look.' He held the label in front of Thabo's face so he could see it. 'Now. What you say?'

'Good evening, sir.' Thabo bowed his head along with the carefully pronounced English words.

'And what do you do?'

Thabo held his hand out to shake and Fezile beamed a proud smile back.

'You're a good-looking boy.' His eyes shone with the love that had grown between them. 'A clever Bantu.' Fezile held his emotions back and clipped Thabo round the head quickly. 'Go well,' he said, with more than a little wonder that the moment they'd worked for had at last arrived.

'Stay well.' Thabo's head bowed in respect for the man who had led him by the hand to the day he'd dreamed of all his life, and he turned towards the city of Cape Town.

Thabo rounded a corner of the high winding road that led behind Table Mountain and his eyes settled nervously on the rising white buildings of Rondebosch suburb below. He hadn't been back to the area since meeting Fezile and he jumped back as a car sped round the corner. It came from the direction of Cape Town University and a group of students waved enthusiastically.

'You want a lift?' they yelled as they ground to a halt ahead of him. Caught totally by surprise, Thabo glanced round quickly. He was looking for the white person they'd called but he was alone and his hands lifted in the air nervously as a blond-headed youth jumped out of the car.

'You want a lift? Come.'

Crammed between the young boy and a girl in the back of the car, Thabo felt very awkward. For the first time he'd noticed how black he was. The girl's arm had moved over his, as she leaned across to her friend and her skin shone white against his.

'Shall we take him with us?' she asked, as though Thabo wasn't there. 'Why don't we?'

'OK.' The youth beside Thabo looked at him with an open smile. 'You want to come with us? We're going to a party.'

'I go to school.' Thabo's English was suddenly fractured as everyone's eyes turned on him.

The driver glanced at him in the mirror, calling back in surprise, 'School? At this time of day?'

'I go to night-school.'

'For Matric?' The girl beside him tilted her head forward, peering up into his eyes. Hers were a clear blue and they glowed with curiosity. 'How old are you?'

Though Thabo sensed the students' questions were well-intentioned, he felt very stupid. 'I get out here.'

'What for? We'll take you wherever you're going. What's the name of the school?'

'No.' Thabo wanted nothing more than to get out of the car. He was drowning in the white youths' good intentions and he wanted to run before he cried.

'We're fighting to stop the Government barring you people from UCT. They're pigs, the lot of them!'

'Did you hear about that march we made on Parliament yesterday?'

'Norman Bromberger made a great speech, hey. Did you hear it?' Thabo's head rattled as they all tried to explain their liberalism at once.

'And how do you think apartheid is going so far, Dr Verwoerd?' The girl in the front seat leaned over with a giggle, pointing an imaginary microphone at the mouth of the boy beside Thabo. 'He's pretending to be Verwoerd,' she informed Thabo quickly.

'Very well. Agh man, yes. It's *lekker*!' The young man spoke in heavily bastardised English. 'Our black people love apartheid. Ask them! Let that Paton man write his books that nobody reads, hey. And that Communist Engelse priest, Huddleston. Like Mr Strydom said, "There is here and there a little whipping of the blacks, and that sort of thing, but you'll find that anywhere in the world, hey!?"'

Thabo's entire body was rigid with tension as roars of laughter engulfed him.

'And now you are to become our Prime Minister, Dr Verwoerd?' the girl asked, not noticing Thabo's reaction. 'What will you do?'

'Drive all the bloody kaffirs into the sea!' The young man collapsed with laughter and the car shook. Thabo tried to smile but his lips were glued to his teeth.

'Are you all right?' The laughter stopped and the young girl beside him touched Thabo's arm gently. 'I'm sorry.' She looked away, embarrassed by her own stupidity. 'We didn't mean to upset you. I'm sorry.'

Unable to handle the sudden waves of sympathy, and the guilt that carried them, Thabo reached for the car door.

'I get out now,' he said quietly. 'Thank you.' With his head bowed politely he smiled, climbing out of the car quickly.

Turning off the main road, Thabo made his way towards the night-school Fezile had organised and tried to reason with himself. The white students had meant well. They'd tried to make contact across the racial barriers erected by the Government and he knew why he'd been unable to respond. He himself had once told his grandmother that it wasn't white that made people smart, it was school. Hanging on to that truth tightly, Thabo's step quickened and he walked swiftly over the small bridge that crossed the Liesbeek canal and led to the promised land of education.

'Hey.' He glanced down as he spotted a group of street children arguing over a sixpence. 'Here!' He tossed them a penny and with squeals of delight they pounced on it. Lifting his new brown shoe, Thabo rubbed it down the back of his trousers and smiling at its shine he moved on with an extra bounce in his step.

'Pass.'

Thabo didn't hear the policeman's voice. He hadn't seen the police car that had pulled into the kerb ahead of him either.

'You.' He felt the sudden snatch of a hand on his arm and swung round in surprise. 'I said pass!' A white policeman held his hand out grimly, his pale eyes daring Thabo to argue. '*Dompass!*'

In an instant Thabo had leapt off the bridge into the canal below as his instinct for survival surfaced.

The street children yelled as he pushed through their pile of small change, the sixpence rolling away with a penny as coins scattered under his feet. A police whistle had blown like a hunter's horn and the children, like Thabo, knew that every cop in the area would be after him.

'Catch,' a child yelled in Xhosa. A knife somersaulted through the air towards Thabo and the small boy vanished in a hole in the canal wall.

'Hey you!' Thabo looked up as a policeman slid down the bank towards him. Behind him, Alsatian dogs strained at their leads, bared teeth glistening with saliva as they reached for him and Thabo's eyes moved to the knife in his hand.

'*You a stupid Bantu?*'

Fezile's face flashed in front of him and quickly Thabo tossed the knife to one side, ducking low as he tried to run. But a heavy black boot was there in front of him. His body flew forward, crashing into the dry hollow of the canal and the boot pressed down in the small of his back.

'Go for a bladdy knife, hey kaffir!' An Alsatian dog growled beside Thabo's face and he realised he was crying.

*

'I'll get it,' David called. The phone rang incessantly from inside the house and he ran the last few steps to the front door, wondering why Constance hadn't answered it. He snatched it up quickly, 'Yes?' David listened as he watched Constance through the slightly open door of the sitting room. She sat alone in there, peering intently into a photograph album. 'Who? Oh yes, Thabo. Yes, I do know him, why? No, he was here a few years ago, but we haven't seen him since. Yes.' David's attention was drawn away from his wife and back to the phone. 'I see. I'll be there as soon as I can.' He put the phone down and moved to the door of the sitting room. 'Why didn't you answer the phone, Constance?'

Constance looked blankly over her shoulder at her husband, the photograph album still open in her lap. 'Was that the telephone?' she asked in surprise.

'Didn't you hear it? You never answer the phone any more — why?'

'Who's this?' Constance pointed to a faded snapshot of Macaroni in the album that was spread on her lap. It was as if David hadn't said a word. 'That — who is it?'

'You know who that is.' David watched his wife carefully as recent fears knotted in his stomach.

'Who?' Constance was looking up at him with a wide smile that revealed she had no idea.

'It's Macaroni.'

'I know that's Macaroni.' She closed the album quickly. 'Who was on the phone?'

'The police. Thabo's been arrested for not having a pass and he gave them this number. He's in jail. I'll get Rebecca to come with me and we'll bring him back.' Busying himself with the matter in hand, David tried to ignore his wife's strange behaviour.

'Thabo?' Constance's face was puzzled.

'You know who Thabo is, don't you? You remember him, Constance?' David knelt down in front of her, his hands holding hers tightly as he reached deep into an abyss to find her. 'Thabo's Miriam's son. Remember?'

'You look so worried,' Constance laughed. 'Of course I know who Thabo is and you'd better go if the police have got him.' As David left calling for Rebecca, she wondered again who Thabo could be.

Stepping through the door that led from the police cells, Thabo's eyes dropped to the floor. He was dressed only in his underpants and a young white woman stood beside David Conrad. Her eyes were dark. Masses of black hair fell around her face and she was truly beautiful. Quite suddenly she smiled and as her wide mouth spread its joy to her eyes, Thabo recognised Rebecca.

'Hullo, Thabo,' she said, and quickly he looked round for a way out. He was more trapped than he'd been in the police cells five minutes before and he felt deeply ashamed.

'His things are in this bag.' The police sergeant pushed a brown paper bag towards David. Thabo's clothes were stuffed inside it, a shoe poking out as if trying to escape. 'Probably stolen. But no one would want them now he's had them.' The policeman let the brown bag go and, wiping his hand down his trouser leg, he removed the touch of a black man.

'Why did you take his clothes from him?' David asked calmly, aware of Thabo's near-nakedness beside him.

'If one of these blokes hanged themselves we'd get the blame.' The policeman nodded at the clothes. 'There's a tie in there.'

'Thank you.' David turned towards Thabo. 'Come on, Thabo. Let's go home.'

'Wait a minute, mister!' The policeman watched David's hand as it squeezed Thabo's shoulder. 'This boy belong to you, does he?'

'I'm taking him home,' David said simply, and Thabo kept his head lowered. He was aware that Rebecca's eyes still held him in the dark uneasy gaze he remembered so well and he felt totally naked. His bare toes curled on the marble floor and he wished he'd been allowed to dress. The failure of the years that had passed between them was laughing in his face.

'What do you mean, you're taking the boy home?' The policeman was watching David with the same look of distaste he'd reserved for Thabo. 'You got his pass, have you? Can I have it?' He held his hand out to the Englishman in front of him with a note of challenge.

'I've paid the fine and now I'll take him home. His mother's waiting for us.' David's voice was quiet but firm and he moved to go.

'Not without a pass you don't.' The policeman had switched to Afrikaans and his eyes narrowed as he watched the Englishman who'd dared question his authority over a black.

'I'm afraid I don't speak Afrikaans,' David said calmly.

'He wants to know about Thabo's pass,' Rebecca said quickly, her eyes flickering back to Thabo. Still he hadn't lifted his eyes to hers and a lump rose in her throat. 'I'll wait outside.' She ran through the doorway quickly.

The stone grey walls of the church that stood next to the police station reached up towards Table Mountain behind, but Rebecca didn't even see it. Her mind was fixed on Thabo, on his averted eyes and the shamed bow of his head. On black legs that stretched bare from worn underpants as he was forced to wait, naked and no more than a police exhibit. Quite suddenly Rebecca's tears ran freely down her cheeks and she gazed up at the mountain as a wave of despair covered her. The pain she'd felt inside Thabo screamed inside her, and through the brick wall that separated them, she could hear his silent cries. The hope she'd seen in his eyes on the morning he'd left Bonne Espérance had vanished. The bright-eyed friend who'd shared so much of her life had gone. Every right due to a human being had been stripped along with his clothes.

The green folds on the far side of Table Mountain deepened into dark and threatening crevices as the sun dipped behind it. The stretching branches of oaks pushed grabbing hands towards Rebecca and she shivered as Thabo stepped outside, handcuffed to a policeman.

'Where are you taking him?' she asked, following as they walked towards a police van. Thabo carried the brown paper package in one hand and still he was almost naked.

'They're sending him back to the Transkei.' David had been unable to secure Thabo's release and shame prevented him from looking at either his daughter or Thabo.

'He's going back to the Transkei where he belongs.' The policeman pulled the large van door open. 'They know they're not allowed to come here.'

'Can't you even let him get dressed?' Rebecca's indignation raced up the mountain, sweeping back down over the rooftops that nestled comfortably below. 'Let him go, you bastard! He's a person, not an animal.' She lunged towards the policeman, grabbing his arm. The man's eyes reflected his distaste as he shrugged her off dismissing her without another word.

'Thabo!' Rebecca reached instinctively towards him, but this time it was his look that stopped her. Thabo's eyes had lifted and in one brief moment they'd met hers. His face was filled with rejection and he held her firmly at bay.

CHAPTER NINE

The twenty-sixth of February, nineteen fifty-eight had been a turning point in Rebecca's life. Until that day, when she'd come face to face with the truth of Thabo's life, the remote beauty of Bonne Espérance had protected her from reality – the reality of racial laws scored across the face of the country daily as apartheid tightened its grip.

All non-Europeans had been wiped from the voters' roll. The Group Areas Act had forcibly removed thousands from their homes as areas were declared 'for whites only'. The Native Amendment Bill, introduced by the Minister of Native Affairs, Dr H. V. Verwoerd, had removed citizenship from all South African blacks and Grand Apartheid had become the Government's god. With strict separation of the races rigorously enforced, the greed and fear that had conceived apartheid strangled a nation.

But the laws hadn't come into being without dissent from many Europeans. Ten thousand ex-servicemen had marched by flaming torch-light to the Houses of Parliament. Pledging themselves to fight the disenfranchisement of coloured people, they'd accused the Government of being the same men who'd supported the Nazis in the last world war. The MP Helen Suzman fought a lonely battle inside Parliament while women like Mary Butcher, Margaret Ballinger, Helen Joseph and Sophie Williams stood alongside the black population in the streets. Father Trevor Huddleston and Alan Paton, leading opponents of the Nationalist Government, campaigned for international sporting boycotts to resist the reign of terror, and Albert Luthuli, leader of the African National Congress, called for mass defiance of the apartheid laws. Luthuli was immediately banned and confined to Natal. In reply, an up-and-coming ANC leader, Nelson Mandela, advocated that the movement go underground, while the ANC's Zulu leader, Mangosutu Buthelezi, fought from within the law to become a constant thorn in the Government's side.

War had been declared between black and white, but Rebecca had been touched only by the eyes of one man. Even as she climbed the steps that led to her Cousin Lydia's house in Cape Town later that day, Rebecca was still haunted by her last sight of Thabo. She felt alone in the land. Alone with millions of people whose dignity was stripped daily by laws that were written in her name.

'This is a surprise.' Lydia's bright smile greeted Rebecca as the door opened. Since the day they had met at Katinka's funeral, Lydia had encouraged Rebecca's friendship and it had blossomed over the years. 'I didn't expect you. Come in.' Rebecca felt the arms of Lydia's four-year-old son Joe wrap around her legs.

'Come, Becky.' The small boy's hand reached into hers but Rebecca pushed it away.

'I need to talk to you, Lydia.' Her voice bubbled on the rage of helplessness that swelled inside her and the small boy stepped back as if his fingers had been burned.

'Come on in.' Lydia turned into the house with her son clinging to her skirts. 'Excuse the mess.' Nodding at the spreading branches of bougainvillea that covered every inch of the room, she wondered why her young cousin was so upset. 'I was about to dry them,' she explained. 'It's so hot. Do you want a drink?'

'Thabo's gone.' Rebecca's voice was quiet and Lydia turned to her with a vague smile. Tears of frustration pushed at the calm exterior Rebecca presented, but she said no more.

'Who?' Lydia asked.

'Thabo's gone.' Rebecca repeated the words she'd said to Lydia four years earlier and her mind leapt backwards in time.

Then Rebecca had gone into the bedroom with Lydia while she fed her new baby boy. Joe had been born just two weeks earlier and Rebecca had been twelve and a half years old.

'Is Thabo a little friend of yours?' Lydia had always been wonderfully vague and Rebecca loved her. She smelt of lavender and rose petals. Dressed in loose flowing kaftans with her dark hair caught loosely on top of her head, Lydia was everything Rebecca wanted to be. She represented freedom to a young girl trapped in a pubescent body and Rebecca had grabbed at it.

'Tell me about him,' Lydia had said. 'Thabo – is that his name?'

'He's black.'

'That's nice.' Lydia had been lost in the magic of her new baby's face. 'Why don't you get the button box.' She'd changed the subject, quickly leading Rebecca into the wonderful world she kept in a small wooden box. Each pearl dress button, collar button and shoe-button told a tale. 'You see this?' Lydia had pulled out an exquisite mother-of-pearl buckle. 'Our great-great-great-grandmother was Danish but she married a Frenchman and she wore this on her belt for Queen Victoria's anniversary!'

'And this one was on Jean Jacques' army uniform. He was our great-great-grandfather.' Rebecca had singled out a round brass button and she'd held it up to Lydia with a flourish. It was the only button that interested her that day.

'Jean Jacques was in the Cape Coloured Mounted Rifles and this button was on his uniform.' Lydia had looked at Rebecca blankly, as though she hadn't spoken at all. 'And Granny Cat had a brother,' Rebecca added. 'A half-caste brother who didn't look white.' She watched Lydia carefully.

'Look at this.' Lydia had held out a small button-hook. 'They used this to do up their shoe-buttons in the old days.' Lydia had smiled absent-mindedly as she avoided what Rebecca had said and Rebecca had suddenly felt furious.

'You don't know about Jean Jacques because you don't want to. Because he wasn't white – and that's why you don't want to know about Johannes Villiers either!'

The silence that had followed Rebecca's well-aimed accusation had been long and Lydia had changed the baby's nappy without lifting an eyebrow. Rebecca had raised a subject which had never been discussed in Lydia's family. Her mother, Elizabeth, Katinka's second child, had never mentioned it at all, but Lydia had known the truth ever since her mother had died. It was locked in a small drawer in the sitting room now but she had no intention of admitting it. In Lydia's arms lay her newborn son, and his future could depend on her silence.

'You don't understand what I'm saying.' Rebecca's voice had been desperate. 'I'll never be able to marry Luke because I'm not white.' She'd blurted out her deepest fears and Lydia had kept her eyes averted. 'Can't you see? Granny Cat told me that Luke isn't Uncle Paul's son, that he's not really part of the Beauvilliers family. So he really is white!'

'Of course you're white, Rebecca. Don't be so silly.' Lydia had laughed to hide the discomfort of Rebecca's words.

'No, I'm not. And nor are you!'

Rebecca had buried herself deep in one corner of the room. The life she'd dreamed of with Luke on Bonne Espérance had been forbidden by law, and even the old key to the original Beauvilliers home in France could never turn the lock on that fact.

'Where do you get these stories from?' Lydia had put the baby down to sleep and moved to Rebecca with a chuckle of amusement, lending no truth to the words her young cousin had spoken. 'People like Estelle say these things just to upset you.'

'But it's true,' Rebecca had yelled, running to the front door. Pushing it open against the howling south-east wind, she'd stood at the top of the stone steps that led down from Lydia's house. It perched high above the city of Cape Town and through the wrought-iron curls of the gate, she'd peered into the streets below. They led in winding lines from the sea to the base of Table Mountain and she knew that Johannes Villiers had once lived somewhere amongst them. It was his dark reality that had threatened her.

'I hate you!' she'd screamed up at the towering flat-topped mountain that had so arrogantly taken the place of her ant hill. She'd longed for the wind to pick her up and blow her deeper into the heart of Africa. Back to 123 Z. Back to the time she'd been free of the sudden longings and unexplained despair that had gripped her body in puberty, while laws forbade her deepest desire.

'It was as if Thabo had died, Lydia.' Now Rebecca tried to explain what had happened. 'The police pushed him into a van that day. They took him to some place he's never been before and said that that was his home. He wasn't allowed in Cape Town, they said – just because he's black!' Rebecca's eyes were filled with Thabo's reflected pain as she gazed at her cousin across the room. 'He was waiting for us to do something, Lydia, but we couldn't. Thabo looked at me, begging for help, but I was scared.' Lydia watched as her beautiful sixteen-year-old cousin broke down in front of her. 'Don't you see? I've finished school and Thabo hasn't even begun. All he ever wanted was to go to school.'

Lydia knew well that the mysteries of the button box wouldn't begin to stop Rebecca's tears this time. She'd grown up and come face to face with the reality of their country and no words could explain away what had happened to Thabo. It was a reality Lydia herself had never dared examine too closely and even now she wanted to avoid it.

'Most of us have no idea what goes on out there.' She moved closer to Rebecca and Joe followed his mother cautiously, sensing the invisible tripwire of tension that stretched between his two favourite people.

'Isn't that because we don't want to know? Because we look white and have the privilege of being white?' Rebecca's eyes were filled with the knowledge of her own inadequacy. 'Is that our excuse for doing nothing? How can we stand by while humiliation is heaped on people just because they aren't like us?'

'We don't know the whole truth.' Lydia kept calm in the face of Rebecca's rising emotion. She didn't like being forced to look at things she'd avoided all her life, and dug her heels in hard. 'None of us knows the truth. Not even you.'

189

'Thabo does.' Rebecca's dark eyes centred on Lydia again. 'Why should he need a pass just to live where he was born? All he wanted was to go to school – like Joe.' Lydia touched her small son protectively, as if Rebecca's words held an axe over his head, and Joe looked from one woman to the other, his future trapped somewhere between them.

'It isn't as simple as all that.' Lydia pulled Joe closer.

'Then tell me.'

'It's not something I'd like to make a judgement on. You see, politics don't really interest me.' Lydia turned away.

'Does that mean you'll bury your head like an ostrich?' Rebecca's voice was filled with amazement. 'People are suffering out there, Lydia! They're being bulldozed out of the only homes they've known, pushed out of their country in the name of apartheid.'

'What can I do about it? It's the law,' Lydia shrugged, trying to keep calm.

'And that makes it right?'

'You're beginning to sound like one of those students at UCT! What do they call it – "Moscow-on-the-hill".' Lydia tried to collect her thoughts. She'd looked over the particular precipice Rebecca was aiming at once before and she'd seen the long drop. She could remember the cold chill that had run through her the day she'd married Stan. Lydia had knowingly broken the law. Her husband came from an upper-class Afrikaner family and as her pen had hovered over the marriage licence, Lydia's eyes had settled on the section that questioned her race. It was a question used to satisfy the law prohibiting mixed marriages and she'd signed herself *European*. Though nobody had ever mentioned the fact, and she herself had never even wondered about it before, her mother's death had revealed it wasn't true.

Among the papers she'd kept in a secret box all her life, Lydia had found something Elizabeth had never dared reveal when she was alive. It was clear-cut evidence of a person called Johannes Villiers; a descendant of Jacques Beauvilliers and the slave, Eva. Johannes Villiers was a non-European whose place on Lydia's family tree had been wiped by carefully nurtured forgetfulness.

Though her journalist husband, Stan, was a liberal and an educated Afrikaner, whose mind had never been censored by rising Nationalist ideologies, Lydia had kept her past hidden even from him. Fear of the law's obsession with race had closed off an entire area of herself, even to Stan, and the gap in their relationship had been filled by fantasy: a horror that she would one day lose her husband to the truth had driven a silent wedge of secrecy between them.

'You don't know what's right any more than I do, Rebecca.'

'I know what's wrong.' Rebecca tossed her head back arrogantly. 'It's their country and they're being locked out of it.'

'*Theirs?*' Joe's bottom lip trembled as his mother exploded. 'We took all this from them, did we?' Lydia whipped back the heavy lace curtain that covered the window, pointing down at the miles of buildings that spread low to the sea. 'That was all there, was it? The docks? The houses?' she demanded. 'They cleared the bush, built the city and we just waded in from the ships, plonked down our suitcases and took it? Is that what you're saying, Rebecca?'

'I'm saying we need each other. They needed the white man's knowledge and we needed their labour. We still need each other. Isn't that the point?'

'And you think they would accept that, the blacks?'

'You're beginning to sound like an Afrikaner.'

'Maybe because I'm married to one.' Lydia's voice was razor-sharp, riding high on the anger Rebecca had stirred inside her. 'My Afrikaner husband was out there carrying a torch alongside "Sailor Malan", being spat on by pigs. He demonstrated against apartheid while you played with your little white dolls, Rebecca.'

'I didn't mean Stan.' Rebecca quickly defended herself from Lydia's anger. She could still remember her thoughts of Stan being an enemy. 'It's people like Luke's mother I'm talking about. There are thousands like Estelle.'

'You mean Stan's not like an Afrikaner? "He's not bad for an Afrikaner"?' Lydia's voice was tight.

'Yes.'

'What the hell is an Afrikaner?' Lydia screamed.

'They're not all like Stan.'

'And blacks are not all like Thabo.' Lydia suddenly quietened and turned to her small son. 'Can we stop talking about it now?'

'Like you stopped me talking about Johannes Villiers before? Like you don't want to know about our great-great-grandfather being coloured because you've buried him along with everything else that threatens you?'

Joe looked through the sudden silence that followed Rebecca's words and his bottom lip trembled once again. He was engulfed in passions that divided people more effectively than apartheid itself and he didn't know the way out.

'You can hide from Johannes Villiers' dark skin, Lydia, but he won't go away. Johannes Villiers was born, he existed, and he'll never go away.'

In total silence Lydia moved to the bow-fronted chest that stood under the window and Joe pressed his tiny body back against the wall, watching wide-eyed as his mother took an envelope from the top left-hand drawer and handed it to Rebecca.

'What is it?'

Lydia's eyes passed over Rebecca's face without answering as she went to her son, took his hand and walked away.

The envelope bore an official stamp and Rebecca opened it carefully, pulling out the folded pages of the document inside. It was an official copy of the last will and testament of Sarah Westbury. She was Katinka's mother, Elizabeth's grandmother and Lydia's and Rebecca's great-grandmother. In it Sarah Westbury testified to the birth of a son, a dark-skinned boy who had been born secretly in the Wynberg home of Mr and Mrs James Robertson. It stated that the newborn baby had been placed in the care of a Catholic convent and Sarah Westbury had told her family she'd miscarried. The child's name had been Johannes Villiers.

'Why didn't you tell me about this before?' Rebecca's voice was hushed as she joined Lydia in the kitchen. Joe peered at her nervously over the top of the round pine table and turned to his mother quickly. 'Why did you hide it?' Lydia stirred a small pot of soup without answering. 'How long have you had it?' Rebecca's eyes searched Lydia's back. 'Why didn't you tell me, Lydia? Why have you avoided it for so long?'

'Records are easy enough to come by.' Lydia poured soup into a small bowl and she sat down beside her son at the table. 'The problem is, they don't record the pain that forced Sarah Westbury to give up her son. Isn't that the real truth of it?'

'What about his pain? Johannes Villiers was discarded, as if not being white is some kind of sin. Didn't that hurt him?' Rebecca was aware of the fear that now gripped them both. 'This document proves we're living a lie, Lydia. It proves that we're no more white than Johannes Villiers was. That's the fact, isn't it.'

'Maybe.' Lydia's eyes settled on the document that threatened her with the same laws Rebecca had challenged her to face. She held a spoonful of soup to Joe's mouth but, watching his mother carefully, he didn't take it.

'Drag Johannes Villiers from among the dead and hold him up to this family if you want to, Rebecca. Give truth to the words Estelle yelled at you. Go ahead and martyr yourself to apartheid but then tell me this: whose would be the lie?'

The two men who shared Fezile's room snored in the joy of sleep as he looked at the round face of the alarm clock on the table beside him. Picking it up he held it close to his nose, peering over his glasses as he read the time in the light of the candle that burned on an upturned fruit box. It was ten minutes to midnight and still Thabo had not come home.

'He didn't come here.' Sibonda's voice was firm as Fezile spoke to him earlier that night. 'My nephew is no longer my responsibility. Many years ago you took him, Fezile. Against my wishes you took him and he was in your care.'

Sibonda's eyes were dull as they followed the slow smoke rings that curled from his pipe. His mind had gone back to his son, Ceba. Back to the naked body he'd found lying on a slab in the morgue. *Bantu* was all it had said on the small label tied to his child's big toe and Sibonda had learned then what happened when a young man without a pass tried to earn a living in white cities. His son had been one of many who'd died over the years as they fled from the police in an effort to escape arrest. Some, like Ceba, had leapt off buildings and met their death impaled on iron railings.

'He will be in the mortuary, Fezile.' Sibonda had stated Thabo's whereabouts as a matter of fact, but Fezile hadn't gone to the mortuary then and now he stood at the door of the single men's hostel in Langa, his eyes moving slowly down the dark and deserted street. The old cockerel, held back on its string lead, clucked as its flat feet scratched in the litter surrounding the hostel door. Echoes of laughter punctuated the still night and a dog's howl swooped over the gently smoking tin rooftops that crowded around him. Although Fezile knew Sibonda had spoken from experience, still he refused to believe him. Picking up the old cockerel, he wound the string lead around his wrist and, tucking the balding bird under his arm, he turned back through the door.

'We sleep now.' He moved into the low brick building behind him. Fezile had decided to look for Thabo in the morning in the only way he knew how.

'What do you want?' The slim white man in police uniform spoke in Afrikaans without looking up from his newspaper. Fezile was standing erect at the battered counter of the police station and his shiny black shoes pinched a reminder that they were his Sunday best. He'd dressed in all his finery for this visit to the police station in the white suburb of Cape Town, and even his teeth shone as he smiled, politely lifting a brown homburg hat from his head.

'It is about my friend.' Fezile spoke to the policeman in careful Afrikaans. It had become the language of the oppressor and he used it only when necessary, but he used it well. 'My friend has not come home. He was in this area last night and he didn't come back.'

'Did he have a name tag on his collar?' The policeman laughed loudly at his own joke and Fezile joined him. Lifting his shoulders high his body shook, his mouth cracked wide with false laughter and his teeth threatened to drop out. Laughing at policemen's jokes was something Fezile had learned early in life and a smile stayed glued to his teeth as he sucked them tight to his gums. As if they too were aware of the importance of the occasion, they remained in place.

'I think maybe my friend . . .' Fezile hesitated, unsure how to explain that Thabo didn't have a pass. 'I think maybe my friend he get in trouble with the police last night.' He snapped his teeth together in a firm bite as they dropped free of his gums, adding quickly, 'Baas!'

'*Dompass!*' The policeman held out his hand and Fezile dug into his jacket pocket to find his pass. Pulling out a well-worn square of paper in a plastic cover he presented it proudly for inspection. It showed the all-important official stamp that permitted him to remain in Cape Town for twelve months, on condition he stayed in the employ of Peninsular Security Guards.

'I work for Peninsular Security Guards. Ten years I am there, baas.'

The policeman stared at him blankly. 'Where do you live?'

'Zone Eighteen, Langa. Single men's hostel. Nice.' Fezile smiled.

'You run a business? You got a licence?' The policeman was searching for some reason to challenge the black man who'd dared intrude on his time.

'No, baas.' Fezile's downcast eyes caught sight of a guilty chicken feather that had lodged in the turn-up of his trouser leg. 'I got no business.' He wondered how to remove the feather without giving himself away. 'No licence, no business,' he grinned, pushing the toe of his left shoe into the turn-up of his right trouser leg. 'I think maybe my friend he in jail.' The feather stuck to the toe of his left shoe. 'His name is Thabo Sogaka.' The policeman stared at him silently and Fezile smiled his appeal. 'You look see if my friend in jail?' The fine down of the feather waved its presence from the toe of his left shoe. 'You find my friend in jail please, baas.'

'Bladdy cheek!' The policeman's hand was suddenly on Fezile's arm. 'You think I've got time to waste on every layabout kaffir in town? You can look for yourself!' Fezile brushed the toe of his shoe against his trouser leg as he was led towards the cells and the chicken feather floated to the ground unseen.

'Why you lock me up, baas?' he argued, but didn't resist as he was pushed into an already overcrowded cell. 'Thank you, baas,' he called politely as the door slammed closed behind him.

Fezile's shoes were tucked under his arm and his teeth rattled their shame in the darkness of his pocket, but he had achieved his end. A bribe might have achieved it more easily, but having no money he'd taken the more difficult route to find out what had happened to Thabo. Being thrown into jail for daring to enquire after his friend, had allowed him to see for himself that Thabo was not there.

As a lonely black body was pushed back into the anonymity of the steel drawers of Langa mortuary, Fezile took a deep breath. The wizened attendant, looking as if he'd just climbed out of a drawer himself, gazed at him without expression.

'There will be more tomorrow. Come back.'

For a week Fezile checked through the collection of unclaimed bodies and finally he accepted the responsibility he'd taken from Sibonda.

With the money Thabo had saved for his mother, Fezile started the twenty-mile walk to Bonne Espérance early one Sunday morning. Reaching the gates much later in the afternoon, he stopped in amazement as his eyes settled on the enormous white house at the top of the drive.

Thabo had described Bonne Espérance to him many times, but the Cape Dutch house was much bigger than he'd imagined. It looked like a colour photograph he'd seen on a calendar once. The vineyards buzzed with the gentle heat of late afternoon, nothing stirred for miles and Fezile wanted to cry. He'd never seen anything as beautiful in his entire life. Even the sky seemed wider as it spread a canopy over the mountains. It was a brighter blue than he'd ever seen in Langa and the white buildings stood starkly against it. Moving his eyes on to a group of small white houses to the left of the house and with his shoes tucked under his arm, Fezile walked towards them. His hand clutched the tight roll of pound notes Thabo had saved for his mother, and his mind searched for the least painful way to break the news.

'I accept your anger that I did not protect your son, Sisi, and I give you now his wages.'

Miriam's fingers pushed at each corner of the bundle of crisp pound notes Fezile handed her and her dark moist eyes settled on the man she remembered from the village of Herschel.

'My son is safe, Fezile. Thabo is in our village with my mother, Sophie.' A sudden light of understanding shone in Fezile's eyes as she explained the whereabouts of Thabo. 'I thank you for caring for my child, *Tatomkhulu*.' Miriam bestowed the title of respect due to an older man and Fezile nodded silently. A gentle smile of relief had touched his lips and his body swayed as if pushed by a slight breeze.

'Will he return to Cape Town?' Fezile was answered only by Miriam's shoulders as they lifted in a vast unknowing shrug. He missed Thabo's company more than he thought was possible. Thabo's determined search for education had allowed Fezile to live vicariously the life he'd never achieved for himself, but now it was over. 'Thank you, Sisi.' Fezile took the bowl of food Miriam shared with him. 'I think one day he will come back.' He coughed and with amazing sleight of hand removed his teeth, slipping them into his pocket before he ate.

'Maybe he'll come back.' Miriam's shrug had reflected what was happening in black family circles. The young people had begun to question their elders' wisdom and everything was changing. African traditions had been made unworkable as men abandoned their families to seek employment in the cities and apartheid had broken the family unit, leaving nothing in its place.

'Thabo is a good boy.' Fezile reassured Miriam that her son was different and he pushed a round ball of mealie pap into his mouth, his bare gums pounding it to a mush. 'You have a good son,' he told the woman who had yet to accept that Thabo's life was his own to live, that her son might indeed still join the angry young men who now challenged their parents' subservience to the white man. 'Yes, he is a good son, Sisi.' Fezile examined a fresh ball of mealie pap carefully before he pushed it into his mouth.

Rebecca looked back as her horse Salu stretched out in long cantering strides that carried her down the slope towards Bonne Espérance. Simon rode on a pony behind her and his face was alive.

'Pull him up, Simon!' she called as Salu trod down on to the driveway, turning towards the stables.

'Again?' Simon's eyes glowed with accomplishment as he tugged on the reins to bring the small pony to a halt. 'Come, Becky.' He turned on the pony's back, pointing over the rustling green vineyards to the mountains beyond. 'Up there!' he yelled in excitement.

'OK.' Rebecca spent every afternoon riding with Simon and she didn't resent a moment of it. Once on the pony's back, he became one with the animal under him. In spite of his physical disabilities, he looked almost normal and saw himself as perfect, finding peace inside his body at last.

'Good day.' Fezile walked down the driveway towards them, removing his hat with a bow of his head. 'Miss Rebecca?' He'd recognised her as the white girl Thabo had talked of with a mixture of love and despair. 'Master Simon.' His eyes moved on to Simon and he bowed again. Thabo had told him how the children had stolen Simon to protect him and Fezile smiled warmly. 'Thabo has told me much about you both.'

'Thabo?' Salu lifted his feet impatiently, scattering loose stones on the driveway as Rebecca watched Fezile curiously. 'Do you know Thabo?' She slid off the horse's back quickly. 'Have you seen him?'

'I know Thabo.' Fezile wished he hadn't taken his teeth out to eat Miriam's food.

'Is he here?' Rebecca peered into the gentle brown eyes that were trying to connect the beautiful young woman in front of him with the small girl Thabo had talked about. 'He's not here, is he?' She spun round towards Miriam's small house in excitement. 'Did Thabo come back with you to Miriam?'

'Thabo not come back here, missy. Thabo in his village.'

'Thabo!' Simon chanted the name as his mind searched the storehouse of feelings that were his only memory. 'Thabo!' he said, with the sudden surprise of recognition. A wash of warmth had passed over him, declaring itself to be Thabo.

'The child. He remembers!' Fezile's eyes lit with a moment of wonder as Simon's face spread into a wide lopsided smile, his tongue pushing out in a moment of forgetfulness. Turning on the pony's back, he strained to look towards the gates of Bonne Espérance, expecting the feeling that was Thabo to come back the way it had gone. The heavy lines on Fezile's dark face creased round his eyes as he smiled. 'He remember! Like Thabo remember him.'

Rebecca moved closer to the man who'd brought Thabo back to Simon and her eyes searched his face in puzzled glances. Fezile's quiet dignity, impossibly combined with humility, was a quality that always drew her. It was the quality of so many African people she knew. A special people, sifted through the fine sieve of oppression till only a core of pure silver remained.

'Why didn't Thabo come here? When he needed help why didn't he come back? We would have helped him. Is there anything we can do now?' Fezile was quite suddenly at a loss in the unfamiliar territory of a white person's care as Rebecca spoke and he didn't know how to respond. He wished he was back in the police station where he knew how to handle white policemen.

'I'm sorry.' Rebecca stepped back. She'd seen the humble dignity of the man in front of her crumble under the unaccustomed weight of her kindness.

'You like chicken, Miss Rebecca?' Fezile's eyes narrowed as he peered into hers keenly, snatching at the only means of regaining his pride. 'The boy, Simon, he like chicken?' He waited silently for the answer that would enable him to give of himself.

'Yes.' Rebecca watched him, wondering at the sudden light in his eyes.

'Then I bring you chicken.' Fezile bowed low and plonking his hat on his head he recaptured his dignity beneath it. 'Next week I bring you chicken.' He curled the brim of his hat with a quick twist of his hand. 'Next week Sunday!'

The gentle African man had cast aside Rebecca's guilt as he held out the gift of a chicken.

'Thank you. But I don't even know your name,' she called after the barefoot figure that had walked away down the drive, his shoes tucked under his arm.

'Fezile,' he called back. His shoulders were straight and his head high. 'A good fat chicken I bring to Thabo's friends.' He walked on with a sweeping wave of his hand. There was a lightness in his step and a gentle swagger in his stride as Fezile began his long walk back to Langa.

'I'm not sure you should eat that chicken. It's a black chicken!' Rebecca smiled at the young man who sat across the dining-room table from her. Her eyes sparkled with arrogant humour and she cupped her chin in her hand as she watched Andre Bothma.

He was twenty-five years old and the great-grandson of Pieter Bothma. Suzanne Beauvilliers' marriage to Thys Bothma, three generations earlier, had brought their bloodlines together. Andre had called in at Bonne Espérance to meet the family on his way to join the police force in Cape Town and lunch had become a family occasion as Lydia joined them with her son, Joe. But the meal had been long and arduous as Andre spent it explaining his belief in apartheid.

'Black?' Andre's eyes twinkled as he looked across the table at Rebecca. 'The chicken had black feathers? Is that what you say?' Andre Bothma's English was heavily accented and his eyes teased Rebecca as she watched him closely. He'd decided she was quite beautiful for an English girl but had quickly sensed that she didn't like him and deliberately provoked her. 'A "kaffir" chicken. That's what it is, is it?'

'A kaffir chicken!' Rebecca observed André's fork move to his mouth, laden with juicy white breast. She watched the soft meat disappear into his mouth and leaned forward with a smile. 'I hear some people want milk and cream apartheid. All white cows to be separated from non-white cows – yet you eat kaffir chicken!'

The point of Lydia's shoe dug into Rebecca's leg and she turned to reassure Andre with a smile. 'She's only teasing.' The meal had become unbearable. Tension danced on the gleaming wood table between them and Lydia wished she could leave the room as Constance had done earlier.

Rebecca's mother had left even before lunch had begun. She'd appeared confused by André's presence and David had gone out of the room with her. It was obvious to Lydia then that something was wrong with Constance, but Rebecca had appeared not to notice.

'Let's forget about chickens, shall we?' Lydia tried to restore a little order to the family occasion. 'Whatever it is, it tastes good.'

Rebecca appeared to abide by Lydia's call for a truce as she lifted a crispy wing to her lips, sucking on it gently. 'Problem is though, while it's feathers were white the chicken most definitely was not.' She grinned at Andre. 'I saw the kaffir whose chicken it was when he brought it!'

'Stop it, Joe!' Lydia turned on her small son as he spat a mouthful of beans on to the table, joining the rebellion that had gathered steam around him.

'Kaffir chicken!' He added a mouthful of spithsoaked chicken to the beans, grinning at Andre to impress him with his bravery.

'Fezile!' Simon shouted suddenly. 'Fezile bring the chicken. And Thabo!' His eyes had lit with the achievement of memory and he stared at Rebecca.

'That's right, Simon.'

'That's right, Simon.' He echoed Rebecca's words and Joe collapsed in a heap of laughter.

'I'm so sorry about this.' Rebecca's attention moved back to Andre Bothma. 'Thabo's also black, you know. Just like the chicken.' She smiled. 'He's our friend. The only problem is, he's one of the natives your Government keeps pushing away on to reserves. South Africa empty of Africans – isn't that the grand plan?'

'I think you've said enough, Rebecca.' Lydia was caught between Joe's bad behaviour and Rebecca's attacks on Andre Bothma. 'I'm sorry, Andre, I really do apologise. This simply isn't the place to talk politics, Rebecca!'

'No problem.' Andre wiped his mouth with his napkin. His hands were broad and deeply tanned. 'I'm sorry we don't agree.' He looked at Rebecca with a smile behind his eyes, pushing his rolled napkin into its small silver ring.

'Don't you want to know why I don't agree with you? What I think of apartheid?' Rebecca's anger was no longer concealed by humour. 'It's evil. And so is everyone who supports it.'

'You know what it means, do you, apartheid?' Andre had kept calm throughout Rebecca's attacks and still he smiled.

'Greed,' Rebecca snapped. 'Fear. You want to hear more?'

'Apartheid means separate and equal development of the different cultures in our country.' Andre Bothma's beliefs were firm and based on generations of Afrikaner heritage. Passed down through the Dutch Reformed Church, they'd become part of his everyday life. 'It was ordained by God.'

'Now he's blaming God!' Rebecca turned to Lydia in amazement.

'If you read the Bible you would see that God told His people to separate themselves from the heathens in the land.' Andre placed his knife and fork together on the plate.

'What heathens? Most Africans are Christians just like you probably say you are. So you tell me why the Bible also says that God condemns any nation that brings misery by its decrees.' Rebecca stood up. 'You can find that in Psalm ninety-three, unless the Psalms have been banned by your church – like everything else that contradicts apartheid!' She snatched her plate. 'Excuse me, I can't stand any more of this.'

'Why are you so angry?' Andre asked, still eating. 'Could it be because you know I'm right?'

'You're as right as Adolf Hitler was.' Rebecca slammed her plate on the table.

'Hitler!' Joe slammed his plate on the table in imitation of Rebecca, and Simon followed his lead. Bringing his plate down in a thundering crash he looked at the smashed pieces in amazement and Joe howled with laughter.

'Look, Andre!' he yelled at the man he was trying to impress. 'Simon broke his plate, see?'

'Rebecca, please!' Lydia was beside herself as Simon hurled bits of food and plate at Joe, carrying on his cries of 'Hitler!' as Joe hurled them back. They were swept up in the anarchy that had overtaken lunch and were totally beyond Lydia's control.

'Excuse me again.' Rebecca left the room quickly, dragging a reluctant Simon away with her.

'I'm so sorry.' Lydia tried to apologise as Simon held a chicken bone ready to throw, challenging Joe to follow. 'They're not usually so badly behaved.' She tried to excuse the entire family. 'Why don't you go outside and look around?' Lydia smiled at Andre with a shrug. 'Lunch appears to be over.'

Standing back from the house, Andre Bothma's eyes passed slowly over the clean lines of white gable that reached above the front door. The sweeping Cape Dutch architecture moulded into the gentle folds of the mountains behind, becoming one with the land. Bonne Espérance was a part of the rich earth that surrounded it, expressing the wealth of the land it dominated ... and the arrogance of the English people who occupied it, Andre decided, and turning away he thought back to his own family home.

Doornfontein was a farm built generations before by his ancestors, Thys and Suzanne Bothma. It had been burned to the ground by British soldiers during the Boer War, but the house had been rebuilt over the years. It was a square white building with an extending porch, shaded by masses of purple bougainvillea. Long lines of salted meat hung in strips from the *stoep* roof as they dried under the constant attention of buzzing flies, and, though equipped with running water at last, its simplicity was stark in comparison to Bonne Espérance.

Quite suddenly, Andre felt uncomfortable. Automatically he pulled a stick of biltong from his pocket and the salty taste of dried venison carried him home while the words his father had spoken before he'd died rolled round his head.

'*Bonne Espérance belongs to us too, my son.*'

Though the words had been quiet they'd been clear and Andre had never forgotten them. Pieter Bothma, his great-grandfather and the son of Thys and Suzanne, should have inherited Bonne Espérance along with Jack Marsden, but it hadn't happened and Andre thought he knew why.

Suzanne, his paternal great-great-grandmother, had become Afrikaans when she'd married Thys and he knew that was the reason his family had been cut out of this inheritance. Since the day Willem Bothma had been hanged by the British, the Afrikaner side of the family had been ignored.

With his interest caught by the miles of spreading vineyards ahead of him, Andre turned his thoughts back to the land. His family farm at Doornfontein was bigger, but the land was hostile and Andre had spent many years fighting back the bush that continually reached to regain it. Drought and flood were an ever-present threat to crops that earned them a meagre living and Bonne Espérance was a Garden of Eden by comparison.

Once again drought had ravished Andre's home. He'd been forced to move to the city in search of a living while his mother stayed behind to look after her other children. With an Afrikaner Government in power, Andre had lost the insecurity of being a 'poor white'. His people had united under the Nationalist flag and he intended to regain the 'pride' of his inheritance as his people had regained their country. Squatter camps of poor white Afrikaners outside Cape Town had been cleared overnight by a proud Government. Thousands of uneducated white Afrikaners had been given safe employment in the railways and police force. Their humiliation at the hands of the British wiped out, they'd pushed even further to create a pure white *volk*, their feet now treading on the heads of blacks.

'*Yiza!*' Andre called a greeting to the curly black head that had suddenly popped up among the wide leaves of vines ahead of him. '*Ndifuna uku thetha nawe.*' He moved towards the young Xhosa labourer, asking if he could speak to him.

Miriam listened in silence as she stacked the lunch dishes in the sink. She didn't like her kitchen being invaded by arguing outsiders and wished Lydia and Rebecca would leave so she could get on with her work. White people, though they spoke more quietly than her own, seemed personally destructive.

'I thought you'd grown up, Rebecca. Good grief, Andre's part of the family! No wonder there's such a divide between Afrikaner and English. You insulted him. Your manners were worse than the kids.' Lydia wiped Joe's mouth hard with a dishcloth and he banged his feet under the kitchen table in frustration.

'How could I keep quiet while he shot his mouth off like a typical Afrikaner?' Rebecca tried to pull away from Simon as he attempted to squeeze forgiveness out of her from behind. 'He's one of the people who've brought South Africa to where it is now. He's joining the police force, Lydia. Just imagine him with power. He's a racist.'

'And you?' Lydia's eyebrows were raised as she glared at Rebecca, pushing a loose strand of hair back on top of her head. 'Would you have said the same things if he hadn't been an Afrikaner?' Joe sucked his cheeks in and out to check they still worked after his mother's scrubbing hand had flattened them.

'Simon, please!' Rebecca tried to get away but he grabbed her again and slipping in front of her he hugged her tight. 'OK, OK.' Her arms wrapped round him, unable to resist the apologetic love that poured out of him.

'Simon sorry,' he mumbled into the soft warmth of her body.

'I don't know why politics has to come into everything nowadays. Apartheid's got nothing to do with lunch. It's all so boring!' Lydia dropped the dishcloth into the full sink and Miriam wiped the small bubble of soap that spouted into her eye.

'Maybe black people don't think it's boring.' Miriam's bottom lip pushed forward as Rebecca tried to draw her into an argument she didn't want to hear. 'Do you think apartheid's boring, Miriam?'

'*Out!*' Miriam clapped her hands suddenly. 'Out of my kitchen! *Everybody out!*' She asserted her authority and pushed them out with their politics.

As Rebecca sat at the piano later, picking out a tuneless song with one finger, she stared blankly at the yellowing ivory notes. She'd been upstairs to see her mother and had found her asleep. David had insisted nothing was wrong, telling her that Constance was just tired, but he'd gone quickly to the cellars on the pretence of work.

'What's wrong with my mother?' Rebecca kept her head turned away as Lydia came into the sitting room. 'There's something wrong with her, isn't there?' She prodded a rising line of notes, bouncing them round the room in aggravating procession.

'Why don't you go outside and talk to Andre?' Lydia avoided Rebecca's question. She hated disagreement and worked always for peace. 'He's not bad-looking. In my time I'd have quite fancied him – even though he is an Afrikaner!' Lydia chuckled, remembering Rebecca's ideas on Afrikaner men. 'Anyway, it would be better to talk to him than do that to the poor old piano.'

Rebecca dropped the piano lid slowly and turned round on the stool to look at her older cousin. Her aggression had vanished and she was a small girl once again.

'My mother's sick, isn't she?' She looked down at her hands, examining them carefully.

'She's not young any more, that's all.' Lydia indicated for her to move up on the piano stool. She didn't know how to reassure her but knew she must try. 'Your mother didn't recognise Andre, that's all. I didn't know who he was either, not till he explained. It's not surprising. She's never met him before, has she?'

'She didn't remember Elize or Uncle Paul either. She got a letter from them in England and she didn't know who they were.' Tears had formed in Rebecca's eyes and she moved away to the window. The afternoon sun stared at the glass in front of her, revealing smudgy half-circles where Miriam's cloth had missed. Everything was still. Ring doves cooed quietly in the eaves of the house and she heard the distant laughter of labourers in the vineyards, but nothing moved, as if Bonne Espérance itself was a grave. 'My mother's going to die, Lydia.' She turned to look at her cousin as her mind went back to 123 Z. 'She used to dress so well. You know all Mum's clothes were from England. I loved watching her pull her nylons on.' Rebecca fell silent as the grandfather clock in the hall chimed a slow five through her life.

'Heavens, it's time I went.' Lydia went towards the door, keen to get away from the rising emotion in Rebecca. 'Stan will think I've left him.' Lydia had no answer to Rebecca's questions about Constance.

'Oh God, I wish he was here.' Rebecca turned back to the piano and lifting the lid again, she banged the notes.

'Have you heard from him?' Lydia stopped at the door and Rebecca looked up blankly. 'You were talking about Luke, weren't you? Is he coming down to see us?'

'I don't care if he never comes back.' Rebecca ran her finger over the keys and the notes screeched in rippling protest. 'And I suppose you still think I should apologise to that Nazi. What shall I tell him – that he's wonderful and so's apartheid?'

'Rebecca?' Their relationship had changed since the day Rebecca had challenged Lydia with Johannes Villiers and Lydia was tense. 'It's Luke that's the real problem, isn't it?' Rebecca didn't answer and Lydia took her hand, forcing her to meet her eyes. 'It wasn't just a crush, Rebecca. True?'

Pushing her way through the rows of vines, Rebecca's face grew puzzled as she spotted Andre. He'd removed his jacket, hanging it over a trellis as he examined a vine. He was listening attentively as Samson, a young black labourer, explained the procedure of grafting. They spoke to one another in Xhosa and there was an understanding between them that excluded Rebecca as Samson stepped back politely the moment he saw her.

'Madam.' He touched the woolly cap on his head.

'Hullo.' Andre's face had warmed in the sun and everything about him seemed suddenly different. He was no longer the man who'd defended apartheid over the tasty carcass of Fezile's chicken. His feet were firmly planted on the ground and he was entirely at ease with a black man. 'Samson was telling me how you graft vines. Not much different to any fruit, from what I can see.'

'You were speaking in Xhosa.' Rebecca's eyes reflected her confusion.

'That's his language, isn't it?' Andre wiped his hands on a handkerchief and his eyes moved over the vines as he picked his jacket off the trellis, pushing the hanky back in a pocket. 'You've got a beautiful piece of land here.' Andre turned towards Samson and his hand lifted in a wave. '*Dimkile*,' he called, turning back to Rebecca's scrutiny. 'Is there something wrong?' He looked down as if checking he was properly dressed. 'There's something else I've said that you don't like?'

'I just don't understand you.' Rebecca shrugged. Her mind had gone back to Granny Cat. To the fire that had killed her son and to Pieter Botha's death at the hands of I Titus. 'The way you treat Samson – it isn't what I expected, that's all.' She remembered clearly her hatred of the Boer farmers who'd hanged I Titus just because he was black.

'You think I hate the blacks?'

'Don't you?'

'No, why should I?' Andre was looking out over the miles of land. 'My family used to farm here, you know,' he said reflectively. 'The Bothmas, in the last century, before the Boer War.' He walked deeper into the vineyards and Rebecca followed, plucking a large dark grape as she went. 'Till the British hanged Willem Bothma, of course.' He looked at her with a smile. 'But we won't talk about that.'

'I'm sorry.' Rebecca rubbed her thumb over the cloudy mist on the grape. 'I had no right to speak to you like that at lunch. It wasn't called for.' She peered at him, screwing her eyes tight against the sun.

Everything about Andre was masculine, and as he looked at her Rebecca felt uneasy. Feelings were pushing their way to the surface inside her, the same feelings that came each time she thought of Luke. Holding the grape out for him to take, she moved on, her slim body threading its way through the gnarled wood of the vines.

'You didn't ever meet Luke Marsden, did you?' she called back casually, putting enough distance between them to avoid the feelings his masculinity had aroused. 'I think you'd have liked him. His mother's Afrikaans like you.'

'Do you?' Andre's voice was quiet, almost gentle. 'Like him?' He pushed the grape into his mouth as he waited for her to answer.

She wanted to shout aloud, 'I love Luke!' and her voice trembled as she said quietly, 'He's OK.'

'I've never met him.' Andre bent down and taking a clump of earth in his hand, he allowed it to run through his fingers in a dusty red stream. 'The soil's good here.' He caught a few grains between his thumb and fingers, rubbing it gently into a fine red smudge. He was at one with the earth and Jacques Beauvilliers, their common ancestor. 'This is what it's all about, you know – land. The land our original family claimed.' He glanced towards the graveyard in the distance. 'Is that where our ancestors are buried? The Beauvilliers family?'

'Most.' Rebecca turned towards the graveyard, pulling herself free of a deep longing for Luke that Andre's presence had stirred. 'I'll show you. Come.' She glanced at him as he reached her. 'You're not so bad after all.'

As Rebecca stood beside the low white wall that surrounded the graveyard, she suddenly remembered the night she'd dug the key from under Clara's stone. 'You see that grave over there?' she said to Andre. 'That's Clara Beauvilliers'. It's odd, but when I met you I thought of Clara. She hated everybody – blacks, even Afrikaners!' Rebecca pointed to Katinka's marble headstone. 'And that's my grandmother's grave. She loved everybody but she died on our way down here.'

Andre had stopped beside the old stones that marked the graves of Emily, Prudence and Clara and he peered at them, trying to read the worn inscriptions.

'They're not all here, of course.' He turned to Rebecca. 'Suzanne's missing. My grandfather told me she ran away from Bonne Espérance when she married Thys Bothma. He said she became an Afrikaner. Did you know that one of your forebears was an Afrikaner?'

'And one was an ape according to Darwin but that doesn't mean I eat fleas.' Rebecca was suddenly angered by his arrogance and ran her finger along the top of the low white wall, blowing off a film of fine dust as she turned to him. 'I also know that it was the British who began apartheid, Andre, but that doesn't make it right. No more than British soldiers burning down your family's farm during the Boer War was right! My grandmother told me about it.' She smiled. 'And that's the only reason I'm being nice to you.'

'Did she tell you about my great-grandfather, Pieter Bothma? That his wife died in a British concentration camp? That he lost three children in the camp also and that the British put fish-hooks in their bread? Did you know that thirty thousand Afrikaner women and children died in those British concentration camps?' Andre's eyes were alight with accusation as he looked at her; as if everything he talked about had happened only the day before.

'I know what happened when your great-grandfather came here to burn down Bonne Espérance.' Rebecca was equally angry. 'He came here for revenge! Did you know that?' Her cheeks burned as she remembered what her grandmother had told her about the fire at Bonne Espérance and Andre was quite suddenly Pieter Bothma. 'I suppose you think setting fire to a house with a child locked inside was right!'

'That's a lie! Pieter Bothma tried to help that Englishwoman.' The brief moment of friendship vanished in the face of the past as Andre remembered the story of his great-grandfather's return to Bonne Espérance. It was a story he'd been brought up on, as had his father before him.

'Pieter Bothma came back here to find his own family – the Beauvilliers. He was looking for the part of himself that had been destroyed when his family was wiped out by the British.' Rebecca listened in amazed silence as the story of Pieter Bothma came back at her through Andre's eyes.

'A black man had set fire to the house and Pieter Bothma saw it burning as he rode over that hill over there. He found a woman trying to reach a child who was trapped in the house. The roof was collapsing but the woman kept trying to get in. He tried to stop her but he couldn't, so he pushed her away to get to the child himself, and then a black attacked him. It was the same black who started the fire that killed my great-grandfather when he tried to save that woman's child.'

'That's not true!' Rebecca's eyes burned with accusation. 'Pieter Bothma set fire to the house and that "black" you're accusing was I Titus. He tried to stop your great-grandfather killing my grandmother. And after that you Boers killed I Titus. You Boers killed him just because he was black! The same way your Government's trying to do now!' Rebecca was suddenly back in time. She was beside Thabo outside the police station. He was near-naked and handcuffed, his eyes begging her to bear witness to his degradation as he was dragged away. 'What you've just said is a pack of lies, like everything else you say about black people.'

'Lies?' Andre's temper had risen to equal hers as they faced one another across the family graveyard, each balanced on their own truth, and each demanding it be absolute. 'That black wanted to kill your grandmother but you people never believe it! That's the truth of what happened and all the fairy tales you make up will never change it!' Andre knew the British always took the side of Africans over Afrikaners and it angered him beyond measure. 'My great-grandfather tried to save your grandmother's child and he died doing it!'

'Never!' Rebecca glared at him. 'You only want to believe that because I Titus was black!'

'I just know what black people are under the European clothes we've given them. It's people like you that have to be protected from themselves. You treat blacks like civilised human beings, as if they're equal to whites, and then you scream for help when they hold a *panga* over your head!'

'So that's why you came here today.' Rebecca's body shook with rage and false laughter. 'That's why you joined the police. You're going to protect innocent whites from marauding black savages – is that it?' A picture of Fezile as he'd held the chicken out to her filled Rebecca's mind and she screamed in frustration. 'If that's why you came here, Andre Bothma, you can get out. We don't need you, or your kind.' She swung away to run to the house.

'I came here to take what's mine.' Andre's quiet words stopped Rebecca in her tracks. 'Bonne Espérance is mine as much as it is yours – more, maybe.'

Rebecca responded by turning away with a dismissive laugh and Andre's temper flared. 'Don't you turn your back on me!' His fingers dug into her shoulders as he gripped her. 'Don't ever do that again.' He wrenched her round to face him.

'But I do turn my back on you, Mr Bothma. You *and* your kind.' Rebecca held her head high. She was terrified but wouldn't give in. 'You're not good enough for the dust of Bonne Espérance to touch your shoes. This place was built on the blood of people who challenged your kind. It was built on love, and you surrendered your right to the whole of Africa the day you mistook hatred for pride.'

'And where do you belong, Rebecca? In Africa? Will you stay here when things get rough, or will you run home to England?' Andre shouted after her as she turned to go. 'Tell me that!'

For the first time in her life, Rebecca truly knew where she belonged and Bonne Espérance had become a part of her being, but still she couldn't answer his question.

'Perhaps Africa belongs to the Africans,' she said in defiance of her own insecurity.

'And I am an African.' Andre's voice was firm. 'What are you?'

CHAPTER TEN

The high white walls that surrounded the convent couldn't hold back the laughter of children playing inside. Rebecca stood with her finger held tentatively over a brass button as a heavy clanging bell sounded. She pressed it and the children's laughter stopped at once; a row of tiny brown fingers appeared along the top of the white wall and five solemn faces peered down at her.

'Hullo.' Rebecca smiled up at them. 'Can someone let me in?' With their chins propped on top of the wall, the children clung tight with their fingers and stared at her in silence.

'Down!' A smart clap of hands signalled the children into instant retreat and their faces disappeared over the wall. A key grated as it was pushed into the lock and the gates groaned back against their hinges to reveal a luminously white face, outlined by the blue of a nun's short veil.

'Yes?' The nun was tiny. With her body doubled in a permanent crook under her flowing robes, Sister Paulina pushed her head forward and up to see Rebecca. 'You wanted something?' An Irish lilt sang a melody of curiosity and tiny black eyes peered into Rebecca's. 'You rang the bell?'

'I need help.' Rebecca's voice was tight in her throat as the nun's habit challenged her reasons for visiting the convent. Through the slightly opened gate she could see a cluster of children's heads, popping up and down as they peered over one another to see. 'I need information about a child who once lived here.'

The heavy wooden gate creaked a little wider and the nun took two steps back, pushing the gate with her behind.

'May I come in?' Rebecca asked, and the nun's eyebrows lifted as her body strained against the weight of the gate.

'I wish you would.'

Sister Paulina darted searching glances over Rebecca's face. 'The child you are looking for – there's a name? It would help.' The heavy crucifix around her neck swung in a wide arc over her sandalled feet as they trod the gravel drive towards a vine-covered building up ahead.

'Johannes Villiers.' Rebecca glanced at her. The nun's eyes closed and her lips moved silently through a list of memorised names.

'No.' She opened her eyes and looked directly at Rebecca. 'No.'

A small brown hand stroked the full skirt of Rebecca's dress and she looked round. A tiny half-caste girl, her head tipped sideways, peeped under the skirt at the miles of stiff petticoat that held it wide before she darted away with shrieks of glee.

'Johannes Villiers would have been here about ninety years ago,' Rebecca said and Sister Paulina stopped. Like a bent top she turned to Rebecca and her face crinkled in a mischievous smile.

'Then we must ask Mother Francesca.' Taking a sharp turn to the right she stepped on to a cobbled pathway that led to another large white building ahead of them. 'Dead or alive, every child that's been behind these walls, Mother Francesca knows them all.' A laugh rumbled under her flowing habit. 'But perhaps this time we'll be catching her out.' There was a certain anticipation of delight in her voice.

Aware that they were no longer being followed, Rebecca glanced back. A semi-circle of children stood at the top of the cobbled pathway they had taken. Though their tiny bare feet hovered over the path, as if they might step on to it at any minute, none did.

'Are you of the faith?' Rebecca was surprised by Sister Paulina's sudden question. 'You are Catholic? That's why you've come to our convent?'

'No.' Rebecca's answer was cautious as she looked ahead at the building they approached. Surrounded by wide verandahs with intricate iron balustrades woven like fine lace, the heavy front door stood wide. A beam of sunlight reached through it, spreading its bright warmth across a gleaming yellow-wood floor before flaring into a broad pool of light at the feet of a plaster Madonna.

'You're not sounding that certain.' The nun had stepped back as they reached the steps that led on to the verandah. 'Sister Helena!' she called and a young nun looked up through the small square pane of a window she was polishing from the inside. 'Is Mother Francesca in her office?' The rosy-faced nun shook her head. 'Is she at prayers?' The nun nodded. 'Of course!' Sister Paulina glanced at Rebecca. 'Come.' The tiny nun stepped on to the gleaming wood of the hall floor and tilted her veiled head towards a closed door. 'You will wait in there.' Her fingers wound round the rosary that disappeared inside her habit and she pulled it free. 'Ninety years!' she muttered at her reflection on the highly polished floor as she trundled away.

Alone in the room, Rebecca looked round it cautiously and wondered if the schoolmaster, James Robertson, had once waited there himself. Had he brought the unwanted baby, Johannes Villiers, to this very room? It had been easy enough to discover who James Robertson was. His had been the school at which John and Sarah Westbury, the parents of Rebecca's grandmother Katinka, had first met. James Robertson had become something of a legend in Cape history. His strict English boarding school had produced many famous names, not least among them being Rebecca's great-grandfather, John Westbury – the politician and target of an assassin's knife.

Rebecca had read through all the old letters Lydia's mother had kept with Sarah Westbury's will. They were written by an old man who'd gone home to die in England, but who'd never forgotten the baby he'd handed to an orphanage in Cape Town. James Robertson's letters had been locked away, unanswered either by Sarah Westbury herself or Lydia's mother, Elizabeth Marsden. Those letters threatened the lives of their family in a country which had become obsessed by the colour of a person's skin.

'What good would it do to find out, Rebecca?' Lydia had tried to stop Rebecca's search for Johannes Villiers. 'You're nearly sixteen and a half years old and you should be out having fun, not living in the past. What about boyfriends, haven't you got one yet?'

'You're scared.' Rebecca was scared herself, but since Andre Bothma had challenged her, she'd been driven by a strong desire to trace her own African heritage. 'You gave me the information, Lydia. What are you frightened of now?'

'You.' Lydia looked at her coldly. 'You're the one who cried about "not being white" when you were twelve years old. Do you remember that? Because you'd decided you were half-caste, you said Luke couldn't marry you.'

'Luke's got nothing to do with it.' Rebecca turned away quickly, revealing that he had everything to do with it. In the years they'd been separated, her feelings had never changed. Though she'd grown from a child into a beautiful young woman, still Luke possessed her; still she believed in the power of the old key she'd dug from Clara's grave.

'What are you trying to prove?' Lydia persisted. 'Proving you're not quite white would satisfy you would it?'

'I don't care what colour anybody is! Johannes Villiers was our grandmother's brother, Lydia, and we can't sweep him under the carpet any longer.'

Lydia had picked up a book and was casually flicking through the pages of it as Rebecca spoke quietly. 'What are you so ashamed of, Lydia?'

'When's your birthday?

'Did you hear what I said?' Rebecca watched her cousin in amazement. 'Are you ashamed of who you are? Does Andre Bothma's Government frighten you?'

'That doesn't frighten me, no.'

'Then what does?'

'Losing my husband.' Lydia had looked up from the book and her eyes reflected her innermost fears. 'Stan knows nothing about Johannes Villiers.'

'So what? He won't stop loving you just because he finds out you're not pure white!'

Rebecca flinched as Lydia advanced on her. 'Oh, so you're quite sure about that, are you? You who believe in the power of some stupid old key, who thinks Luke will marry you just because of a key.'

'It's not *just* an old key, Lydia!'

'No, it's magic, *you* said! It's the key of our Huguenot ancestors' house in France which they brought with them when they fled Catholic persecution. The key to the door of the past!' Lydia's voice had risen in denial. 'But not my past! Do you hear me, Rebecca? Not mine!' Rebecca had touched a fear that lurked deep in her cousin. 'When I married Stan I had to lie about my race because somewhere in my veins is spot of non-white blood and *now* you expect me to reveal it? I love my Afrikaner husband Rebecca.'

Lydia eyes had moved back to the book in her hand as she pulled away from the thoughts that frightened her. 'Your birthday's on January the third and you'll be seventeen right?' She'd once again immersed herself in the irrelevancies of birthdays and Rebecca had watched her in silence.

'You were looking for a child?' Mother Francesca interrupted Rebecca's thoughts as she stepped through the convent doorway now. A rosary climbed up and over her heavy bosom before tumbling across her wrists. 'His name is Johannes Villiers, I hear.'

'Yes.' Rebecca had got to her feet and she curtseyed politely. 'I'm sorry to trouble you. Maybe your records don't go that far back and I'm wasting your time.'

'No.' Mother Francesca's raised eyebrows conveyed her assurance that the records certainly did go that far back and Rebecca trotted after her as she left the room. 'You will keep your silence, please,' the nun scolded Rebecca's echoing footsteps as they stepped into the hall.

Tiny cracks led under the short clean nail of Mother Francesca's finger as it stopped at one name listed among many others. The wide page of the leather-bound book recorded Johannes Villiers as having arrived at the orphanage on 21 July 1868. The name that had haunted Rebecca since her grandmother died shouted its reality in black ink and Mother Francesca's mouth moved in silent words of concern: 'Are you all right, child?'

Rebecca pulled herself free of the name that had haunted her since Katinka had uttered it. 'I'm fine, yes.'

Mother Francesca's stubby finger jabbed at a small red star beside Johannes Villiers' name and the enormous book fell closed, its leather covers flopping together as she got to her feet. Running her finger along a row of faded spines in a large bookshelf, the Mother Superior pulled another book free and those on either side fell together quickly, ashamed of the sudden gap in their ranks.

'Confirmations,' Mother Francesca announced as she sat beside Rebecca on the hard wooden bench under the window. She flicked through the pages and her finger jabbed at a name, Johannes Villiers. His confirmation into the Catholic church was recorded in careful lettering and the finger moved on to accuse the small asterisk after the name.

'The child ran away from the orphanage.' The book snapped shut and Mother Francesca's eyes fixed on Rebecca. 'That's all we have, I'm afraid.'

'But don't you know where he went?' Rebecca stared at her blankly. She stood on the edge of a mystery that concerned her entire life and her eyes pleaded for more information.

'I said he ran away.' Mother Francesca's cold gaze kept Rebecca firmly outside her Catholic world and the secrets it protected.

'But I've got to find him.' Rebecca lowered her head as failure stared at her.

'Why? What does Johannes Villiers mean to you?' Mother Francesca's eyes were like wet stones and her words were careful as she prodded for the truth.

'I think he was my grandmother's brother.' Mother Francesca's face was puzzled. 'Maybe.' Rebecca shrugged as the nun's eyes fixed on her like searchlights. Stripped naked by her look at last, Rebecca spoke the words she now knew to be true. 'Johannes Villiers was my grandmother's brother.'

The hint of a smile touched Mother Francesca's lips as pride shone bright behind her eyes, softening the wet stones of before. She stood up and replaced the book among the others. Pushing her hand deep into the pocket of her habit she moved to a small desk in a corner of the room and turning a key in the lock of the top drawer, she pulled it open. Silence stretched between them but she made no effort to fill it. Keeping her back to Rebecca, the Mother Superior pulled out a very old book. She moved a loose piece of paper from among its leaves, snapped the book shut and pushed it back into the desk drawer.

'Your family is Beauvilliers?' Mother Francesca's words caught Rebecca by surprise but still the nun didn't look at her.

'Yes.' Rebecca's voice crept out on a whisper. 'Beauvilliers was the family name.'

'Then this is what you're looking for.' Mother Francesca placed the folded piece of paper into Rebecca's hand. 'When Sister Veronica died she asked that this was never lost and her prayers have at last been answered.' Tucking her hands under the rosary as it hung over the step of her bosom, the Mother Superior walked to the door without looking back and Rebecca stared at the paper in her hand.

In the throbbing silence of late afternoon, Rebecca could still hear the sweet melody of children's voices as she walked away from the convent. She glanced back at the stone walls of the church as her feet crunched the gravel of the drive. The delicate notes of a hymn danced on the grey slate roof and she clutched the paper tightly, its words running through her mind.

This is to certify that the boy, Johannes Villiers, whom I brought to this convent ten years ago, is the child of John and Sarah Westbury. That Johannes Villiers is a direct descendant of the family Beauvilliers of Bonne Espérance.

A tiny blot spread in a circle at the foot of the page, and a scrawled signature stated that James Robertson had sworn his statement on oath in London.

As Rebecca stepped through the convent gate children's voices slipped momentarily outside with her. Johannes Villiers had been carried through those same gates ninety or so years earlier, but until that moment his identity had remained locked behind them.

Pushing the evidence of her own African identity deep into her skirt pocket, Rebecca walked slowly away. She knew that the hopes and prayers she held in her hand might yet kill her own deepest desires.

'Why do you keep asking me the same question, Lydia?' Stan's voice was soft as he lay back in the brass four-poster bed. A gentle man, his wife's refreshing innocence of the practical always amused him. Stan Liebenberg was a political journalist: an educated and caring human being. He was a real Afrikaner whose love of the land enabled him to share it, but Lydia knew nothing of Stan's other life – his political beliefs which went directly against Government thinking. He'd protected her from the deepest reaches of himself and lived a double life, writing provocative newspaper articles under an assumed name.

He watched her with a smile as Lydia sat straight-backed on the edge of the bed. 'I fancy you,' he said quietly, but she didn't answer. 'If you think it'll help Rebecca, then of course I agree. Bring Luke down. Just leave his mother where she is, OK? What do you say?' He kissed his wife's neck gently, longing to ease the pain inside her.

'Are you sure you don't mind?' Lydia spoke in Afrikaans as she always did with her husband. As she did when her own insecurities could be lost in a foreign tongue. She'd seen Rebecca earlier that day and had been confronted by the piece of paper that declared Johannes Villiers to be a member of the Beauvilliers family.

'Johannes Villiers was our grandmother's brother, Lydia. James Robertson risked everything to tell the truth, and Sister Veronica prayed for a day like today.'

Rebecca's voice had ridden an emotion she wasn't capable of controlling. She'd fulfilled her grandmother's last wish but cast herself headlong down a path of self-destruction, pulling Lydia with her.

'What exactly does all that mean to you?' Lydia was observing her closely. 'Are you looking for Johannes Villiers, or a way out of your own worst fears?' Rebecca flinched as Lydia touched on the truth. 'You're afraid Luke doesn't want you — isn't that it? You're beginning to think that maybe he never did, that he was just a childhood fantasy and now you need an excuse to face up to it.'

'Stop it!' Rebecca shouted, but Lydia had gone on quickly.

'It's because — "I'm not white! See, I have the proof right here!" Or, "It's only because the law says we can't marry!" Those are the excuses you're looking for instead of facing the fact that no amount of old keys dug out of graves will make your fantasy come true.'

'You're wrong!' Tears streamed down Rebecca's cheeks as she argued against the truth of Lydia's words. 'It's you who's looking for excuses. Excuses for apartheid! Excuses for being married to a bloody Afrikaner.' Rebecca's head snapped back as Lydia's hand whacked her across the face. 'It's the truth!' Rebecca had screamed in her face.

'*It's fear.*' Lydia had taken her by the shoulders and held her tight. 'Digging people out of their graves and using them as an excuse for failure? That's fear, Rebecca, and *that's* what led to apartheid!'

'How old is Rebecca going to be this birthday, anyway?' Stan examined the back of Lydia's nightdress now, looking for some opening that might lead him inside it. 'What is this thing — a tent?'

'I think it would be good for Rebecca to see Luke again, now that she's grown-up.' Lydia still neglected to mention Johannes Villiers' presence in her family to Stan and she ignored his efforts to find a way into her

214

nightdress. 'It'd be a lovely surprise for her birthday if Luke will come. Stan, what are you doing?'

'Opening my Christmas box!' He tweaked at the miles of cotton that made up the voluminous Victorian nightgown in which she'd hidden herself. 'One of us was born in the wrong century, and it sure wasn't me.' At last he found an entrance and his hand stroked her naked body. 'That's nice.' Stan knew that the best way to distract Lydia was by making love and it was all he wanted to do.

'Luke's twenty-one, you know. I can hardly believe it.' Lydia ignored his caresses. 'Estelle can't stop him coming to Cape Town. No!' She pushed Stan's hand away and heaved herself over, rolling herself into a cotton cocoon beside him. 'Joe's still awake,' she warned, going back to her thoughts. 'Do you think I should tell Luke his visit is our birthday present to Rebecca? I said no, Stan.' She laughed as he found his way into the nightdress again. Her resolve to ignore his advances vanished as he held her down, pulling the nightdress up over her head as his lips moved over her naked body.

'What you doing?' Their son's voice crept towards them through the brass railings at the foot of the bed and they froze.

'Stan!' Lydia's muffled voice pushed its way from under his body. 'Do something!'

'Hi, Joe!' Stan rolled away and, pulling the covers over Lydia casually, he smiled at the wide-eyed boy who stared at him from between brass rods. 'You want a wee or a drink? How about a scotch?'

'What you doing?' The question came again and Joe's large round eyes moved on to the lump of Lydia's body as she hid under the bedclothes.

'Who? Oh, your mother. That's her under there!' Stan offered his explanation hopefully. 'I'm just cuddling her, like we cuddle you.'

'But why you take your clothes off to do it?'

'You might as well go on writing that letter to Luke,' Stan murmured and turned away, pulling the cotton nightdress over his head to hide.

A train ticket dropped from between the folded page of a letter and Luke looked down at it curiously as it lay at his feet.

'Uh, uh!' With an outstretched leg he stopped the dog picking it up and he spread the letter on the desk in his bedroom.

Dear Luke, you probably don't remember me after all this time but . . .

Luke turned the page over and saw Lydia's name at the bottom. A vague image of his aunt stood on the boundaries of memory and he studied her signature carefully. He'd always liked Lydia though his mother hadn't, and turning the page over again he read on quickly. Lydia's name had brought with it a sudden and clear picture of Bonne Espérance: of the vineyards and misty blue mountains that surrounded the only place he'd ever felt at home . . .

It's Rebecca's birthday on 3 January and Stan and I would like to give her a surprise. That's what the ticket's about. Luke bent down to the floor and picked it up. It was a railway ticket to Cape Town – second class, return. A flutter of excitement ran through his body and he turned back to the letter quickly.

. . . Rebecca will be seventeen and she's grown into such a lovely girl. I'm sure she'd like to see you. Anyway, we thought . . . Luke put the letter down and pulled open the top desk drawer. His hand fumbled through a collection of oddments till his fingers touched the glossy surface of a snapshot. He'd never looked at the photograph clearly before and now he gazed at the small girl as if seeing her for the first time. The pert face was broken in a wide smile and Rebecca's dark eyes were lit with fun. It wasn't the face that loomed in front of him each time he was with Althea – then Rebecca's eyes smouldered with accusation. But now she looked different as he stared at the photograph and in some curious way he knew he had to see her. Good or bad, Rebecca was a large part of his bond with Bonne Espérance. She'd stepped into his life in a moment of time that he'd never forgotten.

'I'd only be away for a week, and I'm owed leave anyway.' Luke pushed a forkful of stew into his mouth and watched his mother across the table. He was nervous and his jaws ached as he chewed, but still Estelle didn't say a word. Since he'd told her about Lydia's letter and the ticket to Cape Town, his mother hadn't said anything.

'How boring!' Naomi wiped her mouth with her napkin and glanced at Luke. She was seventeen years old and had grown into the brittle young woman promised by the child. 'When's her birthday?'

'On the third of January.' Luke glanced at his sister. Everything about her was immaculate. Her features were perfect and her skin crystal clear but her eyes were empty. She'd left school in standard eight and found work in a Johannesburg hairdressing salon. Every moment of Naomi's life was devoted to her appearance and Luke wondered if Rebecca was similarly absorbed by her own image now she'd grown into a woman.

'May I leave the table?' He rolled his napkin tightly and pushed it through the silver ring.

'She's been after you since you met, you know that, don't you?' Naomi looked at her brother as he stood up. Luke was tall and handsome. If he'd been wealthy too she'd have understood Rebecca's interest, but never would Naomi understand Luke's. 'Rebecca obviously thinks you're a good catch. From what I hear there are no decent men in Cape Town.'

Though Luke's hair had darkened, his eyes were the same clear blue and the clean line of his jaw was strong as he looked down at his sister.

'What does she look like now anyway? Have you got a picture?' Naomi's tongue ran quickly over her lipstick and she pushed at the corners of her mouth with her napkin. All she remembered about Rebecca was that she didn't like her. 'Hey, did I tell you Arno wants to take me to Durban this weekend?' Naomi's thoughts centred back on herself as she turned to her mother. 'His dad says we can use the plane.'

Luke stopped at the door on his way out, Estelle's continued silence disturbing him. 'So, I'll write and tell Aunt Lydia it's OK?' A question mark lifted his last word.

'No.'

Estelle still had the ability to make Luke feel like a small boy and he held firmly to the door handle, as if holding on to himself.

'No what?'

His mother pushed her napkin to one side, her eyes opening with amazement as she looked at him. 'After all that's happened you can still ask?'

'What's happened?' Luke shrank as Estelle's eyes pinned him in the doorway, just as they had when he was a child.

'Doesn't it matter what *I* feel about it? That it might not be what *I* want?'

'Ma, please!'

'Ma, please *nothing*!' She pushed her plate away and Naomi smirked. Her mother's knife and fork had dropped on to the white tablecloth and a pea rolled a slow gravy trail across it. 'What's there for you to go to anyway? It's not a happy place for any of us. That family is your father's family, and there's no reason for you to go there at all.'

'Simon's there.' Luke's voice was quiet and Estelle looked away. 'I want to see my brother, Ma. And I want to see Bonne Espérance.' He tried to hold tight to his twenty-one years as they disintegrated around him and Luke's mind leapt back to the moment the small mongol child had revealed his mother's true nature.

'That poor child.' Estelle's words lifted on a tidal wave of emotion. 'You know why that family took Simon, don't you? So they could use him as a weapon against me!'

Luke's shoulders slumped as the familiarity of defeat crept over him. 'They didn't take Simon away from you,' he whispered, but his voice was drowned by Estelle's.

'It was that girl who put you up to it.' Her mind was back in Bonne Espérance, back with the old woman Nombeko as she'd held Simon out to her. 'That girl dragged a black heathen into our home.' Her voice hit a screech of terror. 'She left my child in that black woman's shack!' Her eyes drove into Luke like needles and his thin skin of protection peeled back. 'That family kept him there against my wishes! Like a circus freak they kept my poor helpless child to be gawped at ... laughed at ... pointed at by blacks. And your father agreed to it.' Her body shook with emotion. 'I wanted my child cared for in a home. I wanted him protected because he couldn't protect himself.'

'I was there, Ma!' Luke's cry came from the roots of his soul. The deformed figure of a small boy stood between them like a battered punch-bag and he turned to the door.

'Don't go, Luke.' Tears pushed at Estelle's voice. 'Don't walk out on me like your father did. Don't shame me again with that half-caste family. What do you want to see that coloured girl for? Please don't leave me!'

The tendons on Luke's neck knotted as he held himself together. 'I'm not leaving you, Ma.' Ripples of tension ran up Luke's cheeks. 'I'm not shaming you, and I'm not leaving you.' He faced her. 'And I'm not Dad,' he said simply as his hand tightened on the controls of his life. 'But I *am* going to Bonne Espérance.' Luke had made the first decision of his life. He'd gone directly against Estelle's wishes and he watched his mother in surprise as she said nothing.

'What about Althea?' Naomi's voice danced towards him from the table in simpering delight. 'Maybe she'd like to go with you.' She squeezed past him in the doorway and quite suddenly Luke felt absolutely free.

Althea hadn't even entered his head. As he'd argued with his mother about going to Cape Town, he hadn't thought of Althea once. Bonne Espérance was a part of his life that Althea had never occupied, and it was exactly where he wanted to be.

For the briefest moment Estelle's silence touched Luke with a warning, but he held tight to his newly gained confidence. He'd cut himself free of the hold his mother had had over him all his life, and slowly he walked away.

As her son left the room, Estelle stared down at her hands. Her knuckles were white with tension and slowly she stretched each finger to relax them. Lifting her head she carefully scraped the leftovers of dinner on to plate, stacking the dishes neatly together. Her mind had latched on to the source of Luke's confidence and she was quite calm. Glancing at the straggling gravy trail the pea had left on the cloth, she wondered how best to remove it.

Tucked under Table Mountain, with Lion's Head and Signal Hill towering above it, the city street plunged between terraces of double-storeyed cottages in a bumpy strip of tarmac. District Six in Cape Town was alive with bustling crowds. Children ran helter-skelter in and out of permanently open front doors and their mothers screamed after them in a high-pitched mixture of Afrikaans and English – the language of the Cape coloured people.

Cars and heavily laden lorries were parked haphazardly down the sides of the narrow street and hawkers yelled the delights of mangoes, lichees and grapes as their horse-drawn wagons squeezed and rattled their way down the road.

The ramshackle rows of gaudy Victorian houses, their tin roofs running rusty red sheets over open verandahs, were alive with music and chattering voices. Over the elaborate wooden balustrades, bright sparkling washing hung like waving scarecrows, reaching across the street to touch one another's shirt-cuffs in greeting. Tall poles carried crisscross cables alongside the houses and black and white circled lamp-posts stood guard.

'You look like you lost, girlie.' A plump woman leaned over a balcony that bent with her weight as she called down to Rebecca in a singsong voice. Her skin was a light golden brown and her dark slanted eyes revealed a mixture of Malay and white blood. '*Boetjie!*' she screamed to a small boy as he rushed out to join his friends. 'Don't forget the chips!' She turned back to Rebecca and her plump face wrinkled in a smile that buried her eyes, revealing two front teeth to be missing. 'There's tea in the pot if you want a cup, dearie.' She'd guessed at once that the girl was a stranger, and English. Distinguishing race and language had become a fine art in the mixed community of District Six in Cape Town.

'I'm looking for the Anglican church,' Rebecca called up, holding her small pillbox hat on her head as the south-east wind threatened to tear it off. She'd been surrounded by children, all of them grasping for her white gloved hands and each swearing they'd show her the way better than the other.

'*Foetsek!*' a child's voice yelled, and a small dark boy held on to Rebecca's hand tightly. '*Foetsek!*' he spat at the other children again and his mouth stretched a firm line across his teeth. 'I take you to the *kerk*, madam.' He claimed her and walked on, dragging her behind him. 'You English. I speak English! I not speak that *Boere Hotnottaal*.' He pulled her on as the other children chased them down the narrow winding streets. 'There is it.' The small boy skidded to a stop in front of a sprawling patch of land. Covered in weeds and litter, it separated the houses from a small white church. 'You got money for me to go to the bioscope?' The child's dark face spread in a grin as his creased yellow palms opened in front of her. 'One shilling enough for a film.'

'Where do you live?' Rebecca looked into the dark face that grinned up at her. 'Here?'

'Here?' The boy's eyes widened like astonished marbles. 'District Six is a dangerous place to live, madam,' he informed her. 'Skollies and pimps here. No!' He straightened his tiny body and stood to his full three and a half feet. 'I not live here.'

'Then where do you live?' The fear with which Rebecca had entered the mixed-race area of District Six, regarded as a den of thieves by most white people, had vanished in the face of the small boy. He could have been Johannes Villiers. 'Do you have a home?' She held a shilling out. 'Where do you live?'

'You know the Houses of Parliament?' The child grinned, snatching the shilling. 'Good steps and big doors. I live there – with the Government!' He nodded back across the wasteground. 'And there the *kerk*. OK?' Before Rebecca could answer he was gone.

The cool dark of the church rang with the chattering voices of women as they spread tables with beautifully embroidered cloths, placing elaborate flower arrangements in the centre. The smell of incense, mixed with the ripe hot scent of curry, invaded Rebecca's nostrils as she was swept up into the land of Johannes Villiers.

'Can I help you?' a tall Indian youth called to her as he moved down the aisle. A Tony Curtis curl was planted on his dark forehead, his white teeth shone and a gold filling sparkled its value between smiling lips. 'Are you looking for Father David?' His English was immaculate.

'Yes.'

'Come this way, please.' He turned, moving back up the aisle and Rebecca followed him as he passed the altar. Automatically bowing his head he moved on to the right and ducked through a low arched door.

'I want to trace someone in the church register,' Rebecca called after him as she ducked through the door behind him, her voice echoing in the cool stone passage.

The plump, grey-haired priest ran his fingers under the tight white collar around his neck and closed the large book on the table in front of him. 'Perhaps we'll find something among the baptisms.' Father David turned away from Rebecca and moved to a cupboard.

'But you said he couldn't have been married in the church because there's no marriage recorded.' Rebecca watched the Anglican priest as he emerged from the cupboard, books tumbling round his feet like leather butterflies.

'That doesn't mean there wasn't a child baptised.' Father David's eyes were alight as he lowered the heavy volume on the table in front of Rebecca. He loved sifting through the past. 'Villiers, you said?' His finger ran down a page. 'There are many Villiers, of course. It's a common name in the district.'

'Johannes was his Christian name.' Rebecca had already been through the records of the Catholic church in Cape Town and she'd found nothing. 'He was a Catholic but he wasn't married in the Catholic church either so I really don't understand why you should look for a child.'

'But if he had a woman and that woman was an Anglican . . .' he paused and looked at her as his voice rose on a note of triumph '. . . then the child would be recorded in the Anglican church. Ah!' He pointed at the Registration of Baptism. 'Villiers. Thirteenth of January, 1890. A boy child and the parents' names were . . .' he squinted as he peered at the page '. . . Elizabeth and Nathan Villiers. Uh, uh, you said Johannes.' He hummed, mumbling 'Johannes' to his own tune. 'Ah.' He buried his face in the page in front of him. 'There!' He pointed proudly at an entry.

Elsie Villiers was recorded as having been baptised on 26 September 1887 and beside the entry, written in immaculate black ink, were the words, *Parents: Frances Boesak and Johannes Villiers.*

'It's him!' Rebecca's face was alive with excitement. 'He would have been in his twenties then. It could easily be him.' The priest scrutinised her. Father David had listened to Rebecca's story of her search for Johannes Villiers and he'd enjoyed his own scrummage in the past, but he didn't fully understand. No white person had ever been in his church to trace their ancestors among the coloured folk he served.

'Is there some reason a dead half-caste man is of such importance to a young European woman?' Father David smiled, trying to conceal his very real concern for his flock.

'Elsie Villiers could be his daughter and she could still be alive!' Rebecca's cheeks were flushed with excitement and she'd completely missed the priest's concern. 'I might be able to find her or one of her children.'

'And then?' Father David's question was quiet and he watched Rebecca keenly as he waited for some answers. His head spun with those he wanted to hear but didn't believe he would. 'Elsie Villiers would be a relation of yours, isn't that right?'

'Yes.' Rebecca was suddenly uncomfortable and wanted to get out 'Thank you for your help. You've been very kind.' She got up to go but Father David had already stood up. He smiled and gently took her by the hand, leading her to the vestry door. Opening it wide he looked into the church. The women were still busy, carrying large pots of curry and rice to the tables.

'It's for the poor,' Father David explained. 'A feast for alcoholics and drop-outs. Some are white, you know. White down and outs.' He looked at Rebecca and smiled. The women had stopped their work and stood quite still, watching them. 'They wonder why you're here.'

Held in the women's silent gaze Rebecca felt suddenly unsure of her reasons.

'Why *are* you here, Rebecca?' The priest's eyes begged her for the right answer. 'Is it just idle curiosity, a quick peek into your past?'

'Johannes Villiers was my grandmother's brother – I told you.' Rebecca turned in the doorway, putting on her white gloves.

'You said that, yes.' Father David waited. 'But I wonder where his granddaughter is now? Here in District Six, would you think? Well ...' he shrugged and smiled. 'Maybe not. None of the people will be in their homes soon. Did you know the area's been declared a slum? Odd, isn't it?' He smiled but an edge remained in his voice. 'Seems they've declared this "slum" a white area! Curious, don't you think?' Rebecca watched him in total silence as he went on: 'What will you do if you find Elsie Villiers, Rebecca? Her daughter or her granddaughter, perhaps? Will you cross the border of privilege your white skin affords, or will you simply wave from your side of the fence?'

Rebecca left District Six quickly and walked the streets of Cape Town for hours as she waited to meet Riaan du Toit for the drive home. Father David had forced her to look clearly at what she was doing and Johannes Villiers was no longer just a name. He'd become the victim of a system and Lydia had been proved right. There was no route back through the past, and Johannes Villiers could never regain his place in the Beauvilliers family.

'Rebecca!' The sixteen-year-old Riaan du Toit leaned out of the window of his father's old van and tooted as he spotted her. 'I can't wait here,' he yelled, moving on in erratic leaps as irate drivers shook their fists at him.

'I polish your shoes, lady?' Rebecca glanced down at the young half-caste boy who held a shoe-brush in each hand, his smile as wide as their wooden backs.

'No, thank you.' Rebecca ran towards Riaan as he crawled the car round the edges of Church Square. She didn't know that the young boy sat exactly where Johannes Villiers had once sat, shining an old colonel's boots.

It was a wet and cold Monday morning in 1876 as Johannes Villiers waited on a wooden box under the flopping black wings of an old umbrella. Pouring rain had kept his usual customers away and his polishing brush sat unused in the small tin he carried. As his eyes followed the heavy blobs of rain that slid off the umbrella to fall in slow water bombs at his feet, he wondered again about Colonel Stringer's words on the day he had cleaned his tall black boots for the last time.

'A young lad like you could make something of yourself in the Army.' The old man with sparkling blue eyes had observed Johannes keenly. 'Mark my words, Johannes, the time's coming when Her Majesty's Government will be crying out for the likes of you to serve against the Boer.' Colonel Stringer had been found dead in his bed the next morning, and word had spread quickly among the street children of Cape Town. The striding figure of the old Army colonel had become part of their lives as he rode high on their admiration. He had relived times past with anyone prepared to listen for a penny piece and Johannes had always been ready. Colonel Stringer had talked of his escapades in the British Army, conjuring up the glory of a people destined to run the world. English people who lived in a land of green fields and castles, whose extending arms embraced the southern tip of Africa.

'The Queen herself would welcome you to Buckingham Palace, my lad.' Colonel Stringer had shown him a picture of Queen Victoria and Johannes Villiers had examined it very carefully. He hadn't been that sure he'd like to be welcomed by her, but he'd smiled anyway.

'You say so, baas!' and Colonel Stringer had answered with a hard slap on Johannes' back.

The vibrancy of the old man's presence had stayed with Johannes for the rest of his life. He'd taught the scrawny street child to reach for impossible dreams. The trick was to discover what those dreams were, he'd told him, and at sixteen Johannes Villiers discovered one. It was Frances Boesak, a young girl who lived in District Six and wanted to be a schoolteacher. She was the most beautiful girl Johannes had ever seen, but her parents would not accept the attentions of the shoe-cleaner-cum-tap-dancer, so Johannes had changed his life to suit them.

Making his way through the gates of Cape Town Castle one morning, Johannes held himself erect as Colonel Stringer had taught him.

'Tie yourself by a string to the sky!' Colonel Stringer had lifted the small street child by the hair and his bare feet had dangled over his shoe-cleaning box as the colonel exploded with joy. 'You've grown six inches!' His words had helped Johannes Villiers to stand very tall as a British officer questioned him.

'You speak Dutch?' Johannes Villiers spoke Dutch, English, German and French. Language was an important part of his shoe-cleaning trade and he'd never stopped to wonder which was his own.

'You knew Colonel Stringer?' The British officer was impressed, and listened intently as Johannes embroidered himself into the colonel's war escapades, earning himself a place in the Cape Coloured Mounted Rifles.

The uniform met with more success than he'd expected, and Frances Boesak's parents made immediate wedding plans. But wedding plans were not part of Johannes Villiers' dreams.

'I'm going to England.' This hasty excuse fooled nobody, including himself. Even as Frances gave birth to their daughter Elsie, he kept just one step ahead of matrimonial ties.

'I'm going to England!' he'd shrieked again as he returned home with papers that proved his words. His repeated tales of Colonel Stringer's bush warfare tactics had found their way to the land of castles and queens. They'd been attributed to 'the native intelligence of the Cape Coloured' and, as war loomed between Boer and British, Johannes Villiers had been seconded to British Intelligence. Waving a sad goodbye to Frances and Elsie, he'd sailed away to meet Queen Victoria in Buckingham Palace and had never returned.

'Are you sure your father didn't mind you using his van?' Rebecca asked as she climbed into the passenger seat beside Riaan du Toit. His hair shone with Brylcreem, slicked back in a rollercoaster wave.

'Pa said I could.' Riaan's nose was almost pressed flat against the windscreen as he gripped the steering-wheel tight, trying to avoid each small bump in the road out of Cape Town. He wasn't sure what frightened him most – being alone with Rebecca, or driving his father's van. So many things had changed. Rebecca no longer invaded their territory with her black friend as they played war games and Riaan often watched her from afar. She wasn't a child any more. None of them were and Rebecca was truly beautiful. Curiously silent and aloof, she suggested his inferiority without words and he'd accepted his place. He was happy just to watch her as she sat under the shade of a tree day after day rereading Luke's letters. But now they were alone and he was very nervous.

'You want to go to the dance next week? If you do I'll take you.' Riaan neatly shifted his desire to partner the beautiful Rebecca Conrad on to her. 'If your parents say yes, then I don't mind,' he added, but Rebecca wasn't listening.

Her mind was back in District Six among the ramshackle houses and dark-skinned people. They held a small part of herself in their midst, but Father David had challenged her to look again at her reasons for digging Johannes Villiers from his grave.

'Why wouldn't you come into District Six with me?' Rebecca knew that underneath the greased hair and long trousers, Riaan was still a small boy, the one who had called Thabo a pikkanin as they'd hurled abuse at one another, along with stones. 'Have you ever been there?'

'What for?' Riaan's nose moved closer to the windscreen as a toot came from behind and a car flew past. 'It's full of bloody Hotnots.' He wound his window up quickly against the dust that ploughed back at them from the passing car. 'Why'd you go there anyway?' His English was as sloppy as his jaw.

'To see my cousin.' Rebecca laughed as he turned and looked at her with an expression of absolute amazement. Then his mouth curled up in a smile and his eyes twinkled the hope that she was fooling.

'Watch out!' She screamed as a car flashed past. 'Keep your mind on the road, stupid,' she shouted over the screeching horn of the car that had just missed them. 'Don't worry, I was only kidding.' Rebecca needed Riaan for days like this and she had no intention of breaking the spell she held over him.

'You want to go to the dance?' he asked again over the drone of the engine as they drew closer to the blue haze of mountains up ahead.

'Why don't you turn off the road here?' Rebecca nodded at a narrow dirt road that cut off to the left and Riaan's Adam's apple stood out in surprise.

'You mean that?' He glanced at her nervously. He'd stopped breathing and his voice had slipped off its pitch. 'You want to stop here?' He swung the wheel and the car skidded off the road, bumping its way across the hard shoulder till it juddered to a dusty stop. His tongue ran over his front teeth quickly and he wished he hadn't bought the hot garlicky samosa from the Indian trader in Green Market Square. 'You sure?' His heart drummed loudly and he hoped she couldn't hear it.

'It's what you want, isn't it?' Rebecca's body was tense, but she was determined to go ahead with her plans. It didn't seem that long since she'd gone into the cellars late one afternoon when her parents were asleep. She'd been nearly fourteen years old and her tiny new breasts had prickled as she'd spotted Riaan's father, Christian du Toit.

He'd been standing beside a vat, drawing off a little wine for blending and everything about him had been masculine. She'd wanted just to be near him, as Althea was near Luke, and she'd spoken nervously.

'What are you doing?' She'd stepped back the moment he'd turned to her. Christian du Toit was dark. His eyes glowed when he looked at her and she was certain the winemaker of Bonne Espérance secretly loved her.

'How's school?' Christian asked the same question he always asked and Rebecca had tossed her head back, fixing him with a look.

'How's work?' she'd retorted, moving a little closer.

'Riaan was looking for you earlier.' Christian had gone back to the vat as if she hadn't been there at all. He hadn't even seen her and had passed her on to his thirteen-year-old son.

'I don't play with Riaan. He's only a child,' Rebecca had pouted, glancing up at him from under thick dark lashes. 'Why don't you like me being here?' Her mind had leapt back to the pages of Emily's diaries, to the night Emily had found Prudence in the same dark cellars. Something strange had happened, Emily's diary said, and Rebecca had guessed that the winemaker M. Claudelle had been responsible. She wanted to know what happened between men and girls when they were alone. She was certain Althea was often alone with Luke in places as dark as cellars.

'Do you like me?' Rebecca asked, and Christian du Toit laughed. 'Don't laugh!' Every part of her had reached out to him as a woman but pulled back as a child. 'I'm nearly fourteen!' She'd run out of the cellars quickly. The body she'd imagined as round and full with the allure of a woman, had reverted to the angular collection of stretched limbs she saw in the mirror each day. The two delicate buds on her chest were no more than angry pimples and Rebecca had felt deeply ashamed.

'What are you waiting for, Riaan? Don't be scared.' She wondered if she'd be as frightened if Riaan had been Luke, but quickly she pushed the thought away. It was Luke she was trying to exorcise. Trying to break herself free of a promise he'd never really made. Rebecca had guessed that Althea was not just a friend, and alone in her bed in the dark of night, she'd burned with a jealous anger. She wanted Luke to feel the same anger: the same jealousy and pain that she felt each time he mentioned Althea in his letters. But more than anything, she longed to break free of a childhood dream and Riaan could help her do it.

'I am scared.' Riaan was staring at the outline of Rebecca's right breast as it pushed against the cotton of her bodice. A small button had snapped off and her delicate pink skin was clearly visible. 'Can I touch it?' His hand moved nervously towards her breast and his face loomed closer to hers. Closing her eyes quickly, she felt the tickle of his seedling moustache and against her pink eyelids she drew a picture of Luke. Luke was tall and handsome. Luke's hand was reaching for her breast. Luke's mouth was on hers and she pushed her breast forward against his strong wide hand.

'What's wrong?' Rebecca's eyes flew open. Riaan had pulled his hand away as if burned by fire and Luke vanished in the face of the terrified boy beside her.

'Shit!' Riaan pushed the van door open and jumped out. He walked away from the car with his thighs apart, peering down between his legs uncomfortably. 'Shit! Shit! Shit!' He spat at a small stone, stubbing his toe as he kicked it.

'It doesn't matter, Riaan.' Rebecca leaned back against the lumpy van seat and a silent laugh rumbled deep inside her. Pimpled, insecure and unable to control his own body, Riaan was her reality and Luke just the dream of a small girl on an ant-hill. Lydia was right. Johannes Villiers had been merely the excuse for her dreams being untrue.

'Let's go home,' she said quietly. Her longing for Luke had vanished in one fumbling moment and she spoke gently as Riaan looked at her shamefaced. 'It's all right.' She realised how close she'd come to destroying an adolescent boy along with herself. 'I'm sorry.'

As Riaan dropped her silently at the gate of Bonne Espérance, Rebecca saw the soft glow of light in the sitting room and she ran towards the safety of her family. Her smile turned to a quiet giggle as she remembered Riaan sitting half an inch off the driver's seat all the way home. The inadequacy of the moment had made her face up to herself and at last she was free of Luke.

'Mum?' The word crept out of Rebecca's mouth on a whisper of astonishment. As she ran to the house, she'd been met by a mixture of sights and sounds she'd never experienced before. The sitting-room curtains were wide open and her mother was in her father's arms. Old-fashioned music scratched its way through the loudspeakers of the gramophone and a deep male voice crooned *Honeysuckle Rose* as David led Constance round in a curious dance.

Her mother was smiling at her father. She looked hideous but she was smiling as if he'd just said she was beautiful. A bright silk scarf was tied tight across her forehead and its long ends streamed behind her as she twirled in David's arms. The glimmering gold lamé dress she wore was too tight, reaching inches short of her chubby red knees.

'The Charleston!' Constance jumped up and down like an overgrown child. Her knees twisted and her hands waved like the blades of a broken windmill. Lipstick was smeared in a bright arch across her top lip and blue paint smudged its way round her eyes. 'Another Fats Waller song. Do you remember *Black Bottom*? Play that one!'

'One at a time,' David said, and Rebecca stared at her father. He was smiling as he changed the record, dropping a scratchy needle on to another as if nothing was wrong at all. He was still smiling as he moved back to Constance while she danced in front of him. The roll of her stomach was accentuated by the tight short dress and her hips pushed the skirt up to reveal the dip of sagging pants below its hem.

'Shall we dance?' David beamed at Constance, moving his hands and legs in the same pigeon-toed movements she performed. 'The *Windsor Castle*'s a nice boat, isn't she?' he called over the music. He was still smiling, but his smile was empty. 'I'm going to Cape Town to see how I like it. I might even go further north in Africa to settle. Where are you going?' he asked his wife, as if she was a stranger.

'Dance!' Constance yelled, her body twisting in ungainly shapes as her legs kicked out clumsily.

Rebecca pulled back from the window as her lungs snatched for the ice-cold air surrounding her and she realised she was looking in on a nightmare. She rubbed at the water on the glass that distorted her view and peered through it again but it was her own tears she'd tried to wipe away, and they were still there.

'Do you remember Charles Barlow? That chap who had dinner with us at the Captain's table last night?' David asked her mother, his voice casual but his eyes desperate.

'No.' Constance hadn't stopped dancing though the music had ended. 'Why do you keep asking me if I remember people I don't even know? Dance! I remember the music and it's lovely. Dance! Dance!'

Rebecca spun away from the window and ran. She ran away from the house. She ran far away from the strange people who had once been her parents. She ran far enough not to hear the music, see her mother's terrifying display of insanity or hear her father's constant questions.

'Oh God!' She turned her face up to the darkening canopy of sky and a distant star flickered before vanishing behind a cloud. 'What's happening?' she screamed into the night that had at last hidden her mother among its dark folds.

CHAPTER ELEVEN

A heavy mist hung low over Bonne Espérance, as if hiding it from the shame of the night before. It seeped under the huge arched doors of the cellars and crept silently over the cobbled courtyard as Miriam and Simon's feet trod softly through it.

'I give it her now.' Simon clutched a small brown paper parcel tightly to his chest and achievement shone in his eyes. 'Rebecca seventeen!' He said proudly as they walked towards the house. The dark thatch of the roof was lost in the mist and even the white walls had melted away. 'Her birthday!'

'That's right.' Miriam had woken early that morning to find Simon already in her room and together they'd wrapped the small horse he'd carved for Rebecca's present. They'd used the brown paper Miriam always salvaged from the rubbish, ironing it till it shone like new. Miriam had taught Simon to carve, as her father had taught her. She'd watched him swell with pride as a horse appeared in the piece of wood they worked on and his eyes had lit with wonder at his first small creation. He'd decided at once that it was for Rebecca.

'What you say when you give it?' Miriam asked, as she'd asked every morning that week.

'Happy birthday.' Simon clutched his gift tightly.

'And what you sing?' Miriam smiled. Simon's pride had warmed the morning and her voice rose with his in a curious duet as *Happy Birthday* lifted into the mist before being swallowed by the cotton-wool silence around them.

Rebecca stood at her bedroom window, gazing into the swirling damp clouds outside. She could see the shimmering shadows of Miriam and Simon in the distance but she didn't register them. Her mind was on the strange scene she'd witnessed the night before.

'She remembered nothing.' David sat on Rebecca's bed, gazing blankly at the floor as his daughter listened. His voice was hollow with despair and behind his eyes was a sadness Rebecca had never seen before. 'I tried to take your mother back to the night we first met. The music, the Charleston ... the dress.' David shook his head. Though an image of her mother still danced grotesquely in her mind, Rebecca pushed it back and waited for him to go on. 'That dress,' he looked up at her, his eyes reflecting total loss. 'She wore that dress the night we met. On the boat. She wore it then and all these years she kept it.' His head dropped into his hands and his voice fell to a whisper. 'But she remembered nothing.' David looked up at his daughter from a pit of despair, but he said no more. Everything had been wiped out.

'Missy Rebecca?' Miriam stepped into the doorway with Simon beside her. His mouth was pulled straight to hold back the beaming grin of pride that strained to express itself as he clutched the brownpaper parcel.

'Not now, please.' Rebecca turned away from the door impatiently and Miriam took Simon by the shoulders, moving him out as she did. He looked round in surprise, his mouth open for a rendering of *Happy Birthday* but he was dragged quickly away by Miriam.

'We sing soon,' Miriam tried to reassure the puzzled boy as she walked him back to the kitchen. 'They busy.'

'The horse.' Simon held the brown-paper package up to her as if it no longer belonged to him. 'For Rebecca's birthday.'

'The cake!' Miriam clapped her hands and all of her shook as she led Simon to the kitchen table in a show of excitement. A large cake, covered in white icing, sat on the table. It was usually Constance who made the family birthday cakes but only Miriam had remembered this one. 'You want to put the candles on? You can count to seventeen?' she asked Simon, placing a box of used candles in front of him like a prize. 'How many is seventeen?' But Simon's shoulders had lifted in an uninterested shrug and he clutched the brown-paper package to himself in silence.

'You want Rebecca have candles on her cake?' Miriam's voice scolded, though her heart ached. She'd felt the rejection as Simon had, but was determined it wouldn't spoil the occasion. 'There's seventeen candles.' She laid the candles on the table one at a time. 'Like this you put them on the cake.' She stuck a small candle into the white icing, handing another to him. 'Simon put on the candles while Miriam work.' She moved to the kitchen door. 'I come get you when Rebecca ready.'

As Simon sat alone at the kitchen table, his hand pressed against the hard wood of his carving inside the package. He longed to take it out. When he looked at the small wooden horse he'd made he saw himself on its back and he didn't really want to give it away. He wanted to keep it

230

for ever. To look at it always and see himself riding majestically on its back.

Footsteps on the wooden floor outside caught his attention and he moved to the kitchen door quickly. Standing to the side, he peered through the gap between the door and the wall. David was alone and he walked straight past him to the front door.

'Rebecca!' Simon called in a secret whisper towards her bedroom. 'You there, Rebecca?' he called again. But still she didn't come to her door and he couldn't understand what was wrong. Birthdays were days to get presents like wooden horses. Days of jellies, ice creams and cakes. 'Rebecca!' The small brown-paper package reached towards her as she stepped out of her room, but she moved away without seeing him.

'Where I wear this, madam?' Miriam's voice was filled with amazement as she examined the gold lamé dress Constance had given her. As if she might find the answer to her question in the seams, she pulled at them, her fingers tugging at the fine gold mesh as she peered at it. 'Where you wear this dress, madam?' She looked at Constance in amazement.

But Constance sat silent and still in front of the dressing table. Watching Miriam through the mirror, she was trying to understand what the black woman in the room was talking about.

'For my sister's child maybe.' Miriam's concentration was back on the dress. 'My sister say Zinzi dance well – like Missy Rebecca.' In a moment Miriam's soft round body was twisting and heaving in a bizarre rock jive. Her behind swung independently of her body and her feet twisted squeaky circles on the polished wood floor. 'You do that, madam?' She collapsed in a bubbling heap of chocolate laughter. 'In that dress?' But as Miriam looked at Constance in the mirror her laughter died. Her mistress' face was devoid of expression and the strange sickness seemed worse today than the day before.

'I go make you breakfast now.' Miriam pushed herself off the floor, hanging the dress over her arm like a gold dishcloth. 'You all right?' She glanced at Constance, her voice a gentle lilt of concern.

'Yes.' Constance didn't know why the black woman in her room had danced so suddenly and she wished she'd go away.

'Missy Rebecca!' Miriam looked at Rebecca as she came into the room. She wanted to help her mistress but didn't know how. 'I bring you breakfast up here with your mother?' she asked. 'You stay with her? – keep her company?' On the tip of Miriam's tongue sat the words, 'Happy Birthday,' but she held them back for Simon to say first. 'I get breakfast.' She left the room quickly.

'Why don't you join us in the dining room today?' Rebecca moved to her mother, wrapping her arms around her from behind. 'Do you remember when we used to have breakfast outside in the summer and ...'

'Why does everyone keep asking if I remember? Of course I remember!' Constance got up and went towards her bed.

'OK.' Rebecca held back the swell of fear that had filled her throat as she'd seen her mother's feet. She wore a slipper on her right foot and a shoe on the left. Dark hairs stood out on her legs like the stubble of a forest fire and her skin was a dull flaking white. The immaculate woman she'd watched pulling on shiny nylon stockings which came from England was gone. Everything about her was different. 'I'll change these for you.' Rebecca pulled off the shoe on her mother's foot as she lay down on the bed.

'Someone keeps hiding my slipper.' Constance closed her eyes and turned away. As if she needed it for comfort, she tugged at the candlewick bedspread. 'It's probably that black woman. She's always in here nosing around – and she stole my gold lamé dress.' Constance's eyes flew open as Rebecca pushed the left slipper on to her foot. 'Where did you find that?' She kicked the slipper off like a petulant child. 'I don't need slippers when I'm on the bed.' The slipper tumbled to the floor and Rebecca held tight to her own composure.

'You're as bad as Granny Cat.' She didn't notice the sudden flicker of recognition in her mother's eyes as she spoke. 'Do you remember when Granny and I were supposed to bath in Bulawayo station? Well, she didn't.' Rebecca kept her voice light. 'She just sat on the toilet and made splashing sounds in the water.' Rebecca stopped talking. Silent tears were running down her mother's cheeks in strings of liquid beads and she knew that she *had* remembered. Constance was back on the train. She was looking at her mother's body as it lay quite still on the bottom bunk of a small compartment.

'We shouldn't have brought her.' Constance's whisper called from a mislaid past. 'I never told her it wasn't to punish her. That we weren't taking her back to Bonne Espérance because she wasn't ...' Constance's eyes had quite suddenly fixed on Rebecca as if seeing her for the first time. 'What's happening to me?'

'Don't cry, please! It's all right.' Rebecca pulled her mother into her arms as tears, built up over the years without release, released Constance's grief. 'Dad's here. It's all right.' She tried to comfort her.

David stood in the doorway behind them, watching in bewilderment as the roles were reversed and his daughter comforted his wife.

'Everything's all right now.' Rebecca looked at her father and smiled. 'We're going home.'

Miriam had tried to keep Simon occupied all morning. He insisted with each passing minute that it must be time to give Rebecca her present and sing *Happy Birthday*, but she had to keep delaying him.

'Maybe after lunch,' she said.

But after lunch the right time had still not arrived. Rebecca and her father had been in the sitting room for hours. They'd made phone calls. They'd argued, and still there was no conclusion in sight.

'I know we left because of me, Dad, but I also know it's the only place Mum might get well. She loved 123 Z. We all did.' Rebecca was trying to convince him that they must go back to the small mining town for her mother's sake. In some way they had to retrace the steps they'd taken which had cost Granny Cat her life and which now threatened her mother. Perhaps then Constance might find herself again. 'Uncle Dewi would love us to come.' Rebecca also knew how much her father would like to go back. She knew that nobody really wanted to leave the obscure little town that still held their hearts in its dusty streets. They'd left too quickly to say goodbye to so large a part of their lives. Each one of them had memories still buried in the land of ant hills and squat trees.

'What about you?' David could see his small daughter clutching a baby in a tree on top of an ant hill and he recalled the ugly faces of the women, accusing her of something they didn't understand themselves as a shade of skin cast his daughter to the outer realms of loneliness. But David was already back in the hoisthouse of Stork shaft. His feet had already trod the fine golden sand of Z Avenue and he knew that in many ways he'd never left.

'It's going to be all right, Dad,' Rebecca said and her father's face lightened as the years lifted. He smiled and she saw once again the man who could mend a bird's wing at the same time as he healed a child's heart. 'I want to go home too,' she said simply. 'I think I understand now.'

Rebecca looked up as Miriam gave Simon a gentle push in the back. They stood at the entrance to the sitting room but Simon didn't move as his weight leaned back against Miriam's hand.

'What is it, Simon?' Rebecca vaguely remembered that he had been somewhere close by her all day. He'd wanted something, but she didn't know what.

'Tell her, Happy Birthday,' Miriam whispered in his ear but Simon stood silent, clutching his small package in his hand. As some people sensed rain in the far distance on a bright summer's day, so Simon had sensed tears.

'Good grief!' David hit his forehead as he suddenly remembered what day it was. 'Happy Birthday, darling.' He pulled Rebecca into his arms. 'Happy Birthday.' He held her tightly and only then did Rebecca's tears break. They ran in slow streams down her cheeks and buried themselves in her father's jacket. 'Say "Happy Birthday" to Rebecca, Simon.'

But Simon had turned away. With the small wooden horse still clutched in his hand he walked slowly out of the room.

As the train rattled relentlessly through miles of spreading scrubland that met the hot white sky in an invisible horizon, Luke stared at his reflection in the carriage window.

'Like Australia.' The flat North of England voice of the large lady beside him rambled on. 'But they haven't got the Afrikaners there, of course. Or blacks. Just aborigines. Or is it Maoris?' Luke tried to hold his mind back from the buzz of sleep that tugged at it. 'They killed theirs off, of course. Like the Americans killed the Red Indians.'

Caught in the twilight zone on the borders of sleep, Luke saw a group of Africans, dressed as Red Indians. They raced beside the train across the dusty plains of the Karoo, their feathered headdresses stark against the sky. 'That's why they wear corks in their hats, you know — because of the flies.' A cowboy with corks dangling from his stetson chased the Africans while a swarm of flies chased him. 'You asleep?' The sharp dig of an elbow in his side sent Luke spiralling down a well on the end of an elastic band. 'You awake?' Luke jumped as the elastic band snapped back just before he reached the bottom. 'You fell asleep!' He stared at the woman blankly as she scolded him. Her powder-puff cheeks had buried her eyes as they met the corrugated folds of her forehead in a smile. 'Not much else to do, is there?' Like a turtle in a turquoise hat, her neck pulled into her body and her chin buried itself between the tweed lapels of her jacket.

Luke glanced at the magazine in his lap but didn't read it. His thoughts were back where they'd been since the train had pulled out of Johannesburg station the night before. He was thinking again about Bonne Espérance, a place that still called him back, its voice carried on the whispers of memory.

Estelle hadn't come to see him off. She hadn't spoken to Luke in all the time that had passed since he'd told her he was going, but the woman next to him had made up for that when she'd asked to share his compartment. With her lips slightly parted, she shivered as each breath slipped down the embroidered front of her blouse and Luke leaned his head against the carriage seat, his mind relaxing back among the mellow folds of Bonne Espérance. It was an island of hope in a life of storms and its call grew stronger the closer the train drew to the Cape.

A gentle squeak announced the passing of wind between the leather seat and the woman's corseted behind and Luke smiled. Turning away he gazed through the window again, wondering how much longer before the steep sides of purple mountains would rise alongside the train.

A rubbery underwater puncture bubbled between leather and flesh and the woman's shivering lips snatched a quick guttural snore. Watching her carefully, Luke listened as a rumble of flatulence preceded a salvo of machine gun farts and she dropped deeper into sleep. Quickly, before the compartment ignited with her fumes, he moved into the rattling corridor outside. Lurching for the window, he stuck his head into the dry stream of air that rushed at him.

'You all right, sir?' Luke pulled his head inside as a steward stood behind him with a tray balanced on his hand, his spread feet steadying him in the swaying corridor. 'Coffee or tea, sir?'

'No, thank you.' Luke's face was still spread with a smile as they were plunged into sudden darkness, the thunder of steel wheels churning the solid black air around them.

'Won't be long now,' the steward's voice shouted through the noise as Luke stared into the blackness.

Charcoal brick walls flew past his face in a sweep of smutty air, mixing into a gentle clatter as the darkness of a tunnel vanished in the face of the sun. The high granite walls of mountains ran a solid curve up ahead and the train snaked its way towards them. Far below, a valley spread itself wide in the richest of greens and the soles of Luke's feet tingled as they sensed the red earth of home.

Rebecca walked towards the vineyards with Simon's small wooden horse held tightly in her hand. She wanted to be alone. The entire day had been spent planning their journey back into Central Africa but she knew that 123 Z was no longer her home. Bonne Espérance had taken its place.

The small attic room that snuggled under the thatch, the room in which Emily had found her mother's diary and had kept her own, that room had claimed her. It held her heart with Luke's alongside the heart of Jean Jacques and Bonne Espérance.

Turning Simon's small horse in her hand Rebecca studied the yellow veins in the dark wood. They wound round misshapen legs to form a thick neck that reached forward in a clumsy head. The carving was the most beautiful thing she'd ever seen. She'd found Simon in the stables beside the pony he always rode and finally he'd handed her his present. The pony on whose back he'd built an image of himself.

'It's beautiful, Simon.' Rebecca had run her hand down the back of his head as Simon watched her, but he'd pulled away from her touch. 'Is it your pony?' He'd stepped further back as if warning her not to come too close. 'Or is it Salu?' Rebecca asked.

'You leave Simon!' he shouted, his eyes firing arrows of accusation. 'You go away from Simon!'

'But you're coming, too. We're all going, Simon.' Rebecca pulled his body close to hers, allowing her own very real fears to join his. 'Mr du Toit is going to look after Bonne Espérance when we're away and very soon we'll be back.' Rebecca smiled through the lie she'd held up even to herself. She knew it was possible they might never return to the place that had claimed her heart. 'And Miriam will stay here too while we're away. And your horse ...'

'Thabo.' Simon's eyes filled with the warmth that was Thabo as he spoke his name. 'Thabo come too?'

'He's coming back soon.' Rebecca fought to keep her voice light. She'd heard from Miriam that Thabo was still in the Transkei. 'Do you know there are ant hills in Northern Rhodesia?' She tried to interest Simon. 'Did you know the ant hills on the other side of the Zambezi are the biggest ant hills in the world? As big as houses!' Simon had listened in silence and the glow of Thabo had slowly left his eyes. Sadness had descended on him like a cloud and he stared through it at the small wooden horse in her hand.

'There horses?' he asked quietly. 'Horses there?'

'No. There's tsetse fly in Northern Rhodesia so they can't keep horses. They'd get sleeping sickness, you see.'

Simon had pulled away and ran out of the stables before Rebecca had finished, realising that this time, the tears he'd sensed in the distance were his own.

'I'll see you up at the house.' Luke climbed out of Lydia's car as it stopped in front of the huge white arch that held the gates of Bonne Espérance wide. As she pulled away, driving slowly up the long drive that led to the house, Lydia's small son, Joe, waved at him through the back window, but Luke didn't see him. He was gazing across the miles of spreading vineyards that nestled at the feet of the most glorious mountains in the world. He was walking back into his own childhood and felt a sudden rush of water over his body.

A black face grinned down at him from the roof of the stables as Thabo held a bucket high over his head.

'*Wowa!*' he shouted, dropping the bucket in fright before scrambling over the thatch of the stable roof to escape Luke's mother, Estelle.

'What's wrong now?' Luke heard his own voice calling in his head. He'd called to a little girl with a mass of dark hair that fell over her face to hide her eyes. She was struggling with the weight of a small boy she carried on her back and her face was suddenly in front of his own. Her eyes were very dark and they peered into his soul.

'*The key will keep us together on Bonne Espérance.*'

Luke found himself running. He was running through rows of spreading vines and his spirit soared with the release of at last being back where he belonged. Not among memories. Not with the children who were a part of those memories. He was home and free of memory at last.

It wasn't a small girl or an old key that made Bonne Espérance his home. It wasn't a mongol child or a black friend who had welcomed him. It was the land itself. The rich red earth trodden down by countless feet before his own, yet still alive with hope. He was surrounded by a feeling so extraordinary he knew he could never explain it to anyone else but it no longer mattered. Bonne Espérance had welcomed Luke back like a mother.

'I'm home!' he shouted, his voice racing ahead of him as it skipped over the low canopy of spreading green leaves. 'I'm here!' His words raced up the sides of the purple mountains in front of him and a gentle echo answered, 'I'm home! I'm here!'

Rebecca looked up as she sat alone under the shade of a huge tree on a slight rise beyond the vineyards. She'd heard a voice calling in the distance and she'd seen a man running through the vines. His legs took long leaping strides and his jacket flew back, his tie whipping over his shoulders in a flapping wave.

'Riaan?' she mumbled to herself, but immediately she knew it wasn't Riaan. It was a man. She'd never seen the man before and he'd stopped at the edge of the vineyards. He'd turned to her.

'Hullo,' his voice called across the wide stretch of land between them, and Rebecca wondered why she wanted to run – she wanted to run away from this stranger who was moving towards her. He was walking towards her and now she wanted to run towards him. But he'd stopped. He stood still and totally silent. She could make out the outline of his face against the setting sun and she peered at it, her heart beating in the hollow of her chest. The man's face was strong and the angle of his cheekbones was accentuated by thick, dark-blond hair cut short into his neck. He was walking towards her again and again she pulled back instinctively. The hard bark of the tree dug into her back and her hands gripped the rough wood for security.

'What do you want?' Rebecca's puzzled voice called to him nervously. 'Who are you?' A part of her ran ahead of her thoughts towards him and she pulled back against the tree, terrified by her own impulses. 'This is private property. You're trespassing,' she shouted, trying to chase the curious longings from inside her.

The young woman in the distance was quite suddenly clear in Luke's vision and he stopped walking. Her hair was long and dark and her body slender. She was beautiful. Though he'd never seen her before he walked a little faster towards her and then he found he was running. His body leaned towards her, his mind reached out to take her and as her eyes touched his in a moist glance of disbelief, Luke stopped breathing.

'Rebecca?' His voice rode a question mark as he stared at her. 'Is it Rebecca?' She nodded and her eyes sparkled as she reached for him.

'I don't believe it.' Her words were as quiet as the gentle breeze that pushed at the vines in rustling recognition as she ran towards him. 'Luke!' Her spirit lifted as she reached him, pulling back as his eyes held her in a steady gaze.

'Happy Birthday,' Luke said. But he didn't move any closer.

'Thank you.' Rebecca's lips were touched by a smile. With the small distance left between them still uncrossed, their spirits met. They were balanced on the edge of time, held still by an emotion that neither had felt before.

Simon hadn't spoken to Miriam since he'd given his present to Rebecca. His world had come to an end with the news that they were going to a land without horses and the only person he wanted was Thabo. He needed the warmth and security his name conjured up. He'd seen Lydia's car drive up to the front of the house, and he'd seen her small son clamber out of it. Joe had rushed through the front door calling for him, but Simon hadn't answered. He'd hidden in his bedroom instead; surrounded by the junk piled high on the floor of the large cupboard, he'd stared into the darkness. He could feel the button eyes of a teddy bear fixed on him and the hard metal of a train set dug into his bare legs as he sat on it, but he didn't move.

'Where are you, Simon?' Joe looked around the bedroom curiously. Miriam had told him that Simon was there but his friend was nowhere to be seen and he wondered if perhaps he'd magicked himself away. Simon was very special, his mother had once told him. Though he looked a little stupid, she'd said that Joe must always remember Simon was not stupid. It was then Joe had decided that the boy with the peculiar swollen face and lolling tongue was not only not stupid – he was a magician.

'Simon,' he called cautiously, his eyes searching the deserted room as he wondered if perhaps Simon had magicked himself to death, 'it's me.' Joe threw his voice into the emptiness around him but only silence answered. Wondering if Simon had made himself invisible, Joe pulled back to the door in terror. He could feel him. He could hear his heavy breathing. Turning in a tiny circle of fear, Joe shouted, 'I can see you, Simon!'

'What!' Simon's amazed voice crept under the wooden door of the cupboard and Joe stared.

'I can't see you.' Joe's bottom lip trembled and all the proud years of his life vanished. 'Where are you?' His voice melted into dripping tears as he stared into the empty space around him.

'I not here,' Simon's disembodied voice came again. 'Go away!' The cupboard door creaked open and a battered teddy bear rolled out, landing on its ear with just one button eye fixed on him.

'Mommy!' With his heart in his mouth, Joe backed towards the door. 'Mommy!' he screamed louder as Simon stepped out in front of him, his legs apart and his body swaying to find its balance. An old and very large Army jacket sat heavily over Simon's shoulders, its long red arms hanging to the floor like crumpled windsocks. Tattered gold epaulettes stood out in frayed fringes on the broad shoulders and rusty brass buttons swung from stretching threads to touch the floor.

'Sshhh!!' Simon moved to Joe. 'Ssshhh!' A spray of saliva shot into Joe's face and he screamed again. 'Sshh!' Simon clamped his hand firmly over Joe's mouth. The small boy's eyes were circles of terror as the monster who'd emerged from the cupboard held him back. With a sharp bite he brought his teeth together around the edge of Simon's hand and the red jacket tumbled from his shoulders.

'It's you!' Joe gawped as Simon stood back innocently, sucking his hand as the crumpled red monster lay at his feet. Seeing Joe's very real terror, Simon wrapped his arms around the small boy quickly and held him tight. Patting him on the head like a comforting parent he repeated a salivary, 'Ssshhh.'

'What on earth's going on?' Lydia stood in the doorway. An army jacket lay at the children's feet like a dead soldier and they both looked at her innocently. 'Don't scream when you play, Joe.' She moved to her son, taking his hand to lead him away. 'Supper's nearly ready and Rebecca will be cutting her cake.' Joe tugged against his mother's arm with his eyes fixed on Simon.

'We playing.' All he wanted to do was to join Simon in his game of soldiers.

'Then don't scream.' Lydia glanced at the jacket. 'And tidy up this room when you've finished.'

'Yes, Mommy.' Joe's face shone with innocence, determined his mother would never know how frightened he'd been.

'And you'd better come out to see Luke soon, Simon. He's come all the way for Rebecca's birthday and you must come and say hullo.'

Simon had no idea who she was talking about.

'I take it in here, Miss Lydia?' Miriam asked, meeting Lydia on her way to the sitting room. She was carrying Rebecca's birthday cake on a large tray, and her dark face glowed with pride.

'Isn't that beautiful, Miriam! Where is the birthday girl anyway? Does she know Luke's here?'

'Miss Rebecca outside, madam.' Miriam trundled off with the cake. 'I lay it with the dinner. Yes?'

'Yes.' But Lydia's mind was outside where she'd left Luke – where Rebecca had apparently gone. When she'd met him at Cape Town station Lydia hadn't recognised her young nephew.

'I don't believe it,' she'd exclaimed as he held out his hand to her politely. 'You were no bigger than a tickey on a brick when you left.'

On the drive from the station to Bonne Espérance, Lydia had noticed a reserve about Luke. He'd asked questions about his brother, Simon, about the vineyards and about his horse, Salu, but he hadn't once mentioned Rebecca.

'Lydia,' David called, putting his head round the sitting-room door. 'Can I see you for a moment?'

Miriam glanced up as the door closed behind Lydia and David. She knew what they would be talking about. The same thing David had told her earlier in the day and about which she'd been wondering ever since. Wondering if she'd ever see the family again.

'Miriam!' She stopped as a headless red jacket moved towards her. Two tiny bare feet shuffled underneath it and long empty sleeves polished the wooden floor. Simon was guiding the apparition from behind and he grinned at her sheepishly.

'Boo!' The red jacket fell to the floor, revealing the small figure of Joe. 'I do magic like Simon,' he said proudly.

But neither of the children knew that the dead soldier whose jacket they played with, meant something to Miriam. It was a small part of the story her people told of the murder of Jean Jacques Beauvilliers. Though it had happened a hundred years before, it was the very beginning of a journey the family was about to make back into Central Africa.

'You see your brother Luke yet?' Miriam asked, and Simon wondered again why everyone wanted him to see Luke. He couldn't place his name among his feelings at all.

'Come!' he called to Joe, scooping the jacket off the floor as he dragged him away to avoid more talk of someone he didn't know.

Lydia listened quietly as David explained their plan to return to the small

240

mining town. Although she couldn't see the sense of such a journey, she said nothing.

'I'm sure it'll be very good for Constance,' she smiled. 'And for you. To be honest, I don't think you ever settled here.'

'It's not really my kind of life.' David tried to hide his true feelings behind a smile. 'But we're not going for good,' he added quickly, as if he knew Lydia had guessed that they were. 'Christian's going to run Bonne Espérance. He's going to move into the house with his family ...'

'And Simon?' Lydia looked at David, her head tilted to one side.

'He's coming with us, of course. Where is Luke, by the way?' David moved to the window, trying to escape Lydia's questioning eyes. 'What's he like now? I was quite fond of the lad, you know. I've no idea how he's survived that mother of his.'

'She's Simon's mother too, David. You'll need Estelle's permission to take him.' Lydia fell silent as he turned and looked at her. In many ways David had blamed Simon for his wife's illness and she knew it. Constance had devoted much of her time to the child in the years before she'd become ill, and David had often resented his intrusion into their life.

'We adopted him legally. She didn't complain then, so why now?' The sudden threat of Estelle pushed David's discomfort about Simon to one side. 'Legally we can do as we like, and we can live where we like.' As Lydia nodded David knew that Simon was not really the issue; he waited, aware that she was on the threshold of the truth – his real reason for taking his wife back to Central Africa.

'In all this time Constance has never seen a doctor, David.'

'No.' David's eyes lit with sudden challenge. 'If the medical profession had come up with the cure for a broken heart, I might have thought about it, Lydia. But no.' He turned back to the window, stopping as he saw Luke. He was with Rebecca and as she waved he noticed the slight brush of Luke's hand against hers.

'They look good together,' Lydia said quietly, her eyes settling on the young couple outside. Luke and Rebecca were gazing into one another's eyes.

'I think it's time Simon said hullo to his brother.' Lydia left the room, knowing that David would still not face up to his wife's illness.

Though Rebecca kept a small distance between herself and Luke, their senses reached across to touch one another. An electric current had passed between them the moment they'd met and it was still there.

'When did you arrive?' Rebecca glanced at him as he walked beside her. She was drawn to him in a way she couldn't understand and longed just to touch his hand. It was as if she'd never met Luke before. Her childhood memories had been replaced by an inexplicable urgency.

'Did you come by train? How long are you staying? Imagine Lydia doing that! It's wonderful!' Her words tumbled out meaninglessly as she held back the powerful longings that burned inside her.

'Lydia met me at the station.' Luke allowed himself to be drawn into the mystical glow of Rebecca's eyes and goosebumps rose on his skin. He'd stepped back into the circle of Rebecca's presence and had been captured. He'd become a part of her, yet he knew nothing about her.

'Hey!' They turned to the side of the house as Joe's voice called. 'Come see Luke, Simon!' Joe stepped around the corner of the house but Simon didn't follow him. Luke's name meant nothing, though he'd gathered it should mean a great deal. He'd hunted for some feeling that matched the name but all he'd felt was a deep loss and Simon hung back behind the white wall of the house rather than face it.

'I'll get him.' Rebecca moved towards Joe. He was tugging at Simon's hand but Simon still didn't emerge from round the corner of the house. 'He might find it hard to remember you,' she called back to Luke. She could feel his eyes on her and as she reached Simon she waited for the rush of heat in her body to subside.

'Come and say hullo.' Rebecca took Simon's hand, leading him unwillingly to Luke. 'This is your brother. It's Luke.'

As the tall man with dark hair and striking blue eyes looked at him, Simon felt nothing but emptiness. It engulfed him and he wanted only to run, but Rebecca held tightly to his hand.

'Hullo, Simon.' Luke stepped towards him. 'Don't you remember me?'

Simon shook his head and his tongue lolled out of his mouth. He was lost in a moment of darkness. The man who stood in front of him and spoke his name, was somewhere in that darkness.

'I'm your brother. I'm Luke.' Simon gazed back and Luke knew he was talking into a vacuum. His eyes were dead and his tongue moved in slow searching sweeps across his bottom lip as he stared at a total stranger.

'Say hullo so we can play.' Joe gave Simon a swift kick on the leg. 'You stupid!' Joe taunted him. But Simon was lost in the darkness that surrounded Luke and he said nothing at all. He was searching for a clue that might shed some light on the moment in time of which Luke was a part.

'Luke was Thabo's friend,' Rebecca said quickly and Simon's look fixed on to her. Holding tightly to the feeling that was Thabo, he dragged himself away from the darkness that was Luke.

'Thabo!' he called, running away towards the gates of Bonne Espérance. All he wanted was to climb back into the safety that Thabo's name brought with it. On the last day he'd seen him, Thabo had gone through the gates.

'Come back.' Joe went after him.

'Joe, come and wash your hands now,' Lydia called from the house.

'Coming!' Joe ran on after Simon, nothing further from his mind than washing his hands.

'I'm sorry,' Rebecca said quietly. Luke was watching Simon's back and his eyes reflected a deep sadness. Simon's body lurched from side to side in an ungainly run and Luke knew he was running from him.

As Lydia stood still in the doorway of the house and watched, the feeling between the young couple was so real she could almost touch it. And Lydia longed to. It was a feeling she missed deeply.

'Supper's ready,' she said quietly, aware she'd looked in on a moment of first love.

'I'll bring the children inside, Lydia.' Rebecca pulled herself free of the force that gripped every part of her as she looked at Luke. 'I'll get the boys.' She felt a rush of heat in her body and then froze as Luke's hand took hers.

'I'll come with you.' He was unable to let her go even for a moment.

Constance had joined the family for the birthday supper and Lydia watched her in amazement. She was totally at ease. It was as if the gracious woman Lydia had first met had returned to Bonne Espérance after a long and curious journey.

'I can hardly believe you're seventeen today, Rebecca.' Constance smiled at the beautiful young woman who sat beside the blue-eyed man at the dining table. 'Potatoes for you, David?' She glanced at her husband and he nodded. As though any noise might break the mystical moment in which Constance had stepped back into their lives, nobody at the table spoke. 'The day you were born could be yesterday, Rebecca. That mine hospital was really very good, you know. Even Sister War was kind when I went into labour.'

Rebecca felt the soft flannel of Luke's trouser brush against her leg and the joy with which she watched her mother was momentarily lost in the pulsating urge aroused by his touch.

'Do start, everyone, please.' Constance smiled at them all as she lifted her knife and fork. 'Oh!' She bowed her head. 'For what we are about to receive, may the Lord make us truly grateful. Amen.' Constance smiled again and began to eat. 'And how's Stan these days, Lydia?'

'Stan?' Lydia had been caught by surprise. Constance had never asked about her husband before but she'd asked today. And today Lydia wasn't sure. 'He's fine. Yes,' she glanced at Joe nervously. 'Mind you, I don't see much of him. He's always working. And when he gets home he still works. That's why he couldn't join me today.' Lydia looked down as her own very real fears jumped to the forefront of her mind. Stan hadn't come home at all the night before; as he hadn't come home on many previous nights in the last few months and she was certain she knew why. Every nerve in her body had been on edge on the last morning he'd eventually turned up, armed with a barrage of excuses. But Lydia had believed none of them. Stan had changed and she'd sensed that a woman was the cause. She'd tried to believe him when he'd explained that he'd stayed on to work in the office, but each time he'd tried to touch her, Lydia pulled away, trembling with unspoken anger. Night after night she'd lain alone in bed, telling herself that her husband was where he'd said he'd be, but her heart had seethed, compounding her growing feelings of inadequacy.

'What's wrong, Lydia?' She could remember the last time Stan had tried to make love to her. How his hand had run up the length of her thigh and how she'd wanted to scream. Where once his touch had sparked such desire, Lydia had felt nothing but repulsion. He'd reeked of aftershave and had taken to chewing strong mints, but nothing concealed the smell of adultery. Lydia had seen the woman in her mind's eye. She'd been beautiful and young as her imagination sketched her. She'd also been pure white.

'What about you, Luke? What news of the family?' Lydia tried to draw herself and everyone else away from the problem that consumed her. 'How's your mother and Naomi?'

'They're fine.' Luke could feel Rebecca's thigh close to his and his eyes swept quickly over her face.

'Do they like Johannesburg?' Lydia went on, but Luke was lost inside Rebecca's smile.

'Yes.' He tried to pull free of Rebecca's eyes. 'Sorry. What did you say?'

'You obviously don't like Johannesburg.' David leaned back. The change in his wife's behaviour had reassured him that his decision to return to the small mining town was right.

'Maybe it's because I still think of Bonne Espérance as my home.' Luke's attention returned to Rebecca. She watched him intently. 'I know now that this is the only place I want to be.' He leaned closer to Rebecca. 'I've got something for you,' he whispered, held by her look and with no desire to break free.

'Do you remember him yet?' Rebecca hastily turned to Simon. The curious tremor she felt in Luke's presence was more than she could bear, and she was certain that everybody knew what was happening inside her. 'It was Luke, myself and Thabo who . . .'

'Thabo!' Simon stared at Rebecca. He couldn't understand why Thabo hadn't been at the gate when he'd got there. He didn't know why the feeling that was Thabo had suddenly been surrounded by the same darkness he'd felt when he'd looked at Luke.

'Of course Simon doesn't remember Luke, Rebecca.' Constance had recognised the moment of darkness Simon was lost in. It was the darkness in which his mother, Estelle, had abandoned him and Constance had been lost in it herself. 'He was only a baby when they left. Eat!' She smiled at them all. 'Miriam's cooked a lovely supper so don't let it spoil.'

Luke picked up his knife and fork, concentrating on the dinner of roast beef and potatoes that Miriam had prepared for Rebecca's birthday. The moment he'd reached the house he'd gone into the kitchen to say hullo and Miriam had been overcome with shyness.

'Thabo big like you, master Luke. He grow!' She clapped her hands as she spoke and Luke tried to remember the black friend who'd taken his place in Simon's heart.

'How is he?' he asked, unaware that it had been one of the many laws he translated for a living that had cost Miriam her son. Those laws were part of a job that had cost Luke his freedom, too. 'Rebecca says he's in the Transkei.'

'That right.' Miriam had smiled and in her smile Luke had seen Thabo, recognising him instantly. 'You remember Sophie? Thabo look after my mother now.'

'Of course I remember Sophie.' But Luke had felt strangely uncomfortable with the mention of Miriam's mother, Sophie. He remembered the hours of his childhood he'd spent seeking comfort against her soft bosom and it was a part of his life that the apartheid laws had covered with guilt. 'She's well, I hope.' Luke had backed away to the door, discomfort overwhelming him. 'I'll see you later.' He'd moved quickly back to Rebecca. She was beside the open doorway as he stepped through it, and Luke immediately felt safe.

Though Rebecca had been in bed for three hours, sleep still hadn't come. Luke filled her every thought and his image played in front of her eyes constantly. Even when she'd switched on her bedside light to break free of her thoughts, he'd still been there. He wasn't the same boy she'd given an old key to so many years ago. Luke was a stranger and the feelings that engulfed her now were strangers too.

'Who's that?' She jumped back against the headboard, pulling the bedcovers under her chin. A small stone had hit her window. Her curtains were closed but the moon shone through them, casting shadows that danced on the wall beside her bed.

'Rebecca?' It was Luke's voice. It was coming from just outside her window and she couldn't move. Her body was shaking and her throat had closed in a mixture of excitement and terror.

When Rebecca had climbed into bed that night she'd wondered if he might come to her window as he had when they'd stolen Simon. She'd hoped he would know that she'd moved downstairs to a bigger room. She'd waited for this very moment all night but now it had come, she couldn't move.

'Can I see you, Rebecca?' Luke's voice was soft but it rang clear through the still night and she wanted to run to the window, to climb through it into his arms. But she couldn't move. She didn't know if Luke had come for the reasons she'd dreamed.

'Rebecca.' Luke called again. 'Can I come in? Please.'

'What is it?' She jumped out of bed, suddenly afraid he'd go before she reached him and, pushing the curtains back, she froze. Luke looked at her from the other side of the glass and she could neither speak nor breathe.

'Come, Rebecca.' The electric current raced between them again and quickly she ran to the door.

The sweet smell of hay and the warmth of Salu's breath against her neck became a part of the tight circle that held Luke and Rebecca together in the stables. It was a circle of inexplicable hope, firm in the knowledge that it was more real than the world around them yet so delicate it was hardly there. Though neither had experienced anything like it before, both had welcomed the overpowering excitement between them. It had sprung up like a long-lost friend. Until that moment, Rebecca had known only a childish passion and Luke just an obligation to a small girl's belief in a key.

'Do you remember this?' Luke held the old key in his hand and Rebecca laughed in surprise. It shone, glowing brass in the swinging light of the bare bulb above them.

'Your mother's polished it.'

'She polishes anything that doesn't move – remember?'

'Even something I gave you?'

'Maybe that's why.' His eyes settled on hers as she reached for the key. But she couldn't speak any more. Luke's little finger had touched her hand.

'What's happening?' Luke's eyes fixed on her face and his hand held hers with the key flat between their palms. 'Rebecca?' he breathed, afraid to say more in case no words came. Moving closer, the key pressed hard between them and Rebecca wanted to bury herself inside him.

'I couldn't sleep.' Luke felt her words through the softness of her body

246

as it pressed against his own with no more than a fold of cotton between them.

'Rebecca.' His breath drew her name on the thread of a whisper. He could feel the rise of her breasts against him and her supple body bent back with his. It was as if the cotton of her nightdress had vanished as she pressed against him, the length of her legs running close to his as her breath flowed in waves of longing.

'I love you, Luke. Oh God, how much I love you.' Rebecca peered into his face, every part of her clinging to him. A dull ache throbbed between her legs, pushing deep inside her and her body screamed, calling for Luke as a flood of warm moisture soaked from the depths of her desire. Luke's hands were running down her back, feeling her body and touching her soul. Her skin tightened and quite suddenly she felt herself snap. Rebecca no longer knew or cared what was happening. Luke's mouth was on hers. He'd pulled her hips hard against his and his chest pressed on her breasts. Everything had suddenly changed. Short gasps of shallow breath were the only sounds and their bodies drew closer with a force neither could control.

'No!' An unexplained warning came from somewhere Rebecca had never been. It shouted between them and she pulled away, the key dropping to the ground. But Luke moved after her; wrapping his arms round her from behind, he pulled her into him again. She felt the hard push of his longing against her and she gasped. Swinging round to him she curled into his arms and tears brushed against his neck.

'No. Please, no,' she whispered, begging him to go on: to take her wherever he was leading, to fill her aching body with every part of himself. She could feel Luke's hand slipping under her nightdress, running up the line of her stomach and she wanted to scream for the world to stop and the moment never to end.

But Rebecca couldn't scream. Luke's mouth was on her mouth. It was on her neck, on her breast: his tongue stroked gently and her nipple ached as it rose hard in his mouth.

Rebecca's body had swelled to fill the curves of the woman she'd always longed to be, the woman Luke's touch had sparked into life. She was swallowed by the magic she'd been drawn into and the child had become a woman in Luke's arms. She'd left the real world in a moment of passion that had shattered her senses and stripped her bare. She'd offered the centre of herself to Luke and begged him to fill it.

But Luke had pulled away. He'd wrenched himself away, keeping his back to her as his body shook.

'What's wrong?' Rebecca's skin tingled as her heart reached out for him. Just the sight of him, the scent of his body and the touch of his skin had swallowed her alive and she pulled him back against her. 'Luke?'

'I'm sorry.' Luke held her away, his hands gripping her tightly as if hanging on to their passion even while rejecting it. In a split moment of truth Luke had seen the purity of their love and it had stood clean and aloof from the sex he'd shared with Althea. As Rebecca had responded to his deepest longings, Luke had recognised the sparkling fragility of first love. It had tied them together with a silk cord that reached beyond the longings it roused.

'You must believe I love you, Rebecca.' Though he held her away, Luke's body throbbed for her. 'I know now that it's you who's been hidden somewhere inside me, promising everything I've ever wanted. But not now. We mustn't.' His face brushed her cheek and his breath stroked her hair. 'I want you forever, not just like this.'

Salu prodded Rebecca in the back with his nose so her body fell against his and they laughed. For the first time in their lives each had found peace with the other, understanding the laws of creation that were written in love. Luke's mother had gone. Johannes Villiers had gone. Althea had never existed and Rebecca had cast off the shroud of a lifetime's loneliness. Nothing existed that had existed before and they were held secure in a pure and abiding love.

The outline of the three horses on the horizon was clear against the sky and David glanced at them as he moved to the cellars with Christian du Toit. David hadn't missed Rebecca and Luke's growing attachment. At first, driven by his memory of Estelle, he'd tried to ignore what was happening, hoping that nothing would come of it. He knew, as Rebecca did, that Luke wasn't really a member of the Beauvilliers family, that the shadow of an ancient love between a white man and his Malay slave had not cast itself on him. David was also aware that Luke worked for a Government whose eyes had narrowed on to colour and had been blinded to anything else, but he knew his daughter best of all. It was as if Luke had lifted the heavy shutters that constant rejection had slammed down on Rebecca's life. He'd revived the bubble that was her; and laughter had found a home in his daughter once again.

'Who's the young man?' Christian had spotted Luke and Rebecca riding with Simon when he'd arrived for work early that morning. He'd often wondered why a legion of young men hadn't battered a path to Rebecca's door.

'Riaan's nose is going to be out of joint.' Christian grinned at David as they moved together through the dark arch of the cellar doors. 'By the way, I spoke to Pa and the boys, and they're only too happy to move in while you're away. But I reckon I'll keep it quiet about Rebecca's new boyfriend.'

'Thanks, Christian.' David's attitude was completely different from the day he'd told the winemaker he was taking the family to Northern Rhodesia. His tension had gone and his eyes were bright. 'You wouldn't believe how Constance has changed since we decided to go. I can't pretend I know why, but there it is.'

'It's obvious.' Christian du Toit moved towards the huge steel vats and his image bent double, staring back at him from gleaming silver skins. 'No matter what way you look at it, a person's home holds the soul. So far as I can make out it's the soul that holds the mind too. Whatever ... it's good. No?'

'Maybe.' David's image in the shining steel vat bent to a shadow of Christian's as he stood next to him. He'd never spoken to the Afrikaner winemaker about South African politics, or mentioned the coloured blood that ran through the Beauvilliers family. Though Christian didn't know that the Westbury house his family lived in had once concealed the lie of that coloured blood, David knew the bitter secrets woven into Bonne Espérance had touched them all. Clara Beauvilliers' hatred had spread from a family into a nation and finally, enshrined on the altar of apartheid, it governed them all.

As Simon's pony raced past Rebecca and Luke, his spirits lifted on the wind of triumph. The sturdy little animal beneath him had galloped its heart out, as if it knew its small passenger needed to win.

'I'd never have believed Simon could ride like that,' Luke called across to Rebecca as they rode after him. Her hair was flying in the wind and her cheeks glowed in the early morning light. 'You're not that bad on a horse yourself now.' He pulled Salu a little closer to her horse as they slowed down and their legs touched.

'Is it good to be riding Salu again?' Rebecca watched Luke carefully. Her body had filled with longing, as it did every moment he was near.

'Did you teach Simon to ride?'

'Yup. I had a good teacher myself.' Rebecca looked towards Simon as he sat totally still on his pony in the distance. 'You won!' she called and Luke reached out, taking her hand.

'Rebecca.' He'd been in command of his emotions since the moment he'd recognised the love that seemed to be born fully grown between them. 'I want to marry you.'

'What?' Rebecca's heart had turned a somersault as she heard his words and she was unable to say anything else. Only her eyes spoke as they reached out to him.

'Come!' Luke's hand wrapped round her arm, swinging her off her horse and on to his. Buckling under the added weight for a moment, Salu snorted his annoyance.

'Tell me,' Luke turned Rebecca towards him in the saddle. 'Will you marry me?' Her face tilted up to his and their lips were so close she could feel his breath. 'What do you want, Rebecca?'

'You.' Like a curling kitten she turned her body into his and as his mouth found hers, she murmured, 'I want you.'

They'd fallen off the world once again and their spirits soared as it spun away without them.

Pawing at the sandy ground under its feet, the small pony Simon rode wondered why the race had come to such an empty end. Simon was still on his back but the excitement he'd felt in the small boy's body had vanished. He was no more than a dead weight as he stared back at Luke and Rebecca. Their shapes had become one as they sat on Salu's back and Simon sensed he was no longer a part of Rebecca's world.

'Thabo,' he murmured quietly, trying to find the other person he'd lost and needed to find. 'Thabo!' he called into the emptiness around him and the pony's ears pricked against the answering silence.

'You do know we're going back to Northern Rhodesia, Luke,' David said simply as Luke faced him in the sitting room two weeks later. Rebecca and Luke had spent every moment of their time together and he'd seen the strength of their love. He was aware that even when they lay alone in their beds, their spirits met in the night air. It was as if his child had already become one with another man and David was on edge, unsure how to handle his own feelings. The hidden truth of Luke's birth concealed a threat to his daughter; but he couldn't be the one to reveal it. He was trapped between his care for Rebecca and a truth which could blow everything apart.

'Rebecca told me you were going back, Mr Conrad.' Luke was nervous but he tried to hide it. He'd worked out what he knew of his blood relationship to Rebecca and as first cousins once removed they were free to marry. 'There's nothing to stop us marrying.'

'No, no. Of course.' David hesitated. 'But she's only seventeen, Luke. Rebecca's a child.' Turning away towards the window David watched his daughter outside. She sat with Simon, swinging slowly on a hammock strung between two trees at the side of the house and she really was just a beautiful child. But even at this distance, David could see that something about her had changed. 'Are you certain you know what you want, Luke? In such a short time?' David turned back to him.

'We know, Mr Conrad.' Luke was very sure of his feelings and David felt a little naive as he held back the questions that plagued him. 'We're going to get married no matter what. Not yet, but soon. If you give your permission, of course. When you're back from Northern Rhodesia . . .'

'I can't answer now, Luke.' David moved away restlessly. He didn't know how to tell the boy that they might never come back. 'Rebecca's mother isn't well and, I'm sorry, but that's the most important thing in our lives right now.'

'Rebecca told me.'

'Then you understand?' David observed him carefully. 'None of us are thinking clearly at the moment. It's just not the right time.'

'I didn't ask to fall in love with your daughter, Mr Conrad. I didn't expect it and I didn't want it, but it happened. I love Rebecca and I want to be with her for the rest of my life. If you stay up North, then I'll go up North. If you come back here, I'll come back. For the first time in my life I know what I want, Mr Conrad.'

The directness of Luke's words wiped David's mind clear in an instant. The young man who stood in front of him was asking for his daughter's life. A life he'd been unable to protect adequately himself would be taken over by someone about whom he knew very little.

'What about your work, Luke? You're in the Civil Service in the Transvaal, aren't you, translating laws, – Government bulletins?'

'I'm leaving my job, Mr Conrad –'

'But tell me about it,' David interrupted. 'Politics isn't something any of us talk about easily in this country. I'm sorry, but I must know where you stand.'

'Beside your daughter.' Luke's eyes centred on David's and his voice was firm. 'She's pulled me free of a trap, sir, and I've made my decision. Apartheid's not my job. What I did, it was no more than a way of earning a living. I had to care for the family when my father left. They were my responsibility and it was the only way I could find. And . . .'

'What now?' David had tensed with Luke's mention of Paul.

'Now my responsibility is with Rebecca. Only with her.'

'And your mother?' David's words caught Luke by surprise. The surprise was that he felt nothing at all with the mention of Estelle. No moment of fear and no resentment.

'What will your mother say when you tell her you want to marry Rebecca?' David asked again. 'You do know how she feels.'

'I'm twenty-one and I don't need my mother's permission any more, Mr Conrad.' Luke wasn't talking about his age and David understood that. He was secure within himself, brimming over with the confidence he'd found in Rebecca. 'I want to marry your daughter. That's all I want and all I ask.'

'There is one more thing.' David paused and though Luke longed to run outside and lift Rebecca off her feet, wanting only to hold on to her spirit of absolute peace, he waited in silence for David to go on. 'If ever you hurt Rebecca. If you ever hurt my child, I'll kill you.'

In the pause after his words David smiled and he pulled Luke towards him, hugging him.

Though a vast area of uncertainty was still there between them, David trusted the love Luke had expressed. He knew the small girl on an ant hill had found happiness, and he had no intention of standing in its way.

CHAPTER TWELVE

With his spindle legs stretched out in leaping strides, a small black boy raced towards the rugged mountains in the distance. He carried a swinging black pot, a white envelope was tucked in the waistband of his raggedy short pants and a pair of men's shoes swung from laces looped round his neck.

'Thabo!' he called into the wide space of the Transkei as his feet flew effortlessly over the ground. 'A letter!' he squealed in Xhosa, glancing down at the flapping envelope in his shorts. It had arrived with the bus from Cape Town the night before and had passed through the hands of every villager before being given to him to deliver.

Lunga had spotted the bus winding its way up the mountain pass hours before anyone else and a small crowd had soon gathered on the road to wait for it. People who returned from the city of Cape Town often had luggage to carry and he'd earn a few pennies heaving it up to their small village. Consisting of a few mud-brick houses with a large and special rondavel in its centre, the village nestled on a steep mountainside in the district of Herschel in the Transkei. A fire burned all winter in the rondavel and everyone met there to cook and eat. They would sit far into the night, talking round the open fire and it was those dark evenings of winter that Lunga loved best of all.

He would never forget the night that Thabo had come back from the city. When he'd arrived, their grandmother Sophie had told Lunga that Thabo lived in Cape Town. Before that, he'd lived on the wine farm called Bonne Espérance, where she and Thabo's mother worked; Lunga had stared at the visitor in amazement.

Thabo had talked of lights that came on with a flick of a switch, fires that burned without smoke, and boxes that talked. Thabo had even brought such a box with him, and when he'd switched it on Lunga had been startled. He'd crept towards the radio secretly, in the hope of catching 'the small people' who talked inside it and Thabo had laughed. But though Lunga had laughed with him, the small boy hadn't yet worked out how the people always vanished just before he pounced.

'It's a letter for you,' Lunga shouted towards the huddled shape of Thabo in the distance. As Thabo went through initiation into manhood, the small boy was his contact with the outside world and he knew his older cousin would read him the letter out loud. On the back of spoken words he would be carried into a land of glass buildings, blue roads and white people and Lunga could hardly wait.

'You're early today,' Thabo called down as he watched the child clamber up the rocks towards him. Naked except for a brightly coloured blanket wrapped tightly round him, Thabo sat on a barren outcrop of rocks halfway up a small mountain.

'It's a letter from your mother.' The shoes scraped across the rocks as Lunga crawled towards him on all fours, the letter in his outstretched hand reaching Thabo before he did. 'It's from Cape Town.' He dropped to his haunches and the shoes swung in front of his heaving chest as the pot dangled from his hand. 'Read it.' Lunga had never understood how blue squiggles on paper translated into spoken words, but he knew Thabo did. 'What she say?' His sharp elbow dug into Thabo's side and Lunga stared at the envelope in anticipation.

Luke is here. Miriam's letter had begun without greeting and Thabo read it to himself in silence. *He's a man now.* Thabo closed his eyes and smiled. Initiation had made him a man himself. The boy had been cut away with the sharp knife of circumcision, and the physical sign of childhood had forever gone. In the company of three others, Thabo had been taught the responsibilities of manhood by clan elders. They were men of status, *Bahlankana abafana*. They passed down the ancient culture of their people to the younger generation, leading them on a spiritual quest for the inner man. The people of Transkei were deeply religious and served God under the guidance of their *Amaqirha*, but Thabo had not found his answers in their beliefs and he'd searched for his own truth.

His thoughts had turned to Fezile and his talk of the great God, Jesus Christ, whom he worshipped: the God of white men that Fezile considered to be his father, even though he was black. But Fezile's God had also eluded Thabo and the truth he sought remained firmly out of his reach.

'Tell me!' Lunga couldn't bear the silence of Thabo's thoughts as the letter vanished inside his head. Until the day he'd been given the responsibility of caring for Thabo during initiation, Lunga's time had been spent herding his family's goats near the banks of the Tele River.

With other small boys, each in charge of their own herd, Lunga had passed the time hunting mice and rabbits among the echoing caves in the mountains and his life had been complete. But Thabo had shown him a glimpse of another world and quite suddenly it had been all he wanted.

'They still clean.' He spat on the toe of a shoe and rubbed it before holding it out to Thabo. 'See – I take good care of them.' He hoped his smile might encourage Thabo to give him the shoes one day. 'Look.' He swung the small black pot in front of Thabo, lifting the lid with a quick grin. Lunga knew that neither man nor boy ever refused the thick mealie meal porridge his grandmother Sophie made. 'You want to eat now?' Thabo shook his head and Lunga wondered what was required to bring him back from wherever he'd hidden with the words.

'Thandi says . . .' Lunga looked down as Thabo turned to him. Examining his small wriggling toes, he tried to regain his composure. 'Thandi, she make you something.'

'A hat?' Thabo looked at the small boy carefully. He knew the beautiful Thandi liked him and his body had often reminded him of the long days he'd spent with her. She was the most beautiful girl he'd ever seen and the day he'd first spotted her was clear in his mind.

A crowd of young people had gone down to the river to swim and they'd leapt naked into the swirling waters. But Thabo hadn't noticed Thandi then. It had only been as he lay in the sun to dry that he'd seen her. She'd stood absolutely still beside him, and he would never forget the sight of her gleaming brown skin. With her head held high she'd gazed at him steadily and her beauty had driven deep into his soul.

Thabo knew that once he'd passed into manhood, the elders would expect him to take Thandi as his wife. A hat would mean she wanted marriage, too.

'A big hat.' Lunga stretched his arms as wide as a tree. 'What your mother say?' A dusty black shrug of his shoulders dismissed all girls.

'I'm going back to Cape Town.' Thabo's voice was quiet and the small boy listened carefully, waiting for him to add the magic words: 'and you will be coming with me,' but he didn't. 'When the ceremony is over tomorrow I'm going back to Cape Town.'

Lunga cast his eyes downwards. Thabo had already disappeared into the world of white men and he'd left him behind. 'When you go to school, you must learn well, Lunga.' Thabo's eyes fixed on the small boy, drilling his words into his head. 'You must be a man here, first.' He tapped the small boy's head and Lunga wondered why grown-ups always did that. He wished he hadn't brought Thabo the letter from Cape Town. 'The people who come here from the towns, you mustn't listen to them, Lunga.

And you mustn't listen to girls, either. You must listen only to your own heart: it's with that you will see clearly.'

Lunga knew what people Thabo referred to. He'd often seen the men who returned to the village from the city with silver radios and straightened hair. They dressed in smart clothes and they spoke in raised voices. They talked of 'revolutionary struggle' and called his elder brother Comrade though his name was Themba.

'Education is important,' Thabo went on. 'You must find your own respect and that can be found only in here.' He tapped the child's head with a hard knuckle once again and Lunga wondered if his skull had maybe chipped a little. 'You must tell Thandi that I will not marry her, Lunga.'

'What?' Though the skin hat on his own tiny penis was still there, Lunga could see for himself what a girl as lovely as Thandi could do to a boy. 'You not marry Thandi?' he said in amazement.

'I am going back to Cape Town.'

'You want I go with you?' Lunga's eyes lit with the remnants of hope.

'No.' Thabo gripped the bony shoulder of the child whose name meant 'sweet boy'. In his own mind Thabo had already covered the hundreds of miles by slow bus to Cape Town and he held tightly to the promise he'd made to Fezile many years before.

'I am going to school, Lunga.'

'Don't forget to write,' Luke called through the carriage window. He reached down to clasp Rebecca's hand between his as a shrill whistle announced the train's departure for Johannesburg and the clatter of slamming doors echoed round Cape Town station.

'I can't hear you,' Rebecca shouted as the train moved forward, drowning Luke's voice under grinding wheels.

'I love you.' Luke's voice rang suddenly clear as the train stopped and a slow hiss of steam bounced his words in echoing calls against the domed station roof.

'I heard you,' Rebecca smiled as the wheels rolled forward once again, turning slow steel somersaults down the line. 'Luke!' She ran beside the train as it gathered speed and the stone grey platform raced under her feet. His face was blurred behind tears she wasn't quite sure were her own. 'I love you,' she shouted as the reality of his departure stretched the length of their reaching arms, pulling them apart.

'Hey, Rebecca!' She turned at Riaan's excited shout behind her. Beckoning with agitated waves he raced down the platform towards her. 'Come on.' His hand gripped hers, pulling her back as the train threaded its way through a maze of shimmering lines. 'Get in.' He pushed her into the lumpy front seat of his father's old van and jumped in himself, starting the engine before the door had closed.

'What are you doing?' Rebecca wiped at her tears as the van spun in a semi-circle of dust and squealing tyres. 'Stop!' she screamed as the rusty old vehicle, piled high with sacks of compost, drove a rattling path between parked cars and scattering pedestrians.

'Hold tight!' Riaan's excitement was heightened by the fact that neither Rebecca nor Luke had guessed why he'd offered to drive them to the station that day. 'It's OK,' he chuckled. The elderly van was threatening to snap clear of its wheels as it raced into a sprawling industrial site on the outskirts of Cape Town, the station and swooping gulls of the dockyards left far behind.

'Look over there.' The van sped clear of factory yards and a train appeared like a silver mirage alongside the road. 'Hey!' he shouted, pushing his hand flat on the horn in a long cry for attention. 'Hey!' he called again, 'Luke!' The van tore down the road next to the train.

'Luke!' Rebecca exploded in excitement as she realised what was happening. 'Luke!' she yelled, her voice mixing with the wailing horn and rattling wheels as two small boys looked down at her from a carriage window.

'Luke!' they called in mimicking unison as the pile of sacks slid from side to side on the van that raced down the wrong side of the road beside them.

'Rebecca!' Luke's head pushed out of a window beside the boys. 'Look out!' he yelled as an oncoming car scraped past the van, its horn a rising howl of accusation.

'I love you,' Rebecca shouted.

'What?' Luke called back.

'She loves you,' a giggling duet of boys' voices answered.

'She says she loves you,' Riaan echoed as the success of his plan filled him with confidence. He wanted only to please them. 'See you at Belville!' he yelled as the train picked up speed and pulled away from them. 'It's the first stop.' Riaan's voice chased Luke. 'Go get him, baby!' he encouraged the rattling hulk of rust around them and, pressing his foot hard on the already flat accelerator pedal, the bags of compost slipped slowly backwards.

Luke glanced at a small swinging sign as he hung on to the iron railings of the carriage steps. The deserted station into which the train had pulled was Belville, and a whirling cloud of dust announced the van's approach. Running with the train in great stretching strides, Luke released his grip and swung back to land on the platform.

'Rebecca,' he whispered as her solitary figure stood out against the dark shape of Table Mountain in the far distance.

'Kiss her,' the boys encouraged in a fervour of excitement as Luke ran towards her. 'Go on, kiss her!'

But Luke had stopped just short of Rebecca. As if a moment of time had been snatched back from an enemy, they gazed at one another.

'Come with me,' Luke whispered. 'Come now, Rebecca.' He was back in the circle of her presence and afraid to step outside it again.

'I can't.' She fought the strong urge to go with him, to climb on to the train, wave goodbye to Riaan and never be outside the reality of the love she'd found. 'I can't.' She threw herself into his arms. Her mother's needs cried out to her and she shrank from the familiar space of loneliness. 'I love you so much,' she whispered as he took her face between his hands and his lips moved to hers. A chorus of cat-calls erupted from the two small boys and Riaan looked away as the conductor blew into the silver whistle round his neck.

'Bye.' Rebecca's breath brushed over Luke's face and she stepped back.

'Come on!' the small boys called over a sudden spurt of steam and judder of steel.

'It won't be long.' Luke challenged the slow march of time that spread between them with the roll of steel wheels. 'I'll love you always, Rebecca,' he called.

'Here,' one of the young boys shouted down to Luke as the train gathered speed. 'Hold on.' He stretched his hand to reach him from the steps and Luke grabbed it. 'Help!' The boy's tiny hand was swallowed by Luke's fist. 'Let go,' he shouted in terror as Luke's legs swung free before climbing on to the steps beside him.

'See you in Touwsrivier, the next stop!' Riaan shouted as the tail-end of the metal snake whipped away. 'Hold on, Rebecca.' He forced the old van faster along the narrow strip of tarmac that led towards the deep purple mountains up ahead.

'Put your foot down,' Rebecca yelled as the train called back a hooting challenge.

'Go on!' Riaan wondered why the old van was slowing down. 'Get going!' He banged the rusty sides of the cab, whipping it like a dying race-horse as the sacks of compost slipped slowly forwards.

'What's wrong?' Rebecca watched Riaan as the van leapfrogged down the road before wheezing to a slow halt.

'Shit,' Riaan muttered as the sacks moved forward in a sliding pile behind the cab. He banged the steering wheel in frustration. A spidery needle on the petrol gauge indicated an accusing zero and success disintegrated around him.

'We've run out of petrol.' Rebecca laughed, leaning back in her seat as the train curled away towards the horizon.

'I'm sorry.'

'What for?' Rebecca's voice was gentle and as Riaan looked at her, her smile lit the darkness of his failure.

'Have they run out of petrol or something?' The shorter of the two boys stood beside Luke at the rear of the train. Sucking aggressively on a flattened white straw that led from his mouth to a Coke bottle, he gazed at him. 'You reckon they've run out of petrol?'

'Something like that.' Luke was watching a flickering gleam of sunlight on metal far behind them. It was all he could see of Rebecca.

'That's stupid.' The small boy blew into the straw and sucked a quick stream of bubbling Coke. 'You really love her?' Luke nodded and the boy's teeth let go of the straw, his face reflecting total amazement. 'Why you going away then?' The soggy straw poked his nose as his mouth searched for it.

'I have to.'

'Why?'

'Because.'

'Because why?'

Luke had begun to wonder why himself and was suddenly irritated by the boy's incessant questions.

'You sure your mother's not looking for you?'

With the straw firmly between his teeth and his cheeks sucked in like sticky dead balloons, he shook his head. 'Nope.' The word clung to the straw before exploding in a loud burp.

'Go away.' Luke dismissed him.

The van was no longer even a glint of sun on metal and his mind rolled back down the silver tracks to the long warm days he'd shared with Rebecca. Her laughing voice called as they raced their horses down a wide white beach.

'Do you still love me?' Her eyes lingered on his as she curled her body into the curve of his arms and Luke knew there'd never been a moment he hadn't.

'And when I'm old?' Rebecca screamed as a blue wall of seawater rose behind them. 'When I'm drowned?' she spluttered as the wave spread a cloth of salty bubbles over her golden skin.

'I'll never stop loving you.' Luke heard his own voice as they lay together on a warm flat rock. It clung tight to the side of Table Mountain and the Cape peninsula pushed a prodding finger between the Atlantic and Indian Oceans far below. The longing inside Luke was something he'd never known before. He wanted not just Rebecca's body, he wanted her soul.

The house had been a hive of activity ever since Simon woke that morning and he gazed at Miriam suspiciously as she buttered crisp white rolls on the kitchen table.

'The chicken smells good.' Rebecca was packing a large wicker basket with food. She'd spent the entire day with Miriam preparing for the five-day car ride northwards the next morning. Though she was tired, the practicalities of packing had filled the emptiness inside her, the void which hadn't filled since the day Luke had left.

'There.' Miriam closed the crusty lid on the last buttered roll and packed it with the others in the top of the basket.

'Will you take this outside and give it to Dad?' Rebecca asked Simon, holding the basket out to him. 'What's wrong?' Simon hadn't taken the basket. His arms were crossed over his chest and reaching behind his back, his fingers groped for each other, locking in a tangle of white knuckles.

Simon had watched his clothes being packed away in trunks. He'd seen his toys being tidied away into a cupboard. Worst of all, the small horse he'd made for Rebecca had been pushed into the dark of an airless drawer and he himself had suffocated.

'Dad's packing the car.' Rebecca tried to encourage him. 'Go on, Simon.' Turning him by the shoulders, she placed the basket in his hands and pushed him towards the kitchen door.

'He not happy.' Simon heard Miriam's whisper to Rebecca and he stopped in the hall on the other side of the door. He wasn't not happy – he was mad! With a scream he flung the basket on to the hall floor. Hard-boiled eggs rolled across the gleaming yellow-wood floor, chased by soft buttered rolls, and he jumped on them all, stamping them into a squidgy mess of yellow and white. Then he made a dash for the door.

'Simon!' Rebecca ran after him with Miriam on her heels.

'He bad.' Miriam's eyes fixed on the floor she'd only just polished. A long line of egg-yolk footprints stretched through the open front door.

'Leave him,' David called to Rebecca as she ran out of the house. Simon had darted into the stables. 'Just leave him.' David was packing the old Humber Super Snipe and a large trunk was strapped to the roof.

Alone in the straw twilight of the stables, Simon's back slid slowly down the rough brick wall behind him. He could feel his pony just a few feet away but he didn't look at him. His entire body was shaking and he rattled with emptiness. Every feeling which governed his life had vanished and there was nothing left to hang on to. Locked inside his deformed body he was incapable of expressing his grief and a howl of helplessness lifted to the stable roof as he threw himself forward. His feet kicked, his body scraped against the rough cobbled floor and his head banged from side to side. Frustration foamed in his mouth and his tongue stretched in sweeps across the floor, as if reaching for unknown words.

'Where Simon?' he called quite suddenly, his eyes peering round the stables in loss. Crawling on all fours he moved towards the pony's feet. 'Simon?' Straw hung from his tongue as he gazed up at the drooping grey curve of the pony's belly. 'Simon?' he called again, and looking for himself on the pony's back, he pulled himself up against its legs.

'Simon,' another voice called behind him and Simon froze. His mouth opened and shut involuntarily and he stared at the pony's flank. 'Simon,' the voice came again and his mind prodded a familiar feeling. The voice had come from the door and he twisted his head under his arm. Peering back through the dim light he searched for the source of warmth that had touched him and his eyes settled on a dark figure in the doorway.

'Thabo!' he shouted as strong black hands lifted him, holding him high.

The excitement of Thabo's unexpected return had raced through Bonne Espérance on Simon's voice and Rebecca stared in amazement as she saw him. The tall black man whom she'd last seen stripped of all dignity in a police station, stood in front of her with a proud smile.

'You should have told us you were coming back,' Rebecca said as they sat round the kitchen table later. Simon sat beside Thabo, his body glued to his side. 'Luke's only just left. I can't believe you missed him! Did you know we were getting married?' she said all at once and Thabo nodded. Though still extraordinarily beautiful, Rebecca looked different. She was a woman, and a flush of pink had touched her cheeks when she'd mentioned Luke's name.

'My mother told me.' Thabo's smile was as wide as the country he'd just left and his eyes shone as he turned to Simon. 'OK?' Simon nodded, moving closer. Thabo hadn't understood why Simon clung to him so tightly but he didn't care. The child's love had welcomed him back in a way he hadn't expected.

'Tell us about you.' Rebecca cupped her chin in her hands. 'Miriam said you were in the Transkei, going through initiation or something. Is that right?'

'And I'm a man.' Thabo laughed. It was a deep laugh, filled with the echoes of running streams and Simon instinctively pulled closer. 'The key? That why you and Luke marry?' Thabo's mind had raced back to the night Rebecca had dug the key out of Clara's grave. 'You remember?' He chuckled, remembering all too clearly the fear which had pumped through his veins as Rebecca had clawed her way under the gravestone.

'I remember.' Rebecca smiled. 'Nombeko too! The thorn in my foot and ... do you remember the car?' She was back on the night they'd taken Simon to Nombeko and they were both laughing. 'I thought it was a bat. Do you remember how I screamed?' Miriam stood back proudly, watching her children.

'And Luke's bag? He dropped it,' Thabo reminded her.

'I dropped it.' Rebecca's laughter quietened and she looked at him seriously. 'Luke remembers too, Thabo.' Rebecca had noticed he hadn't asked about Luke any more than he'd answered about himself. 'You are OK?' she asked and he nodded. The elders had taught Thabo never to reveal his deeper feelings too clearly. If a friend became an enemy they could be used against him.

'You going back to Cape Town?' Miriam asked quietly, fear filling the silence that had suddenly descended.

'Tomorrow.' Thabo looked at Rebecca. 'And this time I get a pass.' There wasn't a trace of bitterness in his voice and Rebecca felt suddenly humble.

'Oh, Thabo, I'm so happy for you.' She watched him as his eyes turned on to her. Even they were free of bitterness.

'And this time I go to school.' Thabo's voice was firm but a smile lingered in his eyes. Until the moment he'd stepped back into the circle of Bonne Espérance, Thabo hadn't known it was his home too.

'Come!' Miriam stood at the kitchen door waiting for her son.

'You've got to bath now, Simon.' Rebecca held out her hand to him.

'He come with us.' Miriam had seen her son's presence heal Simon like anointing oil, and she took his small hand in her own. 'Simon sleep with Miriam and Thabo,' she said, leading them both away.

The shadowy figures of David and Rebecca moved to the car as dawn broke the chill of darkness and Thabo looked away from the window. The night had been long. It had been punctuated by Miriam's exclamations of joy or sorrow as he'd passed on news of the village while Simon waged war with sleep till at last it had overcome him.

'Simon?' Thabo looked down at his tightly curled body on the bed now. Though he hadn't understood the deep affection the mongol boy held him in, he'd made a vow. He would care for him as he'd been taught to care for all children. He would be responsible for Simon for the rest of his life.

But Thabo sensed deep problems on Bonne Espérance and he didn't understand them.

'What's wrong with Rebecca's mother?' He'd asked, when Miriam explained that Constance was the reason the family were going away.

'She's gone.' Miriam's voice was as quiet as Simon's breathing and she looked at her son questioningly, wondering if the elders might have explained such a curious thing to her son. 'Inside her body there is no one, Thabo. They say it is because the old lady died. That they must take her back to where her mother was alive.' Miriam's face was puzzled and she sighed. 'Maybe.' Her shoulders lifted in a huge shrug. 'But I think she's very sick.' Her face set like flint.

'And Luke?' Thabo still hadn't understood why Luke had gone away when he and Rebecca were to marry. He'd left Thandi himself, but his reasons were good. He didn't love her. 'Why's Luke gone back to Johannesburg?' Miriam's answer had been no more than another shrug and Thabo's mind had pulled back quickly as memory threw up a threatening glimpse of Estelle.

'Don't go to Cape Town,' Miriam had said, as if sensing his fear of Estelle. 'It's bad there now, my son.' Her people's growing defiance of white laws terrified Miriam. The Government had issued passes for women and because such things were contrary to her people's own laws, they had defied them. 'What now?' She'd shaken her head slowly as she talked to herself. 'It's not good,' she'd said quietly as Simon and Thabo slept.

'Simon.' Thabo shook the warm crumpled body that still slept. 'You have to wake up now, Simon. You going!'

Deep in the dark swirls of sleep Simon gazed up at the black face that looked down at him and he smiled. Then, closing his eyes, he settled back into the comfort of Thabo and slept again.

'Simon!' Thabo shook him a little harder. He'd heard his mother call from the house and he pulled the child into his arms, moving with him to the door. Miriam met Thabo at the kitchen door, leading him towards the car with Simon still asleep in his arms. The engine ran slowly and a whirl of blue smoke pushed at the grey mist of early morning, the slow throb of the car's engine wrapped in silence.

'Maybe it's better this way.' Rebecca laid Simon in a sleeping ball between packages on the back seat. 'Well.' She turned back to Thabo. Though her smile was wide it was meaningless and Thabo understood why. She was going away for her mother's sake, but, like Miriam, Rebecca knew it was useless.

'Let us know where you are this time, Thabo. I'll be back soon.' Rebecca climbed into the car quickly.

'You tell me when you marry.' Thabo reached his hand through the car window and took hers. Though both had become adults, the childhood friendship was deeper than ever before, glued fast by Simon.

'Luke will want to see you at the wedding. You'll have to come.' Rebecca was aware of tears welling behind her eyes and she let go of Thabo's hand before they broke. 'See you soon.' She pulled the car door shut quickly.

'You'll be OK, Miriam?' David called as he climbed into the driver's seat and Constance gave them all a slow wave. Though she'd appeared to know exactly where they were going and had acted accordingly, Miriam knew that her mistress' actions were no more than the obedience of a lost soul. Her heart wept for the white lady she loved and served.

'I be fine, master,' she called cheerily. 'I look after Mr du Toit too. You not worry. You take care of madam!'

'We will,' David called back as the car pulled away and Thabo watched Rebecca wave through the rear window.

'*Hamba Khale!*' he called after her, glad Simon was still asleep.

'*Hlala Khale,*' Rebecca called back that he should stay well and then Thabo froze.

Simon's small face had appeared at the rear window of the car and his fist banged on it as he disappeared into the swirling morning mist.

The gentle ping of Estelle's cup on a saucer broke the silence that had fallen between Luke and his mother. He'd told her he loved Rebecca. He'd said he would be working out his time before giving up his job in the Civil Service and then he would return to Bonne Espérance to marry her.

'I'm not sure what to say, Luke.' When she spoke Estelle's voice was careful. As he'd talked of his love for Rebecca there'd been no doubt in his words and no question as to how she might feel about it.

'Whatever you say it wouldn't make any difference, Ma.' The completeness Luke had found in Rebecca placed him on sure ground, though his legs had weakened the moment he'd faced his mother. But there was something different about her. There was a note in her voice that he hadn't heard before and it had thrown him into confusion. 'I'm sorry if it's not what you'd want, I'm sorry but I love her.'

'I can see that, Luke.' Estelle's emotion released itself in her eyes and Luke was confounded by the gleam of tears. 'Don't you know how much I want you to be happy? I want what you want.' Estelle paused and Luke tried to straighten his thoughts as she wiped her eyes. 'I'd never stand in the way of your happiness, Luke. You must know that.' Luke's mind raced through the possible explanations for his mother's behaviour. At any other time Rebecca's name would have launched her into a tirade of abuse about the girl whose coloured blood ran so clearly through her veins. But today his mother said nothing. 'Oh, Luke.' Her head dropped back against the small embroidered cloth on the chair and she closed her eyes. 'How much you need your father now.'

'Ma, please.' Luke tried to regain the authority he'd found in Rebecca. 'I don't need Dad to tell me what I feel.'

'You need your father, Luke.' Estelle repeated. She opened her eyes and leaned towards him. 'You need him now as you've never needed him before.' Tears ran down her face freely. 'Oh, God, that it had never happened!'

'Dad's got nothing to do with it.' Luke was totally confused.

'I'm talking about *your* father, Luke.' Estelle got up and pulled the curtains closed, wiping out the last beam of sunlight that entered the room. 'You have to know the truth.' Plunged deeper into the half-dark of the unknown, Luke watched his mother very carefully. 'You see, Luke,' she paused. 'Paul wasn't your father.' Estelle kept her back to her son. 'Till now I've tried to keep the truth away from you but I can't lie any more. Your father ... he was somebody I loved but he abandoned us.' She turned round. 'Your father denied you, Luke!' She moved to him suddenly, wrapping her arms around her baby and clinging to him. 'I didn't want to tell you before. I wanted to keep it away from you but I can't any more, not now. It's the truth and you have to know it.'

Luke didn't say a word. As his mother smothered him with emotions he'd never experienced before; she was wiping him out.

'Luke.' Estelle held him closer. 'Your father was ...'

'No!' Luke stepped back. He was trying to distance himself from the curious sensation of a mother's tears; fighting to hold on to himself as he resisted the love for which he'd longed all his life.

'Your father ran away when I got pregnant. We weren't married ... but I was expecting his child. He denied you, Luke. He abandoned us both.'

'It's a lie. I don't want to hear it!' Luke bolted for the door, trying to escape the insecurity that had swallowed him alive as her words closed round him.

'But you have to know.' Estelle's voice chased her son as she chased him to the door. 'It's Althea, Luke. You've got to listen to me!'

Like a lasso round his neck, Althea's name swung Luke back to face his mother. His head was spinning with the confusion of facts she'd thrown at him, but the name of Althea had driven a steel knife into his inner being.

'Althea's pregnant.'

Luke had heard the words long before Estelle said them, but he remained silent.

'She's having your child, Luke ... you can't abandon her. You can't do to your child what your father did to you.'

Luke hadn't heard any more. He'd run out of the house and across the stretching lawn to the garden fence. He'd ducked through the small gap between the wooden slats and the dog had watched him from the other side. He'd raced across the bare patch of ground and stopping beside the small clubhouse near the bowling green, Luke had stood absolutely still. Staring ahead of himself he'd tried to face what his mother had just told him.

'Althea's pregnant ...' Her words trod through his mind. 'Paul's not your father ...' A picture of Paul loomed in front of him, crumbling the moment his inner eye settled on it.

'No,' Luke whispered. His body shook as his mind turned inside out in its search for Rebecca. She had to be somewhere in the dark that surrounded him.

'Your father denied you!' Estelle's words filled his head and Rebecca was nowhere. Althea's having your child and you can't do to your child what your father did to you.'

Estelle had laid a trap and it had closed neatly around Luke's life.

Althea waited until everyone in the house had left for the day, and then she closed her bedroom door. Her eyes moved to the bottle of pills she'd found in her mother's drawer and she walked slowly towards them.

'You don't really imagine my son will marry you!' Estelle's voice still rang in her head as she sat down on the bed and opened the small bottle. The pills were tiny and very carefully she examined one. It was covered in a shining white skin and rolled in her palm like the embryo of a lost pearl.

'It hardly surprises me, of course.'

Estelle's face had been filled with distaste as she'd spoken and it had been then that Althea realised she'd never really seen Luke's mother before.

'I'd have thought you'd have known better than this. What do your parents say?'

Althea hadn't told her mother and father she was pregnant. Since the day she'd sat between the four white walls of the doctor's surgery and heard that she was, she had spoken to no one but Estelle. She'd been looking for Luke.

'So what are you going to do about it?'

Estelle's voice pushed through the walls of the doctor's surgery which Althea had built around her mind.

'Aren't you ashamed?'

Her words joined the doctor's. Althea had not just insulted her family, he'd insinuated, she'd insulted the entire Afrikaner nation.

'You want me to have an abortion?' Althea's own voice sounded in her head and it was filled with fear. The fear which had led her to steal the small bottle of sleeping pills from her mother's drawer.

'Abortions are easy to get nowadays, I'd imagine. Your parents will know what to do.'

Estelle's precise Afrikaans words had cast Althea back into the arms of parents who had fed her on fear and weaned her on guilt. They were emotions her father had used with immaculate precision as he led his daughter down the narrow route of Calvinism.

'It's all right, Luke. My period's due tomorrow.'

Althea's mind leapt further back, back to the day she'd conceived the life now hidden in her womb. Perhaps Luke's mother was right, she decided, and put the small pill in her mouth. Washing it down with a sip of water from the glass on her bedside table, she looked at the glass as if she'd only just seen it. A picture of Westminster Abbey was printed round its curve and a fine gold rim circled its edge. Her Aunt Marie had brought the glass from England and Althea could still remember her talking about the old buildings, bustling streets and green fields. She'd wanted to go to England herself one day and had talked about it with Luke.

'You've tried to trap my son but I won't allow it!'

Luke's mother had been right, Althea realised that now. She had intended to marry Luke.

'He'll deny that the child is his!'

Althea hastily tipped the small bottle of pills into the palm of her hand. 'That's strange,' she said out loud as she stared at them. She didn't feel anything. Not even the fear she'd lived with since the moment she'd understood what the word fear meant. It had meant black men then – Millions of black men who, her father told her, wanted only to rape and kill.

Gently Althea touched each pill. Pushing them one at a time into a small hailstone pile with her thumb, she counted them. There were sixteen, and opening her mouth she pushed her palm flat against it allowing them to roll on to her tongue. They settled for a moment in a sweet heap against her palate and then they were washed down like flotsam.

For the first time in her life Althea had taken responsibility for her actions and she felt strangely secure. She was warm and totally calm. Every muscle in her body had relaxed and she lay back on the bed, gazing up at the ceiling.

'I should have done that,' she said to herself. Althea was staring at the shade that covered the light bulb in the centre of the room. Her mother had told her to wash the shade the day before and she'd meant to, but somehow it had slipped her mind. Her mind was slipping. Althea was slipping into a deep warm peace.

'Althea?' It was Luke's voice. He was calling from a long way off and she called back.

'Althea?' Luke obviously hadn't heard her and he'd called again. He was shaking her. Luke was shaking her and she wanted to tell him to stop. But she couldn't. She was so tired. Couldn't he see she was tired? She had to rest because she was pregnant. She needed to sleep. Her baby was asleep too and Luke mustn't wake the baby.

'Why are you screaming?' she called to him inside her head and at last she knew Luke had heard. He'd stopped screaming. He'd stopped shaking her and she was sound asleep with her baby.

In the four hours since the ambulance had arrived to take Althea to hospital, Luke had tried to understand what had happened. His life had been wiped out by the lie of his own birth, rewritten in a moment by an unborn child.

Frustration had climbed on the back of rage and he'd fought to find Rebecca among the debris of his life. But she'd remained firmly outside it. She'd stood on the edges of the darkness into which he'd been plunged and she shone with a pure light. Rebecca had called Luke to move into that light, but he'd been unable to. Though he'd tried to reach out to her he'd held himself back. She wasn't a part of the dark world he'd found himself in, and love had stopped him pulling her after him.

'She's going to be all right.' The Afrikaans doctor's voice was a mixture of care and concern as he spoke to Althea's father later that day. 'And the child.'

'Child?' Jan Strydom's face crumpled in confusion that teetered on the brink of shame as he looked at the doctor.

'Your daughter's pregnant, Mr Strydom. And the child is alive.'

The doctor's words broke into Luke's thoughts and he felt suddenly sick. He was no different from his own father, after all. Whoever the man was, whose existence he hadn't known of till then, was himself. Luke had wanted his child to be dead.

As he stepped into the small hospital ward, Althea turned her head away from Luke, burying her shame in the starched white pillow.

'Althea,' he said quietly, but she didn't answer. The squeak of a nurse's shoes as they pulled free of the polished lino floor was the only sound, the rippling white of spreading sheets, the only movement as she made up the bed next to Althea's.

'It's me, Althea. It's Luke.' He felt the nurse's eyes touch his back in accusation and he lowered his head. Luke was suffocating in guilt. His own dark wish that the child would be dead pointed a finger directly at him, accusing him of being his own unknown father.

'I'm sorry.' Though Althea's voice was clear and Luke knew she'd turned to look at him, he kept his head down. He had yet to take the last step away from Rebecca, the only person he'd ever loved. 'I didn't mean this to happen.' Althea's hand reached for his. 'You don't have to marry me, Luke. I understand,' she said, and he pulled her into his arms.

Luke couldn't explain that whatever Althea did was no longer the point. It was he who had to free himself from Rebecca. Free her from the tight grip of a love that might pull her after him into the darkness.

'It's going to be all right, Althea.' Luke's throat closed, fighting back the words that formed in his mind. 'I want our child.' Though the words were true, Luke knew he was stepping into another lie. 'I want to marry you.' He whispered a promise his own father had never spoken.

CHAPTER THIRTEEN

Simon's aim was immaculate, proudly, he watched the stream of urine that ran into the hollow metal handle of a serving ladle. Forming a rising yellow pool in the shallow bowl, it lapped over the edges and tumbled in smelly waterfalls before sinking into a sack of mealie meal. Bending down quickly, he examined the edges of sackcloth on the red polished floor and waited for a damp patch to appear.

'I can hardly believe how you've grown up, Rebecca. You're quite the young lady!' Mrs Bernstein's voice was polite but nothing could hide the amazement behind her words. 'And I hear you're getting married.' The woman with the beef-roll neck stood quite still – an astonished monument to the past.

'I'm marrying Luke when we get back to Cape Town.' Rebecca stood on the other side of the scrubbed counter between them and smiled.

'I'm so pleased.' Mrs Bernstein conveyed to Rebecca how incredible she found the news. 'When exactly is the big day to be?' The smile on her face reached no further than her bright red lips and pinhead eyes challenged Rebecca for the reality of a date.

'The moment Luke's worked out his time in Johannesburg.'

Rebecca had gone to Mrs Bernstein's shop soon after they'd arrived back in the small mining town. It had been an attempt to lay the ghosts of time past, but an immediate whiff of Eau de Cologne 4711 had assured her that nothing had changed. The perfume monster was still alive and only Mrs Bernstein's grey hairs revealed the time which had passed.

'I see.' The woman's mouth formed a cracked lipstick ring round the tip of a cigarette. 'You'll be living in Cape Town, will you?' She peered through smoke and melting mascara towards Simon, who stood with his back to her at the far end of the shop, watching the bottom of the mealie meal sack.

'That little boy's your cousin, I hear.' Mrs Bernstein hadn't been surprised to discover the Conrad family had returned with a strange child. 'It runs in the blood,' she'd assured Wally Craine, the policeman. 'And that's not *all* that's in the blood!' she'd added.

'Come here, Simon.' Rebecca turned and held out her hand, but he hung back. 'He's a mongol, of course – what they call a Down's syndrome child now.' With that, Rebecca quickly informed Mrs Bernstein that she was right: Simon was *not* normal. 'Would you like to meet him?' she asked, and the shopkeeper's chins ducked under each other in panic as Rebecca led Simon towards her. 'Say hullo to Mrs Bernstein.' Simon propped his chin on the counter, his tongue flopped out and he stared at the curious painted lady in front of him.

'Hullo,' Mrs Bernstein said carefully, her eyes fixed on Simon's wandering pink tongue as it reached towards a slab of bright yellow cheese. 'No, dear,' she said, pulling the cheese away. 'Good grief!' She shrieked in alarm, whipping her hand away as Simon's teeth closed round it in a quick bite.

'Simon!' Rebecca pulled him back and the slobbery thread that stretched from his tongue to the cheese snapped in a small burst of spit. 'I'm so sorry.' She tried to control the laughter that bubbled inside her.

'It's hardly amusing, Rebecca! The child should be locked up, surely.' Mrs Bernstein wiped at the sticky spit streaks on the counter.

'I don't think children should be prisoners, Mrs Bernstein.' Rebecca's words were polite but pointed. 'I'm sorry we bothered you.' She moved quickly to the door with Simon and Mrs Bernstein closed it behind her.

'What on earth were you doing, Simon?' Rebecca asked as she got him outside, her face burning with a mixture of anger and shame.

'Want to go home.' Simon kicked his heels against the rough edge of the pavement. He clung to the flaking pillar that held up the verandah roof and had once balanced Rebecca's bicycle. 'Go home! Don't like her!' He glared at Rebecca through hot angry eyes.

'You've made that obvious from the moment we arrived.' Rebecca wrapped her arm around his shoulders and pulled him into her. She knew Mrs Bernstein would be watching through the shop window. She also knew it wouldn't be long before she'd phoned her friends to tell them what had happened. 'Do you want a milk-shake?' she asked, dragging Simon away towards the café on the corner.

'No!'

All Simon wanted was to get back into the shop and pee into the mealie meal one more time. Since the day they'd driven the last few miles of the long journey from Cape Town, he had been impossible. As the narrow strip of road drove a straight line through squat trees and tall brown grass, quite suddenly revealing the small mining town, he'd wanted nothing but to go home. He'd picked up a feeling of insecurity in the air around him and his every move had been destructive. Even the ant hill hadn't impressed him.

'Ugh!' he'd commented as he'd stared up at it from beside Rebecca. They'd discovered that 123 Z was empty and the whole family had gone straight to see it, as if seeking the part of themselves it still housed.

'It's the ant hill. You remember, I told you about it. Isn't it wonderful?' Rebecca had tried to share her pleasure with Simon but he'd hurled a stone at the huge mound in front of him. Covered in earth warts and pitted with dark-snake holes, the ant hill looked nothing like the one Rebecca had told him about. That had been spun by ants on gossamer thread.

'Let's climb it.' Rebecca tried to encourage Simon to climb with her, but he refused as his eyes settled on the tree at the top. Its roots clung to the heap of earth like dead arms and he'd spat at it quickly.

'Wait till you see what it's like from the top,' Rebecca had persisted and Simon hurled himself to the ground in refusal. Making himself a dead weight against her hand, he'd screamed till the pale faces of curious neighbours had peered over the hedge in alarm.

'I'm sorry.' Rebecca had smiled at them as Simon screamed louder. 'Dad!' She'd called her father out of the empty house to help, knowing that word of the mad Conrad child would quickly spread on the long tongues of gossip.

Inside the house, David had calmed Simon down and the family wandered through empty rooms in echoing silence. Each person was soon deep in their own past, and no one noticed Simon creep outside.

'Look!' Constance's voice called to Rebecca and she ran into the kitchen with David. Her mother was standing quite still in the empty room, staring at the base of the Bendix washing machine, which was still nailed to the floor. 'I remember that man. He was from Ndola and he was so stupid!' Excitement had lifted Constance's voice with the familiarity of memory, and it was then that Rebecca realised Simon wasn't with them.

'Simon! Where are you, Simon?' she called as she walked through the house, a small tornado of dust at her feet. 'Simon?'

There was no answer. She'd stopped in the doorway of the empty room that had once been her bedroom. Her eyes passed over the smudgy white walls that were half as big as she'd remembered, and in the corner a clump of hard grass pushed its way between the floor and wall as Africa reclaimed her past.

'You can have it,' she smiled to herself, calling again for Simon.

'He's not here.' Her father's footsteps echoed on the bare concrete floor. Dry red polish streaked patchy lines across it and a crack divided the room in two.

'You horrible little boy, stop that at once!' a woman's voice screeched from outside the window of Granny Cat's old room, and Rebecca chased her father towards the sound.

With his back arched, Simon's small body was teetering on the edge of the tin roof of the garage, a powerful yellow stream curving in a spluttering arc before dropping over the hedge into the neighbour's yard.

'You didn't do that in Mrs Bernstein's shop, did you?' Rebecca couldn't stop a smile as she watched Simon now. Sucking noisily through a straw he poked the popping dregs of milk-shake in the bottom of the glass and shrugged.

'Did you wee in Mrs Bernstein's shop, Simon?'

Though Rebecca's voice was more demanding than he'd heard it before, a slow innocent shake of Simon's head denied the truth. There was no way he would let on about the many spots in which he'd exercised the only power he had over the small town he hated.

Though it hadn't changed in appearance, the town had lost its heart. With the exception of Mrs Bernstein, the people there had welcomed the family back with familiar warmth and generosity, but there was something wrong. Northern Rhodesia was on the verge of independence from Britain and uncertainty stalked the wide sand streets. Fear of the unknown twisted the hearts and minds of the white population and no one talked of anything but the future. To stay or leave was the only question asked and it sat on the lips of all those who were still there.

'You wouldn't last out the winter,' Dewi Hawkins scoffed, for even he and his wife had argued about it from the moment Rebecca's family had moved in to stay with them. The rotund Welshman with permanently rosy cheeks wanted to pack up and leave for South Africa, but his wife talked only of going home to Wales.

'How long before South Africa goes the same way – before they too have a black Government?' she demanded, and Constance quickly retreated inside her own head. Though Rebecca's mother had found a small part of herself nailed to the kitchen floor of 123 Z, each day's arguments about the future upset her a little more. The small town, which had represented a moment's reality, was teetering on the threshold of oblivion, and Constance was aware that she stood on that same threshold. It soon became apparent that Simon's secret weapon was no longer necessary to bring about their departure.

'So you're going back?' Dewi Hawkins said. It was two weeks later, and they were all sitting on the verandah talking into the warm black night as it crept between the spread wings of moths that clung tight to the gauze. 'Well,' he finished his beer quickly. 'It's more than likely we'll join you down there ourselves.'

'Over my dead body!' His wife nodded her determination to return to Wales. The town had been shaken to the core the day before and whether they would leave or not was no longer the question. A white woman and her children had been murdered on the Ndola road. A massing crowd of Africans with the word *Kwacha* on their lips as they screamed for freedom had surrounded the family's car and burned them alive.

'I'd rather die of cold.' Mrs Hawkins passed a decisive nod to her husband. The barbaric killing had shattered the belief that no African would ever dare attack a European. Already people had begun to trickle out of the small town, leaving nothing but fear behind.

'Where's Rebecca?' David asked quite suddenly. He'd realised there was no place for his family in the small town any more and his mind was on their return to Bonne Espérance.

'She's still in her room, reading the letter that arrived for her from Johannesburg. It takes hours to read letters from your fiancé, David, you should know that. What do you think you'll do in South Africa anyway, Dewi?' Mrs Hawkins turned her attention back to her husband and the only problem that concerned her. 'You're not qualified for anything but hoist driving. At least we'd have the pension back home – unless you plan on pulling a rickshaw, that is!'

'Might not be such a bad idea.' Dewi drained his glass of beer and held a hand out for David's. 'I hear a lot of folk have gone down to Durban. What's it like?' he asked, his mind still searching for some place that wouldn't mean leaving the shores of Africa.

'Excuse me.' David stood up, going towards the bedroom Rebecca shared with Simon. 'Rebecca?' he called outside the door. 'It's Dad. Can I come in?' He turned the handle and stepped inside.

Rebecca was standing at the window. She was staring blindly at the gauze and she didn't react to her father as he moved closer.

'How's Luke?' he asked, glancing down at the letter which she held tightly in her hand. 'Was the letter from him?' But before David had finished speaking, Rebecca had spun round and buried her face in his chest.

'He doesn't want me.' Tears soaked through David's shirt and his daughter's body trembled in his arms. 'Luke doesn't want me any more.' Her words were drowned in grief and David held her tight. 'He's married someone else,' she sobbed, and David's heart burned with anger. He'd warned Luke he'd kill him if he ever hurt his daughter, and in the rage that consumed him now, he was capable of doing it. But his mind had filled only with the moment of hesitation in which he'd held back the truth of Luke's identity. It was that hidden truth that had led to this moment.

With her life scattered among the sand-browns of wide avenues, Rebecca sat on the ant hill and her eyes searched the small town. Luke's letter had wiped out the glory of love which had supported her and once again she was a small lost girl. She could see the deserted railway line behind the row of houses on stilts, and its abrupt end still haunted her. Her life had come to the same end. Against the buffers of Luke's letter she'd been forced into a lonely world once again.

Though his letter explained clearly what had happened when he'd returned to Johannesburg, Rebecca didn't believe him. He wrote that she was the only person he'd ever love, that he would love her always, that it was because he loved her so deeply that he'd had to let her go. Rebecca knew it wasn't true.

'*Lies!*' she screamed into the silence around her, and the word skimmed over the red tin roof of 123 Z as she threw the old brass key after it. She'd carried it with her ever since Luke had left Bonne Espérance, but now it had been proved worthless. The heat of midday powered its way through the branches of the tree and the hard crusted surface of the ant hill buzzed underneath her.

'It's all lies!' Rebecca's voice raced back into the past, searching for those same lies among the grown-ups who had gathered on the lawn below her years before. Their whispered words reached up like dancing demons now, as Luke's reached from the pages of his letter.

Paul's not my father.

Luke had explained that his real father had been an Englishman who'd abandoned him even before he was born.

I can't do that to my child, Rebecca! It's my fault and I'm responsible for him. I can't do what my father did.

Though love filled every word of Luke's letter, it passed Rebecca by as lies. She knew he'd rejected her only because she was not white and he'd discovered that he was.

'*I hate you!*' she screamed into the burning white sky that spread over the face of the small town that had stolen her life once again.

'Donna Rebecca?' A voice reached among the branches of the tree and Rebecca peered down through the leaves to find it. A tall black man gazed up at her, crinkle-eyed. He was exactly where Macaroni had been on the day she'd hidden on the ant hill with a stolen baby in her arms; but this time there was no baby. There was nothing. 'You come home, Donna

Rebecca.' The old man's voice came again and Rebecca raced down the ant hill towards him. Only then, as Macaroni held her in his arms, did he understand the urgency which had driven him back to 123 Z that day.

Macaroni hadn't known why the bush surrounding the small village he lived in had buzzed with electricity from the moment he'd woken. It had been alive with the crackling of a familiar presence, and the old man had sensed that he had to go back to the small mining town, though he didn't know why.

He'd taken his stick and, leaving his grandson in charge of the Coca Cola stand, he took long barefoot strides back to 123 Z. With the slow tread of an ancient elephant he'd returned to the place that had called him, his stick poking the sand before each foot trod on it. Macaroni had gone straight to the ant hill and there he'd peered up among the branches of the tree, uncertain what he was looking for but knowing he would find it.

'Why you cry?' he asked gently. His eyes were covered with a film of pale blue and he couldn't see Rebecca, but he knew that the child he'd loved since the day she was born was the one who wept. 'You not happy to see Macaroni, Donna Rebecca?'

'Oh yes.' Rebecca stood back and looked in wonder at the man who'd stepped out of the past. 'How did you know I was here?' Macaroni's ebony shoulders lifted inside the tattered shirt that was neatly tucked into baggy short trousers. His legs trembled like gnarled sticks, chewed at the knees and brittle with age as he shook his head with a smile.

'Who told you I was here, Macaroni?' she asked, wondering how the past had found her so easily.

'I know.' The dark skin on Macaroni's face creased in a smile, burying his eyes in a small moment of delight. 'The family? They are well?' But then, as if an iron had passed over it in shame, his face fell. 'What happened, Donna Rebecca ... when they kill those white people in the car.' He lowered his head. 'My people. They not killers!'

'I know.' Rebecca's voice was a whisper as she felt him reach out for her understanding.

'Forgive them,' he begged quietly.

'*Baba*,' she touched him with a word from the past. 'Granny Cat's dead.'

The old man nodded and his mouth dropped open, just a little. Turning away, he gazed into the burning white sky above them, looking for the old woman he knew he'd one day meet again.

'I go,' he said simply, and turning back to Rebecca, he smiled. 'Good-bye.' Crooked black fingers curled round her hand and his bottom lip pushed forward. 'I tell mama her child is well. That she is a woman now.'

Turning away, Macaroni's spreading bare feet flattened the small holes his stick dug in the sand ahead of him and then he stopped. He'd felt something jar against his stick and slowly his body curled forward to reach for it. Picking up the old key, he held it between his fingers and then he turned back to Rebecca. He couldn't see her. He couldn't see the key. But he smiled.

'You lost this, Donna Rebecca?' As Rebecca took the key from his hand, Macaroni turned away once again. Without another word, like an elephant following in its ancestors' footsteps, he walked out of her life.

'Goodbye, Macaroni,' Rebecca whispered. A large part of her was still tucked in his pocket and she knew he'd walked away for the last time.

'All gone.' Simon grinned at Mrs Hawkins as she stepped into the doorway of the room he shared with Rebecca, indicating with a proud gesture that everything which didn't belong had been removed. 'Simon go home now.' He put his arms round her and squeezed. He'd guessed it wasn't his well-aimed terrorist attacks that had made the family leave the small town so quickly, but he'd decided he'd remember them anyway. Just in case they ever came back.

'So.' Mrs Hawkins smiled as she stood beside the car in the driveway of their house later. 'Well!' She wondered if perhaps Dewi was right after all. She hadn't realised how much she envied the family who were returning to a secure place in South Africa. 'Take care won't you, love.' She smiled at Rebecca as she sat in the back of the car. Mrs Hawkins had seen the young girl crumble in the face of her loss, but she'd said nothing and wouldn't now. 'It's goodbye then.' She turned to Constance in the front seat. 'You get well now, dear, you hear?' Mrs Hawkins touched her friend's hand, her eyes filling with concern. Constance's illness had taken on a more threatening hue when cast against the insecurities of her own life. Mrs Hawkins wondered if she looked as old as Constance and pushed her hair back quickly, glancing at Dewi. 'We're all getting on. Maybe it's time to settle down in a country we're used to.' She wondered if Dewi was right when he said that one winter back in Wales would kill her. 'From what you've said about Cape Town it sounds very nice.' She smiled at her husband with a hint that perhaps he was right after all.

'Just keep your ears open.' Dewi spoke quietly to David on the other side of the car as the engine started. 'If you hear of anything, let me know.'

'It could be OK here,' David said. 'What's wrong with a black government?'

From the moment David had climbed into the car his eyes had been fixed on his daughter in the rear-view mirror. Since Luke's letter had arrived, he'd remained consumed with anger. He'd read it through himself several times, and though he could see Luke's words were true, his daughter had been hurt and only bitterness surfaced in his heart.

'South Africa's not all good, you know. There are problems there too — bad ones!' he added quickly.

Though David knew the truth of why Luke had left Rebecca, he also knew it was apartheid that had confirmed her childhood rejection.

'You OK, Rebecca?' he asked, aware that the bubble of love inside her had gone. 'Constance?' David's hand touched his wife's knee. Though she wasn't sure why they were going or where they were going to, she waved as Dewi banged the car roof in farewell.

'Home,' Simon hummed, watching Rebecca as she sat silently beside him. The feeling of loss that surrounded her was familiar and he pushed it away quickly. Turning to the rear window he shouted his goodbyes, his arm moving in sweeping waves that passed from Mr and Mrs Hawkins to the entire town.

'Goodbye,' he called to the ant hill, wondering why Rebecca had ever liked it. 'Goodbye!' he yelled to Mrs Bernstein's grocery store. 'Goodbye,' he called again as thick bush closed tightly round the small town that receded on a narrow tail of tarmac. There was only one thing Simon regretted. He wished he'd had another chance to pee right through the mealie meal sack.

Lydia tensed as she felt Stan crawl quietly under the bedclothes beside her, the illuminated hands of the small clock beside the bed hesitating between 4.30 and 4.35 in the morning.

'Are you awake?' Stan's breath brushed her cheek as he leaned over her. She could smell alcohol and nicotine lingering under the antiseptic lie of a mouthwash. More than that, she thought she could smell perfume. 'We must talk, Lydia.' But before she could stop herself, Lydia pulled away and climbed out of bed.

'Don't come near me!' The shout that erupted from deep inside her body didn't seem to belong to her. It was a stranger's voice, the cry of a woman so deeply hurt she was no longer in control. 'Do you think I don't know where you've been? Where you go every bloody night of your life, you bastard!' Lydia's voice rose to a scream as Stan reached for her hand. 'Let go of me! You reek of alcohol and that woman's stench is all over you!' She struggled to free herself but Stan held on tightly, his eyes reflecting confusion and pain.

'We must talk.'

'I've heard enough of your lies — I don't give a damn any more.' A knot of pain had pushed Lydia's stomach into her throat as months of controlled bitterness erupted. 'I hate you!'

278

Grabbing her shoulders, Stan swung her round to face him. 'You have to listen to me!' Tears filled his eyes but they did no more than add to Lydia's rage. 'I've tried to protect you but . . .'

'I don't need your bloody protection or your lies. Ask her to listen to you!' Before she could stop herself, Lydia's arm had swung free of Stan's grip and her hand smacked him hard across the face. 'Now get out!'

For a long moment Stan didn't move. He stood totally still and then, very gently, he released his wife from his grip.

'I'm sorry.' His voice was quiet, the look in his eyes one of total bewilderment, and as Lydia watched him she felt herself break. Like a small boy who no longer knew where to turn, he was reaching out to her, but she couldn't move. A steel rod drove its way up her spine and she watched in silence as he left the room, their life in tatters at her feet as love drowned in suspicion.

Thabo had returned to Langa township soon after he'd arrived back at Bonne Espérance and he'd gone straight to the single men's hostel in Zone Eighteen.

'Aye aye!' Fezile exclaimed as Thabo surprised him in the doorway of the hostel. The squat man with an indomitable spirit had been outside to watch the crowd gathering for a meeting. He'd argued that the people should go back to their houses, but they hadn't listened. All public meetings had been banned by the Government but the people had ignored the order and a nationwide demonstration against pass laws was to be held on 21 March.

'Inside!' Fezile had dragged Thabo quickly into the hostel. 'No bail, no defence, no fine. That's what they say we must do.' Fezile glanced up at Thabo and his gums closed together in a toothless grin. 'Ah!' He'd peered into Thabo's eyes. 'So you're a man now.'

'And this time I'll get a pass.' Thabo wrapped his arms round Fezile in warm greeting. 'Where are your teeth?'

'It's not Sunday.' Fezile patted him on the back with a laugh, but it was obvious that Thabo's friend had not been happy to see him at that particular time.

'You can't stay here,' Fezile explained later that night as they sat together under the concrete table in the dining room. It was the place Thabo had slept before. 'They say we must burn our passes, that we must fill the jails. On the twenty-first of March they say that we must close the white man's water pipe. No passes, no permits, no water pipe. Against guns?' He looked at Thabo in wide-eyed amazement. 'They tell us to challenge the white man's guns?'

Robert Sobukwe, Afrikanist leader of the Pan African Congress, had assured the black people that the demonstrations would be peaceful, but Fezile knew better. He knew his people's helplessness had been stirred to bitter anger and he'd seen the tense preparations at Langa police station. Extra police had been moved into the area and one particular white policeman, Andre Bothma, stood out from the rest.

'Cop Bothma', the people had quickly nicknamed him, unsure how to react to his apparent friendliness. The white policeman spoke fluent Xhosa and had assured the township people that he was there to help them – but Fezile was not fooled. Andre Bothma knew too much about his people, and he'd felt an instant mistrust for the white policeman with black ways.

'You must go to Cape Town,' Fezile whispered to Thabo. 'The police will be there also, but there you can hide from them and our people. They will force you to join them if they find you, and then you will be killed!'

Fezile had seen his fellow Africans stirred into an unwieldy crowd and they frightened him as much as Andre Bothma did. 'We can't do this thing with the passes that they want us to do, Thabo. Education is what we need – not this!'

Fezile was no different from other men of his age in the township. The older generation's lives had changed dramatically as the youth were led to defy their elders. The cracks in their ancient culture, brought about by apartheid as it divided families, had widened into a gulf of mis-understanding and it threatened everyone. Fezile knew that in many ways the young people were right when they accused their elders of subservience to the white man, but he also knew that the children themselves could destroy his people more quickly than any white government.

'Go on,' Fezile said early the next morning, as he pushed Thabo on to the train to Cape Town. 'Go to school!' he shouted after the thundering steel carriages as they pulled away.

But Thabo did not find things easier in Cape Town, and on the eve of the planned pass demonstrations he was still without a pass, a job or a place to live. Fezile had warned him that any black man loose on the streets would quickly be hauled away by either the police or his own kind, and Thabo was desperate, with nowhere to hide.

'Do you want something?' Thabo woke on the morning of 21 March to find the clear white face of a priest gazing down at him. He'd fallen asleep on the hard wood of a church pew and jumped with fright as Father Jamieson's hand touched his shoulder. 'It's all right.' His voice was soft and his eyes reflected a peace Thabo had never seen before.

'Are you hungry?' Father Jamieson watched him calmly across the table as Thabo ate sausages and baked beans. 'That was a stupid question.' The priest nodded at an overall that lay across the back of the chair beside Thabo. 'When you're ready you can try it on.' He stood up and moved to the door. 'Then I'll show you what to do.'

The way in which the priest had taken over his life still bothered Thabo as he lay back in a warm bath of water later that day.

'You'll sweep the classrooms when the children have gone home,' Father Jamieson's voice called through the bathroom door, and Thabo wondered again why he had been compelled to go into the church the night before.

He'd been looking at the school buildings attached to the church, wondering if he'd ever achieve his dream, now his people had resorted to anger. It had been then that a gentle nudge had pushed him into the Anglican church that was reserved for white worship. Thabo had never felt so curiously 'led' in his life. Something inside him had warned him not to resist the unknown voice in his head, and he hadn't.

'Here. The priest knows you're coming.'

Thabo had looked round the empty church for the source of the voice that had seemed to be part of himself.

But the voice was wrong. There was no priest in the church that night. Though Thabo had walked right up to the altar, peering curiously towards the dark doorways to the side of the building, he'd seen nobody. But something deep inside him had stirred and he knew he had to find the voice that had called him inside. It was then that he'd lain down on the hard wood of the pew and in some curious way, Thabo had felt welcome.

'Why you do this?' he asked as he stood in front of Father Jamieson, dressed in the fine blue overall with white trimming. 'You know me?' Though he knew the question was ridiculous, Thabo repeated it. 'You know me?'

'No.' Father Jamieson turned to the door, indicating that Thabo should follow him out of the manse and towards the school buildings outside. 'But I've been waiting for you.'

'Why you wait for me?' Thabo caught up with the priest halfway across the brick square that spread in front of a long line of classrooms. 'You not know me but you wait for me?' His English faltered in his attempt to understand what was happening. 'Why you wait for me when you not know me?'

'The Lord knows you. Now: these are the classrooms and cleaning them will be your responsibility. I'll organise you a pass in the morning,' the priest went on, as though nothing at all was untoward.

'A pass?' Thabo stared in amazement at the man who had known him without knowing him and talked of a pass as if it was easy to get. Had a voice spoken to him, too? He was totally confused by the priest who seemed capable of so many impossible things.

'I've been looking for someone to clean the classrooms,' Father Jamieson explained as he walked away, his head bobbing forward as if looking for lost coins on the ground.

'You give me a job?' Thabo called after him in surprise. 'Where I live? Where I sleep?'

'Here.' Thabo watched curiously as the priest pushed open the door of a small room. A bed was made up in the corner and his eyes were immediately drawn to an open book on the small table beside it. It fascinated him, but he didn't know why.

'You can move in whenever you like and the job's yours if you want it.' The priest left without another word and Thabo stepped further into the room. Very carefully he moved towards the open book, unsure why he felt drawn to it.

I am the door: if anyone enters by me, he will be saved and will go in and out and find pasture. I am the Good Shepherd.

Thabo stared at the Bible in amazement. Had he found the invisible being who'd guided him into the church the night before, he wondered. His fingers pushed hungrily at the flimsy pages and words jumped at him through flicking paper.

Awake all you who sleep. Arise from the dead and Christ will give you light.

Thabo's heart beat a little faster. Somehow he knew he was treading in ancient footprints; following feet that had long since left a trail across his heart.

Before I formed you in the womb I knew you. Before you were born I sanctified you. I have called you by name and you are mine.

Thabo's throat choked with tears as his spirit stirred in recognition of the power that surrounded him. His body shook, his pulse raced and his arms reached out for the glory that covered him, even as tears streamed down his face.

Hemmed in on all sides by a supernatural power, Thabo felt a peace that was beyond his understanding and yet familiar. He'd felt it brush against him in fleeting moments of time past. He'd heard its call and glimpsed its light as he'd walked blindly on in the dark. But now it left no gap for escape.

I am the Alpha and the Omega, the Beginning and the End. I will give of the fountain of the water of life freely to him who thirsts. He who overcomes shall inherit all things and I will be his God and he shall be My son.

The Almighty God Whom Fezile worshipped had dipped His hand into the universe and touched Thabo. The light of His being shone on him. Reaching beyond the curling edges of a mind closed by reason, it woke him from the dead.

On the eve of 21 March, 1960 Philip Kgosama addressed crowds of thousands in the townships of Langa and Nyanga. He told them to heed his call for a national anti-pass demonstration the next day, and his voice swept over the rusty rooftops on a note of challenge.

'How long shall we starve amidst plenty in our fatherland? How long shall we be a rightless, voteless, voiceless majority in our homeland?' His words had sunk deeply into the hearts and minds of an oppressed people and the Pan African Congress had moved ahead of the ANC's planned demonstration for later that year. Everything had appeared to be in the people's favour.

Harold Macmillan, the British Prime Minister, had warned the white Government that winds of change were blowing across the African continent. Momentum had gathered for international sports boycotts and as the morning of 21 March dawned, six thousand people gathered in the rain outside the men's hostel in Langa.

Fezile peered through a misty window as the crowd marched towards the police station. He knew the police were ready for them: he'd seen the Saracen armoured cars and mass reinforcements arrive in riot gear and carrying Sten guns. Fezile had also seen 'Cop Bothma'.

'Look at the bastards,' Andre Bothma whispered to the policeman beside him. He stood in a solid line of uniforms that faced the swelling crowd who moved towards them in a black tidal wave. Despite the warnings and several baton charges, the people kept on coming forward and there seemed no way left to stop them.

'Bloody kaffirs!' Andre Bothma's hatred was fuelled by fear. He knew the Africans who advanced towards him were angry. He also knew there was not one among them who would hold back from killing a white policeman, and his fingers closed round the gun in his hand.

'God!' Andre's knees weakened under a storm of stones and hatred. His finger trembled on the trigger as the swarming black crowd surged closer. 'Get back!' he screamed in Xhosa, raising his gun, his eye centering on the forehead of a black man. 'Get back or I'll fire!'

Someone did fire but Andre wasn't sure it was him. Though his finger was still on the trigger and a small puff of smoke rose from its muzzle in eerie silence, Andre didn't know what had happened.

Quite suddenly, the crowd had split in a fragmented mass of fleeing people and rattling gunfire pierced the air as screams raced between rows of ramshackle houses.

'Well done – one less to lock up.' A policeman turned the body of a black man over with his foot and Andre stared at the face of death that gazed up at him.

'Come on! It's chaos,' another policeman shouted as he ran past, snapping Andre Bothma free of the confusion that paralysed his mind. Houses blazed and telephone wires sang as they were cut. Road blocks had been pushed together and hundreds of black people fought to keep the police back while Langa burned.

Watching through the grubby window of his hostel bedroom, Fezile saw the flames lick high into the sky and his hand pushed at the tears on his cheeks. His people's dreams were floating away on dark clouds of smoke as silence fell in a shroud of ash.

But somewhere the crackle of a radio pushed through the silence and Fezile pricked up his ears. There had been a disaster during a demonstration in another township called Sharpeville, the white man's voice said in clean English. It was a black township near Vereeniging in the Transvaal. Although the police had warned the people to disperse, and low-flying jets had flown over them in an effort to bring order, sixty-nine African people had been killed.

Lydia stood quite still in the kitchen, staring at the small pot of potatoes that bubbled to a sticky mush on the stove in front of her. A radio played on the counter and the announcer's voice was hushed as he reported the murder of sixty-nine people.

'No!' she cried and Joe looked up from the floor in surprise. The tiny matchbox car he scraped on the lino between his legs stopped and he stared at his mother, unsure what he'd done wrong.

'Lydia!' She swung round to the door, bound by immediate tension as she heard Stan's voice. He stood quite still in the doorway and he was trembling, his face pale with fright, but Lydia didn't move to him. In the void that followed the news on the radio, her mind had already heard his unspoken words and fear filled the silence. 'I'm leaving.' As Stan moved closer, Lydia pulled back, her breath held tight in bursting lungs. 'I'm sorry I haven't told you before but I've been trying to protect you . . .'

'There's no need to explain.' Lydia's voice was paper-thin, her body rigid as she tried to face the moment with dignity. 'You don't have to worry about us. I'll take Joe out while you pack your things.' She turned to go as she felt a crack appear in the icy calm behind which she hid.

'Listen to me, Lydia.' Stan grabbed her arm and swung her back to face him.

'To more of your lies?' As her shell of protection broke, Lydia screamed. 'Are you going to tell me you're leaving for my sake? For Joe's sake? That you're sorry but you love someone else and you can't live without her? Damn you to hell, you bastard ...' As Lydia's fists lashed out at him, Stan pushed her hard against the wall and held her.

'I love *you*. There is no other woman.'

'Liar!' Lydia's voice rang round the kitchen and Joe's bottom lip trembled, uncertain how to stop the anger that had flared between his parents. 'I *know*, Stan. I know the truth!' The woman who'd stolen her husband was more real to Lydia than Stan himself, and tears of fury poured down her face. 'Tell your son your filthy lies. Tell him, and then tell him you love him!'

Lydia's head snapped back as Stan's hand held her chin firmly, stunning her to silence.

'There is NO other woman and NO other love but my country. That's the truth, but those people who've just murdered sixty-nine Africans don't believe it either. To them I'm a traitor. You're a traitor — our son's a traitor ... Are you listening to what I'm telling you, Lydia? Can you hear me now?'

Lydia stared at him as his words swept aside the images that tormented her.

'The only woman I've been with is the wife of a black man who died in that slaughter today. The mother of all the dead children in this country! The only lies I've told are to protect *you* from people who are so afraid, they'll kill rather than listen!' Lydia remained silent as she shared the agony he'd suffered alone till then. Tears ran down her cheeks but now they came from shame as her husband revealed what she could not have imagined in her wildest dreams. The secret hours of Stan's life had been exposed by the tragedy of Sharpeville and he himself was wanted by the secret police.

Among a small group of journalists, their lives under constant threat from covert forces, Stan had been warned many times for publishing articles under an assumed name as he spoke out against the Government. He'd met clandestinely with black leaders in an effort to find a way forward for their country, trying to avert the catastrophe that had happened that day. But Stan had been met only with accusations of terrorism and high treason, his life openly threatened. Finally, with the ears of the Government firmly closed to the cries of bleeding people, the mass of black South Africans had taken the situation into their own hands that day. They had demanded the right to be heard and been answered by bullets.

'Passive resistance is futile resistance, Lydia — that's what the blacks are saying now. Don't you see? It's exactly what the Boers said before they took up arms against the British. This country can't survive if the Government won't listen to reason. Those people who died in Sharpeville didn't want violence, not in the beginning. They've had violence from whites all their lives and they were trying to be heard – like the Boers tried. But nobody listens any more.'

Stan slumped wearily in helplessness and Joe pushed the small matchbox car up his father's leg with throbbing engine sounds.

'Our son deserves a country. This is his home, too, and we've got to make sure it's still here for him, and for all the children out there. We've got to make them listen before it's too late!'

It had taken Lydia many hours to calm down after Stan's sudden arrival home. She'd driven him to Cape Town station and then had returned home with her small son to wait for the knock she knew would come. Stan hadn't told her where he was going, but she'd understood why he'd left and quietly she sat with Joe in the sitting room.

The secret police arrived quite suddenly, rapping loudly on the front door. They asked to see Lydia's husband, Stan Liebenberg and she told them he was away on business. That he'd been out of town for several days, and she had no idea where he'd gone.

'Daddy's gone on the train,' Joe added innocently, and the police pushed their way past him into Stan's study.

Locked in the nightmare of her husband's truth, Lydia stood back silently as they walked out of the study a little later. They were carrying a large box of papers.

'What are you doing with those?' she asked, following them closely. 'Those papers are my husband's – put them down at once!' Her diminutive figure was dwarfed by the barrel-chested man she challenged, but she stood firmly in front of him.

'Excuse me.' He gazed down at her with the distaste reserved for traitors. 'Thank you, lady.' She stepped aside and he moved out of the house with the papers, leaving Lydia alone in the land of discovery. Discovery that her husband was not who she thought he was. That his only other love had been for people less fortunate than himself. In one short day Lydia's love for Stan had grown deeper than ever before and she was filled with pride.

'Why did they take Daddy's things?' Joe asked as she tucked him into bed.

'Because he's special.' She kissed her son, knowing it was also his future for which Stan fought. 'People always want what special people have and some of them just take it.'

It was only much later that night as Lydia looked into the study and her eyes settled on the upturned drawers of Stan's desk that she realised she was still shaking. Her husband had gone and there was no place left she could hide.

As Luke stepped back into the small flat in Johannesburg that night, Althea was as upset as Lydia had been. They'd rented the flat after their wedding and she'd quickly made it a home, but it was an empty one. Althea had also heard the announcement on the radio that day, but she hadn't registered the number of Africans killed. All she'd heard was that thousands of black people had gathered together in defiance of the white Government and every nerve in her body screamed.

'It's what Pa said would happen.' She paced the room as Luke sat down in a chair with the newspaper.

POLICE OPEN FIRE UNDER HAIL OF STONES, screamed the headline and he stared at it blankly as Althea went on.

'Pa says a white man without a gun is a dead man. He says they'll murder us in our beds!' She was back among her childhood fears of black people, fears which were reanimated each time their existence was rammed home by events like those in Sharpeville. 'I'm frightened, Luke,' she called to the man who always came home but was never 'there'. She watched his face as he read the paper: he hadn't reacted at all, and that was a large part of what frightened her.

'Don't you care what's happening? Don't you care about me or our baby?'

Since the day of their wedding they hadn't slept together at all. Luke had been honest, telling her the marriage was only for the sake of the child, but Althea continued to hope that one day it would be different.

'I want a gun!' she screamed at him suddenly. Pulling the paper down in a crackle of newsprint she stared at him, but still he wasn't listening. Luke was in a distant country. He was with Rebecca Conrad and Althea knew there was no way she could reach him. He seemed to have died inside his body.

'I'm listening.' Luke took her hand between his own as if she was a child. 'I don't want a gun in the house. I don't want to risk an accident — it's not worth it.'

'And if we don't?' Althea's eyes narrowed as she looked at him. 'If you come home one day and find your wife and baby hacked to death by a black?'

Luke shook his head, looking back at the newspaper. He wanted to bury himself inside it: to hide from the truth of Althea's need for a gun — that she no longer trusted him to protect her.

'You know how to use a gun, do you?' He looked up at her again, testing his own feelings of insecurity. 'You could shoot a man? To kill him?'

'Pa would teach me.' Automatically Althea turned to her father where Luke failed her and he tried to keep calm.

'I'm listening,' he repeated, and took her hands again, knowing her fears had been bred into her by the very man she would turn to for help. 'Pa's not right about everything, but OK – we'll think about it – just remember, it's not what I want.' Luke's mind turned to Rebecca, wondering how she felt now she was back in South Africa. He'd written to Riaan for news and knew the family had returned to Bonne Espérance. All he wanted was to be there. To hold Rebecca and step free of the prison he was locked inside.

'My father says you should buy me a gun.' Althea watched Luke carefully. She longed for his blue eyes to smile at her just once, but they were blank. 'Please, Luke. I'm frightened.'

But Luke's mind was still on Rebecca. He could feel the softness of her body against his and he ached for her. Riaan's letter said that she had changed since she went away. That she never talked about him. That she spent a great deal of time looking for someone in the coloured areas of Cape Town and Riaan didn't known why.

'What did you say?' Luke glanced up at Althea as she stood silently beside him. In order to return to his job, Luke had numbed his mind to everything and he seldom looked at Althea clearly. Any more than he could look at himself.

'It doesn't matter.' She walked away.

'If you want a gun I'll get you a gun.' Luke moved after her quickly, trying to pull himself away from Rebecca. 'Althea!' He held her by the shoulders and tried to be gentle. 'I don't want you to be frightened.' He pushed back the shame he felt for the lie of their lives but was swamped by his longing for Rebecca and he moved away quickly.

'I'll get you a gun.'

Father Jamieson had seen Thabo half an hour before Rebecca and Simon knocked on the manse door. After the children had left the school buildings he'd seen him leaning on a long broom, gazing through the window of a Standard Four classroom. His slim black body cast a curved reflection on the classroom window and the priest wondered again what Thabo was doing. He'd seen him outside the Standard Three classroom the previous week, and before that outside Standard Two, but he still didn't know why.

Since the morning Father Jamieson had found Thabo asleep on a pew in his church, he'd known the young African man had been sent. Each time he'd knelt quietly in the presence of God a gentle nudge had urged him: 'Feed my lambs.' And he'd done just that. He'd given Thabo a bed, work and food. Employing him as school janitor, he'd used his influence to get the precious pass Thabo needed to live in Cape Town, and he knew Thabo had found God. But still the priest sensed there was more his Lord wanted from him.

'I'll be with you in a moment.' He smiled at Rebecca as she stood in the open doorway with Simon.

'Wait!' Rebecca held Simon back as he turned to go, wanting only to find Thabo.

Simon's twelve-year-old body had grown strong but his mind was still that of a child and he let go a rubbery blubber of boredom. Every mile of the journey back from the small mining town had seemed endless and only as the white arches that led to Bonne Espérance appeared had he begun to breathe again. He'd sensed such unease in the car that he'd wondered if it really was home they'd been driving to. All he wanted was to see Thabo.

'Hullo, you must be Simon.' Father Jamieson moved to the impatient boy beside Rebecca. 'You wanted to see Thabo?' Simon's hand was lost in the priest's as he led him outside. 'Last time I saw him he was sweeping. Not fast, mind you. But the broom was with him.' He bent down to Simon and looked into the dark slanted eyes that spoke out the secret world of Down's syndrome. Thabo had told him long ago that Simon was his responsibility – a responsibility that he'd taken on as part of his manhood.

'You wouldn't be able to find the way to Standard Four, would you, young man? You know the number four?'

Simon's chin lifted and his eyes peered arrogantly down at Father Jamieson's head as he bent low in front of him. The priest's bald patch was an exact round, a fringed white round that matched the collar on his neck and the black circle of the cassock that spread at his feet. Holding out four fingers, Simon assured the priest he wasn't entirely stupid and quickly he used his fingers for a reassuring scratch, checking that his own hair was still on his head.

'Thabo!' Simon called loudly and ran away quickly towards the long line of classrooms across the brick square ahead of them.

'Miriam told us you've got Thabo a pass.' Rebecca smiled at the priest, unsure what to talk about and wanting only to speak of Luke. To ask somebody why her life had been broken in two.

'Thabo's mother, Miriam, yes.' The priest had uncovered Thabo's family background as he'd gone about getting him a pass. 'And he's told me about you too.' He held a hand out to Rebecca and together they walked across the pale bricks of the schoolyard towards the classrooms.

'Where's Simon gone?' Rebecca looked round in surprise. He was nowhere to be seen. Just a long line of windows, shone a vacant orange in the setting sun as Table Mountain cast a shadow across the tiled roof of the classrooms.

'Don't worry, he'll be fine. You were in Northern Rhodesia, Thabo said.' Rebecca's eyes reflected her absence and he cleared his throat. 'How are things there now? They're on their way to independence, aren't they?'

'Yes.' Father Jamieson had tugged Rebecca's mind back to the day she'd read Luke's devastating letter and she held herself firmly in the present. 'Miriam says Thabo's very happy here working for you, Father.' Though she smiled, Father Jamieson quickly recognised the half-smile of a lost soul.

'Simon?' he called quickly. 'Thabo?' He looked at Rebecca wide-eyed. 'Where have they gone?' Like a suspicious turkey at Christmas, he turned his head this way and that, peering down the long corridors as his hand rubbed his bald patch to a gleaming shine.

Simon had run instinctively into the square schoolroom where he'd found his friend deep in concentration at a small wooden desk. Thabo's long legs were spread wide, his knees pressed against the underside of the desk as he wrote. The broom was balanced against the desk and in his rush to greet his friend, Simon knocked it over. Skating on its bristly end, it sped away and came to a clattering halt against the wall.

'Boo!' Simon shouted as Rebecca stepped into the doorway. He wished the priest had taken longer to find him and squeezed closer to Thabo on the small wooden chair. 'Ssshhh!' he warned them not to interrupt.

'Ah, the broom.' Father Jamieson went and picked it up, carrying it like a straw spear back to the desk. The priest hadn't found Thabo sitting inside a classroom before and he was puzzled. 'What are you doing, Thabo?' His face filled with pleasure as he enjoyed the smell of chalk, ink and paper. He wondered if perhaps Thabo enjoyed it too.

'Arithmetic.' Thabo nodded at the blackboard. Six maths problems were scratched on the board in chalk. The teacher had prepared them for the children's homework and on the piece of paper in front of him, Thabo had written the answers.

'Full marks!' the priest said with a congratulatory nod as he checked them, wondering again about the young man God had led into his church. Smiling at Rebecca, he headed back to the door, needing time to understand the new piece of information he'd discovered about Thabo. 'You may have your friends' company for the rest of the evening.' As the priest slipped his hand under his cassock to tuck the small piece of paper into his trouser pocket, Simon's eyes moved to the floor. He was waiting for the paper to drop out from under the skirt of the cassock but it didn't, and Father Jamieson disappeared, leaving Simon to puzzle out where the paper had gone.

'Why he wear a dress? Where the paper go?' he asked Rebecca, the moment the priest's shiny bald head had disappeared.

'It's a cassock not a dress.' Rebecca moved to Thabo. She'd dreaded seeing him that day. His pity would be more than she could bear and quickly she looked round the classroom, trying to avoid talk of her cancelled marriage to Luke.

'It's better than the one we had, isn't it?' She dragged Thabo back to the small school they'd shared under the shade of an oak tree as children, when Luke was not a part of their lives.

'I'm sorry, Rebecca.' Thabo had approached her even before she'd stopped talking and as his eyes settled on her, she felt her spine bend.

'So!' She shrugged off her feelings. 'The old key didn't work and he married someone else. Better to find out now he didn't love me, isn't it?' She looked at the blackboard to change the subject. 'I suppose you did that lot in one minute flat. How many standards have you worked your way through so far?' She turned back to Thabo but he didn't answer her. He was watching her silently and Rebecca's throat clenched as she held back her emotion. There was something in Thabo's eyes she hadn't seen before and it disturbed her.

'What's this?' Simon had fixed his attention on the small inkpot that was sunk in a hole in the desk. Nobody answered his question so he dipped his finger into it to find out.

'You remember when we were children we talked about God, Rebecca? Do you remember that?' Thabo's eyes had never left her but they were not demanding.

'About I Titus being an angel, you mean?' Rebecca held her head back with a wary laugh. 'You said you didn't believe all that rubbish any more, Thabo. Not now you're a man.'

'There is a God, Rebecca.' Thabo's voice was gentle. 'I know because I have met Him. Because He is alive.'

'So that's what the priest has been telling you. That's why he took you in. Has he convinced you to join the church, too? Is that it?' Rebecca was suddenly tense.

'Maybe.' Though Thabo reached out to the deep anger in Rebecca, his voice remained quiet. 'God is alive, Rebecca.' Simon glanced at them quickly before ducking under the wooden desk-top, looking for the bottom of the inkwell.

'So? Tell me,' Rebecca smiled though it was a brittle smile, 'does Father

Jamieson shave his head at the same time as he shaves his chin, or does he polish them both?'

'God didn't take Luke away from you, Rebecca.' Thabo touched the open sore of her loss and at that same moment, Simon pushed the small inkwell up from underneath the desk. Shooting into the air, it turned a liquid blue somersault and splattered on to the floor.

'Look what you've done!' Rebecca's eyes blazed as she turned her anger on to Simon. Ink dripped a bead necklace from the desk and spread a wrinkled blue puddle on the wooden floor.

'It OK. It not matter.' Rebecca's outburst had fractured Thabo's English and he moved to Simon protectively. 'I clean ink here many times.'

'Because you're a school janitor?' Rebecca wished she could control the burning anger that swelled inside her but she couldn't. 'What's all this got to do with your dreams of school, Thabo? You're in a school maybe, but you're here to clean up white children's mess! Is this what your people are fighting for – what they're dying for? A white priest with a white God and a white congregation?'

The horror of Sharpeville had greeted Rebecca's family just as they'd arrived home, and it exploded once again in a small brick classroom. The murder of whites on the Ndola road was nothing in comparison to the seething anger that raged in South Africa, and nowhere could Rebecca see God's love.

'Who convinced you that this is all your life's worth, Thabo? A broom in one hand, an overall on your back and a Bible under your arm? Was it God or that priest?' Rebecca's words ran on in an angry torrent and Simon stared at her in amazement. Anger had snapped the steel rod in her spine and her emotion poured out faster than the ink he'd spilled. 'If there is a God, tell me where He is now? I can't see Him anywhere! Was He with those people who were murdered in Sharpeville? With the starving people in Cape Town! Or is He in Luke's lies to me!'

Simon glanced at Thabo. He wasn't sure he liked what was happening and his bottom lip trembled with guilt as his eyes settled on the ink that seeped into the wood floor at his feet. Whipping the tail of his shirt out of his trousers, he bent down and wiped it up. He wished he wore a dress like the priest. It would have made a better rag than his shirt, and no one would have seen the blue on the black. 'Clean!' He smiled with a clutch of bright blue shirt in his hand. But Rebecca had turned her back and moved away from them both.

'It OK, Simon.' Thabo took his hand. He felt suddenly unnecessary and wondered why the comfort he'd found in the shelter of supernatural wings hadn't touched Rebecca. 'Do you want to talk, Rebecca?' Thabo saw God in everything and held tightly to his newfound faith. 'With God there is always a reason, even for the bad things.'

Slowly Rebecca turned and looked at Thabo carefully. 'Do you remember when I told you about Johannes Villiers, when I was small? Remember when we looked for him in the winemaker's house?' Thabo nodded but he was unsure what Rebecca was getting at. 'Johannes Villiers is the reason God found to take Luke away!'

Rebecca was just half-alive and her pain was so close to the surface it touched Thabo. He'd also lost Luke and he could pinpoint the exact moment it had happened.

Maybe when we're grown-up we'll meet again.

Luke had said those words on the morning he'd left Bonne Espérance, and Thabo had known then that their friendship was over. Apartheid was a grown-ups' disease – and now, they were all grown-up.

As Thabo went back to his room after seeing Simon and Rebecca home later that evening, Father Jamieson stepped out of the manse to walk with him. The priest needed answers. He had plans but he wanted to make sure they were right.

'That maths you did wasn't easy, but you managed it. Didn't you tell me you'd never been to school?'

'Not school.' Thabo watched his feet push through the darkness that had fallen over the brick paving. 'When we were young, Rebecca she teach me from her school. And Luke.' Since Rebecca's visit, Luke's name sat uncomfortably on his tongue and there were many things he no longer understood about his childhood friend.

'And what is it you want of life now?' Father Jamieson stopped walking and Thabo gazed down at the polished black shoes that peeked out at the world from under the priest's cassock.

'School.' Thabo's English fractured again. 'I want Matric.' His eyes remained fixed on the priest's shoes and Father Jamieson's head tilted back as he looked up into the night with a wide smile. Forming a tent of black silk, the sky was shot through with stars and his eyes followed the lines of the Southern Cross. At last he knew why the young black man had been sent to his door and, turning to the stranger who had become his own, he smiled.

'School?' Thabo was too old to go to school and there was no place for him in the all-white school belonging to the church, but the priest had sensed there was a way. 'Maybe.' He ran his finger round the circular fringe of hair on his head while his mind trod backwards through his life. 'But maybe I'm past it.' Father Jamieson was back in the days he'd taught in Latymer High School in London. It was many years since he'd left teaching to serve God as a full-time minister, but teaching had been a large part of his life and he missed it. 'Why not?' His eyes lit with a sudden smile. 'Shall we give it a go?' he asked the young African man who stood on the edge of a lifelong dream.

Father Jamieson had realised that God, as always, had used the economy of His creation when he'd brought Thabo into the church that night. God had needed no dustbin for leftovers when He'd created the universe, using nothing to achieve everything. He longed to teach, Thabo longed to learn, and the priest's eyes were lit with the excitement of a miracle.

'Come!' The priest turned back to the manse, his head dipping as he searched the ground for the wisdom he needed to fulfil God's will in Thabo's life.

'You say you want Matric? Let's see what we can do about it, lad.' Father Jamieson had already dived back into the world of chalk, desks and ink. 'Mind you,' he stopped, eyeing Thabo challengingly. 'It'll depend on you as much as on me!' He headed on towards the dark classrooms, leading Thabo into a shared dream.

CHAPTER FOURTEEN

The residential suburb of Claremont nestled under the steep green rise of Table Mountain. Winter rain formed lazy streams down its back and heavy folds of cloud rolled over its top. Rebecca was in a narrow street lined by Victorian terraces, knocking at the door of a house. An ancient Indian man had spoken to her on the *stoep* of his home in District Six the day before, and she'd quickly discovered he'd once known Johannes Villiers' daughter, Elsie. He'd told Rebecca that Elsie Villiers' grand-daughter, Lorraine Hendrickse now lived in that particular house.

'Is your mother at home?' Rebecca asked as a young boy peeped at her through a slit in the heavy lace curtains at the window. 'I need to speak to your mother, Mrs Hendrickse.' The child disappeared behind a fringe of white daisies and Rebecca knocked again. In her handbag she had a copy of Elsie Villiers' baptism record and the letter that confirmed Johannes Villiers' identity as a Beauvilliers.

'My mother says she's busy.' The small boy had opened the front door an inch and he eyed Rebecca suspiciously through the narrow gap as she spoke.

'Will you tell her my name's Rebecca Conrad and I've come to talk to her about her grandmother, Elsie Villiers. I've been in District Six and . . .'

A young woman moved into the doorway to close the door and Rebecca pushed her foot against it quickly.

'Excuse me. Mrs Hendrickse?'

'My son told you I was busy.'

The woman was delicate. Her jet-black hair was swept back before tumbling over one shoulder in a thick pony tail and her eyes were dark with fear.

'I have to speak to you.' Rebecca forced her body between the door and the wall. 'It's very important. My name's Rebecca Conrad and we have a common ancestor, Johannes Villiers. He was your great-grandfather and –'

'I'm sorry but you've come to the wrong house.' Lorraine Hendrickse tried to close the door but Rebecca persisted and the small boy stepped back nervously as his tiny sister clung to her mother's skirt.

'I know I haven't got the wrong address.' Rebecca pulled the two pieces of paper from her handbag and held them out. 'Johannes Villiers was my grandmother's brother and his daughter, Elsie Villiers, her baptism's on this church record. She's your grandmother, isn't she? May I come in and talk to you?'

Being so close to finding her own beginnings in Africa, and the 'self' which Luke's rejection had shattered, Rebecca also found the strength to persist. 'If I could explain,' she went on quickly. 'When Johannes Villiers was born he was given to a Catholic orphanage because his father was a white politician.'

'I'm sorry but this has nothing to do with me.' The woman tried again to close the door but Rebecca held it open.

'What's wrong?' She watched Lorraine Hendrickse carefully. Her face was rigid and dark half-moons hung under her eyes. 'Don't you understand why I am here? We're related. You're a Beauvilliers like me, and the place where I live, it's a wine farm near Stellenbosch called Bonne Espérance. It's where your family came from. We're cousins, that's what I'm trying to tell you.' Rebecca challenged Andre Bothma's claims on Bonne Espérance at the same time as she tried to calm Lorraine Hendrickse's fear. 'Please. Just read these.' She held out the papers but Lorraine didn't take them.

'Can I live there, on the place you're talking about?'

'Sorry, I don't understand what you mean. I said you're . . .'

Lorraine turned away, leaving the door ajar as she moved to the sitting room, beckoning Rebecca to follow.

'Did you notice that on your way in?' Pushing back the heavy lace curtain she pointed at a house across the road. It was boarded up with sheets of corrugated iron and stood solitary like an unvisited tomb. 'I knew the people who lived there. They were nice people, family people. But – they were *coloured* people.' Her look fixed on Rebecca. 'I watched them leave. They couldn't sell their house because they were given no time, you see. So I watched them cry as they left before they were dragged out in the name of Group Areas. Do you know what Group Areas means? What happens when your home is suddenly declared For Whites Only – *Net Blankes*? When you have to clear out because you're no longer the right colour, the way they threw people out of their homes in Sophiatown in Johannesburg, naming the new white suburb "Triumph"? Were you there when they bulldozed those people's lives and said it was for the good of the country?' She shook her head. 'I'm sorry.'

Rebecca felt sick with shame and Lorraine went on quickly, her face set as her children watched her nervously: 'My skin looks white too, like yours. Maybe even whiter *than yours*, but according to the law I'm *not* white.' She peered at Rebecca, her eyes filled with the frustration of a lifetime, as were her words. 'Do you think I don't know that somewhere in my past there's a white man? Am I supposed to be honoured that my ancestor is your ancestor too? Do you expect me to thank him for donating a little white blood?' Though she paused in her anger, she didn't breathe. 'I don't thank him, I hate him!'

Rebecca remained silent as Lorraine went on, years of bitterness finding release. 'Have you heard the expression, "trying for white"?'

There were no words left in Rebecca's mind so she shook her head.

'The problem is that when you "try for white" you're really trying to die. I tried, now I can't walk the streets in case I bump into someone from my own family – a coloured someone who somebody else might see me talking to and who could use it to prove that I'm not really white!' Lorraine's voice quietened and her hand pushed into the curly brown hair of her small daughter. 'So my family pretends I'm dead.' She looked at the papers in Rebecca's hand. 'And those papers, they could end my life with the stroke of a pen. Wipe out my white husband and my children because they prove I am Elsie Villiers' granddaughter.' Lorraine held her head back and her being filled with quiet dignity. 'If you told me I would inherit a million pounds by admitting who I am . . . I'm sorry.' Her voice dropped to a whisper. 'How can I?'

As Rebecca told Lydia about Lorraine Hendrickse later that day, she'd still been stunned by the reality of apartheid which had confronted her. Pouring out the story of Johannes Villiers greatgranddaughter, Rebecca had wanted to deny the country they lived in. Lydia listened in silence. Suddenly Rebecca noticed there was something different about the room.

'Where have all the books gone?' She looked around at the bare shelves and Joe gave an enormous shrug as she turned to him.

'We're going,' he said flatly.

'What's Joe talking about, Lydia? Where's Stan?'

'Away.' Lydia stood up and moved to the last few books not yet packed in boxes. Rebecca had been talking about the very things that had driven Stan into exile but she said nothing. 'I was waiting for you to accuse my Afrikaner husband of what Lorraine Hendrickse said about Group Areas.' Lydia kept her back to Rebecca.

'Lydia, please.' Rebecca's mind reeled with confusion. 'Where's Stan gone? What's happened to him?'

'Stan hit a small problem.' Lydia turned to her with a half-smile. 'He opened his mind to something outside Afrikaner thinking and he became a traitor.' She bent down, putting the books with the others in a box at her feet. '*Black Beauty* – that's banned, isn't it?' She glanced at Rebecca with a sudden smile. 'The coffee's not packed. Would you like some?'

Filling two cups, Lydia stirred in the sugar and talked quietly about what had happened on the night Sharpeville exploded in anger and death. She was glad to be able to talk at last, sensing that for the first time, Rebecca really was listening.

'The only thing I can't believe is how much I love Stan now. It's more than before, would you believe that?' Lydia's face filled with confidence. 'Odd what it takes for us to find out who the person we live with really is. That he's "not bad for an Afrikaner"!'

Every thought Rebecca had ever had about Stan jumped into her head and she felt deeply ashamed. He'd risked everything to help those less privileged than himself yet she'd always considered him a part of the Afrikaner Government.

'I'm sorry.' She lowered her eyes.

'Why? We're going to make the most of it. It'll be a fresh start.' Though Lydia knew she would be driving to a small seaside town in South West Africa, where her life would change dramatically, she was smiling. The one-horse town of Luderitz that would hold her family's future was surrounded by the Namib Desert and their living would be eked out by the meagre work Stan would do for the local newspaper. But Lydia's voice was full with hope. 'Do you know, I honestly think it's the best thing that's ever happened.' The cold suspicion that had poisoned her mind when she'd thought Stan was in love with another woman was gone and she'd recaptured feelings as fresh as the day they'd met. But there was still sadness somewhere behind her eyes. Lydia and her family would be leaving the country of their birth for the isolation of exile.

'Do you remember how afraid I was when you started climbing around in our family tree? I never told Stan about it, you know. I hid from him and he hid from me.' Lydia admitted her fear to Rebecca for the first time. 'It's so strange. Now it's because we are *white* that we're in trouble. We're supposed to know better than to defend non-whites!' Her voice filled with laughter. 'Just imagine if they knew about Johannes Villiers!'

Rebecca leaned back in her chair, one of several that waited to be moved out with the rest of Stan and Lydia's life.

'Luke works for the Government, Lydia.' It was the first time Rebecca had admitted that fact to herself. She needed a reason to hate him but still she couldn't. 'So! We're both leaving.' She shrugged, trying to drive Luke's constant presence from her thoughts. 'You know Dad's sending me to Europe.'

'England, he said.' Lydia lifted another cane chair and sat beside Rebecca. In all the time she'd known her young cousin, Rebecca's heart had only been truly free when she was with Luke. 'I know about your mother, Rebecca.' Lydia could still see the pain in David's face as he'd told her that Constance had Alzheimer's disease. At Groote Schuur Hospital he'd heard the words he'd dreaded for so many years and his concern had been for Rebecca. He knew her mother's memory would fade until she could no longer perform the simplest bodily function and David wanted only to protect Rebecca: to hide from her the degradation of Constance's slow slide into a world more lost than the one they occupied.

'London's an exciting place, Rebecca.' Lydia tried gently to push her out of the nest in which thorns had grown. 'You'll have a whole new life. Isn't it strange? We're both getting a second chance.' She took her hand. 'Who knows? Even our country might one day.'

As the South African Airways Viscount raced down the runway of Cape Town airport to begin its two hour and forty-minute flight to Johannesburg, Rebecca pressed her face against the small round porthole. It was six months since Lydia had left for South West Africa and now Rebecca could see her own father waving from the front of the airport building. She could see her mother, too. Miriam was holding Constance on her feet, pointing at the plane as she tried to get her to wave. But Constance didn't wave. Like a tiny shrunken bird that had lost its way she stood quite still behind a film of tears. They flowed freely from Rebecca's eyes as she wondered if this would be the last time she would see her mother. If the fragile shell, all that remained of the strong and loving woman Constance had once been, would be there when she returned. Catching sight of Thabo and Simon beside Miriam, Rebecca tried to wipe away her tears. They waved as if the plane depended on them to whisk it off the ground till finally it disappeared behind swirling cloud. The throbbing of the engines had joined the throb of Rebecca's heart and her thoughts were caught in the whirring power that wiped out her past.

'Aye aye.' Shaking his head slowly, Fezile gazed at Thabo. There'd been so many changes since he'd first met the arrogant and hardened youth beside a dustbin, that he could hardly believe his ears. Thabo told him his dream had come true; Father Jamieson had decided to teach him.

'I have also found the God you worship.' He added the news that meant even more to Fezile than education. 'Now I understand why you praise Him.' His eyes shone with tears as he spoke and Fezile's spirit bubbled, knowing that only tears expressed the touch of God's Almighty love on a man.

'Those teeth you say you buy me,' Fezile spoke in Xhosa, for Thabo's English had been perfect and his own quite suddenly embarrassed him. 'You speak like Shakespeare, so I speak like a Xhosa!'

Father Jamieson had introduced Thabo to the English writer's works and the beauty of his words had reached deep into his African soul. Stories of white tribal warfare in centuries past moulded easily into his ancient culture, living comfortably alongside it.

'You remember my teeth?' Fezile went on with a grin.

'Of course.' Thabo dipped a small ball of mealie pap into the bowl of gravy Fezile had given him, watching the warm brown liquid soak into it. The process of eating was something he'd missed as much as he'd missed African food and, holding the dripping mealie pap ball over his mouth, Thabo caught the sweet gravy drips on his tongue. 'Father Jamieson will know where to buy teeth.' He smacked his lips.

'The priest?' Fezile's mouth opened in an astonished black cave. 'He has plastic teeth?' Fezile's mind wrestled with the image of a priest handicapped by false teeth as well as a collar. 'I put mine back in the undertaker's bin.' Fezile roared with laughter and the empty cave of his mouth opened wider. 'And you will get Matric, Thabo!'

'I'll try.'

'You will get.' Fezile joined Thabo in English for a moment. 'You are one clever Bantu!'

'What about you?' Thabo knew that life in the black townships had grown more difficult for the older generation. He'd heard how the youth had turned against their elders, calling them 'Uncle Toms'. They'd challenged them to stand up to the white man, forcing them to swallow paraffin, raw meat or oil if they'd bought it from a white shop. 'The priest says you can live with me, Fezile. You will be safe there.'

'I live here.' Fezile banged the bed they sat on. 'Here.' A small cloud of dust billowed from the mattress and he coughed. 'This is my place.' Fezile indicated the bedroom of the men's single quarters with a wide sweep of his hand. He was more afraid of the ugliness that was changing the character of his people than he'd ever been of a white man's gun. Though he knew as well as anyone that the system of apartheid had raped his nation, Fezile didn't agree with the methods being used to fight it.

'Our children must all go to school like you, Thabo. Not burn down the school!' His eyes filled with a burning passion. 'We are not a *free* people: no, but we are a *proud* people! And what pride in hatred? Resistance is in the mind! Love! *That* is our weapon!'

The politics of the African National Congress had changed and Oliver Thambo's predictions of ten years before had begun to come true. He'd said that in time there would be only one method left to his people and that day had dawned, as Nelson Mandela encouraged armed struggle against the oppressor. While insisting that the ANC was a non-violent movement, he added that members who resorted to violence would not be chastised. Albert Luthuli, freed from a banning order for long enough to collect the Nobel Peace Prize, had also given tacit agreement to violence.

'Against whom are we going to fight?' Fezile stared at Thabo blankly and then he banged his chest with a rigid index finger. 'We will kill ourselves with our hatred. Is that freedom?' Quite suddenly Fezile chuckled. 'You know what they call themselves, these children? "Comrades." Do you know what that means, Thabo? Is it maybe Russian for "kaffir".' His chuckle turned into a cough and he threw his head back suddenly. *'Uthixo wethu uphethe!'* His shouted words rattled the tin roof. 'Our God reigns!' Fezile translated the words with a wink in honour of Thabo's friend, William Shakespeare. *'Nkosi sikelel 'iafrica!'* His voice lifted in song.

'Maliphame uphondo lwayo. Yiva nemithandazo yethu. Nkosi sikelela thina lusapho iwayo.'

The delicate children's tune of *Incy Wincy Spider* filled out with the mellow harmony of Africa as Thabo's voice joined his friend's. Bursting through the walls of the single men's hostel in Langa their plea rose high above the rooftops.

'God bless Africa. Let its banner be raised. Hear our prayers and bless our children. Descend, O Spirit!' Their voices had covered the troubled township in prayer.

'For your Father Jamieson!' Fezile dropped a plump plucked chicken into Thabo's lap and grinned widely. 'The priest can eat chicken with plastic teeth?'

'Where's Thatomkhulu?' It was only then that Thabo noticed the old cockerel was not in the room.

'Thatomkhulu inkukhu?' Fezile looked at Thabo, a deep sadness behind his eyes. 'Old-man chicken. Uh! He has gone.'

'Where?' Thabo waited silently and quietly Fezile told him. Old-man chicken, the old cockerel who'd escaped the pot for so many years, had been killed by 'comrades'. Slitting the chicken's throat, they'd pushed the bloody carcass into Fezile's bed, marking him out for punishment as the white man's friend.

'You think I will run away from children?' Fezile laughed, his pride rising above the grief he felt for the old rooster. 'I would run first from Cop Bothma, my friend!'

Andre Bothma had been promoted since the Sharpeville Massacre and, posted to a small police station in the black township of Langa, he'd continued to befriend the local people. His beliefs that the country's future depended on the white man had not changed. He believed white rule was in the interests of all South Africans and he'd found a way inside the minds of the African people. To achieve his ends Andre Bothma had become one of them.

His Xhosa was so fluent nobody could tell his voice came from a white man. He listened in on their gossip, spread his own and quickly he'd found his place within the community. He'd assured them he was there to help them, and in many ways Andre Bothma believed what he said. Violence and intimidation threatened everyone, but most of all it threatened the black people themselves.

'Why do you let your children boss you around like this?' Andre had asked the elders many times. 'Where's your dignity? You think your ancestors are proud of you?' He'd used their own culture to convince them he was right and if an elder questioned the sense of an old man taking on the youth, he asked if they were afraid of dying.

'Have you lost your courage? Are you nothing compared to the Zulu who greets death in battle as an honour?' He also challenged them with their fear of the Zulu warrior nation.

'What about you?' the people argued. 'You're a white man! The comrades will kill you before they kill us.'

'Never!' Andre Bothma had laughed in the face of this assertion. 'No black will ever kill me. My great ancestor was killed by a black and it is he who protects me now.' Andre had used the story of Pieter Bothma's death at the hands of I Titus to back his claims of immortality, and soon a myth had grown up around him. The story of Cop Bothma's invulnerability had spread quickly through the townships and its truth had been proved on several occasions. Though youths had attacked him with knives, sticks and knobkerries, he'd emerged unscathed while they died in a hail of bullets.

'They're so stupid they use knives in a gun-fight, and yet you're frightened of them?' Andre had challenged the elders again and quickly he'd found a place for himself as leader of the older generation. Holding up the system of apartheid as God's way in Africa, Andre Bothma used it to serve both his country and himself, striding through the streets of Langa like a white colossus.

*

Rebecca wandered round the airport, drank cups of coffee and looked at every small shop as she waited in Johannesburg to board the South African Airways flight on to London. But there was only one thing in her mind: only one person in her thoughts. *Luke lived in Johannesburg*. She was closer to him now than she'd been since he'd left Belville station and his last words still rang in her head.

I'll love you always.

Pulling her thoughts away, she looked up as passengers for the London flight were called to move into the departure hall. Pushing the luggage trolley forward, she walked to the gate of the International Departure Hall and turned her back on her country.

As Luke stood silently outside a small shop window in the airport, he held down a sudden urge to run after Rebecca and pull her back. He wanted to shout that he loved her, that nothing would ever stop him loving her, but he stood silent and out of sight.

He'd been in the airport building from the moment Rebecca stepped off the Cape Town flight. Riaan had told him she was going to England. He'd also told him the times of her flights and Luke had sensed that the young Afrikaans mechanic had taken their love as his own burden. But, although Luke's eyes had never left Rebecca and his body had ached with her presence, he'd remained out of her sight.

'Passport please.' Rebecca held out the blue British passport she'd come by so proudly and the airport official glanced at the photograph with a quick smile of appreciation. 'Have a good trip,' he said and she moved past him, turning into the long corridor that led to the departure gate. But as she turned, as she moved away, in the tail of her eye Rebecca saw something. A man was standing on the other side of Passport Control and she thought it was Luke. Pushing to get back to him, she tried to call out but was swallowed by the crush of people and dragged away with the crowd.

'I was dreaming,' she told herself as she looked ahead at the silver Boeing 707 she was about to board. 'BLOEMFONTEIN' was written on the side of the gleaming jet and one silver wing reached over her head as she walked towards it.

'May I have your boarding card, please?' A smiling steward held out his hand as she reached the top of the gangway, but Rebecca hadn't heard him. She was looking back. She was still looking for Luke, certain he was somewhere near.

Standing on the other side of the airport building, Luke's mouth was dry and his throat clenched. Rebecca was looking round from the door of the plane. He wanted to run across the heavy blue tarmac to be with her, but his legs wouldn't move.

'It's the tenth row back on the right,' the steward said as Rebecca stepped into the plane. 'Alone, are you?'

'Yes.' For the first time she felt tears pricking her eyes but didn't look back again.

'A sweet?' A smiling hostess held out a basket of boiled sweets and Rebecca took one without knowing why. 'Are you all right?' The hostess asked, and Rebecca nodded. Turning away before her tears broke, she repeated to herself that she must have been dreaming. Through the plane window there was nothing but empty brown land. Dumps of rejected gold-dust sat like blind yellow pyramids and Luke was nowhere to be seen.

With a rising scream of jet engines the plane moved forward. Taxiing slowly down the tarmac, it passed by the silent dumps, and the brittle brown grass of the Transvaal fluttered as it turned for take-off.

'Is your seat belt done up?' The hostess checked as she passed and Rebecca looked back out of the window. The plane was moving, the engines screaming for the release of flight as they gathered speed and only then did she see him. A solitary figure stood on the other side of the airport fence and she knew it was Luke. Peering down as the plane lifted she could just see his tiny figure and her hand pressed against the porthole window as tears ran freely down her cheeks.

'Goodbye, Luke,' she whispered as the unaccustomed power of the plane lifted her free of her own body.

'I love you,' Luke called up to the giant silver bird that flew over his head. As his hand reached to Rebecca in a motionless wave he knew their minds had met.

Lydia glanced up as a single-engined plane swooped low over the small town of Luderitz in South West Africa. Its paper-thin frame shone as it flew towards the setting sun and her eyes moved downwards, settling on the dull red glow of sand that surrounded her.

She knew that Rebecca was beginning her new life that day and wondered if the plane carrying her young cousin to England had passed over the South African border yet. Would Rebecca feel as lost in her new life as she did herself? Though the timeless and shifting sands of the Namib Desert had snatched Lydia's spirit, holding it tight in its remote silence, she hadn't yet found her place. Surrounded on one side by the icy blue of the Atlantic Ocean and with nothing but desert on the other, Luderitz was a lonely monument to its colonial past. German architecture reached into cloudless blue skies and slate-grey turrets hissed as the wind whipped them with fine grains of sand. Each day Lydia swept that sand back from the verandah of the small wooden house Stan had rented, but each night it returned. The wooden walls of the house creaked with the shrinking cold of night as the temperature plummeted and Lydia wondered if the house would collapse one day, buried in steep banks of untrodden sand.

'Joe, come in and wash now,' she called to her son as he whipped his bicycle in a dusty circle on the other side of the small picket fence. Joe's look of fear as they left their house in Cape Town for the last time was something Lydia would never forget, but it was the cold contempt on the faces of the secret police that had shouted her husband's treason across the flatlands of the Cape, and Joe had sensed their hatred.

'Dad will be in soon, so wash up quickly.' Lydia pushed Joe gently towards the house.

'Are the people coming?' Joe asked. Strangers often arrived at night. They would sit with his father, talking till the early hours while his mother served them with food. They fascinated Joe. Appearing from out of the misty haze of the desert so quietly that he wondered if they were real, their faces were gaunt, their eyes hungry and Joe had made up many stories about his father's friends.

'Can I see them tonight, just for a bit?' He was afraid of anything more than that.

'I'll see,' Lydia said, and Joe knew that meant she wouldn't. The men who came to the house were strangely silent when Lydia was around, but at least she knew who they were. They were exiles. Some black, and some white, they were people eking out an existence in the arid heat of a desert that separated them from their own land. They had joined the political movement of SWAPO as it fought for independence in South West Africa and through them the exiles found a way to continue their own fight. They lived in hope that their voices would be heard somewhere clear of the desert.

'What were you talking about tonight?' Lydia asked Stan later. He'd crept into bed quietly and she could smell alcohol on his breath but now she felt only guilt. Now she understood that her husband's secrecy was to protect her, and her suspicious of the past only accused her.

'Nothing much,' Stan said, as he always did, turning away in the bed.

Lying beside her husband, with their bodies not touching at all, Lydia gazed at the ceiling of the small bedroom. She'd tried to make it pretty. She'd draped lace from the rickety frame above the bed and the sheets smelled of roses, reminding her of home. Automatically her body moved closer to Stan. Pressing herself against him she felt the hard warmth of his back and longed for him to turn to her. They hadn't made love for a long time and she ached for him. It was Lydia who had resisted when she'd thought Stan's heart was elsewhere, but since her love had been rekindled by pride, Stan had not come near her.

'Do you remember the day we were up in the mountains near Franschoek?' Lydia's thoughts were on the first time they'd made love, when a whisper was a promise not a threat. 'Do you ever think about that now?'

With a deep sigh Stan turned over to face her and his eyes peered at her through the half-light. Like a loaf of bread, the moonlight was sliced by the bars of shutters on the window and dark shadows fell across Lydia's face.

'I'm sorry,' he said quietly.

'Why?' Lydia ran her hand down his body, holding the firm rise of his buttocks against her palm. 'I love you.' She kissed him on the tip of his nose. Every part of her body longed for his touch and she was moist with the passion they'd once shared. Each long and lonely day of their exile her mind had teased her body as she thought about making love and, pushing herself up on her elbows, she looked down at her husband. Even in the half-light she could see Stan's eyes were dull though hers were burning. 'I want you,' she whispered and Stan looked away. He'd been surrounded by fear since the day of the Sharpeville riots. Fear that his actions would destroy his family long before they destroyed their cause; that he'd never again see the country he loved. But, as if waking from a long and distant sleep, Stan felt his body warm as the silk of Lydia's fingers threaded through the hairs on his chest.

'Is Joe asleep?' he whispered and Lydia's back arched as his hand moved down her leg.

'Yes.' She pulled the tent of her nightdress over her head and as her arms reached high the night light streaked across her naked body and Stan gazed at her in wonder. She was truly beautiful. He longed for her and his mouth moved to her breasts. Running familiar and teasing circles around her dark nipples, his tongue searched for the wonder of his wife and he pulled her naked body into his arms as Lydia's breath quickened.

'It's been too long.' Her voice was a whispering wind. The same wind that brushed over the desert, calling a welcome to the invisible creatures that hid in the sand. So Lydia's voice had called a welcome to the love Stan had buried in fear.

'I thought I'd lost you,' she said as their bodies pressed together and carefully they sought the way back.

Rebecca stared at the glass of lukewarm orange juice on the rickety table in front of her. It was the middle of the night and the air around her was warm and solid, the only sounds the scrape of chairs and the tread of tired feet on the lino floor. She sat in the sparse lounge of Brazzaville airport, a sleepy fly buzzing just above the rim of her glass while a group of black children gazed at her through the grubby airport windows. It was the last time Africa would breathe its wonder into her soul as the small black faces peered at her from enormous eyes. She knew it was the silver bird the children had come to see and the magic of its descent was still reflected in their faces. They were waiting for the plane to rise again, like a dodo that had found its wings. Rebecca smiled but she wanted to cry. It was the last time she would breathe the same warm African air as Luke breathed, and the tangy scent of frangipani promised that nothing would ever smell as sweet again.

'We're boarding now, Miss Conrad.' A stewardess stood beside her. 'Did you miss the call?'

'I'm coming.' Rebecca tried to dismiss her last moments in Africa as the hostess did.

'You'll get a sleep on the next leg.'

'Where do we land then?'

'Athens. Then Rome, Zurich, Paris and London.' As if they were bus stops the hostess listed names Rebecca had only heard of in distant geography lessons. 'It's what we call the milk run. I'll be leaving you in Rome.'

Stepping on to the gangway, Rebecca tried not to react as her foot lifted off African soil.

'Do you stay in Rome?' she asked the hostess, wishing that she herself would be staying in Rome, ready to return home. Rebecca was certain it had been Luke at the airport and she'd thought about nothing else since the plane left Johannesburg. In a curious way that small glimpse had been more devastating than anything else.

'Are you going on holiday to England or to study?' The hostess fitted Rebecca's bag into the hold above her head.

'Study.' Rebecca pulled out the South Africa Airways Boeing 707 safety sheet and stared at it. She hadn't thought about safety. Her mind had been far away and not even the sudden turbulence on landing in Brazzaville had worried her. In many ways she was already dead.

'If you wait till we've taken off you can stretch out and sleep.' The hostess handed her a blanket and Rebecca wished she could sleep. She wanted to sleep all the way to England. To forget she'd gone. The sight of Luke had rekindled the flames of a lost love and the image of her mother, standing so helpless, was a picture Rebecca would never forget.

As the plane lifted into the sky she gazed down on the black might that tried to conceal Africa and a cluster of lights assured her no darkness could ever hide it. People like Macaroni would be sitting round open fires and Rebecca knew the old man would be singing. He wouldn't know that she had gone.

CHAPTER FIFTEEN

From the moment she arrived in England, Rebecca shrugged off the collective guilt of South Africa and turned her back on the past. Forcing herself to accept that Luke would never be a part of her future, she began a life that deliberately excluded Africa and all it meant to her.

London had long since become Paul and Elize's home and very quickly Rebecca made it her own. But, although they'd welcomed her warmly, Paul and Elize were another part of the past, and she soon looked for her own space, finding it in a bedsitting room tucked into the grey terraces of North End Road. Tiny, and containing only a bed, chair and a gas-ring, it became her home as she began her new life, attending a three-year Art and Design course.

The Beatles had shaken a slumbering nation awake and England had become the centre of hope for a generation born into the nuclear age. Nothing was impossible and there was nothing to lose. Dreams were the beginning of reality, and everywhere the age-old barriers of the English class system had come tumbling down. It was an unprecedented time of opportunity and Rebecca snatched at the freedom it offered.

It was among the people on the Circle Line tube and crowded pavements of London that she discovered herself. Distanced from her home, she was able to look back at the creeping State controls she'd escaped, and quickly she realised she'd only been half-alive. Her spirit had been bound, as every thought and word was measured against a heavy backdrop of laws. The heart of a colourful and vibrant nation had been bled dry like her own as artificial separation forced people to exist in the twilight vacuum of false ideology, while hostility and self-interest fed one another in an atmosphere of arrogant isolation. But now, like a released bird, Rebecca had found her wings. Accepted unconditionally, she blossomed;

but alongside her own, there still remained the heartbeat of Africa and an abiding longing for just one man.

It was a wet Monday morning and London's streets were held down by heavy skies as people hurried back and forth under battling umbrellas. Working for an advertising agency in her first job since completing her studies, Rebecca had pulled up in the King's Road, Chelsea and she peered through the foggy windows of her battered Renault Dauphine car at the tailor's shop for which she'd been searching.

Once inside, she was to convince the retailer to display her advertising material. However, the particular shop she'd called on that day was totally out of keeping with the rest of the street. The paintbrush of the 1960s had passed it by and its grubby exterior presented a daunting façade.

'Good morning.' Rebecca peered round the door with a bright smile and an old man looked up from behind a stacked counter. Samuel Netherby was as grey as the day outside and he struggled to hold back a rusty smile as he saw her. As if it was a tie, he straightened the measuring tape that hung round his neck and watched as she manoeuvered her way inside. A large box of posters was tucked under one arm and a cardboard sheep dangled from her other hand. She smiled and the old tailor stared at her blankly from behind smudged glasses as she dripped in the doorway.

'Wet, is it?' His mouth pulled straight across his teeth and his glasses slid to the end of his nose.

'A bit.' Rebecca looked at him through the semi-dark of the cluttered shop, which smelt of damp and gas. A fire spluttered in one corner and the windows hid behind years of grime that defied daylight to enter. Every inch of space was packed with toppling bolts of cloth, and fitting frames were strewn on the floor like fragile wire corpses. In one corner an old-fashioned male mannequin leaned drunkenly against the wall while another lay flat on its back in a cloth grave, but Rebecca felt only an unexplained excitement.

'You must be Mr Netherby.' She held out her hand as she moved towards the counter, clambering over a bolt of tweed as he eyed her suspiciously.

'If you've a mind to park that animal in here you've come to the wrong place.' Samuel Netherby peered at her between dusty spools of thread but he didn't take her outstretched hand.

'It's OK. I'll find somewhere for it.' Rebecca's presence had lit the shop with a moment of spring and the old tailor adjusted his glasses to see her more clearly. Long legs stretched from a mini skirt, disappearing into high suede boots and she was the most beautiful creature he'd ever seen, but Samuel Netherby concealed his pleasure behind a determined scowl.

'From the Wool Board, are you?' He concentrated on the cardboard sheep that leaned against her like a dead dog.

'You guessed!' Rebecca glanced round at the cluttered merchandise. 'Have you ever thought of selling some of this stuff?'

'Yeah!' Samuel was aware that the smile he'd so successfully repressed had escaped and was teasing the corners of his mouth, so he glared at the box under her arm. 'And I'm not sticking them posters in here neither!'

'You don't have to. I will.' Rebecca was unsure where to begin. 'We're having a drive on wool this month, you see. There'll be a TV advertising campaign running at the same time and . . .'

'You're on a hiding to nothing.' Samuel Netherby looked away from Rebecca's friendly eyes. Widowed eleven years earlier, the old tailor had hidden in his shop to conceal his loneliness. His time had gone. Everything had changed and the bespoke tailor had lost his way in a world he no longer understood. It was filled with alien people who didn't want what he had to give. His trade had died and he'd buried himself alongside it in the shared grave of his shop.

'You can stick a herd of them sheep in here but it won't make the yobbos out there buy wool!' He railed at the people who'd driven him out of life, and disappeared behind the counter, trying to avoid the light Rebecca's presence had shone into his dusty life. 'Man-made fibre's what they want nowadays.' He reappeared with an enamel kettle. Pitted with chip-marks, the lid clattered as it bounced on a cloud of steam. 'Don't want nothing made to measure no more.' He tipped a small handful of tea leaves into the kettle and banged down the dancing lid. 'I see 'em walking the road out there all day long. Hair flapping round their ears and rayon flapping round their legs.' His eyes followed the long dark stream of tea that poured into a cracked mug on the counter. 'Wouldn't give it floor space meself.'

'But maybe that's exactly what you should do!' Rebecca stepped back as he fixed her with a piercing gaze and a bolt of cloth rolled across the floor between them. 'Times have changed and we have to keep up with them.' She stepped over the obstruction. 'Isn't that what being in the rag trade's all about?'

'Rag trade!' Samuel Netherby's eyes sparked with the insult of her words but he held his anger back as he concentrated on the kettle. 'Tea?' He turned the pot in slow circular movements to calm his temper.

As Rebecca watched the old man using a kettle as a shield to protect his pride, an overwhelming sadness touched her. It was as if he'd been stranded on the shores of time past and she knew exactly how he felt.

'I didn't say I don't like your shop, Mr Netherby. King's Road is the "in" place and people kill for a square inch of it nowadays.' She tried to undo the damage her words had caused.

'And what's that supposed to mean?' he challenged.

'That you're sitting on a gold mine.'

'Huh!' Samuel Netherby turned his attention back to the tea and the security he found in its swirling leaves. 'I knew that was why you were here – like the rest of them that comes here to get their hands on my place.' But Samuel Netherby had sensed immediately that Rebecca was different. She was nothing like the glib, shifty-eyed agents who wanted to buy his shop, knock it down and lay claim to the precious land on which it stood. 'You want a mug of tea or not?' He shook the enamel kettle in front of her and the lid clattered in a wobbly jig. 'It's leaves. Not them perforated bags.'

But Rebecca was already at the door and she swung it wide on the outside world. 'There's the gold mine!' She tried to encourage him. 'It's nineteen sixty-four, Mr Netherby. The world's on your doorstep and I don't believe you can't see the potential.'

'I can see the heat getting out.' The old tailor sat down behind the counter with his tea and Rebecca closed the door.

'Don't you want to make money?' She moved back to the counter. 'Don't you like money?' She grinned as he glanced up at her.

'I didn't say that, love.' The old man stirred his tea. 'I said there's no room for that sheep of yours.' He peered at her over the edge of his mug as he swallowed a slurping mouthful.

'But can't you see?' Rebecca's mind was spinning with the exciting possibilities that had stirred inside her the moment she'd walked in. 'If you fill this shop with what those people out there want, you'll clean up! Your customers are walking up and down *out*side, just waiting to get *in*side! There's millions of them out there waiting to get in here and they've all got money burning a hole in their pockets.'

'You reckon?'

'Yes.'

'You talk pretty big for someone who can only afford half a skirt!' The old man fixed her with narrowed eyes as he tried to burst her bubble of excitement.

'OK.' Rebecca glanced at the cardboard sheep. 'Not much point in leaving this, then.'

'Not a lot.' The old man watched her struggle to the door. 'Goodbye.' He went back to his tea, dismissing her along with the times.

'I'm not gone yet.' Rebecca fought to keep the sheep under her arm as she opened the door with her foot. 'Not much point either in me telling you this sign on the door says *Closed*, I suppose.'

'What sign?'

'The one that says Open on the other side.' Rebecca tossed her head back with a grin. 'Goodbye.'

'Hey, you!' She stopped in the doorway and the old man watched her back carefully. 'Since you're so altogether smart maybe you should tell me what you'd do with my shop.' He shrugged as she turned to him in wide-eyed amazement. 'Seein' as how it's still raining and that sheep ain't got his mac on.'

Pushing a soggy chip into his mouth, Samuel Netherby listened to Rebecca very carefully as she talked. Their shared meal of fish and chips was spread on a newspaper beside the old treadle machine that stood between them and Rebecca's hands moved in excited gestures.

'Everything will have to go. We'll get rid of the lot and then begin again.'

'Me too?' As the old man watched her, a smile hid behind his eyes. It was obvious to him that Rebecca had a flair for business and her excitement had caught his attention, but he didn't let on.

'Not you! You're going to make the new clothes – minis, midis, maxis, hot pants . . . but that old thing will have to go.' As she glanced at the elderly treadle sewing-machine, the hairs on the back of Samuel Netherby's neck stood on end. 'You don't really sew on that, do you?'

'You don't like it?' Though his eyes had narrowed, the spark of life she'd lit shone behind them. 'Planning on getting one of them modern machines, I suppose. Ones that do self-ravelling seams.'

'The very best! Then in time we'll have a factory and you'll just sit back and count the money.' There was a moment's silence as Samuel Netherby watched her curiously.

'Where did you say you come from?'

'Africa.'

'Ah.' The old tailor nodded his head as though that explained everything.

'You asked me what I'd do with this shop.' Rebecca plonked her hands on her hips. 'Isn't that right?'

'And you told me, love.'

'Well?' A sudden smile lit Rebecca's face. 'Glad Rags!'

'Come again?' The old man pushed the last chip into his mouth and licked his fingers clean.

'The name of the shop – we'll call it "Glad Rags".' She twirled in a small circle of excitement and he watched her in fascination. 'Can't you see it? Pure white, nothing but mirrors, and miles and miles of off-the-peg fashion. It'll be amazing!'

'It would be.' The old man wiped his mouth with a crumpled hanky, rolling it into a tight ball before he pushed it back into his trouser pocket. 'The bills would be and all.'

'It won't be *your* money. Where do you think anyone gets money from, to start a business?' Rebecca moved closer, peering into his eyes. 'You said you've got the freehold on this shop, right?'

'Right.' Samuel's expression grew obstinate. 'And I ain't selling it neither.'

'I didn't say you had to. We use the freehold as collateral and *borrow* the money we need, right? We'll get enough to do the renovations, purchase the materials for stock, and the new machines, with some left over to hold on till it all comes together.'

'Hold on to what?' The old man rolled the oily newspaper into a long paper pipe and tossed it towards a bin. It missed, hitting the floor like a soggy javelin. 'From the big ideas you've got we'd have nothing to hold on to, love.' He went over and picked up the newspaper and pushed it into the bin. 'Be better off selling fish and chips. I'd serve 'em out of a classier newsprint than this mind.' He nodded at the unappetising twist of *Reveille*.

'You haven't listened to a word I've said, have you? How do you think Mary Quant and Biba started? And look at them now.' Rebecca glared at him. 'You've just sat there while I made a fool of myself and you haven't heard one word I've said!'

'Now that's not fair, love.' Samuel Netherby looked keenly into her face. 'I just wondered why a nice-looking girl like you wants to waste her time dreaming.'

'It's not dreams.' Rebecca had felt the old tailor's tread on the fringes of her past and she moved away from him quickly. 'Turning this shop into a money-making concern is no more than common sense. What *you've* been doing is dreaming. Me, I'm facing the facts of life.'

'Yup.' Rebecca looked at the old man in astonishment as he nodded his head slowly. 'And everything you said makes sense, girlie. But it's you I'm asking about. Wondering what it is you left behind in Africa that's still stepping on your tail. A young man, is it?'

'Excuse me.' Rebecca moved to the door of the shop, pulling away from the thought of Luke. 'I don't think there's anything left to talk about.'

'If I'm going to hand over my shop to you, there is.' Rebecca stopped dead in her tracks. 'I need to know what I'm getting myself into, don't I? You're the one who talks about good business and that's good business from where I stand.' Rebecca stood silently in the doorway, staring at him. 'It's what you want, isn't it?' Samuel Netherby shrugged, turning away before she caught his smile. 'A free hand to turn this place into some kind of gin palace for frocks – isn't that what you said you wanted to do? Or didn't I hear you right?' He glanced at her over his shoulder, holding back the forgotten pleasure Rebecca's presence had stirred in him.

Since the moment she'd walked into the dead end of his life with a cardboard sheep under her arm, she'd stolen his heart, but there was no way he'd let on.

'Far be it from me to stand in the way of progress, but if you're going to be in charge of me purse-strings – and it's a pretty big purse from what you've said ... well, it'd be only sensible if I knew what my partner's all about, don't you reckon?'

'Partner?' The word crept out of Rebecca's mouth on a whisper of disbelief and the smile the old tailor had held back for so many years cracked his face. 'Why?' she challenged him for an answer.

'Why's anybody do anything, love?' Samuel Netherby tossed the end of the measuring tape over his shoulder like a silk scarf. 'Can't think of one good reason meself, but I'll bet you can.'

From the day Rebecca had left home, Simon had taken it on himself to look after her mother. Constance's illness had led her slowly back into a second childhood, and he'd held her hand, guiding her into the only world he'd ever known. It was a world of innocence, a state of mind unhindered by expectation, and locked inside it together they'd formed a strong bond of understanding.

'What's that?' Constance peered at the blue oblong of paper Simon examined as they sat together in the shade of the old oak tree.

'A letter?' He turned it over and over in his hand, wondering if that was right. Miriam had given it to him that morning but he hadn't yet found his way inside the sealed blue paper.

'Miriam!' He ran towards the back of the house, skidding to a stop as she came towards him out of the kitchen door. 'This a letter?' He waved it in front of her, walking backwards as she advanced with a large basket of wet clothes balanced on her head. 'What is it?' He asked the same question three times, waving the envelope in front of Miriam's face as she stopped in front of the washing line.

'It's a letter from Rebecca.' Miriam bent forward, catching the basket of clothes as it slid off her head. 'I told you.' Bending over the basket, she spread her legs wide and her bottom formed a broad padded seat behind her.

'It's a letter from Rebecca.' Simon flapped the blue airmail letter under Constance's nose as he sat down beside her again. 'It's for ...' Constance watched him at a loss as he raced back to Miriam again.

'Who's it for?' He pushed the letter under Miriam's nose as she pegged a shirt to the line. Her words struggled round the wooden peg in her mouth. 'It's from Rebecca. For you.' Miriam clipped the shirt to the line and Simon stared at her in astonishment.

'Me?' A wet shirt-tail slapped him in the face and he pushed it back, peering round it at Miriam. Though many letters had arrived from Rebecca in the years she'd been away, this was the first one for him and Simon couldn't believe it.

'It's for me!' He raced back across the cobbled courtyard in front of the house, waving the letter over his head as he reached Constance under the tree. 'Mine!' He held it out for her to look at, his breath coming in heaving pants of excitement. 'I read it to you.' He squatted down beside her and she watched him curiously. 'Miriam!' he yelled again. He was on his way back to the washing line. 'Open it!' He stood back excitedly as Miriam slipped a chubby black finger under the edges. He could see she was angry, as the tight curls on her head were standing on end, so he smiled at her sweetly. 'Please?'

'You want I read it?' She glanced at him and Simon nodded with excitement. '*Dear Simon . . .*'

'That's me.' Simon beamed with pride.

Though he was nearly sixteen, Simon was still a child in a young man's body and Miriam wondered how much Rebecca's letter would mean to him – if he even knew where Rebecca was. But London meant no more to her than it did to Simon and she glanced back at the letter, screwing up her eyes to read the English words.

'*How are you?*'

'Fine,' Simon answered, peering over the edge of the paper as Miriam examined the next words carefully, leaving out the ones she didn't understand.

'*I got a shop. It glad rags.*' Miriam looked at Simon in amazement and her mouth pushed forward as she went back to the letter. 'What!' she exclaimed, peering at the words, her mouth moving slowly as she tried to reason them out. Then she shrugged and handed him back the letter. 'The master he read it when he come home.' Simon snatched the letter and, spinning round in the small hole his excited feet had dug in the ground, he raced back to Constance.

'You want me to read it to you?' Simon slid to a stop beside her. 'You want to hear?' He bent down, peering up at her as she stared ahead of herself. 'It's to me. It's a letter to me and it's from Rebecca.' Constance had no idea what Simon was talking about but she smiled to please him as he held the letter upside down.

'*Dear Simon how are you I'm fine I been to the shop. I bought rags and I'm glad.*' Simon scratched his head, trying to remember what else Miriam had said as his eyes battled with the long line of incomprehensible words. '*The shop sells mealie meal.*' He carried on with his own words as his mind raced back to the only shop he knew well enough to talk about. '*It's in big sacks.*' He dropped the letter to his side and grinned. 'Good?'

'Good,' Constance repeated, nodding in complete agreement.

'*There's an ant hill outside the shop. It's a big ant hill.*' Simon had dismissed the letter completely and continued with his own train of thought. He'd long since decided that Rebecca must have gone back to the small mining town he hated. It was the only place distant enough to keep her away for so long. '*It's a big ant hill and it's got a tree on the top with dead legs.*' He looked up at the sound of a motorbike in the far distance and his interest in Rebecca's letter vanished. Simon had long since learned to pick out the sound of Riaan's arrival and, grabbing Constance's hand, he pulled her out of her chair. 'Quick!'

Riaan du Toit spent the late afternoon of every day on Bonne Espérance with Simon and Constance, sharing his time with them both. He was dismantling the old Humber Super Snipe which David had said he could cannibalise for spare parts and Riaan had discovered something that Simon did as well as anybody else.

He was fascinated by motor cars. Memorising each small part Riaan handed to him, Simon's mind was a meticulous filing system of gaskets, spark plugs, nuts and bolts. For the first time in his life Simon had found self-respect and he made sure Constance shared it. She spent every afternoon beside him, her skirt spread to catch the parts as Simon listed them. Each time she caught one he congratulated her and together they formed a formidable team.

'I got a letter from Rebecca today,' Simon said very casually, his face upside down beside Riaan as he worked under the old car.

'How is she?' Riaan asked, but Simon didn't hear him. He loved the way Riaan's face was streaked with grease when he worked on the car and carefully he wiped his hand across his own brow to give the same effect. 'How is Rebecca?' Riaan asked again.

'OK.' Simon hoped he wouldn't ask him to read the letter and peered at the chassis to change the subject. 'What's that?'

'What did Rebecca say?' Riaan pushed himself out from under the car. It was five and a half years since Rebecca had left for England and Riaan had always made sure that Luke knew exactly what she was doing. 'Is she coming back soon?' He wiped his brow and Simon marvelled at the broad streaks that ran across it as he did so. 'She's not living over there for good now, is she?' Five and a half years was far longer than Riaan had expected

Rebecca to stay away, and he'd found it hard to convince himself she'd ever come back.

'Don't know.' Simon answered all his questions with one slow shrug. He knew Riaan wouldn't be happy with his version of the letter and dug into his pocket to pull it out. 'You can read it,' he said casually and, spotting the two greasy fingermarks he'd left on the blue paper, he beamed with pride.

'You want to go yet?' Simon called as he moved closer to Constance. He'd seen a familiar expression on her face and he knew it meant she needed the toilet. 'Come.' Taking her hand he helped her out of the chair and the spare parts he'd collected so meticulously, tipped on to the ground. 'It not matter.' Simon forgave her, but he stopped as a slow smile of satisfaction spread over her face. Though he knew Constance had wet her pants, he smiled again, leading her towards the house as if nothing had happened. 'I be back soon,' he called to Riaan over his shoulder, turning to Constance with a comforting smile as her wet dress clung to the back of her legs. 'It's OK,' he forgave her again.

As Riaan leaned against the cellar wall to read Rebecca's letter, his heart sank further with each word. She'd written it for Simon's under-standing and its simplicity screamed the truth. Rebecca had found a new life in England. An unexpected flair for business had been proved on the day she'd opened a small boutique with Samuel Netherby and she'd achieved success. Her letter spoke of a time and place that had nothing to do with the wide open spaces of Africa and Riaan knew that Luke wasn't a part of it. Even in the small spaces between Rebecca's words Luke didn't exist and, reading the letter again, Riaan tried to understand why.

Having elected himself guardian of the love he'd witnessed between his friends Riaan felt the familiar weight of failure, the same failure he'd experienced on the day the old van had run out of petrol. Up until then he'd believed that no matter what had separated them, one day Luke and Rebecca would be together. He'd believed their love was an all-conquering force that neither time nor distance could kill. But now he thought he'd been wrong.

Putting the letter carefully on the bonnet of the car, Riaan slid his body underneath it. He needed time to work out what to tell Luke, and there was no better place to think than in the greasy cool shadow of the Humber Super Snipe.

Luke had long since looked down the lengthening shadows of time that stretched between himself and Rebecca. It had been the birth of his son almost six years earlier that had made him face reality and examine his actions more honestly. At twenty-seven years old, Luke was a married man with a young boy and he'd tried to accept the blow fate had dealt him because of that son. Anton was a child whose eyes reflected an understanding of things he couldn't possibly know. A small being, around whom Luke had tried to build a marriage as he determined to forget Rebecca. But Riaan's letter had proved only one thing: Rebecca was still at the core of Luke's being. Just her name ruffled the calm exterior he presented to the world and he'd forgotten nothing.

In the time they'd been apart, South Africa had become a Republic. Severing its connections with the Commonwealth, the grinding wheels of apartheid churned on as it drove a road through people's lives and Luke's was one of them. Though his work supported the very framework of the system, he avoided that fact. Burying himself in the pretence of a marriage, he'd never dared look round in case he tripped over himself. Like hundreds of others in the country, Luke's mind had been numbed by the horrors of the system and he buried his head rather than examine it too closely. He ran the translating and printing firm that Althea's father had pushed him into, supported by Government funds, and the money he earned supported a marriage.

But for Althea things were very different. Though she knew it wasn't love that kept them together, Luke had at least taken her as his wife and she'd accepted her position. She'd become what her father had wanted – a respectable married woman whose demands did not include love.

I don't think Rebecca's ever coming home. Riaan's words rolled in Luke's mind as he walked through the Johannesburg park that day. It was the same place in which he'd spent his lunch hours many years before. He'd sat on the particular bench that he chose now, but then it had been Rebecca's letters he'd read – letters from a small girl who'd grown into a woman behind his back and stolen his heart.

Leaning his head against the hard wood of the bench, Luke tried to think instead about the other news in Riaan's letter. About Simon and his success with motor cars. About Constance's illness and Bonne Espérance. Bonne Espérance ... which Riaan said wasn't the same any more. *Even Pa says things aren't the same now.*

Though it had regained its place as a superior Cape vineyard, producing a successful pinotage and many new wines, Bonne Espérance had lost its soul. Its heart had gone with Rebecca, and David's was no longer there either. He was with his wife, an aggressive and helpless stranger.

Shutting his eyes against the glare of the sun, Rebecca's image danced against the bright pink of Luke's eyelids. She was still somewhere deep inside him and longing stirred her memory. He wanted to snatch Rebecca back from the life she'd found in England. He was jealous and he wanted to hold her close, feel again the excitement that always swelled inside him as their bodies met.

Pushing himself off the bench, he moved away, crunched Riaan's letter into a small hard ball and tossed it at a wire bin. He hadn't noticed the African man who was leaning over the bin, picking his way through the rubbish as he searched for food. Only as the creased white ball of Riaan's letter bounced against the black body and rolled back into Luke's path did he see him. Picking up the letter in irritation, Luke moved closer to the bin and his hand lifted to throw it once again.

'Don't hit me, baas!' the African shouted in terror and Luke pulled back in surprise. Dressed in long baggy trousers, stiff with dirt, the African man crouched in fear, his hands folded over his head in protection. 'No, baas ...' The crumpled shape of a terrified human being backed towards the bushes. 'Not hit me, baas ...' he repeated again and again as Luke watched in stunned silence.

No human being had ever been so cowed by his presence and the hundreds of racial laws that Luke had translated ran in front of his eyes. Every one heaped on the cowering stranger who backed away in fear.

'I'm not going to hurt you.' Luke felt suddenly sick as he went after the terrified man but it was too late. His person obliterated by the laws of the land, he'd vanished like millions of others. The Government had achieved its end as an African man's fragile identity was wiped from the face of South Africa and Luke had recognised his part in one man's destruction.

As if blinds had been lifted from his eyes, he saw the people around him as he'd never seen them before. He saw black people huddled under rough blankets in the cold of night as they waited for a bus to collect them out of the comfortable white areas in which they worked. He saw women and children walking barefoot, their few belongings balanced on their heads as they were moved out of town by police. He watched bulldozers flattening people's lives as they crushed their tin shacks, demolishing the last shreds of their self-esteem. But more than that, for the first time in his life, Luke saw fear. The living that had protected him from his own truth for so many years also protected a system that reduced people to fearful shadows.

'I can't tell you what I'm going to do, Pa, because I don't know. All I do know is that I can't go on with it any more.'

It was four weeks since Luke had met the African in the park and his voice was quiet as he faced Jan Strydom across the sitting room of the house which Althea had tried to make a home. It was a large white house

320

in the suburb of Linden and it sat among tall shade trees in the centre of spreading lawns.

'And what about your family?' Jan Strydom tried hard to hold back the anger he felt as he listened to Luke, but it burned in his eyes. 'You can't just toss your wife and son aside for an ideal, man! It's a good business we've got. What are you going to live on? What are my daughter and my grandson going to live on? Communism – is that what you want?'

Luke paced the room and his small son Anton kept beside him. A nervous smile tilted the corners of the child's mouth and his eyes were filled with questions he didn't know how to ask. Anton had been singed by the sparks of electricity that had filled the air the moment his grand-father had arrived. He'd seen his mother tense as they talked and he'd tried to reach out to her, but Althea had turned away.

'All I'm saying is that I want a change.' Luke's hand pushed through his son's hair as he stood beside him. 'I don't want to go on doing the same thing for the rest of my life. It's time for something different, that's all.' Luke tried to hold back the horror of apartheid that engulfed him.

'What the hell do you think any of us do?' Jan Strydom's face was ruddy with anger and his eyes had narrowed. 'Do you think you're special, man? You think you're above working for a living like the rest of us; is that it?'

'I'm talking about self-respect. I can't go on doing what I do now. I can't support a system that denies blacks a place in their own country!'

'There won't *be* a country if you get your way.' Jan Strydom was rigid with anger and Anton thought he saw smoke coming out of his grandfather's ears. 'Come here, boy.' He beckoned the child towards him but Anton hung back, twisting one of his legs around Luke's. 'I want to talk to you. Come to Oupa.'

'It's got nothing to do with him, Pa.' Luke attempted to keep calm. He could feel his son trembling beside him and fought to protect the security he'd tried to give him inside a loveless marriage. 'My wife and child are my responsibility, Pa.'

'Then behave as if they are!' Jan Strydom's voice was a roar and the small boy concentrated on his leg. He tried to work out how much more he'd have to grow before his leg was as long as his father's and he made a mental note of the many inches still to go. Measuring legs was better than listening to his grandfather. Anton had never seen him so angry, and he was talking about him!

'Here.' Before Anton could slip away, his grandfather had picked him up and held him in front of Luke. 'Have a good look at your son!' Anton looked down at his shaking legs and he knew he was blushing. He felt ridiculous dangling like a puppet from his grandfather's hands and he wanted to cry, but he didn't.

'Can I get down, Oupa?' he said quietly, but Jan Strydom didn't hear him.

'Next you'll be saying the Government should hand this place over to the blacks, like that bastard Mandela! You want that bladdy convict governing your son? You believe what Mandela said at his trial, do you? He's a bladdy Communist – said so himself! Convicted of terrorism and now he talks about peace! While he kills white women and children with bombs, he hides in the pockets of the Russians and says he wants democracy! "I live and I'll die for my ideals," Mandela says. I'll help the kaffir die, I tell you! The man's a gun-toting terrorist, a Commie. He's trying to get his hands on this country just like the rest of them overseas, and what future for any of us then? You think you'll have a job then? You think you'll have *anything*? It's a total bladdy onslaught, man! Look up north! See what happens when those black monkeys get their hands on a country and then tell me apartheid's wrong. Tell me how you'll look after your wife and child when kaffirs are roaming the streets with *pangas*, killing us like they kill each other. Is that the future you want? Is that what our fathers fought for?'

The truth behind his father-in-law's words ran a cold chill down Luke's spine. It wasn't Jan Strydom's mistrust of Africans that disturbed him, it was the fact that he hadn't done anything about such opinions before.

'When did you last look at a black man, Pa? Or speak to him, ask him what he feels?' Luke's anger rose against himself. He could see his childhood friend, Thabo, a friend who'd had no colour when seen through the innocent eyes of a small boy but a friend who was suddenly an enemy. 'Blacks are no different from us, Pa,' Luke screamed against the brainwashing of a life-time, snatching his son out of Jan Strydom's arms. 'If what you say is the truth – if that's the truth, Pa – then maybe we shouldn't be in Africa at all. *We* should get out!'

'Hah, so you're off too, eh, like the rest of them who run with the first sign of trouble. Is that what you're going to do – run? And then what? You going to claim it's apartheid you're running from when it's really the threat of a black Government?'

'I didn't say that.'

'Then what the hell did you say, man, 'cos I'm hearing you!'

Althea looked from her father to Luke and quickly she moved to her son. 'Come.' Her Afrikaans was gentle but the small boy had heard only her inner voice of fear and he clung tightly to Luke. 'I said come, Anton!' Althea screamed, losing control.

'Let him stay – let him hear his Pa.' Jan Strydom had spotted Luke's vulnerability and now he went in for the kill. 'Tell your son the future you're planning for him, Luke. Tell him what kind of a country you want to hand on to him – a country reduced to ashes by a Communist takeover without even a bladdy drop of water to drink!'

'Excuse me.' Luke tried to leave the room but Jan Strydom went after him.

'It's still that woman, isn't it.' Though his voice was a whisper it carried on the arrow of his anger and Althea flinched as it pierced her.

'Come.' She tried to drag her small son away again but he screamed, holding tightly to Luke's hand. 'Anton!' Her hand flashed towards his face, catching him across the cheek in a hard slap.

'I've said all I've got to say, Pa.' Luke grabbed his son, holding him tightly as Jan Strydom eyed him. 'I don't want any part of the Government any more, but it's still my country.' As Luke moved towards the kitchen door with Anton in his arms, Jan Strydom made to follow him.

'Leave him, Pa,' Althea yelled, but her father had heard nothing except his own truth.

'You're still after that bladdy Englishwoman, that's what all this is about,' Jan Strydom wanted to shake the life out of Luke. He wanted to kill him. 'It's her ideas you're full of. *Kaffir-boetie* ideas . . . that's what you're saying, dammit. That Englishwoman's still got you and you're dancing to her bladdy tune!'

'Rebecca Conrad has nothing to do with my decision.'

As Luke spoke Rebecca's name Althea felt her legs tremble.

'Are you trying to tell me you've never given her a thought since you married my daughter? Don't lie to me.' Jan Strydom's mind leapt back to the day Althea had tried to kill herself. 'You wanted my child and my grandchild dead!'

'Pa!' Like the wail of a wounded animal Althea's cry broke between them and, snatching Anton away, she dashed out of the room.

'You listen to what I'm going to say to you now, boy.' Jan Strydom was beside himself, his face quivering with rage as he stared at Luke. 'If you ever do anything that harms my child or my grandchild – so help me – if anything happens to them because of you, your life won't be worth living, boy!'

It was several minutes after Jan Strydom had left the house that Luke looked round the suddenly silent sitting room. It was immaculate. The carpet was as clean as the day it had been laid and each piece of furniture gleamed with the constant rub of Althea's polishing rag. The entire house smelt of polish, a smell that took Luke back to his childhood, covering the stench of death as apartheid did.

'Was Pa right?' Althea stood in the doorway and she watched Luke, her eyes betraying the fear her father's words had brought with them.

'Why must you look for some other reason, Althea? I told you why. I can't go on supporting apartheid.' Luke went towards her, but feeling the tension that ran through her, he stepped back. 'Where's Anton?' he asked suddenly. A sense of unease had touched him and he was afraid for the child though he didn't know why.

'What happened wasn't good for Anton, Luke.' Althea's eyes settled on his face as though she might find the answer she needed there. 'Is it Rebecca?' As she spoke the name, she felt the same agony of loss she'd felt when she first heard it. 'Are you leaving me, Luke?' She couldn't control the tremor in her voice and it cracked on tears. 'You're going to her?'

'I'm not going anywhere!' Luke's temper flared with guilt as she touched his deepest longings, but Althea's eyes were filled with the same deaf condemnation as her father's and he was helpless in the face of their blind ignorance. 'I don't want to do the Government's dirty work any longer. There's no justice for blacks in this country and I intend to change that the same way Isie Maisels tries. I'm going to do what I should have done in the first place – study for a degree in law. Do you hear me now? Are you listening to what I'm saying, Althea? People are being obliterated out there and I've been part of it. My work feeds my child by starving other men's children and I can't go on. This has nothing to do with Rebecca. I just will not be a part of what's going on in this country any longer.'

'So Pa's right – you think blacks should take over.'

'I didn't say that.' Luke's voice was quiet with frustration. Confronted by the brainwashing of generations, he no longer knew his own truth. He'd finally stood firm against a system that had once fed him, but as yet he had little idea how to change it. Staring into her eyes, his voice gave each word equal weight as he spoke. 'I – don't – know.'

Though Althea nodded, Luke knew she still hadn't understood his longings for justice; for a country in which every man, woman and child would have access to the law regardless of race. All she'd heard was his silent cry for Rebecca; a cry that had risen from deep inside him the moment Jan Strydom said her name.

'I'm sorry.' Althea walked away. She poured him a whisky as she did every evening, approaching him with a repentant smile. Holding the small tumbler out, she allowed her finger to touch his hand as she tried to contact him.

'There has to be another way, Althea.' Luke's eyes searched hers for just a hint that she might feel the way he did. 'There must be!' She nodded with a bright smile. 'Can you trust me to find it, Althea – some way to live here in Africa that doesn't destroy? For us and the black people of our country to live together?'

Though Althea's face was still spread with a smile, her eyes flickered with fear. Luke's words had brought with them the reality of millions of Africans. He'd brought 'black' inside the home she'd tried so hard to protect.

'Why are you frightened?' Luke held her hand between his as he looked into her eyes. He'd spent his life trying to calm Althea's fears but knew he'd achieved little.

'Anton!' Althea had spotted her son in the doorway and she leapt at the chance to avoid what Luke wanted from her. 'What are you doing here, darling? I put you to bed.'

'Doesn't Oupa like you any more, Pa?' Anton's pyjama bottoms had slipped over his tiny hips and hung like creased concertinas round his legs as he looked from his mother to his father, his world threatened by the tension between them.

'You're supposed to be in bed.' Luke picked him up, holding the delicate body close as blond tufts of hair tickled his chin. He ached with love for his son and wanted to comfort him but he didn't know how. No fairy tale could be spun around the lie of his life any longer.

'Why's Ma scared?' Anton's eyes were expectant and as round as blue saucers as he looked at his father.

'I know one thing for sure.' Luke looked at Althea and she looked back silently. 'Ma won't be scared if you aren't. You think you can do that?' He lowered his son to the floor, walking with him to the door. 'When our Mas are scared it's up to us to make them not scared. That's what being a boy's all about. We've got to show them that there's nothing to be scared of — you think you can do that?' As he spoke, Luke's words filled him with the cold chill of a life without Rebecca but he encouraged his son with a smile. 'Can you?'

'Yes.' Anton's determined answer reached through the door to Althea as his father led him out of the room and she was even more afraid than before. Luke didn't understand. It was her job to protect her son from a threatening world. She'd tried once to protect him even before he was born, but then she'd failed.

CHAPTER SIXTEEN

Althea watched Naomi carefully as she sat at the far end of the large dining table, her voice running on in a meaningless stream of hollow words. Though nothing had been said between herself and Luke since that night many weeks before, she knew she'd now completely lost her husband. Luke had changed. He'd become a total stranger and every move he made threatened her child.

Naomi wanted to know what Luke was planning to do since he'd given up the company he'd once run with Althea's father, but she didn't wait for his answer. Like a runaway train Naomi chattered on and Althea thought her head would burst. She was always uncomfortable when they visited Luke's sister, seeing herself inferior in every way. Naomi had married a wealthy businessman and she'd taken on his English language as well as his money. Dick Davidson had cornered the Republic's fast growing record market, and wealth dripped from every inch of the Houghton mansion in which they lived. It dripped from Naomi too but she was empty. Behind the façade of beauty, Naomi was ice cold.

'I almost forgot.' Naomi stood up, making her way across the pure wool carpet and through the pillared archway that led from the dining room to the sitting room. The house was always tidy and Althea wondered how many servants Naomi had to keep it that way. It was as immaculate as her clothes and face. Even her lipstick was always perfect and never once did she leave a trace on a cup, glass or napkin. Naomi's looks intimidated Althea as much as her constant use of English.

'Have you seen this?' Naomi tossed a glossy magazine on the table in front of Luke and glided back to the dining table. 'Who on earth would have believed she had it in her?'

Althea saw Luke's reaction before she saw the magazine itself. 'What is it, Luke?' she asked anxiously, but he stared silently at the cover without answering and Naomi chattered on.

'I wouldn't have recognised her myself. Didn't I say so, Dick?' Naomi didn't wait for her husband's answer, knowing he was as bored by Luke and his wife as always. 'I said I would never have known it was her. She was quite plain as a child – a long face and always so miserable. Don't you agree, Luke?'

Althea leaned across to look at the magazine. On the cover was a photograph of a very beautiful young woman in a London street. GLAD RAGS TO RICHES was the headline and Althea felt the prick of a steel knife run the length of her spine as she saw the name Rebecca Conrad.

'And she was so dark! Her complexion was always much darker than mine, isn't that true, Luke?' Naomi talked relentlessly on, unaware of either Althea or Luke's reaction. 'It's hardly in the family, is it? I have to sit in the sun for hours to get the teeniest touch brown!'

'Not bad.' Dick Davidson had moved round the table, surprised to discover his wife's brother had taste in women after all. Standing behind Luke with a bottle of wine in his hand, he gazed at the magazine in open appreciation. 'Not bad at all. A chain of boutiques in London must be worth a bomb now.' Luke still hadn't spoken and Althea had begun to shake. 'If I'd got my end away with a bird like that I'd have stuck with it, Luke.' Dick laughed and moved to Althea. 'Wine?'

'No, thank you.' Covering her glass with her hand, Althea tried to smile but her hand was shaking and quickly she dropped it into her lap. Since the day her father had confronted Luke with Rebecca's name, Althea had never asked about her again. She'd tried to hide her fears, the same fears of rejection that had shadowed her childhood; she'd buried them rather than face them. For the sake of their small son, Althea had decided to pretend Rebecca had never been a part of Luke's life but now the lie had crumbled. 'I'll just check Anton's OK.' She stood up and Naomi waved her to sit.

'Do leave the child, Althea! We don't want kids running round making a noise, do we. Nanny's looking after them.' Dismissing her with a wave of her hand, Naomi turned to Luke. 'If you keep staring at that picture we'll have reason to wonder about you and Rebecca, darling.' She retrieved the magazine and took it back to the sitting room. 'I've had enough trouble keeping it from Mother. She can't abide Rebecca, as you know,' Naomi chuckled as she disappeared through the white archway.

'Luke?' Althea whispered. She wanted to go but couldn't move from her seat.

'I do think you should go and see Mother one day soon, Luke.' Naomi's disembodied voice drifted back to the room on a waft of perfume. 'You can't live in the same town and ignore her forever. After all, she is your mother no matter what. We're thinking of doing up that little place in the garden for her to live in. Mind you, she'll probably say it's no better than servant's quarters. You know what she's like and . . .'

'Excuse me.' Luke stood up and abruptly left the room.

'Luke!' Naomi hid her sudden irritation behind a laugh. 'You're not usually in such a hurry to see Mother.' But Luke had gone and she turned back to Althea with a cold stare. 'You spoil him, you know. And the child. It's not good for them if you fuss all the time.'

'I'm sorry.' Althea was totally intimidated. She longed to get away as Luke had, but her body had lost its strength. She wanted to check that her small son was all right. Anton had been made to eat with Naomi's two young children. Out of sight of the grown-ups, he was in the kitchen under the care of a black nanny and Althea was disturbed.

'Luke doesn't really mean to try for a law degree after all this time, does he? He's far too old. He'd look ridiculous pretending to be a student.' Naomi leaned across the table with an intimate whisper to Althea. 'If you're not careful he'll sell the house from under your nose, and then what? If I were you I'd make sure he goes back to your father's company. After all, it was a good job and it must have been lucrative.'

'Any Government work's lucrative.' Dick Davidson lounged back in his chair, tossing his napkin on the table. 'Why do you think they've tied the whole thing up? Apartheid's a licence to print money if you're a Dutchman.'

Althea was suddenly unable to breathe. The walls of her chest felt like pressed steel and her heart battered against them.

'Excuse me.' She glanced at Naomi with a weak smile, knowing she had to get outside quickly. The doctor had put her on Valium tablets to calm her nerves but they didn't work any more. She needed twice as many just to feel normal and she needed one now. 'Do you mind if I go to the toilet?'

'No one's stopping you,' Dick smiled and a hot flush of embarrassment spread from Althea's neck to her cheeks. Her face burned, her mind was buzzing and she wanted to run, but her legs wouldn't hold her. They were quivering like jelly and she was unsure where she was.

'*Ek is jammer,*' she apologised again, snatching for the safety of her own language as she pushed herself up against the dining table. Her insides danced and her head reeled as she forced herself to the door through which Luke had gone. The ground was rolling under her feet and as she reached for the handle, the round ball of brass spun in front of her.

'What on earth's wrong with her now?' Naomi's voice chased after Althea as she guided herself through the doorway, hanging on to the frame. Hollow terror gripped her and Naomi's words dug deep as ice-picks.

'Shit, your family's boring,' Dick Davidson muttered. 'Stupid bloody woman.' His words clanged in Althea's spinning head.

'Rebecca's the reason she got herself pregnant in the first place and everyone knows that.' Naomi's defensive voice echoed in the emptiness of Althea's skull as she leaned on the wall outside the room, trying to catch her breath. Her body screamed for the melting comfort of a tiny Valium capsule and pushing her hand blindly round the inside of her bag, she searched in desperation.

'Althea?' Luke was in the passage and he stood beside her. 'Anton's OK, I've checked.' He stopped talking as he looked at her. 'Are you all right?'

Luke's words vanished in a vacuum of terror and his face swam in front of Althea's eyes. Luke was laughing. He had the magazine in his hand and he waved it in front of her face with a jeer of triumph. Rebecca's cool beauty peered at her from glossy paper and she was laughing too.

'It's her!' Althea's scream stepped out ahead of her thoughts. 'You love her!' Her cry rolled among the scattered débris of her life and her being shattered into a million small pieces. She was looking up at Luke and Rebecca from among those pieces. Pieces of herself were lying at their feet and they were laughing as they made love in front of her. 'I hate you!' A scream ripped through Althea's body and her hands clawed at the image of Luke's face as it danced in front of her in the arms of another woman. Years of buried truth had erupted, casting her headlong into the dark of hell as her mind snapped.

'Coffee?' Naomi smiled across the table at her husband as Althea's screams touched each crystal glass with a high-pitched twang. 'Sorry about this, darling.' She lifted the small brass bell on the table in front of her and the clear tinkle of its ring mixed with Althea's screams.

'Must you keep asking them round? She's pig-ignorant and your brother's not much better.' Dick stood up to leave the table.

'It's hardly my fault, Dick. Clear the table!' she snapped at the white-uniformed servant who stepped into the doorway. The African man's face was devoid of expression, as if he didn't hear Althea's hysterical cries reaching out from the insanity that gripped her.

'Coffee, madam?' Samson placed the words carefully in the minefield of emotion that surrounded them.

'Two.' Naomi didn't look at him as she got up from the table, tossing down her napkin as she followed her husband to the sitting room.

'Yes, madam.' Samson bowed and moving to the door he prepared to negotiate his way back through the drama outside it. The pain in Althea's voice was familiar, but he ignored it. 'I will bring the coffee into the sitting room, madam,' he called quietly after Naomi. Samson's position as head of the household servants didn't allow for involvement in their private lives and he bowed again as his masters dismissed him with their backs.

'Can't she even speak English? I can't stand that bloody Afrikaans!' Dick Davidson had no intention of involving himself in Althea's problems now. Afrikaners were simple people, he'd decided, and best left to sort themselves out – like Africans. 'Brandy?' he asked his wife as she sat down.

Jan Strydom had gone straight to Luke's house when the doctor phoned him later that day. His wife Adriana had run ahead into the bedroom to their daughter and Luke waited outside with his son. Terrified of breaking the fragile truce of silence between his father and grandfather, Anton concentrated on his shoelaces as he tried to rethread them.

'Have you got nothing to say, man?' His daughter had been reduced to a gibbering wreck and Jan Strydom knew Luke was responsible. 'Your wife's having a nervous breakdown and you say nothing?'

'I'll help you.' Luke bent down to his small son, taking the lace from his curling fingers. 'In that hole there, see?' Anton glanced up at his grandfather; the small boy knew he was very angry.

'I do it.' Anton turned his attention back to his shoelaces. Nothing had been the same since he'd heard his mother screaming in Aunt Naomi's house and he wasn't sure what had happened. He'd gone obediently to the car when his father fetched him and he'd sat silently outside while the doctor visited his mother. But still he didn't know what was wrong.

'It's you who's done this to my daughter, and so help me, you'll pay for it!'

Luke closed his eyes. His father-in-law's words were partly true. The moment he'd seen Rebecca's face on the cover of the magazine, his feelings had been confirmed: Rebecca possessed every part of him. The sight of her after so many years had proved only that he'd never stopped loving her, and Althea had read his feelings accurately.

'Is Ma dying?' Anton peered into Luke's eyes as he stood up, his own awash behind a well of tears. 'Will she be dead, Pa?'

'Of course not.' Luke took his son's hand and walked him towards the bedroom door. He wanted to comfort the child whose life was balanced on the truth of his love for Rebecca. It had broken through the façade of his marriage and caught Anton's inner eye.

'Don't you care, man?' Jan Strydom's voice stopped Luke at the door, his eyes pinning him down. 'You're driving my daughter insane. As sure as God you'll kill her one day.'

'Excuse me.' Luke stepped into the bedroom. His father-in-law's presence had stirred feelings of resentment he could no longer handle and he moved to Althea's bedside quickly. 'There, you see? Ma's fine.' He smiled at Anton.

Althea was lying quite still in the bed as Adriana tidied it round her. Jan Strydom's wife looked tiny. Stooped under the weight of her daughter's sudden illness and her husband's demands, her body was bent almost double.

'I'll leave you.' She moved away from the bed with the humility of a servant. 'Althea wanted to see you, Luke.' She'd heard her husband's angry shouts and felt sorry for her son-in-law. 'I'll be just outside.' She ducked through the door as Anton stretched his neck to see his mother in the bed.

'Are you sleeping?' he asked. 'Is she sleeping?' He turned to Luke, begging for reassurance that the strange happenings in their lives had come to an end the moment his grandmother left the room.

'Anton.' Althea's voice was quiet but he heard it immediately and jumped on the bed.

'Ma!' He covered her with kisses. The anger he'd felt between his father and grandfather had been more than he could bear and he burrowed for a hiding place beside his mother, but still he could feel the tension. It was in his mother, and slowly the small boy glanced round at his father for some kind of reassurance.

'I'm sorry.' Althea tried to smile as she looked at Luke. Her mind was numb and her body felt like lead, but terror had vanished in the sweet comfort of sedation.

'It's not your fault.' Luke moved closer and took her hand. 'It's not your fault,' he repeated, as if words could ever express his guilt. Althea shook her head and slowly she smiled. It was a smile that begged forgiveness and Luke didn't know how to respond as heavy lids closed over her eyes.

'She sleeping now?' Anton looked at his father urgently, trying to ensure that his mother hadn't died, for the panic that gripped him threatened death. But Luke was trapped somewhere in the past and couldn't free himself, though he knew he had to. For the sake of his son he had to find a future, but for him there was no future without Rebecca.

'We'll find a way out of this, Althea.' Her eyes opened and she looked at Luke as he spoke. 'I know what it's costing you and I know what selling the house means, but I have to try for what I think is right.'

Luke did know what the house meant to Althea and he'd used it to evade the real issue. The security of love that he could never supply meant the house was all she had. It afforded protection from black people who'd terrified Althea as they began to fight back, threatening to force her into the twilight world of 'poor whites'.

She'd come from an Afrikaner family who'd once earned a living under British rule as *bywoners*. Less than slaves, they'd worked on English farms in return for the tenancy of a tiny piece of land, but they'd pulled themselves out of that poverty. They'd fought for their land and built a united Afrikaner nation to which she clung, but now Luke was wrenching her free.

'It's going to be all right, Althea. I promise.' He held her hand and Anton snuggled between them, giggling though he didn't know why. 'One day we'll buy another house.' Luke concentrated on everything except the constant presence of Rebecca, as she stood between them in his mind, calling him. 'When I'm qualified it'll be easy. Have you ever seen a poor lawyer? You want a house as big as Naomi's?' He nudged Althea, trying to make her smile as he drew her away from the truth.

'That's not what I want.' Althea's other hand reached out and touched his.

'Pa?' Luke hadn't responded and Anton wondered why the sense of warmth he'd wallowed in had so suddenly seeped away. It had vanished in the wide sea of half-truth that lay between his parents and he knew his mother was floundering in its depths.

Simon had never felt quite as proud in his entire life. He was beside Miriam in the pew of an Anglican church and Thabo had just been ordained into the ministry. Dressed in a smarter navy-blue suit than he'd ever dreamed of wearing, Simon felt as if he'd been ordained himself. His face was spread with the widest smile he could achieve without cracking in two and it was all he could do not to clap. The rustle of cloth as Thabo passed him in the aisle, his robes billowing out behind him, was more than he could bear and he glanced at Miriam to check how she contained her excitement. But Miriam's eyes were lowered and Simon could hear her weeping.

'Shh!' He pushed his new hanky into her hand but didn't look at her. He couldn't understand why she was crying on such a special day. 'You must be happy,' he whispered and Miriam sniffed, rubbing her tears away quickly. Thabo had stopped beside them and his eyes were fixed on them. They were the warmest of warm browns and in them Simon saw a reflection of himself. He could see his own smart blue suit and he wanted to shout out loud.

'This is Thabo! He's my friend!'

But he didn't. Instead, Simon held his mouth tightly closed and breathed through his nose as Rebecca had taught him.

'Rebecca come back now?' he whispered to Miriam as Thabo moved past them in a line of newly ordained ministers. Miriam had always said that on the day Thabo was ordained, angels would sing in heaven. 'Will she come?' He was certain Rebecca would have heard them singing, even from so far away.

'Shh!' Miriam's lips pushed forward to silence him.

'She will!' Simon's voice rose with certainty and his words echoed against the high grey walls of the church. He was aware people were looking at him, so he smiled at them all. He remembered the day Thabo had got his Matric results. They'd all gone to the High School in Langa and that day had been just as exciting as this. The school was an enormous building and there'd been two other men waiting outside. Simon remembered that they were both in the church now and he looked round to find them. Craning his neck over the top of the congregation, he searched among faces that stared silently back.

Fezile and Father Jamieson were standing together at the back of the church and they both looked happy, which surprised Simon. When they'd been outside Langa High School they hadn't seemed to like one another. They'd scowled at each other then, as if they were fighting over Thabo.

'Fezile and Father Jamieson are smiling,' Simon whispered to Miriam, and then he stared in amazement. She was crying even harder than before. His new hanky was a soggy ball in her hand and he wasn't sure he wanted it back.

'You can keep it,' he said but Miriam didn't react, so he shouted. 'I said, you can keep my hanky!'

A giggle chased its way through the congregation, erupting in a wave of skipping laughter as everyone turned and looked at Simon. 'It's all full up,' he explained with a nervous shrug and Miriam nudged him into silence with a soft black elbow.

'You must be proud of your son.' Father Jamieson was talking to Miriam in the large church hall. It was crowded with people and Simon had spotted a table at one end of the room. Spread with short snacks and long drinks, it was a place he needed to avoid at all costs.

'I say "Thanks to God", Father.' Miriam lowered her head as she spoke to the priest. She knew the white father was a kind man. He'd saved her son many years ago, but still she was embarrassed in his presence. Father Jamieson spoke as if she was an equal and her legs bent in a shy curtsey as she moved away, unable to take his open friendship.

'And you, young man? What do you think of all this?' Simon looked round as he suddenly realised Father Jamieson was speaking to him. His mind had been so occupied with the peril of eating snacks in front of so many people that he hadn't paid attention till then. He'd never yet managed to balance one of the salty little fish on its wedge of bread and was sure he wouldn't now.

'I not hungry.' Simon smiled innocently. He'd seen Miriam move to the table of food and knew she'd be bringing some for him. She'd already told him off for talking in church and he was certain he'd be in more trouble when he ate. Strangers watched him very carefully at times like that. It was as if they'd never seen anyone eat before and they stared till he got so nervous he spilt his food. He couldn't hide behind his hanky because Miriam had that, so he'd decided to avoid eating. Instead he would slip some food into his pocket when no one was looking and then he'd eat it in private when he got home.

'Can God hear you think?' Simon's question jumped out from among his thoughts and he scrutinised Father Jamieson as he waited for his answer. He still remembered the first day he'd discovered he could talk inside his own head without anyone else hearing. It had been the most amazing discovery of Simon's life. But now he needed to clear up what God could hear. Miriam had said God heard everything, but he wasn't sure she'd told him the truth, so he asked the priest again. 'When I think, does God hear?' He kept a wary eye on Miriam as she piled a plate high with food at the table.

'He knows our thoughts even before we have them.' Father Jamieson wrapped an arm round Simon's shoulder and Simon wished he wouldn't. He didn't understand why people told him off for crumpling his suit and promptly did just that themselves.

'Thabo says he take me to see my mother one day.' Simon changed the subject as quickly as he could. Thabo had promised him that when he'd finished his studies he'd take him to see Estelle, and Simon could hardly wait. He was certain his mother was the most beautiful woman in the world.

'That's wonderful.' But Father Jamieson wasn't looking at Simon any more. He'd moved away to another priest across the room and Simon thought his behaviour was very strange. The priest wasn't the only person who went away the moment he said Thabo was taking him to see his mother in Johannesburg. David always moved away. And so did Miriam.

'Hullo.' A slow African voice caught Simon's attention. Fezile was beside him and his mouth was packed full of teeth. They were the whitest teeth Simon had ever seen and he stared at the greying African man in wonder. 'How your horse? He all right? And Missy Rebecca, she come back soon?' Simon wondered how Fezile expected him to answer so many questions at once. 'You come to Thabo's church in Langa? You come see us there?' Still Fezile didn't stop asking his questions and Simon decided perhaps it was the fault of his teeth. 'You pleased your friend a priest now?'

'Yes.' Simon slipped the word in quickly, hoping it would cover all

Fezile's questions at once and he went off to join Thabo. He'd wanted to feel the white collar round his neck from the moment he'd first seen it.

'Does it hurt?' As he reached Thabo, Simon fitted his own hand around his neck and squeezed, coughing loudly as he choked himself. Without looking at him, Thabo patted Simon on the back and continued talking to the man beside him. Thabo always did that. He was always aware of Simon even if he didn't look at him and Simon liked it that way. Nobody else ever ignored him the way they did other people. First they stared at him and then they pretended they hadn't seen him at all, but always their eyes showed they were just a little bit scared.

'This is Peter Maname, Simon.' Simon turned to the man beside Thabo. He wore the same sparkling white collar that Thabo wore and Simon held his hand out. He loved shaking hands with Africans. They had a special handshake that Thabo had taught him many years before and Simon's mouth dropped open in an expectant smile. Taking his hand in his own, Peter Maname locked thumbs and in a flash he swallowed Simon's hand in three quick grips.

'You Xhosa!' Peter Maname exclaimed with a laugh and the entire room shook. It was a rumbling laugh that held within it all the warmth and mystery of Africa.

'Can God hear what I think?' He hadn't believed Father Jamieson any more than he'd believed Miriam so he asked his question again.

'He knows our thoughts before we think them, child,' Peter Maname answered and Simon stared.

'So!' He tilted his chin up in challenge. 'If God knows what we think, why must we pray?' He'd only just offered up a quick prayer. Miriam was making her way towards him and in her hand was a plate piled high with slippery snacks, so quickly Simon had asked God to make her give them to someone else.

'And you *not* hide the food in your pocket for later. You eat it now,' Miriam warned as she reached him and Simon was devastated. God hadn't only listened to his prayer, but his thoughts. Worse than that, he'd let Miriam in on them.

'He's not hungry.' Thabo rescued Simon quickly and with an arm around his shoulder, led him away. 'We'll get some for your pocket when no one's looking,' he whispered. 'What you think of that, huh?'

But Simon's mouth remained firmly closed. He wasn't thinking. He'd decided never to think again as long as he lived.

Slipping the small grey gun Luke had bought her into her handbag, Althea snapped the silver clasp shut.

'A white man without a gun is a dead man!'

Her father's words roamed her head and her heart banged like a hollow drum. It was almost a year since she'd broken down in Naomi's house and although Althea had subsequently pretended she was all right, nothing had changed.

Looking round the bedroom of the small flat in Hillbrow that Luke had rented when their house was sold, she quite suddenly spotted one of Anton's socks. Tucked behind a leg of the bed, it hid, as she wanted to hide. Picking it up, she flattened the sock against the back of her hand and laid it carefully on the chest of drawers in front of her. Broad yellow and red stripes ran into narrow blue ones and it was one of Anton's favourites. She'd been looking for it for two days.

'You ready, Ma?' Anton stood in the doorway of the bedroom and watched his mother. He knew she didn't like living in the small flat in Hillbrow, but he did. He watched through the windows every night when she thought he was asleep and the streets were always full of people. All kinds of people. But still he hadn't worked out where they were going so late in the day. 'My sock,' he shouted, as if he'd found a long-lost, favourite friend.

'Wait by the door!' Althea's voice was shrill with nerves and Anton felt confused. He'd thought his mother was happy that morning. The moment he'd woken up she'd told him they were going for a picnic. 'Wait outside,' she said again, and obediently he walked out of the room to the front door, his head bowed.

Looking towards the bed, Althea felt a curious warmth fill her body. It was the warmth of sheets that hid her from reality in the dark of night: the only time she ever felt safe. The only place that her mind stopped its wild dance as she drugged herself with sleeping pills. But then she remembered the cold chill that crept between the sheets after her ... Luke's dressing gown was hanging on the door and her hand moved to it. Rubbing it gently between her fingers she smiled and in her mind's eye she saw Luke's face. He was sadder than anyone she'd ever seen and she held the cloth tightly against her cheek to comfort him.

'It'll be all right,' she whispered into the striped cloth of the gown and the chattering echo of lying words filled her head as darkness descended on her mind.

'I got the sandwiches.' Anton was struggling to lift a large picnic basket. He was seven years old and had been in school for a year. 'It's not as big as my satchel. See, I can carry it. You want me to wear the socks? I got the other one.' All Anton wanted was to please his mother.

'Not now.' Althea turned the front-door lock and the narrow hardboard door squeaked back against its frame. 'Go on.' She watched Anton's blond head pass under her arm and then she froze. His eyes were the brightest blue she'd ever seen as he looked up at her.

'I love you, Ma.' Thick dark lashes closed over his eyes and one foot rubbed his leg as he scratched his behind in embarrassment. Anton had said the words in obedience to his father. Luke had told him that his mother needed their love now more than ever and he could see she'd been weeping.

'You mustn't cry, Ma,' he said. He wanted to wipe all her tears away, but he didn't know how. His mother's tears weren't always wet. Most times they were so silent and dry, nobody saw them but him.

'Come!' Althea pushed him gently through the door.

'You got the key?' he asked, as his father might have.

'Yes.' She closed the door behind them firmly.

The drive seemed longer than Althea remembered. When she and Luke had visited the dam all those years ago, it was in her father's old van and now she was driving a car. Yet the journey still seemed longer.

'Can we swim in the dam? Is there bilharzia there?' Anton had been watching his mother every moment of the long drive. There was something different about her. Different even from the first day she'd got sick and though Luke had told him she was just unhappy, he wasn't so sure. His mother looked scared and Anton knew that her happiness was his responsibility.

'You mustn't be scared, Ma.' His small hand reached over and clasped hers on the steering wheel. 'I'm not,' he said. 'There's nothing to be scared of, see.' He'd remembered Luke telling him that if he wasn't scared his mother wouldn't be either and he clung tightly to the shiver that threatened to give him away.

'It's all right.' Althea tried to smile although the touch of her child's hand had sent a chill through her body. She couldn't bear him to be so close and she pulled her hand away, pretending to adjust the rear-view mirror.

'Anton!' Her voice lifted on a note of warning as she stared into it. Althea could see a car behind her. It was an old car, packed with Africans and they were laughing. She could hear the Africans laughing and they were all looking at her. Black faces stared at her, black fingers pointed at her and she screamed: 'Don't look at them, Anton! Keep down! Get down!'

'Who?'

'Don't look at the blacks!'

'What blacks?' Anton had turned to look at the car behind them and inside it he'd seen an old man with a woman beside him. 'They're not black, Ma. Look – they're just white –'

'*Don't!*' Anton lurched in his seat as Althea pulled the car off the road. 'I told you not to look at them! I told you!!' She was hysterical and her face pressed so close to his he could feel her screams. '*Don't look at them!*'

'Sorry.' Tears of shame formed behind Anton's eyes and he tried not to let them fall. 'I didn't look, Ma. I'm sorry.' He didn't understand why Althea had screamed. His mother's voice was different and she was seeing things that weren't there. 'Ma?' he spoke carefully. 'You mustn't be frightened, Ma.'

But Althea stared through the windscreen in silence. Her breath came in short snatches and she hadn't heard anything he'd said. She knew only that she had to get to the dam and, patting Anton's leg, she tried not to let him see her terror. 'Nearly there!' She turned the car back on to the road and drove on.

The solid dark water that spread an inland sea in front of Anton looked as deep as forever and the stillness of its surface threatened him. But he pulled his bottom lip under his teeth, determined to hide his fear as he went back to his mother. She was still sitting in the car even though they'd arrived at their destination.

'I bet there's crocodiles in there. Come and see, Ma. If one comes, I'll kick it in the teeth!' His mouth turned down in a grim scowl and he ran to the car, but still Althea didn't get out. She sat totally still, staring at him blankly through the windscreen.

'Ma?' Anton called to her brightly. At that moment she frightened him even more than crocodiles but he couldn't let her know that. 'We can take the picnic over there, see? Past that big tree.' He pointed across the dry grass that ran a blond fringe round the damn; bending double, it dipped into the water like a line of thirsty scarecrows. 'Or do you want to stay here?' Anton knew crocodiles sometimes slept in the grass and they certainly ran faster than him, so he nodded comfort to his mother. 'We'll stay here. We can sit here, see?' Leaning on the open car window as casually as he could, he grinned and his chin dropped on to his forearm.

'It's hot so we'll eat in the car.' Althea's voice was calm for the first time and she smiled as she looked at her small son.

'But it's hotter in the car.' As Anton argued he remembered that his mother hated spiders. He'd even had to kill one for her once and he'd thought it would grab him by the ankle as he did, so he decided not to argue. 'OK, we'll sit in the car.' He ran round and jumped into the seat beside her. 'I'll get the food.' He leaned over to heave the basket off the back seat but it was heavier than before and he groaned loudly as he struggled with it.

'Not yet, Anton.' Althea was staring into the wide open space that surrounded the car: everything in it seemed to jump. Lit by an unreal light, the bush was dancing around the car, alive and threatening. The still-spreading water in which she'd once swum with Luke was black, and the branches of the trees were dark as their twisted arms reached out to her.

'Anton?' Althea's hand clutched the bag in her lap and as he watched her his throat dried. His mother had a gun in her hand.

'Ma?' The small boy could no longer hide his fear. His father had warned him about guns. Luke hated guns and he'd told him never to touch one. He'd even shown him the gun that was in his mother's hand now and he'd told him not even to look at it.

'Do you know I love you, Anton?' Althea's eyes were lit by a mysterious light but it turned to darkness the moment it touched him. 'You must believe I love you.'

Anton didn't say a word. He wanted to tell his mother he believed her, but he couldn't. His mind raced as he searched for an explanation for what was happening, but he couldn't speak.

'It's no good, Anton!'

'Why?' The word shot out of the child's mouth as he looked at the woman beside him. She was nothing like his mother. A total stranger was in the car beside him and the gun she held was pointing at his head. 'Ma?' His voice searched for his mother.

'Trust me, Anton.' Althea was in a place of intense darkness; separated from light by a foreboding that picked at her flesh, she could find nothing to hold on to. All around her was the deep of an empty dark and she was locked inside it with her child. 'We're not safe, you see. They'll kill us like they killed Dr Verwoerd!' Althea's mind had leapt backwards in time, back to the day the Prime Minister had been assassinated. Her father had said that Dr Verwoerd represented the only security for the white man in Africa, but he'd been killed.

'They'll kill us all!' Althea's eyes fixed on her child and he couldn't breathe. He was trying to 'think brave' but he couldn't think at all as her look choked him.

'Pa!' he said suddenly. He decided that thinking about Luke was the only way he wouldn't feel scared. 'Pa will be waiting for us!'

'Pa's not waiting for us, Anton.' The words were hollow and they slipped out of Althea's mouth without expression.

'Pa will be coming home now,' Anton argued, but still his mother wasn't listening. She'd moved closer to him and his eyes fixed on the gun in her hand. It was shaking. Everything was shaking. The whole world was as scared as he was and he no longer knew how to convince his mother that he wasn't. Words were clanging inside his head. They were words he'd been taught at Sunday School and his mouth moved involuntarily as they found their way in whispered speech.

'Gentle Jesus meek and mild. Look upon a little child . . .'

'*Don't!*' Althea screamed as his words touched her and the muscles in Anton's neck locked with tension.

'You mustn't be scared, Anton.' Althea said the words he was supposed to say and the small boy tried to smile. It was a shaky smile. He couldn't move his lips properly but he forced himself to speak.

'I'm not scared.' He stared at his mother as his breath came in shallow gasps and he reached for the gun.

'No.' Althea's voice was loud but Anton didn't hear.

'Don't touch it,' Althea screamed. She knew she had to stop her son being hurt. She had to protect him from the gun. The gun was dangerous and he was grabbing it.

'See?' Anton's hand held the cold metal barrel. 'There's nothing to be scared of, Ma.' He tried to pull the gun free of his mother's grip but she held on to it tightly.

'Ma!' he shouted, and in that moment Anton saw his mother's face clearly for the first time. It was lit by a circle of white light and surrounded by smoke. Her eyes were large and her mouth was wide open in a scream. It bounced without sound inside an explosion that had sucked him into its centre.

'It's all right, Ma. I'm not scared,' Anton called with a laugh of sudden surprise. He could hear his own voice and his fear had vanished in the light that surrounded him.

'Anton?' Looking down at the small boy's head as it lay quite still in her lap, Althea was aware of warm liquid soaking through her skirt and on to her legs. A curious smell of sulphur filled her nostrils, the hard edge of the car seat dug into her neck and somewhere out there in the dusk, a dry twig scraped the side of the car. Somewhere out in the darkness, a finger was prodding her. It was challenging her with the words of the child's prayer as Anton's remembered voice played in her head. *Gentle Jesus meet and mild. Look upon a little child . . .* They were words that came from somewhere in her own distant past, and were filled with a curious comfort.

'It's all right now, Anton.'

Althea's hand stroked the child's tousled head to comfort him and then she stared. The warm liquid that ran down her legs was blood. Her child's life was seeping back into hers, binding them together.

'It's all right now.' Pushing the gun into her mouth, Althea closed her eyes. The metal was cold and hard but she was no longer afraid. She could hear her son's whispered words and she knew he was somewhere in the pure light that shone just beyond the darkness.

CHAPTER SEVENTEEN

A summer storm ripped wide the heavy night sky as lightning splintered the dark, with thunder rattling its tail.

'Come on!' Luke stood alone on a small rock outcrop to the north of Johannesburg, challenging the heavens to reach down for him, as they had Althea and his son. 'What are you waiting for?' His voice raced across the face of pure light that divided the sky with a sheet of power. 'Take me too!'

A thundering roar shook the earth in answer and a cry rose from the depths of Luke's soul.

'Rebecca!'

Staring into the darkness of her bedroom Rebecca listened intently, but there was no sound. The only light was a pale shimmering beam that stretched across the carpet from the street lamp outside, yet she'd been shaken wide awake.

'Zanu?' Looking towards the open door of her bedroom Rebecca's eyes peeled back the layers of darkness as a Great Dane curled round the doorframe. His head was tilted to one side and one ear flopped over his face as he watched her from still brown eyes. 'Good boy.' Rebecca tried to calm herself as she calmed the dog. She didn't know why she'd woken so suddenly, why sleep had been shredded by an urgent longing, so deep it consumed every part of her. Switching on the bedside light to settle her thoughts, her feet reached towards the thick white carpet and her slippers. The dog tilted its head to one side and an enormous paw plonked in her lap as a bony tail brushed the carpet in expectant sweeps.

Ignoring the dog's hopes that it had been woken for a walk, Rebecca crossed the bedroom and went down the steep steps that led to the lower floor of her London mews house. Switching on the hall light, she pulled the soft white dressing gown tighter around her body and entered the kitchen. Only the hollow clatter of footsteps on the pavement outside revealed that she wasn't alone in a sleeping world.

Pushing a heavy china bowl with his nose, Zanu looked up as it skidded across the kitchen tiles to Rebecca's feet. The dog's face was a picture of expectancy, but she hadn't seen it. Her mind was back on the moment she'd woken, on the silent cry of her name that had shaken her from a deep sleep. An urgent longing still gripped her but a sense of loss followed on an incoming tide of dread and she moved to the telephone quickly.

'Dad?' she whispered as her father picked up the other end of her thoughts, thousands of miles across the world. 'It's Rebecca.' Her voice was thin and her fingers twisted the curling telephone lead. Tense with the anticipation of bad news, her mouth formed words she hardly dared speak. 'Is Mum all right?' Zanu stretched his body at her feet, dropping heavy jowls on crossed paws as steady eyes watched his mistress.

'I'm fine, Dad. I was just thinking about you.' Rebecca's voice became reassuring. 'Are you sure everything's OK?' An ice-cold finger had prodded her again, suggesting David wasn't telling the whole truth. 'There's nothing wrong with Mum?' Rebecca smiled, her hand loosening its tight grip on the telephone. 'I know, yes. It's late here too. Dad?' Her voice reached down the miles that stretched between them. 'There's nothing else is there?' An image of Luke had leapt at her out of the blue to fill her mind. 'Give Simon my love. Mmm . . . Bye. Love you. Bye.'

Rebecca laid the phone on the cradle and the dog's eyes flickered at the gentle *ping!* that disconnected her from her father. Though Zanu had sensed uncertainty in his mistress, he knew there was nothing amiss in the world he guarded, so he closed his eyes.

'Milk?' Rebecca moved to the fridge. A dim light shone on Zanu from the inside of the cold cupboard he often dreamed of raiding, and he was tense with expectation. He leant casually against her leg, as if passing time was his only ambition; as if the long stream of pure white milk that poured into his china bowl was no more than an interesting apparition.

Zanu had taken over Rebecca's life from the day Samuel Netherby had bought him for her Christmas present. The enormous black dog filled a gap in her life, but tonight the gap had widened and even he couldn't close it. Watching the dog lap the milk with swipes of his wide pink tongue, Rebecca leaned against the fridge door and it snapped closed behind her. She couldn't understand what had happened, how the urgent longing for Luke had broken into her life again with such unexpected force.

Glancing round the sparkling kitchen she allowed reality to pull her back and she examined her life. Rebecca had everything. Samuel Netherby had purchased the beautiful mews house in Wilton Row near Knightsbridge in London. He'd said it would be a good investment for the company, but she knew he'd bought it for her. She ran a chain of boutiques called *Glad Rags*, built on the foundation of the old tailor's shop, and her lifestyle would once have eluded even her imagination. But it was empty. The life she'd fought so hard to achieve had been shattered by an invisible touch from the past that had reached across miles of spreading sea, and called her home.

Going down to the swirling brown river that threaded its way through Bonne Espérance, Miriam was looking for a small black girl. Portia was a township child. The illegitimate daughter of an African mother and a half-caste father, she'd been rejected by both sides of her family and Thabo had taken her in. Unable to look after him himself, as he had his large parish in Langa to care for, Miriam's son had asked her to take in the child and she'd agreed immediately. There was something special about Portia. Like a tiny space traveller, just here to check things over before reporting back, she watched the world in serious silence.

But Miriam had spotted Luke even before she'd seen the little girl. He was sitting on the river bank and the small black child, her feet pressed into the river's mud skirt, watched him as he watched her.

'Luke?' Miriam's whisper reached no further than her mind. Her eyes were screwed tight and she peered towards the man on the river bank, wondering again if she really did need glasses. '*Luke!*' Her voice exploded in recognition as he turned to her and the small girl, Portia, stared back from wide serious eyes.

'Why are you here?' Miriam's words raced ahead of her. Though Luke's face was without expression, behind his eyes she could see all the agony of a fallen world. 'Nobody's here, Luke. They all gone out. The madam she go to the hospital on this day every month, and ...' Miriam's words dried in her mouth. Luke had lifted his head and the tracks of a million unshed tears traced a path down his cheeks.

In Miriam's mind he'd remained one with Rebecca since the day she'd first seen them in each other's arms. Their love had encompassed anyone who stepped within its circle and she'd been within that circle.

'Missy Rebecca not here, Luke.' Miriam stared at him but he said nothing. 'Missy Rebecca away.' No words passed Luke's lips but Miriam had heard his cry. Two pebbles clicked together as their hard whiteness bumped one another and Miriam looked down at the small girl who'd dropped them at her feet.

'Go into my room. Inside, Portia.' Miriam switched to Xhosa, needing to protect the child from Luke's pain as it lapped round the pebbles at her feet. Though he'd turned away from her, though Luke had stood up and walked away, Miriam was surrounded by his grief as she'd once been by his love for Rebecca.

'My son's dead.' Luke's voice touched her with the sharp flick of a whip and Miriam was aware that Portia had stopped in her tracks.

'Go on,' she muttered and the small girl placed one muddy foot in front of the other, moving obediently towards the house.

'They're both dead.' Luke's voice was also dead. There was no sign of life among his words though he was looking directly at her as he spoke. 'Althea killed herself and my son.' His voice lifted on a note of disbelief and Miriam wrapped him in her arms. Pulling him close into her soft heaving body, she cried his tears as she held him.

Luke didn't know why he'd gone back to Bonne Espérance that day. It was more than a week since he'd come home from university to find a policeman at the door of the flat. He was a young officer and, unable to find the words to explain what had happened, he'd asked Luke to accompany him to the station.

There, Luke had stared at his son's tiny body in the steel drawer of a mortuary and he'd buckled under the full weight of tragedy. Since the day he'd found Althea in her bedroom, pregnant with his child, Luke had sensed that death stalked her. He knew she'd never really lived at all. Crushed under the weight of her own sense of inadequacy, she'd listened only to the taunts of fear that had raised her. But Anton had been a gift. He'd stepped into the emptiness of her life and their marriage, claiming them both as his prize.

Luke had expected his son to sit up. The tiny boy had seemed alive. Even a smile had tipped the corners of his mouth, but his chest, ripped to pieces by a bullet, was covered with a plastic sheet.

Luke didn't know how he'd got himself away from the mortuary. He hadn't heard Adriana Strydom's rending sobs as she stared at the bodies of her daughter and grandson. He hadn't seen the silent condemnation in his father-in-law's eyes and he hadn't answered the police sergeant's questions. It had only been as Luke stood on a small outcrop of rock, looking down at the city of Johannesburg as a storm raged around him that he'd woken up. There'd been a vast empty cave at the centre of his being and he'd known only one person who could fill it.

Luke had driven immediately to Bonne Espérance. The miles of land that had held him at bay for so many long years had disappeared under balding tyres and quite suddenly he'd found himself on the banks of the river. Nearby had been a small black girl and she'd been the same age as his son.

'Where will you go, Luke?' Miriam looked at him as he sat across the rickety table in her room. She'd known he was lost among childhood memories that still lurked there in her room. Memories of Sophie's soft bosom as she'd rocked him to sleep while Miriam herself stood to one side. She'd been a young woman then, unsure of the small white boy who'd claimed her mother's love.

'I don't know.' Luke's words were as empty as their meaning and Portia watched silently from the place where Miriam had once stood – on the edges of a love that had nothing to do with her.

'You want to see Thabo, Luke?' The name touched Luke's senses and he stared at Miriam, but he said nothing. 'Thabo is in the church now. He's a priest.' Miriam's head dropped in a humble bow as he looked at her. 'It is God you need. Only God can help you, child.' Standing against her talk of a God he knew was dead, Luke moved to the door and Portia watched him, unsure how to react to the white man who wasn't like the others she'd met.

'Don't say I've been here, Miriam.' Though Luke's voice was calm it stirred a note of warning inside her, but before she could answer he'd gone. Closing her eyes, Miriam rocked her body backwards and forwards in the old wooden chair. She'd tried to hide her feelings from Luke but in his absence they broke free in a heavy sigh. She'd sensed there was only one person in the world who could help him, but Miriam knew that Rebecca had cut herself off from her past.

'What's wrong?' Portia's quiet Xhosa words touched Miriam gently as grief rocked her.

'My heart is sore, child.'

'Why?' With a slow sweep Portia's eyes moved across the room to the window. She could see Luke driving away through the gates but she sensed that the white man hadn't left Bonne Espérance at all.

'What do you think of it?' Samuel Netherby stood beside a gleaming Mercedes 250 SL. A smile pinned the corners of his mouth to his ears and the old man's feet shuffled an excited tap-dance on the hard grey of a London pavement. 'Not bad, eh?' He looked totally out of place beside the immaculate white car as he leaned on it casually.

'Are you sure you could drive something that fast, Sammy?' Rebecca chuckled as she moved to the door of the Glad Rags offices in the King's Road. Exquisitely dressed, everything about Rebecca revealed the confidence of success they'd found together. Her beauty had matured with her twenty-six years, but the lonely child still lurked behind her eyes and Samuel Netherby had seen it. Though her life was far removed from Africa, ant hills and 123 Z, Rebecca still bore the stamp of an exile. Since the night she'd been woken by an unheard call, her mind had been filled by Luke. She'd gone out with many other men in an effort to drive him away, but she hadn't found love with any of them. She'd buried herself in Somerset House, searching for Johannes Villiers' descendants in an effort to convince herself that their love could never be, but still, even as Rebecca had uncovered Johannes Villiers' family in America, she'd wanted only Luke.

The company she'd started with Samuel Netherby had grown and she'd opened the offices of *Glad Rags* on the floor above their first shop while Sammy occupied the top floor. He'd lived in that building most of his life and had no intention of ever moving out.

'You'll kill yourself in five minutes flat driving that car, Sammy.'

'You think I'm daft, don't you?' the old tailor grinned as he gave the sleek car a quick wipe with his elbow.

'Definitely!' Rebecca stopped at the door of *Glad Rags* and watched him. She'd allowed her love for Luke to fall on the old man instead and he'd grabbed at it. 'You'll get a parking ticket too if you leave it there.'

'You want me to send it back?' Samuel Netherby's chin lifted as he eyed her from behind new glasses, through which he couldn't quite see. 'You know how long I've waited for this?' Pushing the specs to the end of his nose, he gazed at her over the rims.

'I'd say about nine months, from the way you're looking at it.'

'Six!'

'So?'

'You don't like it?'

'I didn't say anything about not liking the car, Sammy. It's beautiful. But for someone who insists on living over the shop and washing in the sink when he could be living anywhere he likes, well . . .' She shrugged. 'It's not quite your style.' She moved to take his arm but he pulled back.

'Not my style? What is, then – a number seventy-three bus?'

'You said it!'

'And what about yours? Not your lifestyle neither, I suppose.' Rebecca had turned away but at his words, she stopped. Swivelling round, she fixed her eyes on his.

'Now hold on a minute, Sammy. I already have a car, and I've told you before that company profits are not to be spent on luxuries like this.'

'Who said anything about company funds?' Sammy had seen Rebecca's eyes flicker over the car in appreciation and he wanted only to please her. 'Who said *I* can't buy you a present? It's my bleedin' company and my bleedin' money and I can do what I damn well like with it!' The old tailor was on the defensive.

'But Sammy . . .'

'No "But Sammy's". Look at it!' He snatched her hand and led her back to the car. 'You can't kid a kidder, kid. I seen you eyein'' 'em in the street every time one whizzes past.' He swung the car door open. 'Now, get in and drive it and let's see the poncy nobs round here gawp!'

Samuel Netherby's life had become totally entwined with Rebecca's and he'd never felt such care for another person. She'd become the daughter he hadn't had and everything he did was for her. The riches that had poured into his lap since *Glad Rags* had caught the imagination of the public had only ever been used for one purpose: Samuel Netherby wanted nothing more than to make Rebecca happy.

But even now, sitting beside her as the sleek white car with a dipping roof streaked down the new M4 motorway, the old tailor knew he hadn't achieved his purpose.

'Something you don't like about the motor?' He watched her as she drove. Her profile had always fascinated him. The arrogantly classic line of her face was tinged with vulnerability. Like everything else about her, Rebecca's beauty had nothing to do with the world. 'Why you stopping? Not fast enough for you, then?'

Rebecca had turned the car into a slip road, pulling up in a lay-by. Switching off the engine she leaned back in her seat and Samuel was aware of a stillness he'd never seen in her before.

'I want to go home.'

'What?' The old tailor bought himself time to think. Rebecca had never talked of going home before and he was momentarily threatened.

'I thought I'd cut myself free, but I haven't.' Rebecca watched the silver body of a plane as it circled Heathrow airport and she wondered if it had come from Africa.

'Africa, you mean.' The old tailor's eyes lowered and he fiddled with the edge of his jacket. His suit held the pride of his craft within its seams and he needed something to hold on to. But he didn't know what to say, aware only of the strong leather smell of a brand new car.

'Your mother, is it?' Every day of the time he'd known Rebecca he'd expected her mother's illness to call her home. But more than that, he'd known there was someone else who called her. 'Anybody'd miss rushin' around the bush with a bow and arrer!' He glanced at her with a smile that acknowledged defeat. 'So, you don't like your present?'

'I love it, Sammy.' At any other time the beautiful car would have meant much more to Rebecca, but today it was worthless – like all the possessions she'd accumulated over the years as she tried to fill the gaping hole that Luke had left in her being. But she smiled at the old man who occupied so much of her life. 'I think you'd have done far better getting a Rolls Royce for yourself.'

'A Roller?' Samuel Netherby stared at her, wide-eyed. 'What would I want with a fast lorry! I ain't got a licence.' The old man's eyes danced with humour, but then his smile faded and he patted her hand gently. 'I know you've got to go, Becky. I'll take care of the shop.'

Samuel Netherby spoke of their business as he always did, as if it was still just a small outfitting shop. The success they'd achieved together meant no more to him than it did to Rebecca and he'd heard her cry for Africa.

Andre Bothma watched Thabo carefully as he stood outside the small corrugated iron church in Langa. His long black cassock was covered in township dust and the hem was worn ragged from miles of unmade roads. The tall African priest, whom Andre had come to despise, was talking to a black boy and their quiet Xhosa disturbed him. There was a confidence about the black man that never faltered and he was asking the child if he remembered seeing anything unusual on the previous night. Thabo wanted to know if the boy had seen who'd killed his family; who'd started the fire that had destroyed their shack in the vast squatter camp of Crossroads.

'Don't know.' The child's angular black shoulders lifted in an expression of determined ignorance. He'd watched his parents, his two brothers and three sisters, burned alive in the inferno of their home – but he'd also seen Cop Bothma.

'Is there a problem here?' Andre spoke in Xhosa as he reached Thabo and the black child.

'No problem.' Thabo used careful English as he faced the white policeman. 'There's no problem when a black family is burned alive is there, sir?' His eyes settled on Andre Bothma's. 'Unless the child's a problem to you, of course?'

Andre Bothma switched his attention quickly on to the child in question. He wanted to avoid Thabo's steady gaze: the total calm in the priest's eyes angered him beyond belief.

'Was it your family?' Andre moved close and spoke in Xhosa as a fly buzzed round an open sore on the child's face. 'Where were you last night, boy? Was it you set fire to your family? You like the rest of the "comrades" round here? Tell me!'

'Leave him.' Thabo stepped between the white policeman and the black child and quickly Andre pushed him away.

'Don't mess with me, kaffir!' His eyes were alight with hatred and it was all centred on Thabo. The touch of black skin on his arm was an insult he wouldn't accept.

'I won't mess with you.' Thabo smiled. 'It's the Lord who will do that, sir.' Curling the flat of his hand around the small boy's head, Thabo led him towards the rusty tin door of the church.

'Bladdy nigger priest!' The words crept from Andre Bothma's mouth as he turned away.

In the time since Thabo had opened his church in Langa, Andre had lost some of his power. Township people flocked to the services each Sunday. Songs of worship filled the smoky township from morning till night, African voices rising in harmony to reach beyond the drudgery of lives lived out on the foothills of white carelessness.

'Here!' Andre called to a middle-aged black African further away and Sithole moved to him with a dipping bow of his head. 'Did you know about that boy?'

Sithole shook his head nervously. He knew what Andre Bothma was doing in the township but he'd decided it was for the good of his people. The shack he'd helped the white policeman set fire to the night before was the home of two known 'comrades'. The small boy's brothers had terrorised the elders in the township for months and Sithole had helped Andre mete out justice.

'Find out what he's going to do – and make sure he doesn't spread his bladdy liberation theology again.' Andre Bothma was certain the township children were being brainwashed by both the church and militant black leaders like Steve Biko. He'd seen the result of their attacks on older blacks. He knew the violence in the townships was part of a Communist onslaught; he himself was certain that Africans wanted only to live in peace with the Europeans. They *wanted* apartheid.

'Keep an eye on him!' Andre never allowed himself to be seen speaking to a black for too long and he threw his words back at Sithole as he moved away. The myth of Cop Bothma's invulnerability was something he had to preserve with the utmost care. His life depended on it.

With eyes as wide as saucers, involuntary expressions of shock crept from Miriam's mouth in a stream of exclamations as Thabo walked down the driveway of Bonne Espérance. Her son, with his cassock raising a sand-storm at his feet, was followed by nine black children. Each one had a brown package balanced on his or her head, and all of them shone like squeaky black leather.

'Thabo!' Before Miriam had collected her thoughts, Simon rushed towards the black Pied Piper he'd seen approaching the house. 'I be back just now!' he called to Constance as she sat under their tree. 'Who they?' He walked down the long line of children who followed Thabo, examining each one curiously. 'What's this?' He knocked the brown package off a small girl's head and her eyes stared down at her spilt possessions in shame.

'Uh, huh, Thabo. Uh, huh!' Miriam was shaking her head in answer to a request Thabo hadn't yet made and Portia walked silently beside her. The small girl was shaking her head too, her expression one of serious agreement with Miriam. 'There's no room, my son. No room for all these children.'

'Just for a while?' Thabo wrapped an arm round his mother as she reached him. 'Hullo, Simon.' He watched him as he balanced the patched-up parcel back on the child's head and the children trailed into Miriam's room behind him, Simon restoring dignity as he ushered them into line. Forming a silent circle around them as Thabo talked to his mother, the children's eyes moved round the room in wide-eyed curiosity and Simon stood back in the doorway with Portia.

'I want to send them to the Transkei. They're no longer safe in Cape Town, Mama.' Miriam kept her mouth firmly shut as her son spoke. She'd quickly worked out the cost of bus fares to the Transkei and her head shook from side to side. 'They can live in the village with our family. Grandmother will look after them.'

'Sophie is old now, Thabo.' Miriam held her head back in refusal. 'And where do you think we get the money for the fares and the food to feed them? Who pay for that, Thabo?'

'You worry about that?' Thabo chuckled as he turned his mother to face him. 'First the Lord sent Portia to our door. Now these. And next?' His face was alight with a joy Miriam couldn't resist. 'God knows what we need to care for His children and He will supply it.'

Miriam's face lit up with the same joy that illuminated her son's eyes. She'd prayed since the day Thabo was born that God would use him for His work.

'And there's Zola.' Thabo's grin widened and he went on quickly, 'My Cousin Zola will help with his wife Christine and Petrus, with the child, Lunga. They will all help.'

'No, Thabo.' Miriam tried to be firm within the watching stare of the children.

'We are Christ's hands and feet, Mama.' Thabo's voice was serious as he argued, but still he was smiling. 'We are His people and it is to us that He has sent these children.'

'Yes!' Simon shouted. He'd picked out Miriam's resignation to Thabo's will as she raised her hands in defeat and, pushing his way between the children, he cheered. Simon remembered the day Portia had arrived at Bonne Espérance in much the same way and his self-esteem had grown daily under her serious but admiring gaze. 'They sleep with me.' Simon wrapped a choking hold of possession round two startled black boys.

'Miriam!' David's excited call pushed its way into the small room and

Miriam stood up, dusting away the tiny black fingers that touched her skirt.

'Stay!' she called back to Thabo as she rushed out of the room, breaking into English as she prepared to meet David. 'Yes, master?' Miriam skidded to a stop. David's face was alight with excitement and the years his wife's illness had added to his age were gone.

'She's coming home! Rebecca's coming back!' David was more excited than Miriam had ever seen him. It was as if the world had stopped turning for a brief moment and she felt her feet loosen their grip as his excitement caught her. She didn't know whether to cook dinner, breakfast, tea or mealie pap and all she could think of was Luke.

'Portia?' David was watching the small girl quizzically as she stood alone in front of Miriam's room. As Simon and Constance's playmate, Portia had become part of Bonne Espérance but there was something different about her. She was smiling. 'What's happened to Portia?' David turned to Miriam and a slow shrug lifted her shoulders as a trail of black children stepped out of her room. 'I see.' As he looked at the children David smiled. Thabo and Simon had appeared behind them all. 'I might have known you were here, Thabo.' He went towards him with his hand outstretched. David was constantly amazed at the change in the young black boy who'd once lived on Bonne Espérance. Dignity filled every part of Thabo and his eyes reflected a peace that defied the white laws designed to break him.

'Thank you.' Thabo took David's hand warmly between his own in a gesture of total trust. Though David had aged more than he should have over the years, Thabo could still sense a shred of hope in a man who should have lost it. He had a gentleness that reflected great strength and the promise of Rebecca's return shone in his eyes.

'She's coming home, you said? Rebecca?' Thabo's look searched David's face as he nodded.

'She's coming home.'

'Rebecca's coming home!' Simon shouted his excitement and his attention turned back to Constance as she sat alone under the tree. Snatching the hands of two children he dragged them towards her. 'We got more friends to play with – see. And Rebecca's coming home!' The children looked back at Thabo for help as Simon pulled and Portia pushed from behind. Glancing back at Miriam, the small girl's face expressed her determination that Thabo was absolutely right.

Andre Bothma had spent all day waiting outside the church in Langa. Sithole had told him he'd seen Thabo taking children out of the squatter camp that morning and Andre was sure he now had ammunition enough to deal with the arrogant black priest.

'Good day, Father.' His voice was filled with contempt as he watched Thabo climb off the packed bus from Stellenbosch. The sight of a black in a priest's collar angered Andre, as he believed it angered God.

'Good day, sir,' Thabo nodded with a smile, moving straight past Andre and towards the church at the bottom of the dirt road.

'Where the hell do you think you're going? I'm talking to you!' Thabo stopped. 'I'm told you took some children away.' Thabo moved on again without a word and Andre followed in the dusty trail of his cassock. 'You had the necessary papers to do that, did you?'

As he reached the doors of the church, Thabo turned back to him. 'You're coming in?' He spoke in English despite Andre's Xhosa. 'There is something you want of God that you're at the door of His church, sir?'

Andre had never understood how Thabo could make the word 'sir' sound so insulting and pushing his face closer to Thabo's, he sneered his contempt. 'It's you I want, kaffir.'

'Yes, sir?' Thabo's voice was soft. There wasn't a trace of bitterness behind it and his eyes had filled with delight. 'Come in.' He turned into the church and his feet echoed on the bare concrete floor as he moved between rows of wooden chairs. 'You are following me to speak to me, but God is here. He is listening so I think we speak to Him.' As Thabo paused, Andre stopped in the narrow gap between the chairs. Though the African priest had been polite, Andre had heard a note of victory in his voice and he clung tight to his temper.

'There are legal methods of adopting children, Father. Perhaps you didn't know that.'

'Please sit down.' Thabo held his hand out to a crooked line of chairs.

'There are welfare organisations in the townships who look after orphans. It's a legal procedure and their care is the concern of the Government.' Andre didn't sit down.

'But I was sent the children, sir.'

'You were sent no children, damn you!' Andre couldn't control the anger that Thabo's composure stirred. 'You *took* those children and I have witnesses!'

'But I too have a witness.' Thabo smiled. 'And I ask you to leave if you have nothing to say to Him.' Waiting beside Andre for a moment Thabo looked deep into his eyes. He could see the hatred behind them but he ignored it. 'There is a prayer meeting in one hour and I must eat now. Unless you will join our prayers? Excuse me, sir.' Thabo bowed his head, turning towards the wooden altar at the far end of the church. It was covered in tin cans and each one held a tiny wild flower. A rough wooden cross was pinned on the wall and it looked suddenly different as Thabo reached it. He could see the man who had once hung from a cross in his place and he could hear the voices of people like Cop Bothma who had screamed for Christ's blood. Thabo wanted to turn back and face the white policeman behind him. He wanted to call hellfire and damnation down on his head, but instead he knelt at the foot of the cross. Silently he asked forgiveness for his anger as Andre Bothma's footsteps echoed into the distance and out of the church.

'You can't keep doing this. You crazy?' Fezile had been waiting for Thabo all day. He sat in the small room behind the church where Thabo lived and he was nervous. 'Cop Bothma wants the "nigger priest". I've heard him talk. He paints his face black and thinks we don't know it's the white cop who stirs hatred.'

Thabo remained silent as Fezile spoke out his fears. He knew his old friend was right but there was nothing he could do. Thabo's commission was to help those in need, and vengeance belonged to God.

'The children are gone to the Transkei, Fezile. Their families have been killed and they have nobody to care for them, so they are gone! He can do nothing.' Thabo shrugged. Some of the children had seen their parents hacked to death by *pangas* and all Thabo could do was pray that they would forget.

'And you?' Age had softened the armour of Fezile's courage. Andre Bothma represented the worst side of man and he knew Thabo's church robes wouldn't protect him from the white cop's anger.

'Why are you worried, Fezile?' Thabo had felt Fezile's fear himself for a moment, but the overshadowing power of Almighty God had surrounded him; casting out fear as a stranger he had no need to acknowledge. 'The children were sent to me and I have done only what I believe is right. Food?' He glanced at the bubbling pot of mealie meal between them.

'Aye, aye aye.' Fezile shook his head and Thabo watched him carefully. His friend's cheeks were hollow and the sparkling white teeth Thabo had bought him with his first month's wages were missing. Tipping Fezile's face up with a finger under his chin, he challenged him. 'Where are they?'

'What?'

'Your birthday present.'

'You worry about teeth with Cop Bothma after you?' Fezile tried to change the subject as he pushed Thabo's hand away, but Thabo waited in silent demand for an answer and Fezile shrugged, beaming with a new thought.

'If God had wanted us to wear false teeth we would be born with clips on our gums, my friend.' Thinking he'd won the argument, Fezile grinned, but still Thabo waited. 'You think He wants me to choke on them?'

'I think He wants you to tell the truth.' Thabo gave the pot of mealie meal a slow stir.

'OK.' Fezile stood up with a sigh of exasperation. 'OK, Father. You want the truth.' His mind itched with fear of what Andre Bothma might do next, but he knew Thabo wouldn't give up till he answered. 'They said it was a good horse. They said it would win even if it went backwards.' Fezile stamped his feet in a small war dance of frustration. 'But it lies down!' He stared at Thabo in open-mouthed amazement and Thabo's mouth turned up with the slightest smile on which Fezile swiftly capitalised. 'He lie down this way,' Fezile lay flat on the floor. 'Then this.' He rolled the other way. 'And then he kick his legs in the air. That horse — he laughing at me!'

'Where are your teeth?' Thabo watched, unamused, and Fezile got to his feet very solemnly.

'The woman who bought them,' he pursed his lips as if deep in thought and a slow whistle of appreciation joined the rising steam from the pot between them, 'I think God be pleased she has again the wonderful smile He gave her!' As Thabo chuckled Fezile smelt victory and he went on quickly: 'Her children they got their father back. God, He waste nothing, Thabo. That's six children you not have to send to the Transkei!'

Thabo's laughter filled the small room and the mealie meal bubbled in the pot with squirting bursts of pleasure. But Fezile watched him in amazement. He knew what he'd said wasn't that funny.

'You OK?' he asked tentatively.

'I'm not worried about Cop Bothma.' The small room echoed with laughter as Thabo patted him on the back and made a plan to get the false teeth back. 'That white Xhosa has no chance with you, my friend!'

With yellow beaks snapping and rubber red beards swiping one another, two cockerels fought it out in a small wooden coop on the roof of a bus. Thabo, Miriam and Fezile stood back while the children moved past them in a pushing line to climb inside. Fezile grabbed one by the arm.

'With this you buy a day-old chick.' He pressed a sparkling five-cent piece into the child's hand and turned to the next. 'A good-looking hen for the roosters up there. Nice and plump!' He pressed another silver piece in the open black palm in front of him.

'You all right?' Miriam touched the small girl, Portia, as she reached the door of the bus. A fluffy toy lion was tied to her back like a baby but, unlike the others, Portia wasn't smiling. Just a small tilt of her head said goodbye as she clung to Fezile's five-cent coin, shrugging the lion higher on her back.

'You look after my grandmother, Sophie.' Thabo moved to a window of the bus as two small boys pushed their heads through it. 'And you go to school. Every day you go to school. You hear me?'

'Yes, Father.' The boys grinned and Thabo banged their tight crinkly heads together gently.

'God bless you, children. And remember: it is our God who reigns!'

Father Jamieson had raised the children's fares to the Transkei from his congregation, and the family at Bonne Espérance had taken on the cost of feeding them. But Fezile knew he'd made the biggest contribution of all and gazed proudly at the two squabbling roosters on the roof.

'Quiet!' He clapped his hands sharply. Staring down at him from under dishevelled headdresses, the roosters' feet spread flat like old men's toes as they clucked in quiet frustration. 'That's better. And you, you drive carefully!' He banged on the cab of the bus and the driver gazed down at him blankly. 'Be careful of those birds up there and I give you more when you come back.' He pushed a ten-cent coin into the driver's hand and empty pockets hung out of his trousers.

'Hamba Khale!' the grown-ups called as the bus drove away, the roosters skating in terrified circles on the floor of their coop as it rolled from side to side.

'Hlala Khale!' the children called back from the windows, and Miriam watched as Portia gazed at her from the back seats.

'You take care now. You be good, child!' Miriam ran after the bus while Portia watched her very seriously. She'd never seen Miriam run before. 'You look after yourself, you hear!' Portia held her hand flat against the window and watched in silence as Miriam disappeared in a cloud of dust.

'She'll be all right.' Thabo wrapped an arm round his mother. He knew she had grown to love the small girl and he wiped away a tear on her cheek. 'They'll all be just fine.'

But Miriam wasn't sure. She remembered the day she'd seen Luke with Portia by the river. She could still feel his pain and felt threatened herself, though she didn't know why.

'You did right, my son.' Denying her own fear, Miriam patted Thabo's hand.

Thabo had ensured the children caught the bus from Kraaifontein before Andre Bothma had time to question his authority. He knew it wasn't the children's welfare the white policeman was protecting. He was challenging Thabo himself, and as he returned to the church with Fezile later that day, he knew Cop Bothma would be waiting.

The church was surrounded by screaming people as Thabo pushed his way through them to the doors.

'These people want their children back, Father.' Andre was smirking as he reached him and he pushed the church door open with his foot. 'They say you've taken their children. They want those children back, Father.'

'I know none of these people.' Thabo didn't look at Andre as he made to go inside the church but was prevented. Andre's arm stretched across the open doorway in front of him and stale nicotine blew in Thabo's face.

'But they know you – and they say you are not the father of those children. Not even in those fancy robes of yours are you their father.'

'You want your children?' Thabo turned to the crowd and Fezile stood back in dread. 'You are the mothers and fathers of those children? Where were you when I found them starving? Where were you when they were taught to throw stones instead of to read? Where were you when they were naked and crying?' Thabo held a flapping clutch of flimsy paper in his hand and his anger rose to new heights as it centred on Andre Bothma. 'I believe this is what you want, sir.' He pushed the flimsy Bible pages into Andre's hand. 'You talk of the law? Read God's law!' Knocking Bothma's arm aside, Thabo strode into the church without looking back.

'You hear what he say?' Fezile moved in front of Andre, his face lit with a challenging smile as Thabo's courage fed his own. 'You still understand English, Mr Policeman?' He grinned and walked through the church door with a swagger. But the moment he disappeared from Andre's sight, Fezile's face clouded over and he ran quickly after Thabo.

'What was that you gave him?' His inquisitive Xhosa chased Thabo as Fezile ran after him between the wooden chairs. 'Where'd you get the papers? Those children have no papers – they have nothing. They are not even born, according to Bothma's law!'

'But today they were born.' Thabo dropped to his knees in front the altar and Fezile knelt beside him.

'Today they were born?' he repeated in quiet amazement.

'As God's children.' Thabo smiled at his friend warmly. 'And Cop Bothma has the words of the Bible that prove their birthright.'

CHAPTER EIGHTEEN

Samuel Netherby stood to the side of Rebecca's front door in Wilton Row and the Great Dane watched as his mistress climbed into a taxi. Zanu had seen Rebecca packing her cases. His china bowl had also been packed in a plastic bag and the dog had sat quite still as Samuel took it from Rebecca. He hadn't even objected when the old tailor had slipped on his lead. It was only as Rebecca stepped into the London taxi cab, her cases stacked beside the driver that Zanu had known something was definitely wrong. She'd forgotten him, and a gentle whimper carried a reminder of the giant dog's presence.

'I'll be back soon, Zanu.' Rebecca tried not to look at the dog as she pulled her Afghan coat tighter round her body. 'Are you sure you don't want to move into my place while I'm away, Sammy?' She pushed the cab window down and leaned out to him. 'Zanu might be better behaved if you stay here with him.'

'No mutt orders me around, love.' Samuel Netherby eyed the dog. 'Right?' Tossing the old man a dismissive glance, Zanu turned his attention back to Rebecca.

'You've got my number?' she shouted over the sudden rattle of the cab as it moved forward. 'You haven't forgotten it?' She tried hard to conceal the excitement with which she had awoken. Africa had dawned with the morning and she'd been filled with a hollow quiver of expectation from the moment she'd opened her eyes.

'Got your number right here!' Sammy bellowed after the cab, tapping his pocket. He'd gazed at it so often as he tried to imagine the kind that called his young friend home that he knew it off by heart. 'So long.' He waved, as if she was only going to the end of the road. 'Don't worry about anything this end. I'll take care of the shop!' he reassured her as the taxi mingled with the heavy London traffic and disappeared.

'OK, mate?' Samuel glanced at the dog beside him. A quiet whine sounded in Zanu's throat and his ears hung limp velvet blinds over his eyes. 'Can't she even go home to her family?' The old tailor was speaking as much to himself as to the dog. When he turned to go, the lead jarred him back. 'Move yourself.' He stared at Zanu and Zanu stared back with a whispered growl. 'Up you get, good boy!' Even with this change of approach the dog remained glued to the pavement, his head turned away in arrogant dismissal.

Sitting down beside him on the bottom step that led up to Rebecca's house, the old tailor gazed into the dog's eyes.

'You want to talk about it? So! Maybe it *is* a fella she's going back to — what business is it of ours?' He'd always known it was something more than a country that had called Rebecca home, and now he looked down at the pavement, tracing the line of cement between the stones with his foot. 'Not to say there's not plenty of 'em here. Like bees round a honeypot — Englishmen an' all! But she's not interested in 'em, is she?'

Samuel thought of the young man Rebecca had left in charge of *Glad Rags*. Richard Statten had all the arrogance of youth and the old tailor had little time for him. He had been Rebecca's assistant for two years now, and Samuel Netherby hadn't missed the constant attention he paid to her. 'Not one of 'em ever gets past first base. Load of louts, mark you. Wouldn't hold a candle to a white hunter.' He glanced at the dog. 'So! We're lumbered with each other and we'd better make the most of it.' The dog turned away, his thick neck reaching upwards as floppy jowls trembled. 'Opening time.' Sammy looked at his watch and stood up, his mind already inside his King's Road local. He nudged the solid black flank of the dog with his knee but Zanu ignored him. 'I've got to get back to the office, mate. They'll be needin' me.' But Sammy knew nobody would be needing him now Rebecca had gone. Although he owned the business she'd created from his shop, Rebecca was the only person who pretended he was necessary. A factory had long since taken his place on the manufacturing side and he understood little about the business. Money meant nothing to Samuel Netherby except as a means of making Rebecca happy. 'Come on, fella!' He moved off but the dog's lead tugged him back sharply once again.

'Looks like he wants a carry,' laughed a postman as he pedalled his bike past them.

'And you look like you'll be stitching them postbags yerself soon, mate!' Samuel yelled after him, turning back to the dog in a rage of inadequacy. 'You're making a mug of me.' He gazed up and down the street as if the dog had nothing to do with him. 'We've got better lamp-posts down the King's Road, I can tell you. If we get there sharpish you can hose one down.' But the dog bridled with a majestic tilt of his head.

'So, right, as usual, is she?' The old tailor dug into his pocket and pulled out a bunch of keys. 'Wouldn't be seen dead with you down my way any road, you East End mutt.' He turned the key in Rebecca's door and Zanu's tail whipped his leg with pleasure.

Miriam had begun cleaning even before the sun had pulled itself over the slow curves of mountains that morning, and the entire house smelt of soap, Brasso and polish. She'd washed the curtains, scrubbed every mark off the white walls and each door handle shone like a gold bubble. An air of expectancy filled Bonne Espérance and even the wind whispered the excitement of Rebecca's promised return. But Miriam knew that many things had changed since Rebecca had left. No amount of spit and polish could hide the truth of her mother's illness. It had consumed all David's time and money, and Bonne Espérance had disintegrated as Constance had. Even Christian du Toit had left for a more successful estate, but still Miriam hoped to conceal the ravages of time.

'Can I do that?' Simon asked as her behind swung from side to side in front of him. Miriam was polishing the square red flagstones on the front porch, her feet pushed under the straps of large floor brushes as she shimmied her way back and forth, side to side. 'Let me do it.' Simon tugged at her swinging skirts. Stepping off the brushes, Miriam glanced at him and her spreading bare feet moved to the front door.

'Till you see your face shine in the floor!' She disappeared into the house and Simon pushed his feet under the straps on the brushes. His toes curled round the hard edge of wood expectantly, he moved forward gingerly and both feet shot out from under him.

'Hey!' he shouted, landing with a bump, his trousers polishing the floor as he slid across it. Pulling himself up on the window sill, he stared down at his feet in amazement, wondering how Miriam had made it look so easy.

'Polish.' Miriam's hand pushed out of a window and a dusting cloth blew a small cloud in his face. 'Till you see yourself!' The cloth disappeared inside and Simon's mouth twisted with determination. One foot slid forward and his tongue poked out as he concentrated. Though fully grown, he was as engrossed as any small child and his feet slid slowly forward in a polishing dance.

Rebecca gazed at the streaks of colour that stretched across the horizon as the plane sat on a flying cloud mattress. It was eight hours since she'd left Heathrow airport and she knew that Africa was hidden somewhere underneath her. The vast continent had tightened its grip with each moment that drew her closer and she was aware of its tug on her soul.

Leaning back in her seat she tucked a blanket higher under her chin and closed her eyes. Sammy had insisted she went first class and he'd bought the ticket himself to ensure that she did.

'If a yobbo like Adam Faith goes first class, so do you.'

But in spite of the comfort, Rebecca hadn't slept at all. She was constantly aware of the urgent longing that had woken her so suddenly in her London house. She didn't know why she'd thought Luke had called her. He was no longer part of her life. He'd been as far removed from her as ant hills and 123 Z were removed from Wilton Row, yet all she'd thought of was him.

A beam of light tapped at the thick cold glass of the plane window and Rebecca pressed her face against it. Driving a path between the clouds, the sun pushed down to reveal miles of distant brown land below. Like a million tiny pinheads, trees clustered in the wide flanks of a still army that guarded a rift in the earth and Rebecca felt herself reaching down to touch it.

Dragging her mind quickly back to London and the rich life she'd found there, Rebecca tried to free herself from its pull. She tried to remember instead the intense dry heat and hard stubble of her homeland. She forced herself to look back into the space of loneliness that had been her childhood, but the silent rhythm of Africa tugged at the core of her being and wouldn't let go.

David had spotted the gleaming wings of the South African Airways jet long before anybody else at D F Malan airport, and as the fragile glimmer of the plane disappeared in a glare of sunlight he closed his eyes. He hadn't realised he was nervous until that moment. The years Rebecca had been away stretched a vast distance between them, but now she was crossing it.

It was a phone call that had disturbed David. That morning, Luke's sister Naomi had called from Johannesburg and though she'd tried to sound casual, her voice had been too polite as she'd asked if David had seen Luke.

'I'm hardly likely to have seen him, Naomi.' He'd been angry with even the mention of Luke's name: the anger as alive as it had been so many years before. But then, as Naomi went on to tell him about the tragedy of Althea and Anton, he'd felt sick. He'd often read of family suicides in the newspapers – it was a South African phenomenon, one in which entire families of white South Africans were wiped out by one desperate parent and nobody ever discovered the reasons – but never before had the full weight of such a tragedy touched David personally.

'I'm sorry.' He tried to conceal his emotion and listened silently as

Naomi explained that as Luke hadn't been seen in Johannesburg since the day his wife and son had died, she wondered if he'd gone back to Bonne Espérance.

'Luke wouldn't have come back here, Naomi.' David hoped he wouldn't; he still resented Luke so much.

'I don't want Rebecca to know anything about what's happened,' he told Miriam later. 'Luke's part in her life is over. He has nothing to do with her any more.'

He insisted that if Luke ever turned up, she was to send him away. At this, Miriam was close to tears. All she could remember was the day Luke had been back to Bonne Espérance and all she could feel was his loss. But Miriam had seen no reaction in David's face. Like most white people, he'd spoken as if it were possible to remove a person's presence in his life quite painlessly.

'But Luke loves Rebecca, master.' Miriam was unable to hold back her feelings and at last she told David what Luke had urged her not to. 'He came here when his child died. Luke needs Missy Rebecca, master. He has nothing.'

Miriam's culture was based on the care of extended families and when one of her people hurt, they all hurt. She didn't know that David was doing the same thing, but in his own way. He was trying to protect Rebecca. To him, she was still a small lost child on an ant hill. Both he and Miriam had felt the first love that once flowed between two young people to warm the air, and though neither said another word, they both knew it was still there. The love between Luke and Rebecca was alive. It filled every nook and cranny of Bonne Espérance and they knew Rebecca would sense it.

Sitting quite still as the plane taxied towards the airport buildings, Rebecca's eyes fixed on the granite form of Table Mountain that loomed from among distant clouds. The loud snap of releasing seat-belts and the clatter of overhead lockers opening didn't reach her. She'd spotted her father in the doorway of the airport building and he was exactly where he'd been on the day she'd left.

'Daddy,' she whispered as childhood called her. She could feel the comfort and quiet strength that expressed itself in her father's love.

'Your bag, Miss Conrad.' A steward lifted down her large travelling case and Rebecca looked round in sudden embarrassment. The plane was empty.

'Thank you.' She moved after him to the door, but stopped as she reached the wide opening. Mellow Cape air had wrapped her in its arms and she was enclosed in the magic blue haze of mountains.

'Rebecca!' David's voice reached across the tarmac between them as he ran towards the plane. Her father was climbing the wide steps of the gangway, taking her in his arms and wrapping her in the firm grip that told her she was back where she belonged.

Dressed in the same smart blue suit he'd worn for Thabo's investiture, Simon walked tall beside Rebecca. Though he wanted her to notice how much he'd grown, he didn't want her to spot the shrunken jacket, and so he clutched the cuffs tightly between curled fingers.

Simon had studied photographs in the family albums from the moment he'd heard Rebecca was coming home.

'You've grown,' she said seriously, and only then did he recognise the beautiful woman dressed in blue jeans and cowboy boots. She threw her head back and laughed as they walked through the vineyards. Rebecca's laugh was filled with remembered mischief and Simon's toes curled in his shoes as he recognised the feeling that was her.

'I just remembered what you did in Mrs Bernstein's shop!' Rebecca's dark eyes lit with familiar challenge and he nodded. Simon recalled events in the small mining town and was still secretly proud of his triumph. 'And do you remember the horse you carved for my birthday?' Rebecca could see the tiny wooden horse where it stood in pride of place above the Adam fireplace in her London home. 'Every time I look at it I see you on its back.'

'Yes.' Simon wasn't at all surprised. He knew he was on the back of the small wooden horse he'd carved, even if nobody else noticed him there. 'I was little when I did that,' he reminded her.

'I can't get over how much you've grown, Simon.' Rebecca watched him as he walked beside her. Simon was well built. His shoulders were back, his head high and though his legs moved awkwardly, his strides kept up with hers. 'You're a man, of course – almost twenty.' She kept the distance he'd placed between them.

'Nineteen.' A small shrug of pleasure hitched Simon's shoulders higher and the child he still was peeked out from the man's body. 'You mustn't be cross.' His tongue pushed out of his mouth in a moment of forgetfulness as he tried to find the right words for his thoughts. 'She not know who you are, that's all.' Simon was talking about Rebecca's mother and she looked away from him quickly.

Rebecca still found it hard to accept what had happened when she'd first seen Constance. Her mother looked far older than Rebecca had expected. Frail and vulnerable, she'd looked physically older than Granny Cat. A curious anger hid behind Constance's eyes and there'd been nothing familiar about the woman who'd once been her mother.

Overwhelmed by sudden compassion, Rebecca had run to her but Constance had pushed her away. With angry slaps of her hands she'd fought her daughter off and turned to Simon for comfort.

'She only wet her pants.' Simon tried to explain Constance's frustration at being trapped inside a forgetful and decaying body. It was something he'd grown used to and he led Rebecca's mother out of the room with warm reassurances that all was well. Miriam had rushed quickly to clear away the wet cushion on which she'd sat and Rebecca had felt totally unnecessary.

'She likes your present. She thinks it's nice.' Simon tried to reassure Rebecca now and he grinned, but it was a fixed grin and Rebecca knew that none of the presents she'd brought home had been successful.

The silk dress had been for her mother – a dress from England like the ones Constance had tried on in 123 Z, but this one had been made with great care by Samuel Netherby.

'She didn't like the dress, Simon.' Rebecca remembered how her mother had let it drop to the floor without interest. 'And you don't like your present either.' As she turned to him, Simon's eyes lowered. Rebecca had brought him a cassette player. She'd watched him open the parcel carefully, each layer removed and folded neatly before going on to the next. Then Rebecca had pressed a button to surprise him, but as the Rolling Stones played, Constance had banged the floor in protest and Simon had rejected her gift.

Miriam hadn't really liked hers either. Though she'd made all the right noises as she held the swirling pink negligée in front of her, she considered only how many children it might have fed. It was then that Rebecca realised how far she'd strayed from her own beginnings, losing sight of the simplicity that ruled the world in which she'd once lived.

The vineyards that stretched a canopy of green up the slopes of purple mountains hid the part of herself that had gone missing. A child to whom a rusty old key had held out so much hope. A young girl who'd found that hope in love.

'I play with her in the days.' Simon's thoughts were still on Constance and he talked as if Rebecca's mother was his child. 'Sometimes I read her your letters.' He shone with pride and shrugged as though he'd achieved nothing much. 'We do work on the cars with Riaan too.'

'Riaan?' The name snatched Rebecca back to the day long ago when Luke had left Cape Town on the train. To the last time she'd ever seen him as he waved from a curling steel snake.

'Riaan says I'm clever with cars. He says he get me a job with him in the garage in Stellenbosch!' Simon's entire body smiled. Every part of him, until that moment awkward and clumsy, had gained a momentary dignity, but Rebecca was no longer listening.

Riaan was deep in an inspection pit under a large truck in the Stellenbosch garage when Rebecca found him later that week. He hadn't heard her arrive as the lorry's engine roared over his head, dripping oil on to his face as he worked.

'Why'd you turn it off, Amos?' Riaan yelled in Afrikaans as the engine cut out. 'Hey!' He pulled himself up over the side of the pit, looking for the Malay mechanic at whom he'd shouted. And then he stared. An exquisite pair of legs had stopped in front of his face.

'You've run out of petrol again, Riaan.' Rebecca's voice was balanced on a smile as she reached down to him.

'Hell's teeth, it's Rebecca!' Riaan pulled himself up and the oil marks on his face stretched wide with a smile.

The Stellenbosch restaurant was immaculate and Rebecca sat with Riaan at a small table under spreading bougainvillea. Though he'd scrubbed himself from head to foot before leaving the garage, Riaan still felt uncomfortable. It wasn't the crisp white cloth on the table that bothered him, it was Rebecca. If anything she was even more beautiful than he remembered. Exquisitely dressed, like women who belonged only in magazines, she was perfection and her voice held the cultured tones of a British accent.

'You know that's why there's a drought in the Free State,' Riaan tried to joke as he nodded at her short skirt. Afrikaner farmers had blamed the arrival of the mini skirt for their shrivelled crops. To them it was a sign of depravity and the day it had reached their shores, the Dutch Reformed Church had condemned it.

'It's good to see you again, Riaan.' Rebecca's hand reached to touch his over her plate of mussels. 'You haven't changed at all. You're just the same.'

Though Riaan was a man, she could still see the nervous boy who'd made a fumbling pass at her so many years before, the dusty child whom she, Simon and Thabo had faced in a replay of the Boer War. And though neither of them mentioned him, Luke was still right there between them.

'I don't know where he is.' Riaan's words were unexpected and quiet. He wasn't sure how to tell Rebecca the news he'd only recently heard himself. He'd discovered the tragedy when one of his letters to Luke had been returned unopened. 'Nobody's seen him since –'

'Since what, Riaan?' The silent cry that had woken her in London was ringing again in Rebecca's ears and her eyes held his, demanding an answer.

'Haven't they told you?' Riaan wished the ground would open up underneath him. He wished he was where his father was, miles away from Bonne Espérance and free of a past that dragged the future back.

'What haven't they told me?' Rebecca's fingers touched the back of Riaan's hand and he was lost for words. Glancing down at the white tablecloth, his eyes followed the looping trails of thread that wove it.

'It's his son.' Riaan struggled to find the English words that might express the truth without the guilt it aroused. 'Luke's wife, Althea.' Riaan's hand wiped his mouth, as if wiping the words he had yet to say. 'She killed herself, Rebecca – and the child. Miriam knows about it. He came to Bonne Espérance.' The words tumbled on to the table between them and the moment of insanity in which Althea had taken their lives jeered its triumph. It raced through Rebecca on a wave of nausea as Luke's face flashed in front of her eyes. He was desolate as the face of a small unknown boy looked up from a grave and Rebecca ran. She ran from the restaurant without turning back. She drove home and as Miriam faced her, her eyes closed in silent prayer.

'Luke was looking for you, Missy Rebecca.' Miriam watched the beautiful woman who sat across the wooden table between them. 'He came here to find you.' Miriam no longer cared what David would say. Her mind had gone back to the day the children had stolen Simon. To the moment Rebecca had faced Estelle's anger. To the way in which both white children had defended her son, Thabo. 'He still loves you, child.' Miriam pulled Rebecca into her, holding her as though even now she was that small girl.

Unseen by either his mother or Rebecca, Thabo had stepped into the small room. On either side of him stood two small black girls, their arms reaching up to him as they clung to his hands. 'So much pain in our country now, Missy Rebecca.' Miriam's head leaned against Rebecca's as her eyes passed over the faces of the two small children with her son. She knew why they were there and she could see the ugliness that surrounded them all, but Rebecca saw only Luke.

'Rebecca?' Thabo's voice was quiet and she turned to him slowly. She'd recognised the deep brown touch of his words and she gazed silently at the tall black priest who looked back at her. The dust that clung to the hem of his cassock, powdering his worn black shoes a dull brown, that dust was a part of her life and she'd recognised it too. The African priest who stood so still in the doorway was a part of a land that had called her home. With all its problems and pain, Africa was hers and Thabo embodied it.

*

David didn't turn round as Rebecca's voice reached him with words he'd expected since the day she'd first arrived home.

'Why didn't you tell me, Dad?' She was watching him from the arched doorway that led into the cool dark of the cellars. It was the first time she'd been into the cellars since she got back and the dank smell of failure greeted her like a clammy hand.

'I didn't think you needed to know.' David's voice was quiet, unprepared for the silent anger that poured from his daughter.

'I'm not a child any more. Don't you know that every time the doorbell or the phone rang in London I thought it was to tell me Mom had died? Don't you know how I hated leaving?' Rebecca peered at her father through the semi-dark of the cellars, her emotions in total confusion as she accused him of her own guilt. 'I left everything I loved and now it's all dying!'

'Go back to London, Rebecca. You've got a life there and you don't need all this.'

'All this *is* me, Dad!'

'What about your business and . . .'

'*This is me!* Can you hear me? It's me . . . Luke is me.' The look that flashed from Rebecca's eyes made David hesitate but he went on.

'I'll never forget what he did to you, Rebecca. I'll never forgive Luke for what happened. Is that what you can't accept?'

'That you didn't trust me enough to tell me about Luke's wife and child – that's what I can't accept, and what hurts so much.'

In the silence that stepped between them David watched his daughter and for the first time he faced the truth: Rebecca was a woman. She no longer needed his protection – what she needed was his trust.

'I'm not going back to London.' Her tears gone, Rebecca looked at her father. 'I know where I belong; I just didn't know how easy it would be to admit it.' David felt the touch of her hand on his arm. 'This is what I want, Dad. Not a business, not money. I've been trying to prove something but now I don't even know what it was. Who was I trying to impress? I never impressed Sammy.' Rebecca pictured her old friend. 'He didn't need me because he knew who he was.' Her eyes passed over the cellars and the same excitement filled her as on the day she'd first seen Sammy's rundown shop in the King's Road. 'I can bring this place back to what it was, Dad!' Her thoughts had flown to the pages of Emily's diary. Though she hadn't read them for many years the words were engraved on her mind.

Even though Bonne Espérance seems to have died, Father's spirit is still here. It's held in the earth he loved. He was part of the land. Part of the 'mother that never dies', and it will live again.

Rebecca knew her father was as lost as Jacques Beauvilliers must have been when Emily had written those words. David was as out of place as Samuel Netherby had been when she first met him. The hoist-house that reached for hot white skies in the centre of Africa was part of a bygone age, but David's heart was still locked inside its steel walls.

'We can make Bonne Espérance live again, Dad. Prudence Beauvilliers did it and we can do it — together!'

'Why?'

Rebecca didn't really know why. Bonne Espérance was no more than an African vineyard. It had claimed her on the same day she'd claimed Luke, yet even now it held her.

'For him?' David peered into her eyes as if he might find the answer there. 'Luke's gone, Rebecca.'

'Yes.' Her voice was quiet.

'Then why?' David demanded an answer. She'd claimed his trust and now he claimed hers.

'Because this is my home.'

'And you'll be able to live here now?'

Rebecca knew what her father was asking. She'd gone back to District Six soon after she'd arrived. She'd stood in the windblown desert under Table Mountain that had once been a vibrant community. The homes of Johannes Villiers' people had been flattened by bulldozers and ghosts now stalked the streets. The church in which she'd found the baptism record of Elsie Villiers stood as a lonely monument to 'orderly progress'. District Six had been declared a 'white group area' and non-whites had been pushed out to the flatlands of helplessness.

The Group is Killing My People had been scrawled on a crumbling wall and as Rebecca read the words, her mind had raced back to Lorraine Hendrickse. She'd gone immediately to the house in Claremont, but Elsie Villiers' granddaughter had disappeared and her home was occupied by white strangers.

Marching on down the road of Grand Apartheid, South Africa had ignored the winds of change that were sweeping across the continent. Rhodesia had declared unilateral independence from Britain and a bloody bush war raged in the buffer state. Aided by newly independent black states, ANC guerillas fought for their people's freedom in South Africa and the rest of the world turned its back.

The Government's racial policies had sapped the strength of a nation and the heart of Bonne Espérance bled dry with the country. The earth itself seemed drained of hope and the vineyards had slowly died, their thirst for the love of Jacques Beauvilliers unquenched.

Rebecca didn't know that as Luke had taken his first faltering steps to stand against apartheid, he'd been thrown off-balance by his family's suicide. All she knew was the love she still felt for him and it was as deep as her love of Africa. The smell of sweat and earth, horses and vines excited her as he did. She was a part of Luke – and a part of Jacques Beauvilliers, Eva and Jean Jacques. Like a spider's web, Bonne Espérance clung to her, wrapping her into its centre as she discovered her own African heartbeat.

'I am an African,' she smiled. 'And old enough to accept whatever that might mean.'

Samuel Netherby stood back in the large Goods Hall of Heathrow airport, watching the giant black dog being loaded into an enormous wooden crate. Printed in bold red letters on the side was a label that read: *Live Dog*, and a white-jacketed man looked Zanu firmly in the eye as he closed him inside.

'Going to South Africa? Huh! Right colour anyway, ain't he!' he chuckled as he moved to Samuel Netherby. The enormous dog had lifted his head in disdain, watching them arrogantly through the wooden bars. 'Give 'im a cap an' he'll fly the bleedin' plane hisself!'

'He don't need no cap to do that.' Samuel Netherby reached a hand through the bars and patted the dog. They'd formed a curious relationship of mutual mistrust since Rebecca left and he knew he'd miss Zanu, but not nearly as much as he did his mistress.

'OK, mate? Be good now, but never forget you're a Londoner!' Zanu's tongue wiped his jowls with a wide pink chamois leather and he stared back at the old tailor in silence.

Rebecca hadn't asked Samuel to send the dog to Cape Town. She hadn't even said she'd be staying in Africa, but between the lines of her letters Samuel had read the truth. She'd talked of Bonne Espérance, saying she'd have to stay for a while to help rebuild the vineyard. She'd talked of her hopes of what it could be, what it had once been when Jacques Beauvilliers had built it, and excitement had shone in her words. Rebecca wrote of her mother, of Simon, of her father and of Miriam, but nowhere did she mention the man. Samuel Netherby knew he was somewhere among the words she'd left out.

'When you get there,' he cautioned Zanu, 'you can just forget all about lamp-posts! Shouldn't think they've got 'em there, anyway, and if you try hosing down one of them huts you'll start a mud-slide. And watch your p's and q's out there in the bush, mind. Them cats aren't like that ginger poofter next door. They'd have you for breakfast! Get it?'

A slow whimper answered, as if the dog wanted to reassure the old man that he'd miss him, despite everything.

'Take him away!' Samuel Netherby walked off without looking back. He'd always known Rebecca was only on loan, and the time had come to hand her back and pick up his own life. *Glad Rags* was meaningless without her and the old tailor had decided to sell it and return to the only trade he knew.

As the enormous black dog raced across the wide open spaces of Bonne Espérance, Rebecca laughed out loud. It was as if Zanu had come home, too. The freedom he'd found was visible in each stretching stride and his ears lifted like wings as his tail propelled him from behind.

'This way, Zanu,' Simon yelled across the vineyards from the back of his pony. The dog skidded and his body twisted back to the man who played with him like a child. With his legs flying in all directions, a deep warm bark echoed against the mountains behind them and Zanu galloped back to Simon.

Life had returned to Bonne Espérance and Rebecca knew the old tailor had forced her to make the right decision. *Glad Rags* was a part of time past, a time that had served its purpose for both of them. In the tail end of his life, Samuel Netherby had reclaimed himself and the bespoke tailor of the King's Road was back at his old trade.

You remember me old treadle machine? The one you thought I'd got shot of? Rebecca could hear Sammy's hoarse chuckle among the words in his letter. *It still goes like the clappers!*

Rebecca's car arrived at Cape Town docks several weeks after the dog, and she went to collect it with Simon and Zanu. Lost in the meccano world of the docks, they watched an enormous crane swing the gleaming white Mercedes Benz high over their heads. Moving to it quickly as it was broken free of its packing, Simon gazed at the car in admiration.

'Wow!' he declared, and Rebecca smiled as Zanu sniffed a wheel, promptly lifting his leg in recognition of ownership.

'What's that?' Simon peered through the car windscreen in puzzlement and the dog stared with him. His jowls quivering, Zanu growled his caution, backing away on shaking legs.

'You old devil!' Rebecca laughed as she looked into the car. Sitting in the front seat was the cardboard sheep.

CHAPTER NINETEEN

A narrow beam of light pushed its way into a small mud hut in the Transkei. An open fire in the centre of the earth floor puffed clouds of swirling smoke between the threading grass of a thatched roof. African voices harmonised their grief in song and Thabo's grandmother wept as she rocked backwards and forwards. Sophie didn't know how she was going to tell her grandson what had happened the day before.

In full spate, the Tele River had spilled down the mountain to claim the life of the small girl Portia. She'd gone down to its banks to fetch water as she did each day, but this time, Portia had drowned.

Lunga, the child who'd taken care of Thabo during his initiation, had run back to the village with the news. He was now sixteen years old, and had been put in charge of the children Thabo had sent to the village. His screams still rang in Sophie's head. Lunga had cried out that the river spirits had taken Portia, but Sophie knew differently: God had taken her. From the moment the serious little girl had stepped off the bus to join them in the Transkei, Sophie had known that Portia was not of this world.

Settling her eyes on the dead child in front of her now, she watched as two women painted the tiny body with brown clay. A loincloth of strung beads was tied round her waist, a bead bodice covered the child's chest and, very carefully, black and white dots were painted on her cheeks. Then, turning to Sophie in silence, the women retreated, acknowledging her right to complete the preparation for burial. With her aging body bent double and legs crippled by arthritis, Sophie's spreading bare feet pressed down the earth floor as she moved forwards. She carried two traditional white blankets with black edging, and she laid one carefully in the bottom of the child's coffin. Stepping back, she watched as the small body was placed carefully on top of it and spreading another blanket, she tucked it under the child's chin. Taking a small carved stick from the woman beside her, she laid it next to Portia and finally, placing two fifty-cent coins beside it for the child's journey, she lowered her head in prayer.

'*Yima*.' She told the women to wait as they moved to close the coffin. Holding the fluffy lion in her hand, she laid it carefully beside Portia's face and then stepped back once again. She watched as the rough wooden lid covered the body; the women placed a jug and a suitcase on top of the closed coffin and Sophie had completed her part in Portia's return to God.

Lunga was as lost as everyone else as he stood with Zola outside the mud hut in which the women prepared the body. Sophie's son and Lunga's uncle, Zola had once been a policeman in Cape Town and it was he who'd stopped Lunga going after Thabo to the city. Zola had told him he'd seen many young men arrive in Cape Town from the Transkei. They'd gone in search of riches but had found only an empty and difficult dream that often killed them. Zola was a powerful man and his presence usually filled Lunga with awe, but today the uncle who wielded so much authority in the village was broken and he wept like a woman.

Portia's death had covered the entire village with a cloud of despair. Echoing laughter had been replaced by mourning and nobody understood why she'd been taken.

Father Jamieson was silent as he read the letter which had carried the grief of an African village all the way to Cape Town. Composed by Sophie, it was written in the careful hand of Zola and addressed to Thabo. Thabo sat silently in a wooden chair beside the priest, staring at the rough cross above the altar of his corrugated iron church and Father Jamieson knew that guilt had touched him alongside grief.

'The deeper things of God are not within our understanding, Thabo. We must accept them by faith.' The priest reacted as Thabo's eyes turned on to him. They were lost, spilling over with the confusion he'd often seen in the eyes of English parents whose children had died.

'When we accept Christ into our lives we accept His divine instruction and pain is a necessary part of it.' Father Jamieson pulled out a chair beside Thabo. The legs scraped on the concrete floor, echoing against the iron walls of the rusty church before dropping back with a dull thud as he sat on it. 'He delivered us from the power of darkness and translated us into the kingdom of His love.' Father Jamieson paused. 'We can't understand such love, Thabo. It's beyond our understanding. The fullness of God's love gave us His son even before we cared.' The priest's eyes settled on the wooden cross above the altar and the majesty of Christ's suffering reached down to him. 'Can we face the risen Christ unless the spirit has strived within us?'

'I failed.' Thabo's voice was quiet, reaching out to the white priest. 'A child He sent me to care for has died.' Thabo turned and looked at the man through whose door God had led him so many years before. He wanted to accept the truth he'd spoken, but guilt clung to his mind with suffocating darkness.

'He who is in you is greater than he who is in the world.' Father Jamieson placed the living word between them. 'A seed must die and fall to the ground before it brings life.'

'Why?' Thabo struggled to accept the truth.

'It's not for us to demand an explanation of the mysteries of creation, Thabo. But God demands of us that His name be exalted in all things. That His light shine in the darkness though none comprehend it. That glory be given to Him in all things – even the death of a child.'

Without another word Father Jamieson stood up and moved out of the building. He'd felt the supernatural presence of God descend on the small church that sat so incongruously in the centre of a sprawling township. Thabo was weeping and he knew the African priest had broken under the full weight of God's presence.

As if stalking the dark continent of Africa, death had also visited Bonne Espérance, but Simon hadn't recognised it. He'd sensed something was missing the moment he'd walked into Constance's bedroom that morning, but he hadn't known what. Constance wasn't missing. She was there and he'd called gently to wake her.

'Time to get up.'

But Constance hadn't woken so Simon had encouraged her with breakfast. Passing a bowl of her favourite Maltabella porridge under her nose, he'd tried to tempt her.

'I put three sugars in. Smell – it's nice. You like it!'

Then Simon had blown in Constance's ear very gently, the way he remembered being woken himself when he was small. It was his favourite discovery of a new day and he tried it on her.

'The sun's up. Open your eyes and say hullo.' He'd touched her hand. 'Why you so cold? It's not cold.' Simon had blown on to his own hands and held hers between them to warm them. But he was puzzled. He didn't understand why Constance seemed to be missing although she was there. It was only when Miriam came in to dress Constance a little later that Simon realised something was definitely wrong. Miriam had looked at her mistress curiously, then she'd touched her, and then she'd cried.

'Outside, Simon. Outside!' Miriam had pushed him out of the room quickly as she tried to hold her own emotion under control and Simon had fought to get back. But he hadn't been allowed. He'd stood outside as Rebecca and David had run into the room, and they'd cried as much as Miriam. Then a doctor had arrived. Later still, other men had been led into the room and Simon had watched in silent puzzlement as they'd carried a large wooden box away. Only then had he got back into Constance's room and all he'd seen was an empty bed.

'Where's she gone?' he yelled as he ran out. Simon had never known anyone die before and Constance's sudden departure baffled him completely. 'Did they take her away?' he asked Rebecca later.

He listened as Rebecca tried to explain that her mother was dead. She was weeping, hardly able to speak, and Simon had never seen Rebecca cry before, He'd never seen a man cry either, but David had cried, and still Simon didn't understand why.

'Why you all crying?' he bellowed in confusion.

'Do you remember when your pony died, Simon?' Rebecca tried to explain again, but he refused to believe her.

'No!' he argued. 'She didn't say she was going!' Simon had understood when his pony had left for heaven without a word; he knew the pony couldn't talk, but he'd been unable to believe Constance would have gone anywhere without saying goodbye – not even to heaven. It was only the empty space inside him, which he'd felt in her room for the first time that morning, that finally convinced Simon she'd really gone. The space reserved for her among his feelings had remained empty ever since. Constance had walked out of it without a word.

'Hullo Simon.' Simon looked at the young man standing beside him. Several people had arrived at Bonne Espérance and they all apparently knew him, but he recognised none of them.

'I'm Joe, your cousin. Your Aunt Lydia's son – remember? My mother's over there. See her?' The young man pointed to a woman who stood near the piano with Rebecca, and Simon stared at her blankly. There was a blonde child beside Lydia. 'That's my sister, Tarcie. You won't know her 'cos she was born after we left for South West Africa. You didn't meet her. Hey! You remember that day you hid in the cupboard and scared me with that uniform when we were kids?' Joe tried to remind him who he was but Simon stared back in silence. 'Anyway, I'm glad to see you're OK.' Joe shrugged off his embarrassment at not being recognised and walked away. He wasn't aware that Simon's eyes were still on him. Joe hadn't sensed the anger that followed him as Simon's heart burned with rage. Everybody who'd come to the curious ceremony in the family graveyard appeared to have known beforehand that Constance was leaving. Everyone had known she'd planned to go; except him.

'What's Joe going to do now he's finished Matric?' As Rebecca asked her question she wondered why there was a curious detachment about Lydia. 'Will he be going to UCT?'

Exile had taken its toll. Everything about Lydia was different. The sparkle that had once shone from her eyes had gone. Her clothes were limp and the wonderfully fresh style that had been her trademark was nowhere to be seen. Even the small blonde girl beside her spoke loudly of poverty.

'Please tell me if I can do anything to help, Lydia.' But Rebecca's offer was rejected with a small sigh of amusement.

'Like what?' Lydia tried to hold tightly to herself, hoping that at least a scrap of her former dignity remained. 'Everything's fine.' She had tried to dress as well as possible before returning to the country that had banished her husband, but it hadn't been easy. Stan had lost the meagre living he'd first earned on the local newspaper in Luderitz and Lydia had struggled to make ends meet on her own.

'Joe won't be going to university. He wants to be a journalist like his father.' Lydia smiled at Rebecca as she spoke but her smile was distant. Her mind was back in the desert of South West Africa. Back with a husband whose passion for his country had been rendered impotent by exile. Lydia had watched Stan sink deeper into a stupor of helplessness as his voice echoed unheard in the miles that separated him from the battle for his country. She'd tried hard to rebuild his confidence in himself and his own Afrikaner nation, but with each determined step his people took on a road to a disaster, Stan found comfort only in drink. In an effort to blind himself to his own inadequacy, and the growing shame of his Afrikaner heritage, Stan had been unaware of the trap that had closed around him.

'How is Stan?' Rebecca asked as she sensed the Afrikaner she'd once misunderstood so completely lurking behind Lydia's eyes.

'Stan's fine,' Lydia lied, her hand running down the length of the skinny blonde pigtail that trailed over her small daughter's shoulder. Rebecca's question had locked Lydia's mind into a ghost-town not far from Luderitz. Kolmanskop had once been a thriving community of Europeans but now it lay still and silent among rolling pink dunes. Steep banks of fine sand pushed through the doors and windows of wooden houses, telling of the day life had been wiped from the town. The people of Kolmanskop had known nothing of the trucks driving through the night from Johannesburg to move them out. Only when they'd woken in the early hours, ordered to leave their houses with nothing but the clothes they wore and their Bibles, had they realised the truth. To prevent theft, the open cast diamond mines had been closed without warning and the people had been driven away from the only home they'd known. Diamonds had proved more valuable than life itself and the town had been left to the whistling wind of the Namib Desert.

The creak of an open piano, groaning under the weight of folding sand, had spoken to Lydia just as loudly as the words she'd heard that day. She'd gone to Kolmanskop to meet Stan's South African contact in the exiled anti-apartheid movement. One of their own had been assassinated and everyone's life was in danger – except Stan's, the man had said. It had been inside buildings occupied by nothing but sand that Lydia had first heard the truth about her husband. The secret police no longer considered Stan a threat. They'd watched him sink into alcoholism and, standing back, they'd decided to let him kill himself.

'Stan's fine,' Lydia said again in defiance of memory, and she smiled. She could picture the man she loved, drinking himself blind to what he saw as the failure of his life. She could smell the bitter stench of alcohol that seeped through his pores and Lydia knew she'd heard the truth on the day she'd visited Kolmanskop. The aim of those who'd decided to stand back and watch her husband kill himself was more accurate than any assassin's bullet.

'Joe might need your help though, Rebecca.' Lydia dragged herself out of the pit of despair in which she'd lived for so long. She knew Joe's determination to be a journalist wasn't to emulate his father but to prove himself against Stan's failure. 'He wants to join the television service here when it starts up – as a cameraman.'

'Then I'll help him as much as I can.' Rebecca turned to the small girl Tarcie who stood silently beside her mother. A familiar space of loneliness surrounded the child and Rebecca felt suddenly protective.

'Why don't you send Tarcie back here sometime for a holiday, Lydia? Would you like that?' She smiled at the small girl whose eyes had lit with surprise.

'You want me to stay with you?' Tarcie's voice was filled with astonishment, balanced on the possibility of Rebecca's words being as empty as most grown-ups'. Nobody had ever asked Tarcie to stay with them. The people in the small town of Luderitz ignored her. Her father was never well and her mother was too busy washing other people's dirty clothes to pay her any attention.

'Of course I want you to stay.' Rebecca put her hand on the child's shoulder and felt the delicate bones lift with delight.

'Thank you!' The excitement that bubbled in Tarcie spoke of the moment she'd been conceived, and Lydia recognised it instantly. It was a moment of love that had been snatched from alcohol.

'I'm sure Simon would want you to stay.' As Rebecca spoke, Tarcie glanced across the large sitting room towards the door. It was open and

Simon stood in the hallway. Leaning against the wall he watched the people inside with such anger that it made the small girl shiver. She'd seen Simon the moment she'd arrived at Bonne Espérance and there was something so solitary about his eyes that the man/child fascinated her.

'Simon thinks my mother went away without saying goodbye to him you see, Tarcie.' As Rebecca talked of her mother's death she suddenly realised why she'd felt such a curious relief. The stranger she'd come home to was gone, and with her the pain. In death Rebecca had reclaimed her mother as she'd once been – a strong woman, a woman whose anger at the people of the small town had often terrified Rebecca herself, but Constance had been a mother who'd loved far more than she'd been capable of expressing and only now did Rebecca remember her.

'Maybe you could help Simon understand?' She turned back to Tarcie. 'My mother would have wanted that.'

Tarcie's eyes remained fixed on Simon and then she turned her slow gaze on to Rebecca.

'What if he doesn't want to?'

David held himself firmly in control as Andre Bothma talked. They were in the kitchen and Miriam stood silently at the sink, trying not to listen. She could feel anger building in her master; it was mingled with grief that hadn't yet been released and she knew it was dangerous. Miriam had thought a great deal about the two deaths that had touched her so recently. She'd gazed down at the ironing board as she'd ironed David's dark suit for his wife's funeral, and her thoughts had been punctuated by sharp bursts of steam. Thabo was right: Portia's death must be used to glorify God, but she wasn't certain about Constance. Her mistress' death had pushed Simon into an isolated world of rejection, and Miriam wondered if Bonne Espérance would ever be the same.

'I'm not sure I understand what bothers you, Andre,' David was saying. 'Rebecca stood to inherit Bonne Espérance according to the original Beauvilliers will, and nothing's changed. The estate was passed down by my wife's grandfather and grandmother as you know, and now it goes to Rebecca – together with Paul, of course.'

'Which original Beauvilliers was that?' Andre Bothma's face was devoid of expression as he watched David. It was while he'd stood beside Constance's grave in the small family burial yard that Andre had found his passions re-aroused. Once again his eyes had passed over the stones that commemorated the Beauvilliers girls and they'd excluded his own great-great-grandmother's name, Suzanne Beauvilliers. Like all Suzanne's descendants, Andre had been excluded from Bonne Espérance, and he thought he knew why: she'd married an Afrikaner. Suzanne Beauvilliers' marriage to Thys Bothma had cut the family out and Andre burned with the bitterness of dismissal as he'd watched Rebecca beside her mother's grave.

Rebecca was an extraordinarily beautiful woman but even in grief Andre seemed to feel the distance of superiority that she still placed between them.

'Maybe it's time the original will was looked into.' Andre smiled at David but he retreated as Rebecca's father moved very close to him.

'If there's anything you have to say, Andre, I suggest you get yourself a lawyer.'

'I intend to.'

'Good.' David made to go but Andre's voice stopped him in his tracks. 'A lawyer who's familiar with the race laws, of course.'

The hideous ring of truth in Andre's words stung David and he swung back on the man who'd sicked apartheid into his home.

'Get out!' David's voice was quiet and Miriam moved hastily to the door. She'd heard the distant thunder that warned of a storm between the two white men and she wanted to escape.

'What are you two doing tucked away in the kitchen?' Rebecca stepped in brightly, but was greeted by a wall of tension. 'Is there something the matter?' It was the first time she'd seen Andre since she'd come home but she recognised the white policeman instantly. 'Is there a problem, Andre?' She glanced at her father. 'What is it, Dad?'

'Nothing, Rebecca. Andre was just going.' David tried to remove Andre before the reason for his presence exploded in her face.

'But I haven't even spoken to you yet, Andre.' Rebecca sensed that her father was covering something. 'What is it?'

'My lawyer will be in touch.' Andre swivelled on his heel but Rebecca stepped in front of him. The young girl whose anger he'd faced once before was now a woman and she was no longer even slightly afraid.

'Lawyer?' Rebecca watched him carefully, her mind back on the moment in the family graveyard years earlier when Andre had first expressed the rights of his family to the Beauvilliers heritage. 'What about? Your family's right to Bonne Espérance?'

'That could be relevant.' Andre tried to speak Rebecca's language clearly. He was aware that the English despised Afrikaans and it angered him as much as the confidence with which she faced him. 'Goodbye.' He tried to get to the door but she stopped him once again with a gentle touch on his shoulder.

'Relevant means there's something else, Andre.' In London Rebecca hadn't only gained confidence but a belief in herself. She'd lived free of the shadow of apartheid and that freedom showed in her clear dark eyes.

The humiliation heaped on her as a young girl had been shrugged off and Rebecca had accepted who she was.

'We don't need to go on about it, Rebecca. It's hardly the time.' David opened the kitchen door, keen to get rid of the poison Andre had brought with him.

'But what is it, Andre?' Rebecca held firm, her eyes challenging him. 'What exactly will your lawyers be looking into?' Her anger hadn't been stirred by the man but by the bitterness she'd recognised in his heart.

'I think you know what I mean.' Though Andre's voice was as quiet and threatening as his daughter's, David was smiling. He'd relaxed. For the first time in her life he'd seen his daughter stand firm, free of shame in her own identity.

'I think I do know what you mean, Andre.'

Rebecca's mind had leapt back to a small prefabricated house in the Cape flats. It was one of a vast plain of identical houses. They spread like lines of thirsty ants in the bowl of a spoon as it scooped its way up from the sea to reach between folding mountains. Rebecca had gone there to find Lorraine Hendrickse and she could still smell the degradation that had greeted her.

Lorraine's coloured blood had been discovered when a schoolteacher complained that her son was too dark for a European. The clumsy wheels of bureaucracy had moved forward in a relentless search for the child's race and inevitably Lorraine Hendrickse's had been run over. Everything she'd lived for had been wiped out as a pencil pushed its way into her child's hair. The pencil had lodged firmly in his tight curls and it had pointed directly at his mother. The Immorality Act had declared her marriage to a white man illegal and, charged with 'Unlawful Carnal Intercourse', their love had been annulled. Banished with her children to an area designated for non-whites, Lorraine's dreams of 'white' had been wrecked on the rocks of apartheid as her European husband killed himself in shame.

'Yes, I know exactly what you mean, Andre.' Rebecca's voice was quiet.

'Then my lawyer will be in touch.' Without another word he turned away but Rebecca's voice stopped him once again.

'Are you sure you should do that?' She longed for some kind of light to break through the blinkers on Andre Bothma's mind but he ignored her and didn't turn back.

Only after everyone else had left Bonne Espérance that night did Rebecca allow herself to react to what had happened. Standing alone in the vineyards, she gazed towards the mountains that hid in the dark and she thought of her mother and Granny Cat. They could no longer be hurt by Andre Bothma's prejudice, nor could Jacques Beauvilliers, the man with whom everything had begun. His love for the slave, Eva – a love that had blossomed on Bonne Espérance a hundred and fifty years before – had hatched Clara's hatred in its warmth and it lived on. It had set the Beauvilliers family on a path of destruction that still reached out to touch them.

'What are we doing here, Zanu?' Rebecca reached down and touched the giant dog who leaned heavily against her. She knew she could start her life again in London at any time, and every part of her railed against the sickness that spread in the hearts of people like Andre. His hatred was so deep it touched both the oppressor and the oppressed, and quite suddenly she wanted to be free of it.

But it was the African people who had called her back as much as anything else. These were people who had held on to their dignity under the heavy hand of oppression. Their humility had been a strength she'd never seen anywhere else. It spoke of an inheritance more valuable than Bonne Espérance, and it was rooted in Africa. Like her love for Luke, which still rang clear no matter how the years denied it, the African people had bound her with cords that could never be broken.

'I love you, Luke.' Rebecca's whisper lifted from the past and disappeared unheard into the night. Though the whitewashed house stood still and silent under the dark thatch of the roof, she could see Luke and Thabo climbing up to her bedroom on the night they'd stolen Simon. She could see Thabo in his iron church, embodying his people's ability to forgive. His uncluttered humility held within it the power of one who'd sacrificed his life as he reconciled man to God. But the giggling taunts of time past still raced round Bonne Espérance. The agony of a divided family had carved its image on every tree and Clara's curse dominated every inch of the land, touching the entire country.

I'll love you always, Rebecca.

Luke's voice was quite suddenly somewhere among the others in Rebecca's thoughts, but a giggling screech quickly drowned it.

He's white and you're not!

Rebecca held herself erect, holding her mind firm against the reality of Andre Bothma's heavy step back into her life.

A shrill whistle skipped over stretching miles of whispering maize and Luke lifted his hand against the sun as he looked up. A white glare burned red dots against his eyes from directly overhead and he knew Ouma Malan had called him in for lunch. It would be a simple meal of stewed meat cooked in a three-legged pot. Ouma Malan would watch him across the table as he ate and, as if counting each mouthful, her eyes would fix on Luke's. But she would say nothing. The gnarled old lady cared little for idle conversation and even less for other people's problems. Every moment of her life was filled with activity. She found constant fascination in the busy life that went on in the apparent emptiness of her land.

Luke could hardly remember when he'd first arrived on the austere Afrikaans woman's farm, 'Drie Koppies'. His brief visit to Bonne Espérance eight years earlier had begun an endless journey. Luke had been searching for something he knew no longer existed. Time itself hadn't existed as he banked his mind against it. Taking any work he could find to feed himself, he'd moved on constantly in an effort to wipe out the past. And Rebecca. But she'd always been there. Though he'd buried himself among the gold mines' caverns of hell, hidden from light like a rat as he earned a living, the past still tagged him. He'd tried to leave it behind in the cold deep of underground but it always climbed out after him. No matter how far Luke had run, what he ran from was still etched in his eyes and Ouma Malan had recognised it instantly.

A white envelope slid across the table towards him and Luke looked at it as it bumped against his plate. The letter was addressed to Luke Marsden, care of Drie Koppies, and a tiny splatter of gravy smudged the corner to conceal the stamp.

'Yours?' Ouma Malan's Afrikaans was quiet and Luke pretended not to have heard her. He'd recognised the handwriting as his sister Naomi's, and the old lady's eyes were fixed on him, the edge of her silent questions prodding him. But Luke said nothing. When he'd first arrived on the farm, he'd told Ouma Malan that his name was Jakes and she'd never asked his surname. She'd never told him her Christian name either, and acceptance had settled a contract of silence between them.

'Who's it from?' Ouma Malan asked as Luke spooned another mouthful of hot stew into his mouth, packing it tight with a hunk of bread. The directness of her question surprised him. 'It says Luke Marsden,' she went on. 'You know him?' Luke could no longer avoid the truth her eyes demanded and he nodded. In all the years he'd worked on her farm the old lady hadn't been vaguely interested in who he was or where he came from, but she was interested now. 'He says there's been plenty of these letters, the postmaster, Oom Johannes.' Ouma Malan nodded at the envelope and the young African man Julius, who sat beside Luke at the table, watched silently. 'Oom Johannes says there's been plenty of letters to that name!'

Julius had arrived on the farm when he was a child. Starving and alone after his parents had been burned as witches in Venda, the small boy had gone to every white farm in the vicinity to beg for food. Chased by dogs, white men, black men and geese, he'd moved nervously on to the last farm. Drie Koppies was owned by a strange woman about whom the little boy had heard many dark tales. Nobody had been certain the white farmer was a woman at all. Ouma Malan had the reputation for wielding a *sjambok* better than any man and Julius had been terrified.

'What you want, pikkanin?' the tall figure dressed in khaki trousers and a shirt had yelled at him from the front door of her small square house.

'You got dogs, baas?' Julius had yelled back, standing close enough to a tree to escape snapping teeth.

'If I had dogs would they eat you, pikkanin?' she demanded, and the child collapsed in giggles. In that moment Julius had become part of Ouma Malan's life.

'Why they looking for you?' The old woman's eyes were still fixed on the letter that sat on the table between her and Luke.

'Nobody's looking for me.' Luke went back to his food.

'Oom Johannes at the post office says it's not the first letter to that name,' she repeated, and Julius pushed a last mouthful of food into his mouth. He'd learned that when Ouma Malan latched on to something she never let go.

'Excuse.' Julius ducked out of the kitchen quickly.

'Who's looking for you?' Ouma Malan stared at Luke, as if she hadn't been interrupted by Julius' sudden departure.

'It's my sister.' Picking the letter up Luke pushed it into his pocket and moved to the door. 'Julius,' he called as he stepped outside, but the young African was already safely away and sitting in their jeep.

'I think you got a problem,' Julius assured him in perfect Afrikaans as Luke slid into the torn seat beside him. 'Ouma won't give up now. What you going to do?'

But Luke didn't answer Julius either as his hand moved round the sweatband inside his wide felt hat. Pushing it on to his head, he reacted to the broad strip of shade that fell across his eyes. It cooled memories that had flooded back with the arrival of Naomi's letter.

Pulling her hands out of the deep pockets of her khaki trousers, Ouma Malan began to collect up the dirty plates from the table. She'd never wondered till then where Luke came from. When he'd arrived at her farm she'd taken him in without question, considering him no different from the pikkanin who'd arrived long before, but the postmaster, Oom Johannes, had worried her. Apparently, he'd started by mailing all the letters addressed to the unknown Luke Marsden *Back to Sender*, but they'd kept returning. Finally, in frustration, the postmaster had written the name of every farmer in the district across each one and sent them on.

A sudden bark attracted Ouma Malan's attention and she looked out of the window. A barrel-chested baboon sat on top of a rusty tractor and called to her again as he saw her. His snout tilted arrogantly in the air, yellow teeth threatened from wide jaws and long dark fingers scratched his behind as he shouted for attention.

'Wah!' The small kitchen echoed as the old lady answered his call with a deep grunt. But, pretending he hadn't heard her, the baboon's deep-set eyes followed the path of a fly as it buzzed round his head. He was the elder of a troop of baboons that shared Drie Koppies with Ouma Malan, and each day the same battle ensued between them. It was an opportunity of name-calling that neither would miss as they claimed the land to be theirs.

'What you want?' Pushing the creaking gauze door open with a well-worn boot, Ouma Malan plonked her hands on her hips and barked another insult at the baboon. But there was no reply. Instead, turning his angry red behind to face her, he sloped off into the bushes with a dismissive glance over his shoulder. The old woman smiled. She knew he'd be back at sunset and the entire troop would be with him. Striking up a chorus of tuneless barks they'd wait till she went outside with food and a line of hairy delinquents would squat in front of her to eat. Rubber fingers would push scraps between bared teeth and once again they'd all live to fight another day.

The baboons were so uncomplicated in their needs that they'd become a welcome part of the old woman's daily routine. She'd pointed a gun at the leader once. He'd simply covered his eyes as he waited to die and she'd never threatened him again. Ouma Malan seldom ventured across the wire fence that secured the miles of spreading maize fields which had once been her father's. She'd long since decided that life outside her borders was too complicated and she knew nothing of politics. Time had stopped for her father on the day her mother had died, and it had never moved on for her.

Living a life rich with wide silences that cracked with any sign of life in the surrounding veldt, Ouma Malan found more of interest on a delicate stem of grass than in an entire city. She lived at peace with her surroundings, but somehow she knew the letter in Luke's pocket was threatening.

'Why's she looking for you?' She challenged him again that night and the hard slats of the wooden bench on which Luke sat beside Julius, dug uncomfortably into his back.

'Who?' He closed his eyes and leaned back to avoid Ouma Malan's question, allowing the cool of night to calm him.

'What's your sister want?'

'Nothing.'

'Huh!'

Silence fell between them once again and the old lady walked away into the surrounding night. Her figure was tall and scraggy. Like a long piece of biltong, with grey hair sprouting in a wire crown, she was outlined against a moonlit sky.

'You didn't tell me you had a sister.' She kept her back to Luke but spun round suspiciously as Julius tried to creep away.

'Good night,' he yawned, trying to convince her of his innocence in the matter. 'Good night.' Julius nodded at Luke quickly.

'You don't answer the pikkanin?' Though it was twenty-two years since Julius had arrived on the farm, Ouma Malan still called him a child and she kicked Luke's boot with her own. 'You don't like pikkanins? If you don't like blacks, boy, you're living in the wrong country! Who's looking for you?'

'Nobody's looking for me!' Luke yelled. He was suddenly angry and wished the old woman would get off his back.

'Who's the letter from?'

'My sister – I said.'

'Why'd she write if she's not looking for you? You don't go missing from a sister, huh?' The old lady's voice had risen in argument, each word given emphasis with a quick kick of her boot. 'What's wrong with your sister that she's not looking for you?'

'Nothing.'

'Then what's wrong with you?' Ouma Malan demanded an answer to the question that had plagued her since the letter arrived. 'You got people out there?' She pointed into the black night that clung around the small house as the moon hid behind a roll of twisting cloud. 'Are there people *there* looking for you *here*?' Ouma Malan hadn't said so many words to another human being in years and she felt suddenly tired of being one herself. 'I want nobody from *there*, *here*! You hear me? No *people*!' Her eyes fixed on Luke and she brushed her hand over the top of her wiry head as her lips twisted to one side. 'It's a woman, isn't it.' She'd seen for herself what an attractive man Luke was, and she persisted in her search for the truth.

'Do you want me to go?' Luke looked up as she towered over him, demanding an answer. Her sunburnt face was so deeply lined that it buried her eyes in leather folds and remained expressionless. She was defending exactly what Luke himself wanted, but he could never tell her. He needed the lost world of Drie Koppies as much as she did, but he knew the time had come to move on.

'You got a wife as well as a sister?' Ouma Malan kept mining for the truth with relentless digging. She could see a woman hiding behind Luke's eyes and pursued her aggressively. 'You running away from a woman? What woman? A wife? A fancy woman? What woman is it?'

'I'm not running away from anybody!' Luke stood up and turned away from her as he moved back to the house. 'You've got nothing to worry about. There's nobody.'

'And when "nobody" comes to my land looking for you?' Ouma Malan had caught hold of his shirt and swung him back to face her. 'What do I tell them, huh?'

'*Nobody* is looking for me!' Luke stared into her questioning grey eyes. 'And that's why I'm here, Ouma. *Nobody* is looking for *me*, the same way *nobody* is looking for *you*!'

Long before dawn the next morning, Ouma Malan woke up to find the baboon rattling the gauze on her bedroom window. Bared yellow teeth expressed his excitement and leather lips pulled back in a humourless smile.

'OK, OK.' Ouma Malan's bones creaked in harmony with the wire bedsprings as she got up. 'I'm coming,' she shouted back as her hairy friend banged his forehead against the window in a suicidal attempt to hurry her. The icy chill of night pricked her skin as her bare feet touched the stone floor and she dragged the bedcovers round her body as she moved out of the room.

'What is it?' she asked as the old baboon bounded round the house to meet her at the front door. 'What?' she repeated, as he scampered away into the dark with excited barks. Galloping away on flat rear feet and the backs of his hands, he screeched for her to follow.

'Wait, you old fool!' Screwing her eyes tight, Ouma Malan tried to drive a path through the darkness to see him, but only the heavy black sheet of night faced her. 'Get out of there!' she yelled with sudden fright. The baboon had exploded out of the blinding dark in front of her and he rushed past her into the house. 'Hey!' Her hand was raised for a whipping as she shakily pursued him, but she stopped. Bouncing on gangling hind legs outside the closed door of a room, the old baboon screeched with hysterical laughter. But there was no ring of joy in the sound as his deepset eyes challenged her.

Pushing the door open with her bare foot, Ouma Malan peered round the solid wood frame. Luke's room was empty. He'd gone and she felt only the heavy nudge of guilt. She knew she'd sent him back into the same world from which she'd run. It was a world she'd vowed never to be a part of, but she'd helped it recapture Luke.

Stepping into the open doorway of the sitting room, Naomi glared at the man who stood with his back to her. He was well built. The solid line of his shoulders spoke of years of hard work and she knew at once that he wasn't the kind of man who usually called on her. Pulling tighter the belt of her long silk gown, Naomi automatically pushed her hair back before she spoke.

'What do you want?' She used Afrikaans, as she always did with tradesmen. Her eyes settled on the man's dust-covered boots and she noticed the dirt on his jeans; it matched his long unkempt hair. But Naomi's real anger was with her black maid. Avril had banged on her bedroom door a little earlier. She'd quite obviously known what her mistress was doing in bed at that time of day; she'd known that Naomi wasn't alone. Avril's understanding of what was going on in the house she cleaned irritated Naomi beyond measure, but neither had said a word about it.

'Did the girl show you into the house?' Naomi's annoyance was clear in her voice but as the man turned to her she fell silent. Bright blue eyes looked directly into hers in a way she'd long since forgotten.

'Luke!'

'You wrote to me.' As Luke spoke Naomi pushed her hair back in amazement and embarrassment.

'I don't believe it!' She was aware of the added years that must show on her face as they did on her brother's. 'I never thought I'd see you again, Luke. Can you wait a moment? Just give me time to dress.' She tried to hide her sudden shame in his presence. 'I had a headache, I'm afraid, and I was lying down. Wait here and I'll call the girl to get you some tea. Or do you want coffee? Can you wait a moment?'

'You said there was something we had to talk about, Naomi.' Her brother's voice was deeper than she remembered. Its tone had warmed with maturity and the unquestionable charisma of mystery charged the atmosphere between them. Nowhere could Naomi see the lost and insecure young man who'd last been in the house with his wife and child. Facing her now was a mature man and his look searched her soul.

'Yes, we must talk.' Naomi had heard the footsteps of someone on the stairs outside and she quickly closed the door. 'It's about Bonne Espérance.' She licked her lips, pushing her finger into the corners of her mouth as she tried to cover the traces of where she'd been. She was certain the passionate lovemaking of ten minutes earlier was obvious to Luke and she tried to hide her guilt with a bright smile.

'Did you know Constance Marsden is dead? Rebecca's mother?' Naomi noticed a flicker of reaction in Luke's eyes. She pulled the soft silk of her gown tighter across her bare breasts; the footsteps had stopped outside the door and she was on edge.

'I'm off.' A young man poked his head round the door, waving an airborne kiss in Naomi's direction. 'See you on Thursday – OK?'

'A friend of the family.' Naomi felt her face burn and looked down as the door closed behind the source of her embarrassment, but Luke hadn't looked at all. He'd moved away to the window. His shoulders were broad, his neck thick with muscle and his back expressed a renewed strength that disturbed her. 'He often drops in to see Dick. Just to say hullo.' Naomi had taken Luke's reaction as a form of accusation and once again she tightened her gown, her body tingling with remembered guilt. 'Good grief, Luke, I don't have to lie to you, surely. It's enough the way that maid of mine looks at me. Breeds like a bloody rabbit herself, then accuses me! I tell you, those blacks are getting damn cheeky nowadays. Anyway, Dick knows about it. We both know what's going on and we're both adults, for heaven's sake. Dick has his bits on the side, so ...' Defending herself with a long trail of empty excuses, Naomi was unaware that Luke wasn't listening. 'After all, I'm hardly old enough to disappear into the woodwork, so why should it be different for me? Dick certainly enjoys his life – why shouldn't I?'

Naomi's words trailed to a halt as Luke turned to face her. He was watching her silently and his face expressed no condemnation at all. Just one unspoken question sat on his lips.

'Yes, Luke. She's back.' Naomi caught the tiniest spark of light in the blue of his eyes and she smiled, her guilt dismissed. 'Rebecca's at Bonne Espérance.'

'What did you want when you wrote to me, Naomi?' Luke pushed her chatter aside. 'Your letter said it was important.' Touched by the memory of his son as he'd thought of Rebecca, Luke shut her out of his mind quickly.

'It is important. It's about our inheritance.' Naomi moved a little closer and smiled. 'Bonne Espérance does belong to us, after all. We didn't sign away our rights when Rebecca's family moved in, Ma's assured me of that. Constance might have shared it with Dad, but now she's dead, so – I think it would be sensible if we contacted Dad in London to see what he wants us to do. It's obvious he's never coming back, so the least he can do is to give us our rights as his children.'

'Paul's not my father, Naomi.' There was no bitterness in Luke's voice. Nothing about him suggested the confusion Naomi had witnessed when Estelle had faced him with the truth of his identity.

'Wait, Luke!' Naomi moved after him but she didn't touch him. His masculinity had reached out to her and she wanted to, but she'd sensed he was unobtainable either as a brother or a man. 'Are you staying in Johannesburg now? You must leave us your address.' Naomi tried to break free of his charisma. 'You've no idea how hard it was to find you. I had to employ detectives – would you believe that?' She watched Luke carefully. His eyes had never moved from hers and the strange power behind them confused her. 'Mother will be thrilled you're back. Oh, of course, you don't know she lives with us now, do you? Dick doesn't much like it, I'm afraid. They never did get on.'

As Naomi chattered to avoid the constant pull of his presence, Luke allowed his thoughts to find Rebecca. He could see her dark eyes watching him, drawing him into her as they always had. He could feel the urgent pull that had held him since the moment they'd met as man and woman, and he longed to step back into the circle of her being. To feel her body next to his. To hold her tightly as their skin touched, sparking feelings he'd never experienced before or since.

'There are parts of my life that are over for ever, Naomi.' The truth of Luke's words shone crystal clear in his eyes and Naomi knew he'd included her in his statement. But still she wouldn't give up. Though her brother's quiet strength was something she'd never seen in another man and she was aware its source was far outside her world, all that concerned her was Bonne Espérance.

'We have to make certain we don't lose what's ours, Luke! Why else do you think I hunted you down? Good heavens, the estate's worth a fortune and we can't ignore our rights.'

'*Your* rights, Naomi,' Luke smiled. 'But if you want to see me you'll be able to get hold of me. I'm not hiding from you or anyone else.' Luke was no longer running away and Ouma Malan's last words were firmly in his mind.

If you don't like blacks you're living in the wrong country.

He knew now that he was in the right country. Luke was in the world Ouma Malan dreaded, but he'd re-entered on his own terms. The house he shared in Johannesburg was a 'safe house' within the white perimeters of the city. Annie and Tertius Marais took in people of any race who needed help and Luke had been one of them. Carefully the white Afrikaans minister and his wife had pieced him together. They'd taken away the shame he felt, shining a wider truth into his life: that the real shame was to stand back.

Waging daily battles against both the white Government and radical black youth, the Afrikaans couple had placed themselves and Luke in the front line of a private war. They'd held white police back while black children clung to them, helicopters whirring their threat overhead. They'd saved the life of a young black man who'd been attacked by 'comrades', only to find him murdered by 'vigilantes', but they'd never given up their search for justice.

Total darkness had enveloped a divided nation and Luke had come face to face with a tragedy far greater than his own. His country was dying; its suicide no less deliberate than Althea's. Luke's eyes had turned away from himself and he'd realised he was no longer part of his family either.

'You've come back for that woman, have you?' Luke turned with the familiar edge of his mother's Afrikaans words. In her late sixties, Estelle was the same cold woman he remembered and she stood rigid between the pillars that led into the dining room, her eyes passing slowly over her son.

'Hullo, Ma.' Luke studied the taut figure framed in the white archway. Though his mother looked much older, nothing else about her had changed. Bitterness bound her spirit and the resentment of a lifetime dug deep lines in her face. But Estelle no longer touched him. He felt nothing but pity for this woman who'd once dominated his life, and he went towards her with a smile. 'How are you?' He watched as Estelle side-stepped him, going on into the room without a word. Her silence spoke the language of rejection that he'd felt so often as a child, a feeling that had thrown him off-balance more times than he could remember, but he smiled again. 'Good to see you, Ma.'

'Is it?' Estelle turned back as she reached a chair, one hand gripping its wooden arm tightly. She'd sensed immediately that her son had stepped out from under her control and Luke's unruffled presence disturbed her. 'Are you trying to help us get back what's ours, or are you running back to that woman now your responsibilities as a father are buried with your son?' Estelle's words rode high on a note of accusation but still Luke didn't flinch.

'Ma, he's come back.' Naomi knew their mother had lost her power over Luke and she used her own tactics to recapture him instead. 'He's promised to let us know where he is. We'll have him back in the family. Isn't that wonderful?'

'Don't bother.' Estelle's eyes slid off Luke, settling on Naomi like sucking snails. 'Aren't you going to dress before your husband comes home, girl?' Though she'd dismissed her son completely, his presence still filled the room and Estelle knew he'd won.

CHAPTER TWENTY

Rebecca sat on the verandah of the Lanzerac Hotel in Stellenbosch. One of the first Cape vineyards, the hotel grew out of ages-old surroundings, its Cape Dutch architecture rising brilliant white against a blue sky. Set around a courtyard, the buildings nestled at the feet of rugged mountains that reached up in granite folds behind them. The mountains held light in silver streams which fed the heavy green foliage of the vines and lit the secret gardens that hid behind high white walls and heavy arches. Popping orange pumpkins, runner beans and broccoli tangled round one another in a scramble for the sun, and dripping blue wisteria hung clusters of tiny grapes overhead.

High in the opposite wall, Rebecca noticed a pure white dove. Its nest was built into the round base of a port-hole window, and its feathers fluffed a perfect curve over its eggs. Watching her with velvet eyes, the dove looked out from among the paper-thin petals of orange bougainvillea and Rebecca's nerves melted.

She'd gone to the Lanzerac Hotel because she'd received a letter from an American woman named Amy Jackson. During her time in London, Rebecca had traced Johannes Villiers through British Army records. She'd discovered that he'd gone on to live in America after World War One and her search had reached across the Atlantic from the shores of England. There she'd unearthed his existence with a death certificate; then, at last, she'd discovered the legal marriage of Johannes Villiers to Emma Jones.

Advertising in the US press as she looked for his descendants, Rebecca had been answered by his great-granddaughter, Amy Jackson. She'd written to Rebecca in London and they'd begun a long correspondence as family history drew them together.

However, *Glad Rags* had quickly taken up Rebecca's time and she'd lost sight of what had first caused her to look for Johannes Villiers among the dead. Only as she'd faced Andre Bothma on the day of her mother's funeral had her attention been drawn back to the extended Beauvilliers family – the hidden descendants of Jean Jacques whom she'd first discovered in Emily's old diaries.

Rebecca knew nothing about Amy Jackson. Their correspondence had revealed her to be a vivacious and educated woman, but nothing else. A person of substantial finance, Amy Jackson ran a real estate business in Mississippi and she'd written the previous month to tell Rebecca of her proposed visit to South Africa.

You can blame that book, Roots. *It never entered my mind to go trace my own in darkest Africa before.*

A Southern drawl was audible in Amy Jackson's letters and Rebecca had longed to meet the woman who'd emerged from Johannes Villiers' past.

'You wouldn't by chance be here to meet Amy Jackson?' Rebecca looked round on hearing an American voice behind her, and met with the curious gaze of an elegant negress. The darkest of ebony browns, Amy Jackson's eyes shone with humour. 'My.' Her face was a picture of astonishment. 'Nobody told me my great-grandpappy was so pale!'

'Nobody told me you were the wrong colour, either,' Rebecca laughed and for a brief moment racial conflict was wiped out as two members of the Beauvilliers family embraced. But their meeting, captured in the peace of a dove's eyes, was set against a backdrop of unprecedented violence in South Africa.

What had begun as a protest about Afrikaans being the language used in black schools, had quickly developed into a state of emergency. A schoolboy called Hector Peterson had been shot as police fired on chanting schoolchildren in the streets; driven to a clinic by the journalist, Sophie Tema, the child had been found to be dead on arrival. Subsequently, offices, cars and people had been torched and beer damped down the dusty streets as bottles were smashed by chanting youngsters.

'Less liquor, better education!' they'd cried, and in response all black schools were closed down. Police reinforcements were rushed in, but the spiral of violent rebellion had still not been contained.

Then the President of the South African Students' Organisation, Steve Biko, had died on the stone floor of a police cell in Pretoria, having been held in detention for twenty-six days without trial, stripped naked, manacled and beaten. His death had shaken the country.

The South African lawyer Sydney Kentridge had taken on the Security Forces in legal proceedings, clashing with Colonel Piet Goosen, Head of the Port Elizabeth Security Branch. Sydney Kentridge had asked under whose authority Biko had been kept in chains for forty-eight hours.

391

'I have the full power to do it,' Goosen had answered smugly.

'I'm asking you to give the statute,' Kentridge demanded, and two white South Africans had faced one another across the divide of apartheid.

'We don't work under statute,' Goosen replied eventually, and Sydney Kentridge smiled.

'Thank you very much. That's what we've always suspected.'

Steve Biko's death, like the Soweto riots, led the country further down the path of social and economic disaster. The problem had been met only with a further tightening of security by the Government of John Vorster, and Europeans had fled in droves for Australia, Europe and North America. Cries for the release of the political prisoner Nelson Mandela had grown louder both inside and outside the country, but one black and one white woman had met on the verandah of the Lanzerac Hotel in Stellenbosch and a divided family was reunited.

'Who do you say this Andre Bothma is again?' Amy looked up from reading the lawyer's letter. 'What kind of cousin is he?'

'You see that name there?' Rebecca placed her copy of the family tree on the table between them. 'Suzanne Beauvilliers. She was the daughter of Jacques and Emily Beauvilliers, the sister of Clara, Prudence and Emily – the one who kept the diaries I told you about – and, of course, half-sister of Jean Jacques Beauvilliers. He was Johannes Villiers' grandfather. So Suzanne is Andre Bothma's great-great-grandmother! You see?'

'Lordy!' Amy's wide black face spread in a glorious smile. 'You telling me this here entire family was white?'

'Except for Jean Jacques.'

'My!' Amy chuckled. It was a deep chuckle, filled with the warmth of a woman who'd long since come to terms with her own identity. 'With all them honky ancestors, my great-grandpappy ended up marryin' a buck nigger!' Amy reached across to Rebecca and touched her hand. 'Do you need this kind of trouble, honey?'

'I need a country,' Rebecca smiled.

The lawyer's office in Cape Town was on the third floor of a large building in Church Square. Its windows overlooked the spot where Johannes Villiers had once polished the boots of the British soldier, Colonel Stringer, and Amy gazed down on it without knowing how close to her 'roots' she was. Her mind was elsewhere, on the whispered voice of a young white secretary who spoke to Rebecca at reception. The girl was nervous, unsure how to handle the situation as she queried Amy's presence in the lawyer's offices.

'I think perhaps you'd better tell Mr Bothma and your boss Mr Cheyney that either he sees Miss Jackson and myself together or not at all.' Rebecca spoke quietly and Amy realised with a smile that the problem was the colour of her skin. Her legitimacy in the all-white offices of a legal firm in South Africa was obviously questionable, but she didn't react. It wasn't that long since black children had been bussed to white schools in America and she'd been one of them. Amy could still remember her fear of the angry white faces which had surrounded the buses in protest. Her child's heart had wondered why so many strangers hated her, and she hadn't found the answer yet.

Amy's childhood had been spent in the humble Mississippi home of her parents, a home in which nights were spent in the dark for fear of Ku Klux Klan bullets ripping through lit windows. But Amy's people had been held by a vision, – the vision of Martin Luther King. He'd fought for the dignity of his race as he looked beyond bitterness to hope, and Amy wondered if such a man would ever emerge in South Africa.

'You coming?' Rebecca was beside her.

'Do I leave my gun outside?' Amy whispered, linking her arm through Rebecca's.

Andre Bothma stood on the other side of the door as they entered the offices of Cheyney and Morrison's firm of attorneys, and his eyes averted the moment he saw them. He couldn't understand how Rebecca could share the company of a black and had no idea why Amy was there at all, although he had little intention of treating her as if she was. The black woman was in his white world and it was that world he intended to snatch from Rebecca.

'I must admit to finding all this rather strange.' The attorney, Mr Cheyney, looked up at Rebecca. 'Your family is and always has been considered European, Miss Conrad. According to the law as well.'

'What law's that?' Rebecca asked and Andre reacted as Amy smiled at him, leaning back in her chair. He knew blacks were no different one from the other and wondered why Amy seemed so at ease. The Africans he ruled with a *sjambok* and gun in Langa township would never be so cheeky in the presence of whites. Despite her American accent, Andre Bothma knew Amy Jackson was no different from the rest.

'I'm talking about race classification, Miss Conrad,' Mr Cheyney explained with a smile he hoped was pleasant. 'According to the Population Registration Act, you . . .'

'You mean I can prove myself to be white if I choose? How does it go again?' Rebecca had memorised the legal requirements for a person to be classified white and she reeled them off. '"One who is generally accepted as a white person and is not in appearance obviously not a white person and not generally accepted as a coloured person".' Rebecca grinned. 'Or

393

the other way round, just to make sure we all understand! "A person who is obviously white in appearance and not generally accepted as a coloured person. Whose habits, education and speech and demeanour and deportment shall be taken into account." It's quite a mouthful, but yes, I guess I'd pass. You were saying?'

'Exactly.' Mr Cheyney was pleased Rebecca had seen sense and he turned to Andre. 'As I told you before, Mr Bothma, I doubt very much that Miss Conrad could be evicted from Bonne Espérance on racial grounds. She and her family have been accepted as European over many years, as will undoubtedly be proved.'

'But I have no intention of proving any such thing, Mr Cheyney.' Rebecca was wide-eyed in apparent surprise as he turned to her. 'I'm not ashamed of who I am – are you?' Her eyes turned to Andre and silence fell as they looked at one another. 'There's some problem with that?'

'Unfortunately, since there's been a query by Mr Bothma, your race must be classified to verify this matter, Miss Conrad – just to stay within the letter of the law.' Mr Cheyney's arms were elbow-deep in the dirty washing Andre had dumped in his office and he turned to him hopefully. 'But I'm certain Mr Bothma would be willing to accept part-ownership of the estate in question without any further legal procedures.'

'Good! Now. What about my claim on this here Bonne Espérance?' Amy smiled brightly and the lawyer turned to her, blank-faced. 'I guess my race don't need no classification!'

'Sorry?' Mr Cheyney was totally lost.

'I'm talking about my rights of inheritance, honey. Seems to me you're goin' to split everything down the middle and I'm here to ask 'bout my share. *As a Beauvilliers.*'

Rebecca allowed a stunned silence to descend on the room. Slowly, she pushed the legal document in front of her back across the desk to Mr Cheyney.

'You've made an omission on this document, I'm afraid. The Beauvilliers family is incomplete.' Rebecca pulled the letter that confirmed Johannes Villiers' identity as a Beauvilliers out of her bag and she laid it between them alongside her own family tree. 'The omission is the continuing and existing line of Jean Jacques Beauvilliers. I'm sorry to have to tell you that every one of his descendants has the same claim to Bonne Espérance as your client, Andre Bothma.'

'Indeed we do.' Amy glanced at Andre with a wide smile. 'You were quite right layin' that claim on behalf of us all, Andre. It was real nice of you, honey. Thanks.'

'I don't have to stand for this.' Andre switched to Afrikaans as he turned to leave the room.

'Why are you running away, Andre?' Rebecca followed him.

'Don't count on me running anywhere, Rebecca.'

'Oh boy!' Amy looked at Andre wide-eyed and in that instant he saw the face of every black person he had ever met. 'Nothin' like good family feudin' to get things goin'.'

'Don't shit your kind of crap in my country and think you can get away with it.' Andre spoke in Afrikaans once again and Amy's eyebrows lifted as she turned to Mr Cheyney.

'Could I have a translation?'

'You want to live like a white, get back to your own country and do it there, lady! We don't fall for that crap in South Africa.' Andre had switched to English as he stared at her. Her presence angered him beyond belief and his person smouldered at the edges.

Rebecca appeared calm but she wanted to scream, to beg Andre to push off the choking hold apartheid had on his mind, to look clearly at the world they all shared. 'Are you really going to take this all the way to court, Andre?'

'Damn right I am!'

'But what about the shame?' Rebecca prepared to play the card she'd held close to her chest till that moment. 'If you want to fight we'll give you a fight, I promise. Every last one of us. But where will that leave you?'

'You still OK, honey?' Amy had turned to the lawyer with a smile. 'If you ask me, this could be a real expensive case. The Beauvilliers family fighting for its inheritance between two continents. Lordy! It'll be a mighty pile of dollars that pays you.'

'Do you still want to go on, Andre?' Rebecca tried to find a way through the bigotry that blinded him. 'If you do, it won't just be Amy you'll have to accept as family, it'll be all of us.'

'Like hell!'

'Yes – like hell.' Rebecca watched him carefully. 'You've missed the point of the can of beans you've opened, Andre. To have a claim on Bonne Espérance means proving you are a direct member of the Beauvilliers family – and that includes Amy Jackson, Lorraine Hendrickse and dozens of others – people who aren't recorded on that pure white family tree of yours! Johannes Villiers didn't disappear because he was brown. He's still right here among us, and I can prove it beyond any doubt.'

'Imagine the publicity this'll get in the States.' Amy kept her concentration on the lawyer. '"Nigger claims rights to white farm in South Africa. Black challenges Afrikaner kith and kin." Oh boy, it'll be worth every cent!'

Mr Cheyney knew what the truth of Rebecca's revelation meant to

Andre and he observed him in silence. The presence of blacks in Andre's family was something against which his entire being raged in ungovernable fury, and Rebecca kept prodding it.

'Your problem is your friends in the police force and everywhere else. Unfortunately they're just like you, Andre.' She wanted to shake him, to rattle him free of the chains on his life. 'Would your own kind believe the coloured blood skipped you completely? No smoke without fire – no tarbrush without splash?' Rebecca reached out to touch his arm but he jerked back.

'When you first came to Bonne Espérance it was the *land* you wanted, Andre. What's happened since? Your heart was in the earth then, like our common ancestor's, Jacques Beauvilliers. The land's still there, but where are you?'

'You think I believe you'd go that far?' Andre pushed at the liberal guise he was certain Rebecca hid behind. She too had an image to protect and it was her image he envied as much as anything else. Success in London had lifted her above apartheid and its spillovers. 'Smart cars and wine estates don't hide who you are, Rebecca.' He turned his eyes on Amy but she knew he didn't see her at all. 'Don't count on your American lawyers getting anywhere in this country, lady. You'd never win that game here.'

'But I don't want to win, honey. I can't stand grapes.' Amy's eyes were still wide with innocence, but she suddenly felt tired and defeated. The hatred that touched her came straight from Andre Bothma's heart, and it had taken its toll.

'You got laws in your country to prove you're racist, and we got 'em in ours to prove we ain't.' She pushed her hands into her gloves. 'Don't it all just go to show how far we've gone and strolled from the Garden of Eden?' Amy looked up at Andre again. 'I reckon we just lost our way, honey. Problem is, to find it, we're gonna need each other.'

Amy's presence in South Africa had shone a light into the darkness that threatened to swallow the land, and she had speedily become a part of Bonne Espérance. She'd wandered through the vineyards with Rebecca, listened in amazement to her explanation of wine-making, and as she studied the grapes she so despised, the giant dog had held her wrist in his mouth.

'He planning on a meal?' Amy glanced at Rebecca nervously. 'You told him I ain't no wild boar, did you?'

In the company of David, Simon and Lydia's small daughter Tarcie, Amy had gazed up at the surrounding circle of mountains in wonder while they in turn had listened as she'd talked of her world.

'I guess Disneyland's the most real place in America, kids,' she'd laughed.

Together they'd leafed through Emily's old diaries and there Amy had seen her very beginnings recorded in 1820 with the birth of Jean Jacques Beauvilliers. She'd stared at the faded writing in wonder. Their shared ancestor had taken his place in a world dominated by fear, and little had changed in either of their countries.

But Amy had been filled with curious delight as she peered into the past. Both sides of her family originated in Africa and at last she'd discovered them. The slave trade had removed her ancestors to America, but Andre Bothma existed there too. Her people's negro spirituals told of their longings. Their songs were the same as she'd heard among the African voices in Thabo's church: a cry for recognition as a human being. A longing to be free of a look that sat behind the eyes of Europeans – a blind gaze that said they didn't exist.

'I'll tell you one thing, honey.' Amy turned to Rebecca as they sat with Simon and Tarcie on the white sands of Camps Bay. A mountain range built a high wall behind them; reaching down from the sky it plunged steeply into the ocean. Formed by the ages into the shape of a dozen faces, the twelve apostles gazed silently over the depths of the Atlantic Ocean while the sea rose and fell in sweeping waves. It washed endless white sand, pushing Africa deep into Amy's soul.

'It's not only a beautiful place, this tip of Africa. You've got the smartest, fastest blacks on earth,' Amy chuckled and Rebecca watched her curiously. 'They outsmarted and outran them there slave-traders when *my* lot got caught!'

Amy's laughter echoed against the mountain wall behind them, skipping across the sand as Simon watched her. When she talked of her own people it seemed to him that she knew them, but Simon no longer knew his. Since Constance's death he'd wanted nothing more than to find his own mother, and then himself.

'You take me to Jo'burg now, Thabo?' Simon demanded, scrutinising him across the kitchen table. Amy had returned to America that day and Tarcie sat close beside Simon, but he ignored her as he had done since the day she'd arrived for a holiday.

'Where you going?' Tarcie asked, one end of her blonde pigtail disappearing into her mouth as she chewed it. 'You taking him somewhere?' She turned to the black priest as she spat hair from her mouth. Thabo often called at Bonne Espérance as he delivered children to be moved on to the safety of the Transkei. Since Portia's death the family of displaced children had grown fast and a charity named 'Portia's Khaya' had turned the small girl's death into victory. A 'village house' for children had grown to God's glory and He had honoured it with ample provision.

'You going to take Simon to Portia's Khaya too?' Tarcie asked.

'Shh.' Simon silenced her as he held his attention on Thabo. 'You taking me to my mother now?'

'What's going to happen, Thabo?' Miriam spoke to her son in Xhosa, excluding Simon. She was worried. Violence in the black townships around Cape Town had erupted once again as the people formed themselves into opposing groups of 'comrades' and 'fathers'. Everybody knew Cop Bothma had stirred the anger and mistrust; rumour said that he blacked himself up, adding fuel to the flames of their tribal differences.

Andre's claim to be immortal had been proved time and again and he'd become a faceless myth as township blacks spoke of him in awe. Finding a hero's route, Andre Bothma had driven an accurate wedge along the line of people's differences. He'd fanned the flames of hatred while Thabo scooped up the remains of broken families, but Miriam wasn't sure how long it could go on.

'What we're doing is right. It's all we can do.' Thabo touched his mother's hand as they continued their conversation in Xhosa. 'Did you hear about the water? Do you see how the Lord is spreading His love through Portia's Khaya?'

Miriam nodded and her face cracked in a wide smile. Her mother, Sophie, had written of the day not long ago when Zola had returned to the home in Transkei that was Portia's Khaya.

It had been a day clouded by heavy mountain mist, through which Zola had peered ahead at the strangest assortment of men he'd ever seen. A group of Africans, with one white among their ranks, had congregated on horseback in front of the large mud hut in which the children lived. The village of Herschell was close to the border of Lesotho, and Zola was accustomed to Sotho ponies carrying blanketed riders, but there'd been something different about these men.

'What do you want?' he'd called to them nervously, slipping naturally into the Sotho language.

'We want to know who's responsible for this place.' The white man spoke fluent Xhosa as he looked down at Zola from his horse. 'Who's in charge here, do you know?'

Zola was aware of children peeping at him through the dark doorway of Portia's Khaya and he answered quickly: 'I am.' But his heart had beaten faster as the stranger watched him and he'd added quickly, 'Also my sister Miriam in Cape Town. My mother. My mother's grandson, the Langa priest, Thabo. A white priest, Father Jamieson. White churches in Cape Town. White people in the English churches . . .' Zola had hoped the number and variety of those involved might shift the responsibility from his shoulders. And then he'd added the name above all names; the only name of real authority. 'This place is the responsibility of God,' he stated firmly, and the children climbed on to one another's backs as they strained to hear better what was going on.

'And where do they get their water?' The white man had removed his hat and peered inside it, as if looking for something before putting it back on his head.

'From Tele River, where everyone in the village gets their water,' Zola replied.

'But a child was drowned in that river, isn't that true?' Zola nodded, unsure what the man was getting at. 'It's not safe for the children to go to the river for water.'

'But it's what we have to do.' Zola noticed that none of the other horsemen had said a word and their steady gaze hadn't faltered. 'The village has been here since long before I was born and always we've had to go to the river for water. What village round here has water? You tell me!'

'That is why we're here.'

The white man turned to look at the children and they shrank quickly back into the darkness of the hut. Zola gazed down. He was certain that bureaucracy had caught up with Portia's Khaya and he was unsure of what to say next. There was no way he could stop the children being carted back to the battlefields of Cape Town by officialdom and his heart had sunk deep into the soft sand at his feet.

'What you want?' Sophie's ringing voice broke through Zola's thoughts and he looked round as her bare feet stomped in angry strides towards him and the men. 'What are you doing here on your horses? You tramping our mealies! You scaring our children!' She glared up at a black and he stared back in terrified silence.

'We've come about water,' the white man addressed her in Xhosa.

'What?' she yelled, glaring up at him, her eyes meeting those of his horse, which pulled back in terror.

'Water,' he repeated politely.

'What water?'

'We're here about water,' the white man informed her for the third time, but Sophie continued her attempt to unnerve him. She cupped an ear in her hand.

'You speak Xhosa too quiet, boy! In Xhosa you must talk loud or the ancestors they think you talk about them.'

'We're here to pipe water into the village, old woman!' the white man bawled. He had explained their visit at last and Sophie fell totally silent.

'We're bringing you water — in pipes. You hear me now?' He looked round at the gathering crowd as he felt the edge of Sophie's suspicion crumble. 'We're going to put a tap right there.' He threw his stick like a spear, and it dug into the ground in front of the children's mud hut. 'You going to yell "what!" again, old lady?'

But Sophie was stamping the ground, raising a dust-cloud of excitement at her feet as her bent body moved in a swinging dance of delight.

'We got a great God!' She raised her hands high in the air as her bare feet banged the ground. 'We got a God who hears our prayer for water! We got a God who cares that these children are safe!' Sophie's eyes were screwed up tight and fine shafts of light fell on the faces of the surrounding villagers. 'Tell me now that the river spirits took our child away. There is only one God and He has given us a tap!'

Sophie knew that her grandson Thabo had stepped out in faith each time he'd sent more and more needy children to the village after Portia's death. At last she'd seen his faith realised. God had sent streams of living water into a wasteland and Portia's death had given birth to life.

'We will kill a sheep tonight, Zola.' She linked her arm through her son's, turning back to the strangers. Pinning her eyes on the white man in their midst, she smiled. 'You are invited to our celebration, my friend.' Her pink tongue pushed into the corner of her mouth with delight. 'You too are welcome to Portia's Khaya.'

'You said you'd take me to see my mother in Johannesburg.' Simon's determined voice broke through the warmth of Miriam's recollections.

'Who's your mother?' Tarcie tilted her head to one side and a skinny pigtail tickled her bare knee as she leaned forward. Though Simon had consistently ignored her, Tarcie was besotted by him. He'd tried hard to be a man, determined never to play with her, but she'd found a friend and was determined to help. 'You taking him to see his Ma, Thabo?' She made sure Simon knew she was on his side. 'If you said, then you must,' she insisted. 'You promised.'

'Yes,' Thabo nodded with a smile.

'When?' Tarcie persisted and Simon watched in amazement. She was doing his work for him and he was most impressed. 'When will Thabo take Simon, Miriam? When will he take Simon to his mother?' Tarcie reinforced her persistence by bringing Miriam into the matter.

'No, no, no! Not to do with me.' Miriam sidestepped the issue, clapping her hands. 'Out of my kitchen, all of you.' But nobody moved.

'If Thabo said he was taking Simon to see his mother, he must.' Tarcie turned her attention back to him and her eyes centred on his collar. 'It's a lie if you don't and then that thing will choke you!' Simon's mouth fell open in total amazement.

'OK,' Thabo grinned.

'What?' Simon turned his open-mouthed stare on to Thabo.

'How you take him to Jo'burg? You can't go on the bus,' Miriam argued. 'How you go? On two buses, one white, one black? He white, you black. You blind? You can't go. No!'

Locking himself in his room in protest and refusing to eat, Simon couldn't understand why no one would allow him to go. He blamed them all. To him the impossibility of travelling with Thabo on public transport was just an excuse, and his inability to express his longings began to affect his health. No amount of reasoning through the closed bedroom door could explain why Estelle was to remain an unrealised dream. He couldn't understand why 'the beautiful and loving mother' Rebecca had built up to protect him should be denied, and slowly Simon lost the will to live.

'Don't you see? It doesn't matter what his mother's like,' Tarcie pleaded with the rest of the family in an effort to help Simon. 'Everyone says my dad's a drunk but I still love him.' Tears filled the small girl's eyes as she blurted out her secret. 'Everyone's got a mother except him.' Weeping openly, Tarcie tried to explain what Simon could not. 'Even if she hates him, he loves her and if you stop him going he'll think it's his fault, that he can't have a mother 'cos he's a mongol. He'll die 'cos no matter how hard he tries, everyone still thinks he's no good.'

As Tarcie's words touched on a truth that outweighed all fear, Rebecca, Miriam and Thabo pointed out to David that in one of Naomi's letters she had said that Estelle *wanted* to see Simon. Unaware of Naomi's motives, the family finally agreed. Even the problem of transport was solved and ten days later Simon gazed proudly at Rebecca's gleaming Mercedes Benz. He'd often wondered how many spare parts he'd have had to file in his head if Rebecca had ever allowed him to take the Mercedes apart, but now he was in it. He was going a long way and he'd be alone with Thabo when he met his mother. It was more than Simon had ever dared hope for – even in his dreams.

'Don't forget your *padkos*.' Miriam pushed a picnic basket into the back of the car. 'And drive slow, Thabo.' She'd seen the car streak up the drive many times with Rebecca at the wheel and she hid her fears behind that. 'Thirty miles an hour is all.'

'We can go faster than that,' Simon whispered to Thabo.

'Why's it got a dent in the roof?' Tarcie stood on tiptoe before ducking down to the window and Simon. 'You got a dent here.' She ran her hand along the dipping car roof.

'It's a Mercedes SL coupé,' Simon informed her with disdain as he leaned back in the passenger seat. Though he remembered asking Rebecca exactly the same question, his attitude denied it as he stretched his legs, folding his arms proudly.

'Don't forget to keep that letter I wrote giving you permission to use the car, Thabo. Leave it in the glove compartment just in case.' Rebecca had tried to ensure that Thabo wouldn't get into trouble if he was stopped. She knew no white policeman would accept a black man driving such an expensive car. 'Take care, won't you.' She tried to ignore the very real danger of what might happen, pretending it wasn't Luke's mother they were going to see.

'If I see Luke?' Thabo glanced at Rebecca, stepping into her thoughts. Though she'd never spoken to him about Luke since her return from England, he knew her heart was still his.

'You won't see him, Thabo.' Rebecca touched his hand as it rested on the window. 'And I'm not looking for him anyway.' She attempted to believe her own words and Thabo's smile chased away her fears. 'Now you be good, Simon.' Rebecca watched him as he sat smugly in the passenger seat. Tarcie was gazing at him through the other window and Rebecca winked at her. She knew the small girl felt suddenly abandoned. 'It'll be good to get rid of them for a while, eh, Tarcie?' Rebecca banged on the car roof and Thabo pulled away.

In the rear-view mirror Simon could see Tarcie's hand lift in a wave and he felt suddenly sad. It had taken till that moment to realise how much he liked her.

'I'll miss you!' he yelled as the car drove away.

'You too!' Tarcie called back, her wave growing in excitement with Simon's words of care. 'Come and see me when you come back, Simon! Come and see me in Luderitz!'

Miriam stood silently in front of the house. Though she'd said nothing, Rebecca knew Thabo's mother was worried.

'What is it?' she asked, and Miriam's soft black shoulders lifted in a shrug.

'I worried when Thabo he go to Cape Town. Now Jo'burg!' Miriam's lips pulled under her teeth and she shook her head slowly. Though her voice had given the entire city an aura of terror, Miriam was thinking only of Estelle Marsden, Simon's mother.

'Nine!' Simon grinned at Thabo as the car raced down the road that drove a straight line through the flatland of the Karoo. 'Your turn!' He called for Thabo to carry on with the game they played with passing number plates. Each oncoming car was checked for its number and they took turns in collecting them, one to ten. It was a game Simon loved. It had passed long hours on their journey to the small mining town many years before and now he could play it with Thabo.

'Five,' Thabo shouted as the approaching car offered the number he needed, but his mind wasn't really on the game. It was on the many problems he could face as a black man driving an expensive car, and he glanced at Simon seriously. 'Who am I?'

'Thabo.' Simon wondered why he'd asked such a stupid question and shouted as a car flew past, 'Ten – I won!'

'Who am I?' Thabo persisted and Simon leaned back in his seat, his chin tucked into his chest. He could feel bristles on his chin and hoped that Thabo would help him shave as Miriam did. Or perhaps, he thought, he could even grow a beard. That way his tongue could hide when it occasionally slipped out without his knowing.

'I'm your driver,' Thabo informed him firmly.

'No, you're not. You're a priest.'

'Who's driving this car?' Thabo knew the only way he would be accepted by policemen or anyone else was as Simon's chauffeur and he repeated firmly, 'I am your driver. Understand?'

'You my driver. Your turn.' Simon was interested only in the game and had no idea why Thabo was so concerned.

'When I leave you with your mother, I'm going on to Soweto to see my cousin. Then I'll come back to get you in two days. OK?' Thabo had rehearsed the plan many times, always ensuring he wouldn't have to spend any time with Simon's mother and sister.

'You're not playing,' Simon complained as another car flew past. 'Don't you want to play?' His face changed and he prodded Thabo's arm accusingly. 'Why you got that jersey on? No one will see you're a priest with it on.'

'It's cold.'

'It's not cold.'

Simon didn't know that Thabo had seen his priest's collar arouse as much anger in white Christians as it did in Andre Bothma himself. The Anglican Dean of Johannesburg, Desmond Tutu, had challenged the proposed reforms of the Prime Minister, P. W. Botha, and black priests had become the focus of derision.

'I don't need to show the collar.' Thabo knew it was not his priest's collar that would protect him but his faith. 'Who am I?' he asked once again as he ran his finger round the polo neck of his sweater to check his collar was hidden.

'My driver.'

'Good.' Thabo peered at an approaching car, screwing his eyes tight to read the numbers. 'My turn.'

CHAPTER TWENTY-ONE

The Mercedes pulled into the kerb of a wide avenue in the Johannesburg suburb of Houghton and Thabo looked out. Behind steep white walls, Naomi's house perched like a fortress and no sound dented the silence that enclosed it.

'This is it.' He glanced at Simon as their long journey from Cape Town came to an end. Although the exterior of the house immediately flooded his mind with memories of Estelle Marsden, Thabo hid his tension behind a wide smile.

'My mother lives in there?' Simon stared excitedly at the heavy wrought-iron gate which was all that separated him from the person he'd looked for all his life. He glanced at Thabo hopefully. 'You coming?'

'Maybe it's better if I don't. Go on, ring the bell.' Thabo tried to sound casual, as if common sense held him back and not fear. Estelle had been capable of destroying him with no more than a look, and an uncanny sense of disaster nagged him.

'But you must come!' Simon wanted to share his mother with Thabo and he trembled in anticipation. 'I not go in without you. *Please.*'

'All right, but then I've got to leave you – you understand?' Though Thabo felt uncomfortable in the no-man's-land that separated his people from Simon's, he knew he had to see him inside before he could leave.

'OK.' Simon leapt out of the car and ran to the gates as Thabo collected his small case from the back seat. 'This the bell?' he yelled, his chubby hand hovering over the gleaming brass button that stood proud on the white wall. 'Do I push it?' he asked as the soft pad of his finger pressed down hard.

'Who is it?' a disembodied voice bubbled in the metal box beside the bell and Simon jumped back.

'There's somebody in there,' he whispered.

'Hullo?' Thabo pressed his mouth against the speaker. 'I've brought Simon Marsden to see his mother. Mr Conrad from Bonne Espérance wrote and . . .'

The metal gate swung wide in front of them and Simon stared in amazement. An immaculate brick path led to an enormous house and squeaky green grass spread a carpet under the mist of a hissing garden spray.

'Come on.' Simon tugged Thabo's hand but he hung back, searching the wide garden for the dog whose bark his acute hearing had picked from the silence. 'Look out, someone's coming,' Simon warned him as a black maid walked towards them from the house.

'Madam's waiting for you.' Holding her hand out for Simon's small case, Naomi's maid Avril glanced at Thabo coldly. 'You his driver?' She spoke in Tswana, her eyes moving curiously to the Mercedes behind them.

'Yes.' Thabo made a move to step through the gates with Simon.

'Wait here.' The maid dismissed him and turned away.

'But he's coming with me.' Simon stood quite still and the maid stared back at Thabo in wide-eyed surprise. 'He's coming to see my mother too,' Simon repeated. 'Please,' he added quickly, disconcerted by her silence.

'You're coming inside?' The young woman revealed her astonishment as she gawped at Thabo.

'That's what he says.' Answering Avril in her own language, Thabo moved through the gates with Simon.

Dropping back the fine net curtain that swept across the large sitting-room window, Estelle turned to Naomi beside her.

'Let him in!'

Though Estelle's Afrikaans was commanding, her walk was slow as she moved away to a chair, her body bowed under the weight of rekindled bitterness. The sudden clutch of memory that Simon's re-entry into her life brought with it held her like a vice. 'Get rid of that black before he comes inside.' Her voice dropped to a whisper. Estelle had seen Simon's hand in Thabo's and she held tight to the wooden arm of her chair as the image cast her headlong into the past, to the day Nombeka had held Simon out to her – the day a black had challenged her to love the deformed being who was her child.

'What are you waiting for, Naomi?' Estelle glared at her daughter. 'What did you expect – a normal human being?' Her voice rode a tightrope of bitterness that was strung high over a sea of guilt. 'When those people took him from me they brought him up with blacks and he's one of them now.' Estelle tried to free herself from the dark thoughts that invaded her, but her mind had latched uncomfortably on to the day Simon was born. A human reject had been placed in her arms instead of the beautiful child she'd expected for nine months, and the love she'd felt for her unborn baby had soured in an instant.

'Go on — let him in before that black sets foot in the house!' Estelle spat on a note of defiance.

'Isn't it you who should show him in?' Naomi had observed Simon's cautious tread, his short spread legs carefully balancing his body. His face was flushed, his cheeks puffed and vacant eyes gazed at the house as his tongue searched the air for a welcome. Naomi had never before tried to imagine Simon as a man and the reality startled her. His body was fully developed but controlled by the mind of a child, and she was repulsed.

'He's come to see you, not me.' Naomi tried to detach herself from the situation as she walked away to the dining room. 'Remember we've got people coming round for a *braai* later. Dick won't want Simon hanging about embarrassing our guests.'

'You invited him here and you will let him in!' Naomi turned as her mother's grating voice snatched her attention. 'You said you wanted Bonne Espérance back!'

Holding his foot clear of the marble floor beyond the front door, Simon balanced on one leg. Unsure where to put his feet, he peered at Thabo nervously as the maid stepped inside ahead of them.

'Hullo, Simon.' He swung round in fright as Naomi's voice reached him. The rubber sole of his shoe squeaked on the shining surface as he tried to keep his balance and he stumbled forward, falling clumsily. 'Whoopsie!' Naomi spread her arms wide as if to catch him, but then stepped away quickly as he struggled to his feet. 'Good heavens, how you've grown. You're a man now,' she exclaimed with empty amazement, gingerly holding out her cheek for a kiss. But Simon pulled back quickly, choking on the strong smell of perfume.

'Naomi?' he said quietly. Though Rebecca had described his elder sister, he'd expected something entirely different. 'This my friend.' Simon held Thabo tightly by the hand and watched Naomi cautiously, hoping she wouldn't offer him her cheek again. She was nothing like the gentle creature about whom he'd dreamed and he hesitated as she beckoned him towards the sitting room.

'Mother's in here. Come along.' Naomi glanced back at Thabo dismissively. 'You can go now, boy,' she ordered without acknowledging his presence and the maid tossed him a knowing glance.

'Thabo come with me.' Simon held his friend's hand defiantly, catching Naomi by surprise.

'Pardon?' Her voice was filled with amazement. She hadn't recognised Thabo by sight or name. All blacks were boys and one looked much like another in her eyes. 'Come along, Simon.' She tried not to react to the anger in the squat being who'd challenged her and she held out her hand to take his.

'No! He come too! He come to see my mother too.' Simon's words were disjointed by the sudden terror of being left alone with strangers in an ice-cold house.

'Let the boy go, Simon,' Estelle's voice demanded from the sitting-room doorway, and he turned to look at her. Her body was rigid and Simon's mouth dropped open as he stared.

'You my mother?' Disbelief filled the distance between them and his tongue swept his chin to catch a sticky streak of saliva. The woman before him was not the mother for whom he'd come looking. 'This my friend.' He stepped closer to Thabo, holding tightly to the only person he trusted. Estelle's look had touched him with the stroke of a dead hand and he wanted to run.

'I said, let go of the boy, Simon!' Estelle's voice was harsh and her eyes dared him to argue. 'And make sure he washes his hands before you bring him in to see me, Naomi.' She walked away without looking back.

'Simon.' Thabo tried to remove his hand from Simon's grip. He peered at him, warning silently of the trouble his continued presence in the house would cause.

'Come along.' Naomi snatched Simon's arm quickly before he could go after Thabo. 'You do know how to wash, I hope.' She dragged him away towards a door. 'There's soap and a towel beside the basin and the hot water's marked with a red dot.' She pushed him into a small and immaculate bathroom. 'And don't forget to lift the lid.' She closed the door on him quickly.

Naomi was very angry. Her attempts to keep the pretence of a marriage alive, and with it the comforts to which she'd become accustomed, were threatened by Simon's reality.

'You could have warned me.' Her voice crept back to Simon under the closed door as she stalked across the hall to her mother. 'He spits, for heaven's sake! I can't expect Dick to have him here – we've got people coming. You'll have to do something about him. I'm not having it!'

Naomi's rejection filled the small room in which Simon stood, and his stomach churned the juicy sweet milkshake Thabo had bought him for lunch. Simon's imagination had created a beautiful world of mothers and sisters but it had crumbled at his feet along with his dreams.

'I told you those people left Simon to blacks to bring up. He's been raised like a kaffir and he behaves like one!'

Estelle's words crept under the door after Naomi's, curling round Simon's ankles as his jaw locked wide, launching the milkshake towards the lavatory. Pink goo spread a shallow lake across the closed lid and his body shook as he stared at it. Lifting the seat quickly as Naomi had warned, he leaned over and his stomach emptied once again. Stretching slivers of vomit dripped from the lavatory bowl and Simon stared in terror as they landed on the thick white carpet at his feet.

'Thabo?' He turned in a small helpless circle, trapped between four tiled walls. 'I want to go home.' His voice choked in his throat as he glanced up at the freedom of daylight that shone through the window above the lavatory. Banging the seat down, he climbed on to it and looked out, and then he froze. Just outside straining at a heavy metal chain, a large dog bared its teeth and a deep growl sounded in its throat.

'Good boy,' Simon whispered, wondering if the dog could reach him as he laboriously heaved himself out of the window and down on to the ledge below. 'Nice boy.' He stared at the crazed animal, tugging at its chain. Reaching for a drainpipe, he launched himself on to it, hanging like a terrified monkey as the dog leapt and snapped up at him. 'Sit!' Milkshake dripped from Simon's chin as he plunged down among the orange and blue spikes of a strelitzia. 'Stay!' he shouted back at the demented dog, struggling to get free of poking proud plants. 'Thabo!' he shouted as the dog leapt after him, spinning in an ungainly somersault as the chain yanked it back.

'Wait for me!' Simon screamed as he raced towards the wrought-iron gates. He'd spotted the gleaming white of Rebecca's Mercedes pulling away from the kerb. 'Thabo!' He hauled himself up the slippery ironwork, launching himself across it as metal spikes ripped his trousers. 'Come back!' he yelled, throwing himself off the gate to land in a heap on the rough pavement, leftover milkshake turning to liquid pink tears that ran down his chin. 'That's not my mother,' Simon wept, unaware of the Mercedes reversing towards him.

'Oh, my God!' Naomi's voice rang through the house as she stared at the once-immaculate toilet. A stench of sweet vomit engulfed her and her voice was nasal with disgust. 'Look what he's done! My carpet!' Her interest centred only on the mess Simon had left behind him and she swung round at Estelle. 'He's nothing but an animal. He shouldn't be allowed out!'

'I told you.' Estelle's voice was quiet. Thabo's presence had given her the way out of the shame rekindled by Simon's presence and she snatched at it quickly. 'He's been brought up by blacks!'

As the Mercedes turned into the dusty streets of Soweto, Thabo glanced at Simon sitting beside him. Simon hadn't said a word since Thabo had picked him up outside Naomi's house and in many ways Thabo felt responsible for what had happened. It was his presence that had touched Estelle's anger, depriving Simon of the mother he was looking for. He also knew that taking him into the vast township of Soweto during a time of unrest wasn't sensible. But for a black man with a white teenager in tow there was no place in the all-white city of Johannesburg.

'Are you all right now?' It had been difficult to get Simon clean. They'd pulled up at a garage and Thabo had pretended to be the chauffeur, but he'd been unable to go into the 'white' toilet with Simon.

'This is Soweto,' Thabo said casually a little later, as if the word alone explained the black people who thronged the streets. The township was as noisy as the white suburb had been silent. Chattering voices cracked wide with laughter, calming Thabo's fears as his eyes skimmed the rows of small brick houses that lined the streets.

Children played happily among piles of rubbish and lines of washing waved their cleanliness, denying the poverty that surrounded them. But although Thabo knew it was that poverty which had created the violence, and that a white like Simon could light its fuse without reason, he felt only the warm curiosity that watched the car.

'Samuel will let us stay in his house,' Thabo smiled. 'If I can find it.' He glanced at an address scribbled on a piece of paper, his eyes searching the dusty streets for signposts that didn't exist. 'Excuse me, can you help me, please?' he called out in Tswana, smiling as a tall black woman turned to look at him. A baby peered at him from her back in wide-eyed wonder as he asked for directions and then a small boy ran to the car.

'Here!' he called to Thabo, tiny black fingers curling round the edge of the window as he pulled himself up, his head nodding directions like a small black puppet as his words rattled in breathless Zulu.

'Thank you.' Thabo patted the child's head and slipped a five-cent piece between his curling fingers.

'OK!' The little boy grinned and ran in front of the car, moving backwards as he beckoned Thabo to follow his whirling gestures. 'Voetsek!' He waved his arms the other way to shoo the children who'd joined him and Thabo laughed, following them into a maze of narrow streets.

'Where we going?' Simon stretched his neck to watch the dusty trail of children who guided them.

'Samuel's house. They know him.' Thabo turned a sharp corner and suddenly he slammed on the brakes. The children had stopped. They stood quite still in staring silence. Ahead was a sand clearing packed with people. Chanting voices rode high on the still air and terror claimed Thabo.

'What they doing?' Simon asked curiously, peering towards the crowd who danced round a bonfire. 'What they burning?' His head pushed out of the window to see more clearly.

'Keep down!' Thabo grabbed Simon and pulled him back. The smell of burning rubber filled the car and a man's terrified screams violated the warmth that had surrounded them. 'Keep your head down!' Thabo reversed the car quickly into a side street. He'd heard rumours of barbaric killings in the townships and knew he should drive away fast but he couldn't. The man's agonised cries had trapped him, calling him to help. 'Stay in the car,' Thabo ordered Simon as he climbed out, torn between the man's screams and the very real danger of his actions. 'Lock the doors and don't move.' The children had scattered and Thabo was alone in the deserted street as pillars of black smoke hung a heavy tent over the chanting crowd ahead.

'No, Thabo.' Simon hadn't kept his head down. He'd seen the people Thabo was running towards and they were strangely threatening. 'Wait for me,' he shouted, clambering out of the car to help his friend.

But Thabo didn't hear him. He'd pushed his way in among the crowd, whose eyes were glazed by dagga as they danced around the cause of their celebration. A man was burning alive. Flames licked orange tongues round his face, reaching up from a burning body that was held tight by scorching tyres.

'Let him go!' Thabo pushed his way through the swaying black mass whose dancing steps rose from the centre of darkness. 'In the name of God, stop this killing!'

But his cries went unheard and the heavy stench of burning flesh choked him. Like open graves, wide throats screamed for death and dancing feet grew faster in frenzy. Quite suddenly their cries turned to howls of delight and the crowd turned, sweeping forward on a black tide of hysteria. Only then did Thabo see what had attracted them.

'Simon!' he screamed as a flash of white skin shone among black bodies. 'Leave him alone!' He pushed his way forwards as Simon stared at the crowd that held him, his eyes large and puzzled. 'That is God's child! You cannot touch him!' Thabo wrestled his way between the bodies but he fell, dragged to the ground by scrambling people. Stamping feet shot bursts of sand into his face and murderous cries rose on a wave of hatred that surrounded them all. The crowd was screaming for the blood of 'a white witch' and Thabo could no longer think. His head ached with each kicking foot and his mind was numb, but then he became aware that he was praying. Words he'd never heard before raced through the confusion, springing from his lips in an unknown language.

'Thabo!' Simon implored as strong black arms held him. 'Thabo!' He sobbed in terror as a tyre was pushed over his head, holding him tight beside the smouldering remains of what had once been a man. 'Help!' Simon gagged as petrol was poured over him by screaming black men. He didn't understand why they hated him. The Africans who had so suddenly surrounded him were no longer beautiful like Thabo. They were hideous. He was held tight by the evil that had twisted their souls, and he shrank back as a burning stick moved towards him. He could feel its heat and his skin stung as it drew closer, his heart pushing into his throat like a swelling drum. 'Thabo!' Simon cried again, for the only person who could help. His mind had filled with fire. Flames were swallowing him in enveloping arms as they wrapped his body in white heat. And then, in the centre of that heat Simon saw Thabo.

Thabo was moving through the fire towards him and strange words sounded on his tongue. His hands were lifted high and the crowd had fallen silent. Only Thabo's voice remained as the unknown tongue he spoke reached past man's understanding, lifting above the flames in intercession. And then the crowd gasped.

Thabo had ripped off his sweater to smother the flames that licked around Simon's body. The priest's collar stood bright against the clinging darkness and he pulled the burning tyre from around him. Curiously comforting words were falling on Simon's body like drops of living water as Thabo lifted him clear of the flames and the crowd moved back in sudden fear.

'God, to whom vengeance belongs, shine forth!' Tears of rage mixed with Thabo's cry as he challenged the surrounding darkness with the light of God's word while Simon hung limply across his arms. 'This one lives!' Thabo lifted Simon's body higher and the people covered their faces in shame. 'But you will fall into the hands of the living God for what you have done!'

Turning away quickly, Thabo ran towards the car. He knew it wouldn't be long before the crowd woke up as the truth of his words fell on dead hearts. Pulling the car door open, he pushed Simon into it, roaring the engine into life. The car spun in a circle of dust and flying stones and the children who'd guided them watched in silence.

Cheated of Simon's blood, the crowd suddenly woke up to what Thabo had done and they were running towards the car. Their cries for revenge skimmed the dusty ground, wrapping themselves round Thabo's heart as the tyres spun uselessly on loose earth. Clutching black hands reached for the gleaming white body they tried to reclaim but the car had slipped through their fingers.

'Simon!' Thabo shouted as they sped away through the narrow streets. The smell of petrol and burnt clothes filled the acrid air. Simon was totally still. 'Talk to me!' He reached over to touch him as they raced back through Soweto, crowds scattering as the car cleared a path between them. But even now Thabo didn't know what to do. Though Simon needed medical help, apartheid had made it impossible for Thabo to take him even into a white washroom. There was no way he could take him to a hospital, and Thabo was weak with helplessness.

'Answer the bell, will you!' Naomi instructed the maid as she served snacks to a crowd of partying people around the pool. The sun shone down from an empty sky. Coloured shades sprouted like gaudy trees round a rectangle of clear blue water and Frank Sinatra's voice crooned from loudspeakers fixed in the trees. 'How's the meat, Dick? Do you need more?' Naomi called to her husband. But Dick Davidson was barbecueing and didn't hear her as he joked with another man.

'Could spend all day on one of those.' His eyes were fixed appreciatively on the bobbing bare breasts of a young woman in the pool.

'I do like your hair.' Stretching out for a tiny sausage on a silver tray a woman behind Naomi complimented her.

'Excuse me, Patricia.' The bell was still ringing and Naomi was irritated. 'See to that bell,' she hissed at Samson as he moved through the crowd. Brandy and Coke had already dulled Naomi's mind and a gentle throb in her temple warned of a screaming headache. But she smiled brightly as her friend Patricia repeated her compliment.

'Your hair – who styled it?'

'Nathan.' Naomi tossed her head, allowing a neat wedge of bleached hair to fall over one eye with practised precision. 'He's so clever, darling. He trained with Vidal in London, of course.'

But then Naomi stopped talking. She was aware that a hush had fallen on her guests and she'd seen Patricia's attention fix on the house behind her. Removing her sunglasses carefully, she turned and looked towards it.

'Oh, my God!' Naomi's words were a mixture of shock and embarrassment. Standing on the patio in front of the house was Thabo. Simon's body hung limply in his arms and one hand swept the gleaming marble floor as liquid ash dripped from his fingers.

'Simon's hurt.' Thabo's voice trembled as a multitude of hostile white faces stared at him. There was no sound except the gentle swing of Frank Sinatra's voice. 'He was attacked. He needs help.' Thabo's voice rose on a note of desperation as nobody moved to him. 'Simon's dying!' he

413

shouted at the silent faces that expressed only resistance to his presence.

Suddenly Thabo was surrounded by nervous people peering at Simon in horror. Hesitant white hands reached at his burnt clothes and wary glances swept over Thabo. But all he saw was Naomi's husband. Dick Davidson stared at him and without a word he took Simon and moved away into the house.

It was hours instead of minutes that ticked by as Thabo stood alone outside. Everybody had gone into the house and he'd heard the loud clanging of an ambulance bell in the driveway. He'd heard angry talk of his responsibility for what had happened and a warning voice urged him to leave. But he waited, standing silently, his fears pushed aside by his deep care for Simon.

'What happened?' Dick Davidson's voice denied he'd asked a question at all as he stepped back in front of Thabo. His eyes passed coldly over Thabo's face, then settled on the clerical collar around his neck. 'Who did this? Where did you take him?' Quite suddenly, the white man's hand banged against Thabo's cheek. Challenged by his silence, Dick Davidson was rigid with anger. 'You people burning whites now – is that it? Not good enough to kill your own, you want to kill whites!' Thabo's head snapped the other way as Dick cracked him again. Though he wanted to explain what had happened, to tell him of the shame he'd witnessed among his own people, Thabo couldn't speak. The violence behind the white face that glared at him now was no different from that which had danced round a burning body.

'It's all right now, everyone,' Naomi's voice sang from the house as she stepped outside but her husband was oblivious to her. His attention was centred on the silent African in front of him, and alcohol fuelled his rage. 'The boy can wait at the back now, Dick. The police are coming.' Naomi pressed her hand against her temple. A sharp pain dug its way behind her eyes and she wanted to calm things down so the party could continue. 'They've taken Simon to hospital and the ambulance men say he'll be fine. He was very lucky, apparently.' She smiled at the small crowd around her, unaware that her husband had ignored every word she'd said. 'Take the boy away to the back, Samson.' She nodded at the African servant who stood back nervously. 'What's happened to the music?' She wanted to get the party going again.

'I think I should take this off for a start!' Dick Davidson's eyes had centred on the clerical collar round Thabo's neck and his anger wallowed in a bellyful of liquor as his fingers gripped it. 'You think this hides the bloody savage you are, you murdering bastard!' He ripped the priest's collar from around Thabo's neck, pushing him backwards and knocking him to the ground as he tripped him with a foot behind his knees.

'Oh, for heaven's sake, Dick! Leave it to the police and don't spoil the party.' Naomi went over to her husband to halt any further embarrassment, but then she stopped. Dick's friends had surrounded him, their faces alight in anticipation of a fight, cheering him on.

'Think you're smart like that monkey Tutu, eh?' Pushing his foot on the back of Thabo's head as he lay face down on the ground, Dick yelled, 'You want this country, nigger boy? You want to destroy it like the rest of the niggers up north? You want it? Come and get it! Take it from me – come on!'

Thabo felt the prickle of grass against his face as it was shoved into the earth once again. He could see the angular legs of a grasshopper just beside him. Its tiny green body looked enormous and one glassy black eye peered at him before spiked legs pushed it clear of an enormous boot. Thabo could hear men laughing above him. He could feel the toe of a leather shoe dig into his side and he gasped as a sharp heel pushed down into his back. But still he held tight to Naomi's words.

They've taken Simon to hospital and they say he'll be fine.

'Get up, kaffir!' A foot levered under Thabo's stomach, rolling him over on the ground.

'You heard the bwana.' Leering white faces peered at him over swelling pink stomachs. 'Get up!' The stench of alcohol choked in Thabo's throat and a lump of spit splattered on his cheek. 'Where's your *panga* now, Zulu boy?' A man's bare foot was over his face. Toes dug into his eyes and grit burned Thabo's skin as hard yellow skin pressed his nose in aching circles. 'I'll make it nice and flat for you!'

'Hell, he's a dirty kaffir,' a voice laughed somewhere and Thabo felt himself being dragged across grass. The hard surface of bricks bumped under his back and quite suddenly his head was hanging over a spread of crystal clear water. 'Wash, kaffir boy!' A hand was around Thabo's throat and water rushed over his face. Through the rippling surface he could see white faces looking down at him from the sky. He couldn't breathe as water pushed up his nostrils but still Thabo didn't struggle. He could hear the distant chug of a pool cleaner underneath him and bubbles rose in streams of clear balloons in front of his eyes as Naomi's comforting words played in his mind.

'Shit!' A splash in the water was followed by echoing liquid laughter as Thabo was dragged deeper under the swirling blue surface. White bodies splashed around him and his lungs ached as he was pushed deeper, his cheeks lifting in front of his eyes to form skin bubbles as he slid into oblivion.

Hauled out by his hair, Thabo was suddenly flying through the air, tossed like a limp rag doll on to hard red bricks. He watched a stream of warm liquid run out of his mouth and a rock banged against his head. A circle of sky spun a dance behind the spread of green trees and a stretching black cable reached across his mind. He tried to hold on to it but he couldn't. He was falling back. He was sinking into a dark tunnel but still Naomi's words comforted him.

'Stop it!' Naomi pushed to get through the huddle of white bodies that surrounded Thabo. All she could hear was the thud of feet digging into flesh and the crack of a skull on bricks. 'You'll kill him!' Naomi's words were lost among the insane babble of obscene shouts that surrounded Thabo. 'Leave him alone!' She hammered her fists uselessly against the fleshy backs of the men who rained a never-ending stream of blows on to the crumpled black body beneath them. 'Somebody stop them!' Naomi swung round to the other guests who stood back silently. Though their faces reflected horror, it was mixed with pleasure and pushing her way impatiently through them, she ran to the house. The thundering in her head reached a crescendo as she picked up the phone while her mother watched from a chair.

'No, Simon's all right, Luke. They've taken him to hospital and they say he'll be fine, but it's the black man. I think they've killed him. You've got to do something, Luke! He could be dead for all I know.' Naomi tried to speak calmly into the phone but her head was exploding and fear clutched her throat. 'How on earth would I know who he is – he's black! You've got to come, Luke! *Please!*'

'Why?' Estelle's voice was cold.

Miles away on Bonne Espérance, the sharp ring of a telephone skipped across the cobbled courtyard between the house and the cellars and Rebecca glanced at her father as he moved to the arched black doors.

'I'll get it.' David glanced back at Rebecca with a smile as he slipped outside. 'You two are doing great things. Keep it up.' He turned and ran towards the house as the shrill ring of the phone hurried him. David was happy at last. Through Rebecca he'd found peace on Bonne Espérance since his wife's death, and their energies had combined to make it permanent.

'What do you think?' Rebecca turned to the young man beside her. Neil Sanderson had been trained in viniculture in Europe, and Rebecca had employed him as winemaker in her effort to rebuild Bonne Espérance. She wanted to restore it to its former glory as Prudence had done, as she had Samuel Netherby's old shop, and every penny she had was sunk in the earth.

'Rebecca!' David was calling from the house and there was a note of horror in his voice. 'It's the police.' He met her in the doorway, trapping her between the cool dark of the cellars and the burning heat outside. He was flushed and spoke between snatched breaths. 'The police have got your car in Johannesburg and they want to speak to you. Something's happened and they need to ask you about it.'

'My car?' A chill gripped Rebecca. Simon and Thabo's faces flashed in front of her eyes and her legs weakened. 'What's happened?' She ran towards the house with David though she couldn't feel her legs at all. 'Are they all right?' She overtook him, racing through the front door. 'Hullo? It's Rebecca Conrad here,' she gasped into the phone.

The policeman's English was interspersed with Afrikaans and Rebecca listened attentively as his words covered the distance between Johannesburg and Cape Town. Simon had been attacked by Africans in Soweto but he was all right. He was in hospital in Johannesburg and the doctors were certain there'd been no real damage, the policeman told her. But he didn't offer any further details and went straight on to the matter that was uppermost in his mind.

'It's about the Mercedes.' His voice was careful. 'The car we have here is registered in your name, lady.' His amazement was evident – as though the car was more important than anything else.

'Where's Thabo?' Rebecca shouted in frustration. 'Where's the man who was driving the car? What's happened that you're ringing me about the car? Thabo was driving it with Simon. Where is he?'

Rebecca stared at her father in silence as she listened and David wrapped an arm round her protectively. In her face he saw only confusion and pain. His daughter's eyes reflected the tragedy of a country which she'd reclaimed as her own and he wondered how long it could hold her.

Arriving at Naomi's house soon after the police, Luke had found them pushing the bloodied body of an African into the back of a van. Naomi's friends had returned to their party and once again music played from speakers perched in the trees. Two black gardeners scrubbed the brick paving on their hands and knees, silently removing Thabo's blood while the party continued as if nothing had happened.

'We'll have to empty the pool.' Dick Davidson's voice reached Luke. 'I'm not getting in after a nigger.' As Naomi's husband sniggered, Luke approached the policeman beside the van and spoke to him in Afrikaans.

'Is he still alive?' Luke looked at the African whose body was face-down in the van, and his eyes settled on the pool of blood that had spread over the rusty floor. 'Aren't you going to do something? That man needs urgent help.'

'Oh Luke!' Naomi's voice stopped him as she rushed out of the house. 'I'm so sorry I called and wasted your time like this. Everything's all right now.' She shone a bright smile. Naomi had changed more than her clothes. The arrival of the police had dispelled her fears and her headache had vanished with her problem. 'They say he's still alive so there's nothing to worry about.' She linked an arm through Luke's to lead him away, reacting as he pulled free. 'The police are taking him to the station to charge him with attempted murder and Simon's fine. He's in hospital so there's no problem any more, Luke.'

Naomi had discovered that the police knew all about the African practice of burning people as witches. It was a system known as 'neck-lacing' and the barbaric murders had spread from the rural areas to the townships. Necklacing had become a political weapon used between warring factions, but the facts had been kept away from the public. Afraid of panic, the police had kept silent, but now they had Thabo and had assured Naomi there was little to worry about.

'Come and have a drink.' Naomi smiled at her brother sweetly. She was pleased she could show Luke off to her friends, hoping he'd wipe away the memories of Simon's crude interruption.

'Excuse me.' As if he hadn't heard a word Naomi said, Luke moved back to the police van and pushed past the surprised policeman. Inside the vehicle a man lay bleeding. Though Luke had no idea who he was, he'd gone to help another victim of his country's insanity.

'What on earth are you doing?' Naomi stepped back as he climbed out of the police van with Thabo over his shoulder. Thabo's face was battered beyond recognition and his body dripped blood down Luke's back.

'You can get my address from Mrs Davidson here.' Luke turned back to the policeman. 'And then, if you still want to question this man, you can come to me to do it.'

'You can't take him away, sir.' The policeman spoke in Afrikaans. 'It's a police matter now and we'll take care of it.'

'Then you can come and get him from me,' Luke shouted, turning away. Thabo's feet brushed against the policeman's face, touching his pride.

'That man's charged with attempted murder and you're interfering in police business.' The officer pursued Luke angrily but he stopped as Luke swung back on him, his eyes alight with anger.

'Yes.' Luke spoke in English. 'There has been an attempted murder. This man has been beaten up with intent to kill him, and it will be *me* who lays charges against those responsible – the people who thought they'd get away with it because he's black and they're white!'

'Don't be so silly, Luke,' Naomi interrupted quickly. 'What on earth are you talking about?'

'Attempted murder, Naomi.' Luke held tight to Thabo's body, as if gaining strength from the helpless man on his shoulders. 'What do you think it is — some kind of game?'

'What's going on here?' Dick Davidson pushed his way past his wife and stopped in front of Luke. His face was red with anger and he reeled forward drunkenly, grabbing for Luke's arm. 'Don't bring your liberal crap into my house, *bootjie*! Your sister might stand for it — she's liberal with black cocks for all I know — but don't try your *Verligte Afrikaner* shit on me!'

'What are you trying to say, Dick?' Luke's eyes turned on to him slowly. 'Are you speaking in defence of what's happened?' The rage that burned in Luke came from the core of his being and was aimed directly at his sister's husband. 'Or are you trying to say it was an Afrikaner who beat this man to a pulp?'

'Get the hell out of here!' Dick Davidson lurched at Luke as he touched on the truth. The Afrikaner Government, whose laws he'd hidden behind while disclaiming them, had begun to give way. Black nationalism was rattling apartheid's chains and Dick Davidson's true feelings had been revealed in the blows Thabo had taken.

'This man's annoying me.' Dick turned away from Luke quickly. 'Do something,' he yelled at the policeman beside him.

'Why don't *you* do something?' Luke's voice commanded the attention of everyone as he challenged Dick Davidson again. 'Or will you wait till we meet in court?' Luke turned to the gates with Thabo's blood soaking through his shirt and he walked away. He was walking away from his family for the last time, but it was a time he'd known would come as he took his place in Africa.

Dick Davidson swung round on the policeman in an inadequate fury. 'That *kaffir bootjie* Afrikaner's made a bloody ass out of you. Do something!'

'He could be right, sir.' The policeman shrugged Dick's insults away, turning to the van. '*Tot siens*.' He left behind an Afrikaans 'goodbye' as he climbed behind the wheel. 'But don't worry, sir. We won't forget what's happened here today.' The police van drove away through the gates and Dick Davidson turned back to his friends.

'Anyone for a drink?' he called, as if nothing had happened, while Peggy Lee's voice whispered a gentle melody among the trees. 'Shit,' he laughed. 'What the hell else can you expect from a bloody Afrikaner!'

The fine net curtain once more fell back against the sitting-room window. Estelle felt totally alone. When Thabo had brought Simon back to her, she'd kept herself well under control. There'd been a moment when some impulse within her had cried out to go to her child, but Estelle had resisted it.

Bound tight by hurt pride, she'd denied emotions she'd thought were long since dead. She'd watched Simon being carried away to the ambulance but hadn't gone to him. She had also watched the brutal beating of Thabo. She'd watched her son, Luke, accuse his own family of a crime against humanity, but still she hadn't allowed herself to react.

Once again, an African had picked up the leftovers of Estelle's life, and once again she'd rejected him. Rejecting life itself, she'd watched Luke turn his back on his own kind in defence of a black man and she clasped the shining brass doorknob tightly as she turned it. She longed to be free of the bitterness that had held her prisoner all her life. She knew that freedom stood just beyond the walls she'd built to protect herself, but Estelle had lost the will to break free.

Simon's body was swathed in bandages, but he smiled as Rebecca and David approached his bed. They'd come straight to the hospital from Johannesburg airport and the warmth behind their eyes scattered the fear that still surrounded him with flames.

'Where's Thabo?' Simon whispered. He could remember nothing but the image of Thabo moving into the fire that had licked around him. He could still hear the strange language that had come from his friend's lips, but Simon hadn't found him.

'We'll get Thabo soon.' Rebecca stroked his forehead gently and her eyes filled with tears. What had begun as a search for Simon's mother had ended in tragedy, as if any move she made vaguely close to Luke was doomed before it began.

Although Rebecca had the address to which Thabo had been taken, she hadn't been told that it was Luke who'd dealt with him. The police just said that they didn't know the man. They'd talked with contempt of his threat to lay 'charges of attempted murder' against whites but they refused to give further information. Thabo's position as a cleric and friend of the Conrad family had surprised the police, and they'd realised they were without the clout even to lay a charge of car theft against Thabo. And so they'd stepped back rather than admit the truth of what had happened, leaving Rebecca with no more than an address.

'Where Thabo?' Simon's eyes held Rebecca's as he pleaded with her again. 'Fire!' He stared in terror from the memory that surrounded him as he looked around the ward for his friend. 'Thabo!' he cried, and David turned to Rebecca, nodding for her to leave.

'But I've got to know what happened,' Rebecca argued, and she quickly turned to a coloured nurse who'd walked into the ward, and had gone over to make a bed in the far corner. The nurse's shoes squeaked on the gleaming lino and Rebecca followed her quickly. 'Excuse me, can you tell me if anyone came with Simon to the hospital?'

'No.' The nurse glanced at her coldly, walking back towards the ward door.

'Please!' Rebecca ran after her, catching her up in the corridor outside. 'Somebody must have brought Simon into the hospital. Was it his mother, Mrs Marsden?'

'Nobody brought him in.' The woman's dark eyes were scornful. 'Looks like you people don't like his kind any more than you like ours.' Her eyes were filled with resentment and she started to walk away again.

'I've got to talk to you, please!'

'What do you want with me, lady?' Behind the anger in the half-caste woman's eyes Rebecca saw fear. 'Didn't your white police tell you what happened?'

'I'm trying to find out the truth.'

'It's only us coloureds that lie, is it?' the nurse said sarcastically. 'That helpless creature in there was attacked by blacks – that's what happened, lady! Blacks tried to burn him alive with a tyre round his neck.' Her expression contained the same horror Rebecca had once seen in Lorraine Hendrickse. 'They burn a mongol, they burn each other and they going to burn us coloured people, too! You got your white police to protect you, but what about us? You going to protect us when blacks want to burn my kind, too?'

The nurse swung away and Rebecca stood still in the vacuum of fear that divided all the people of South Africa.

'Rebecca?' David appeared from out of the ward behind her.

'What's happening, Dad?' Her voice was carried on a note of helplessness. 'Why?' David saw once again the small girl he'd found hiding on an ant hill with a stolen baby and he held her.

'I'll tell you what's going to happen, Rebecca.' He wrapped his arms tighter around her. 'You're going to get Thabo from that address the police gave you, and I'm going to stay here with Simon.' He tucked her under his shoulder as if she was a small bird whose broken wing he was trying to fix.

'Whoever took Thabo must have wanted to help him, so you're not alone, my love.' David tilted her face towards him. 'Simon's asking for Thabo. Go and find him and then we'll all go home.' David's voice had filled the word *home* with the peace of a refuge.

Walking towards a ramshackle house set back in a wide bare garden, Rebecca checked the address the police had given her once again. She had no idea why she felt so nervous. A taxi waited in the road behind her.

The police had told her nothing about the man who'd rescued Thabo and their curious silence disturbed her. She'd heard the distaste in their voices and had no idea what to expect.

'Hullo?' she called into the silence. The door of the house was open and a thin ginger cat welcomed her with a creaking 'meeow' as its tail brushed her leg.

'Is there anybody at home?' Peering round the door, Rebecca could see nothing. 'Hullo?' She stepped into the cool darkness and reacted as a floorboard squeaked beneath her. Broken windows stared at her like jagged blind eyes and slim shadows moved deeper into the dark room. 'Excuse me?' she called as her eyes grew accustomed to the sudden shade. She'd picked out the shapes of people who stood silently in the dark of the room. They were black and as the darkness lifted they stared at her from unblinking eyes. 'I'm looking for someone. May I come in?' Rebecca took a cautious step closer.

'Can I help you?' She swung round with fright as a door on the other side of the room opened. A blonde woman stood in a shaft of light but she didn't smile. 'My name is Annie Marais. You said you were looking for someone.' She spoke with an Afrikaans accent and for a moment Rebecca didn't answer. She'd sensed another presence; Rebecca knew there was someone else near her – someone she hadn't yet seen. It was someone she knew; a familiar presence filled the house.

'I'm looking for an African man the police say was brought here.' Rebecca moved closer to the woman, determined not to be stopped by the familiar sensation of urgency that engulfed her as Annie Marais stepped to one side.

In a beam of light that fell across the floor of the room ahead of them, Rebecca picked out Thabo. He lay quite still on a mattress on the floor, his eyes closed and his face puffed by swelling raw wounds. Swiftly, she knelt beside him and the horror of his beating touched her. But then she tensed. The presence was coming closer. It called to her and her heart beat faster as it consumed her.

He stepped out of the shadows and into the stream of fading light that reached across Thabo to touch her. 'Rebecca?' Luke spoke on a whisper of disbelief, his eyes filled with wonder. The world around them disappeared as they came face to face. Feelings that had bound them together across the years wrapped round them in silent longing.

'Why are you here?' A note of tension touched Luke's voice as his eyes took in Rebecca's sudden reality. She was even more beautiful than he remembered and he could hardly breathe.

'Don't you know why?' Rebecca's eyes reached out to him. 'It's Thabo.' Though she longed for Luke's touch, every part of her trembled and she was afraid. Though only a short distance was between them, she couldn't cross it. Time separated them with miles of unknown living, concealing the secret of who Luke was now.

'Are you the person who took Thabo away?' Luke nodded and his eyes moved down to Thabo as he lay between them. The priest was still unconscious, as he had been from the moment Luke found him. But now, as he looked at the bleeding and swollen face of the man he'd helped, all Luke saw was a childhood friend – someone with whom he'd shared colour-blind dreams that were out of reach of apartheid. He could hear children laughing. He could smell the air of Bonne Espérance. He could see the three of them as they'd once been, as they'd stolen Simon. And he could feel her in his arms. She was the ghost of a mislaid past.

'Why did you help him, Luke?' Rebecca searched for the man he was now. The years had given him a physical strength she'd not seen in him before, but she was looking for the inner man – the beliefs that made up the person who stood in front of her now.

'He needed help.' Luke's voice was quiet as he drew back from the explanation for which she asked. He was aware that Rebecca's time in England would have opened her eyes, as his had been, but he no longer knew who she was.

'Why, Luke? He was just another black, wasn't he?' Rebecca pressed on, searching for a sure sign of the man Luke was now.

'Yes. He was just another black man.' Luke moved his hand to Thabo as he stirred and in the same moment Rebecca reached out, sparking electricity as their fingers touched.

'Why?' Her voice was balanced on a fine thread of longing. As they'd touched, a swell of desire had swamped her but still she held it back. 'Tell me!' Her voice lifted in demand of an answer and Luke's eyes settled on hers.

'Are you asking me a question or accusing me, Rebecca?' All he wanted was to move to her. To hold her in his arms and let loose the love that still filled him. 'Did you come here to accuse me or to help Thabo?'

Rebecca's eyes flew to meet his in sudden anger and his look held her still as mistrust stepped between them, neither able to cross the divide of misunderstanding.

'What about you?' Love poured across the rift between them as Luke spoke but neither dared acknowledge it.

'Me?' Rebecca's eyes filled with feelings she was trying to deny but her voice was flat. 'I'm still not-quite-white.'

'And I still want you.'

As the love they tried to deny burst through the walls of protection they'd built around their hearts, Luke pulled her into his arms. The warmth of his body pressed against hers and he drew her into the depths of that love.

'What are you staring at?' Annie Marais turned to the circle of black children who'd crowded round her in the doorway and she clapped her hands. 'Shoo!' She pulled herself free of the emotion that had filled the room behind her as she chased them away.

Rebecca was buried in the circle of Luke's arms and his lips passed over her face in a million silent words. His body curled tightly around hers and the house had filled with recaptured love.

CHAPTER TWENTY-TWO

Luke and Rebecca had been reunited by tragedy but with their love had come an extraordinary peace. Settling on them gently like healing rain, it softened the scars of time past and together they went to the Central Johannesburg police station to lay charges on Thabo's behalf.

'Is that it, sir? Nothing else?' The police officer's Afrikaans carried a smile behind it. He leaned on the counter casually, taking down the particulars in detail as Luke gave them, but his mind had already consigned Thabo to apartheid's black dustbin.

'You don't really imagine they'll take that man to court?' Annie Marais, the woman Rebecca had first met in the house where she'd found Luke, laughed when they told her what had happened. 'They'll think your brother-in-law's a hero, don't you know that?'

Annie Marais had seen blacks arrested and jailed for no more than an insulting glance at a white man but she'd never known the situation reversed. The scales of justice were balanced on white prejudice, coming down with thundering regularity on the heads of blacks, and she knew nothing had changed.

The country was still gripped by violence and 'People's justice' had taken charge of township streets. Kangaroo courts sentenced innocent blacks to be 'necklaced' with burning tyres, their bodies left as a smouldering warning to others.

'What good freedom now?' Fezile had gone to Bonne Espérance the moment he heard Thabo had returned. They sat under the oak tree, dapples of shade dancing at their feet as Fezile's words reached out from a crushed spirit. He'd witnessed many gruesome killings in Langa himself while police quirts, tear-gas and bullets had taken a further toll on his optimism.

'What good freedom when our people are no longer people but savages?' Fezile's eyes were shaded by heavy cataracts and he stared blindly at Thabo, his finger searching his mouth for the lemon pip that had escaped his ice-cold drink. 'You must get back to your church, Thabo.' Fezile trapped the pip against his gum and examined it carefully, surprised to find he could see it. 'Our people are dying!' With his toe he dug a small hole in the ground and pushed the pip into a sandy grave. 'They need God to lead them from death to life.' His worn shoe brushed dirt to cover the pip and his eyes screwed tight as he blew his finger clean. Though he couldn't see Thabo against the light, Fezile challenged him. 'You must take the truth of God's forgiveness back to our people – remind them that vengeance belongs to Him!' The old man's toothless jaws snapped together in an exclamation mark. His mind had looked back at the words Winnie Mandela, wife of the jailed leader, had recently spoken to the crowds. "Together, hand-in-hand with our sticks and our matches, with our necklaces, we shall liberate this country.' Her words had shocked Fezile as much as they had shocked the world, and now he defied them.

'God will scatter the darkness, Thabo.' His voice dropped to a whisper, as if he'd already seen the curling edge of evil that crept towards them. The ugliness that gripped his people was something Fezile wouldn't accept any more than he accepted white brutality. That hid behind the gloss of civilisation but was no less demonic.

'And when will *you* get yourself a wife?' Fezile tried to shake Thabo out of the silence in which he sat. He hadn't missed the joy that rang round Bonne Espérance. Plans for a wedding strung excitement over the vineyards like bunting and he searched among the debris of man's frailty for some fragment of hope to give Thabo.

'Do you Rebecca Olivia Conrad take this man. Luke Derek Marsden to be your lawful wedded husband, to have and to hold, for richer for poorer, in sickness and in health till death do you part?'

'I do,' Rebecca whispered in answer to the priest's question, and two words brought years of emptiness to an end.

'Why's Uncle David crying?' Simon whispered to Miriam as they sat together in the cool dark church. He'd seen David bow his head as he stood beside his daughter. When Simon turned to Thabo, who was on the other side of him, the young priest's eyes were fixed on the cross that stood stark against white walls and in them too, Simon saw tears.

'Don't cry,' Simon murmured, but Thabo didn't hear him. He was aware only of the love that radiated between Luke and Rebecca. It was a love that had survived separation and disaster to prove its all-conquering power, but Thabo had yet to understand the pain that went with it. He could still see remembered flames in Simon's eyes, while his own beating had in many ways killed him. Unforgiveness sat in Thabo's heart like a boulder, holding him earthbound and separating him from God.

'Do you Luke Derek Marsden take Rebecca Olivia Conrad to be your lawful wedded wife, to have and to hold, for richer for poorer, in sickness and in health till death do you part?'

'I do.' As Luke spoke he looked into Rebecca's eyes. They were the same dark pools that had always drawn him so inexplicably to the hidden person of her heart and the past had vanished inside them.

'Shh,' Simon cautioned Miriam as an almighty howl of emotion released itself. Her body shook like a chocolate blancmange under her smart new dress, her feathered hat tipping forward to hide the tears that flowed down her cheeks. Simon had never seen so many people cry at once in his entire life and pulling out his hanky, he pushed it into Miriam's hand.

'Not too much,' he warned. He'd heard the threat of a sago explosion in her nose and remembered the last time he'd lent her his hanky. 'You OK?' He glanced at Thabo cautiously, hoping he had his own handkerchief.

'Simon?' A whisper from behind caught his attention and he twisted his neck in a folding pink corkscrew to see who it was.

'Hi!' Tarcie smiled and Simon's mouth dropped open in amazement. She was beautiful and sat between her mother, Lydia and her brother, Joe.

'What happened to you?' Simon's words were round with amazement and his tongue swept his chin in awe as the pretty blonde girl behind him smiled again. Her eyes were a deep sea green and nowhere could he see the pig-tailed stick insect who'd once hounded him.

'Shh!' Miriam gripped Simon's arm and he felt the sog of his hanky push into his hand.

'You can keep it,' he whispered loudly and Tarcie poked him in the back with a prodding finger.

'I'm going to catch Rebecca's posy,' she said, as if he should know why. But Simon had no idea why and felt suddenly threatened. Rebecca was walking back down the aisle on Luke's arm and his eyes moved straight to the posy in her hand. It looked innocent enough but he decided to keep an eye on it, just in case.

'You still here?' Rebecca whispered, turning to Luke as they reached the church doors. His eyes had never left her and behind them was the love for which she'd longed. The touch of his skin against her hand. The firmness of his body beside her and the brush of his dark suit on the flowing white satin of her dress, sent sparks through her body and for the first time in her life Rebecca felt complete.

'So this is the white hunter!' Rebecca's eyes opened in astonishment as

Samuel Netherby stepped in front of her outside the church door. 'What's happened to his *sjambok* and safari suit, then?' The old tailor's smiling face and polished head looked totally out of place against the rising wide landscape of Africa. His skin was luminously white and the pure wool suit on his back steamed in the afternoon sun.

'Sammy! How on earth did you get here?' Rebecca's face flushed with the surprise of his unexpected presence and he shrugged, his finger searching his ear for a tickling hair.

'They called it a plane. Wouldn't be so sure meself though.' His look moved on to Luke. 'Took you long enough, mate. Could have lost her to a red-neck Anglo Saxon if she'd ever given 'em a second glance.' Rebecca threw her arms round the old tailor and he held her. Buried in the white of her dress, time had come full circle and Samuel Netherby had caught up with it once again.

'Throw the posy, Rebecca. Go on,' Tarcie called, and Simon watched nervously as she prepared to catch it, her weight passing from foot to foot in anticipation of success.

'Why's Rebecca going to throw her flowers away? They not dead,' Simon asked Miriam casually, as if it didn't matter at all, and she smiled her agreement.

'The person who catches the bride's posy will be the next one to get married,' David whispered as he stood beside him and Simon's eyes flashed back to Tarcie in alarm.

'Catch!' Rebecca tossed the flowers and Simon's hand shot out in desperation. Snatching them before Tarcie could reach, he galloped away round the side of the church, his legs a spreading tangle of terror.

'Simon!' Tarcie chased him through silent gravestones. 'Who you going to marry?' She careered round a heavy grey cross, trapping him between two rising earth mounds. 'Tell me,' she demanded, and Simon wondered if he should leap into a grave himself.

The night was still and very dark, lit only by a flickering candle that stood on a table beside a crisp double bed. Rain fell gently outside the hotel and somewhere somebody laughed, but all Luke saw was Rebecca.

She'd stepped out of the bathroom in a white towelling robe belted tightly round her body. Her hair was pushed up on top of her head, wet strands clinging to her neck while her face shone, scrubbed clean of make-up.

'What time is our flight in the morning?' She moved past Luke quickly, making for the bed as she glanced at an envelope of tickets on the table. 'Do you know how long it will take to get from Durban to Mauritius?' Her inconsequential questions passed Luke by unheard. The front of her gown had opened a little as she walked and he was aware only of the line of her body. He wanted to hold that body, to allow her skin to touch his as they dived back into the love they'd found so many years before.

'Rebecca?' Luke approached her and Rebecca concentrated on the immaculate stretch of the bedspread in front of her. She could sense Luke's breath on her hair; she could feel his hand pull the collar of her gown lower as his lips touched the back of her neck and she longed to turn into his arms, but she retreated, pulling the bedcover back.

Their wedding night was something neither had thought would ever happen but now that it had, Rebecca was avoiding it. She'd loved Luke for so long that she no longer knew how to express it. Aware only of the fuller curves the years had added to the young girl's body that he must remember, Rebecca was consumed by inadequacy.

'I can't believe it's still raining.' She folded the bedspread very carefully in front of her and Luke watched her with a puzzled smile.

'Where do you reckon they keep the hoover?' His eyes lit with humour and Rebecca pulled the cover close to her body in protection. She ached with longing but she couldn't move. 'Hold on to your end.' Luke took one side of the bed cover and walked away with it. 'Don't crease it, now.' He stretched the bedspread wide, shaking it in billowing waves as he held on. 'Right.' With the cover between his outstretched arms, he moved to her, wrapping it quickly around her body. 'Anything else, madam?'

As Rebecca laughed Luke's smile faded and the bedspread dropped to the floor around their feet. Her eyes were the same deep pools of longing he remembered and he no longer resisted their pull. His hand moved to the belt of her gown and, pulling it free, he allowed it to fall. He could smell the warm fragrance of soap on her skin. He could feel the slight damp of her body as he pulled her against him and his hands gripped her back.

'No ghosts, Rebecca.' Luke's voice was gentle as he pushed the gown off her shoulders, his lips touching her neck with a stroke of silk. His mouth was moving over her breasts and as his tongue touched her skin, Rebecca was back in the stables of Bonne Espérance. She was seventeen and begging him to stop. But now Luke hadn't stopped. He was exploring every part of her and her senses had locked on his touch as emotion bubbled inside her. It was a longing so deep it controlled every part of her and Luke felt the skin tighten over her body. The swell of her breasts reached for him; she was crying out for him. Warm and moist, Rebecca was clinging to him as they sank into the soft folds of the bedspread at their feet.

Rebecca could see nothing but Luke's face as he leaned over her. She could feel only his weight as his body pushed down on to hers; his eyes reassuring her she was still the most beautiful woman he had ever seen. His hands moved down the line of her stomach and Rebecca gasped as her body erupted with his touch. She was alive with longing and gripped his back, forcing her hips against his as his lips brushed her face.

'Luke!' Rebecca had opened wide to draw him into herself, deeper and deeper, to fill the gaping void inside her that yearned only for him as he pushed his way inside her.

'I love you.' Luke's mouth moved against hers as he whispered her name and their bodies locked together as one.

'I still can't believe it's all come true.' Rebecca felt herself melt as Luke gazed at her. The crystal clear waters that surrounded Mauritius reflected their colour in his eyes, lapping gently around their bodies as translucent fish swam a zigzag game of tag around them. The water's touch was as gentle as the stroke of night air on bare skin and she was lost in the magic of a tropical island.

'What are you thinking about?' Luke's eyes passed over her body as he held her afloat in front of him. Her skin gleamed the warmest of golden browns, tiny drops of water stood proud on her body and her dark hair spread across the water in strands of stretching silk.

'Guess.' She smiled up at him. The strong line of Luke's face was even more pronounced. Tanned a deep brown by the sun, he was broad and strong, his hair flecked with grey. Everything about him was real and the touch of his hands under her back shot excitement through her body as it had every moment they'd been together. 'I want you.' Her voice dropped to a whisper and Luke's mouth pressed down against hers as he cradled her in his arms. Her entire body reached for him and her mouth opened as his tongue pushed between her lips.

'Coconut oil? Beads? Pareos?' A bright-eyed boy popped up suddenly in the water beside them, yards of fabric trailing their colour in the water as he held his wares high in the air. 'You like?' White teeth flashed against brown skin and a smile cracked the young man's face wide. 'OK?'

'OK.' Luke tipped Rebecca into the water and pulling her under they swam away.

'No problem.' The young boy waded after them, his waterborne display of goods skimming the surface as he chased two gleaming shadows that fled under water.

'Do you think this is paradise?' Rebecca leaned back against Luke as she watched a boat chug away from the small island called Isle aux Cerfs, making for the rounded white curves of Le Tousserok Hotel. 'That maybe we're dead?' Every part of her body was alive with Luke's touch and her mind was locked on the wonder of being his wife. 'Put me down,' she laughed as Luke heaved her over his shoulder, carrying her along winding pathways heavily scented with frangipani. Over a delicate wooden bridge that swung from side to side as they crossed, he carried her into a cool white room. Vast windows gazed out at miles of still blue water and the Indian Ocean rolled white crested waves against the coral reef that held it back. The extraordinary beauty of Mauritius had become a part of their love.

'Has anyone told you you're even more beautiful now than before?' Luke's voice was filled with wonder as his eyes ran over Rebecca's body. Her skin shone gold, her breasts pushed against the black bikini that drew a soft line across them and he longed to take her, but he held back. He allowed himself instead to sink deeper into the beauty of Rebecca's gentle spirit. A delicate thread stretched between them, so fine it threatened to snap at any moment. It was a thread that had held them together across the world through both tragedy and success, expressing itself now in rising passion.

'Shells? Coral necklace? Dodo? You want I show you?'

The slim brown youth had reappeared in a circle of white froth that bubbled in the water outside the window. Waist-deep in the sea he grinned as he held his goods over his head.

'Honeymoon?' His English struggled through a French Creole accent. 'Your wife?' He beamed as Luke moved to the window. 'Nice!' The curtains swished across the smiling brown face in the ocean. 'No problem,' a voice assured Luke from behind the heavy folds of material that had blotted him out and Rebecca fell back on the bed with gales of laughter.

Leaning over her, Luke's fingers tugged at the fine black laces of the bikini. Her stomach rose and fell on a gentle pulse; her breasts were full and every part of her reached for his touch. Brushing his lips down the warm lines of her body, his fingers tugged on the tight black bow that reached across her pelvis, and she moaned.

'Luke!' Rebecca ached as he pulled her into his arms. Naked, she curled against him, pushing her face into his neck as he rocked her. 'I love you.' The warm wet of Rebecca's welcome called him to her again and he pulled her closer. She throbbed with an abandon that had hidden beneath the surface of her will since the day they'd met and her hands gripped his shoulders. 'No ghosts, Luke!' Her bare body pressed against him as her back arched and their skin touched. Every ounce of energy was concentrated on one another and they were lost in the magic of their love once again.

Luke's lips searched her body. Pushing her down on the crisp white sheet, his tongue ran down the long line of her neck. Her nipples were

431

hard as her breasts pressed against his chest. Her head was back and her eyes brushed his face with sweeping love calls as her hips thrust against his. They'd claimed again and again their impossible dream and time had stopped. It stood still as the crystal waters of the Indian Ocean lapped sandy white shores. It ticked the world by without moving on from them.

Joe Liebenberg peered through the lens of his camera, searching for a way down straggling pathways that snaked through the squatter camp of Crossroads outside Cape Town. Surrounded by filth and squalor, trapped among black plastic shacks that huddled together between deep puddles of rain, Lydia's son shivered. Damp air clung to his skin with the chill of a wet winter and Table Mountain hid behind clouds of shame.

Joe's camera had settled on a child's shoe, a tiny blue and white sandal. Its buckle clung desperately to a thread and it was all he saw as screams were crushed to silence by the thunder of bulldozers. All around him police uniforms shone starkly against a sea of poverty as they dragged people from refuse-bag homes while black hands hurled stones in hopeless defiance.

'Hey you!' Joe swung round in surprise as a hand grabbed him from behind. 'Get rid of that bloody camera!' His camera was knocked to the ground and an elbow dug into his stomach as a white policeman pushed past him.

'Bastard!' Joe's scream chased the man. It was the first time he'd been in the black squatter camp of Crossroads and curiosity had turned to blinding rage as its shame gripped him. 'These people need help!' Joe grabbed the policeman's jacket and pulled him back. 'They need food, not bulldozers!'

'You want to help them?' Joe was suddenly on his back in stinking mud with Andre Bothma's boot pressed down on his chest. Neither had recognised the other and only anger stood between them. 'If you want to help these people, get your camera out of here and let us do our job.'

'What job?' Joe scoffed into the face of white arrogance that challenged him. He was unaware that their fight had begun a century earlier on a farm called Bonne Espérance, its fury still burning as fiercely now as it had then. 'Is this what you call protecting your country, you stupid bastard? You're starting a war!' Joe pulled his head back as a stone hurtled past his face.

'If that had hit you it might have knocked some sense into you.' Andre yanked Joe brutally to his feet. To him, the young man he held by the collar was no less than a traitor. Journalists had helped outsiders undermine his country with pictures that told only half the truth. 'You go and cry to the people who pay those kids to throw stones – the Commies! The

Yanks! Tell them to look at those kids!' He swung Joe round to face a group of black children. Their faces were twisted with anger as their arms curled back to heave stones powered by hatred. 'They want this lot to run the country – and do you know why? 'Cos they've already bought it from them. Why the hell else do they give terrorists money? It's an onslaught – get that into your head!' Andre's boot came down on Joe's camera, grinding it into the ground with a crackle of breaking glass. 'Take pictures of the white baby these coons killed with a stone yesterday! Show your newspaper friends a two-month-old baby with a broken head and see if they print that! You want freedom for this lot? Why – so they can burn their parents for another dollar?' Joe felt the hard leather of Andre's boot press down on his back as a confusion of gunshots and screams gathered momentum around him. But then, out of the corner of his eye, Joe saw a tiny black girl, her face spread by a glorious smile. She'd picked up the shoe and her joy at finding it shone briefly in her eyes before a bullet split her head in two.

'In all honesty, I don't give a shit, Joe.' The American journalist Martin Bradley smiled, took another sip of his pink gin and leaned back in his chair. 'If you'd got a shot of the kid being killed it might have meant something.' Martin Bradley sat with Joe at a round table in the bar of the Mount Nelson Hotel. He'd tried to listen as Joe's youthful ideals reached out to him but he was bored. 'Guilt isn't news, kid – we all live with it. It's shit, so forget it!'

'But what you want isn't the whole truth.' Joe had tried to keep calm as he'd told Martin Bradley what he'd seen in Crossroads, but he couldn't any longer. He'd seen African people wading in poverty as they defended the meagre possessions that made up their lives, while police trampled them. 'Glorifying the violence won't change it, Martin. It's like selling pornography – the public only want more. We've got to get to the roots of what's happening, make both sides turn round and look at each other.'

'Sounds great.' The other man smiled as he chewed on a purple cocktail stick. 'But I'm here to tell it the way it's happening, kid, and that's all I want from you.' He was irritated by the young South African's idealism but still he smiled. 'Just doing my job. Same way you're paid to.'

'So's that white cop.' Joe was suddenly very angry. 'Doing his job!'

'Hey, kid. Come the revolution the blacks will kill him, but meantime I've got a family to feed so I'll deliver the goods I'm paid to deliver.'

'He's delivering the goods he's paid for, too! We're talking about people's lives, Martin.' Joe knew the media fed an overseas public which hadn't heard the real cries that came from both sides of his country and newspaper reports did no more than enrage the stubborn resistance of a

Government that was too afraid to change. The masses of African people, whose identity had been denied them for so long, weren't hungry only for power; they hungered for dignity and hope. But it had to come from the hearts of their own countrymen. It was a vision Joe hadn't yet grasped but he'd glimpsed the glow of its outer rim and he struggled to hold on to it.

'Maybe we can help find the way, Martin. There *is* a way. It's face to face and man to man.' Joe tried to filter through the confusion of his thoughts. 'Maybe we could do our job better by touching people's hearts instead of their anger.'

During his National Service on the Angolan border, Joe had seen hideously broken bodies, but only in Crossroads had he seen a child's joy shredded by a bullet.

'That cop believes what he does is right. Those kids believe they're right, too. Don't you see, they all believe other people's dreams! But what about us? Where do we stand?'

'At this precise moment, without a camera!' Martin Bradley smiled his boredom. Deep down he felt the push and shove of the idealistic young man he'd once been himself, and quickly he drowned him in another pink gin. 'This is what sells papers, my friend.' He pushed a newspaper across the table. 'And that's what I employ you to get.' On the front page was a picture of a smouldering man. 'Call it pornography, call it murder. It's what is wanted and you either get it or you clear out of the kitchen.'

Lydia had just finished work in the Kapps Hotel and stepped into the main street of Luderitz with a letter from Joe clutched in her hand. She screwed her eyes tight against the sun, peering into the bustling life that thronged the sidewalk. The motley crews of fishing boats poured out of the crayfish factory and into shops that stayed open to serve land-hungry men. Tipping their wages on counters, they bought everything they could carry before being bussed out; driven away to leave the small town asleep and silent under the gaze of white sand and sea.

Joe's letter overflowed with ideals and hopes that had once driven his father, Stan, a man who still poured alcohol down his throat from bottles hidden along the path that led to his grave. Though Lydia felt pride in her son, the reality of what was happening across the border in South Africa frightened her. She had recognised, but didn't know, the white policeman her son had come face to face with in the snaking avenues of Crossroads. Similar men had come to her door in Cape Town when they'd been looking for Stan many years earlier. They'd turned their house and life upside down as they searched for any slim evidence of treason. Silently, those same men had watched them leave the country and their expression had been one reserved for the dregs of society. It was they who still hounded the Luderitz bars; intent on picking up any drunk words from Stan that might lead them to more important quarry as they waited for his suicide.

Lydia understood Stan's hopelessness. Movements that had sprung up worldwide under anti-apartheid banners offered no real hope. Given birth by the cries of suffering people, they'd been hijacked by greed, carving highroads of opportunity through man's conscience. Nor could Lydia see hope in the self-righteous calls for economic sanctions that came from neighbouring black states to the north. Their people's hopes had also been crushed. Under the weight of corruption on which Communism thrived, only the colour of the oppressor had changed with Independence. It had been Stan's realisation that opposition in itself was not an answer that had driven him to drink, and Lydia wondered where it might lead her son.

Staring out towards the ice-cold Atlantic that lapped the desert shores, her eyes sank into the fog that hung low to hide the sea. It concealed the screaming gulls which swooped after emptying buckets of unwanted crayfish. It silenced the meeting place of sand and water with clouds of rolling mist, enshrouding the shores of a land which had once been joined to America. Wrenched apart millions of years before, the Namib Desert had formed diamonds from the dust of ages; and it was those diamonds that people fought for now. But they called it freedom.

Army boots and the tracking bare feet of bushmen trudged blindly past the 'desert roses' that lay in their path. They tramped the beauty of perfectly formed stone flowers as they sought the 'enemy'. Blind to blossoms shaped by time, they killed one another, and Lydia wondered if her son still searched for those roses made of stone.

Stepping hurriedly back from his bedroom window Simon pushed himself against the door of his cupboard and held his breath. He'd been looking for Thabo, but it wasn't his old friend he'd seen moving towards the house. It was Naomi – and her unexpected presence on Bonne Espérance had sent him hurtling back in time. Great drops of sweat trickled down his temples as he hid and the dog Zanu watched him from puzzled eyes.

Eighteen months had passed since Rebecca and Luke's marriage. Though the country writhed under terrorist attacks and the government's heavy-handed counter measures, a curious peace had settled over Bonne Espérance. Together with Thabo, who still hadn't returned to his church, Simon, Luke and Rebecca had forged again the friendship that had once bound the four children together. Even David had become a part of their small band. He'd let go of the steel hoist-house that called him back to the small town in Zambia and with Luke, he'd stepped into a new life. The red earth of Bonne Espérance had drawn them back to its mystery.

David no longer went to his wife's grave to mourn. When he sat beside Constance's tombstone now he smiled, telling her of his joy as he waited for their first grandchild. Like Ouma Malan, the family had cut themselves off from the world outside their boundaries. As international sanctions threatened to bring to an end the living they earned, they went on regardless as they built a new life.

But bitterness still held Thabo away from God and now it had touched Simon with memory's red edge of flames. Nobody had told him Naomi was coming to Bonne Espérance. Her name had been mentioned only when Luke had told him of the death of Simon's father, Paul Marsden. But Simon had ignored that and what touched him now was very real terror. Naomi's heels clopped on the flagstone floor of the house and even Zanu growled an instinctive warning.

'Thabo?' Simon's voice trembled as he searched for his friend among snatching memories. Flames sucked his body, hideous black faces screamed for his life and vomit dripped from a lavatory. 'Thabo?' Simon burst into tears as the only person he trusted appeared in the doorway.

Running into Simon's room, Thabo held him in his arms, rocking him gently to comfort him.

'It's all right.' Thabo had seen Naomi's taxi pull up outside the house and quickly he'd run inside through the back door. 'It's OK.' He tried to calm Simon, knowing he was back among screaming black faces and flames.

'Naomi ... she get me ... she take me back!' Simon's terror raked the air and the dog whimpered his sympathy.

'No, Simon, she won't take you. You're coming with me to Cape Town. Come!'

Simon's terror had brought Thabo face to face with himself. The hatred that had swelled inside him since the beating he'd taken from Dick Davidson had cast him headlong into a private hell. Hatred was still alive inside him and Thabo knew he'd kept it alive himself.

'We're going in Rebecca's car.' Simon tried to pull away from Thabo but he held on to him, peering into his eyes to chase away the flames that he knew still burned there. 'What happened is finished, Simon. It's over and we're going to prove it by going in the car.' Thabo led Simon to the door of his room and the dog loped after them hopefully.

'Don't be so ridiculous, Luke.' Naomi's brittle, arrogant voice reached them as they stepped into the hall. 'What on earth would Simon have to say about it? He's a simpleton.' Her words challenged Thabo as he led Simon quickly past the sitting-room door, the dog following them in arched-back silence. 'He's not fit to run his own life, let alone make a decision like this. Good grief, Simon's an idiot and if you used him against me you'd be laughed out of court.'

Thabo whipped round as Rebecca emerged from the sitting room, catching them at the open front door.

'Go on,' she whispered encouragingly. She'd guessed why Thabo was taking Simon away and she smiled. 'Take the car.' She held out the keys but quite suddenly she doubled up, clutching her abdomen as tearing pain ripped her insides. 'Go on!' She shooed Thabo away with the car keys, trying to hide the fear that shone in her eyes. Rebecca was eight months pregnant and the child inside her fought to be free of the tension that choked it.

'Must I make tea?' Miriam's face appeared around the kitchen door, her voice balanced on a question mark that dared Rebecca to answer 'yes'. 'Out!' she ordered the confused dog as he backed away through the front door with Simon and Thabo. 'Where you go, Thabo?' Miriam switched her attention quickly to the figures disappearing with the dog. 'Simon, Thabo – come back!'

'Tea please, Miriam.' Rebecca smiled and Miriam reacted as she saw the pain in her face for the first time.

'You all right?' Miriam cared more about the tiny human being growing inside Rebecca than she'd ever thought possible, and was suddenly protective. 'Madam must go to her room, lie down. I bring you tea now.'

'Tea for Miss Naomi first.' Rebecca's hand touched her arm gently. 'Please.' She walked carefully towards her bedroom, trying to hide the agony that threatened both her child and herself.

'Don't be so ridiculous – of course it's what my father would have wanted! It's his will, Luke, and you've read it yourself!'

Naomi's shouted words had excluded Luke as Paul's son and they chased Rebecca on her way to the bedroom.

'My father did no more than follow Jacques Beauvilliers' original intentions that Bonne Espérance stay in the family. It's the same as Rebecca's mother did, and there's nothing to argue about. I'm selling my share – I told you,' Naomi continued.

A dragging pain pulled at Rebecca's insides. Her body doubled over and her nails scraped against the brass of the bedpost as she reached for it.

'I don't want Bonne Espérance. I'm not a farmer. It's worthless to me as it is and I need money.'

Rebecca stared down at her feet as water dripped between her legs while Naomi's words attacked her. A large smooth puddle sank slowly into the carpet and she couldn't hear Naomi any longer. Her mind was clinging to the baby that was coming too soon.

'Madam!' Miriam stepped into the bedroom and with a clatter of china, dropped the tea tray she was carrying and ran to Rebecca.

'Don't tell me what I should do, Luke.' Naomi's voice was everywhere. 'You insulted my husband. You treated Dick as if *he* was the black. Good grief, it's because of your behaviour that Dick left me. The whole thing's your fault!'

'Close the door,' Rebecca gasped as the brass bedpost slipped through her sweating hands. Her insides were burning. Searing knives drove angular paths through her back and she whispered as the solid wood door shut out Naomi's words, 'It's the baby!' She tried to draw a deep breath but her body crumpled in agony. The base of her spine was splitting in two and her pelvis pulled wide as her insides prepared to drop. 'My baby!' Her voice clung to the words like a lifeline as she sank to the floor.

One half of Miriam's mind had already run out of the room – for David, for Luke, for doctors – for anyone who could help, but the other half of her mind had stood still in a mud hut in the Transkei. Her mother Sophie was right beside her and it was Miriam herself on the floor. She was crying out in pain as Thabo pushed his way to life before time.

'Breathe, madam.' Miriam leaned over Rebecca, lifting her head off the floor. 'Breathe deep.' She stared into Rebecca's wide empty eyes. 'You must help the baby.' She pushed Rebecca's legs wide, ripping off the soft silk pants that clung to her skin with warm red blood. 'Push! Push!' The words Miriam's mother had called to her blew softly against the terror she felt. She knew how much the child meant to Rebecca and it had been called into the world ahead of time, with the noose of Naomi's words tight round its neck.

'It's coming!' Miriam's voice drove through the pain that gripped Rebecca. Every part of her writhed in agony. Her insides dragged as the baby forced a path into the world. The ceiling spun over her head and the hard wooden floor had turned to jelly underneath her. 'I see it! *Thyala!* Push!' Miriam stared at the tuft of hair that had appeared on the edges of life. 'The baby's coming,' she whispered. '*Thyala!*' She tried to break through the deep silence of Rebecca's pain, her hands held under the child's head. 'Yes,' she encouraged as a slippery infant wriggled free. '*Yes!*' she shouted as quite suddenly it fell into her hands. Tiny pink fingers clawed the air, creased feet kicked the nothingness that surrounded them and Miriam's tears rolled as free as the Tele River as the baby screamed.

'*Sikwakele.*' Her mouth opened in a quiet call of thanks as the tiny round belly rose and fell on a gentle flight of breath. '*Sikwamkefe!*' Miriam welcomed it into the world and, crawling on her elbows and knees, she held the scrap of humanity out to its mother, still tied by a fleshy pink cord. 'It's a girl, madam.' The baby's slippery skin touched Rebecca's cheek as Miriam's voice rang out in song.

'*Uthixo usiphe isopho!* God has given us a gift,' she sang to the world. Her panic had vanished in the face of the newborn child who stroked Rebecca with its breath.

Unaware of the drama being played out behind them on Bonne Espérance, Thabo glanced at Simon as they drove towards Cape Town. Rebecca had often tried to make him drive her Mercedes again but he'd refused – until today. Simon's need to be free of the past had challenged Thabo to cut loose himself, and the car, normally only polished by Simon, was the way to do it.

'You OK?' He glanced over at Simon. A science fiction comic was in his lap, but it was upside down. 'What's the story?' Thabo turned the comic the right way up. 'Is it good?' He tried to keep Simon's mind off Naomi's arrival on Bonne Espérance.

'Don't know.' Simon's voice was as blank as his face as he gazed at the comic book astronaut who hung high over the earth. 'Why you not talk to me about God any more?' he demanded of Thabo, watching him out of the corner of his eye. He'd never understood why Thabo hadn't worn his priest's collar since that day in Soweto but he thought he knew now. 'Is God dead?'

'No. He's just a breath away.' Thabo looked at his hands on the steering wheel. He could see the tension in his own fingers as they gripped it tightly and he made them relax. 'So what do you want to know?'

'About Jesus.'

'What about Jesus?'

'Why they killed Him.'

'I told you before.'

'Tell me again.'

Thabo searched the faith he'd been hiding from: the belief that opened up the fourth dimension to reveal eternity. He'd seen through the veil of flesh and stepped into God's kingdom years before but now he was lost. Thabo knew he had to find a way to tell a story he'd once preached with total conviction. It was the story of God's forgiveness as He reconciled himself to man through His Son, and it was a story Thabo had hung back from until now. Now it confronted his own unforgiveness.

'Right.' Thabo glanced at the comic in Simon's lap. 'You see that man? He's in a spacesuit, huh?' Simon nodded and Thabo cleared his throat. 'What if our bodies are spacesuits?'

'What?' Simon stared at him, his eyes alight with sudden laughter. 'This is me, not a spacesuit.' He prodded his leg and laughed again as he pointed at the astronaut. 'That's a spacesuit.'

'How do you know? Maybe the world's a spacecraft.' Thabo grinned. 'Maybe our bodies are really spacesuits, what do they call it – 'life-support?'

'Then why's he got a spacesuit on?' Simon pointed at the comic astronaut again. 'See,' he called in triumph.

''Cos he's gone to another planet. He's left the world so that's another spacesuit on top of his body spacesuit!'

Collapsing in laughter, Simon banged the comic on his knees in flapping beats of hilarity and Thabo watched him with a smile as he went on.

'Then let's pretend our bodies are spacesuits, and the Bible's the rule book that tells us how they work.'

'What? That's silly. I'm me.' Simon guffawed with laughter once again. 'Me.' He pulled his shirt and kicked his legs. 'This isn't a spacesuit, it's me.'

'That's what he thinks.' Thabo nodded at the comic-book astronaut with a grin. 'He thinks that spacesuit's him too. He polishes it. He washes it. He really likes it. He's got so used to it he's forgotten that his body's inside it and now he thinks the spacesuit's his body.'

'What?' Simon gawped at Thabo. He was totally lost and Thabo wondered if he understood himself. He was preaching the strangest sermon he'd ever preached, but in some curious way it fascinated him and he went on quickly.

'So, the astronaut, he throws the rule book away. *Hamba!* Out! He doesn't understand it, see? It tells him about a body he's forgotten exists 'cos he can't see it under the spacesuit.' Simon watched Thabo cautiously. He knew his friend was as ill-informed about outer space as he was about the parts that made up a car, and, leaning back in his seat, he closed his eyes with a smile. 'Then he turns off the radio,' Thabo went on. 'The voice that keeps giving him orders on the radio doesn't make sense. He thinks he knows best, you see. His spacesuit's fine and he's not listening to anyone talking about the body inside it because he *knows* it doesn't exist.'

'So?' Simon peered at Thabo through one screwed-up eye.

'There's someone in charge back on earth where the astronaut comes from. Well, he knows he's got to do something or the spaceman's body will die inside the spacesuit. He'll get lost, too. But it's a dangerous job, see. Not just anybody can do it. So the boss, he puts his son in a spacesuit just like the man's and he tells him to go and remind the astronaut who he is and where he comes from. He must tell him before the man gets lost and dies.'

Simon opened his other eye. 'Does he believe him?' He didn't hold out much hope for Thabo's story but he was worried about the astronaut.

'*Hayi Khona!*' Thabo shook his head. 'He says he doesn't believe him. The astronaut says, you go away! *Hamba!* He thinks he knows exactly who he is, see. He knows what he's doing.'

'Does he? Does he go?'

'*Hayi Khona.* The son tries to remind him about his body that's inside the spacesuit. He says he mustn't just feed his space suit, he must feed his body inside the spacesuit or it'll die. He says he must turn the radio on again and listen for directions before he gets lost.'

Simon leaned forward in his seat. Thabo's new angle on comic-book stories had caught his attention and he waited for him to go on with renewed interest. 'What then?'

'The astronaut says no. He knows who he is, he says. Like you!' Thabo grinned. 'He knows his spacesuit is his body and it's OK. It's good and shiny. All polished. What's wrong with it?'

'Does he leave him to eat the polish?' Simon hoped he didn't. He didn't want the astronaut to die and he smiled with relief as Thabo shook his head. 'Did the boss' son kill him then?' Thabo shook his head again and Simon stared.

'The astronaut killed the boss' son!' Thabo announced. 'He tore his spacesuit to bits and pieces. He didn't believe he was the boss, you see, because he didn't behave like a boss.' Simon watched Thabo in horror. 'But . . .' Thabo paused, adding drama to his story, 'he was *still* there! He was *still* alive, even though his spacesuit was dead.'

'What?'

'The astronaut just couldn't see him. He didn't believe in bodies any more, remember, so he couldn't even see him. All he could see was spacesuits.'

'Did he kill him back then? If the son was still alive did he kill him?'

'He fed him. He guided him, too. He really wanted to help him, you see, even though he'd tried to kill him.' Thabo shrugged. 'That's why they killed Jesus. But just His spacesuit.' Simon was laughing and the comic book fell apart in his hands as he banged it helplessly on his knee. 'What's wrong now?' Thabo asked, grinning.

'You're stupid, Thabo. Jesus is God's Son so He doesn't need a spacesuit!'

Thabo smiled and then he laughed as his faith bubbled to life inside him. Simon had said words he could only have heard from God.

'And this is me! Ow!' Simon yelled as he pinched himself. 'Hey, why you laughing?'

Thabo couldn't explain why. The Holy Spirit had reached deep to dislodge the boulder of his unforgiveness and once again he was aware of divine reality.

'The baby's going to be fine.' Dr Trueman's presence had brought the white calm of a hospital into the bedroom and he tucked a freshly laundered sheet under Rebecca's chin. 'A little premature, but beautiful. Like her mother.' He turned towards Miriam as she sat in a chair beside the window, nursing the newborn infant in her arms. 'But I don't know what you'd have done without Miriam.'

Her heart bursting with the doctor's words, Miriam gazed down at the child in her arms, pressing her cheek against its face. It was hers. It would always be hers and it was safe.

'I'll be taking you to hospital of course, Mrs Marsden, just to check things out.' The practicality of the physician's words built blocks of calm around Rebecca and she looked at Miriam as she nursed her child.

'Can I see her?' Rebecca's voice was cautious as Miriam held the tiny bundle possessively in her arms. It was as if the baby's life had drained out of her own and Rebecca longed to hold it, to share their lives once again. 'Where's Luke? Does he know yet?' she asked, as Naomi's demands on Bonne Espérance flooded her mind.

'He not know yet, madam.' Miriam's eyes shone a deep black and her face spread in a glorious smile as she laid the newborn child in Rebecca's arms. 'I get master Luke.' She turned to the door, glancing back at Rebecca with another proud smile, but Rebecca was lost in the wonder of the tiny baby that was hers.

Wide and clear, the child's eyes gazed back at her from the depths of a secret knowledge, of the place she'd left. In her face, Rebecca saw a reflection of something so beautiful she could only stare at the miracle that lay in her arms.

'Hullo,' she whispered as tiny fingers curled through her hair and moist warm breath stroked her neck.

'Rebecca?' Luke appeared, looking pale. 'Why didn't someone call me?' Naomi's demands had claimed his attention, holding him back from the birth of their child and he moved to Rebecca quickly, pulling himself free.

'Somebody wouldn't wait.' Rebecca held the child out to him. 'Your daughter.' She smiled, but Luke's face reflected little joy. 'She's ours, Luke.' Rebecca's voice reached out to him but for a split second he held back. He'd seen Anton in the tiny face. The son who'd kept him away from Rebecca in both life and death was in her arms. 'No ghosts, Luke,' Rebecca whispered and Luke's eyes looked only at hers as he took their child in his arms.

442

'Did she tell you her name?' he asked, with a smile.

'Not yet.'

'Tea?' Miriam's voice sang brightly as she stepped back into the room, a freshly laid tray balanced on bosoms held high by pride. 'You want tea?' She looked round at David as he hung back in the doorway nervously. 'What you scared of, master? You must hold your grandchild,' she scolded him with a laugh and, balancing the tray on one hand, she led him to Rebecca. 'You take it, master – like this.' She plonked the tea tray down on a chest of drawers and, tut-tutting with disapproval, she indicated how he should hold his arms. 'Now you show me,' she insisted, before daring to lay the baby in such a trembling cradle. 'Not so high.' She lowered his arms, watching him suspiciously before taking the baby from Luke to lay it in its grandfather's arms. 'Now, you be very careful.'

'Has Naomi gone, Luke?' As Rebecca spoke Miriam turned on her.

'The old master he hold the baby. You be quiet!' To Miriam, grandparents held a position of great respect but still she watched David very carefully. 'Not squeeze. It very new.' Her part in the birth of the child ensured her protection and she nodded as David held it carefully. 'Just look,' she instructed with a proud nod of approval.

'What happened?' Rebecca's voice was quiet and her breath brushed against Luke's cheek as she reached for the only answer she needed now. 'I have to know, please.'

'We're going to lose Bonne Espérance.' Luke's grip on Rebecca tightened as he felt her pull back from his words.

CHAPTER TWENTY-THREE

It was three weeks since the birth of Rebecca's child and Simon studied his reflection in the bonnet of the Mercedes very carefully, examining in detail the new line that had appeared in the corner of his eye. His face shone as the car did. No spot of grease detracted from the old Mercedes' perfection and it remained a symbol of hope.

But Simon didn't understand all the other changes that had come about on Bonne Espérance. He knew nothing of Naomi's intentions to sell her share of the wine farm over everyone's head and he'd decided it was the birth of Rebecca's child that had made such a difference.

'Go to sleep, little girl. Shh, Thalitha.' As David's voice sang towards him, Simon looked up from his reflection. Being a grandfather had changed his uncle completely. David sat under the shade of the old oak tree, on the swinging seat Luke had made for him, and his foot rocked a wicker cradle as a lullaby rolled on singsong soprano notes.

'She doesn't like it. She not sleeping, she screaming,' Simon told him. He'd never before heard such bellows of anger from anything so small, and his mind reeled at the thought of what Thalitha would be like full grown. Even the old dog had covered his ears with his paws and moaned as he hid in the shade of the car. 'You want me to get Rebecca?' Simon asked hopefully. He knew David wasn't too familiar with babies. He'd heard him talk to Thalitha as if she understood every word and then he'd answered his own questions in his new grandfather voice. Becoming a grandparent seemed to Simon to be one step from madness and quickly he'd decided to give it a miss. 'I'll call Rebecca.' Knowing she was the only one who could quieten her child, he ran to the house before David could object. Rebecca would disappear with it into her bedroom, he thought, undoing the front of her clothes as she went and then there'd come a glorious silence. Simon had often considered asking Miriam what it was that Rebecca kept in her shirt, in case he could pass the tip on to David, but he'd resisted. The day he'd asked where the baby had come from, Miriam had pushed him out, tut-tutting and dismissing the subject forever.

'You find out when *you* have a baby!' Her words had silenced his curiosity and he'd prayed fervently that babies weren't catching.

'Where's Rebecca?' As Simon stepped into the hallway with Zanu beside him he instinctively leaned back on his heels, keeping the curly rubber imprints of his soles off Miriam's polished floor.

'Outside.' She shooed him away with a shake of her polishing cloth and the giant dog slid backwards on folding legs. 'You not hear the baby yell? You deaf, boy? Tell Grandad to call Rebecca!'

The arrival of the baby had changed David's name as well as his voice and Simon shook his head in amazement. With the dog loping beside him he moved out towards the cellars and the only answer he knew.

'You want your baby, Rebecca?' Stepping into the cool dark room, Simon held his breath against the smell of fermenting grapes. He hated the cellars. The great wooden vats that lined the walls, unused and neglected, depressed him; and the enormous steel vats stared down at him, promising to explode at any moment. He'd never understood why such a dark and forbidding place fascinated Rebecca and he'd decided it was just one more secret best ignored.

Rebecca was deep in conversation with the wine-maker, Neil Sanderson, and such a gloom hung over them, that Simon stood back at the door rather than move into it.

'Your baby's crying.' His voice was thin as he held his nose between two squeezing fingers. 'You go fetch her from Uncle David, Rebecca.' He ducked away quickly, making for the only place in which he felt safe. 'Phew!' he breathed a sigh of relief as he reached the car and climbed inside it, the dog crumpling into a heaving heap on the seat beside him.

'But I don't see how we can keep Bonne Espérance, Luke. There's no way we can match the offer Naomi's had for her share and you heard what Neil said about the vineyards. We can't manage any more.' Rebecca cradled Thalitha in her arms, unbuttoning her blouse as she sat on the bed. The baby's tiny pink mouth clasped her nipple and its cheeks shivered as it sucked excitedly. Looking down at the small face that pressed its nose flat against her breast, Rebecca was covered with a peace that denied the very real threat Naomi held over their future. Like the country itself, Bonne Espérance had been claimed by the greed of outsiders, and as yet no way forward had been found.

'Stay with me, Luke.' Rebecca patted the bed as he moved to go. 'Do

445

you like her hairstyle?' She smiled, stroking the baby's fine black hair so that it stood on end in an Indian head-dress. 'We could always go and live in England.' Rebecca's voice was cheerful, denying her dread of ever leaving Africa again. 'I'm sure we could make a go of it there. We could start another shop and Samuel . . .'

'How long is it since I told you how beautiful you are?' Luke propped his chin on her shoulder and gazed into her eyes, refusing to be drawn into a future he'd already rejected. Rebecca's body felt warm and soft to his touch and everything about her had mellowed with Thalitha's birth. Motherhood had made her even more vulnerable and Luke knew he couldn't protect her from what frightened her most. Running his finger down the full curve of her breast as their child drank, he whispered, 'I want you.'

'Right now?' Rebecca laughed as Luke wrapped her and his child in his arms. She knew the loss of Bonne Espérance was something he hadn't dared examine too closely, any more than she had herself, avoiding the country's slow fall into anarchy as well.

Under the new tricameral Parliament that once again had excluded blacks from the voters' roll, violence still stalked the townships. Though President Botha had discarded many forms of petty apartheid, his promised reforms had come to a halt and, challenging the world with a wagging finger, he'd demanded the right to govern without interference. But the economy was on the verge of collapse. A State of Emergency had given the police far-reaching powers as they held a heavy lid on the turmoil, but still the country groaned under the weight of bodies piled high in mortuaries. Archbishop Tutu had risked his life to save a man from the fiery hell of a 'necklace', crying out against the mindless killing that had taken captive his people's hearts, but nobody had listened. A sense of helplessness covered the nation, but still Thabo preached the victory of the Cross.

' "He was wounded for our transgressions! He was bruised for our iniquities! The chastisement of our peace was upon Him and by His stripes we are healed!" '

Isaiah's words rang out from the pulpit of his tin church in Langa but they too fell on ears that were deaf to God's voice. The collapse of Communism in Europe and the rest of Africa had revealed the suffering it had brought to millions of people as it imprisoned them in the name of freedom, yet Communism was still being preached in South Africa.

Luke didn't understand how his friend held on to his faith when events denied the very existence of God, but in many ways he envied Thabo. He wanted him to be right.

'We'll find a way here, Rebecca.' Covering her bare shoulder with kisses, Luke clung to the love that Paul's unexpected death had threatened, as it threatened Bonne Espérance.

'But perhaps we should leave, Luke. Maybe it's time to move on.' Rebecca filled her words with hope she didn't feel and lifted the baby off her breast. 'I'll write and tell Sammy what's happened, anyway. Maybe he'll have an idea.' Though Rebecca's mind held back from leaving Africa for the low skies of London, she tried to encourage Luke. 'I could show you my old haunts in England.' Ignoring what she'd said, Luke turned her face to his and his lips moved to hers. Rebecca's mouth opened and her body surged with the passion his touch always roused. Love-making had never lost its wonder as their bodies touched but she knew he had yet to face the truth. 'We have to admit we can't keep Bonne Espérance, Luke.'

Luke stood up and went over to the open window. A gentle breeze blew a curtain against his face as his eyes passed over the miles of sloping vineyards. He remembered the day he'd been dragged away from Bonne Espérance by his mother and he knew that once again Estelle was behind Naomi's moves to destroy them, but he no longer had weapons to fight back.

'Doesn't that mean anything any more?' He turned round and indicated the old brass key that hung above their bed in glowing pride. Taking it down and holding it out in his open palm he looked at her. 'Do you remember what you said about this key, that it would keep us together forever on Bonne Espérance?'

'Of course I do, Luke. But we were children then.'

'And when you threw it away, Macaroni gave it back, you said?'

'Yes. But Luke . . .'

'Macaroni was right! Wasn't he?'

Looking down at the sleeping baby in her arms, Rebecca wanted to cry. She knew that taking Luke away from Africa would be like removing the salt from the sea but she could see no option. The key was no more than a relic of the past – an old piece of brass without the power to change anything.

'I'm not joining the "chicken run"!' Luke's voice was firm as he knelt in front of her, his eyes gleaming with determination. What had begun as a slow trickle of Europeans leaving South Africa for more stable shores, had turned into a flood, graffiti reminding the last person leaving to turn out the lights. 'People like Naomi aren't running away because of apartheid, Rebecca. They're running because apartheid might *end* – because we might be forced to live together as one nation. Will we leave for the same reason?'

As Rebecca shook her head a single tear rolled down her cheek, dropping on to the baby's face. 'Then what will we do, Luke? When we lose Bonne Espérance, what then?'

For a long moment Luke watched her. But he had no answer to her question and, moving away, he hung the key back on the wall without a word.

Samuel Netherby's eyes pierced their way through the darkness of his old shop, as if searching for something he'd lost in its past. The moment the old tailor had sold *Glad Rags*, he'd restored the building in the King's Road to its former dignity as a dusty bespoke tailor and the drunken mannequin was back, leaning against the wall in a pure wool suit. In his hand Samuel held a letter from Rebecca and he didn't know why it disturbed him so deeply. In it she talked of her baby, Thalitha, of Simon, Zanu and the aging Mercedes. Joy bubbled in every word, even as she told him they were losing Bonne Espérance, that Naomi was selling her shares in the estate and they couldn't afford to buy them. But Samuel didn't believe that joy. Her letter said that they were considering coming to live in London and, although it was something he'd often wished for he knew it was wrong. Despite the horrifying violence in South Africa's black townships that blazed across his television screen every night, still the old tailor knew that Rebecca and Luke must never leave their country.

Calls for the release of the jailed black leader, Nelson Mandela, were more intense than they had been for the son of God, and in his efforts to discover the truth, Samuel Netherby had studied the country's history carefully. He'd read Mandela's speech, made as he was sentenced to life imprisonment on Robben Island, and he'd found him to be a man of courage. But Samuel Netherby had read of the courage of many white South Africans, too. He'd discovered unknown heroes who'd faced the Government's wrath as they stood on the side of the oppressed. Churchmen like Beyers Naude, Michael Cassidy and Nico Smith. Young doctors like Wendy Orr, who'd risked everything as she challenged police brutality, and Ivan Thoms, who'd gone to jail rather than wear an army uniform, putting at risk the work he did in black squatter camps.

The old tailor had also learned of Britain's part in the introduction of apartheid: the hideous truth of 1906 – a time when black African hopes of freedom had been crushed by colonial troops. Under their leader, Bambatha, blacks had resorted to armed insurrection against British rule and Bambatha's head had been hacked off in barbaric reply. Three thousand Africans and thirty whites had died in the bloodbath and Bambatha's rebellion had been halted as British troops held his severed head high in triumph.

Now, in his late eighties, the old tailor still resisted the pressures of an

448

apparent economic miracle in his country. Although the square footage of his London shop had become more valuable than gold, he held tightly to his independence and refused to sell. Worship of the Gross National Product had evaded him as he resisted offers of retirement with a bagful of paper money for company. Samuel Netherby had come to the end of a life lived independent of the times, and he challenged them still as he set about buying a future for Rebecca and Luke.

'It's a farm in Africa and I want to buy it.'

'A game park, you mean?'

'I said what I meant, mate. A farm.' Samuel watched the young lawyer, James Morgan, very carefully. He'd taken over the firm of financial advisers that he and Rebecca had once used for *Glad Rags*. 'It's in South Africa.' Pushing his finger under his collar, Samuel loosened his tie and smiled. 'You got a problem with that?' he enquired of the youth who'd taken over his country on a binge of borrowed money.

'South Africa's not a country I'd advise you to invest in.' James Morgan leaned back in his seat.

'Why? Been there, have you?' Samuel Netherby tried to hold his bubbling anger in place as he smiled in apparent surprise.

'I wouldn't set foot in it!' James Morgan's self-righteousness swelled and quickly Samuel Netherby pricked it.

'Then how you planning to return what you owe the blacks, mate? Have to make quite a few trips to cart the Albert Hall back brick by brick!'

Though Samuel Netherby hadn't come any closer to an understanding of Rebecca's country himself, despite all his reading, he understood the hypocrisy of his own, and with a flourish he put his pen to a contract that purchased Naomi's share of Bonne Espérance. He smiled as he paved the way to the old folk's home he'd always shunned.

'Like a drop of the old vino, do you?' Samuel Netherby glanced up at James Morgan with a twinkle, completing his signature with a fancy 'Y'.

'Not South African, I can assure you.'

'Hah! You could be drinking "vin crocodillo" without knowing it by the time I've finished, matey!' Poking a full stop after his name, Samuel Netherby gave up a lifetime's independence as he bought Naomi's shares in Bonne Espérance for Luke and Rebecca.

At a road-block just outside Crossroads in Cape Town, Lydia's son Joe Liebenberg was stopped and turned back by the police. Civil war raged in the sprawling black squatter camp as the older generation of Africans formed themselves into groups of 'fathers'. Armed with *pangas* and knobkerries, they roamed the streets to hunt down militant young 'comrades', and peace remained as elusive as Government attempts to move the squatters on.

Though the media had been banned from the area with enforced censorship laws, Joe was determined to gain access. He'd heard rumours that the anger of the elders, whose lucrative 'protection' business had been hijacked by the radical youth of the UDF, was being fuelled from the outside. Tales of white involvement in the violence were rife, but as yet no one had come forward with evidence. It was that evidence Joe was after.

Control of Crossroads had been taken over by *Amaqabane* – young comrades who'd heeded the ANC's call to burn schools rather than attend them. The accusation of being an informer led to a 'necklace' death, handed down on parents by radicalised youths as children seized power. Zwelakhe Sisulu, son of the jailed ANC leader Walter Sisulu, had stood out against the 'comrades'. He'd told them intimidation was wrong, that power didn't lie in the hands of kangaroo courts, but neither the 'fathers' nor 'comrades' had listened and civil war raged.

As Joe crept through the bushes that skirted Crossroads, even the air was tense with the expectation of sudden death. A pall of smoke hung over raggedy lines of burnt-out shacks and among the shadows that lay heavily between them, he saw someone dart for cover. Only a dog's persistent barks reminded him he was treading among the ashes of people's lives, and an ear-piercing whistle shredded the silence.

Joe swung round, but all that confronted him was a puff of curling smoke among dying embers. 'Come out and talk to me!' It was as if a ghost had passed by and, pulling his camera out of his jacket, Joe tried to concentrate as nerves stretched his skin taut. He peered through the camera lens, knowing he was surrounded by unseen people – invisible men with white headbands that revealed their loyalty to the 'fathers'. The *witdoekies* were somewhere near and somewhere else were the comrades – PAC youths who chanted 'One settler one bullet!' as their eyes burned with hatred.

'I want to help,' Joe called towards shapes that melted into a curtain of blue smoke. 'I want to understand what's going on – tell me what's happening!' A hail of stones rained down on him from behind a burning shack and he swung round as a slippery shadow darted away. 'Unless people know what's wrong here, nobody can help! Will you talk to me?'

'Leave, white man. We don't want your kind here.' Though the voice that had called him from the shadows was Xhosa, the sentiment was not, and Joe turned towards it very carefully.

'Who are you? Come into the light and talk!' Though Joe's words was filled with bravura his bones had chilled. His legs had lost their strength and his body shook. He'd sensed a closing circle of unseen people but he couldn't move. Forcing himself at last to break free of the terror that paralysed him, he lifted his camera to his eye and the glare of the camera flash lit the bushes. A black man was moving towards him. With his hand raised high he held a bloodied *panga*, ready to swing it down as he ran straight for Joe. With bloodcurdling Xhosa screams, the hideous face of death loomed in front of him and Joe held his finger firmly on the camera trigger.

He didn't see the gleam of the blade as it sliced down on his head. He didn't hear the obscenities that poured from the mouth of his attacker. All Joe saw as he fell to the ground was a smudge of black paint. It had spread on his skin as a black hand held him down while another sliced a *panga* through his neck.

Andre Bothma's stomach emptied itself into the rusty tin can at his feet. He could still see Joe's eyes. Joe was looking up at him in puzzlement as the *panga* came down on his neck and in those dying eyes, Andre had recognised himself.

The black paint on his face stung as he rubbed his eyes in an effort to wipe away the image that haunted him. His attack on the white journalist had been scored by the police as a 'vigilante hit' and Andre had escaped the scene quickly. Running back to the small room he kept in the single men's hostel in Langa, he'd tried to clean himself up. He hadn't noticed the African child who watched him through a crack in the door.

The boy's eyes had been round in amazement as the black paint peeled off Andre Bothma's face. Andre had done what he himself had often dreamed of doing – he'd washed the blackness away to become white. Quickly the child ran off to report the magic he'd witnessed, and the fact of Cop Bothma's involvement in the killing of the white journalist was quickly confirmed by others.

But Andre was immune. Doing only what he believed to be right, he felt no concern at being identified. It was war. He'd killed an enemy of the people to save his country.

Andre Bothma had seen many middle-aged Africans die at the hands of their own children and he'd stepped in to fight back. Uneducated and unemployed, the youth chanted Communist slogans while politics brutalised their minds, completing the work apartheid had begun. Andre believed firmly that killing the few to save the lives of many was the only way. As Joe had believed apartheid was wrong, so Andre believed it was not only right, but God's will: black people needed white rule to protect them from themselves, and he'd never wondered if his beliefs had come from the slow drip of brainwashing. Like Thys Bothma's mother, a century and a half earlier, Andre believed the black people were his God-given responsibility and nothing would change his mind.

Andre Bothma's beliefs had been passed down from the mouths of his forefathers for generations. Preached from the pulpits of the Dutch Reformed Churches, they had become a part of his life.

Ever since the day that Constance had disappeared so inexplicably from the storehouse of his feelings, Simon had reached a better understanding of death. The Great Dane, Zanu, had also died, his soft brown eyes fixed on Simon as his breath slowly ran out. Now, on the day of Joe's funeral, Simon remembered what Thabo had told him then. He'd said that Constance and Zanu would be with God. That God was only a breath away. That beyond the skin of the spacesuit Simon wore, was God. He was reached through Christ's Cross as death freed man from the shadows of this world into the reality of eternity.

But Joe's death had devastated the entire family and Simon was no different. As Lydia, Stan and Tarcie stood in the small Luderitz graveyard with Luke and Rebecca, their grief was surrounded by oceans of sand and silence. The tragedy that was their country had reached out to touch them even in exile and Simon wished he could explain to Tarcie what Thabo had told him. But Tarcie was beautiful. Even though she was crying she was more beautiful than anyone he'd ever seen and he watched her silently as she stood beside her brother's grave.

The funeral service was in German and although Simon didn't understand a word the Lutheran minister said, he knew for sure that Joe did. He wanted to tell that to Tarcie, to comfort her as he'd once needed comfort himself. Luke's hand was firm and reassuring under Rebecca's arm, understanding that her mind was back in a Cape Town house with Lydia's small son. Lydia's apparently calm denial of her son's death puzzled Rebecca. Watching her cousin now, as Lydia stood with Tarcie and her husband beside Joe's grave, Rebecca sensed a new remoteness in her. It was as if Joe's death had forever stilled her life. As if, swallowed alive by the miles of sand and icy seas of her place of exile, Lydia had died herself.

A cold wind whipped at the dunes that surrounded them and spirals of fine sand danced whirling circles across the endless horizon.

'Lydia hasn't cried at all.' As Rebecca spoke, Luke glanced at Lydia, reacting to the coldness that had touched his wife. Standing beside Stan, a man whose inner being had been sucked out of him like marrow from a bone, Lydia was as dead as her son.

'Justice will be done, Lydia,' Luke told her quietly.

'Will it?' Lydia's voice was as cold as her eyes as she turned to him. 'I want that man dead.' Her mind was filled only with an image of Andre Bothma, the cousin she'd once defended to Rebecca. A man whom her son, Joe, had tried to impress over a lunch table when he was a small boy, the man who'd killed that child and walked away a hero. Holding her head high, Lydia moved out of the graveyard that hid Joe without another word, her husband and daughter following behind like lost shadows.

Time had stood still on Bonne Espérance since the day of Joe's funeral and Luke had spent every moment of it trying to bring about the justice he'd promised Lydia. But nothing had come of his efforts. Rebecca had given birth to a son in the months that had passed justice by and she'd buried herself in her family. She knew that Joe's murder had begun inside that family on Bonne Espérance, and across the divide of a nation the Beauvilliers inheritance had reared its head once again.

This is the key our father's ancestors brought to this land when they ran away from the Catholics in France. It's the key to the home that belonged to the Beauvilliers in Nîmes and it's a house that we will claim one day as our right.

Rebecca read to her daughter from Emily's old diaries. They sat in the shade of the oak tree while her small son slept in a cradle beside them and the constant buzz of a million crickets echoed loudly against the mountains. The diaries were delicate and crumbling with age, their contents apparently confined to history. But Rebecca knew the story they told must be remembered by her children – the next generation.

We swear this day to wipe out the stain of our father's son, the half-caste boy, Jean Jacques!

As Rebecca read Emily's remembered words of Clara's oath, made to her younger sisters over the family Bible a century and a half before, they covered every part of Bonne Espérance with the tread of a visiting ghost.

'What key?' Thalitha's small voice sang through the crickets' scratchy chorus and she tugged at her mother's skirts. She didn't understand why Clara wanted to kill her brother, Jean Jacques. He hadn't done anything bad enough to die. 'What he do?' Thalitha eyed her own brother suspiciously and, picking her nose, she watched a bobble bounce as it hung from an elastic thread on her finger. 'What key?'

'Use a hanky!' Rebecca smacked her daughter's hand and wiped it clean, the practicalities of teaching manners overtaking the promised murder of Jean Jacques for a moment.

'It's mine!' The tiny girl looked on in horror as her mother squashed her prized possession with a hanky, but curiosity about the story got the better of her and, with her mind locked on the story in Emily's diary, she forgot the slippery yo-yo she'd found in her nose. 'Tell me 'bout the key!'

'Rebecca!' Simon's voice hollered from the front door of the house and Thalitha tugged at her mother's skirts with renewed demands for information. 'There's a man, Rebecca. He's from the newspapers and he wants to see you.' As if giving the words flight, Simon waved his arms with each one to hurry her inside.

Chased outside to take care of the children while Rebecca talked to the visitor, David and Fezile sat together on the swinging seat under the oak tree. It was Fezile who had brought the truth of Joe's murder to Bonne Espérance. Determined that the family should know it wasn't a black man but the white cop, Andre Bothma who was responsible, Fezile had arrived at Bonne Espérance frightened and exhausted. Being in danger from vigilantes, police and comrades. Luke had insisted Fezile stay on with them and a curious friendship had developed between the two old men.

Watching Thalitha without comment as she poured sand over her sleeping brother's face in an effort to find out when he'd stop breathing, the old men, one white one black, pondered the reasons the young journalist had called on Rebecca. Not much happened in the slow march to the end of their days and together they enjoyed their moment of puzzlement to the full.

'What do you think?' David rocked backwards and forwards on the seat that swung them in and out of deep shade. Do you know why?' He turned to Fezile with a slow twist of his head, his eyes puzzling as Fezile's empty mouth pushed forward in loss. 'Didn't he say he was from the newspaper?' David tried to reassure himself he'd heard correctly, his finger squeaking a waxy circle in his ear to make sure he heard now.

'Mmm.' Fezile hadn't yet grown accustomed to sharing a swinging seat with a white man, let alone being asked his opinion, so he handed the question back to David with a smile. 'Why you think?' A small nod of Fezile's head gave David credit, as a white man, for knowing the answer better than he. Then Fezile's mouth dropped open as wide as David's and he studied David's teeth, wishing he'd persevered with the ones Thabo had bought him. But they were locked away in a small box and left to Thabo in his will. Fezile was determined the teeth wouldn't end up in the undertaker's bin.

'It's probably about that Andre Bothma again.' David nodded to himself. Both men had long since given up hope of hearing that Luke's efforts to have Andre charged with Joe's murder had succeeded.

'Look, Grandad,' Thalitha interrupted and the two old men stared at the small mound of sand that popped empty bubbles over the baby's nose.

'There, there, there.' Laying the baby over his shoulder David patted it on its back as Fezile calmly picked sandballs from its nostrils.

'Why did you do that, child?'

454

'Clara did,' Thalitha shrugged and David placed the now screaming baby back in its cradle as Fezile wiped the sand off his fingers on the sleeve of David's jacket.

'Won't be any different news from usual.' David turned to his friend as they sat down again. 'What do you think?' he shouted over the baby's rage.

'No different.' Fezile shook his head in agreement. Both men knew that Luke's attempts to get justice through constant publicity would prove useless. Though the film in Joe's camera had clearly revealed his attacker was not black, Andre had remained untouched.

'Andre Bothma's been charged with the murder of Joe Liebenberg, Mrs Marsden!' Rebecca remained silent as the young journalist gave her the news she had never expected to hear. 'What do you think of that? Your husband's got the justice he was after. Andre Bothma's going to be charged in a court of law!'

'I heard you.' Rebecca's voice was quiet and she turned away, wondering why she suddenly felt so empty. 'Now it suits them, they're making a scapegoat out of Andre – is that what you mean by justice?' She turned back, observing the young journalist who could himself have been Joe; his belief in the rule of law not yet floundering on the rocks of South African reality. 'Will he be found guilty? Maybe that's the question we'll have to ask when the all-white court tries Andre.'

Gazing out of the window, Rebecca watched her small daughter as she pushed the swinging seat with shrieks of glee. The two old men chuckled their delight and her small son, Michael, slept. The world seemed at peace, but still fear nagged at Rebecca's consciousness.

'P. W. is talking about releasing Mandela as well. Did you know that?'

'On what conditions?' Rebecca wanted to react to the hope she heard in the young man's voice, but couldn't. There'd been talk of releasing Nelson Mandela many times before. The world's most famous prisoner had been offered freedom if he would renounce violence, but time and again he'd refused. With each passing day the Government had dug its heels in deeper and the aging black prisoner had taken another step closer to martyrdom.

'Don't you think it's possible we're running out of time? Out of conditions? Black or white?' Rebecca knew she was crushing the young man's hopes for the future of his country but she went on. 'Maybe it's too late for everyone – not just Andre Bothma.'

It was too late for Rebecca. As she'd read the family history to Thalitha she'd known it was still unfolding and an old key locked them all inside it.

*

Lydia stared at the woman who sat across from her in the sitting room of Bonne Espérance. In her early sixties, Andre Bothma's mother wore drab clothes, worn thin by constant washing. Her fingers knotted one through the other as she spoke in a heavy Afrikaans accent and her face was drawn, her lips dry, held slightly apart as she breathed.

'I can only beg you. Please, help my son.'

Lynette Bothma could feel the sticky warmth of sweat on the palms of her hands and she pressed them down on her skirt. She was shaking. From the soles of her feet to the top of her head, her body trembled as she pleaded with the only person who might yet save her son from the gallows.

Several years had passed since Andre had killed Joe, and suddenly the country had moved in a new direction. 'I know what I ask.' Lynette Bothma's voice dropped to a whisper, her words slipping out from somewhere deep within her. They hid her son among hopes that faded with each moment and she knew they needed no translation. 'Please. Help Andre!' Her head hung forward but the curve of her neck remained rigid. 'Don't let them hang my son!' The tears Andre's mother had tried to hold back from Lydia broke free, covering her cotton skirt in spreading circles of emotion.

Though nobody had expected Andre to be convicted, quite suddenly he'd been sentenced to hang and all appeals for clemency rejected. 'My son did only what they said – what they asked of him. You're his last hope and I beg you to help him.'

'They told him to kill Joe?' Lydia's voice was icy and her face a cool mask of contempt. 'Where were your tears when my son died, Mrs Bothma, when my son was murdered by yours? When your son brought a *panga* down on Joe's neck, were you crying then?' Lydia pushed herself out of her chair and walked away from the woman who'd hauled Joe's murder back into the present. Standing tensely beside the window, Lydia saw nothing. She didn't see Rebecca outside the house with the children. She didn't see David and Fezile as they stood further away on the edge of the vineyards, gazing silently towards the mountains. From opposite ends of South Africa's divide two old men had discovered one another through tragedy. It still played out in the house behind them, but Lydia had found only renewed hatred.

'Would you be here now asking my forgiveness if your son had got away with killing mine – if Andre hadn't been charged, found guilty and sentenced to death?' Lydia's voice rose on a note of hysteria and she swung round on the woman who'd pleaded with her. 'Where were you when they buried Joe? When Andre wore a hero's crown on his head while his Fascist friends cheered? Did you come to me with your tears then? Did you need my forgiveness then, Mrs Bothma? No! I cannot forgive you or your son! Never!' The sorrow that Lydia had held back for so long broke as she screamed, 'My son is dead, and you ask me to help yours? You dare ask me to give you Andre's life while Joe lies in a grave? Get out! *Get out of here!*'

As Lydia's voice raced through the house and across the cobbled courtyard outside, a crack ran the length of Rebecca's spine. She'd heard those cries somewhere before. They were recorded in Emily's diaries and they were a part of the air they breathed now.

Andre Bothma was due to be hanged the following morning and Rebecca knew his broken neck would never ease the pain that screamed from the house.

'My son's life is in your hands. Please help him,' Lynette Bothma pleaded. 'I beg you!'

'I want him dead.'

The chill of Lydia's bitterness surrounded Rebecca and she pulled her own small son close to her and held him.

'Will breaking my son's neck bring yours back?' Lynette's scream followed Lydia's and Rebecca turned to the house quickly.

'Come, Thalitha,' she called to her daughter as she sat playing further away.

'I'm busy.' Thalitha didn't look up from the tiny black ant she studied in cross-eyed fascination as she tried to avoid the pain screaming from the house.

'I said, come here!' Rebecca's voice echoed the tension and Thalitha turned to her mother in amazement. She'd seen the thin Afrikaans woman arrive earlier and she'd watched her Great Aunt Lydia tense as they'd met. 'Come here at once, Thalitha!'

'No!' Thalitha screamed and Rebecca's hand clipped across her face. 'I hate you! I hate you!' Her pride stung to shame, the small girl stamped angrily on the ant she'd examined with such fascination a moment before.

The emotions that charged the atmosphere had exploded and she wanted only to be alone with Simon. No matter what, she knew Simon would be happy. He'd take her hand in his and, like a top with legs, he'd drag her away to a place where a small girl could enquire about spiders, chameleons and ants. Simon would lead her into a world that paid no attention to grown-up anger, or do diaries that told stories of the same pain she felt today.

'What happened was not an accident, Mrs Bothma.' Lydia's high-pitched words reached from the house again, snatching at Thalitha's fleeing figure. Lydia's need for vengeance had found expression and she hurled it at Mrs Bothma. 'Andre painted himself black. He pretended to be black and he murdered my son.' Her need for revenge had been touched by a woman with whom she'd never wanted to come face to face, and now it was uncontrollable. 'Do you think I wanted any of this to happen? I didn't *want* my son killed, I didn't *want* yours to hang – but now I do!'

'Please no. You can stop it. *Please.*'

Through the sudden silence that filled the room Lydia stared at Lynette Bothma. Her eyes were blinded by the tears she'd held back since the day of Joe's death. Though years had passed, her bitterness hadn't and Lynette Bothma was no more than a glimmering reminder of her loss.

'You told me your son wanted peace in our land.' Lynette's emotion flowed on her words as she still reached out to touch Lydia's heart. 'Your son stood for justice. You said Joe wanted to help the ones who were hurting.'

'Yes.'

'So did mine!'

Lynette Bothma had spelt out the misunderstanding of a nation and Miriam stood outside the door of the sitting room with a tea tray in her hands, but she didn't go in. Beyond the closed door lay the pain of centuries. Of black mothers who'd lost sons without number.

'Leave it, Miriam,' Rebecca whispered as she entered the house, touching the soft black of her arm to calm her.

'It not good, madam.' Shaking her head slowly, Miriam went back to the kitchen. The tray was immaculately set and the delicate silver spoons rattled nervously. 'She must forgive, madam. She must.' Miriam's plump back disappeared through the kitchen door and the words of Emily's diary jumped back into Rebecca's mind.

Forgiveness is God's greatest gift.

But forgiveness was nowhere on Bonne Espérance that day. Lydia's heart had hardened to a degree Rebecca couldn't have imagined possible and she moved quietly past the sitting room, needing to be alone, to understand her place in a family still torn apart by its beginnings. Then Rebecca stopped. The sitting-room door had opened and the fleeting shadow of Lynette Bothma ran out of the house.

'Don't go!' Rebecca ran after her. 'There must still be hope, Mrs Bothma,' she lied.

'Not for Andre.' Looking round as Rebecca's hand on her arm, gently held her back, Lynette Bothma's words were quiet, but then she lifted her head, looking directly into Rebecca's eyes.

'If it had been her son, if her boy had murdered mine, I too would want him dead.'

Only Rebecca had seen Lydia standing in the sitting-room doorway and as Andre's mother walked on through the front door, Lydia ran after her.

'Come back, please!' Lydia's cry lifted towards the dark thatch on the roof as she reached out to her enemy. *'Come back! Please!'*

A black hood dropped over Andre's eyes and his mind spun with the terror that sang in the whispered voices around him. The image of a young man with a *panga* slicing his neck danced in the blackness; words danced in his head too.

Joe Liebenberg's mother has appealed against your death sentence, Bothma.

But the prison governor's words had been followed by others the following morning.

The appeal's been turned down.

Now, one hour later, Andre's life stood in front of him like a closed book and he was wrapped in its covers. Wrapped in the black folds of death's hood, he waited for his neck to be broken by the country he had served so loyally.

'Is there anything you want to say?'

Andre could think of nothing and all he could do was breathe. But he wanted to shout. To shout his misunderstanding out loud as death coiled over his head in a hangman's rope. Terror clung to him. Fear of forever falling. Of snapping free of life as his neck broke to hurl him face to face with a God he no longer knew. Andre Bothma knew nothing any more. The wood on which he stood had juddered in a moment that never came to an end.

CHAPTER TWENTY-FOUR

With the radio playing quietly at their feet, David and Fezile were sound asleep on the swinging seat under the oak tree. The voice of the newly appointed president, F. W. de Klerk, was drowned by their snores. Spurts of released breath spluttered through Fezile's wide empty mouth and David's lips hissed a slow leak in reply. It was 2 February 1990, and President de Klerk spoke words that promised to change the course of the country's future, but the white walls of the house stood still and silent, its shutters closed as Bonne Espérance dozed.

Only Rebecca's two children and Simon were awake. Out of the shade they'd been told to share with their grandfather and Fezile, the children sat under the glare of a burning sun, watching a chameleon as it chewed on a grasshopper.

'Ugh!' Rebecca's small son, Michael, backed away as the grasshopper's last green leg disappeared into a smiling, wide mouth. 'Mummy!' he cried out in horror, his feet turning him in a terrified circle as the chameleon's eyes swivelled in satisfaction. Michael's proud two and a half years had vanished in the face of a grasshopper-eating monster and he wanted to run.

'He's got to eat, silly.' Thalitha held her brother back by his pants and his short legs ploughed the air uselessly as Simon ran towards them from the car. 'You eat chickens, don't you. Do you think they like it?' Thalitha turned to Simon in frustration as he reached them. 'Tell him, Simon. Go on, tell him!'

As Simon explained the chameleon's eating habits, President de Klerk talked of a new dispensation, of building a country in which there would be a universal franchise, ensuring a place in the sun for everyone, regardless of race. The President's words called for an end to centuries of apartheid under British and Afrikaner rule, but they passed Bonne Espérance by.

Missed by sleeping adults, they were ignored by the children, who listened only to Simon.

'One tribe was losing the war, see?' Simon's eyes were wide, his voice filled with the danger his story promised. 'The chief, the one that was losing, he send a message with the chameleon to the chief who was winning. "Tell him I give in. Hands up – you win!"' Simon stuck his hands in the air and his head hung in defeat. 'But ...' he straightened an accusing finger at the chameleon and its protruding eyes turned in searching circles. Careless of the myth Simon spread about it, it hunted only for another grasshopper.

'He walk too slow, like this.' Howling with laughter, the children watched as Simon's right foot hovered in the air before the left tugged itself free. 'The chameleon he go so slow, the enemy kill the chief before he get there! And when the chief die ...' Simon fixed the children with an intense and meaningful stare '... he curse the chameleon *for ever*!' Ending his story with a smile, Simon folded his arms proudly across his chest. 'That's why he eat grasshoppers now.'

'That's silly.' Thalitha groaned her disgust at Simon's conclusion. 'He eats grasshoppers 'cos their legs are nice and crunchy.'

'No!' Michael shouted.

'What was that?' David awoke with a start. He'd gone to sit outside with Fezile for a special reason, but now he couldn't remember it. Sleep still dragged him back to the warm comfort of its arms but an Afrikaans voice on the radio prodded him.

'Why did we bring the radio out here?' David nudged Fezile and the swing shook against its chains.

'What?' Fezile was surprised to find he was alive after the plummeting dive through sleep into which he'd been nudged. 'What you want?' He peered at David, wondering why he was looking at the radio so intently.

The country and the world had been waiting to hear President de Klerk's speech and at that instant, both men realised they'd slept right through it.

'What did he say, Simon?' David called past the deep line of shade that separated him from the children, and Simon shrugged. Afrikaans voices were discussing the President's speech on the radio and David turned to Fezile in frustration. 'What are they saying? Can you understand?'

'Mandela he free!' Fezile stared at David in surprise as he translated the words which had welcomed them into a waking country very different from the one they'd left for sleep. 'It's a new South Africa.' Fezile was unsure exactly what that meant.

The quietly spoken Afrikaner president had held out the first glimpse of hope. Pointing a way out of the dead end the country was in, his words were based on his Christian commitment, and the birth pangs of a nation had begun.

Nelson Mandela's release was greeted by multitudes of cheering people. As black Africans entrusted him with their dreams, white ones wept. Though the aging prisoner spoke without bitterness, his words were tinged with threats of continued violence and quickly they cooled the euphoria that had lifted a country in hope.

'Why?' Thabo's eyes glistened with tears as he faced the congregation of his tin church in Langa. Though black and white leaders had begun to search for a way forward together, the townships still wallowed in anarchy as gangs of youths raped and pillaged their own people. Black councillors were intimidated, stabbed and burned alive, labelled Uncle Toms by a radicalised youth who were beyond the control of their leaders. Innocent people fled as Mafia-style political groups burned down the homes of those unable to meet their demands, and oppression no longer came from 'white' hands, but their own kind.

'Where have our people gone?' Thabo cried Fezile's cry of long years before. His people fought among themselves for power and money while accusations of a third force rang round the country. The strengthening right wing of white Afrikaners itched for civil war, knowing the might of the white Government could obliterate the blacks. Promising to talk to the ANC only over the barrel of a gun, they stirred the white nation with fear of black domination. They believed President de Klerk was selling his people out to heathens and Communists. A traitor to the *Afrikaner volk*, they wanted him dead.

'It is not Buthelezi, Mandela, de Klerk or Treurnicht we must turn to! It is God. We must humble ourselves and bow to Him in repentance. We must own our sin and lean on the mercy of Our Lord Jesus Christ!'

Thabo's voice cracked as he spoke words he knew to be the only way – a way obstructed by opposing forces of evil. As the people struggled to build a life free of oppression, they died in strife-torn townships. The police force was as divided as the country and Thabo knew that Andre Bothma represented only some.

Zola, the man who'd helped him build Portia's Khaya in the Transkei, had just been killed while serving with the police in Natal as they tried to hold back the slaughter of innocent people. Black politics had rekindled tribal war and the man who'd cared for so many needy children had been wiped out. He'd met a violent death in a hail of bullets, killed by the same people who'd cried out for freedom a short while before. Like hundreds of others, Zola's life had been sacrificed to greed.

*

'Hey, he's got Thabo's name!' Thalitha's shout drowned the television news as Thabo Mbeki appeared on the screen. Every night the family watched the drama of their emerging country unfold and quickly Rebecca silenced her daughter. 'But he's got Thabo's name,' Thalitha argued, moving out of the room to escape.

As white and black leaders met for the first time, the charismatic black leader, Thabo Mbeki talked with white minister, Pik Botha. Both men spoke of a miracle. They spoke of their amazement at finding the other side was human. Exiles were granted permission to return. Political parties were unbanned and an era of negotiation dawned.

But quickly the euphoria turned to despair and Thalitha was a very worried little girl. Her parents talked only of an uncertain future and nothing was what it seemed. Like the other side of Alice in Wonderland's looking glass, her world was distorted. Grown-ups were more afraid than children, asking one another in whispered terror if they planned to stay or leave as hope and despair tipped the balance of a bizarre see-saw.

Much of Thalitha's time was spent with Miriam, whose love and comfort were unshakeable. Xhosa tripped off the child's tongue as naturally as English, and through Miriam's African friends she discovered the grotesqueness of their world, too.

Cecilia, a maid from the next farm, talked in terrified giggles about gangsters in balaclavas who roamed the Macasar area of Khayelitsha township, where she lived. Claiming to be ANC, they demanded money for protection, burning down the shacks of those unable to pay. Determined that the 'scollies' would not burn her meagre possessions, she'd locked everything she owned in the concrete toilet outside her shack, asking God to remain there with them.

Thalitha had spent many hours worrying about that, wondering what God did in the toilet all night and if He'd be able to get out to protect Cecilia herself. Even Fezile talked only of disaster. He wept as the power struggle between leaders tore the people apart. Though the Zulu chief Mangosutu Buthelezi had led the world's call for the release of Nelson Mandela, the ANC and Inkatha were now at war. As each side blamed the other, Fezile saw only the rising piles of bodies that no one claimed, as none claimed the sin of apartheid. Street politics used millions of uneducated youths as weapons, their future threatened with annihilation once their purpose was served. Deeply hurt by the growing hatred of black for white, her grandfather David hid in the past. He seemed to carry the guilt of a nation that wasn't his own, as if waiting to take it with him to the grave.

But most of all Thalitha worried about losing her home. She couldn't understand why joy had vanished from Bonne Espérance, and secretly she blamed the old key her mother had told her about.

She'd discovered that Rebecca had dug it up from Clara's grave when she'd been a child herself, in an effort to claim Luke and Bonne Espérance. However, to Thalitha the key had brought with it only disaster and the threat of losing Bonne Espérance so, as the words in Emily's diary played in her mind, she made her plan.

Dragging herself up on to her parents' bed, she tiptoed sinking steps on to the pillows, reaching to lift the key from its hook on the wall. But she couldn't. Inches short of the gleaming bronze object that possessed her, her fingers stretched uselessly towards it.

'What are you doing?' Simon asked, his awkward figure quite suddenly at the door as the small girl smudged fingertip-tracks on the clean white wall above Rebecca's bed.

'Nothing.' Thalitha wasn't too sure Simon could keep a secret and she snatched a fly swatter from beside the bed. 'There's a fly!' Swiping it towards the key she knocked it off the wall and shrugged. 'Missed.'

'The key, Thalitha!' Simon backed out of the room quickly. He'd once played with that old key himself and had never forgotten his punishment. It represented danger, and lifting himself above such childish pranks Simon warned her. 'Put it back. Your mother be very angry.' He disappeared before she could involve him further.

Alone in the room at last and gazing at the gleaming key in her hand, Thalitha was amazed by its weight. It was much bigger than any key she'd ever seen before and her mind boggled at the size of the door in France it must once have locked. Pushing it deep into her pocket she moved to go, peering round the door's edge nervously before stepping outside. Although she knew nothing would distract her parents from the latest political news, she wasn't so sure about Simon and crept out of the house as quietly as she could.

Silent and dark, the graveyard seemed to whisper as Thalitha moved towards it, the key clutched in a sweaty hand as her feet pushed through the darkness. Bending down beside a grave, her fingers tugged at the sharp crumbles of rock that lay chipped and loose around the base of a tombstone which bore only a faint trace of the name, *Clara Marsden*. It was a name that sent shivers up her spine. But Thalitha was determined and her fingers pushed into the dirt: she believed the key had been loosed like an evil spirit, free to weave once again its spell on Bonne Espérance.

The overhanging branch of a straggling willow creaked as a breeze pushed it and Thalitha's flesh crept. Her fingers were burrowing towards the dead while limp leaves stroked her neck. Wondering if Clara's skeletal hand would reach out to snatch the key from her at any moment, her breath came short and sharp and her eyes closed against the dancing demons of imagination. The depression of a country in deep crisis, as it wrestled with the future, had touched her as it had Rebecca and she'd felt its clawing threat to her home. Even the horror of delving among the dead couldn't deter her from her claim on Bonne Espérance.

Hidden in the surrounding dark, an owl screeched as she pushed the key deep under the gravestone, back to its hiding place. Pulling her hands away, she examined them for signs of death's touch and quickly wiped them clean on her dress. Though her knees shook with the fright of what she'd done, Thalitha turned and raced towards the house.

'What you do?' Simon's voice snatched at her from the dark of a rhododendron bush and she screamed. Like a rampaging ghost, childlike and grey haired, Simon reeled towards her, his tongue sweeping his chin in terror as he tried to silence her.

'What you two doing out there?' A torch searched the night till it found them both and Miriam stepped out of the kitchen. Her bare feet firmly planted on the path, she shone the torch between them, challenging them to confess.

'The old key – Thalitha bury it in the grave.'

'I didn't, Simon's fibbing!'

They defended themselves, but Miriam was smiling. Though she'd seen the dirt on the little girl's hands she turned back into the house as if nothing had happened.

'Go to bed.' She switched off the torch and went back inside, secretly pleased that the key had been returned to the place where her ancestors had said it belonged.

As Luke lay asleep at her side, Rebecca couldn't quieten the fear that surrounded her.

All sides of the political spectrum had met through a negotiating forum called Codesa, working to draw up a new Constitution, but, as they searched for ways to bring warring factions together in the black communities, the promise of freedom revealed only the darker side of Africa.

While men talked of peace, the country trembled on the verge of civil war and the bankruptcy of uncertainty. Rebecca no longer knew where she belonged. The day on which the letter had arrived from Samuel Netherby, enclosing the gift of Naomi's shares in Bonne Espérance, seemed a lifetime away. The joy which had seized Luke and Rebecca as their home was restored, their promise to one another fulfilled once again, had gone. The country itself was lost in the anarchy of mass action and political murders, leaving no room for hope. Samuel Netherby had died in an old folk's home in England and the gift that had cost him his independence, seemed suddenly worthless. Even the old key had gone missing, as if promising the end of a dream.

'Are you awake, Luke?' Rebecca whispered, curling herself into him as he instinctively pulled her into the sleepy warmth of his body. She thought Luke's comfort was all she needed but still her body was hollow. Somewhere in the far reaches of her mind an ant hill in Zambia called her back with promises of the peace for which she longed. Forty years had passed since Table Mountain had dismissed the most important place in her world as inadequate, but once again it called, promising safety.

'I want to go home,' she murmured as Luke's breath stroked her, his hands moving down the length of her body as he called her into a love that chased away fear. But Rebecca held herself back.

'Home where?' Luke peered into eyes that looked out from behind the veil of a small girl's fears.

'Home.' Rebecca's voice was flat. She cried out for the same inner healing the country yearned for — a longing that somewhere in Africa, freedom might lead to life.

Simon breathed a sigh of relief as the old Mercedes drove out through the gates of Bonne Espérance several months later with Luke, Rebecca and their children squeezed in the back. The car's size had saved him from returning to the small mining town with the family and he'd polished it with the renewed vigour of gratitude. It had been agreed that Simon would stay behind to keep David company, but quickly he'd organised things his way. Fezile was David's friend and he would stay on, while Simon accompanied Thabo.

Moving throughout the country, Thabo preached a gospel of repentance, forgiveness and peace, and not for one moment did Simon doubt his message came from God. There was a beauty and simplicity about the words on his friend's soft African tongue and he'd recognised their truth instinctively. A childlike belief had opened Simon's mind to eternity and he knew now that the image the mirror showed him was a lie. God's were the eyes of morning as they looked on Simon.

Before I found you in the womb I knew you: before you were born I sanctified you.

Though Simon had lived as an oddity all his life, he knew now that he wasn't 'odd' to God.

The closer the old Mercedes drew to the small mining town, after thousands of miles of lonely road, the faster Rebecca's heart beat. She was travelling back in time to meet herself, and she'd already seen the 'big tree'. The tallest of tall trees, it grew alongside the road from Ndola and it had once stood out from squat bush as the first sign of home, but now it was dwarfed by forests of pine.

Lowering herself deeper into the back seat as the car drove through a rusting arch that welcomed them to the place of her mother's birth, Thalitha tried to ignore everything. Wide and curiously empty of trees, the road was pot-holed and neglected. Turning left, Luke drove between shops that her mother had told her were dominated by Mrs Bernstein's grocery store, but they were dilapidated and empty. The painted arrogance of Mrs Bernstein had vanished with the perfume monster and the scent of Eau de Cologne 4711 no longer lingered in the air. The sun stared down only on abject poverty.

Turning the car at last into the sandy wide spread of Z Avenue, Luke glanced at Rebecca as he pulled up. They were beside a line of square houses. Built of tan-coloured bricks, imported from England in colonial times, they crouched under rusty tin roofes. But Rebecca sat in total silence.

'Are we there yet?' Thalitha groaned from the back seat, still wondering how the old key had reached out from the grave to drive them away from Bonne Espérance.

'That your house, Mummy, where you were born?' Michael's nose pressed flat against the car window as he stared with a mixture of curiosity and dread. Picked over and neglected, like an abandoned spaceship, the town was barren. Years of corruption had drained its life and the ant hill had gone.

Rebecca was consumed by an overwhelming grief as she turned to 123 Z. Centuries of labour by millions of ants had been wiped off the face of the earth along with the trees, and her past had vanished in a spread of dry ground.

'Where is it? You said there was an ant hill,' the voices of her children clamoured from the back seat. 'With a tree on top! Where's it gone?' They stared at the flat piece of land on which their mother had said a majestic mud mountain stood.

'You're looking for someone?' As Rebecca climbed out of the car a young black woman emerged from their house. 'There's someone you want to see?' Surprised by the white visitors, the young Zambian woman smiled at Rebecca curiously, her eyes lit by unasked questions.

'I think the person I'm looking for might have gone.' Rebecca turned to the stranger who'd taken her place in 123 Z and, with a warm smile, the African woman released the grip of the past.

'Dad, can we go now? Dad, I'm thirsty.'

'Shh! I'm trying to listen.' As Luke silenced his children Thalitha sank deeper into the back seat. The words coming from the radio had chased them over thousands of miles to the centre of Africa and still her father listened to them intently.

'Rebecca!' Luke yelled as a voice announced the results of a referendum in South Africa. As the family had left, President de Klerk had placed his future on the line in a courageous step forward, asking the white population to vote Yes or No to a negotiated future with their black countrymen under his leadership. They had answered with a resounding Yes. White South Africa had spoken. Taking their future in their hands they'd declared apartheid dead and risen to the challenge of an unmapped future. The people had silenced Clara Beauvilliers' voice at last, and the hatred that had held a nation ransom to fear had been buried beside her.

'You from South Africa?' the young black woman beside Rebecca asked in smiling amazement and Rebecca said the words she now knew to be true.

'Yes, I'm from South Africa. My home is on a vineyard called Bonne Espérance.' At last Rebecca felt able to claim the gift Samuel Netherby had given them, and her eyes were alight with joy.

'OK!' The woman's face spread in a wide smile. 'Maybe both our countries have a future now!'

Rebecca knew the woman's hope lay in the newly elected President of Zambia, Frederick Chiluba, the man Thabo had pointed out to her before they'd left.

'Chiluba is God's man!' Thabo had felt the wind of the Spirit lift the shadows from the face of Africa and his eyes had shone.

Taking over the reins of a country drained by years of the previous Government's corruption, the new President faced impossible odds in his bid to restore his nation, but Frederick Chiluba had declared that nothing was impossible with God. He'd told a sceptical world that all power lay in the hands of the Almighty God Jesus Christ and in His power he'd taken the first steps to rebuild a nation degraded by greed.

As she saw the hope that lit the face of the black woman who'd taken her place in 123 Z, Rebecca recognised once again the true beauty of the African people. Then, as if in a dream, she was aware of a curious sound. From every derelict building in the small town, African voices were singing. Reaching out from the depths of poverty, the Zambian people praised God and among their voices Rebecca heard Thabo's. He talked of the leaders he believed God would one day raise among black people in their own country. His prayer was that men like Thabo Mbeki and Cyril Ramaphosa would step clear of the Communist domination in the ANC, looking instead for God's dream of the future. That they would stand once again on their Christian faith to share that dream with all the peoples of South Africa. Thabo's voice called the words of Habakkuk over thousands of African miles.

'"Though the fig tree may not bloom, nor the fruit be on the vines; yet I will rejoice in the Lord."' Even as events denied it he cried out to his people, 'Our God reigns!'

'I want to go home, Luke, Rebecca called with joy, the suffocating cloud on her mind lifting with inexplicable hope as he climbed out of the car and she ran towards him. 'I want to go back to Bonne Espérance.' Taking her in his arms Luke spun her like a child on the flat piece of land that had once been an ant hill and they laughed, aware that the small girl who'd lived there had gone.

'Why are they laughing? What are they saying?' Thalitha nudged her brother in the ribs nervously.

'We going home,' Michael shrugged, unsure where 'home' was any more.

'Oh!' Thalitha sat up in her seat, trying to disguise the very real pleasure that had spilled over in a smile.

'Why you smiling?' Michael demanded, wondering why his sister and parents were suddenly so happy.

'I'm not!' Thalitha straightened her mouth in a firm line. Though she knew the power of the key had at last been broken, she denied its existence – in case it might even yet stop their return to Bonne Espérance.

'You are – I saw you!'

'No, I'm not!'

'Yes, you are!'

As her children argued, Rebecca moved back to the car with Luke. 'Are you ready to go home, children?'

'Home where?' Michael asked.

'Bonne Espérance.' Luke smiled. 'Where else?'

'It was nice talking to you. Good luck,' Rebecca called back to the Zambian woman she'd met in a curious moment of understanding.

'You too!' the woman responded through the fine gauze that stretched across the open verandah of 123 Z. For a brief moment it was Granny Cat Rebecca saw in her place; Macaroni was beside her and she was certain they were smiling.